Since her explosion on to the publishing scene over ten years ago, Suzanne Brockmann has written more than fifty books, and is now widely recognised as one of the leading voices in women's suspense writing. Her work has earned her repeated appearances on the *USA Today* and *New York Times* bestseller lists, as well as numerous awards. Suzanne Brockmann lives in Florida with her husband, author Ed Gaffney.

Praise for Suzanne Brockmann's addictive novels:

'Taut suspense, sharp dialogue ... sterling prose and expert plotting' *Publishers Weekly*

'Strikes the perfect balance between white-knuckle suspense and richly emotional romance' *Chicago Tribune*

'Sexy, suspenseful, and irresistible' *Booklist*

'I love this book ... Suzanne just keeps getting better and better' Linda Howard

'Brockmann is an undisputed master at writing military and suspense fiction [with] action, danger and passion all rolled into one' *Curledup.com*

'An action-packed and breathtaking thriller' *Romantic Times*

'Readers will be on the edge of their seat' *Library Journal*

Suzanne
BROCKMANN

Gone Too Far

headline

First published in 2003 by Ballantine Books, an imprint of
the Random House Publishing Group,
a division of Random House, Inc., New York.
This edition pubished in arrangement with Ballantine Books.

First published in Great Britain in 2013 by
HEADLINE PUBLISHING GROUP

1

Cataloguing in Publication Data is available from the British Library

ISBN 978 0 7553 7705 3

Typeset in Palatino by Avon DataSet Ltd,
Bidford-on-Avon, Warwickshire

Printed and bound in Great Britain by Clays Ltd, St Ives plc

Headline's policy is to use papers that are natural, renewable and
recyclable products and made from wood grown in sustainable
forests. The logging and manufacturing processes are expected to
conform to the environmental regulations of the country of origin.

HEADLINE PUBLISHING GROUP
An Hachette UK Company
338 Euston Road
London NW1 3BH

www.headline.co.uk
www.hachette.co.uk

For the brave men and women who fought for freedom during the Second World War, and for the brave men and women in the US Armed Forces who continue that fight today. My most sincere and humble thanks. Let freedom ring!

Acknowledgments

First things first. Thank you, Shauna Summers, for your faith and trust in me, right from the very start.

Thank you, Steve Axelrod and Damaris Rowland. I'm so fortunate to have you on my team.

Thanks to my trusted first-draft readers – Lee Brockmann, Deede Bergeron and Patricia McMahon.

Thank you to Stacey Brown for some really great title ideas. (Well, I liked 'em . . .)

Thanks to Pat White for providing writerly support and truest friendship, and to Ann Slaw for standing ready to help!

Thanks for research help to my experts – Kim Harkins, Michelle Gomez, Rob Bergeron, and to She-Who-Knows-All, aka Kathy Lague. (You all think I'm kidding, but Kathy's better than an Internet search engine.)

Thanks also to Rob for his Word of the Day, and to everyone involved with the RCMP (Radford Cookie Morale Program), a project originating on my Internet bulletin board, in which more than 250 packages were sent to the servicemen and -women on board the USS *Radford* during the 2002 holiday season. You know who you are – and your generosity inspires me!

Thanks to Eric Ruben, who called me up nearly ten years ago to tell me about an article he read on BUD/S Hell Week, because he thought that I might be interested in writing about the Navy SEALs. (Uh, maybe . . .)

Thanks to Melanie for loving me even when I'm grumpy, and

thanks to Jason for thriving and growing taller than me on takeout for dinner. Again.

To all the reader and writer friends I've met on my journeys or through email – thank you so much for your continued support!

Last but not least, thank you, Ed, for too many things to list, but mostly for making me laugh. I love you!

Any mistakes I've made or liberties I've taken are completely my own.

Prologue

Fort Worth, Texas
1984

His lunch pail was empty.

Again.

Roger Starrett quickly closed it and latched it back up, looking around the middle school cafeteria, praying no one had seen.

He'd thought his mother was okay this morning. He'd heard her moving around in her bedroom while he was getting dressed. And there were definite signs of life in the kitchen – a cigarette still smoldering in the ashtray, his beat-up lunch pail standing out on the counter, looking ready to go.

He'd grabbed it on his way out the door, late for school, not noticing – again – that it was unusually light.

His stomach rumbled as he got up from the table, joining the line of kids who'd wolfed down their pb and j and were now shuffling past Mrs Hollings – King's Gate Middle School's own personal Checkpoint Charlie.

She narrowed her eyes at Roger from her perch atop her stool. No doubt she'd noticed him coming into the cafeteria just a few moments ago. She always noticed him. 'You finished your entire lunch?'

'Yes, ma'am.' He opened his lunchbox, exhibit A. Not a crumb in sight. You mean old bitch.

'Go on, then. But I'm watching you.'

No kidding. Roger walked outside, purposely keeping his

1

pace slow and steady until he went around the corner of the building and out of her line of sight.

And then he was free. He broke into a dead run as he hit the cracked asphalt, heading past it and onto the football field, toward the creek and the woods back behind the school.

If he hauled ass, he could make it all the way home, check on his mother, grab himself a quick bowl of cornflakes – he knew there were some in the cabinet because he'd had 'em for dinner last night – and then race back to school before Mrs Hellbitch even knew he was gone.

Noah Gaines had barely sat down on a log and opened his book when he heard the sound of voices. But he didn't look up. He just kept on reading.

Bobby Kemp and Luke Duchamps and several other eighth-grade boys Noah didn't know very well came splashing across the creek.

They were loud, they were stupid, and they would be gone in a matter of minutes.

They were playing George of the Jungle, climbing up into the trees as high as they could go without the slender branches bending – which wasn't very high – and whooping like crazy.

Luke ran past and kicked the book out of his hands. 'Whatcha reading, Einstein?'

'Nothing you'd like,' Noah picked it up and brushed it off and sat back down. 'It doesn't have pictures.'

Oh, man. He was so screwed. He'd actually said that loud enough for Luke to hear.

'What did you say?' Luke circled back around, coming to a stop in front of Noah, catching his breath as he gave him his best Clint Eastwood glare. Which wasn't particularly good. The only thing Luke had in common with Clint was that they were both white. After that, there was no comparison.

'Nothing,' Noah muttered, hating that now Luke would think he was a coward. He wasn't. He just wanted the bigger boy to leave him alone. There were only twenty-three minutes left in the lunch period, and he wanted to spend as many of them as possible with this book.

But Luke pushed him, and Noah sprawled back on his butt, in the dirt.

One of these days, he was going to get his growing on, as his grandmother always said. And then Luke was going to slink across to the other side of the street whenever he saw Noah coming – all six foot four of him, just like his grandfather.

'Come on, Luke,' Bobby called from the creek, moving on, ready to disrupt someone else's peace and quiet.

Luke, however, wasn't done. 'What *you* looking at?'

Noah turned to see that Luke's attention was on the trail, where a skinny white boy stood. He was watching them, his blue eyes wary.

Great. It was that stupid kid from Mrs H's class. It could have been one of the high school kids who lived at the end of Noah's block, but no, it was just Roger, who was barely taller than Noah, whose mother drank too much, who'd brought an empty lunchbox with him to school again today.

Noah had seen his face in the cafeteria, right when Noah was slipping out the door himself, his own sandwich safely stashed in his pocket.

'I'm looking at *you*, asshole,' Roger drawled with a twang that was actually real, gazing at Luke with the kind of expression on his face more suitable for someone at least twelve inches taller and much broader, too. 'I'm wondering why you don't pick on someone your *own* size.'

Yeah, it was Roger, all right. Roger, who was always getting into trouble with Mrs Hollings – who'd actually called her dick breath to her face, in front of the entire class.

'Someone like *you*, maybe?' Luke scoffed. He had to have had at least thirty pounds on the younger boy.

Yes, it was good old Roger, who just didn't know when to keep his big mouth shut. He didn't know that if he'd just shrugged and turned away, Luke would have made a little more noise, maybe knocked the log Noah had been sitting on into the creek, and then disappeared, no real harm done.

'I'm bigger'n *him*.' Roger motioned to Noah with his chin.

'There're kindergartners who could pound *his* ass.' Luke laughed.

'I resent that.' Noah started to climb to his feet, but Luke gave him another shove – one that actually hurt this time as he landed on his tailbone in the dust.

'I resent that,' Luke mocked him. 'No one really talks like that.'

Noah's grandfather did.

'Leave him alone,' Roger tersely ordered Luke. It was much better than Luke's imitation of Clint Eastwood, although Noah would bet that Roger wasn't trying to imitate anyone.

'Why don't you make me?'

'Why don't you come over here so that I can make you, dickhead?' Roger countered.

Oh, no, this was *not* the way to end this quickly and bloodlessly.

'Look,' Noah started to say.

'Come *on*, Luke,' Bobby whined from down beyond the bend in the trail.

Roger looked directly at Noah. *Get ready to run*, he mouthed silently, while Luke called, 'Hold up!' back to Bobby.

'What are you doing?' Bobby complained.

And wasn't *that* what they needed? For Bobby to come and see what was keeping Luke and decide to join in the fun, pulverizing a couple of seventh graders.

'Lukey's trying to talk Einstein here into sucking his dick,' Roger called loudly to Bobby and whoever else was in shouting distance.

Luke turned white and then red, and then lunged at Roger.

Leaving Noah finally free to scramble to his feet.

'Go,' Roger shouted at Noah as he took to the trees to escape Luke's wrath.

Luke was going to kill Roger. There was no doubt about it. He was going to catch him, and then he was going to tear him into pieces. Noah hesitated. How could he run away and leave Roger to that fate?

As he watched, the kid climbed higher and higher into the trees. He was light, he was fast, and Luke didn't have a prayer of catching him up there. Those branches wouldn't hold the bigger boy's weight.

There was a *crack*, and Luke lunged for the trunk of the tree, clinging to it with all of his might.

Noah started backing away. This was where Luke would realize Roger was out of reach and decide to take his anger out on him.

'What are you waiting for, shit brains?' Roger shouted at Noah. 'You're supposed to be back on the school field by now!'

This kid had what Grandpa would call 'a colorful way with the English language.'

'What if he catches you?' Noah called back. *If?* There was no *if* involved. It was inevitable. Roger couldn't stay in that tree forever. And when he came down, Luke was going to kill him.

He hadn't planned this out very well.

Roger was silent, apparently realizing the very same thing.

Bobby made the scene. 'What are you doing, Duchamps?'

'Get down from there now, and I'll only beat you within an inch of your life,' Luke growled up at Roger.

'Yeah, I bet you want to beat me,' Roger taunted, with an accompanying gesture that meant . . . Oh, man, this kid wasn't just asking for death, but a painful and horrific death.

Luke climbed higher, disregarding the danger. As Noah watched, he lunged for Roger and caught his sneaker. He grabbed and pulled and . . .

Crack!

The branch Luke was standing on gave way.

It happened so fast. One minute both boys were in the tree, and the next Luke was crumpled on the ground.

Roger had fallen, too, but he'd managed to catch himself on one of the lower branches. He hung there now, swinging slightly, one sneaker on, one skinny foot bare.

'Luke!' Bobby started toward his friend but stopped short. 'Oh, shit.' He backed away.

Luke moaned and stirred and caught sight of his leg and started to scream.

His leg was broken. It was *really* broken, with a jagged piece of bone sticking out, right through a hole in his pants.

Roger dropped lightly out of the tree, landing beside him. 'Holy *fuck*!'

Bobby hit the ground with his backside, clearly unable to stand. Noah could relate. He was feeling a little light-headed himself.

'He's bleeding bad,' Roger said, kneeling beside Luke. 'Jesus, oh, Jesus! You must have cut a vein.'

'I'm going to die,' Luke wailed. 'I'm going to die!'

'Artery,' Noah said faintly. 'Veins take blood into the heart, arteries take it out.'

'Gee, that's important to know right now,' Roger said. 'Bobby! Run back to school and get help!'

Bobby didn't move.

'I don't want to die,' Luke howled.

'You – shut the fuck up,' Roger snapped, 'and you – Bobby! Get off your fat ass *and run back to school*! *Now!*'

Bobby staggered off.

Roger looked at Noah. 'Do you know how to make a tourniquet, Einstein?'

'Yes,' Noah said.

Roger nodded curtly. 'That's the answer I was hoping for. I didn't pay much attention when we did that chapter on first aid in health class.'

'I did,' Noah said. He took off his T-shirt. There was a tear under the arm, and he put his fingers in the hole and pulled so that it would rip. He needed a strip long enough to tie around the top of Luke's leg.

Except his leg was broken right there, right at his thigh. How on earth were they going to do this without hurting him worse?

'You hear that?' Roger was saying to Luke, who was crying, tears running down his face. 'You got lucky and fucked yourself up in the presence of *the* one person in King's Gate who actually paid attention during health class. I think you can erase dying from the list of things you're going to do today, Duchamps.'

Noah couldn't tear his T-shirt past the side seam. 'Help me with this,' he said.

Roger took the shirt from him and stood up.

'Don't leave me here!' Luke sobbed.

But Roger was just digging into the pocket of his jeans. 'No one's leaving you anywhere,' he said as he came up with a Swiss Army knife and quickly cut Noah's shirt.

Noah must've looked green at the idea of tying that around Luke's thigh, with all that blood, so close to the jagged edge of that hideous bone, because Roger didn't even try to hand the shirt back to him. 'Okay,' he said to Noah, kneeling down next to Luke. 'Tell me what to do.'

'You've got to tie it around his leg,' Noah said. 'As close to his, you know, groin area as you can. There's a pressure point there, right at the inside of his leg.'

Roger nodded, his face pale. He glanced up at Noah. 'Hold his hands,' he said, then waited while Noah came around to Luke's other side and knelt down beside the older boy.

Luke flailed at both of them. 'Don't touch me! What are you doing with that thing?'

'We have to stop the bleeding,' Roger said to Luke, speaking slowly and clearly. 'I know this might hurt you, Duchamps, and I'm deeply sorry if it does, but—'

'I want my mama!' Luke wept. 'Where's my mama?'

'She'll be here soon,' Roger reassured him, his voice surprisingly gentle. 'I just know it. Bobby went to get help and they're going to call your mama and she'll rush right over. She's probably already on her way. But right now I know she

7

wants me to tie Einstein's shirt around your leg so that you don't die.'

'I don't want to die!'

'I know you don't,' Roger said, still using that soothing voice. 'So you just hold on to Einstein's hands. Both of his in both of yours, and close your eyes and breathe.'

He looked over, nodding as Noah got a firm grip on Luke's hands.

Roger took a deep breath and Noah closed his own eyes.

Luke screamed and Roger said a whole bunch of words that Noah had never heard before. At least not all in a row like that. Then, 'How tight do I tie it?'

'It's got to be pretty tight,' Noah said. Man, Luke was nearly breaking his fingers.

'Open your eyes and check this,' Roger ordered. 'It's not squirting so much anymore.'

Noah did. He had to look across that terrible wound, but . . . He nodded, swallowing hard. 'That looks right.'

Roger put his hand on Luke's shoulder. 'You're going to be okay,' he told him. 'You are one tough son of a bitch, Duchamps.'

'Yeah,' Luke sobbed. 'Yeah.'

Noah could hear sirens approaching the school.

'This is almost over,' Roger crooned to Luke. 'Just hang on a little bit longer. Help is coming. Any minute now. They're going to give you something for the pain, and your mama's gonna be there, and you're going to float on home. Any minute now. You're just going to float. Here they come . . .'

And there they were. Paramedics with a stretcher, pushing Roger and Noah aside.

The medics got Luke ready to transport, calling on their radios ahead to the ambulance driver and to the hospital, giving Luke some kind of medication that made him stop crying – just like Roger had promised.

And then they were moving Luke out of there.

It was only then, as they were hustling the injured boy down the trail, that Roger dropped to his knees and threw up in the dirt.

Roger sat outside the principal's office, waiting to find out if he was going to be suspended from school.

Again.

Waiting to find out if his father was going to beat the shit out of him.

Again.

He almost didn't care anymore.

No one was watching him, and he took the opportunity to examine the palms of his hands. He'd torn the hell out of them catching himself on that tree branch. Some parts were already blistered, and others were scraped and still oozing blood. It hurt like a bitch, but it was nothing compared to Luke's broken leg.

The principal's door opened, and Roger quickly hid his hands beside him as the black kid, the scrawny one everybody called Einstein, came out, followed by Mr York. The kid was wearing one of those dorky purple-and-gold King's Gate Middle School T-shirts – his own shirt had been trashed.

York cleared his throat. 'I'm afraid I haven't been able to reach your mother,' he said to Roger.

'She, uh, wasn't feeling well this morning, sir. And my father . . . he's out of town. You know, on business?' His father sold farm equipment and spent more time on the road than he did at home. Praise be to Jesus.

York nodded. 'Mr Gaines here told me how your quick thinking and fast action saved Luke Duchamps's life today.'

Roger didn't dare look at Einstein. Was it possible . . .? He was light-headed from hunger. He'd puked his brains out back on the trail, emptying what little had been in his stomach, and he still felt dizzy.

Not to mention that his mouth tasted like the contents of his gym locker.

Einstein nudged him, and Roger looked up to see that the kid had gotten him a cup of water from the bubbler in the corner of the principal's outer office.

'Thanks,' Roger whispered. Aside from the puking and the pain from his hands, he'd been fine up to now. So why were his eyes suddenly filling with tears?

'Don't chug it,' Einstein told him.

Roger nodded, taking little sips of water and gritting his teeth until the worst of the urge to throw himself onto the office floor and cry had passed.

'Mr Gaines's grandfather is coming to pick him up,' York told Roger. 'He's offered to drive you home, too. I think you boys have had enough school for one day.'

Roger looked up at that. Holy shit. Enough school . . .?

'Or you could come over to my house and have something to eat,' Einstein said quietly, as if he somehow knew the only thing in the cabinet at Roger's house was that last box of stale cornflakes.

Roger nodded. 'Thanks,' he said again.

'We'll wait for my grandfather out front,' Einstein told Mr York. *Told* him. Not asked.

It was amazing. They were going home early, but they weren't in trouble.

Roger followed Einstein to the bench out in front of the school's lobby. 'Whatever you told him . . . thanks,' he said.

Einstein's eyes were a light shade of brown behind his glasses. 'I told him the truth. I'm Noah, by the way.'

'Sorry about, you know, puking like that. I hope I didn't spray your shoes. I was just, you know . . .'

'It was really gross,' Noah told him. 'Luke's leg, I mean.'

Roger laughed. 'No shit.'

They sat in silence for a moment, then Noah said, 'I couldn't have done what you did.'

What could he say to that? 'Sure you could've.'

'I don't think so.'

'Well, I do.' When it came down to it, Noah hadn't run away. Roger was still surprised about that. He was either stupid or brave. And with a nickname like Einstein, chances were he wasn't stupid.

'You like Italian food?' Noah asked, kicking at a crack in the sidewalk with the toe of his sneakers.

'You mean, like spaghetti and meatballs?' Roger countered.

Noah laughed. 'Sort of, but much better. My grandfather spent some time in Italy during World War Two and he learned to cook while he was there. He'll make us something good to eat.'

Something good to eat. It sounded too miraculous to be true. 'You don't have to invite me over, you know,' Roger said. 'You don't even need to drive me home. I can walk.'

Noah nodded. 'I know.' He stood up as a station wagon – a shiny new one in a really nice shade of blue – approached.

The black man behind the wheel was huge. It seemed impossible that scrawny little Noah was related to him. He had a broad, handsome face and a full head of thick black hair despite the fact that he was old. And he had the warmest, friendliest smile Roger had ever seen.

'Hail, the conquering heroes,' the man said in greeting, his voice a booming bass, his accent one that Roger couldn't place. He wasn't from Texas, that was for damn sure. 'You must be Roger. Climb in, young man. I'm Walter Gaines and I'm pleased to make your acquaintance.'

Noah got into the front. Roger hesitated only a fraction of a second before he climbed into the backseat of that car.

After all the blood and shouting that had gone down just a short time earlier, it seemed like a very quiet choice. An unremarkable, nothing-much kind of decision.

But getting into that car was, without a doubt, the pivotal moment of Roger Starrett's young life.

One

Sarasota, Florida
Monday, June 16, 2003

Roger 'Sam' Starrett's cell phone vibrated, but he was wedged into the rental car so tightly that there was no way he could get the damn thing out of the front pocket of his jeans.

At least not without causing a twelve-car pileup on Route 75.

He had the air-conditioning cranked – welcome to summer in Florida – and the gas pedal floored, but the subcompact piece of shit that had been one of the last cars in the rental company's lot was neither cool nor fast.

It was barely a car.

Feeling trapped in an uncomfortable place had been pretty much SOP for Sam ever since he rushed into marriage with Mary Lou nearly two years ago, and he waited for the familiar waves of irritation and anger to wash over him.

Instead, he felt something strangely similar to relief.

Because Sarasota was only another few minutes down the road. And the end was finally in sight.

Sam knew the town well enough – he'd hitched down here from his parents' house in Fort Worth, Texas, four summers in a row, starting when he turned fifteen. It had changed a lot since then, but he had to believe that the circus school was still over by Ringling Boulevard.

Which wasn't too far from Mary Lou's street address.

Maybe he should make a quick stop, pick up a few more Bozos, turn this thing into a bona fide clown car.

On the other hand, one was probably enough to qualify for clown car status.

His phone finally stopped shaking.

What were the chances that it had been Mary Lou, finally calling him back?

Nah, that would be too damn easy.

Although, in theory, this should have been an easy trip. Pop over to Sarasota. Pick up the divorce papers that Mary Lou was supposed to have sent back to him three weeks ago. Put an end to the giant-ass mistake that was their marriage, and maybe even try to start something new. Like a real relationship with his baby daughter, Haley, who after six months probably wouldn't even recognize him. Then pop back home to San Diego.

Fucking easy as pie.

Except this was Mary Lou he was dealing with. Yes, she was the one who'd filed for this divorce. Yes, she'd been compliant right up to this point. But Sam wouldn't put it past her to change her mind at the zero hour.

And it was, indeed, the zero hour.

And, true to form, Mary Lou was surely messing with him.

Had to be.

Why else would she not have sent the papers back to the attorney after receiving them four weeks ago? Why else would she not return Sam's phone calls? Why else would she not pick up the phone even when he called at oh dark hundred, when he knew she had to be there because the baby was surely sleeping?

Sam reached for the stick to downshift as he took the exit ramp for Bee Ridge Road, and came into contact with the stupidass automatic transmission.

Six months ago, this entire suckfest scenario would have made him bullshit. Everything sucked. This car sucked, the fact that he had to come all this way for something that should have cost the price of a first-class postage stamp sucked, and knowing that Haley was going to look at him as if he were some stranger *really* sucked.

But along with his weird feeling of relief came a sense of readiness. Maybe this wasn't going to be easy, but that was okay. He was ready for it. He was ready for anything.

Like, Haley was probably going to cry when he tried to hold her. So he wouldn't hold her at first. He'd take it slow.

And Mary Lou, well, she was probably going to ask him to get back together. He was ready for that, too.

'Honey, you know as well as I do that it just wasn't working.' He tried the words aloud, glancing at himself in the rearview mirror, checking to see if he looked apologetic enough.

But, shit, he looked like roadkill. His eyes were bloodshot behind his sunglasses, and the flight out of Atlanta had been weather delayed for so damn long that he desperately needed a shower.

And he definitely shouldn't start out by calling her honey. She had a name, and it was Mary Lou. Honey – and every other term of endearment he'd ever used, like sugar, darling, sweetheart, *sweet thing* – was demeaning.

He could practically hear Alyssa Locke's voice telling him so. And God knows Alyssa Locke was the Queen of Right.

She'd hated it something fierce when he'd called her sweet thing. So he'd called her Alyssa, drawing the S's out as he whispered her name in her perfect ear as they'd had sex that should've been listed in the world record books. Best Sex of All Time – Sam Starrett and Alyssa Locke, Champions of the Simultaneous Orgasm.

Ah, God.

What was Alyssa going to think when she heard about his divorce?

Sooner or later the news was going to get out. Up to this point, his commanding officer, Lieutenant Commander Tom Paoletti, and the SEAL team's XO, Lieutenant Jazz Jacquette, were the only ones who knew that Sam and Mary Lou were finally calling it quits. He hadn't told Nils and WildCard yet – his best friends in Team Sixteen. Shit, he hadn't told his sister, Elaine. Or even Noah and Claire.

And he sure as hell hadn't told Alyssa Locke.

Who was probably going to think, *Thank God I'm in a committed relationship with Max so Roger Starrett doesn't come sniffing around my door, looking for some play*. Max. The fucker. Even after all this time, Sam was still insanely jealous of Max Bhagat. Despite his new sense of relief and hope, he was feeling neither when it came to thoughts of Alyssa and Max.

'How could you fuck your boss?' Sam asked.

Alyssa, because she wasn't in the car, didn't answer him, of course.

It wasn't too tough of a question. Sam could come up with plenty of answers without Alyssa's help. Because Max was handsome, powerful, brilliant, and, yes, probably great in bed.

Yeah, and who was he kidding with that probably? Max was no doubt *definitely* great in bed. Sam knew Alyssa, and she wasn't about to spend more than a year of her life with someone who couldn't keep up with her sexually.

And as far as the fact that the man was her boss . . .

She and Max were incredibly discreet. In fact, they were so discreet, there were some people in the Spec Ops community who refused to believe that they actually had an intimate relationship.

But Sam knew better. He'd gone knocking on Alyssa's hotel room door about six months ago. And, yeah, it was a stupidass thing to do. He and Mary Lou hadn't even separated back then. He had no business knocking on anyone's door.

But an FBI agent matching Alyssa's description – a woman of color, in her late twenties – had been killed that day, and until the news came down that Alyssa wasn't on the casualty list, Sam kind of lost it.

Except who had opened that hotel room door that he'd knocked on? Well, gee, hiya, Max. Sorry I woke you, man.

And that was it. Game over. It was looking into Max's eyes that did it. The fucker cared deeply about Alyssa – that was more than clear.

And every day since then, Sam tried – he really honestly tried – to be happy for her.

And as for his own elusive happiness . . .

Well, he was done feeling sorry for himself. And he was done letting this divorce take place on Mary Lou's timetable, with Mary Lou running this freak show.

Sam and his expensive new lawyer had worked out a schedule of visits – dates and times that he could see Haley. He wasn't looking for joint custody – that would be crazy. As a SEAL he went out of the country at the drop of a hat, sometimes for weeks or even months at a time.

He just wanted to be able to see his kid a couple of times a week whenever he was Stateside. Surely Mary Lou would agree to that.

To make it a no-brainer for her, Sam was prepared to give her the deed to their house back in San Diego, free and clear. He'd take care of the mortgage and continue to pay the taxes. Now that Mary Lou's sister, Janine, had split up with her husband, Sam's plan was to talk all three of them – Mary Lou, Janine and Haley – into moving back to California.

Where he *would* be able to see Haley every other weekend and once a week on Wednesday nights – instead of some pathetic twice a year bullshit.

Surely the idea of a free place to live would appeal to Mary Lou, who, in one of the bigger surprises of a marriage filled with complete surprises, was a total miser when it came to saving money.

So, yeah, Sam was hopeful that he and Mary Lou were going to be able to work this out.

And who knows? Once he did that, the rest of his life could start to turn around, too. Maybe perfect Max had a perfect sister who was beautiful, brilliant and great in bed, too. And maybe

Sam and the sister and Max and Alyssa could all double-date.

Yeah, right. Just as Max wasn't his favorite person, Sam wasn't Max's. The chances of them ever socializing – by choice – were in negative numbers.

Traffic in the city was light at this time of the morning. He was literally four minutes from Mary Lou's door.

Please be home.

Sam had tried calling his soon-to-be ex-wife from a pay phone at the airport, right after his flight had gotten in. It had occurred to him that she was screening her calls and that maybe she'd pick up if her caller ID gave her a number other than that of his cell phone.

Not a chance.

He didn't leave a message on her machine. He was just going to head over to the house and wait. Sooner or later Mary Lou or Janine would scoop up Haley from day care and come home.

And then he'd do whatever he had to do to get Mary Lou to sign those papers and move back to San Diego.

Hell, if she didn't want to live in that same house they'd once shared, they could sell it and she could buy another. It didn't matter to him as long as she lived in the San Diego area. He was going to move into the BOQ on base either way.

Sure, the bachelor officers quarters were tiny, and there was no privacy to speak of. But since it was highly unlikely that he was ever going to have sex again, privacy wasn't something that he needed.

Sam laughed at himself. That sounded really pathetic – never having sex again – like he was such a loser that no woman would want him.

Truth was, women went for him in a major way. In fact, the girl at the car rental counter couldn't have been more obvious about her interest if she'd used semaphore flags.

'Where are you staying?'

'Are you in town alone?'

'If you're looking for a good hangout, you might want to try

Barnaby's, down by the dock. I go there all the time after work.'

Hint, hint.

She was hot, too. A strawberry-blonde with a lithe, athletic body and a cute little ass. But hot wasn't enough for him anymore. No, thank you.

Sam was finished with casual sex. He was keeping his pants zipped, which actually wasn't as hard as it seemed, even after he'd gone for well over nine months without getting laid.

It sounded like a really pansy thing to say, but he wanted more from life than a fast fuck with an empty-headed stranger.

Because, shit, he'd been there and done that – and ended up married to an empty-headed stranger who was pregnant with his child. And hadn't *that* been a fun two and a half years of his life?

He wanted sex to mean something. He wanted to be fucked for more than his blue eyes and his muscles and the fact that he was a lieutenant with the US Navy SEALs.

Unless, of course, Alyssa Locke called him up and begged him to come over, get naked, and light her world on fire.

If that ever happened, all bets were off.

Alyssa was neither empty-headed nor a stranger, but during the few nights they'd spent together, way back before Sam married Mary Lou, she'd definitely thought of him as only a temporary plaything, which still stung.

Sam leaned over to look at the numbers on the houses as he turned on to Mary Lou's street: 458, 460, 462.

Bingo.

Number 462 Camilia Street was a tiny little single-story Florida-style house with a carport that sat empty. There wasn't a car in the driveway either, nor one parked out in front.

Sam pulled up and sat, air-conditioning blasting, just looking at the house. With flaking paint and shutters that hung in crooked disrepair, it was about half the size of their place in San Diego. The yard was dry, the grass and plants brown, courtesy of the drought that was turning Florida into a desert.

A tired-looking palm tree provided the only shade out front. The door was shut behind the torn screen, and the dark shades on the windows were pulled all the way down and—

What the fuck . . .?

Sam turned off the engine and got out into the sweltering heat, staring across the roof of the rental car.

Were his eyes playing tricks on him, making those window shades seem to shift and move, or . . .?

He moved closer to the house.

Holy Lord Jesus Christ Almighty, those weren't dark shades, those were *flies*. There were so many of them, they seemed almost to cover the windows.

Oh, *fuck*! That many flies inside a house could mean only one thing.

Whoever was in there was dead.

At a little after 1000, feeling unsettled, frustrated, and antsy as all hell, Tom Paoletti came in from the garden.

Kelly, still in her nightgown, was at the kitchen counter, cutting up a small mountain of fresh fruit. She smiled, but he could see her concern for him in her eyes. 'Is the hibiscus going to make it?'

'Yeah,' he said as he washed his hands in the kitchen sink. 'It's going to be fine.' He glanced at her. 'And I'm going to be fine, too.'

She nodded. 'I know. It's just . . .'

'Hard,' he finished for her as he dried his hands on the towel hanging over the handle on the oven. 'Yes, it is.'

He glanced at the kitchen clock: 1006. US Navy SEAL Team Sixteen was now officially wheels up and heading out on a training op.

This wasn't the first time in the six months since Tom had been relieved of his command that they'd left town without him, but it was the first time he hadn't been told precisely where they were going.

Which sounded the death knell for his hope of ever returning as Team Sixteen's commanding officer.

Kelly chopped quarters of an apple into even smaller pieces. 'Maybe it's time to make some . . . alternative plans for the future.'

'Okay,' Tom said. 'Let's start by setting a wedding date.'

She didn't stop chopping, the blade flashing in the bright morning sunlight. 'That's not what I meant and you know it.'

'Yeah, but as long as we're making plans . . .'

'Tom . . .' She sighed and put down the knife. 'Maybe this isn't a good time to talk about this.'

And here it came. Tom couldn't help but smile. Whenever he tried to talk about getting married, she would distract him with creative sex.

One of these days he'd finally wear her down and she'd say yes and set a date. But until then, it was pretty much a no-lose situation.

Because despite being a girl-next-door look-alike with her cheerleader-style blond ponytail and her sweet face with those freckles and wide blue eyes, Kelly could be pretty damn creative when it came to sex.

Tom knew that she loved him. There was never a doubt of that in his mind. She just had cold feet when it came to tying the knot. After a failed marriage that had been filled with complacency and a serious lack of excitement, she had every right to be leery.

She rinsed her hands in the sink before coming over to kiss him. 'Maybe we should save the heavy conversations for later and just . . . enjoy our day off.'

Oh, baby. Right on schedule. She tasted like strawberries and cantaloupe. And she was definitely naked under that gown.

'Don't you think?' She reached down into his shorts, her fingers cool and still a little wet.

He answered her with a kiss. Oh, yeah, this was one way to cure that antsy, frustrated feeling – at least temporarily. Except

21

he had quite a few things that needed to be said first.

But then her nightgown went over her head and onto the floor, and she pulled out her ponytail holder and shook her hair free. She was growing it out and the ends curled slightly around her shoulders. It wasn't quite long enough yet to conceal her breasts – which was fine with him.

It had definitely been awhile since they'd made love here in the kitchen. He loved making love with the sun streaming in from the skylights, with all those counters at exactly the perfect height. It was bright and sunny, even after she crossed the room to close the vertical blinds so that the Hodges, whose backyard abutted theirs, wouldn't get an eyeful from their deck.

Hello, gorgeous naked woman in his kitchen.

Kelly smiled, too, as she walked toward him, and Tom was well aware that he wouldn't be here right now if he'd gone out with the team this morning. And while he appreciated this opportunity given to him by staying behind, it didn't really make his recent realization any easier to deal with.

'Maybe we should both just retire. We can sleep late and then make love all day, every day,' he said.

'Okay.' She levered herself up so she sat on the counter, right next to the cutting board and the piles of fruit.

Oh-ho, this was going to be wonderfully, deliciously messy. She was laughing now, and he was, too. God, he loved her.

And he was wrong – his entire life *was* easier with Kelly beside him.

There was a knife on the counter that was very sharp. Tom moved it into the sink.

She waited until he was watching to crush a piece of peach, dribbling it into her belly button and smearing it down, even lower, before leaning back on her elbows, right in the pile of melon.

Oh, baby. Talk about delicious.

But Tom didn't move toward her. There was something he had to tell her first. 'I think I might be serious about that,' he said. 'About retiring – about *me* retiring, you know, from the Navy. And if I did, we could have kids, Kel. I could stay at home with them.'

She sat up, an expression of incredulity on her face. It would have been pretty funny if this wasn't something he desperately needed to talk about right now.

Even more than he wanted to have fruit-flavored sex.

'You want to go from being the CO of a SEAL team – no, not *a* SEAL team, *the* SEAL team. The *best* SEAL team in the *world* – to being the primary caregiver of an infant?'

'I was actually thinking three,' he said. 'Babies. One at a time, of course, but . . . yeah.'

She was looking at him as if she were ready to whip out her doctor's bag and start taking his vital signs.

'I really want us to have kids, Kel,' he told her. 'I love you, and I'm ready to take our relationship to the next level. I've been ready for a long time. And suddenly it seems as if I'm going to have lots of time on my hands, so . . .'

'But your career—'

'What career?' Ever since six months ago, when he'd ordered his men to take down three terrorist assassins who had infiltrated an open-to-the-public SEAL demonstration at the Coronado naval base, Tom had been pulled off his career track as CO of SEAL Team Sixteen and into the limbo of a Navy desk job.

It would be one thing if he'd been transferred to a position that would allow him active participation in the smooth management of the teams, but as far as he could tell, his new job was meaningless. He did nothing but ridiculous paper busywork that helped no one. Lately he'd started coming in an hour late and going home an hour early, but no one noticed. Or cared.

As long as he didn't draw any attention to himself. As long as he didn't make more waves.

He'd been patient at first, as the Navy and the US Government tried to figure out if he was a hero for saving the President's life – and the lives of thousands of people in that crowd – or a dangerous criminal for violating US law.

The US Military was not allowed to take up arms against civilians. Tom knew that as well as any American. It was written very clearly in a little piece of paper called the US Constitution.

And Tom had, indeed, crossed that line. The Secret Service was responsible for the protection of the President, and the head of the Service hadn't given Tom permission to act in his behalf. There was a tape of their radio communications that day that spelled it all out quite clearly.

'You need to let us take care of this,' Tom had been told, even though the Secret Service men in the sniper towers still hadn't located the suspected shooter in the crowd, and the SEALs in the helos overhead *had*.

But Lt Sam Starrett, one of Tom's most trusted officers, had been in one of the circling helicopters. He'd spotted a weapon on the man in question and shouted, 'Gun!'

Tom hadn't thought twice about giving the order to take down that terrorist shooter, or the two others who had started firing into the crowd. Kelly had been there that day, along with countless other wives and girlfriends and children and mothers and . . .

And his commander in chief, the United States President.

Tom's quick order *had* saved lives – there was no doubt about it. He'd do it all over again, without hesitation. It wasn't as if he hadn't known that his career was over even as the command to fire was leaving his lips.

Some things were worth more than a man's career.

He was relieved of his command within the week, and Lt Jazz Jacquette, his executive officer and a man he'd trust with his life, was given temporary command of SEAL Team Sixteen.

'My career in the Navy's over and done.' It was the first time Tom said the words aloud, the first time he'd voiced what he'd known to be true for a while now.

The first time he'd told Kelly.

Her eyes filled with tears. 'Are you sure?'

'Yeah. I've known for months.' He looked at her sitting there, still naked among all that fruit. 'I guess I kind of killed the mood. Sorry about that.'

She shook her head. 'I had no idea it was . . . Oh, Tom. Why didn't you tell me before this? You're supposed to talk to me about things like that. About . . . *God*.'

'I just kept hoping I was wrong,' he said. 'I'm sorry. I just . . .' He shrugged.

She reached for him, and he went into her arms.

'I'm sorry, Kel,' he said again. 'I guess I thought maybe if I didn't say it aloud . . .' He kissed her and tasted salt.

Kelly pulled back slightly to look at him and to wipe her eyes. 'They're fools for letting you go.'

'Yeah, well, thanks, but—'

'You know, Max Bhagat would hire you in a heartbeat,' she said.

Tom smiled at her ferocity. 'You want me to join the FBI?'

'Yeah,' Kelly said. 'Yeah, Tom, I do. There are a lot of very bad people out there and you're very good at catching them. If the Navy won't let you do it as a SEAL, well, you'll just have to do it some other way.'

'I still want to have kids. Let me rephrase – I want to get married and have kids.'

'Will you give me some time to think about that?'

Like he hadn't already given her a few years? 'Yeah,' Tom said. 'I'll give you twenty minutes.'

She laughed.

'Come on, we could go to Vegas,' he said. 'This afternoon. Or we could schedule something small here on base. Betcha I can find someone to marry us tonight. That license upstairs is still good to go.'

On his birthday, Kelly had wanted to get him a new truck with some of the money she'd inherited from her father. Their financial situation continued to be a prickly spot for Tom, who had drawn the line at comingling their funds until after they were married. They were living together, sure, but this was his house and he was paying the bills. Which pissed Kelly off because not only had she received a huge amount of money on her father's death, but she also pulled in a significantly higher salary as a pediatrician.

But Tom had a stubborn streak, too, and until she became his wife, there would be no *ours* as far as finances went. And even then, he was going to make her sign a prenup to protect her inheritance.

As part of his birthday negotiation, he'd told her he'd accept her gift of that truck *if* she went down to city hall with him and applied for a marriage license. They didn't have to use it, they just had to have it.

So now it was in a file on the desk in his den, ready for Kelly to give in and make this thing between them legal.

'You know, you *could* give me more than twenty minutes to think about it, and we could spend the day doing something else.' She leaned back into the fruit, eating a piece of melon and licking her finger clean.

O-kay. Tom laughed, both at her amazing lack of subtlety *and* his own undeniable response. 'Believe it or not, I'd really rather go to Vegas.'

She ate a piece of apple. 'Really?'

'Really.'

She licked the juice from a chunk of orange. '*Right* now?'

Tom kissed her. He was, after all, human. 'Yes.' Funny how he didn't sound so convincing anymore.

'Not in five minutes?' She reached for him, unfastening his shorts.

He pulled back. A little. 'Five minutes. And then we go to Vegas?'

'Five minutes,' she said, 'and then we talk about this some more.'

Talking some more was a step in the right direction. Tom

kissed her again, this time not on the mouth, and Kelly's laughter quickly turned to a moan.

Oh, man, he loved peaches. And he loved knowing just where to touch and kiss her to drive her wild.

After living together for years, with their ridiculous schedules – as a pediatrician, Kelly had to go dashing out of the house at crazy hours even more often than Tom – they'd perfected the art of the quickie.

'Please!' Kelly shifted on the counter, then, oh baby, he was inside her.

And the doorbell rang.

'Shit!' Tom said.

'Ignore it,' she gasped. 'They'll go away.'

But the bell rang again. And again.

And again.

Double shit. Whoever was out there no doubt had seen both of their cars in the driveway.

Kelly, of course, liked it. Devil woman that she was, she got off on the possibility of discovery. She actually enjoyed the idea of people standing on the front steps, wondering where they were, checking their watches, while Tom was buried deeply inside of her.

'We should probably make sure the phone's working,' he managed to say as the doorbell rang yet again and again. She didn't argue, so he picked her up, her legs around his waist, and carried her over to the telephone. She lifted the handset.

There was a definite dial tone.

She dropped it back into the receiver so she could use both of her hands to brace herself along that part of the counter.

She was moments from climaxing. She was making all those sexy little noises that he loved – those gasps and moans of sheer pleasure that made him teeter on the edge of his own release.

Whoever had been outside had finally stopped leaning on the doorbell, thank God.

If it had been important, they'd come back.

In fact, he'd nearly dismissed them completely from his mind as he focused on the beautiful, brilliant, gorgeous, sexy-as-hell woman he was making love to – this woman he was going to talk into marrying him right after he made her come.

Wham! Wham! Wham!

Whoever had been ringing the bell in the front had come around to the back and was knocking right on the sliding door.

It startled the hell out of Tom, and Kelly's eyes opened as he started to pull back from her. 'Did I even lock that door?'

'I did.' She locked her legs around him, pushing him even more deeply inside of her.

Wham! Wham! Wham!

And she was coming. She was laughing, but there was no doubt about it – she'd gone over the edge in a major way.

Bang! Bang! Bang!

Damn it, now someone else was pounding on the front door, too, and ringing the bell.

Kelly knew him as well as he knew her. She knew just how to touch him to make him come crashing into her – in spite of the crazy soundtrack that was completely freaking him out.

Bang! Wham! Ding-dong! 'Jesus, Kelly!'

The rush of pleasure, so fiercely, privately intense, was such a wild contrast to the kitchen's current Grand Central Station atmosphere.

But then whoever was out front started shouting. 'Lieutenant Commander Thomas Paoletti, please open the door!'

Tom started to laugh, and this time as he pulled back, Kelly let him go. She was still laughing, too. As he used the kitchen hand towel to clean himself up, she wiped a piece of fruit from his chin.

'Don't go anywhere,' he told her as he fastened his shorts. 'I've got plans for you today.' He smoothed down his hair as he headed for the front door. A quick glimpse of himself in the mirror in the hall revealed that there was no question about it.

He looked as if he'd just been having sex with his incredibly hot wife-to-be in his kitchen.

Wife. Man, he loved that word. Today was the day he was going to talk her into getting this thing done.

He opened the door. 'What seems to be the problem, gentlemen?'

Damn, it was the shore patrol, the Navy's version of military police. The two ensigns who stood there were impossibly young and incredibly grim-looking.

'Lieutenant Commander Thomas Paoletti?'

'Yes. Who's in trouble?' Tom asked. Most of Team Sixteen had gone out of the country. But Sam Starrett had taken a few days of leave in order to finalize his divorce and visit his daughter in Florida. Petty Officer Danny Gillman had stayed behind after spraining his ankle yesterday during a routine jump. And Petty Officer Cosmo Richter was also in town, studying for his chief's exam.

Out of those three, Tom would bet his money that Gillman was in trouble. Nicknamed Gilligan, he was even younger than these ensigns and still prone to moments of complete boneheaded idiocy.

'Sir, we've been ordered to escort you to the naval base,' the ensign on the left informed him. 'Please come with us.'

Ordered to . . .? 'What's this about?'

'We're not at liberty to say, sir,' the ensign on the right said.

'Well, see, here's the thing, *Ensigns*.' Tom stressed their significantly lower rank, but still kept his voice even and easygoing. 'I've got something very important planned for this afternoon, so unless you can be specific about why I'm needed on base today – where I haven't exactly been needed in the past six months – I'm going to have to decline your invitation.'

'It's not an invitation, Paoletti. It's an order.'

Tom looked up to see none other than Rear Admiral Larry Tucker, the base commander and the bane of his existence, coming around the side of his house. No doubt Tucker had been the door banger in the back. And it had taken him long enough to return to the front. Tom would bet big money that the sleezebag had found a crack in the vertical blinds and had hung back in order to watch Kelly get dressed. Son of a bitch.

She was standing now, in her nightgown, her hair back up in a ponytail, at the end of the hall, where only Tom could see her.

'What's going on?' she whispered.

He met her eyes briefly, slightly shaking his head before turning to Tucker, forcing his mouth into a smile. 'What's the problem, Admiral?'

'You're needed on base,' Tucker told him.

'I understand that, sir,' Tom said easily. 'My question is why now? As I was telling the ensigns here, I'm a little busy today and—'

'You're in trouble, Commander. Isn't that obvious enough?'

Kelly moved closer.

Tom laughed, but on the inside, his stomach had gone into an instant knot. No. This couldn't be happening. Not today . . .

But why not today? And, of course, Admiral Tucker would choose to be present at this humiliation. From the moment Tom had been assigned to command SEAL Team Sixteen, Tucker had had it in for him.

Hauling the shore patrol out here to escort Tom onto the base . . . It was so unnecessary. A phone call would have brought him in.

'Actually, no, Admiral, it's not obvious,' Tom said, with more of an edge to his voice than he intended. 'Since I haven't done anything wrong, it never crossed my mind that I might be in any kind of trouble. If I'm being arrested, sir, I deserve to know the charges being brought against me. What is it that I've allegedly done?'

'You're not being arrested, Commander,' Tucker said. 'At least not yet. You're being brought in for questioning.'

Not *yet*. 'If this is about the assassination attempt in Coronado six months ago, I've said everything I can say about that.'

'Well, goodness me,' Tucker said. 'Look at that. Apparently you remember at least one incident in which you did something wrong. I wonder, Commander, if there could be others.'

Tom turned to Kelly. 'I have to go in. I'm sorry.'

She nodded. 'I'm going with you.'

'No,' he said. 'I'll be home in a few hours.' He turned to Tucker. 'If you'll excuse me, Admiral, Ensigns, I'm going to take a quick shower and put on my uniform.'

Tucker shook his head. 'You'll have to skip the shower, Commander. You've already kept us waiting long enough.'

'I'll be out shortly,' Tom said curtly, purposely leaving off the sir, but when he went to shut the door, one of the ensigns put his shoulder against it.

'I'm afraid I'll have to accompany you inside, sir.'

God *damn*. There was questioning and then there was *questioning*. What did they think? That he was going to run away?

'Do I need to call a lawyer?' he asked the kid, half in jest, as he led the way back to the bedroom, where his uniform was hanging in the closet.

'Well,' the ensign answered seriously, 'you just might want to do that, sir.'

Mother of God. What exactly did they think he'd done?

Sam went around the back of the house, looking for the kitchen door and praying that he was wrong, praying that Janine, Mary Lou and Haley had gone to visit Mary Lou's mother in northern Florida, and that an animal – a raccoon or a skunk – had gotten into the house and, trapped there, had died.

But, Jesus, there were flies covering every window, even in the back of the house. Especially in the back. Whatever was dead in there was bigger than a skunk.

Sam knew he shouldn't touch the doorknob in case there were fingerprints on it. He had to call the authorities.

Except he didn't know for sure that anyone was dead.

Yet the fact that Mary Lou hadn't returned his call for

three weeks – three *long* weeks – suddenly seemed telling. He'd assumed that she *wasn't* calling him back – not that she *couldn't*.

Please, God, don't let her be dead.

He lifted the clay flowerpot that sat on the back steps – Mary Lou's favorite hiding place – and sure enough, there was a key beneath it.

The lock on the kitchen door was right on the knob, and he knew he could unlatch the door by inserting and then carefully turning the key. He didn't need to touch the knob and therefore wouldn't add to or subtract from any fingerprints that might be there.

The lock clicked as it unlatched, and he gagged. *Jesus*. Even just the inch or two that he'd opened the door was enough to make his eyes water from the unmistakable stench of death. Sam quickly pulled the collar of his T-shirt up and over his nose and mouth and swung the door open.

Oh, God, *no*.

Mary Lou lay facedown on the linoleum floor – although, Christ, she'd been lying there so long in this heat, she probably didn't have much of a face left.

Sam couldn't bring himself to look more closely.

He saw all he needed to see. She was undeniably dead, her brown hair matted with blood and brains and, shit, maggots. She'd taken what looked like a shotgun slug to the back of her head, probably while she was running away from whoever had come to the kitchen door.

Sam stumbled outside and puked up his lunch into the dusty grass.

FBI agent Alyssa Locke answered the phone in her partner's office. 'Jules Cassidy's desk.'

There was a pause before a voice that sounded remarkably like Sam Starrett's asked, 'Where's Jules?'

No, it didn't sound remarkably like Sam. It sounded pathetically like him.

Because *she* was decidedly pathetic.

What in God's name did she have to do to get that man out from under her skin for once and for all? She saw and heard him everywhere. She couldn't so much as see a blue jeans ad in a magazine without thinking about his long legs and his—

'Who's calling, please?' she said, scrambling to find a piece of paper and a pen on Jules's black hole of a desk. Her fault for coming in here in search of a file, her fault for picking up the phone instead of letting Jules's voicemail take the message.

There was the sound of air being exhaled hard, then, 'Alyssa, it's Sam. Starrett. Can you please put Jules on the phone? Right now?'

Holy God, this time it really was Sam.

'Oh,' she said, temporarily startled into silence. Why on earth was Sam calling *Jules*?

'Look,' he said in that Texas drawl that she'd always found either infuriating or sexy as hell, depending on her state of mind. 'I'm sorry if this sounds rude, but I've got a fucking bad situation here and I need to talk to Jules right fucking now. So put him on the fucking phone. Please.'

Whoa. A triple *fucking*. Even in the best of situations, Sam had a sewer mouth, but something definitely had him rattled to make him *that* profane.

'He's not here,' Alyssa told him. 'He's out of the office and he won't be back until Friday.'

'Fuck!'

'What's happening?' she asked, sitting down behind Jules's desk. Aha, there was a brand-new legal pad buried among his junk. She pulled it free. 'Is this call business or . . .?'

She uncapped a pen as Sam laughed. It was the laughter of a man who didn't find anything particularly funny right now. 'God *damn* it. Yes, it's business.'

'Where are you?' And no, she refused to let her heart beat harder at the thought that he was here in DC. That was just indigestion from drinking too much coffee on an empty stomach.

'Sarasota,' he said.

'Florida.'

'Yeah. I'm at Mary Lou's sister's house. Alyssa, I'm really sorry, but I need your help. I need you to call someone in the Sarasota Bureau office and have them get over here as quickly as possible.'

'What's going on?'

Another loud exhale. 'Mary Lou's dead.'

It was a good thing she was sitting down. As it was, she had to hang on to the desk. 'Oh, my God. *Sam!* How?'

'A shotgun slug to the head.'

Oh, dear Lord. Oh, Sam, *no*. Alyssa had suspected that things weren't particularly good between Sam and his wife, but . . . 'Was anyone else hurt?'

'I don't know,' he said. 'I came outside to . . . Well, shit, you know me well enough. I got sick. Big surprise. But I . . . I have to go back in there to look for Haley and . . .' His voice broke. 'Jesus, Lys. I'm pretty sure Haley's in there.'

'Whoa,' Alyssa said. She leapt to her feet, pulling the phone as far as it would go as she went to the office door. 'Wait. Just wait a second, okay, Sam? Don't move.'

Laronda was in the hall. Alyssa covered the mouthpiece of the telephone. 'Has Max left for lunch?'

'About an hour ago. He should be back in about fifteen minutes.'

'*Shit.*' Fifteen minutes wasn't good enough. 'Is Peggy in her office?'

'She's gone, too.' Laronda was eyeing her with curiosity. 'Everyone's out but George. You want George Faulkner?'

George was still new to the team and had even less experience in this type of situation than Alyssa did. She shook her head. It was up to her to talk Sam down from whatever emotional ledge he was on. 'Get me the head of the Florida office in Sarasota.'

'Yes, ma'am.'

Alyssa went back to Jules's desk, speaking into the phone. 'Sam, are you still with me?'

'Yeah.'

'Good,' she said. 'Don't go anywhere. Don't go back inside. Just . . . just sit down, okay? Are you sitting down?'

'Yeah,' he said.

'Where's the shotgun?' she asked.

'I don't know. It was so bad in there, I didn't think to look—'

'Sam, I'm going to call and get you help, all right? But you *cannot* go back into that house. Do you hear what I'm saying?'

'Yeah, I do, but—'

'No buts. You sit still and you talk to me. I need you to make sure that you are nowhere near that weapon when the authorities arrive. Is that clear?'

On the other end of the phone, Sam was silent.

'Sam?'

Nothing. Oh, God, please don't let him have put down the phone.

The intercom buzzed. 'Manuel Conseco from Sarasota on line two,' Laronda's voice said.

'Sam, you're going to need to give me the street address.'

Sam laughed. 'You think *I* killed her,' he said. 'That's really nice, Alyssa. Jesus.'

'Are you saying you didn't . . .?'

'Fuck, no. What kind of asshole do you take me for?' He laughed again in disgust. 'Apparently the kind who would shoot his soon-to-be ex-wife and leave her dead in the kitchen. Thank you *so* very much.'

Soon-to-be *ex-wife* . . .? 'I thought it was an accident.'

'With a fucking *shot*gun?'

'Well, I'm sorry, but you said—'

'It's 462 Camilia Street,' Sam said flatly. 'Sara-fucking-sota. Mary Lou didn't return my phone calls for three weeks so I finally came out to see her – to finalize our divorce. I'm pretty sure she's been dead all that time, and I haven't searched the rest of the house, so I haven't found Haley's body yet. Call whoever you need to call so that the feds get here first. I don't want the local police fucking up the investigation.'

'Sam,' Alyssa said, but he'd already cut the connection.

TWO

Claire knocked on Noah's office door as she came into the room. 'Ready?'

'Hey,' he said. 'Can you give me fifteen more minutes, baby?' He looked up into his wife's face. 'Five,' he amended. 'Five more minutes?'

'You sure you have time for this?' She sat down on the couch across from his desk and crossed a pair of legs that were still just as fine as they'd been when she'd caught his attention back in tenth grade.

She'd gotten dressed up. Skirt, silk blouse, heels. *Heels*. She was wearing makeup, too. She always wore a little, but today she had more than gloss on her lips. She was actually wearing mascara.

And high heels.

Noah *was* a little crunched today, timewise. But he was crunched every day. And with two jobs, two kids – one a teenager, God help them – they hadn't managed to schedule a date night for four months. Claire had suggested lunch and he'd actually put it onto his schedule.

But now he realized that this wasn't just lunch. This was *lunch*. As in, he was gonna get lunched.

'Yes,' he said absolutely. 'I have time for this.'

His intercom buzzed, but Noah hit the Talk button. 'Maddy, hold my calls. Claire and I are taking a long, *long* lunch today and we're leaving in approximately four and one-half minutes.'

Claire started smiling when he said that second *long*, and he knew he wouldn't be back in the office until three thirty, when she had to go pick up Dora and Devin from day camp.

'This one sounds important,' Maddy's voice came back. 'It's someone named Sam or Roger or Ringo – he wasn't too clear on which one it was – and he says to tell you it's an emergency, that Mary Lou's dead?'

'Oh, dear God!' Claire sat forward, her hand on her heart. She gestured toward the phone. 'Speaker phone! Speaker phone!'

Noah pushed the button. 'Hey—'

'Ringo, it's Claire.' She spoke right over him. 'I'm here, too. What on earth happened?'

'I'm not sure.' Roger Starrett's – he'd been calling himself Sam since he'd joined the SEALs – voice was clipped and tight. 'Mary Lou and Haley came here to Sarasota about six months ago, to stay with her sister. We've been, um, separated. We were waiting on a divorce.'

Divorce? Noah met Claire's eyes.

Did you know about this? she mouthed.

He shook his head. Noah hadn't had more than a 'Hi, I can't talk right now' conversation with Sam in far more than six months.

'I lost touch with her about three weeks ago,' Sam continued, 'and came out to see what was up and . . .' He cleared his throat. 'I found her body in the kitchen of her sister's house. I'm pretty sure she's been there for just about the full three weeks.'

'Where's Haley?' Noah asked.

Sam cleared his throat again. 'I'm, uh, getting ready to go back in there to look for her.'

'Oh, dear sweet baby Jesus,' Claire breathed, tears in her eyes. 'Do you really think . . .?'

'Yeah,' Sam said. 'Look, I've called the feds – the FBI – and they're on their way, but I was wondering . . . well . . .'

Ah, Ringo, Ringo, Ringo. Apparently it was still harder than hell for him to ask for help. Even with a dead wife on the kitchen floor. 'Where are you?' Noah asked, hoping he could make it easier.

Sam rattled off an address not too far from Noah's office.

'Hang on,' Noah said. 'We'll be there in five minutes.'

'Max.' Alyssa Locke came out of her office in obvious intercept mode.

'Not now,' he said, even though he took a deep breath as she came close to him. She always smelled impossibly good. 'I've got fifteen calls that need to be returned two minutes ago.'

Lt Cmdr Tom Paoletti, the former CO of SEAL Team Sixteen, who was a colleague – no, a friend – had just been brought in for some serious questioning related to last year's Coronado presidential assassination attempt/terrorism case – a case that was extremely high priority for Max's superiors.

They wanted it solved. No kidding. Max wanted it solved, too. But not badly enough to start tossing around some ridiculous conspiracy theory that would implicate a fine, upstanding, and completely patriotic naval officer with an otherwise impeccable record.

With the breaking news about the al-Qaeda tapes – the confirmed knowledge that there were still terrorist cells with the ability to do a crapload of damage all around the world – this was definitely not the right time to start pointing fingers and pulling one of the best Spec War commanders in the Navy out of the game.

But no. Why be smart when you can make newspaper headlines and maybe gain some public recognition points? Election day, after all, was coming.

And so the word had come down to Max that Tom Paoletti had been brought in for questioning regarding those weapons the terrorists had used, the ones everyone assumed had been smuggled onto the Navy base at least several days in advance of the assassination attempt. Because of the seriousness of the potential charges against him, Tom was going to be held under guard for an undetermined amount of time.

If the theory proved true and Tom did have terrorist connections, they didn't want him out and about. Of course, when the theory was proven to be just more senseless crap, they would have taken away the freedom of an innocent man for weeks, maybe even months, and completely destroyed his career.

The thought of it made Max's teeth hurt. This was America, for God's sake, not Nazi Germany. Still, terrorism created fear. And fear could bring out the collaborator in even the most liberal politicians.

'I heard about Tom,' Alyssa said.

'Then you know why I can't talk to you right now.' Max put his briefcase down beside his desk and bumped his mouse so that his computer's screensaver would disappear. 'I have to make those phone calls.'

Seven new emails. Six of them marked 'Urgent.' He glanced up at Alyssa. 'Close the door behind you on your way out.'

She closed the door, but when he glanced up again, she was still in his office. If this were a porno flick, she'd lock it, too, flash that smile that always gave him a cardiovascular workout, and start taking off that designer suit she was wearing in a slow striptease. They'd have sex, right on his desk.

Yeah, right. Real life was never as good as the movies.

Instead, she folded her arms across her chest and announced, 'Sam Starrett called about ten minutes ago.'

Fuck.

Funny how US Navy SEAL Lt Sam Starrett's favorite word was the first thing to pop into Max's head whenever the man was so much as mentioned.

First things first. 'Are you okay?' he asked Alyssa.

He managed to keep his voice even and matter-of-fact. And not sounding at all as if his blood pressure had just gotten high enough to make it possible for him to orbit the moon should he so much as pass gas.

'Yes.' She looked okay. She seemed as calm, cool, and collected as she always did. Which of course meant nothing because she was as good a liar as he was. 'He called because—'

But that yes was all Max needed to hear. 'Nine o'clock,' he said, then amended it as he looked at the pile of files Laronda had put on his desk. 'Make it ten. Your place. I'll bring the pizza and beer. We'll talk about it then, okay?'

'Someone killed his wife.'

Oh, fuck, indeed. 'Someone,' Max repeated.

She knew where he was going. 'Not Starrett.'

He had to laugh even though none of this was even remotely funny. 'Yeah, *you're* impartial.'

'I thought the same thing at first. But it wasn't Starrett.' She was convinced.

Whatever Sam Starrett had said to her had been effective. God damn it. Max didn't need this right now. *Tom Paoletti* didn't need this right now.

'Mary Lou – his wife – has been living in Florida,' Alyssa continued. 'In Sarasota. He went to see her and found the body. He said she was shot, right in her kitchen.'

In her kitchen, in Sarasota. Which was right down the Gulf coast of Florida from Tampa. Which was the last place on earth Max should go and the one place he was dying to be.

He was being good and had been staying far from Tampa. Crap, going on eight months now he'd been goddamn *perfect* when it came to Gina Vitagliano, and now this. Somewhere, God was laughing His ass off at him.

'Sam and Mary Lou had separated,' Alyssa told him. 'Did you know about that?'

Holy fuck, as Starrett would say. 'No,' Max said. 'I didn't.' How come he didn't know? This was something he should have been told.

She was looking at him hard. 'Are you lying?'

He laughed. 'Alyssa. Please. Why would I lie?'

'I don't know, Max,' she said. 'Why *would* you lie?'

No, thanks. He was not going there. 'So why did he call *you*?' he countered. As if he didn't know.

'He didn't. He called Jules.'

Which was virtually the same as calling Alyssa. She and her partner were extremely close, and Starrett knew it.

'He's going to be looked at as a suspect,' Max said, telling her something that she already knew. Husbands and ex-husbands were always high on the list in murder cases.

This was terrible timing. This was all Tom Paoletti needed – one of the top officers in SEAL Team Sixteen under suspicion of murder. It made the entire team look bad, like they were all killers and criminals.

If one member of a SEAL team could kill his wife, then another could sell weapons to terrorists. Damn it, it was even worse considering that Starrett had been the first to spot the weapon in the crowd on the day the President had nearly been shot. The conspiracy theorists would have a field day with this – saying that of course Starrett saw the weapon because he knew where to look.

Forget about the logic as to why, if he were involved, Starrett would ID the shooter, thus preventing the man from taking out his presidential target.

Logic and people who subscribed to conspiracy theories were often strangers to each other.

But okay. Here they were. There was a dead wife on the kitchen floor and a good man – Paoletti – already under suspicion of wrongdoing. Max had to go down to Sarasota and make sure that Starrett had a strong alibi and was no longer a suspect before the news about this murder leaked to the media. And if it turned out that the SEAL really *had* killed his wife . . .

Tom was royally screwed.

Max flipped through his date book, checking his schedule on his computer, too.

Alyssa knew what he was doing. 'You can't go,' she said. 'You have that meeting tomorrow morning with the President.'

'Where's Jules, again?' he asked. Alyssa's partner, Jules Cassidy, had taken several days off. But that was before all hell had broken loose.

'His mother's getting married today,' Alyssa said.

Shit. 'Call him in.'

'He's in Hawaii,' she informed him. 'Even if you could be that cruel, it'll take him a full day to get to Sarasota.'

'I want someone down there who knows Starrett,' Max said shortly, 'and I'm not sending you.'

The moment the words left his lips, he recognized how stupid and petty and childish he was being. This wasn't about him wanting to protect Alyssa from the emotional pain of seeing a former lover. This was about jealousy. It was fear that if she got anywhere within twenty-five miles of Sam Starrett, she'd never come back.

Alyssa was just standing there, watching him with those eyes that could see through all his layers of crap.

Max stood looking back at her, wishing that he could snap his fingers and make everything go away. Mary Lou Starrett would spring instantly back to life. Tom Paoletti would still be CO of Team Sixteen. The World Trade Center towers would still be standing. Terrorists everywhere would be thwarted at every turn.

And Gina . . .

In his perfect, finger-snap-generated world, Max had never so much as met Gina Vitagliano. If he hadn't, he and Alyssa Locke probably would've been married for a year by now, and his life would be tidy and serene and blissfully satisfying, his meager hours away from the office spent with a woman who was a perfect match for him in every way. His life would be orderly – instead of this current train wreck of near-howling frustration and chaotic anxiety.

He picked up his telephone. 'Laronda, Locke needs to get to Sarasota ASAP. And schedule a flight for me for late tomorrow morning, after eleven, okay?'

'Yes, sir.'

Max hung up the phone. 'I'm sorry if I was—'

Alyssa touched him. She never touched him in the office, but now she touched his arm – just a brief squeeze. 'I'll be okay.'

She thought he didn't want her to go because he was worried about *her*.

He was a total shithead.

Max broke his own rule for what was or was not appropriate for the office between himself and a subordinate, and as usual, when he broke a rule, he completely detonated it. He pulled her hard into his arms and held her tightly.

She was soft and warm and, yes, she smelled too good. Somehow, over the past year, this woman had become outrageously important to him – she'd become his confidante, his best friend. It would hurt like hell to lose her.

In fact, he might very well never stop bleeding.

'Be careful.' It was such an inadequate thing to say, but it was all he could manage.

'I will.' Alyssa kissed him, her lips soft against his cheek before she slipped out of his grasp. 'I'll see you tomorrow.'

She gave him one last smile and this time she shut the door firmly behind her.

Max gave himself a little time – at least ten or fifteen seconds – to regain his equilibrium before he got on the phone and started making those calls.

December 1, 1943

Dear Mae,

I wanted to write this letter on Thanksgiving, to wish you and little Jolee a Happy Day, but I was high over the Rockies, transporting a plane to California.

It was a brand-spanking-new North American P-51D Mustang. (I know, I know, this means nothing to you! Suppose instead that I say that a Mustang moves at 435 miles per hour – what a thrill to fly that fast!) This plane had been used for training out in Iowa, and, boy, this baby could fly. I had some fun, all right. I was sorry to land at my final destination in (CENSORED).

I was sorrier still when I caught sight of a newspaper and saw the casualty lists from Tarawa.

That news from the war in the Pacific has made us all somber, I'm afraid, and it didn't seem as if there was much this year to be thankful for. I know you miss Walt very much, and I'm sure he must be missing you and the baby dreadfully.

Still, I wanted to let you know that regardless of this wretched war, I myself have much to be thankful for this year, and high on my list is my friendship with you and Walter. It's occurred to me as I'm sitting here that I never told you the details of how it was that your husband came to bring me to your house that night more than a solid year ago.

So here goes. I hope it will make you laugh, or at least lighten your heart.

I was flying a clunker of an old P-40 from Memphis to the airfield in Tuskegee. That's always the scariest job — taking up an aircraft that has just been pulled out of mothballs. Forget the normal checklist — I nearly overhauled the engine, checking to make sure that thing wasn't going to fall out of the sky with me inside.

But despite my makeshift tune-up, this P-40 developed a bad case of the hiccups when I was about 130 miles outside of Tuskegee. I pushed on, hoping I'd make it those last few miles. I knew that if it got worse, I could always look for a place, a field or even a flat stretch of road, to set that puppy down.

But I didn't want to do that. After landing somewhere other than an airstrip, taking off again would be a pain in the you-know-what.

I turned on the radio to let Tuskegee know that I was having some problems and — I swear to you — the switch came off in my hand. There wasn't much I could do to fix it. I could only sit back and fly.

But then there it was — the airfield. Right in front of me. I said a quick prayer of thanks. (That 'God is my copilot' thing is no joke!)

I flew by the tower, signaling that my radio was out and that I needed to land immediately.

They gave me the go-ahead, using flags to signal me back, and I turned to come around and land the plane.

Only that P-40 stalled on me. It coughed, and it choked, and then I was in this large piece of metal that was falling fast — too fast — toward that landing strip.

I swear to you, my life — all twenty-eight pathetic years of it — flashed before my eyes. I remember thinking about that too-handsome captain I'd met two weeks earlier in Albuquerque. I remember thinking that I should have danced with him. (And yes, dearest friend, I am being euphemistic when I use the word dance. Oh, how I love to shock you!)

But I wasn't ready to go to my heavenly reward, and I used every trick in the book, and made up a few brand-new ones, to get that engine turning over again. I still don't know exactly how I did it, but I did. I came within thirty feet of the ground, and by now I was going way too fast to land, so I pulled up, hard, and went around again. This time, though, I didn't stall. This time, I brought that POS-40 in and landed it, neat as a pin.

So there I was, climbing out of that plane, shaken to h*ll and white as a sheet, thinking that I've got to go change my drawers. I was ready to kiss that dusty ground and spend about a week in church.

Only this man, this tall Negro man, comes running over to me, spitting fire.

'What in Sam H*ll kind of flying is that?' he shouted at me in his clipped Yankee northern accent. 'How dare you fly so recklessly here! Not only did you endanger the lives of everyone on this airfield and yourself, but you came d*mned close to destroying this plane! We don't have half as many P-40s as we need, and you nearly turned this one into a crumpled piece of

metal, ready to be dragged to the scrap pile!'

You know me, Mae my dear, and it didn't take long for my terror to turn into anger. And so I lit back into him, shouting over him as I pulled off my leather flight helmet. 'I nearly died flying this piece of sh*t! That engine stalled on me when I went into that first turn, and let me tell you, Jack, landing that plane in one piece was a miracle similar to turning water to wine, and now I'm getting chewed out by a mechanic? I demand to see your commanding officer, and I demand to see him now!'

Well.

He'd stopped shouting and now this tall Negro man was staring at me, at my messy, blond, and very female hair. And as I stared back at him, I realized he outranked me by about a mile. This was no enlisted mechanic. No, this man had lieutenant colonel clusters on his uniform, and it said 'Gaines' above the pocket of his shirt.

I looked down at the paper I was holding, and indeed, the name of the CO to whom I was to deliver this plane was Lt Col Walter Gaines.

He was clearly as stunned to see a pilot who was a woman as I was to see a lieutenant colonel and commanding officer who was not white.

I did the only thing I could think of to do in this situation. I snapped into a sharp salute and said, 'Lieutenant Colonel Gaines, I beg your pardon, sir.'

I'd been trying to be a part of this man's Army Air Corps since 8 December, 1941, and I can tell you that although I was a first lieutenant, I was only a WASP, and men weren't allowed to salute me because I'm a woman. But that didn't mean I couldn't salute higher ranking officers if I wanted to. And I wanted to make it clear to your husband that my mistake had been from ignorance, not insolence.

Lieutenant Colonel Gaines gave me an answering salute and a smile.

'I'm glad you managed to land safely, Lieutenant Smith,' he

told me. 'You say you stalled when you turned?'

'Yes, sir. She was temperamental the entire flight, but she completely quit on me a little earlier than I wanted her to.' I took him over to the plane, and we messed around with engine for quite some time.

While we did that, I told him about the Women's Auxiliary Ferry Squadron (that's what it was called back then; it wasn't until last summer they started calling us Women Airforce Service Pilots, or WASPs), and that due to the shortage of male pilots, the Army Air Corps was making use of female flyers for such home front assignments as equipment transport and delivery. In turn, he told me about the Tuskegee experiment – that due to the shortage of white male pilots, the Army Air Corps had begun pilot training for exemplary Negro men. He was the commander of a squadron made up entirely of colored pilots. What an opportunity! I was envious because there was a chance they'd see action, while it was clear that I never would.

As we checked that engine, it was also clear to me that Walter Gaines knew as much about airplanes as I did. And I knew that I'd impressed him as much as he'd impressed me.

Walter shook my hand as I climbed onto the bus that would take me to the white part of the air base, and he said, 'That was some good flying today, Lieutenant.'

That made me feel proud, because clearly he was a well-educated man and a skillful pilot himself, and that should have been that. End of story.

Except later that day, in the early evening, I was sitting on a bench outside of the officers' mess on the white part of the base, and who should come walking along the dusty road from the colored airfield but Lt Col Gaines.

He was taking his time because it was a hot summer evening. He lifted his hand to me in greeting, but he didn't walk any faster.

'Waiting for the bus into town?' he said when he moved into calling distance.

I stood up. 'Yes, sir.' I was supposed to catch a flight back to Chicago, but I'd come in a little late, and the next plane wasn't leaving for three days.

I'm sure he noticed my flight bag, because he said, 'You might have difficulty finding a room in town. It's college graduation tomorrow.' He smiled at me. 'On the other hand, there'll be parties and celebrations going on. You should probably plan to stay back here on base tonight, though.'

'Well, now,' I said. 'That creates something of a problem, sir, seeing as how I've just been informed that there's nowhere here on base for a female pilot to be billeted.' I laughed, making light of it. 'I'll just have to throw myself on God's mercy – find a church in town that has cushions on the pews.' This was not the first time this had happened to me, and I knew for a fact that Walter must have had similar experiences.

D*mn, standing there talking to me, he – a lieutenant colonel – couldn't even sit down to wait for the bus because the bench was marked 'Whites Only'.

I took my flight bag and moved over to the other bench, the one with peeling paint, so we could both take a load off.

'You know,' Walter said, as he looked at me, 'you're welcome to come home with me.'

And oh, Mae, you know me! My brain always finds the nastiest explanation for anything. Or maybe I was still thinking too much about that missed dance with that captain back in New Mexico, because I remember sitting there, staring at Walter in total shock, thinking he'd just invited me to . . .

Well. You know Walt, too. He's a very smart man, and it didn't take him long to figure out where my thoughts had flown, just from looking at the expression on my face. I'm sure my cake hole was hanging open!

Walter quickly apologized. I swear, the man began backpedaling so hard, it's a wonder he didn't end up three counties away.

After he was done clearing his throat, he said, 'I can say with *complete certainty that my wife, Mae, wouldn't be adverse to your occupying the bed in our guest room.'*

Me, I'm sitting there, relieved as all h*ll that I haven't just been propositioned by a lieutenant colonel.

But I hadn't yet answered, and the bus was approaching, and Walt said, 'Unless, of course, you'd prefer to stay in the church.'

And I knew what he was really saying was 'Unless like some of the ignorant folk around these parts you have some kind of problem staying in the home of good, honest, and upright colored people.'

I looked him in the eye, and I said, 'I would not be adverse – in fact, I would be most delighted, sir – to sleep in a real bed in your guest room. Are you sure your wife won't mind?'

He gave me a smile. And he said, 'I'm positive she'll enjoy the company, Lieutenant.'

And that, dearest friend, is how I came to meet you.

I'm out of space and must rush to get this letter in the post.

You and Walt and precious Jolee are always in my thoughts and my prayers. I hope your health is improving – you must think strong thoughts! I'll try to stop in and see you soon.

Happy Thanksgiving!

Love,
Dot

Three

Sam Starrett lay on his back in the grass as the FBI swarmed over every inch of Janine's little house.

It had been hours, but Noah still sat cross-legged beside him, his jacket off, his tie loosened, and his sleeves rolled up. Claire had gone home to pick up the kids from day camp, but Noah had remained. He didn't talk, he just sat there, a solid, large, warm presence.

Manuel Conseco, the head honcho of the Bureau's Sarasota office, had come down to this crime scene himself. His team was taking fingerprints off every surface of that little house. They hadn't yet removed the body, and they probably wouldn't for a while. In fact, Sam had overheard a discussion about doing the autopsy right there in the kitchen.

Because, Jesus, Mary Lou had been there so long that, in order to move her, they were going to have to shovel her off the floor.

The forensics team had arrived, and they'd determined where the shooter had been standing just from the splatter marks of blood on the wall.

They also estimated how tall he was. And, assuming he'd held the shotgun at his shoulder, they figured he was just about the same height as Sam.

And wasn't *that* convenient?

Sam had told his story about forty-eight times, to forty-eight different people, pointing out in forty-eight different ways that he'd been thousands of miles away when the murder had

51

occurred. And yet Conseco had implied that they would want him to come downtown for additional questioning after his people were finished up here.

Sam wasn't sure what else he could possibly say. He didn't know anything about Mary Lou's life here in Sarasota. Was she still attending AA meetings? Did she have any friends? Was she seeing anyone? He didn't know, didn't know, didn't know.

He heard Noah shift his weight slightly, and he knew another FBI agent was approaching them. Time to answer those freaking questions all over again.

'Is he asleep?' a voice asked softly. It was a voice he'd recognize anywhere.

'I don't think so,' Noah told Alyssa Locke.

What the hell was she doing here?

Sam opened his eyes and pushed back the bill of his baseball cap as she sat down beside him. Right in the grass. He'd expected Noah and Claire to risk getting their clothes dirty, but Alyssa?

She certainly got to Florida fast enough.

'Hey, Sam,' she said, as if they'd run into each other on some city street instead of her coming nearly a thousand miles to see him. She took in his beard and his shoulder-length hair – he looked remarkably like Jesus with a hangover these days – without a single comment or so much as a blink.

'I figured you could use a little moral support,' she told him. She was wearing her dark hair short, and with her pretty face, perfect cafe-au-lait skin, and big green eyes, it made her look almost fragile. Delicate.

He knew better. Alyssa Locke was tougher and stronger than most men he knew.

God *damn* she looked good, like she might've actually put on a pound or two in the months since he'd seen her last. She'd been too skinny back then, but now she looked . . . healthy again. Strong and healthy and female. More like the way she'd looked the last time he'd seen her naked.

Which had been too, *too* long ago.

'Have they estimated a date and time of death yet?' she continued. 'Because as soon as they do, we need to get on the phone with Coronado and establish the fact that you were in California when it happened.'

'So I *am* a suspect.' Sam exhaled in disgust. 'That's just great.'

'It's standard procedure, so suck it up,' she told him briskly. 'Don't take it personally.'

He laughed. 'Yeah, right. Go into the kitchen and look at Mary Lou and then come back here and tell me not to take it personally when it's implied that *I* did that.'

She glanced over her shoulder at the house. Glanced at Noah, who was listening to every word they said. 'I'm sorry,' she said to him. 'Are you with the Sarasota office?'

'I'm with Ringo – Sam,' he said. 'I live here in town, and when he called, I came. I'm not a lawyer, but I know quite a few, and I've been encouraging Sam to wait before answering any more questions—'

'I'm on Sam's side,' Alyssa interrupted. 'We've—' She glanced at Sam. '—known each other for some years now. We're friends. Mister . . .?'

Sam laughed. Yeah, right. They were friends and he was having lunch tomorrow with the pope.

She gave him another look.

'Noah Gaines,' Noah said, clearly noticing all of it. Sam's laughter, Alyssa's sharp look.

She held out her hand to Noah. 'Alyssa Locke.'

Now she was the one who was watching for any kind of reaction, which, of course, Noah didn't give her because there was none to give.

When she glanced at Sam again, he shook his head very slightly. Noah didn't know. As he'd promised her, Sam hadn't told anyone about those nights – on two separate occasions – when Alyssa had come to his room and completely rocked his world.

Back before Mary Lou had told him she was pregnant. Back before Alyssa had hooked up with Max. The fucker.

'How's Max?' he asked her now.

'Worried about you,' she answered.

Yeah, right.

'Do you have any idea who might've done this?' she asked.

'No.'

Something flared in her eyes at his uncooperative response. 'Look, I know how hard this must be for you—'

'Yeah, and it's *so* much easier now that you're here.' Truth was, he had absolutely no idea who would want to kill Mary Lou. He had no clue at all. One of the aliens from outer space that his mentally ill neighbor Donny DaCosta saw lurking behind every bush would have been just as accurate a guess as anything else Sam might've been able to come up with.

Alyssa was silent for a moment. Then she said, quietly now, 'I'm sorry you feel that way. Max wanted to send someone who knew you, and—'

'So he could ask you whether or not you think I'm lying when I say – again – that I didn't kill her?'

'I know you didn't kill her.' She usually looked around him, above him, past him, or even through him. But now she looked directly into his eyes and even held his gaze. It was the longest amount of time she'd ever allowed herself to do that – aside from those couple of nights that they both were naked, and he was making love to her. Just remembering the way she'd looked at him back then made his chest hurt. 'I heard you when you said it the first time, Starrett, and I don't need to ask again. Has there been any information on Haley's whereabouts?'

'No,' he told her. She actually believed he didn't kill Mary Lou. Man, now his throat ached, too. 'All I know is she's not in there. Haley's not . . .'

His daughter wasn't decomposing in one of the other rooms of the house.

'Thank God for that at least,' Alyssa said softly.

'Yeah,' he said. 'Thank God for that.' Thank God. His daughter's mother was dead – maybe killed in front of Haley's eyes. And Haley – helpless and completely defenseless – was God knows where. To his complete and total horror Sam started to cry.

He'd thought he was succeeding at being stalwart, but really, maybe all he'd been was numb.

Before the FBI had arrived, before Noah and Claire had rushed over, Sam had gone inside and searched the house, every room, every closet, his stomach in a knot. Behind every single door, he'd expected to find Haley, her face as unrecognizable as Mary Lou's.

Instead, he'd found the kitchen table set for three – with two adult chairs and one booster seat – and toys scattered across the living room floor. There was clothing in laundry baskets, clothing on bedroom floors, clothing hanging in closets and in dresser drawers. Shampoo and soap on the edge of the tub, and makeup and hair gels out on the sink counter.

It was a house that looked lived in and comfortable. Apparently, after she'd left him, Mary Lou had stopped spending every spare minute cleaning.

Sam had found a stack of papers and envelopes on the kitchen counter. Bills and the like. On the top were the papers for the divorce lawyer, signed and dated from more than three weeks ago.

Mary Lou hadn't been messing with his head.

She'd just been dead.

He'd found lots of signs of life in that house as well as potential clues as to the time of day the murder had taken place – shortly before dinner – but he hadn't found his baby daughter's dead body.

The relief he'd felt was short-lived – replaced by fear. Where in hell was she?

'Give me a minute,' he said to Alyssa now as he struggled to get back in control.

Her eyes were wide in her face. 'Sam, my God, it's all right if you—'

'Give me. A fucking. Minute.'

She knew him well enough to stand up and walk away.

But Noah knew him even better. He put his arms around Sam, just like he'd done when they were kids back in Texas.

Just like Walt – Noah's grandfather – had done for both of them more times than Sam could count.

'It's okay,' Noah murmured. 'You don't have to be Superman. Don't freak out just because you're human, Ringo.'

Ringo.

Sam could remember the first time Walter Gaines had called him that. It was the day after Luke Duchamps broke his leg falling out of that tree. Noah had approached Sam – he was Roger back then – after the final bell at school and asked him if he wanted to come over again, this time to check out his grandfather's new personal computer.

Roger was more interested in Walt's cooking after having sampled it the day before. And sure enough, when they came in the kitchen door, Walt was stirring something in a big pot that smelled heavenly. The old man had a bad leg, bad enough to make him limp when he walked, and when he cooked, he often perched on a stool in front of the stove.

'Nostradamus!' he greeted Noah from his seat, with a broad smile. It was weeks before Roger found out that Nostradamus was some kind of fortune-teller and that Walt had started calling Noah that back when he was five for his propensity for saying 'But Grandpa, what if . . .?' Walt gave the pot another stir. 'And his trusty sidekick, Ringo! Who's hungry?'

Roger was. He was starved – and for far more than Walt's cooking.

That was the day he'd met Dot, Noah's grandmother and Walter's wife. The day before, she'd been visiting her stepdaughter Jolee, Noah's aunt, whose own daughter, Maya, had just given birth to Walter's first great-grandchild.

Roger had been shocked when he met Dot Gaines. Shocked but also enormously curious. Enough to ask Noah about her.

'She's white,' Roger whispered, as if it were a secret, even though Dot had gone upstairs.

Noah had nodded. 'Yeah. So what?'

'So . . . you're black.'

'Actually,' Noah said, 'I'm at least a quarter white. My father was half white. And my mother, well, she looked black, but she was probably at least part white, too. Many African Americans are. Have you read much about what it was like to be black in America before the Civil War?'

Roger shook his head.

And Noah had proceeded to give Roger both a lesson in the harsh realities of slavery in America, in which a shameful number of babies born to female slaves were the offspring of their white owners, and a lesson in genetics, in dominant and recessive genes.

'The way I figure it, sooner or later everyone in the world will be the same shade of brown,' Noah told him.

Roger had wandered around Noah's living room, looking at the pictures on the walls.

There was a wedding photo of Walt and Dot with a little black girl standing beside them. And there was a picture of an African-American woman holding a tiny baby. She was very pretty and smiling at the camera as if the person taking the picture had just told a good joke.

'Who's that?' Roger asked.

'That's Mae,' Noah said. 'She was my aunt Jolee's mother. She was married to Grandpa before he married my grandmother. She died during the war.'

'The Civil War?' Roger asked.

Noah didn't laugh at his stupidity. He never laughed at stupid questions. He just gently corrected. 'The Civil War was in the 1860s. Mae died during World War Two – you know, the one against Hitler and the Nazis. That happened back about forty years ago, in the 1940s. Look at this.' Over on the end table next to the sofa was a picture of Walt in a fancy uniform. 'My grandfather was a colonel in the Air Force. It was called the Army Air Corps back then. He commanded a squadron of the Tuskegee Airmen – black fighter pilots. You ever hear of them?'

Roger shook his head.

'Soup's on, gentlemen!' Walt called from the kitchen in his big, booming voice.

Noah smiled at Roger. 'You will.'

Sam Starrett was full of surprises, not the least of them being that his best friend from his childhood was black.

Alyssa sat in the observation room at the Sarasota FBI office, watching Starrett be interviewed by Manuel Conseco and his assistant, a young woman named Emily Withers.

'Mary Lou left San Diego six months ago,' Sam said with remarkable patience, considering he was answering the same question for what had to be the seventeenth time that hour. 'She served me with divorce papers the next morning. It was an amicable parting. We both agreed that our marriage wasn't working and we were taking steps to end it.'

He looked exhausted. His clothes were rumpled and looked slept in, and, with his hat off, she could see that his hair really was as long and shaggy as she'd thought. Thick and brown, it was sun streaked and wavy as it touched his shoulders. It was faintly reminiscent of the style so beloved by teeny-boppers in the early 1970s. He looked like he might've been trying to pass as David Cassidy's bigger, meaner, Navy SEAL brother.

His face – the part that showed above his beard – was tanned.

Whatever he'd been up to in the months since she'd seen him last, he'd been spending quite a bit of time outdoors. And that beard was another clue as to where he'd been – he was sporting a full one instead of the neatly trimmed goatee and cowboy-style mustache that he usually favored. The beard, along with his non-Navy regs length hair, told Alyssa that he'd probably been spending a great deal of time in a country that started with the letter A and ended in 'stan'.

The fact that he hadn't shaved upon his return was another hint that he – and probably the rest of Team Sixteen – were intending to go back there in the very near future.

And yet, despite all that excess hair, he was still striking looking. Tall and muscular, with blue eyes and a killer smile, he was loaded with pure alpha male charisma. It was quite remarkable, actually. Just during his walk from the parking lot into this building, female heads had turned.

Alyssa had stopped counting at seven.

And that was without his smile up and operating.

Alyssa had always thought that Sam Starrett's built-in drool factor was something of an embarrassment to the human race, in particular to the females of the species. She'd hoped that most women were smarter than that – that most women had learned to avoid men like Starrett, who obviously could kick all of the other men's butts and look good doing it, but who had little to redeem him when it came to sensitivity or responsibility.

And then she'd gotten to know Sam.

No, actually, first she'd slept with him. Which proved that she at least wasn't smart enough or strong enough to be able to avoid the biologically preprogrammed Darwinian allure of the alpha male, aka *Homo jerkus*.

The really stupid thing was, she'd hated Sam Starrett's guts for years. He was crude, he was rude, and he was so completely full of himself. She'd needed a bottle of ibuprofen and a day off after spending just five minutes in the same room with the man.

But he *was* gorgeous.

And in his own special redneck, Texas cowboy, foulmouthed

way, he was quite funny. And unbelievably smart.

And had she mentioned gorgeous?

Alyssa had been doing okay keeping her distance from him, though. Until she'd had a family crisis.

Because her littlest sister had died due to complications surrounding a late-stage miscarriage, Alyssa had been beyond frightened when her other sister, Tyra, had gotten pregnant. Alyssa spent nine nerve-wracking months anticipating another tragedy before Tyra finally went into labor.

And upon hearing the news that the baby had been born and both mother and daughter were healthy, Alyssa had had something of an emotional meltdown.

And Sam Starrett had been there.

He'd been both sweet and kind.

He'd gotten her drunk, too, the son of a bitch.

And sleeping with him had suddenly seemed like a really great idea.

Alyssa still dreamed in vivid detail about that first night they spent together. She'd never had sex like that before in her entire life. The night was a blur and some parts of it she still couldn't quite remember, but some of it she would never forget if she lived to be two hundred. The intensity of what they'd shared had scared her to death, and in the sane light of morning, she'd made it clear to Sam that their encounter had been a one-time thing. There would be no repeats.

But then she ran into him again, six months later, in a hellhole of a country where the passengers of a commercial airliner had been taken hostage by terrorists.

And again, he was gorgeous. And funny. And smart.

And rude and horrible. *And* sweet and kind.

And again, she'd been drinking, and going up to his room had seemed like a brilliant idea.

That second time, they'd been on the verge of something more. A real relationship. Alyssa had just started to get to know Sam – and actually found herself liking the arrogant prick –

when he'd received the news that a former girlfriend, Mary Lou Morrison, was pregnant.

He'd rushed off to 'do the right thing' and marry Mary Lou, and that was the end of that.

Except Alyssa had never completely been able to forget about him.

And now Mary Lou was dead.

Or was she?

Alyssa had taken a quick look around the inside of Janine's house before following Manuel and Sam downtown.

Two things stood out.

The first was that, though the house was occupied by three people – two women and a nineteen-month-old girl – there was only one body in the kitchen. Which meant that the other woman, presumably Janine, and Haley were still alive and out there somewhere.

But they'd taken nothing with them when they'd left. There were empty suitcases in one of the bedrooms, and no telltale spaces in the closets or drawers where clothes had once been kept.

Toothbrushes were out in the bathroom. A fairly battered and probably much beloved Pooh Bear was in Haley's crib, staring unblinkingly at the ceiling. An opened bag of Pampers sat on the nursery floor.

Wherever Janine and Haley had gone, they'd left in a hurry, taking absolutely nothing with them.

Which made Alyssa wonder if whoever had shot and killed Mary Lou hadn't simply taken Janine and Haley and killed them in another location.

Although why do that? Why not just kill them all at once in one giant bloodbath?

But if they weren't dead, or if they weren't being held against their will, why hadn't they surfaced? Where had they gone? Why hadn't they told someone that Mary Lou was dead?

The second thing Alyssa had noticed was Mary Lou.

Kind of hard to miss her.

Alyssa had met Sam's wife only two or three times over the past few years. The woman she remembered had brown hair and was voluptuous, not particularly tall, and definitely prone to carrying some excess weight.

She remembered a very young, very tired-looking woman with a pretty face, a slightly upturned nose, and gracefully shaped lips.

The shotgun blast, plus the heat and maggots, had altered the details of her appearance in a very major way. She had brown hair, yes. And was relatively short of stature.

But other than that, the woman on the kitchen floor could have been practically anyone who'd been dead for three weeks' time.

Three long weeks' time.

Alyssa now pushed the intercom buzzer, and in the interview room, Manuel Conseco picked up the telephone.

'Yes,' he said.

'I have a question for Lieutenant Starrett,' Alyssa said. 'And several for you, as well. Will you put me on the speaker?'

'Of course,' Manuel said. He made an adjustment to the telephone. 'Go ahead, Ms Locke.'

'Lieutenant, how positive are you that the woman in the kitchen is your wife?' she asked.

Sam glanced over at the mirrored window that allowed her to see him without his seeing her. Her anonymity was completely unnecessary in this situation, and she hoped he knew that she wasn't in the observation booth by choice. She was there because Manny Conseco had put her there.

'I'm pretty positive, ma'am.'

Ma'am.

There had been a time where Alyssa had been dying to hear him call her that, for him to show her a little respect. But now, after the intimacies they'd once shared, it felt odd.

When they were just having a conversation or standing in the same room together, it was possible for her to pretend that Sam Starrett hadn't licked chocolate syrup from her naked body. But for some reason, when he called her ma'am, she was instantly reminded that he had.

And, worst of all, it was hard to believe that he wasn't reminded of it, too.

Oh, God.

'Well, I don't know how you could be so sure,' she said, dragging her attention back to the situation at hand. 'I went in there, Lieutenant, and saw her. Was she wearing some kind of jewelry or . . .?'

'No,' Sam said. He was emotionally wiped, and it sounded in his voice. 'But she had on this pair of boots I bought for her last year. It's Mary Lou.'

'I have a sister,' Alyssa reminded him. 'She's about my height and weight. Back when we lived together, she borrowed my clothing all the time. What does Mary Lou's sister Janine look like, Lieutenant?'

Sam looked at the mirror again, and his gaze was suddenly sharp. 'A lot like Mary Lou,' he said, and he didn't sound quite so tired anymore. 'Holy Jesus. Where's my brain been?'

'We don't know that it's *not* Mary Lou who's been killed,' Alyssa warned him. 'There are two women missing. There's a fifty percent chance that it is your wife who's dead.'

'Ex-wife,' Sam said. 'She signed those papers I was coming here to pick up – they were right on the kitchen counter.' He turned to Manuel Conseco. 'Are we doing some kind of positive ID thing with Mary Lou's dental records?'

'It's standard procedure, yes.'

'And have we established yet when the death took place?' Alyssa asked.

'We're working on that, as well,' Conseco told her.

'I want a call with that information, as soon as possible,' Alyssa ordered. 'And I want absolutely nothing about this case leaked to the media – is that understood?'

'I believe I am familiar with how to do my job, ma'am,' Conseco said dryly.

Guilty as charged. 'My apologies, Mr Conseco,' Alyssa said. 'This one's particularly important. Max Bhagat will be coming down himself tomorrow.'

Sam glanced at the mirror again at that, but then quickly turned his attention back to Conseco. 'Am I done here?'

'Yes,' Alyssa answered for him. 'Thank you very much, Lieutenant. You've been very patient. If there are any other questions, we'll be in touch.'

Sam looked over at the mirror again as he swept his hat off the table, and she knew there were plenty of questions unasked – but they were questions *he* wanted to ask *her*.

'Can I give you a lift somewhere?' she added. She might as well get this over with, otherwise he'd simply show up later tonight at her hotel. And Lord knows, she wanted to keep this man far from her hotel room.

'Yes,' he said. 'Thank you.'

She stood up, and one of Conseco's assistants led her out of the observation room and back to the lobby.

Where Sam's friend Noah Gaines was still waiting.

He rose to his feet when he saw her.

'Well, I'm impressed,' Alyssa said.

He was a good-looking man, almost as tall as Sam and nearly as muscular, with broad shoulders that filled out his business suit very nicely. He had light brown eyes behind glasses, that, at first glance, made him look as if he might be playing at being a scholar, like a football linebacker who was attempting to prove to the world that he had a brain.

At second glance, and after exchanging a few sentences with the man, it was obvious that he was a scholar who simply took very good care of one very nice body.

It was a very nice body that had a wedding ring on the left hand.

'We were in there a long time,' Alyssa continued. 'I'm surprised you're still here.'

'Is he all right?'

'He's not being held,' she told him. 'But until we can establish that he was miles away from here at the time of Mary Lou's death, he'll be considered a suspect, which doesn't make him very happy. I'm doing what I can to make sure that doesn't take any longer than it has to.'

'He's lucky to have you as a friend,' Noah said. It was obvious that he was curious about her.

'How long have you known Sam?' Alyssa asked. He wasn't the only one who was curious.

'We've been tight since seventh grade,' he replied. 'Although to be honest, we haven't been in touch much since my grandfather died a few years ago. I haven't spoken to him in months. Maybe that's why he never told me about you.'

There was an awful lot loaded in that statement. 'There's nothing to tell,' Alyssa said coolly.

Noah just smiled, and it was clear he'd learned a lot from his childhood friendship with Sam Starrett. He had the same kind of killer smile. 'If you say so.' He turned, because there came Sam, escorted out to the lobby by Manuel Conseco.

'We'll be in touch,' Conseco said.

'I'm sure you will,' Sam drawled, as he put his baseball cap back on, adjusting it until it fit just right.

Noah took out his cell phone. 'I'll call us a cab.'

Sam stopped him with one hand, but waited until Conseco was gone before he spoke to Alyssa. 'Would you mind dropping Noah off on the way to ... wherever it is we're going?'

'Of course not,' she said. It would give her a chance to check out where this guy lived – this childhood friend of a man she couldn't quite believe had actually had a childhood.

'Thanks.'

'You know you're welcome to stay at our place,' Noah told

Sam. 'Claire's probably already got the bed made in the spare room.'

'I know,' Sam said. 'And I appreciate it. I might take you up on it. Just . . . not tonight.'

Noah looked from Sam to Alyssa and back. 'Oh,' he said. 'Sure, uh . . . okay.'

'No,' Sam said, shaking his head and laughing. It was the laughter of a man who was told during a five-mile tightrope walk that hurricane-force winds were approaching. It wasn't about humor, just faintly amused desperation. 'I know what you're thinking, Nos, and believe me, you're wrong. I need to *talk* to Alyssa.' He turned to her, all laughter gone from his voice and face. 'I need to find out why my dead ex-wife is so *important* that Max Son-of-God-Almighty Bhagat is coming all the way to Florida tomorrow. I'd like to know what the fuck is going on that I haven't yet been told.'

Noah shot Alyssa an apologetic look. 'Excuse his language,' he said. 'He's still acting out against his father.'

'That's not funny, fuckhead.' Sam's patience had obviously all been used up. 'And you goddamn well know it.'

Alyssa stood silently by as Noah was contrite. 'Sorry, Ringo. It's late and . . . I didn't mean to make light of you or any of this. You know that.'

Sam nodded, his anger instantly evaporated. 'Yeah. I'm sorry, too.'

Noah took out his cell phone again. 'I'll catch a cab home,' he said. 'The sooner you guys talk, the sooner Sam here can try to get some sleep.'

'That's not necessary,' Sam said, but Noah was already walking away.

'Call me tomorrow, brother. Hey, call me tonight if you want to talk. Or just come on over. You know the way. I'm here if you need me, man. Day or night.'

'I know. Thanks, Nos. Thank Claire again, too.'

'Will do.'

Alyssa could have sworn she saw a glint of tears in Sam's eyes. But then he turned toward her, and beneath the bill of his baseball cap, his expression was grim.

'What haven't you told me?' he asked.

It was after 2100 before the door to the spartan bachelor officers quarters opened to reveal Kelly standing in the corridor with the guards.

'Hi,' she said.

Tom stood up from the desk where he'd been making notes on a legal pad that the lieutenant from the JAG office had left behind. 'Hey. I am so sorry. They wouldn't let me call you.'

'I figured,' she said. She was wearing that dress that he loved – the one with the sweeping long skirt and the print with the tiny blue flowers that matched the color of her eyes. With her hair down around her shoulders, she looked sweetly feminine and barely old enough to drink.

She looked completely harmless. Which was obviously her intention.

'Five minutes,' one of the guards told her now. 'Sorry it's so short, ma'am, but I'm not supposed to let you in here at all.'

'I know, and thank you so much.' She was holding Tom's dress uniform – his choker whites – still under the plastic from the dry cleaners. She brought it inside the room and hung it in the closet as the guard left the door just slightly ajar. She had the box that held his medals, too, and she set that down on the bed. 'I thought you might need these.'

'Yeah,' he said. 'I don't know if it'll help, but it sure as hell can't hurt.'

She stood there then, just looking at him, a flash of color in the otherwise antiseptic room. Worry for him radiated from her.

'Nobody's told me anything,' Kelly said. 'Just that they were holding you here. I couldn't even get them to tell me how long they intended to keep you. And they wouldn't let me in to see you, wouldn't even let me call. Admiral Tucker's been particularly nasty. He says I have no rights – that technically I'm not even allowed onto the base because we're not married.'

'I'm sorry,' he said.

'Tom, what is going on?'

'I don't exactly know,' he said. 'I haven't been able to get many answers from anyone, either. But it's, uh, bad, I think. I haven't been charged with anything, but the implications . . .'

'What do they think you've done?'

Tom shook his head, hating to have to tell her. It would almost be easier to list the things they thought he *hadn't* done. 'I don't know for sure, but from the questions I've been asked, I think they want to try to charge me with providing assistance to known terrorists, theft and sale of weapons and/or government property, conspiracy to assassinate the United States President, and oh, yeah, the big T. Treason.'

Kelly was gaping at him. He'd managed to shock her completely, twice in one day. 'That's absurd!'

'Yeah, well, they don't think so,' he told her. 'There's this senate investigation thing going on and, I don't know, some kind of bullshit-squad fingerpointing antiterrorism subcommittee from hell that's really doing little more than providing some nasty politicians with a whole lot of airtime on CNN.'

'They honestly think you've been *providing assistance* to *terrorists*?'

He motioned for her to keep her voice down, and she glanced back at the open door.

'They can't be serious,' she said more quietly but no less intensely. 'Tom, anyone who knows you—'

'Yeah, that's the thing,' Tom said. 'They kind of waited to do this until Team Sixteen was out of town. And Admiral Crowley's still in the Middle East. He won't be back until the end of the month.'

Admiral Chip Crowley was a SEAL himself. He was the commander of Naval Special Warfare Command, and in the past he'd been one of Tom's staunchest supporters.

'They've been asking a lot of questions about an incident that happened about a year and a half ago,' Tom continued. 'An Army helo went down in a lake in . . .' He didn't know how much of this he was at liberty to tell her. Up until a few hours ago, he'd believed it was still classified information. But if everyone and their uncle in the US Senate knew about it . . . Still, until the word came down his chain of command, he was going to keep it cryptic. Kelly was smart enough – she'd figure out what he was saying without his saying it. 'A country that Team Sixteen visited recently.

'It was carrying certain essential equipment when it crash landed,' he told Kelly. 'The flight crew was rescued by Air Force PJs, but the helo sank. The lake was pretty deep, so Team Sixteen came in to try to salvage both it and that equipment, but it turned out to be too much of an al-Qaeda hot spot. It's hard to run a salvage op in the middle of a firefight, so we ended up scuttling the helo and everything on board. I signed off on it – that all that equipment was properly destroyed.

'No one's told me directly,' he continued, 'but I've been getting a pretty strong hint that some of that equipment has since surfaced.' He could tell from her eyes that Kelly knew damn well that the equipment he was referring to was weapons. 'And I know I'm prone to coming up with the worst-case scenario, but I'm starting to believe that that *equipment* surfaced in Coronado last year, when the President was attacked.'

'What?' Kelly breathed.

'Maybe I'm wrong – no one's telling me anything. But the questions they're asking make me think that's what happened.'

'Could it be coincidence?' she asked. 'Or—'

'A setup,' he grimly finished for her.

'But who?'

'I don't know.'

Kelly started to pace. 'Were you part of the team that did the dive and set the explosives?'

She was going to hate hearing this. 'No, but I was part of the team that went down after to make sure the explosives did the trick.'

And he'd gotten shot on his way back out of the water. It wasn't serious, little more than a nasty nick on his left forearm. Kelly had looked at him hard when he came home, and he'd skillfully avoided all of her questions, letting her believe without flat-out lying that he'd cut himself while climbing into a helo.

Which was pretty much the truth. He'd just happened to cut himself on a ricocheting bullet.

But right now she was distracted by the time – they had very little of those five minutes left – and she didn't connect that op to his injury.

'Who went down to rig the explosives?' she asked him.

Tom was already shaking his head. 'No,' he said. 'No way, Kel. It was Sam Starrett and Cosmo Richter and I'm pretty sure Ken Karmody. And a bunch of the tadpoles. Gilligan, Muldoon, Lopez, and maybe Silverman. Oh, and Mark Jenkins, too. I've been sitting here trying to remember the details of that op. One thing I do know for sure is that those men – any of my men in Team Sixteen – would rather die before letting terrorists get their hands on that kind of . . . essential equipment.'

She nodded. 'I know you believe that, but—'

'What I've been trying to remember is the timeline of the events. When did the Black Hawk go down? How long was the flight crew in the water before the PJs got them out? How long before Starrett and his squad made the scene?'

Tom rubbed the back of his neck. 'One thing I didn't do was order an inventory of the equipment that was submerged in that lake. The cargo area of the helo was intact – I do remember Starrett including that information in his report. His team didn't have to search for stray crates scattered at the bottom of that lake. But we didn't have the time or resources to open boxes or even count them. I had an inventory list that had been made when the helo was loaded. I signed off on that equipment, saying that it had been destroyed, but there were quite a few opportunities for some of that stuff to walk away pretty much anywhere down the line. All I know for sure is that *I* didn't take it, and *my men* didn't take it.' He sighed. 'I've told this to the investigators about fifteen thousand times. But it's not getting through. It's like some kind of witch-hunt, Kel. They only hear what they want to hear.'

'What can I do to help?' Kelly asked.

'I don't know,' Tom said. He reached for her, and she went into his arms, holding him as tightly as he held her. 'I honest to God don't know.'

Four

'What kind of freaking idiots would think for even half a second that Lieutenant Commander Paoletti could be part of a terrorist plot to assassinate the President?' Sam Starrett was incredulous.

Alyssa knew exactly what he was feeling. To anyone who'd worked with Tom Paoletti, the idea was inconceivable. 'The kind of idiot whose job depends on him successfully blaming *some*one. There are a lot of frightened people out there who only know that three terrorists managed to get three very deadly weapons past the high-level security of a United States naval base and discharge those weapons at the US President,' she told him as they headed downtown in her rental car.

The streetlight filtered in through the windshield, casting shadows on Sam's face. This was surreal. That she was sitting in a car in Sarasota, Florida, with Lt Roger 'Sam' Starrett and discussing the fact that Tom Paoletti had been brought in for questioning in connection to a terrorist attack on US soil was completely surreal.

'We're the most powerful nation in the world, and those men came into *our* country, onto one of *our* military bases, and nearly managed to kill our leader,' she continued. 'And here we sit, looking foolish, because we *still* don't know much more about who was behind this attack than we did just a few days after it happened.'

'Don't you think it's possible that those three shooters planned it themselves, without any outside help?'

'Only one of them wore a radio,' Alyssa told him. 'The others didn't. As far as we can tell, the radioman signaled the two other men to let them know that the shooting was going to start by putting on a white baseball cap.'

'Yeah, I know that.'

That's right. Sam had been there.

'Maybe that radio was just a mindfuck,' he said. 'Maybe there was no one else involved. Maybe the real terrorist act wasn't the shooting. Maybe the real terrorism is in the way this investigation has tied up the FBI for all these months.'

Alyssa shook her head. 'No,' she said. 'There's more. We know all three of the shooters entered the base as part of a group tour four days before the President's visit. Someone helped them join that tour. We also found information on their computer hard drive that provides evidence to the fact they had help both obtaining those weapons and transporting them onto the base.'

'But nothing that IDs exactly who it was who helped, right?' Sam laughed. 'If I were a terrorist, I'd leave shit like that behind, too, to confuse the hell out of the infidels.'

'We have an extra set of fingerprints on one of the weapons, belonging to a still unidentified person known as Lady X, believed to be female from the size of the prints.'

'Big deal. All that means is Abdul duk Fukkar got himself laid before he went to his heavenly reward. Just in case there really weren't seventy-two virgins waiting there for him. 'Hey, baby, want to touch my gun?' It's amazing how often that line gets results.'

'Okay, work this into your mindfuck theory, Starrett,' Alyssa challenged him. 'We have a 911 call that warns of the attack. It came in right as the first shots were fired. It was made from a public phone on the base, also by an unidentified female. By the time we located that pay phone, we were unable to get any readable fingerprints – although there are some who theorize the voice on the tape belongs to that same Lady X.'

She glanced at him.

But Sam just shrugged. 'If I were duk Fukkar, I'd leave the gun-toucher a little note telling her what's going to go down. Just to add to the confusion. So maybe that tape is your Lady X.'

'So where is she?' Alyssa asked. 'Why would she make that call and then drop off the face of the earth if she *weren't* somehow involved?'

'Maybe she didn't want to go down in history as the woman who laid some terrorist loser who then tried to kill the President.'

She braked as the traffic light in front of them turned yellow and then red. 'Maybe she loved him. Maybe he conned her into believing that they had a future. Or maybe he loved her, too. Maybe he fell in love with her and left a note to try to explain.'

Sam laughed. 'Yeah, I'm sure that's what happened. No, thanks, I'll stick to my mindfuck theory.'

'It's just that we've traced the shooters' trails back over the past two years of their lives, and we still have no clue as to how they got those weapons onto the base. We don't know much, but we *do* know that none of the three terrorists was a rocket scientist. It's hard to believe they'd be able to mastermind an assassination attempt on this scale. I mean, how did they even know that the President was coming to the base in Coronado?'

'Maybe it was just dumb luck,' Sam suggested. 'Maybe their original target was Admiral Crowley.'

'Or maybe someone else *was* involved. There's a theory out there that the weapons were placed on the base – hidden there, waiting for them. All they had to do was pick them up.'

'I can tell you who *wasn't* involved,' Sam countered. 'Lieutenant Commander Paoletti. He saved hundreds of lives that day. He should get a medal instead of being locked up and treated like some kind of criminal.'

'I'm with you on that,' Alyssa said. And when he looked over at her and into her eyes, she had another flash of unreality. She and Sam were in complete and total agreement about something.

Something that had absolutely nothing to do with sex.

They'd agreed quite passionately, and in rather loud unison, in the past when it came to having sex, but to little else.

The traffic light turned green, and she pulled her gaze back to the road.

'So how can I help him?' Sam said simply.

'You can start by providing a written and verified account of where you spent your time over the past few weeks,' she told him, 'so we can officially cross you off Conseco's list of suspected murderers.'

He understood why, and he nodded. 'I'll do that tonight.'

Alyssa glanced at him again. 'Will you be able to account for all your time?'

'I don't know,' he said. 'Yeah. I think so. I mean, I haven't been doing much of anything. I was either out of the country with the team, or . . . shoot, I don't know. Watching TV.' He glanced at her. 'Either alone or with my neighbor Don DaCosta. Who's mentally ill. The aluminum-foil-on-his-head-to-keep-aliens-from-reading-his-mind kind of mentally ill. He's not the best alibi, but that's what I did. Football, basketball and hockey with crazy Donny DaCosta. Once or twice I went to Nils and Meg's, or Savannah and Ken's for dinner. They always wondered where Mary Lou was. It was . . . weird.'

She knew what he was telling her, and she found it very hard to believe. Sam Starrett without female companionship for six solid months? She purposely kept the conversation directly on topic. 'Then we'll have to provide an alibi from your work schedule.'

'That I can do. I went into the base early and stayed late. And I did some, you know, volunteer shit, too. Believe me, I was never home from the base long enough to get out to Florida and back. I'm pretty sure I can prove that.'

Volunteer shit. Wasn't that interesting? Alyssa had heard through the Spec Op grapevine that Team Sixteen had done some kind of program at an inner city high school in Los Angeles.

She tried to picture Sam with high school students and had to fight to keep herself from smiling.

'You know, I've been thinking about this,' Sam mused, 'and it makes sense that it's Janine, not Mary Lou, who's dead. Janine just split up from her husband – a guy named Clyde Wrigley. Although, Jesus, I met him a few times and he's like some kind of throwback to 1972. A real pothead hippie type. Soft-spoken, you know? I'm not sure I ever saw him get up off the couch. I can't picture him getting closer than ten feet to a shotgun.' He laughed with disgust. 'As far as shotgun-wielding types go, I'm the one who fits that bill, huh?'

Alyssa sensed more than saw him turn toward her in the dim light from the dashboard. His voice was soft in the darkness. 'Thanks for believing me, Lys.'

'You're not a killer.'

He laughed quietly. 'You left off the first part of that – "You might be an asshole, Roger, but you're not a killer."' He did a very decent imitation of her voice.

She had to laugh. 'You said it, I didn't.'

'I made a shitload of mistakes in the past few years,' he told her. 'But none of them involved a shotgun.'

What could she say to that? Alyssa just drove, wishing she knew where she was going. Her hotel was around here somewhere, but she was *not* taking him there. Maybe there was an all-night restaurant they could go to. Have a cup of coffee. Then go their separate ways for the night – and hopefully for the rest of their lives.

Sam cleared his throat. 'This is where you're supposed to tell me you're not seeing Max anymore.'

It was too dark in the car for her to see his eyes. Was he actually serious?

'If Mary Lou's alive, you're still married.' Oh damn, why in hell had she said *that*? It sounded as if she were interested in –

'No, I'm not,' Sam said, still in that same quiet voice. 'She signed those papers. As soon as the lawyer gets them, they'll be filed, and our divorce will be official. I spoke to Manny Conseco about it – those papers are evidence, but they'll get copies notarized and sent to San Diego.'

'Don't you have better things to think about – like the whereabouts of your daughter?' Well, that came out a little more sharply than she'd intended. But maybe that was just as well.

Sam was single again, and, now that it was convenient for him, he wanted to get back into her pants. Like that was a big surprise.

But she only had to keep him at a distance for a while. Max would be in town tomorrow, thank goodness. And if she was lucky, he'd send her back to DC.

Alyssa wasn't one to run away, but this was so much harder than she'd anticipated. And she'd anticipated that seeing Sam again was going to be very, very hard.

'Sorry. I'm . . .' He rubbed his forehead. 'Yeah. I'm just . . . a loser.' He looked at her with eyes that were clearly haunted. 'Do you think there's hope that Haley's still alive?'

'I don't know,' Alyssa had to tell him.

'I haven't seen her in six months,' Sam said wearily. 'I don't even know if I'll recognize her.'

'How could you have let six months pass without even having gone to see your daughter?' Alyssa shook her head both at him and at the disbelief that rang in her voice. 'Don't answer that. That has nothing to do with this investigation. I'm sorry for—'

'Getting personal?' he finished for her. 'Like you said to Noah – we're friends. And you were right. We *are* friends, Alyssa. I value your friendship very much, and what you asked was a very valid question for one friend to ask another.' He sighed. 'I guess I have to tell you honestly that I didn't try very hard to visit. I made plans a few times to come out here for the weekend, but every time I did that, the team either went OUTCONUS or Mary Lou canceled on me.

'I might be a lousy father,' he continued, 'but just for the record, it doesn't mean that I didn't miss Haley.'

Alyssa was silent, afraid that he was going to tell her more, and afraid that he wasn't.

'You know, Mary Lou used to go out to meetings. AA meetings,' Sam said. 'She had one mapped out for nearly every night of the week. I spent a lot of those nights with Haley. And yeah, I know, it was only a few hours compared to the time Mary Lou spent with her during the day, but still . . . We had this agreement, me and Hale. I wouldn't put her in the playpen unless I was in there, too – I mean, who could put their kid in a cage like that? – and she wouldn't crap in her diaper.' He laughed. 'I kept my end of the bargain, but she didn't. You should have seen me the first time I changed one of those diapers, you know the kind filled with that really special type of baby poo? It's amazing how after the fortieth or forty-first time you pretty much get used to it.' He laughed again. 'God, you know you're pathetic when you even miss your kid's dirty diapers.'

He was silent for a minute, and then he said, 'She used to fall asleep just, like, lying on my chest. You know, watching a football game or something. It was . . .' He stopped and cleared his throat. 'It was something I missed very much when she was gone.'

'I'm sorry,' Alyssa said softly.

'Yeah,' Sam said. 'Me, too.' He took a deep breath and blew it out hard. 'I figure I'll take a ride north tomorrow. Mary Lou's mother lives somewhere up near Jacksonville, I think. I'm not sure where it is – I need to look at a map to jog my memory. I doubt that Mary Lou or Janine would've brought Haley there, but she might know something.'

'You should let the FBI handle this investigation.'

'Yeah, right.' He laughed his disgust. 'You've done so well with the whole Coronado terrorist case. I'll just sit back and wait for you to deliver Haley to me. Sometime before her eighteenth birthday.'

Her cell phone rang, and she flipped it open. 'Locke.'

'Conseco,' the head of the Sarasota office said. 'We've IDed the victim as Janine Morrison Wrigley. We've got APBs out on both her ex-husband and the missing sister and kid. I'll keep you posted as we get more information.'

'Thank you,' Alyssa said. She hung up the phone and turned to Sam, who was watching her intently. 'It wasn't Mary Lou.'

'Oh, God, oh, Jesus, thank you,' he said, then covered his face with his hands.

He just sat there, head bowed, completely silent. Alyssa wasn't even sure if he was breathing.

But then he drew in a deep breath, and let it out in a hard exhale as he ran his hands down his face. 'I'm okay,' he said. 'I'm just . . . a little . . .'

'It's all right,' she said quietly. 'You don't have to say anything.'

It was several long moments before he spoke.

'It was Janine?' he asked.

'Yeah,' she told him. 'They're looking for her ex-husband, Clyde.'

'You up for a drive?' Sam asked, finally looking over at her. 'Because I know where to find him.'

Haley was gone.

Mary Lou Morrison Starrett's mood went from euphoric to terrified as she searched the small au pair apartment that she shared with her daughter, and then ran down the hall to Amanda's bedroom and then to Whitney's suite.

The good news was that Whitney wasn't lying dead on the floor, her hair soaked with blood.

In all likelihood, the girl had taken Haley and Amanda, her own daughter – born when Whitney was barely fifteen – to the beach.

Still, Mary Lou's hands shook as she picked up the phone and dialed Whitney's cell phone number.

The girl answered it on the third ring. ''Lo?' Amanda was wailing in the background.

'Whitney!' Praise God. The cell phone signal out here in Nowheresville was spotty at best. 'It's Ma – Constance.' Connie, not Mary Lou. Connie, Connie, Connie. She was Connie Grant, who had a *son*, Chris. Haley had balked at a name change until Mary Lou had suggested she pick one herself. Her first choice was Daddy, which had made Mary Lou pause. Her second was Pooh, which also didn't work. The third time was a charm, thank the Lord, with Christopher Robin, which fit right in with Mary Lou's plan to pass her off as a little boy. 'Where *are* you?'

She never raised her voice to Whitney, and right now it took everything she had in her to keep from shrieking at the teenager.

'Almost home. We're nearly at the gate. We'll be in the garage in about three minutes,' Whitney reported. 'Are you and Daddy through? Meet us down there and take the screaming monster out of her car seat. You know, I don't get it. Chris doesn't have shitfits in the middle of Starbucks.'

'Please watch your language in front of the children,' Mary Lou said, working hard to keep her voice calm and in control, closing her eyes and silently invoking Ihbraham Rahman's gentle spirit. Lord, she missed him so much there were times she doubled over from the pain.

If she lost her temper and let on that foul words in front of Haley and Amanda were a serious problem, Whitney would use them *more* frequently, instead of less.

The truth was, Amanda's misbehaving had more to do with the fact that she had been unlucky enough to be born to a rich spoiled brat who was little more than a petulant infant herself.

Whitney Turlington was the bane of Mary Lou's existence – yet she was also her savior. In the past two years of Amanda's life, more than two dozen au pairs had run screaming from the palatial Florida mansion where Amanda and Whitney lived with

Whitney's very wealthy father, Frank. They hadn't run from Amanda, who wasn't the terror everyone made her out to be, but rather from Whitney, who was.

Barely seventeen and constantly at war with King Frank, Whitney Turlington was a bitch on wheels.

But because of that, King Frank hadn't called a single one of Connie Grant's faked references when Mary Lou had applied for the position. He'd just been downright grateful *some*one had showed up for the job interview at all.

Which meant that, at least for now, Mary Lou and Haley had found a safe place to hide in the Turlington's private little compound just southwest of Sarasota – not twenty miles from the house where Janine lay dead in the kitchen.

No one had found her yet.

Mary Lou watched the local news every night, praying that someone would find her sister and give her a proper, decent Christian burial.

She also prayed that the men who killed Janine wouldn't find her and Haley.

Her ex-husband, Sam, the Navy SEAL, had once told her that the smartest place to hide was back where everyone had already searched. So she'd maxed out her credit card in Jacksonville, making it look as if she were heading north, while at the same time buying everything she hadn't been able to take from Janine's house when she'd left town on that awful evening.

One of her first stops had been at a beauty parlor where Haley's golden curls had been cut boyishly short. Mary Lou had her own hair cut, too, and went blond, telling the beautician to match the shade with Haley's.

The next stop had been Sears, where, while Haley wasn't looking, Mary Lou had bought a brand-new Pooh Bear. She'd given it to her daughter, pretending she'd found it at the bottom of her big purse. Haley had looked suspiciously at the new stuffed animal's gleaming golden fur and clean red shirt, but Mary Lou had chattered on about how she'd taken Pooh to the beauty parlor, too, and had his fur 'done' while they were there, same as Mama's hair.

She'd bought them clothes – Haley's from the little boy's section of the store – and luggage on little rollers. They'd headed to Gainesville, ditched the car, and boarded a bus back to Sarasota, where Mary Lou had seen Frank Turlington's desperate ad for an au pair hanging on the community message board in the grocery store where she used to work. It had been there close to six months ago, when she'd first started as a cashier, and a month later, when she'd been about to take it down, her assistant manager had stopped her. Even though the store managers had a rule against signs hanging on the board for longer than a few weeks, the woman gave her the scoop on the Turlingtons, telling her that King Frank – as he was called by the locals – might as well put in a revolving door at the front of his house. Because a few days after a new au pair went in, she'd come shooting out again.

Mary Lou had been here now for almost three weeks, which was breaking the official Turlington au pair stamina record by thirteen days.

And then word had come down from Mrs Downs, the housekeeper, that King Frank had requested Mary Lou's – Connie's – presence at breakfast today. At 7:00 A.M. He'd even given the royal order for Whitney to wake up early and keep an eye on Amanda and Haley while Connie was meeting with him.

Before she'd made the marathon run to the wing with the dining room, Mary Lou had taken Haley to the bathroom at least two dozen times, cursing the fact that her daughter had been potty trained – early – for a full month now. She tried to put a Pull-Ups on Haley, tried to tell her daughter not to drink, tried to caution her not to ask Whitney for help in the bathroom, told her to wait to pee until Mommy came back.

Haley had blinked at her and then returned to staring at *Sesame Street*.

GONE TOO FAR

Whitney had staggered in at 6:57, and Mary Lou had sprinted to the dining room, risking one of Mrs Downs's 'the hired help moves silently throughout the house' lectures.

She'd arrived at 6:59, dressed in Connie's most conservative beige slacks and a pastel blue blouse. And then she'd sat off to the side and waited for more than ninety minutes while King Frank talked on the phone to someone in San Francisco named Steve about acquiring one of Wyatt Earp's six-shooters for his vast gun collection.

Finally, King Frank got off the phone, ate half a corn muffin, and then turned his attention to Mary Lou.

At first she thought she was being let go, because he told her that he'd decided to send Whitney into a special rehab-type program. Starting in two weeks, she would be gone for three months. And she'd be taking Amanda with her.

But then he gave Mary Lou a contract that, if she signed, would give her five thousand dollars a month – including the months Whitney would be away – provided she stayed a full year. If she didn't stay the year, she'd receive only five hundred dollars a month.

The catch was that King Frank was going to Europe this afternoon. Something important had come up, and he wouldn't be back until August. And Mrs Downs's niece was getting married in Atlanta on Friday. She was leaving tonight, and would be gone most of the two weeks before Whitney and Amanda were scheduled to leave, too.

Starting in just a few hours, Mary Lou would be alone in the house with the devil child and her offspring. The security guards would remain on duty down by the gate, and although they did a daily check of the compound to make sure the two empty guest houses were secure, they rarely did more than walk in a circle around the main house.

Of course, she'd signed. She'd had her pen out and ready the moment King Frank had uttered the words *five thousand*. These next few weeks might actually be easier with no one around for

Whitney to piss off. She'd try plenty, but Mary Lou had learned early on to let it bounce right off.

But now Whitney had taken Haley to *Starbucks*.

Mary Lou ran into the garage just as the convertible pulled inside.

And the reality of the situation hit Mary Lou. That girl had taken Haley all the long way to town. In a convertible with the top down.

Where anyone might have seen her.

You did not have my permission to take Chris into town. Mary Lou clenched her teeth over the words. If she uttered them, then Whitney would know that she'd found Mary Lou's weakness. And then the girl would have the upper hand.

Lord help her, she needed a drink.

'Please ask me next time you decide to take Chris to town,' Mary Lou said instead.

'You were busy and I needed a cup of coffee.'

'There's coffee in the kitchen.' Mary Lou worked to make her voice calm. Unaffected. She lifted howling Amanda out of her car seat and held her close. 'Shhh, honey, it's all right.'

'Yeah, well, I needed a *Starbucks*.'

What Whitney had needed was to see Peter Young, the loser of the moment, the boy who was currently using her for sex.

Had she left Haley and Amanda alone in the car, in the parking lot, while she and Peter had gone into the bathroom and . . .?

Mary Lou wanted to break Whitney's nose.

But there was a gleam in her blue eyes that Mary Lou didn't like. And Whitney's smile was just a little too satisfied.

'You know,' Whitney said, 'Chris had to pee on the way home, so we pulled off the road and—'

Damn it!

'—wasn't *that* a surprise.'

Mary Lou made shushing noises as she hugged Amanda,

crossing around to the other side of the car to get Haley out of the car, too.

'I'm going to tell my father that you're a liar,' Whitney singsonged.

Mary Lou had both children in her arms now, one on either hip. She went to the far end of the five-bay garage and put them down near an open area dedicated to Amanda's Big Wheel. Amanda, five months older, would ride, and Haley would watch, all big eyes.

Now what? The thought of murdering Whitney and hiding the body actually crossed her mind. Amanda wouldn't miss her, and Frank would probably be relieved.

No, she and Haley would have to leave. They'd have to pack up and move on. *Damn* it. Five thousand *dollars* a month. She'd been so close.

Unless . . .

Lord, it was worth a try. She marched all the way across the garage, back to Whitney. 'I need your help.'

Whitney blinked. Probably because no one had ever said those words to her before.

'My ex-husband wants me dead,' Mary Lou lied, saying a silent apology to Sam, who had never hit her and would probably die before laying a hand on a woman. 'I left him before he could beat the life out of me, and now he's hunting me down.'

She hoped that Whitney wouldn't recognize the plot from that J. Lo movie she'd rented last week. The truth of Mary Lou's situation was too complicated. But spouse abuse – now, that was something Whitney could relate to. Apparently Amanda's father had had quite a right hook. 'He's crazy,' she continued, 'and he says if he can't have me, no one will, so I changed my name and got this job here with you so I could hide from him.

'He doesn't know I'm in Sarasota,' she told the girl, who was definitely listening. 'I left a false trail to make him think I was up north. But I used to live in Sarasota, so he might have people watching for me here. Or watching for Chris, who, yes, is a girl.

Our lives depend on our being able to stay here, in this compound, where as few people as possible can see us. So I need you to promise that you will never take Chris anywhere again without asking me first.'

Whitney was silent for a moment. 'What's your real name?' she asked.

'Wendy,' Mary Lou lied, praying she was doing the right thing by telling Whitney this. 'I'm not going to tell you my last name.'

Whitney thought about that a little bit longer. 'I should still tell Daddy.'

'If you do,' Mary Lou pointed out, 'you'll find yourself with a new au pair. One who spies on you and tells your father when you sneak out at night to see Peter.'

On the other side of the garage, Amanda was driving in circles around Haley, who was laughing. Lord, she didn't want to leave. Where would they go?

Early on, she'd found that the key to communicating with Whitney was to always be the one to end the conversation. Always be first to walk away.

'Who wants a snack?' Mary Lou asked Amanda and Haley as she crossed the garage toward them.

Please Lord, don't let Whitney tell.

'So.' Elliot glanced over his shoulder toward the other members of Dennis Mattson's yacht crew waiting for him farther down the dock.

'So,' Gina Vitagliano said, pulling a strand of sea-wind-whipped hair from the corner of her mouth and tucking it back into her ponytail. She was determined not to make this easier for him, the jerk.

Although to be fair, Elliot was the sweetest, kindest jerk she'd ever met.

'I'm sorry things didn't work out between us,' he said, and actually managed to sound like he meant it. Because he probably *did* mean it.

'Yeah,' she said. 'Me, too. I was . . .' Come on, Gina, just be honest. It wasn't like she was ever going to see him again in her entire life. 'I was disappointed that we didn't get together.'

'I'm sorry,' he said again. 'I just . . . I couldn't. Not after you told me . . .'

'Yeah, right,' Gina said. 'Dead horse. I'm glad we were friends, Elliot. Good luck in St Thomas, okay?'

'Thanks.' His eyes were such a warm shade of dark brown, it was impossible to tell where the iris ended and the pupil began. It was his eyes that had attracted her to him in the first place.

They'd reminded her of Max.

'So what's your plan?' Elliot asked her.

It was funny, because other than his dark hair and eyes, Elliot looked nothing like Max Bhagat.

Max wasn't as tall, and he wasn't the same kind of handsome. He was swarthier – his father had been a native of India. And he was older. He had at least fifteen years on Elliot, twenty years on Gina. And Max was the head of an FBI counterterrorist unit. He was an experienced FBI negotiator who spent his days saving lives.

Elliot was the cook aboard a rich man's racing yacht.

But, like Max, he'd listened when Gina talked. Or at least he'd listened to a point. But then Elliot had stopped listening, because he didn't like what she was telling him. He didn't really want to hear what she had to say.

'I'm going to do it,' she told him now, because this topic was relatively safe and he was listening again. 'I'm going overseas. I've got a few more things to do for Dennis here in Tampa, and I'm doing that gig at the jazz club down in Sarasota, you know, filling in for a friend. But then I'm flying back to New York to spend a few days with my family, and after that . . . I'm going to Africa. I actually bought the airline ticket this morning.'

Gina still had enough money from the World Airlines settlement. She could kick around for two, three more years at least without having to make any decisions as to what she wanted to do with the rest of her life.

'That's great,' Elliot told her, his voice warm with sincerity. 'I think that's really great, Gina.'

Across the marina, his friends were getting restless. She smiled at him. 'You better go.'

'I'll miss you,' he said, giving her an awkward hug. 'I think you're the bravest person I've ever met.'

'Yeah,' she said with a laugh, trying to turn it into a joke. 'Brave. That's me. Wonder Woman. Right.'

'I'm serious.'

'Yeah,' she said. 'Well, don't be. Too many people are too serious. Life's too short. Didn't I teach you anything these past six weeks?'

Life was *indeed* too short. And the next time she was thinking about getting naked with a guy she liked enough to get naked with, she wasn't going to blurt out the fact that she'd spent four days as a hostage of Kazbekistani terrorists on a hijacked airliner. And she certainly wasn't going to mention being violently attacked and . . .

'Still, when I think about what you went through . . .'

'It wasn't that bad,' Gina lied. 'Go.'

He went, taking his Max Bhagat knockoff eyes with him.

Gina climbed into the rental car and headed back to the hotel, hoping that sooner or later she'd find whatever it was that she was so desperately looking for.

Or that Max would call her again.

Five

'You sure there's nothing I can do?' Noah asked, speaking quietly so that he wouldn't wake Claire.

'Yeah, I'm sure.' Sam sounded exhausted. 'Look, I gotta run.'

'Run where? Come on, Ringo. Call it a day and get some sleep.'

'I'll call you tomorrow,' Sam said.

'Thanks again for letting me know that it wasn't Mary Lou,' Noah said.

He hung up the phone and slipped out of bed, heading in his bare feet for the kitchen. The light was on under Dora's door and he could hear music playing softly. How had he become old enough to have a kid who stayed up later than her parents?

Truth was, it wasn't old age or fatigue that had put him in bed at such an early hour. It was Claire, making all of those 'Gee, I'm tired, I'm going to turn in early' comments out in the living room.

Noah had grabbed Devin, scrubbed his face and brushed his teeth and read him a quick chapter of the latest Lemony Snicket, all in record time, only to join Claire in bed and find out that she really *was* tired.

She'd rolled over and fallen asleep almost immediately, leaving him wide awake and wondering if maybe they couldn't reschedule that 'lunch' for tomorrow.

Now he opened the refrigerator and stared inside for so long, he could almost hear his grandfather's voice chastising him for attempting to refrigerate the entire kitchen. 'If whatever culinary

89

delight you're looking for isn't there inside that first minute, Nostradamus my boy, it's *still* not going to be there five minutes later.'

Noah grabbed a bottle of beer, twisting off the top as he shut the refrigerator door.

He sat on the mismatched stool at the breakfast counter – the creaky one that he'd taken from the kitchen in the assisted living condo after his grandfather had passed – and drank his beer.

He was such a whiny baby. So his wife didn't want to have sex with him tonight. So she really was tired. As Sam/Roger/Ringo would have said, 'Big deal, fuckhead.'

At least he knew where his wife and children were tonight. And no one had recently gunned down any of his in-laws in the kitchen of their house.

Ever since seventh grade, Noah had compared his life to Sam's and found solid reasons to count his blessings.

It had started early on in their friendship, about three weeks after Roger had started coming over to Noah's house every day after school. And he was Roger back then. He didn't start calling himself Ringo until eighth grade.

It was a Saturday, and he and Roger had made plans to ride their bikes down to the mall. Noah needed a present for his grandparents' wedding anniversary, and Roger was going to help him pick something out.

Only he didn't show.

Noah finally rode his bike over to Roger's house. He'd never been there before, but he knew where it was.

The lawn was freshly cut, and a gray-haired man with a crew cut and a stern face who must've been Roger's father was up on a ladder, repairing the gutter that hung on the edge of the porch roof.

Noah rode into the driveway and braked to a stop. 'Good morning, sir. Is Roger home?'

Roger's father did a double take, then looked at him a good

long time. 'No,' he finally said, giving Noah the back of his head.

It was funny. Kids were required to be polite to grown-ups at all times, but grown-ups could be flat-out rude to kids whenever they felt like it.

Fuming and indignant, Noah got back on his bike and headed for home.

He didn't see Roger until Monday, at school.

And that was a shock, because Roger looked like he'd gone head to head with a Greyhound bus. He had a black eye and a swollen mouth and cut lip, and he was walking like his rear end was on fire.

'What happened to you?' Becky Jurgens asked.

'Nothin',' Roger said.

But Noah knew it wasn't nothing. He stood there, staring at Roger, thinking of something he'd said, early in their friendship. It was about Walt, about the size of his enormous hands.

'Jesus,' Roger had said, 'it must hurt like a bitch when he hits you.'

At the time, Noah had laughed at the absurdity of that. He'd never seen his grandfather hit anyone.

He hadn't thought twice about it, but now it made too much sense.

Roger's father had happened to Roger. There was no doubt about it.

But Roger avoided him all day. It wasn't until after the last bell that Noah intercepted him.

'Why did he hit you?' Noah asked, getting right to the point, sick to his stomach with fear that the reason was one he already knew.

Roger didn't play dumb. He didn't deny that his father had beaten the crap out of him. But he did try to shrug it off. 'He always hits me when he gets home from a long trip. There's always something I've done that pisses him off.'

Noah went even more point-blank. 'Was it because he doesn't want you to be friends with me? Because I'm black?'

'Fuck him.' Roger spat on the ground. 'I'll be friends with whoever the fuck I want.'

Noah had wanted to cry. But Roger obviously wanted to pretend everything was fine.

Still, they took a short cut through the woods and through neighbors' yards to get to Noah's house, instead of walking home on the sidewalk, where they might've been seen.

His own father had died in Vietnam when Noah was just a baby. His mother had died about a year later. Of grief, Grandpa said whenever Noah asked, but he knew she'd died in a car accident, after she'd had too much alcohol to drink. Maybe it was grief, or maybe it was just plain carelessness.

Noah could work himself into a 'poor little orphaned me' funk when he wanted to, but he knew that, compared to Roger, he had very little to complain about. He had Walt and Dot, both of whom loved him dearly, both of whom would die before they took a leather belt to his backside.

The walk home had Roger gritting his teeth. Noah made excuses so they could stop and rest a few times, and when they finally reached his house, he made Roger settle back on the sofa.

'Wait here. There's something I want to show you,' Noah told him, and ran to get the top drawer from the built-ins in the formal dining room.

He carried the entire thing back and set it on the coffee table. There was enough stuff in there that Roger wouldn't have to get up off the couch until dinnertime.

'What's in there?' Roger asked. 'Can I see that?'

Noah knew he was hurting pretty badly because he didn't even lean forward to reach for the photo that was right on top. It was a grainy black-and-white picture of Walt – miraculously young – standing with a group of men next to a WWII fighter plane. Noah handed it over, pulling the entire table closer to Roger.

'It's papers and pictures and stuff,' Noah said. 'My grand-parents saved all their letters from the war. Some of them are pretty funny, and they're all really cool to read. Grandma was really good friends with Grandpa's first wife, Mae, and they saved all the letters they wrote to each other, too. Here, check this out. This one's from Grandpa: *Dear Dot, Whoo-whee!*'

'It doesn't say that,' Roger scoffed.

'Does too. Look.' Noah sat next to him on the couch, close enough so that Roger could see the letter, but not close enough to accidentally bump him and hurt him more.

Roger read aloud, slowly, trying to decipher Walt's cursive. *'We've gone up against the Germans and sent them running, weeping for their mothers! Hah! Finally, at last, we are part of this giant effort, this huge Allied machine, created to fight the Nazis' evil.'* He looked up at Noah. 'Cool. He writes just like he talks. *Oh, I know how jealous you must be, but it's such a thrill, one I can't begin to describe! (One I dare not describe in such detail to Mae.)* So that's kind of weird. He's still married to Mae, but he's writing to Dot?'

'They were all friends,' Noah told him. 'Grandma was a pilot – a WASP, they called 'em. It stood for Women Airforce Service Pilots. Before World War Two, women didn't do much of anything besides stay at home and take care of the house and kids. Then suddenly we were at war, and all the men joined the Army or Navy, and there were all these jobs that *some*one needed to do. So women stepped forward and said 'I can do that.' Grandma knew how to fly. Her first husband was a flier during World War One, and after he died, instead of selling his plane, she taught herself to fly it. Pilots were needed – even just to transport planes from one place to another in the United States – and she was one of the women who could do that. That's how she and Grandpa met. She was delivering a plane to his air base. She told me she and Grandpa didn't fall in love until a few years after Mae died.'

'Yeah, what's she going to tell you? That she was messing around with a married man?'

'No,' Noah said. 'That's not what happened.'

'Okay,' Roger said.

'It's not.'

'I said okay.'

'You said okay like you didn't mean it. There's letters and diaries and all kinds of stuff in here – there's three whole drawersful – that prove—'

'I believe you,' Roger said. 'Read the rest of that thing. I want to hear about how he killed all the Nazis.'

'Well, he doesn't go into detail about—

'Just read it, Nos.'

Noah cleared his throat. *'You should have seen the faces of the crews of the bombers when we landed and they found out that the pilots of their fighter escort – who had fought like the devil and not lost a single plane to the Nazis on that trip into Italy and back – were Negro men.*

'We're damn good, Dot. That isn't false bragging but the truth – our record is remarkable. True, we've flown only three missions, but each time all of the bombers have returned untouched. The bomber squadron COs have started to ask for us by name – a true double victory.

'I'm beyond proud to be part of this. It's true there is still much to overcome. My men – all officers – are billeted in places not fit for animals, while the white officers live in fancy hotels. Segregation is SOP, and disrespect is rampant.'

'What's SOP?' Roger asked.

'It's a military acronym. It's stands for standard operating procedure. And segregation is when white people and black people are kept apart. Like, here's a bathroom for white people only, and here's another bathroom – usually smaller and dirtier – for *colored folk.'*

'That sucks,' Roger said.

'Yeah. And it's weird reading these letters, too. All of them – Mae and Grandma and Grandpa – call black people Negroes or colored. At the time that was what African-Americans were called – it wasn't meant to be derogatory. It was pretty shocking the first time I read it, like, 'Whoa, Grandma, were you a racist, calling Grandpa colored?' But she's probably the least racist person I've ever known. The words are just words. She once told me if when you grow up, everyone points to the sky and says 'Blue,' then you call the sky blue. But if the sky turns around and tells you that it prefers to be called azure and that being called blue is derogatory, then you make sure you stop calling the sky blue. Even if you've been doing it all your life.'

'My father uses a word that's worse than those,' Roger said. 'I get the shit kicked out of me if I use any four-letter words in the house, and then he uses *that* word, like that one's okay with God.' He shook his head, like a baseball pitcher shaking off a catcher's signal. 'I don't want to talk about him. Read the rest.'

'*But when we're in the sky, and those dastardly Germans are trying to shoot down both us and the bombers we're protecting . . . Oh, don't those bomber pilots think of us as equals then!* That's it. He says, you know, *Write back soon, God bless and stay safe, write and tell me how Mae is feeling* – she was sick a lot – *sincerely, Walt.*'

'You know, your grandfather told me to call him Uncle Walt,' Roger said. 'You think that's okay? I mean, instead of Mr Gaines?'

'I'm sure it's okay,' Noah said, 'if that's what he told you.'

'He was a real hero in the war, wasn't he?' Roger asked, shifting on the sofa and wincing despite his attempts to hide how much his backside hurt.

'Yeah,' Noah said.

Roger was silent then, just looking at the picture of Walt and his squadron. 'I'm proud to know him,' he finally said. 'And I'm proud to know you, too.'

Noah wanted to cry. He knew that Roger didn't want to talk about his father, but he had to ask, 'Is he going to hit you again, just for coming over here?'

'I don't know,' Roger said, but it was obvious he was lying.

'Maybe, you know, you shouldn't come here when he's home,' Noah said. 'You said he wasn't home that often—'

'I like coming here.' Roger was trying hard not to cry now, too. 'I *hate* him.'

'I do, too,' Noah said. 'You know, when I turn eighteen, I'm going to join the Navy. I'm going to become a Navy SEAL, and then I'm going to come back to Fort Worth and scare the hell out of your father. I'm not going to kick his butt – that would be lowering myself to his level.' That was something Grandpa was always saying. *Don't lower yourself to their level.* 'But I'm going to scare him so much he messes his pants!'

Roger started to laugh at that, but almost immediately he was crying. Oh, he was pretending that he wasn't. He kind of turned away and curled up into himself and tried to cover his face.

Noah didn't know what to do.

So he did what he always did when he didn't know what to do. He ran to get his grandfather.

Walt came into the living room as fast as he could with his bad leg, but when he saw Roger's battered face, he stopped short and made a sound like someone had punched him in the stomach.

He scooped the little boy up – and at that moment, with tears running down his face, Roger looked every inch a little lost boy. Walt held him on his lap, his big arms around him. He just held him and rocked him and murmured that it was all right, that Roger had found a place to come where he'd be safe.

It wasn't until Walt pulled Noah down onto the sofa and wrapped one of his big arms around him that he realized he was crying, too.

They sat there together for a long time.

'What do I do?' Roger finally asked, in a very small voice. 'I don't want to pretend you're not my friends until he goes back out on the road. But . . . I'm scared of him. I'm such a coward.'

Noah held his breath, hoping that his grandfather understood how terribly hard it must have been for tough-as-nails Roger to admit that.

'We could call the police—'

96

'*No*.' Roger was adamant. 'I won't do that. He's my *father*.'

'Then you should stay close to your home for a week or so – until he leaves town again,' Walt advised.

'Let him win?' Roger scoffed. 'No way. I'm coming over here whether he likes it or not. He can just beat the shit out of me every night. I don't care.'

'But I care,' Walter told him. 'And Noah does, too.' He sighed. 'Has Noah told you why I have this limp?'

Roger shook his head.

'Young Ringo, I'm stunned,' Walt teased. 'Am I supposed to believe that you never so much as asked?'

That got a small smile. 'Well, sure, I asked, sir. But Noah said I had to ask you. And I didn't because I didn't want you to think I was rude. I thought you might not want to be reminded about being wounded in the war—'

'This limp isn't from a war wound, young man,' Walt corrected him. He rubbed his knee almost absentmindedly. 'No, I made it through World War Two with nary a scratch. It wasn't until I returned to the States, in 1945, that I nearly lost my leg.'

'In a crash?' Roger asked.

Walt chuckled. 'Not the kind you mean. But it was certainly a crash – of free-thinking people head on with ignorant ones. You see, I came back from Germany in late 1945 to find that my life – as I knew it   was completely gone. Now that the war was over, there was no longer a place for a black pilot in the new Air Force. After serving for so many years, I was a civilian again. An unemployed civilian. My wife had died shortly after I'd been sent overseas, and my daughter – whom I hadn't seen since she was an infant – was living here in Fort Worth, Texas, with Dot, my wife's best friend, who had opened her own crop dusting enterprise, along with a flight school.

'Seeing Dot again was . . .' Walt chuckled. 'Well, we'd exchanged hundreds of letters during the war, but let's just say she gave me quite a welcome home – the kind that warranted an immediate marriage. When that news got out, her family was less than pleased. A white woman marrying a black man – not a very popular concept, not in this part of the country at that time. We talked about going to California or New York City, but Dot's business was already doing quite well, and my daughter, Jolee, had settled in, so . . . But then Dot's brothers came a-callin'. She had three brothers, two older and one much younger.

'They came and told their sister that she would no longer be part of their family if she married "that nigger". Forget about the fact that "that nigger" was more educated than the three of them combined. Forget that "that nigger" was a former colonel in the Air Force, who had spent years fighting for this country, for freedom, for *them*. By marrying "that nigger", Dot would bring terrible, awful shame upon her family.

'Well. As I'm sure you can imagine, Dot told them in no uncertain terms where they could go and what they could do with themselves when they got there.' He laughed softly. 'Back then she had a mouth that rivaled yours, Ringo dear. She sent them running for their very lives. Or so we thought.

'It turned out that Dot's youngest brother – he couldn't have been more than seventeen – stayed behind. When I came out of the house to see what vegetables the garden might yield for our evening meal, he was there, waiting for me. He was holding a shovel, but I didn't think of it as a weapon. I didn't think to be on guard. He was just a boy. It never occurred to me that out of all Dot's brothers, this one might be the most dangerous.

'He came at me, swinging that shovel like a battle-ax, and it hit me in the leg, right beneath my knee. The blade had been sharpened, and the damage done was severe. There was so much blood – you boys know what that's like. He was shouting to Dot about how maybe she had no qualms about marrying a black man, about the kind of life she'd have with everyone in town shunning her – shunning *them* – but maybe the idea of being married to a *crippled* black man would make her change her mind and save their family from this awful embarrassment.'

Walt rubbed his knee again. 'I was in and out of the hospital for quite a few months. Those doctors had to work hard to save my leg, but save it they did. And I should have known better, but after I came out of my first surgery, I asked Dot if she was sure that she still wanted this, wanted *me*. She just looked at me. Then she walked out of the room and came back about thirty minutes later with the preacher from the Baptist church, who married us right then and there.

'Some months later, I was walking again. With a cane, but I was finally up and about. And I realized some things Dot had been withholding from me for a while – that whenever she drove into town and parked on the street, her car windshield would be smeared with cow manure. That our postbox had been mangled, that a dead cat had been hung from a tree out back, that small fires in the shape of a cross had been started on our lawn, that she'd received obscene phone calls and hate mail calling her a nigger lover and worse.

'It was obvious that her brothers were behind it, but when I called the police I was told, "Boys will be boys."

'Well, when I heard that, I put on my Air Corps uniform with my chestful of medals, and Dot and Jolee put on their best dresses – and boys, I'll tell you, Dot's an eye-catching woman in a pair of coveralls, but in a yellow dress with high heels . . . We climbed into the truck and we went into town.

'We parked on Main Street, and together we did a little shopping, making a point to patronize every store in town. Dot introduced me – even to those who knew me – as her "new husband, Colonel Gaines the war hero". We told everyone of our plans to expand our little airstrip, to acquire more planes, to hire more pilots and mechanics, to expand our flight school – all of which would pump life and money into this part of town. Nearly every shopkeeper jumped at the chance to shake my hand, especially when I opened a business account with them.

'Our last stop was at the hardware store, and by then we looked like a parade. After having spent two thousand dollars on various supplies and lumber – which back then was a substantial amount of money – we had folks tagging along to see what we might purchase next.

'I also think there was some anticipation, because all three of Dot's brothers worked at the hardware store.

'We sent Jolee across the street with some girls from her school, to the soda fountain, and went into the store. The owner was very happy to see me. He had no clue of the trouble between Dot's brothers and me. All he knew was that I was there to spend a pile of money.

'Other people from town *did* know of the tension, and the crowd grew – hoping, I think, that a brawl would break out.

'There was, of course, no chance of that. One does not brawl when one's beautiful wife, dressed in her best yellow dress, is by one's side. Instead, I purchased bullets – both for the side arms I'd picked up in Italy and Germany, and for the double-barreled shotgun Dot kept down at the airfield.

'I bought enough ammunition to supply a small army. Or to fight a small war. Boxes and boxes – and they were heavy, too. I told the store owner I couldn't manage it with my bad leg and my cane. He was more than happy to call his hired help out of the back room to carry our purchases out to our truck.

'The chief of police came in at that point, no doubt to make sure I didn't have murder in mind. "Going hunting?" he asked me.

' "No, sir," I said. "Boys may be boys, but here in America a man has the right to be a man – to protect his property and keep his family safe from harm. We've had a bit of trouble out our way and my intention is to see that it stops."

'Now, all three of Dot's brothers were there, and I knew I hadn't made them happy – they were going to fetch and carry for me, a black man.

'But I had their attention – as well as that of most of the rest of the town. So I told them that when I was first attacked, I hadn't expected that kind of violence. But from now on, I would be ready. And the next time – if there *was* a next time, and I fervently prayed there would not be – I wouldn't be the one lying bleeding in the dirt. "I killed plenty of Nazis during the war," I announced, "and I am not at all adverse to killing a few more."

'And then I turned back to the storekeeper and I did something that made Dot a little angry.' Walter chuckled softly. 'She didn't say anything at the time, but, believe me, Ringo, I heard quite a lot about it later.

'I bought a shovel,' he told them. 'The same kind that Dot's youngest brother had used against me. I paid for it, and I handed it to him. "This is to replace the one you lost," I told him. I thought he was going to soil his pants. That's one thing I've learned about bullies, boys. They scare easily.

'Well, we walked out of that store,' Walt said, 'loaded all of that ammunition into the truck, and went on home. Dot held her tongue until Jolee was in bed, and then . . . Me oh my oh, she was furious. She felt I'd put myself in terrible danger by putting that shovel back into her brother's hands.

'But I told her that I'd made sure I was in a position of power before I did that. I made it impossible for her brother to take a swing at me there and then with the sheriff standing by, and I made it difficult for him to come after me later. Although there was always the possibility that he would. But that was what those bullets were for. We were both going to be armed for the next few weeks – months, if necessary – and keep Jolee nearby.

'You see, my handing him that shovel was a message – as clear as the message that came from our purchase of that ammunition. I was letting him know that if he and his brothers wanted this war to continue, it was no longer going to be fought with shovels. I was telling them that I was not afraid.'

Walt looked at Roger. 'I know you disagree with your father. I know you recognize that his opinions about who should or should not be your friends are obsolete – that they're sorely outdated and just plain foolish and ignorant. But you must be careful. Think before you act, Ringo. Knee-jerk reactions are well and good if you're six feet tall and built like an oak tree. But he is big and you are small, and he can hurt you. Don't put the shovel back into your father's hands until you are certain he won't use it against you again.'

'Let him win,' Roger said, bitterness making his voice thick.

'Ah, there's the magic of it, my young friend. *You're* the one who wins. You know what's wrong and you know what's right. And you carry that knowledge in your heart. He can't touch that, he can't take that. That's yours, forever,' Walter said. 'And the other thing that's yours forever is our love for you. Noah and Dot and I will still be here in a week when your father leaves town again. You will always be welcome here – you know that. But I hope you will be wise and not compromise your personal safety to visit us until it's safe for you to do so without repercussion.'

'Someday me and Noah, we're going to join the Navy,' Roger said, wiping his nose on his sleeve.

'We're going to be SEALs,' Noah said.

'Yeah,' Roger said. 'And that's going to really piss my father off because he was in the Army.'

Walter laughed. 'Ringo, I really like you. Nostradamus here has excellent taste when it comes to choosing his friends.'

Roger got very quiet. 'I really like you, too, Uncle Walt.'

Walt hugged him, hugged Noah, too. It was funny, but this time it was Walter who had tears in his eyes. 'You better head home, son.'

'Yes, sir,' Roger said. He climbed painfully to his feet. 'Maybe he'll go back on the road real soon,' he told Noah.

'When he does, we'll be here,' Noah said, echoing his grandfather's words.

Six

Clyde Wrigley was a freaking crybaby.

But he didn't cry at the news that his ex-wife, Janine, was dead. No, he didn't start wailing until he realized that the FBI thought he might somehow be involved in her death.

Forget about Janine. The son of a bitch was crying because he was scared he might have to go back to jail.

He was right where Sam had expected him to be – parked in front of the TV at the house Clyde and Janine had shared back when they'd first moved to Sarasota. It was the same address Mary Lou had given Sam when he'd called to find out where to send money, after he'd been served with those divorce papers.

Manuel Conseco had made the scene, and he and his assistant – the young blonde who'd helped interview Sam – were questioning Clyde.

Sam itched to grab the son of a bitch by the T-shirt, slam him against the wall, order him to stop sniveling, and tell where Mary Lou and Haley were.

Alyssa surely knew that, too. She was standing close – close enough to grab Sam and keep him from getting himself into trouble.

Of course, he could use a little grabbing from Alyssa Locke right about now.

He experimented, shifting his weight, just a little, toward Clyde. Sure enough, Alyssa shifted just a little bit closer to Sam.

What would he have to do to get a full body block? Although, chances were, if he did that, she'd hustle him out of there and he wouldn't get to hear whatever lame information Clyde *did* spit out.

'Three weeks,' Clyde was sobbing. 'I haven't seen Janine in at least three weeks. At *least*. And before that, it was months. Not since she moved out.'

'And when was the last time you went to her home on Camilia Street?' Conseco asked.

'That was it. It was the first time and the last time.' Clyde couldn't seem to speak without a fresh flood of tears and snot.

Someone give the asshole a Kleenex. Crying was bad enough, but crying in public was freaking humiliating. Sam's face heated as he remembered the way he'd broken down himself just a few hours earlier. Alyssa, thank you God, had quickly given him some privacy – unlike the time she'd barged into his hotel room and come across him weeping like a baby. She'd just stood there and stared. That had been embarrassing – doubly so since he'd been crying over her. He'd actually had to chase her out.

'It was the only time I went to her house,' Clyde was saying. 'I didn't even know where she lived until I ran into Carol.'

'Carol who?'

'I don't know her last name. She was just some friend of Jan's – she worked with her at the dry cleaners.'

Conseco made notes on his pad. 'Which dry cleaners was that?'

'Quickie-Clean over on Clark,' Clyde said. 'But Janine stopped working there – same time she moved out, months ago. I think she quit because she didn't want to see me.'

'Because she was afraid of you?'

'*No*, man! She just . . . I don't know, she said she was tired of lending me money. I'm on disability – half pay. You can't live on that. It's been rough these past few years and—'

'So Carol told you where Janine lived?' the blonde asked.

And Sam couldn't keep it in anymore. Who cared what Carol told him? 'Where's Haley?'

Clyde aimed his teary gaze at Sam. 'Jeez, I don't know, man. I didn't see her when I went over there. I haven't seen Mary Lou or the baby since they all moved out.'

'Let us ask the questions, Lieutenant,' Alyssa murmured, as Conseco glared at them both. She was now standing so close that Sam couldn't help but get a noseful of her every time he so much as inhaled.

She smelled so good. She wasn't wearing perfume from a bottle, at least not the way Mary Lou had, in overpowering amounts guaranteed to overdose his sense of smell. No, Alyssa's scent was far more subtle. It came from her shampoo or soap or maybe some kind of lotion she used or, who knows, maybe it was the perfume from her laundry dryer sheets, used to avoid static cling. Whatever it was, on Alyssa it smelled incredible.

It was enough to distract the shit out of him – to make at least part of his brain start working on the best way to get her naked and wrapped around him, as soon as possible, preferably tonight.

And – he was a freaking genius – now she knew it, too. The past few hours had put him way off-balance and he was far from on top of his game. Not only was he thinking about sex – again – when he should have been thinking only about his missing daughter, but he was enough of an asshole to fail to hide the nature of his thoughts from Alyssa.

Yes, indeed, she knew him well enough to know *exactly* what he was thinking, just from looking into his eyes.

For several long seconds, she just held his gaze, the expression on her face unreadable.

God, making love to her had been exquisite. How could she not want to do that, to feel that, again?

Because Sam had dumped her for Mary Lou, for one thing. Not that that had mattered so very much in the long term. Because Alyssa had told him in very clear English that she'd never intended to have more than a hot, brief affair with him –

just a few months, tops, of that brain-searing sex – with no real emotional attachment involved.

At least not from her.

Now she was in a real relationship with someone she actually loved.

Max. The fucker.

Max wouldn't have gone six months without seeing his daughter. Of course Max was too perfect to have had a daughter with some stranger he'd picked up in a bar in the first place. But if he did have a daughter, he'd no doubt have found her and brought her home by now, instead of standing around with his thumb up his ass, wistfully hoping that the kid was still alive.

Please God let Haley be alive.

'Sorry.' Sam was the one who broke eye contact.

'Keep it zipped,' Alyssa warned him sharply, 'or you're out of here.'

Interesting choice of words and definitely not unintentional.

'Carol didn't know where Janine lived,' Clyde was saying. 'I asked her because . . . because Jan took my Phish CDs when she moved out, and I wanted them back.'

Yeah, right.

'All Carol knew was that Janine just got a new job working as a receptionist at the vet's over in Siesta Village,' Clyde continued, wiping his nose on his T-shirt sleeve. 'She told me that Janine was doing really well, that she was working hard to stay clean. She said they were letting her help take care of the dogs on the weekends, and that she really liked doing that.'

'And you figured she was probably getting paid overtime, so you went to see her?' Conseco knew the truth. Clyde had gone to see Janine to try to borrow some money. And when she'd refused to lend it to him . . .

'He wouldn't have killed her over that,' Sam murmured to Alyssa. 'Not this guy. It's not in him.'

She glanced at him, glanced at Conseco, and then back.

'I'm not interrupting them,' he said softly to her. 'As for the rest of me – I'm zipped.'

Alyssa Locke wasn't the type to blush easily, but she definitely avoided eye contact at that. However, after a moment, she did lean slightly closer to whisper back to him, 'What if he found her with another man – a new boyfriend?'

'No. Maybe he'd go home and smoke an extra doobie or two to deal with the pain, but . . .' Sam shook his head. 'Nah. Besides, where's the boyfriend? Wouldn't he have shown up before this, saying, "I think something's wrong – my girlfriend hasn't answered her phone or her doorbell for nearly three weeks"? I mean, come on. Even assuming he's an asshole and doesn't come see her unless he wants some, three weeks is way too long for a guy to go without sex.'

Alyssa gave him a disgusted look, but then exhaled a short laugh and shook her head. 'Men suck.'

'Some women suck, too.'

'Yeah,' she said. 'I know.'

'No. I wanted those CDs back,' Clyde was sticking to his lame excuse. 'That's why I went over there and waited until she left work. I couldn't find a parking space, so I ended up just following her home.'

'Where you killed her?'

Clyde started crying again. 'No way, man. I didn't kill her. I just, you know, rang the bell and we talked and—'

'Front door or back?'

'Front.' He perked up. 'You know, her neighbor was out in the yard, washing his car. He saw me go in and he saw me come out, too. And Jan was with me when I left. She came out to get one of my CDs from the car.'

'Which neighbor?' Conseco asked.

'The fat guy who lives in the house on the left,' Clyde told him, 'if you're facing Jan's house. I swear to you, I didn't kill her.'

Conseco was silent, just looking through his notes.

'Can you please ask him if he knows where Mary Lou worked?' Sam said to Alyssa, loudly enough for Conseco and Clyde to hear. 'Or where Haley went for day care?'

Clyde didn't wait for the FBI agents to play telephone. 'I don't know,' he answered. 'Honest. The only way I knew Haley was still living with Jan was from the toys on the living-room floor.'

'Can you tell me your whereabouts the rest of that evening?' Conseco asked.

'I came here,' Clyde said. 'And, you know, listened to my Phish CDs.'

'You were alone?'

'Yeah, but I swear, I didn't kill her.' He pointed to Sam. 'Why aren't you questioning *him*? Maybe *he* killed her. The SEAL. You know, before Jan moved out, she and Mary Lou were always whispering about him. Stuff like, "What if Sam finds out?" Like, "He won't find out, how could he find out?" I heard Jan say – more than once – "What's he going to do if he *does* find out? Kill me?" I finally asked her what was going on – I was a little worried he was going to kick down the door in the middle of the night. I thought maybe Mary Lou had stolen something from him when she left. Something more valuable than a couple of CDs, you know? But Janine told me it was nothing – that back a few years ago, she gave Mary Lou a special box of condoms that wouldn't do what they were supposed to do, if you get my drift. It was so that she'd get pregnant and the SEAL would have to marry her. Only now they were getting a divorce, so what did it matter? That's what Jan said.

'But I remember thinking, *Man*, if I'm the SEAL and I find out about *that* . . .'

'Jesus,' Sam said. He'd heard the words Clyde was saying, but they'd stopped making sense. And then they made too much sense. Mary Lou *had* gotten pregnant on purpose. He'd always known that, but he hadn't actually *known* it.

But apparently the condoms they'd used had been tampered

108

with. God *damn* it, he'd always been so careful, so Mary Lou's pregnancy had caught him by surprise. He'd spent hours trying to figure out exactly where he'd failed. It made so much more sense now.

And – perfect – now Conseco was looking at him with renewed interest. As if Sam really did have a motive for killing Janine.

It was so ridiculous, Sam didn't say a word. He just held Conseco's gaze. It was far better than looking at Alyssa, who had to be thinking that he was a total fool. Mary Lou had come to him, pregnant and alone and seemingly frightened to death, and he'd walked away from a budding relationship with Alyssa – a woman that he was crazy about – so he could do what he'd thought was the right thing. He'd taken responsibility for this woman he'd accidentally knocked up.

Only it hadn't been accidental.

Jesus.

Alyssa pulled Conseco aside. She spoke quietly, but Sam still managed to overhear. 'Look, he's exhausted. Tomorrow, he'll be giving you a complete record accounting for his time over the past weeks. If you still want to question Lieutenant Starrett after that, you're welcome to do so, of course. But for right now, I'm taking him out of here.'

Conseco said something too quietly for Sam to hear.

'Absolutely,' Alyssa responded.

Conseco turned back to Clyde, and Alyssa headed for Sam. 'Let's go.'

He followed her out the front door, down the steps, and toward her rental car.

'You okay?' Alyssa asked.

Sam glanced at her. He laughed – a short burst of disparaging air. 'Yeah, you know, that's the best part about being a fucking idiot. You're too stupid to know when you're not okay.'

Alyssa opened her mouth and was about to say something, when her phone rang.

* * *

Alyssa answered after only one ring. 'Locke.'

'Hey, it's me,' Max said, opening the refrigerator and taking out the half gallon of milk. 'How's it going?'

'As well as can be expected, sir,' she answered, 'considering that Manuel Conseco doesn't play happily with us other children.'

'Yeah, I've heard that about him. Other than that, he's very good at what he does.'

'Yes, sir. And his entire team thinks he's God, which makes me the Antichrist.'

'Cut it out with the *sir*,' Max ordered. 'It's after hours.'

'Maybe for you. But not for us angels of Satan. Or for poor overworked Manny Conseco. You know, actually, I feel like I'm one of those commodores on *Star Trek* – the ones who come in and make it hard for Captain Kirk to do his job.'

Max laughed, some of the fatigue of the day falling away. Talking to Alyssa always made him feel better. 'Wow. How come I didn't know you were a Trekkie?'

Crap. The milk was dated over three weeks ago. How did *that* happen? He didn't bother to take a sniff, he just opened it up and poured it directly down the sink.

'When I was growing up, Lieutenant Uhura was a major role model for me,' Alyssa told him. 'A strong black woman on the bridge of a starship . . .?'

'In a miniskirt, answering the interplanetary telephone?' Max looked at the bowl of Rice Krispies he'd already poured. Now what? He'd taken off his suit first thing upon arriving home, and walking down to the convenience store on the corner in his boxer shorts might not go over too well with his neighbors.

'Yeah, well, there were definitely some kinks that needed to be worked out.' She paused. 'Is there a purpose to this phone call?'

'I was hoping for a status report. I figured you'd still be up.'

Max took the bowl to the sink, adding water. It was pathetic, but it seemed less so than eating it dry.

'Up and running,' she told him. 'I'm about to drive Lieutenant Starrett to the home of one of his friends.'

Max set the bowl down on the counter, his appetite gone. Alyssa was still with Sam Starrett. At nearly midnight. There were a million questions he wanted to ask, none of them appropriate. He settled for, 'Is he okay?'

'Yes,' Alyssa said. 'It's been a very difficult day, but . . . yes. I assume you heard that the victim wasn't Lieutenant Starrett's wife after all. It was her sister.'

'Janine Wrigley.' Max *had* heard. He also heard the way Alyssa kept saying 'Lieutenant Starrett.' She called Sam that whenever she tried to pretend she didn't give a damn about him. And the key word there was *pretend*. Apparently she didn't realize that Max had picked up on that a long time ago.

'Since it's not Lieutenant Starrett's wife who's dead, the entire situation's a little less volatile,' Alyssa said, 'so you probably don't need to—'

'Yeah,' Max interrupted her. 'I'm not sure yet whether I'm still coming to Tampa tomorrow. Sarasota,' he quickly corrected himself. *Crap*. He was beyond tired, and he was losing it. The only thing he knew for goddamn sure was that whether or not he went to Sarasota tomorrow, he *wasn't* going anywhere near Tampa. Or Gina Vitagliano.

He cleared his throat and changed the subject. 'What's Starrett's take on the potential Gainesville connection?'

'Gainesville?' Alyssa asked.

Typical of Manny Conseco. Not only didn't he play happily with others, he didn't share his toys. Or information. 'I got a call about two hours ago,' Max told her. 'Apparently, three weeks ago, Janine Wrigley – or someone claiming to be her, because according to forensics she was already dead – sold a black 1989 Honda Civic hatchback to a used-car dealer in Gainesville, Florida.'

'Who does Mary Lou know in Gainesville?' Alyssa asked – presumably of Sam.

'No one that I know of.' Max could hear Starrett's lazy Texas drawl through Alyssa's cell phone. He had to be sitting really close. No doubt because the rental car Alyssa was driving was small. It didn't mean anything.

And pigs could fly. Max knew Starrett was sitting as close to Alyssa as he possibly could.

'Why?' Starrett asked.

'We think she sold her car in Gainesville,' Alyssa told the SEAL.

'When?' Starrett sounded as if he'd woken up, all laziness gone from his voice.

'Three weeks ago.'

'Ah, man, *that* trail's got to be stone cold.'

'A cold trail's better than no trail,' Max heard Alyssa say tartly. 'Don't complain. We're closer to finding Mary Lou and Haley than we were just a few minutes ago.'

'All we know is that – maybe – Mary Lou was in Gainesville three weeks ago. Three *weeks*.' Sam wasn't happy about that.

'Locke,' Max interrupted them, hating the way both Alyssa and Sam had said we. Like they were already a team. Or a couple. 'Will you call me back after you drop off Starrett?'

'Is there something more?' she asked.

'No,' he said. 'I just . . . I wanted to touch base with you at a time when you could, I don't know, speak more freely, I guess.'

'Max, I'm fine,' she said, her rich voice warm in appreciation of his concern.

'Please don't—' Max stopped himself. *Let him get within six feet of you.* What was she going to do? Make him sit in the backseat? 'Good,' he said instead. 'Good.'

'Wait a sec,' he heard Sam say. 'You have a map of Florida?' he asked Alyssa.

'Hang on,' Alyssa told Max. 'In the pocket of the . . . Yeah, in there.'

'I just remembered – Mary Lou's mother. She called me about two months ago,' Max heard Sam say over the crinkling of paper being unfolded. 'Because she didn't have Mary Lou's new phone number, and she wanted to tell her she was moving out of Georgia, down to northern Florida, to . . . shit, where was it? I remember the address, number two Happy Lane in, Jesus, Wallace or Wanker or Wacker or—'

'Max, we might have a connection to—'

'Waldo!' Sam said. 'Fuck me! Look at this!'

Max had to laugh. Most people said, 'Eureka.' Sam Starrett, however, said, 'Fuck me.' Interesting use of the phrase as an expression of jubilation. Sometimes he really had to work to hate the guy.

'Mary Lou's mother lives just northeast of Gainesville in a town called Waldo,' Alyssa told Max, excitement making her voice ring. 'I'd call that a major connection.'

'Can you drive me back to Camilia Street?' Sam was saying to Alyssa. 'My rental car's still there.'

'Whoa,' she said. 'Sam, what are you thinking?'

Max knew exactly what Starrett was thinking. Midnight road trip to Gainesville, ETA ASAP. 'Alyssa, for the love of God, talk him out it.'

'I'm not going to sleep at all tonight,' Sam said. 'I might as well head up to—'

'You're exhausted,' Alyssa said. 'Let's wait until the morning—'

'I can't wait. I'm sorry, Lys.' The SEAL actually sounded sincere. 'I know it's unlikely, but if there's even just a chance that Mary Lou and Haley are in Waldo—'

'Okay,' Alyssa said. 'But it doesn't make sense for you to go by yourself. I promised Manny Conseco that I'd keep tabs on you, so—'

'No,' Max said. 'No, no, no. What are you doing? Damn it, Locke, you suck when it comes to negotiating. You're already caving. Let me talk to him.'

'Max wants to talk to you,' he heard Alyssa say.

Then Starrett's voice directly in his ear. 'Yeah.'

'If you insist on going tonight, she's going to go with you,' Max said. 'You know that. And she'll never admit it, but she's tired, Starrett. Give her a break.'

'I'll drive,' Sam said. 'She can sleep in the car.'

'First thing in the morning, I'll arrange for a chopper to take you up to—'

'Look, I'm really sorry,' Sam said. 'You want to keep me from going?'

Max sighed and said it with him. 'Find your daughter. Yeah, I know.' He sighed again. 'I didn't want to have to say this, but . . . You mess with Alyssa, and you're dead.'

Most people who knew Max crapped their pants when he put that cold edge into his voice. But Starrett just laughed. 'I hear you, and I know exactly where you're coming from.'

Max Bhagat was one of the FBI's top negotiators. He was a professional communicator. He could read a person's intentions clear as day by what that person *didn't* say. And since Sam *hadn't* said, 'Okay, Max, I promise I'll keep my distance from Alyssa,' he was essentially broadcasting his intention to do the exact opposite.

'Listen to what I'm about to say, Starrett,' Max emphasized. 'I can fuck you up but good. One word from me, just *one* word, and you're working a desk job in a windowless office until the day you retire. Don't you forget that for one single second.'

'I can't believe it.' It was Alyssa's voice on the phone now. 'Were you actually *threatening* him?'

Shit. When busted, go with the truth.

'Yeah,' Max said. 'Actually, I was. It didn't seem to be working too well, though. Do me a favor and make sure he heard that part about the windowless office, because I don't think he—'

'Goodbye, Max.'

'Alyssa, wait. Don't hang up—'

But she was gone.

Damn it.

He was definitely going to Tampa tomorrow.

Sarasota.

Sarasota.

Jesus H. Christ.

Max dumped his Rice Krispies into the garbage disposal by throwing the bowl into the sink and breaking it in half. Rubbing the back of his neck, he went into his study and tried to make himself stop thinking about all of them – Alyssa and Sam and Tom Paoletti.

And Gina.

He turned on his laptop and started reviewing his notes for tomorrow morning's meeting with the President, hoping that would do the trick.

It didn't.

'He really loves you,' Sam said.

Alyssa glanced over at him, but she couldn't see his face well in the dim light from the dashboard, especially since he had his hat pulled down over his eyes. She'd thought he was asleep. She should have known better.

'Yeah,' she said, hoping that he wouldn't push the topic. He was talking about Max, and the truth was, Max *didn't* love her. Not the way Sam thought.

She and Max were friends. True, theirs was an odd friendship. And yes, at one point over the years they'd worked together, they'd begun a different kind of relationship. They'd shared lots of dinners. They'd had lots of long conversations late into the night. They'd even kissed more than once. But right before they'd stepped across the line into a sexual relationship, Max shut them down.

Alyssa would have gone there. In fact, she'd wanted to rather badly.

And that was a polite way of summarizing that awful night nearly a year ago when Max had come to her apartment for dinner. Dinner had led to a second and then a third glass of wine, which had led to some of those kisses and some more of those kisses and . . .

The hard truth was, she'd had him half undressed on her sofa, she hadn't thought of Sam Starrett once all evening, and she was so, so ready to get busy with a man who honestly liked her, a man who listened when she talked, a man who wanted to know what she was thinking and feeling – and *whammo.*

Max threw on the brakes.

Because he couldn't get past the fact that she worked for him.

The man had actually had the nerve to ask her if she'd be willing to transfer out of his elite FBI team. If she transferred – and he couldn't have anything to do with getting her placed elsewhere in the Bureau, he'd made that more than clear – then and only then could they become sexually involved.

Oh, he'd apologized left and right. Effusively. At one point, Alyssa had been close to certain that he was even going to start to cry. It was one of the weirdest rejections of her life. It was clear that he wanted to spend the night with her as badly as she'd wanted him to stay, but when push came to shove, he simply could not do it.

She had been half naked herself, and in the process of unfastening the man's pants. The fact that he'd had the strength to say no, to refuse to let his beliefs get overrun by physical desire, still impressed her. It would have been nicer if he'd figured out that it wasn't going to work between them before they wound up on the sofa, but still . . .

The entire incident had made her fall a little bit in love with Max Bhagat.

Which was just her style. She apparently only loved men she couldn't have. Men she shouldn't want.

Max had refused to let the weirdness of that night of almost-sex screw up their growing friendship. The kissing and the romantic dinners stopped, but the long conversations continued.

He'd been relentless about it, continuing to call her and bring over pizza until she almost forgot that she'd been ready and willing to sleep with him.

Almost.

Alyssa was certain that Max hadn't forgotten it, either. But that had nothing to do whatsoever with whether or not he truly loved her.

'So are you going to, you know, marry him?' Sam asked now.

'He hasn't exactly asked me,' she replied with a twinge of guilt. It wasn't a lie, not like the lies she'd told about her relationship with Max in the past, but it was close, because it perpetuated Sam's misinformation. Still, she couldn't afford to let him know the truth.

'If he asks you, are you going to marry him?'

She glanced at him again. 'I'm really not interested in talking about this.'

'What *do* you want to talk about?' he asked. A car approached from behind them, its headlights hitting the rearview mirror and lighting Sam's face. His mouth was tight and his eyes were shadowed. 'The fact that Mary Lou intentionally set out to get pregnant? The fact that I'm never going to use a condom again unless it's one I've bought and taken out of the box myself? The fact that I was played – completely? Jesus, could I be more of a fool?'

Alyssa forced herself to watch the road. 'Not all women are like Mary Lou.'

'Not all women are like you, Alyssa. In fact *no* other woman in the entire world—'

'Stop,' she said sharply.

He was silent for only a few heartbeats. 'I'm sorry, but I have something I need to say—'

'Don't waste the effort,' she told him. 'Because we are not going to have sex. Not tonight, not tomorrow, not next week, not ever. Never again. Listen closely, Roger, and I'll repeat it—'

'That's not what I—'

'Nev. Ver. A. Gain. We played that game, and it was terrible—'

'It was incredible and you know it,' he countered hotly.

'Yeah, right up to the point where it was incredibly terrible,' she insisted.

'There were some bad moments, yeah, but the rest of it – it was worth it,' he said.

'Speak for yourself!'

'I am. Alyssa, look, I know you were unhappy when I—'

'Unhappy?' She was shouting now. 'Sam, for God's sake, you eviscerated me!'

The thick emotion in her voice seemed to echo in the car. Her words seemed to shock Sam as much as they'd shocked her. She hadn't meant to tell him that. *Shit.*

Thank goodness the car behind them on the highway had sped up and gone past and it was once again too dark for her to see his face. She hoped he also couldn't see hers.

What was she doing here? It was insane and absurd. She was helping this man who had once been her lover, whom she'd done shockingly intimate things with, who'd gotten under her skin, and whom, even now, all these years later, she still hadn't managed to shake loose. . . .

And she was helping him find his wife.

Ex-wife, sure, but he was pretty freaking eager to find her, wasn't he?

Okay, that was just petty jealousy talking. Sam was eager to find his daughter. To be fair, his concern was mostly for Haley. But still . . .

'You have no idea how sorry I am,' he said quietly.

'Yeah,' she said, angry at him, angry at herself. 'Thanks. Gee, that makes it *all* better.'

'I want to try to make it up to you.'

'What do you want me to do, assign you a stack of Herculean feats? And after you do them, I'm supposed to say, "Oh, Sam, all is forgiven. Come and fuck me"? Let's be honest here about what it is you *really* want, shall we?'

He laughed in disbelief. 'You obviously have no idea what I really want.'

She laughed, too, with disgust. 'Said the man who ended up married to some bar bunny because he couldn't keep his pants zipped for half a minute.'

She'd pushed him too far with that one.

'You're right. You're abso-fucking-lutely right, you know that? You're always right, Alyssa, and this time you're mega-right. Except, you ever wonder why I went home with Mary Lou in the first place? You ever stop to think that maybe it had something – just a little bit – to do with the fact that you wouldn't have any-fucking-thing to do with me?'

She laughed her anger. 'Oh, that's perfect. So now it's *my* fault? You are so fucking immature!' And now he'd gone and done it again. He'd managed to bring her completely down to his super-crude level.

'I'm not saying that it's your—'

'Forget it. It's fine,' she said. 'Blame me.' She gripped the steering wheel, her eyes on the road, gas pedal to the floor. The sooner they got to Waldo and out of the confines of this car, the better.

'You know, I *do* blame you to some degree,' he countered. 'You used me for sex—'

'Yeah, at the time, you were *really* complaining—'

'—and I was such a fool, I didn't realize it was just sex. I fucking fell in love with you.'

Alyssa's heart stopped. But then, as it started beating again, she shook her head. 'You have absolutely no idea what those words mean. You're like, like . . . ABBA, singing phonetically in a language you don't understand. You fell in love with me. No, excuse me. You *fucking* fell in love with me. Of course. The same way you *fucking* fell in love with Mary Lou the first time she took off her clothes for you.'

119

'You are so wrong—'

'What did you *fucking* fall in love with first, Roger? My breasts or my ass?'

'Your eyes.'

Alyssa laughed. 'That's only marginally better – not that I believe you.'

He laughed, too, in pure disgust. 'Why should you believe anything I say? Since you obviously know better than I do exactly how and what I feel—'

'Do you know how many conversations we had before we had sex?'

'No, but I'm sure *you* do.'

'Only a few. And most of the time we didn't talk, we argued. We *fought*—'

'I *can* tell you, though,' he interrupted, 'exactly how many times and how many different ways I made you come—'

'Who am I, Sam? If you fell in love with me, you should know. But I don't think you have a clue.'

'I do so—'

'Bullshit. Even if you *did* somehow think you knew me back then, well, guess what? I'm not the same person I was two years ago. And neither are you.'

Sam didn't speak, but he was far from silent. Alyssa was aware of him sitting there, breathing. If she didn't know better, she would have sworn he was trying to rein in his temper, to keep himself from saying something stupid or hurtful, trying to bring this crazy argument back to a more civilized conversation.

'You're right,' he said, and his voice was actually quiet. 'I *am* different. I'm very different. I think . . . I think you might even like me now.'

God help her when he said things like that.

Alyssa made herself laugh, tried to make light of what he'd just said, to turn it into a joke. 'I doubt it.'

Sam nodded. 'Yeah, maybe that was a little too optimistic. How about, I think you might not hate me so much now?'

Now she had to fight hard not to laugh. As it was, a snort escaped. 'Please just go to sleep.' Despite her efforts, desperation tinged her voice and she took a deep breath before she said, 'It'll be your turn to drive in an hour.'

He sighed, taking off his hat and throwing it on the dashboard, rubbing his forehead as if he had a bad headache. 'I'm sorry if I freaked you out,' he apologized. 'You know, by saying what I said. It's just . . . I didn't say it soon enough before. I should have told you I loved you before we first—'

'Just go to sleep,' she said again.

He was silent, then, for several minutes. She was on the verge of relaxing, when he said, 'I should have written it on you in chocolate syrup. You know, that very first night.'

When she'd gotten completely shit-faced drunk and handcuffed herself to him so she could be sure he wouldn't sneak out of his hotel room and try to help his friend John Nilsson. She'd lost her mind and spent the night having sex with Sam. And somewhere down the line, they'd unearthed a bottle of Hershey's chocolate syrup, and . . .

The sight of chocolate still made her feel light-headed.

Alyssa kept her mouth closed. If she didn't respond at all, surely he'd consider the conversation over and go to sleep.

The Sam Starrett she used to know sure would have.

But the man sitting next to her sighed. 'No comment, huh? You know, to this day, I can't eat chocolate without thinking about you, Lys.' He shifted in the darkness, and she knew he was looking at her. 'I can't taste it without tasting you.'

Oh, God. 'Go to sleep,' she said, marveling at her own ability to keep her voice sounding relatively cool and reserved. 'Or change the subject. Or I'm turning this car around.'

Sam sighed again. 'All right, you win. I'll be good.'

He was quiet again, then, this time for only about thirty seconds.

'What are the odds we'll actually find Mary Lou and Haley in Waldo?' he asked.

'I don't know,' Alyssa replied. 'It depends on a lot of things.' She was relieved to be talking again. This topic was a relatively safe one, and it kept his words from echoing in her head. *I can't taste it without tasting you . . .*

'I keep trying to figure out why Mary Lou would run.' Sam sounded tired, his Texas drawl more pronounced. 'I keep trying to imagine that day. She comes home after picking up Haley from day care and goes inside, and there's Janine with her head blown open, on the kitchen floor. It makes sense she would get out of the house right away – in case the shooter was still in there. But why not hop in the car and drive to the police station?'

'Maybe she knew the shooter,' Alyssa suggested, 'and wanted to protect him or her.' She took a sip of her coffee, aware that Sam wasn't the only one who was tired.

'Or maybe she came home and the shooter was still there,' Sam said grimly. 'Maybe she got back into her car with Haley *and* the shooter. Maybe wherever she went, it was at gunpoint.' He paused. 'In which case, by now, she and Haley are probably both dead.'

'We don't know that,' Alyssa said.

'Yeah,' he said. 'I know. I don't believe that they are. I don't think . . .'

He fell silent then, for several minutes this time.

But he spoke again. 'You know, when I opened that kitchen door and saw Janine on the floor – and thought it was Mary Lou . . .' He cleared his throat. 'I was sure Haley was in there, too.'

'I know,' she said quietly.

He was silent again, and she couldn't help but remembering the way he'd covered his eyes and desperately fought any kind of an emotional reaction when they'd gotten the news that it wasn't Mary Lou's body that he'd found.

She remembered seeing him cry.

On more than one occasion.

'I was sure she was dead,' he said now, 'and all I could think about was how horrible that must have been for Haley. I mean, it would have been bad enough if she'd been shot and killed, but I kept thinking how *really* fucking awful it would have been if she *hadn't* been. Can you imagine? A nineteen-month-old, locked in a house with her dead mother? Starving to death? Completely traumatized and terrified? Screaming her throat raw?' His voice shook. 'Jesus.'

This time Alyssa held tightly to the steering wheel, not because she wanted to hit him, but because she wanted to reach for his hand. 'That's why you didn't want to wait for Manny Conseco before you went back inside,' she realized.

'Yeah,' he said, his voice tight. 'I had to know if she was in there or not.'

'Hiding in the closet,' Alyssa whispered.

'No, I was pretty sure that if she was there, she had to be dead.'

'I know,' Alyssa said. 'I was talking about . . .'

She heard him shift in his seat, felt him watching her.

'Maybe Mary Lou dropped Haley in Waldo,' she said. 'You know, with her mother.'

'Her mother's a drunk,' Sam said. 'Mary Lou would never leave Haley there. I mean, unless Darlene cleaned herself up. Which is possible, I guess. God, I hope . . .'

'If they're not in Waldo, then tomorrow morning we can go over and talk to that car dealer in Gainesville, see if Mary Lou was with anyone when she sold her car, get a description of him or her . . .'

And then what? Sam didn't say the words aloud, but she knew he had to be wondering. If Mary Lou had continued on north from Gainesville – assuming that it was Mary Lou who'd gone to the car dealer – after three weeks she could be anywhere in the United States. By now she could even be in Canada or Mexico.

'We'll get a sense of how far she could have gotten by how much cash she was paid for her car,' Alyssa told him. Of course, if Mary Lou had been with someone else, someone who was threatening her, all bets were off.

This stretch of the highway was lit with streetlights, and she glanced over to find Sam still watching her.

'Talk to me,' he said softly.

She'd had this very dream, this exact fantasy, too many nights to count. Sam Starrett, sitting there, looking at her, oozing sexuality from every gorgeous pore. And wanting to crawl around inside of her head, to explore who she really was, to listen when she spoke.

'I thought I was.'

He shook his head. 'Who was in the closet, Lys?'

Seven

'W as it you?' Sam asked.

Come on, he wanted them to talk. Alyssa had said he didn't know who she was. Well, hey, she wasn't the easiest person in the world to get to know, considering every time they exchanged more than a few sentences, she started fighting with him, tooth and claw.

Although, okay, it was true that she wasn't always the one who started it.

She glanced over at him now, and he couldn't for the life of him read the expression on her face.

He wondered if she knew how hard he was trying, how determined he was not to let this opportunity – all these hours spent in this car together tonight – pass him by.

Alyssa opened her mouth as if to speak, but then closed it. She glanced at him again, and then, with her eyes firmly affixed to the road, she said, 'My mother died when I was pretty young.'

'When you were thirteen,' he said.

She looked at him in surprise. 'I told you that?'

'Yeah. It was, uh, in that bar, actually. Back in DC. Shortly before you, um, came back to my hotel room and, you know, handcuffed yourself to me. You didn't go into details, but you did say you were thirteen when she died.'

She'd told him, and he'd remembered. It had been years since DC. He watched her face as she came to that realization.

'I don't remember telling you.' Alyssa glanced at him again. Her eyes were enormous, making her look fragile and vulnerable

125

and even a little frightened. It was just an illusion – Sam knew she wasn't afraid of anything.

'I don't remember much about that night,' she admitted. 'Much of what we said,' she quickly corrected herself. 'That whole evening is kind of fragmented. I have, like, these shards of memory that are really sharp and clear but – Do you mind if we don't talk about this?'

'No,' he said. 'Sorry. I honestly wasn't trying . . . The last thing I want to do is make you uncomfortable.'

She shot him another look. 'And why don't I believe that?'

'Because you don't believe anything I say. I think we've already successfully established that.'

Alyssa laughed. Good. Laughter was good.

It was way better than gut-wrenching heartache.

Sam, for God's sake, you eviscerated me!

He could still remember Alyssa's face when he told her he was going to marry Mary Lou.

But then she'd told him, later, after he was married, when they ran into each other during a time-out for coffee while battling terrorists in Indonesia, that she'd never intended their relationship to be anything more than a good time. A short-term good time, as a matter of fact. A hot, brief fling. Hello, hello, hello, hello, good-bye.

That, she'd said over a cup of mediocre mocha matari, was all she'd ever wanted from him.

It was not a scenario that included any kind of evisceration.

'Were you lying?' he found himself asking. 'In that hotel coffee shop, in Jakarta?'

She didn't look at him as she signaled to get off at the next exit. 'What does it matter?' she countered. 'If I'm going to marry Max?'

Ouch. Evisceration usually started with a sharp stab like that. If she *married* Max . . .

'I think you should dump him,' he said point-blank, because, damn it, he'd spent too much time over the past few years not telling Alyssa what he thought, what he wanted, what he felt. 'And we should start over. Start fresh.' He held out his hand. 'Hi, I'm Roger Starrett. Most of my friends call me Sam. It's a nickname I got back when I first became a SEAL. See, people started calling me Houston, because of "Roger, Houston" – that's what the folks in the space shuttle said over the radio while talking to the command center. But Houston's still too much of a mouthful as a nickname, so someone started calling me Sam, because of Sam Houston.

'I also answer to Bob and you probably noticed that Noah calls me Ringo. Bob because there's a character in some book named Bob Starrett, and Ringo because my uncle Walt – Noah's grandpa – started calling me that back in seventh grade when we first met. It was because he liked the Beatles.

'I've seen you shoot,' Sam continued, purposely not letting her get in a word edgewise. 'You're an amazing sharpshooter, I'm impressed as hell. I've been impressed by your work in the Bureau, too, these past years. You're solid, Locke. I'd trust you to guard my six any time. And I'd like very much to get to know you better.'

Alyssa didn't take his hand. She didn't even turn her head in his direction. To his dismay, she just stayed silent as she pulled off the highway into the brightly lit lot of a twenty-four-hour gas station.

She pulled the car up to a pump and cut the engine. 'Do you honestly think,' she finally said, only then turning to look at him, 'that I'm going to be eager to jump back into whatever it was we had going while we're in the process of searching for your *wife* and *daughter*?' The look in her eyes was glacial.

'Ex-wife,' he pointed out. As soon as the word left his lips, he knew it was a mistake. Alyssa had her sense of humor shut down to zero.

'I should have said no,' she told him. 'No, I can't take you to Waldo tonight, and no, you can't leave Sarasota until we verify that you aren't the chief suspect in a murder investigation.'

'But you know I didn't—'

'Hush,' she ordered him sharply. 'It's my turn to talk. Hit on me again, Starrett, just one more time, and I will deliver you into the custody of the local police, who will transport you back to Sarasota.'

She was serious. He followed her out of the car and over to the gas pump, where she was running a credit card through the computer, her movements jerky with anger.

She accused him of . . . And now she was mad at *him*?

'I wasn't hitting on you,' he protested. He knew the last thing he should do was let her piss him off – and let her know that she'd pissed him off – but he was too freaking tired to care. 'If you thought that was me hitting on you . . . *Shit. This* is me hitting on you.'

He grabbed her and pulled her in, hard, so that her body was pressed against his. And it was heart attack time. Alyssa Locke, in his arms again. He faltered then, because she froze, too.

If she'd slugged him, he would have known what to say, what to do.

Instead, time stood still under the brightly lit overhang of the Sunoco as he stared down into her eyes.

'I've dreamed about you every single night, Lys,' he whispered. 'I would sell my soul to the devil to win you back.'

He leaned down to kiss her, and for a moment he'd thought he'd won, because she moved closer to him, stepping between his legs. If he didn't know her so well, he might've misinterpreted it as a surrender. But he *did* know her, and he twisted away in just enough time to hip check her little gift of a knee to his balls.

She pulled free from his arms. 'You are *such* an asshole. You always have to prove that you're right, don't you? So *that's* you hitting on me – thank you so much for the demonstration. Forgive me for my earlier confusion. God forbid you should ever be so subtle as to hit on a woman by only using words. As long as we're clearing things up: Touch me again, and you'll be wearing my shoe print on your ass.'

She thought . . . 'That wasn't . . .' Sam shook his head. 'I mean, yeah, it started out—'

'If you want to go to Waldo, you'll shut up right now!' Alyssa slammed open the gas-tank door and yanked the hose over to the car to fill it up. 'From here on in, you're not even going to *talk* to me. In fact, you're so wide awake, you're driving. I'll be in the backseat. Asleep.'

Aw, shit.

He'd gone too far.

Again.

'Jesus,' Sam said.

Alyssa rubbed her eyes and sat up in the back of the car. Jesus, indeed.

There were some lovely motor home parks in Florida, with well tended landscaping and flowering shrubbery and gleamingly clean double-wides in neat rows.

The trailer park they had just pulled in to was not one of them.

It was like something out of a horror movie, where people with bad teeth who changed their clothes once every six years lived with their twenty-seven vicious pit bulls, most of which weren't house trained.

Sam rolled to a stop, the headlights of the car illuminating a former recreational vehicle, a once white metal container vaguely shaped like a rust-streaked can of ham, with deflated tires. A light was visible through the ragged shades that covered its windows.

'Is this . . .?'

'Number two, Happy Lane,' Sam told her grimly. 'Mary Lou's not here. Believe me. She wouldn't let Haley spend twenty seconds in this shithole, let alone three weeks.'

'People do unusual things when they're desperate.' Alyssa tried to get a glimpse of herself in the rearview as she smoothed down her hair.

He met her eyes in the mirror. 'I thought you weren't talking to me ever again.'

'I'm not,' she said. Being semiconscious for the past ninety minutes hadn't really helped her feel any less exhausted. It had, however, kept the conversation at a minimum. 'I'm talking to myself while you eavesdrop. I think I'll go see who's home.'

She reached for the handle on the car door, but Sam didn't move.

'Fuck,' he swore. 'I know it's stupid, and I know I said I didn't think Haley would be here, but I was hoping . . . no, I was *counting* on her being here.' He hit the steering wheel. '*Fuck.*'

What could she possibly say? *Don't worry, we'll find her?* But Alyssa wasn't convinced they would. If Mary Lou and Haley had been held at gunpoint and taken to some out-of-the-way swamp or bog where they were murdered, their bodies might never be recovered.

Although there was a solid part of her that couldn't believe that they could be dead. Life just wasn't that easy.

And wasn't *that* a terrible thought? Shame on her.

'We may not find out anything helpful tonight,' Alyssa told him. 'But we will tomorrow, when we talk to the car dealer in Gainesville.'

He nodded. 'Yeah. I know. It's just . . . *tomorrow. Shit.* Patience isn't one of my strengths.'

No kidding.

He met her eyes in the mirror again, forcing a smile that faded quickly. 'I'm sorry. I'm just . . . scared to death for her, you know?'

The last thing in the world she should do was touch him. Alyssa knew Sam Starrett far too well, knew that he would get the absolute wrong idea. Still, she reached out and touched his shoulder, trying her best to make it a brief, fairly impersonal squeeze.

He was warm and solid beneath the cotton of his T-shirt, and he reached up to cover her hand with his. But he didn't try to hold on to her. He let her fingers slip out from beneath his as she pulled her hand away.

'I'm sorry, too,' she told him. She was sorry about so many things.

Sam took his hat from the dashboard. 'Okay, let's do this.'

'Let's,' she said. 'Maybe Mrs Morrison – What's her first name?'

'Darlene,' he told her.

'Maybe she knows where Mary Lou and Haley are.'

'Yeah.'

She knew he didn't believe it for a second. As she watched, he took a deep breath and blew it out hard. He turned off the car, and together they climbed out.

'Jesus.' The place smelled like raw sewage – as if the septic system had broken down a long time ago.

There was a collection of trash in the front yard – if you could call it a yard. A twisted bicycle, the remains of what looked like an old swing set in a haphazard pile of candy-striped metal bars, a battered shopping cart, part of a rusting car.

Alyssa tested the rickety steps leading to the troll-sized entrance before she stepped onto them. She knocked, three loud raps on the door. Something mean-sounding started barking inside, quickly joined by something equally nasty, and Sam grabbed her by the elbow and pushed her back, stepping in front of her as the door opened.

'Last call was two A.M.,' a woman said before she even saw who was standing there. 'I keep bar hours.' Her speech was slurred, her voice a strange mix of the sugar of the deep south and the hacksaw baritone roughness of a three-pack-a-day smoker.

She was backlit by the bare bulb that hung from the ceiling of her trailer, her face and form in shadows. She looked to be wearing some kind of robe that hung open in the front.

'Darlene Morrison?' Sam asked.

'That's one of my names, darlin'. And goodness, look at you.

For you, hon, I'll make an exception and open up shop,' she said to Sam. 'Fifty bucks for the works, twenty or a bottle of Scotch for the best hand job in the county – up front, and you provide the rubber.'

Oh, this was charming. Apparently Darlene had never met her daughter's husband before. And apparently Sam hadn't known his mother-in-law turned tricks for a living. He seemed something at a loss for words.

Alyssa stepped out from behind him. 'Mrs Morrison, I'm afraid you've misunderstood. We have some questions—'

'You cops need a warrant to come on my land!' Darlene shouted, as she slammed the door shut.

Alyssa looked at Sam in dismay. 'I purposely didn't say I was—'

'You have three seconds to get back into your car before I set these dogs loose!' Darlene's harsh voice came from the trailer. 'One!'

'Mrs Morrison, we're looking for your daughter,' Alyssa shouted back, but it was clear from the noise the woman was making that talking this out wasn't an option.

'Two!'

Sam had gathered that, too. He was already grabbing for the metal bars of the former swing set. 'Lys, catch!'

'Three!'

He tossed one of the pieces of metal to her as the door opened again and two snarling balls of fur and teeth burst out.

Sam threw himself at both of the dogs, batting one of them back with the metal bar he'd grabbed for himself, kicking at the other with his boot, never letting either of them come even remotely close to Alyssa. His hat fell off and his long hair flew as he spun around, seeming to know just where the dogs would go before they moved.

Alyssa hefted the blue-and-white candy-cane-striped bar of metal he'd tossed her, convinced that the best way to help was to stay out of his way. She'd been in his shoes before and the last thing she'd needed at the time was someone tripping her up.

One of the dogs was bigger and uglier than the other, but they both had lots of sharp little teeth. Neither of them took well to being smacked, although the smaller one was meaner and kept coming back for more.

As Sam kept the smaller dog at bar's length, he grabbed hold of the broken bicycle with his left hand and threw it at the larger dog.

Who turned tail and ran.

The smaller dog was growling low in its throat, ears back against its head, eyes glued to the bar Sam wielded menacingly

'I don't want to hurt your dog,' Sam called to Darlene Morrison, who was still inside the tin can. 'Call him off!'

The shade at the window moved slightly, and Alyssa knew that the woman was watching.

Alyssa made a show of tossing down the metal bar Sam had given her and taking out her side arm, holding it in a two-handed Hollywood Movie Cop stance – unnecessary but visually effective – drawing a bead directly between the dog's eyes.

'I don't give a damn about the dog, but the last thing I want to do tonight is paperwork,' Alyssa called to Darlene. 'All we want to do is talk to you. You're not in trouble. Not yet. But if your dog attacks my, uh, partner again, I'll shoot him dead.'

'The dog, not the partner, right?' Sam said in a low voice, his eyes fixed on the dog.

Alyssa ignored him. 'Once I discharge my weapon, paperwork is going to have to be filed. And as long as I'm stuck filling out reports, you better believe that I'll charge you with aggravated assault, which, by the way, is a felony in this state.'

'I was just protecting my property!' came from inside. 'There's no law against that.'

'But there is against solicitation,' Alyssa pointed out.

The trailer door squealed open. 'Trapper,' Darlene barked. 'Inside.'

The dog backed its way to the stairs, and then, with one last look and snarl in Sam's direction, he slunk into the trailer.

'Step down the stairs, ma'am,' Alyssa ordered the woman. She lowered her gun, but she kept it out and visible.

'You said you just want to talk.'

'We do. But away from the trailer, please.' With that dog securely on the other side of the door. She looked at Sam. 'You okay?'

'Yeah. You?'

'I'm fine.' Like she'd done anything more than stand here and watch. How many dogs would have had to come out of that trailer before he'd needed her help?

'What'd you do to Hawk?' Darlene complained as she came down the steps. 'Hawkeye!' she bellowed. 'Hawk! You get your ass back here, you little coward!'

'He was moving pretty fast when he lit out of here.' Sam reached down and picked up his baseball cap, slapping it on his thigh to shake the dust off of it. 'I'd be surprised if he's back before morning.'

Out in the yard, with the streetlight shining on Darlene, Alyssa could see the family resemblance. And for the first time, she honestly felt sorry for Mary Lou Morrison Starrett, even knowing what she now knew from Clyde – that Mary Lou had gotten herself pregnant on purpose in an attempt to make Sam marry her.

Imagine having a mother who would . . . for *Scotch*. As Sam would say, *Jesus*.

'I'm Lt Sam Starrett, ma'am,' he said now to Darlene. 'Your daughter Mary Lou's ex-husband?'

Darlene Morrison made a sound that might've been a bark of laughter. 'Well, shoot, honey,' she said. 'Why didn't you say so in the first place?'

Tuesday, June 17, 2003

Tom Paoletti was awake and already pulling on his pants when the door to his room opened.

He'd woken up at the commotion in the hallway. Whoever was out there hadn't made any effort to be quiet as they entered the building. There were a hell of a lot of them, too.

His first thought was lynch mob.

His second was that his team was back and had come to break him free.

Both were equally absurd.

But it was probably best to have pants on, whatever the situation really was.

Tom checked his watch as he zipped his fly – it was 0612. That wasn't early at all by Navy standards, but most of the mob that came through his door were wearing suits. He recognized some of them as FBI and searched for Max Bhagat's familiar face.

And came up empty.

The lawyer from the JAG office was there, though. Which was not good news. Well, compared to a potential lynching it probably was.

But it meant this gang was here to question him. And at 0612 in the morning, *that* meant sometime in the night they'd received some kind of tip or lead that had them foaming at the mouth.

'What's going on?' he asked the JAG lieutenant, but the lawyer just shook his head. It wasn't clear if he wasn't telling or if he didn't know, but Tom would've put good money on didn't know.

He made them wait while he took a leak and shaved and put on the rest of his choker whites. It felt like he was dressing for his own funeral. He was picking up all kinds of tension and bad vibes from the various guards and players. The mood in the room was positively spooky.

Then he went downstairs, surrounded by guards who

watched him as closely as they might have watched Osama bin Laden. He was escorted into a car, which drove all the way over to the nearby base administration building, where he was escorted inside, into one of the larger conference rooms.

There were more FBI in there, but still no sign of Max.

Tom sat down and put his legal pad in front of him on the table. Took his pen out of his pocket and lined it up neatly next to the pad. He'd remembered most of the details of that op where they'd scuttled the downed helo, the op he'd been questioned about extensively just yesterday. He'd re-created his schedule to the best of his ability, accounting for his time from the moment the team had gone wheels up in Coronado to the moment they'd returned. He was ready for this.

But the first question completely threw him.

'What is your relationship with Mary Lou Starrett?'

He actually laughed aloud in surprise. Who? 'Excuse me?'

'What is your relationship with Mary Lou Starrett?'

Tom shook his head. 'I don't have a relationship with – Are you talking about Lieutenant Roger Starrett's wife?' Ex-wife by now, wasn't she? Her name *was* Mary Lou, wasn't it?

'How long have you known Mary Lou Starrett?'

Mother of God. What was this about? These weren't just casual questions.

'I don't know,' Tom admitted. 'I have to think about it. I can't say for certain, but I'm pretty sure I met her shortly after she married my lieutenant.'

'Do you know the current whereabouts of Mary Lou Starrett?'

That one he answered without any hesitation. 'No. I do know she left the San Diego area about six months ago. I believe she went to Florida. Lieutenant Starrett informed me at the time that they were separating and that she'd filed for a divorce. To be honest, I was relieved. It was clear both to me and to my XO that their marriage wasn't working out and that that was impacting Starrett's performance as an officer and a SEAL.'

'When was the last time you spoke to Mary Lou Starrett?'

'I'm not sure I ever spoke to her,' Tom said. 'I mean, not to say more than "Hi, how are you?" What does this have to do with—'

'We're asking the questions. When was the last time you saw Mary Lou Starrett?'

'I don't know,' Tom said. 'I repeat, I didn't know her. She wasn't friends with—' *Kelly,* he'd been about to say, but no way was he bringing her into this. 'We didn't run in the same social circles,' he amended. 'I occasionally saw her on base when she came to visit Sam – Lieutenant Starrett.'

'Did you ever exchange written or electronic correspondence with Mary Lou Starrett?'

Jesus Christ. Tom reached down deep for his patience. He was going to need every ounce that he had. Because this was going to be one goddamn long morning.

Alyssa's cell phone rang at 0845.

'Locke,' she managed to say, sinking back with it into the motel bed, praying it was a wrong number.

'Are you actually still asleep at quarter to nine in the morning? Or did I totally blow the math?'

It was her partner, Jules Cassidy.

'I'm not asleep anymore,' she mumbled. Jules hadn't been her first partner straight out of Quantico. But by her third week on the job, after she'd gotten a sampling of potential partners – including two James Bond wanna-bes, four self-important MIBs without Will Smith's sense of humor, a Gunsmoke revivalist who said, 'Let me help you with that, little lady,' at least twice a day, and seven men of the 'Partners should be close. Real close. So why don't we go out and get a drink after work?' variety – she'd found herself requesting, no, *begging* to be paired up with Jules Cassidy.

Almost unbearably cute, with a pretty face, boy-band hair that he dyed or bleached depending on his mood, and a trim, perfect body that was slight of stature, Jules had spent the first few years of his career with the FBI passing himself off as a teenager, investigating everything from gang-related crimes to drug trafficking. Street smart, intelligent, and loaded with experience and a solid sense of humor, he was everything Alyssa was looking for in a partner.

As a bonus, he was gay.

Flamboyantly, out-of-the-closet, shock-your-grandmother gay.

He was the perfect partner, and he'd become a close friend.

'Are you calling from Hawaii?' she asked. It had to be, what, close to 0400 there.

'I'm on a red-eye somewhere over the Gulf of Mexico,' Jules reported. 'Cruising at thirty thousand feet. And spending forty dollars a minute to talk to you on one of these ridiculous phones that are attached to the back of the seat in front of me.'

Alyssa opened her eyes. 'You're not supposed to be back until . . . Friday?'

'Yeah, well, I got a call yesterday from Laronda, saying the boss wanted me back in ASAP – first flight out after Mom's wedding, that is. Isn't Max a romantic fool? But people in my family don't do things like get married without the largest possible dose of high drama. Mom skipped out two days ago, Phil went chasing after her, and they ended up tying the knot in Tokyo. Why Tokyo? Don't ask. Was I at the ceremony after traveling thousands of miles to be with them? Not even close. They weren't coming back, so I hopped the next flight out. Which is why I'm calling you. Can you pick me up at the airport, pretty please, schnookums, at ten-fifteen?'

'Jules, I'm not in DC.'

'No shit, Sherlock. I'm flying into Sarasota. I understand our little mutual friend Sam Starrett's been causing some trouble in the Sunshine State.'

Alyssa sat up. 'You're coming to Sarasota?'

'Me and George and Deb and Yashi and Frannie and the new guy, what's his name,' Jules told her. 'Even Laronda's on her way down.'

She turned on the light. 'Why on earth . . . *Everyone's* coming to Sarasota? What's going on?'

'Hmmm. The mystery thickens. I thought you'd be able to tell *me*.'

'I'm not in Sarasota,' Alyssa told him. 'I'm in Gainesville. Sam and I drove up here last night.'

'To talk to the car dealer.'

'Yeah. That's on the morning's agenda. How much do you know about what's gone down?' she asked.

'Dead ex-wife baking in the kitchen for three weeks . . . whoops, it's not the ex – it's a dead sister-in-law,' Jules recited. 'BOLO sent for both Mary Lou Starrett and Clyde Wrigley, Wrigley found. Mary Lou apparently pretended she was her sister and sold her car lock, stock and barrel to some "We Pay Cash for Your Wreck" establishment in Gainesville three weeks ago and maxed out her credit card at the Orange Park Mall, outside of Jacksonville. Unless you know more, I think I'm completely up to speed on that funfest. So let's get personal now, Alyssa, my pumpkin. You and *Sammy* drove to Gainesville and stayed *where* last night? You know I love Roger Starrett like a brother, but . . . are you out of your fucking *mind*?'

'Separate motel rooms,' Alyssa said.

'Thank God,' Jules said. 'Because if you're going to break Max's heart, I at least want to be in the same state when he gets the news. You know, so I can provide comfort.'

'You know, the only thing funny about that was that I know it's costing you forty dollars a minute,' Alyssa said.

Jules knew damn well that Alyssa and Max were not – and never had been – involved. He'd believed the rumors for a while, but then he'd started to notice little things. Like Max never touched her. Ever. Even the times they'd all three gone out for Chinese food after hours. Even the times Jules had dropped by Alyssa's apartment to find Max over, watching the baseball game.

And when Jules had asked her outright, Alyssa hadn't been

able to lie to him. She'd never been able to lie to him.

And yet, even knowing all that, Jules was still rooting for Alyssa and Max to get together.

'Seriously, sweetie,' Jules said now. 'Was it smart to spend four hours in a car with Sam Starrett, who I'm going to kill for not telling me about the divorce? Did you know I spoke to him on the phone just two weeks ago? He said *nothing*. So, okay, news flash – he's single again. *Red alert!* Run away! Don't get into a car with him again! Didn't your father and I teach you *any*thing? I mean, great sex is great sex, and I'm the last person who should be shaking my finger at you for wanting to get some, but there must be a list of eligible bachelors a mile long – including Max – who'd be more than willing to do the horizontal cha-cha with you, *without* shredding your heart in the process.'

'I'm not going to sleep with Sam Starrett,' Alyssa said. But how many years had it been since she'd uttered those very words to Jules, and then gone ahead and done just that? She could hear his skepticism now, in his silence. 'I really mean it this time. I didn't mean it the last time I said it. But now . . . It's not going to happen. There are too many bad feelings between us.'

'Uh-huh,' Jules said in his best noncommittal therapist voice.

'I mean, yes, sure, he's been dogging me – in fact, he's been pretty up-front about it – but I'm *not* going there again. You know, if the idea of a relationship with a white redneck macho he-man Navy SEAL asshole wasn't already completely crazy, now the man comes with an ex-wife and a daughter vying for his time. I don't need that. I don't need Mary Lou calling up at all hours of the night because her tire's flat. I don't need to go scouring the countryside, looking for her every time she turns up AWOL. And I don't need Haley hanging around every other weekend – because you know sure as hell Sam will get called out, and he'd be like, "Hey, Lys, you don't mind watching the baby for a day or two until Mary Lou can pick her up, do you?" No. No, no, no. This is *not* the life I want.'

'Well,' Jules said. 'That's good. I guess. But if that's the case, I can't figure out what you're doing with him in Gainesville.'

'He's freaking out about Haley. Oh, Jules, I can't even think about the possibility of Sam's daughter being dead. He keeps asking me if I think she's still alive, and I don't know what to say. How do you ever recover from something like that?'

'The same way you recovered when your sister died. With the help of your friends,' he said.

'But losing a *child* . . .'

'Hey,' he said. 'We don't know that Mary Lou hasn't taken Haley and gone on vacation. She may not even know that Janine was killed.'

'Oh, she knows,' Alyssa told him. 'The reason we drove up last night was to go to Waldo, just north of here, to talk to Mary Lou's mother, Darlene. Who, in her spare time, when she's not working her job selling frozen yogurt at the Gainesville rest stop – southbound – is the town whore. I kid you not. Talk about freak show. FYI, the going rate for a hand job in Waldo is a bottle of Scotch.'

'Oh,' Jules said. 'I don't want to know how you know that.'

'When we asked if she knew where Mary Lou and Haley were, Darlene told us that *Janine* called her, just about three weeks ago, to tell her that Mary Lou was dead.'

'Hello!' Jules said.

'Yup,' Alyssa said. 'Darlene admitted that she was skunked when she got the call – she's pretty much always skunked – so she couldn't say for absolute certain that it wasn't Mary Lou pretending to be Janine. Apparently, the two sisters sounded alike, especially over the phone. And maternal contact wasn't high on Darlene's daily to-do list, so it wasn't like she spoke to them often enough to know the difference. Whoever called Darlene said that she was Janine, and that Mary Lou was dead, and that she was going to Alaska. She didn't mention Haley at all.'

'Alaska,' Jules repeated.

'To make a fresh start.'

'My bullshit meter is clicking wildly.'

'No kidding,' Alyssa said. 'But wait, there's more. We're not the only ones who've come calling, asking about Mary Lou. Darlene told us that two men stopped in about a week ago. She told them exactly what she told us.'

'Zounds,' Jules said. 'Mary Lou knows that someone's looking for her, possibly to do to her what they did to her sister, and she's using her mother to spread disinformation.'

Zounds? 'Yeah, that was our take on it, too.' Alyssa's cell phone beeped. 'Shoot, that's my call waiting. I've got to get this.'

'It's probably Ma-ax, checking up on you-oo.'

Alyssa hung up on Jules, clicking over to the other call. 'Locke.'

'Missy, where have you been?' It was Laronda, Max's administrative assistant.

Everyone thought Max's elite counterterrorist group ran super efficiently because of his brilliant leadership skills, and maybe that wasn't so far from the truth. Because Max had found Laronda – a single mother of two teenage boys – in the typing pool, back when he was fresh out of Quantico, and whenever he'd moved upward, he'd made sure she'd moved with him.

'Gainesville,' Alyssa said. 'Max was aware that I—'

'Where are you right now?'

'The Motel Six off Route 75—'

'And you didn't call in and give your location and a phone number when you landed last night,' Laronda scolded. 'Cell phone satellites were out from five-thirty this morning until about ten minutes ago. We couldn't reach you, Locke. Max is not happy. I am not happy. No one is happy—'

'I tried, but it was oh-five-hundred when I got here,' Alyssa protested. 'Which wasn't that long ago. I was getting one of those system-wide busy signals, and I figured since I was only going to have about four hours before I got back on the road, I might as well use that time to actually sleep instead of trying to call in.'

'Where's Lieutenant Starrett?'

'Next door,' Alyssa said. 'Probably still sleeping.'

'Get him,' Laronda ordered. 'Stay with him. Bring him back to Sarasota.'

'What's going on?' Alyssa asked. 'I just spoke to Jules and he said everyone's heading down there.'

'Does anyone ever tell me anything?' Laronda complained. 'I'm Max's message service today. Eighteen years and I'm walking voicemail. Let me read you Max's complete message: "Tell her to bring the son of a bitch—" that would be Lieutenant Starrett "—back to Sarasota ASAP. Tell her not to let him out of her sight. Tell her I'll call her as soon as I'm out of this expletive deleted meeting." An expletive-deleted meeting with the United States President, I might add. So do what the boss says, Locke, and get yours and the son of a bitch's butts to Sarasota. Now.'

Mary Lou had just cleaned up Haley and Amanda after their breakfast and set them up with *The Little Mermaid* video, when she heard the sound of crying.

She followed it to Whitney's room – with all of its pink and white frothy froufrous that had been hand selected by some famous interior decorator.

The door was ajar, and Mary Lou knocked on it as she pushed it open.

'Go away,' Whitney sobbed. 'Just leave me alone!'

And Mary Lou might have – had she not caught a glimpse of the girl's face.

Someone had given her one hell of a bloody lip.

Someone? Someone named Peter Young, the little prick.

Mary Lou went into Whitney's bathroom and wet a washcloth with cool water. She carried it back out into the bedroom, where she sat on the edge of that candy-colored bed and rubbed Whitney's back.

'Come on, honey,' Mary Lou said, with the same gentleness that she used with Haley and Amanda. 'Let's get you cleaned up.'

Whereupon Whitney launched herself at Mary Lou and hugged her with a ferocity that was not unlike her two-year-old daughter's.

Mary Lou rocked her and let her cry, murmuring that it would be okay, it was going to be okay – knowing what it was like to be so desperate for affection that any attention from any man was interpreted as potential love. If true love made you blind, then lonely, self-loathing desperation made you blind and deaf and unable to think clearly – so much so that the seemingly appropriate response to a leering look from a stranger was to sleep with the man.

When the girl's tears finally let up, Mary Lou asked, 'You want to tell me what happened?'

'What do *you* care? You're just being nice to me so that I won't tell my father that your name isn't really Connie Grant.'

Mary Lou had to laugh. 'Go on and think that if you want. Besides, I already know what happened. Peter broke up with you, you got in his face about it, and he backhanded you.' She pressed the cold cloth gently against Whitney's swollen lip.

The girl's eyes welled with fresh tears as she pushed the cloth away, but this time they were tears of anger. 'I caught him with his dick in Sarah Astrid's mouth.'

And this actually came as a surprise?

Whitney wiped her nose with the back of her hand, wincing as she got a little too close to her cut lip. 'He was in his car, and he and Sarah just looked up and laughed when they saw me standing there.'

'Oh, honey . . .'

'So I called him up later and pretended I wanted to see him and, you know, get it on, like I didn't care about what he did with Sarah the slut.'

Whitney wasn't a particularly pretty girl, but she did have a certain something in her eyes that, when lit, gave her charisma. It was on fire now.

'See, his parents were going out of town, so we made plans for me to come over – this was last night. So I bought, like, twenty-five bags of ice and got there before he got home. I climbed in through the kitchen window and I put the ice in his bathtub and filled it up the rest of the way with cold water. And then I lit all these candles in the bathroom and turned off the lights, like we were going to have some kind of big romantic moment, like something out of a movie, you know? And when he got home and saw that, he took off his clothes so fast, he didn't even notice the ice in the bathtub, so I pushed him in and pulled out one of Daddy's guns—'

'Whitney!'

She wiped her nose again. 'It wasn't loaded,' she said scornfully. 'I'm not stupid. Of course, Peter the shithead didn't know that. So I held it on him and made him sit there in that ice water for about five minutes, till his lips started to turn blue. Then I made him get out and stand there, and I took some digital pictures of him with his little, teeny shriveled dick. And I put them on the Internet.'

Mary Lou couldn't help it. She started to laugh. 'Oh, my Lord, girl!'

Whitney was laughing, too, but it faded quickly. 'But then this morning, he told me if I hadn't of done that, he was going to ask me to marry him, but now he wasn't going to. And *then* he backhanded me.'

The tears were back in her eyes, and Mary Lou gave her a gentle shake. 'What are you doing crying over a boy who can't keep his johnson out of Sarah Whatsis's ugly mouth? You think he was serious about marrying you – for any reason other than he wanted to get his hands on your father's money? Here's a hot tip, hon. If a man loves you, truly loves you, he's *not* going to be fooling around with anyone else. And he's sure as hell not going to backhand you and make you bleed. Not *ever*.'

Whitney moved slightly away from her, taking the washcloth and pressing it to her lip, pulling it back to look at the blood. But then she made a face. 'Yeah, what do *you* know about true love, Connie-Wendy-whatever? *Your* loving husband wants to kill you.'

Sam may not have been loving, but he certainly hadn't wanted to see her dead. Mary Lou got a twinge of remorse every time Whitney referred to her fictional murderous spouse. And over the past day or so, the girl *had* managed to bring the subject up an awful lot.

'Actually,' Mary Lou said, 'toward the end of my marriage, I did meet a man who loved me the way true love should be. With grace and kindness and sweet devotion.'

'You cheated on your husband?' Whitney asked incredulously. 'No wonder he wants to kill you.'

'I didn't cheat,' Mary Lou said, then corrected herself. 'Ihbraham didn't allow me to cheat. I would have if he'd have let me. I was that desperate.'

Whitney nodded. For once she had no smartass response.

'I didn't realize I loved him at first,' Mary Lou told the girl. 'He was a gardener and, Lord, he wasn't even white . . .'

'Oh, my God!'

'Yeah. And my husband was this officer in the . . . the—' *Air Force*, she was going to lie, but really, what did it matter? 'The Navy.' She went with the truth. It was easier to remember. 'That seemed so much, I don't know, flashier, I guess. More important. I mean, who wants to say, "My husband is a gardener"? But you know what? It really, honestly, doesn't matter. What you really want to be able to say is, "My husband loves me, and I love him, too." *That's* what matters.' Unfortunately, it was a lesson she herself had learned too late.

'So where is he?' Whitney asked. 'If he loves you so much? What's his name – Abraham?'

'EE-braham Rahman, spelled with an I,' Mary Lou said. 'He was from Saudi Arabia.'

'He's, like, an *Arab*?' Whitney's mouth dropped open. 'Weren't you afraid he was a terrorist?'

'No,' Mary Lou said.

Whitney could smell a lie a mile away. Took a liar to know another liar. The girl just lifted an eyebrow and waited.

'Yeah, okay,' Mary Lou admitted. 'So there was this bad . . . thing that happened, and I thought he was involved, and I left town with . . . with *Chris* because I was all freaked out, and I thought not only was he a terrorist, but that he was a dead terrorist.' It had broken her heart.

'Wait a minute,' Whitney said. 'You thought *what?*'

'I thought he broke the law,' Mary Lou simplified. Yeah, simplified was an understatement. What she'd *thought* was that Ihbraham had been part of a plot to assassinate the US President. She'd thought he'd used her to smuggle guns onto the Coronado Navy base in the trunk of her car. She'd actually seen one of those guns, touched it even. She'd first thought it was Sam's and had been royally pissed that her Navy SEAL husband had left it in the trunk of her car, where she might've gotten into trouble for carrying it around.

But it turned out that Ihbraham had nothing to do with the terrorist plot. He hadn't put that gun there, either. He was just a gardener. Just an American who happened to be born in Saudi Arabia.

Who'd been in the wrong place at the wrong time.

Someone else had used her to smuggle those guns onto the Navy base. Someone who had traced her to Sarasota all these months later and killed Janine. Someone who was surely still searching for Mary Lou.

'There was an . . . incident some months ago,' Mary Lou told Whitney now, trying to explain why she'd thought Ihbraham was dead. 'Terrorists started shooting into a crowd, and yeah, they were definitely al-Qaeda – and they definitely looked it. Some of the folks in that crowd started beating the hell out of anyone who looked like they came from the Middle East.

Ihbraham was there and he was attacked.'

'You can't blame people for trying to protect themselves!'

'No,' Mary Lou agreed. 'You can't. But there's a huge difference between knocking a guy to the ground and searching him for a weapon or re-straining him until the police can come – and kicking a hole in his skull.'

Whitney winced. 'Oh, shit.'

'Yeah. After it was over, he was taken to the hospital, unconscious. No one expected him to survive.

'I filed for divorce from my husband and left town.' She continued with her story, because for the first time ever, Whitney was really, *really* paying attention. 'After I'd gotten to know Ihbraham, it seemed kind of obvious that my husband didn't love me. Not even a little. And I . . . I'd finally found out what real love felt like. There was no point in sticking around in a marriage that had nothing to do with anything real.'

She'd also feared arrest. Sooner or later someone would find out that she'd smuggled those guns onto the base. It had been inadvertent on her part, sure, but her past experiences with the police didn't give her much faith in their ability to see subtle differences in the facts.

'I spent five months thinking Ihbraham was probably dead, and then my sister got sick of me crying myself to sleep every night, and called his business number.' It was the same day they'd moved out of the house they'd shared with Janine's ex-husband Clyde.

Jan had been feeling extremely proactive in affairs of the heart, so she'd called the phone number on the landscaping business card that Ihbraham had given Mary Lou a lifetime ago.

Being Janine, she'd been direct and to the point. She was Mary Lou Starrett's sister and she wanted to know if an Ihbraham Rahman who'd used to work from this phone number was still alive.

'I was at work when she called him,' Mary Lou told Whitney. 'But when I got home she told me that Ihbraham was alive.'

Her voice still shook when she said the words.

At the time, Mary Lou had handed Haley to her sister, locked herself in the bathroom, and cried and cried. Ihbraham was *alive!*

'She actually spoke to him,' she continued. 'He'd been in the hospital for three months, but he was almost completely recovered now and even working again. No, he was not a terrorist. He and his brothers had been questioned by the authorities, but they weren't involved in the shootings. My sister also told me that after Ihbraham left the hospital he spent some time searching for me. But since I was keeping myself pretty well hidden . . . . He asked my sister to tell me that he hoped I would give him a call. But, Lord, as much as I loved him – *because* I loved him – I couldn't do that.'

'Why not?' Then Whitney answered her own incredulous outburst. 'Because your husband would kill *him*, too.'

Mary Lou nodded even though it wasn't Sam who would kill Ihbraham. Sam would probably welcome Ihbraham with a handshake or even a hug. Take my ex-wife, please. . . .

No, it was the terrorists – the *real* terrorists – whom Mary Lou was scared to death of.

One of them was a man, a very American-looking man with blond hair and blue eyes, who Mary Lou had only known as Bob Schwegel – obviously that had to be an assumed name. She'd met him in the library, of all places. He'd told her he was an insurance salesman, he'd flirted with her, and they'd become friends.

Sort of.

He'd certainly had access to her car during the time she'd found that weapon in her trunk.

And, months later, she'd seen him leaving her house in Sarasota with another man.

Her heart had gone into terrified palpitations at the sight of him, and she'd kept on driving, ducking down so that he wouldn't see her, grateful as hell that she and Janine had switched cars several months earlier.

SUZANNE BROCKMANN

Janine's car – the old light-blue-and-maroon wreck that Mary Lou used to drive – had been in the driveway when she drove past. She'd been scared to death for her sister's safety, but with Haley strapped into her car seat in the back, there was no way Mary Lou was going to stop.

Besides, it was possible the two men had rung the bell and simply asked Janine if Mary Lou was at home.

Wasn't it?

In hindsight, Mary Lou knew that couldn't have been the way it had gone down. Bob wanted Mary Lou dead – she had no doubt of that. And there was no way Bob would've gone to the door, talked to Janine, and walked away. Because Mary Lou might've called before she came home, and Janine might've said, 'Some guy came looking for you, girl. Blond, killer cheekbones, movie star face . . .? If you've been telling this man no, quick, call him back so I can say yes.'

At which point, Mary Lou would know that Bob had tracked her – somehow – to Sarasota, and would've been heading north on the interstate to Jacksonville and beyond, faster than she could say *presidential assassination attempt.*

On that awful day, Mary Lou had waited until dark, until Haley was fast asleep in the car. She'd parked on the next side street down from Camilia and had crept up to the house from the back, moving as silently as she could. All the windows were dark, even though Janine's car was still in the drive. The kitchen door was locked, so she'd opened it with her key and . . .

Found Janine, dead on the floor.

Lord God help them all.

As much as she ached to be with Ihbraham, she was not going to call him. He was one of the three people in this world who Mary Lou loved, one of the three who loved her, too.

Janine was already dead because of her. Haley was in danger just by being her child. There was no way Mary Lou was going to put Ihbraham at risk, too.

No freaking way.

150

She couldn't stop herself. She had been strong for so long, but now as she sat on Whitney's bed, in that horrible pink and white bedroom, she started to cry.

And this time it was Whitney – little messed-up demon child Whitney – who put her arms around her and murmured that it was going to be okay, that she wouldn't tell her father anything, that Mary Lou's secret was safe.

Eight

'I've been ordered to head back to Sarasota immediately,' Alyssa said when Sam picked up the hotel phone. No *Good morning*. No *Did you sleep well?* No *Sorry to wake you, but . . .* 'And to bring you with me.'

Sam stretched experimentally. Yep. Every inch of him felt exactly as if he'd spent way too many hours cramped in a car made for people half his size, then fought off a couple of canine attackers without properly stretching out first, then slept in a bed with a gully in the middle of it for far too short a time.

He should have slept on the floor. He would have been more comfortable.

'I'm not going anywhere until I talk to the guy at the car dealer,' he told her, his voice gravelly with sleep.

'Yeah, I know,' Alyssa said. 'That's why you have exactly five minutes to shower and get your ass out to the parking lot. You might want to say a quick prayer that the place opens at nine and that our man works Tuesday mornings. Max's orders didn't include side trips, but I figure the way you drive, we can make it up on the road.'

'Thank you,' he said.

'That wasn't necessarily a compliment.'

'No,' Sam said. 'I meant thank you for—'

'You now have four minutes and forty-eight seconds,' Alyssa cut him off, and cut the connection, too.

Sam hauled ass for the shower.

* * *

152

Alyssa glanced up as Sam got into her car still damp, with his hair wet and slicked back from his face. Thank goodness he still had the full beard. One of these days he was going to shave it off and then he'd look less like a mountain man and more like Sam.

Sam, the irresistible . . .

'Whoa,' he said. 'You showered *and* got coffee and doughnuts, too?'

'I didn't shower,' Alyssa informed him. 'I figured we needed directions to Harrison Motors more than we needed me to smell sweet.' She put the car into drive. 'Don't touch that coffee until you open that map and verify that the intersection of Routes 20 and 24 really is south of here.'

Sam wrestled with the road map. 'It is.' He looked up at the motel's proximity to the highway in front of them and said, 'Take a left out of the lot.' He glanced over at her. 'I happen to think you smell very sweet. I've always thought you—'

'Please don't be a jerk this early in the day,' Alyssa interrupted him. 'I'm doing you an enormous favor here, Starrett. Don't pay me back this way.'

'Sorry. I was just trying to be honest.'

'Can't you just say sorry?' Alyssa asked. 'And leave out all the noisy bullshit for a change?'

He sighed. 'Sorry.'

They drove in silence, but it lasted for only about twenty seconds before he asked, 'Sleep well?'

'No,' she said tersely. 'I woke up to the news that Max is moving the entire office down to Sarasota, and I don't know why. I didn't speak to him directly, but he ordered me to bring you there. I'm not supposed to let you out of my sight.'

'Shit,' he said. But then he laughed. 'Maybe he found out my birthday's coming and he wants to throw me a surprise party.'

Alyssa laughed, too, despite herself. 'Yeah, I'm sure that's it.' She glanced at him. 'Aren't you at all worried?'

'Worried is my new middle name.' He fished through the bag of doughnuts until he found the chocolate-covered one. 'But first things first. First, we find out if there's even a prayer that Mary Lou and Haley are still alive. Then we can go to Sarasota and find out how badly I'm about to get reamed. Depending on the news from Harrison Motors, I might even be willing to speculate how bad it's going to hurt, as we drive back south.'

Alyssa glanced at him again. 'Is your birthday really coming?'

The smile he gave her was slightly strained around the edges, but it was still pure Sam. 'There are so many creative ways I could answer that, but they'd only piss you off. So, yeah. My birthday's next week.' He paused. 'You want to give me a present?' He didn't wait for her to answer because obviously he knew she'd jump to sexual conclusions. 'Help me find Haley. I don't care if the whole freaking FBI is in Sarasota ready to help find her. I trust you. I want *you* working on this case.'

He'd surprised her with that one. But she shook her head. 'I can't pick and choose assignments—'

'Maybe you can't, but Max sure as hell can. I know this isn't your normal counterterrorist assignment, but—'

'I really don't have the power to tell Max what to—'

'Then take time off,' Sam implored her. 'Lys, I wouldn't ask you to do this if it wasn't important. Please. The thought of never seeing her again is . . . I'm dying, here.'

Silence. What could she say?

'Jules is on his way back from Hawaii,' Alyssa finally told him. 'I'm sure he'll be willing to—'

'Yeah,' Sam said, correctly reading her words as a great big no. He couldn't keep at least a little sarcasm from escaping. 'Thanks a lot.'

She was dying here, too. But she didn't dare tell him that. She bit her tongue and clenched her teeth and didn't let the words escape.

He was clearly reining himself in, too. 'Sorry. I didn't mean to sound so . . . You've been really great, and I appreciate your efforts. I honestly do.'

'It's all right,' she said. 'I'll do what I can, Sam, but . . .' She cleared her throat. 'This isn't exactly my dream case.'

He laughed. 'Yeah, no kidding.'

'How long do I stay on this road?' she asked.

Sam made a big show of checking the map. 'Another two miles, it looks like. At least.'

More silence.

Then, when she picked up her coffee, he said, 'Careful, it's really hot.'

God. Alyssa didn't want Sam to be kind or considerate or thoughtful. She didn't want him to apologize or to be sincere or to care whether or not she burned her tongue. She wanted . . .

She didn't know what she wanted.

'Thank you,' she said, not daring to look in his direction as she took a big sip anyway.

It burned all the way down.

April 3, 1943
From the journal of Dorothy S. Smith

I was deep in an argument with Nurse Maria the masochist about whether or not I should be allowed up to walk to the bathroom, when there was a knock on the door to the hospital ward. 'Flowers for Lieutenant Smith.'

'Oh, how pretty,' Maria said to me. 'The delivery boy brought you flowers.' She bustled to the door. 'I'll take those.'

I was taking advantage of the opportunity and starting to swing my legs, cast and all, to the side of the bed, when I heard Walter's voice. 'No, I've been ordered to deliver them personally to Lieutenant Smith.'

A lieutenant colonel in the Army Air Corps had actually been mistaken for a delivery boy. I opened my mouth to set Maria straight when I realized that Walt was dressed in civvies – including the goshdarn silliest cap I've ever seen in my life. He met my eyes and gave me the smallest shake of his head – *no*.

So I shut my mouth and tucked my legs back under the covers. What on earth was he doing here in Savannah, Georgia?

'I have a private message for Miss Smith,' he told Maria, in the absolute worst cornpone deep south faked accent I'd ever heard, 'from Lieutenant Colonel Gaines. I'll be in some real, real hot water if I can't deliver it to her and get me a reply to take on back.'

'It's all right, Maria,' I said. 'I know Walt quite well.'

I think it was the sight of me sitting up in bed, looking as if I was going to be obedient about her order to keep using those ass-freezing metal bedpans, that made Maria the torturer relent.

'Don't let her get out of bed,' she ordered Walt before rushing off to the other end of the ward to torment the poor girl who'd had the appendectomy.

Walt glanced at the girl in the bed next to mine as he approached, and I did, too, but she was fast asleep. For the first time, I was glad I was at the end of the row of hospital beds, as drafty as it was, closest to the door. Across the center aisle, two beds down, Lily Foster was sitting up, doing her nails, waiting to be discharged.

She could see us, but she was too far away to hear our conversation if we spoke quietly.

'What are you doing here?' I asked. I pointed to the chair for visitors that was next to the bed. In all the weeks I'd been here, no one had used it. Until now.

'We heard about the accident,' Walter told me in his regular voice. He set the flowers on the little table beside my bed and pulled the chair closer. 'I came as quickly as I could. I'm sorry I didn't get here sooner.'

'I'm okay,' I told him.

He looked at the bandage on my head. 'You didn't write. Mae and I were worried.'

'I was, um, unconscious for a while.'

'They said you broke a rib which in turn punctured your lung.'

'It wasn't as bad as it sounds.'

Walt nodded, clearly not believing me.

It was ironic – me getting into a traffic accident not a week after I'd brought a plane down in a controlled crash. I'd walked away from that only to end up in this hospital just a few days later. But bad weather and poor driving had caused the Army transport I was riding in to skid off the road.

It sure as hell wouldn't have happened if I'd have been driving.

'Why aren't you wearing your uniform?' I asked Walt.

He was silent for a moment, and I could tell that he was wondering whether or not to tell me the truth. I knew right then that the truth was going to make me steaming mad.

'I tried to get in to see you earlier in the day,' he finally admitted. 'In my uniform. But . . .' He cleared his throat. 'Apparently visitors as well as patients need to be a certain correct color to get through these doors. However, it didn't take me long to note that delivery *boys* could be any color they wanted to be.' He smiled at me, so utterly not a boy, but rather a very full-grown man. 'What do you think of the cap? Nice touch, huh?'

'Almost as good as the accent,' I told him. 'I'm so sorry.'

'Think of it as my last chance to wear civilian clothes for a while,' he said. 'For a *long* while. Until the end of the war.'

I sat up even straighter. 'Are you telling me . . .?'

'Yes, I am.' He was smiling. 'The squad leaves for North Africa in a few weeks.'

He'd come all this way not just to make sure I was okay, but also to say goodbye.

This was the last time I was going to see him – maybe forever.

I was glad I was sitting down because I suddenly felt light-headed.

Walt had wanted to go and do his part for his country for so long. I tried to be happy for him, tried to smile back at him, but all I felt was terrified.

I felt stripped bare.

I'd hidden the truth for so long – not just from Mae and Walter, but from myself as well.

But here it was. No longer something that I could ignore.

I loved him. He was a black man and he was married to my dearest friend, but damn it, I *loved* Walter Gaines with all my heart.

And this was it. It was possibly – probably – the last few moments I'd spend with him.

Ever.

I knew far too many good men who went to fight the Germans and the Japanese and never came home again.

Walter glanced up, and I knew he was monitoring Nurse Maria. I looked, too, but she was still terrorizing the appendixless girl.

There was a whirlwind going on inside my head. Should I tell him? I wanted to tell him. I *couldn't* tell him. He was married to Mae. How could I tell him? How could I betray her that way? But did he love me, too? Yes, I knew he loved me, too. I could see it in his eyes, in his beautiful, beautiful brown eyes.

I opened my mouth, and 'Fight hard, fly harder, and fuck the Germans first' came out.

Walter laughed. 'Yes, ma'am.'

I wanted to kiss him. Was that really too much to ask – just one kiss for an entire lifetime? Because even if he did come back home, he'd be coming back to Mae and little Jolee.

I knew he loved Mae. How could anyone *not* love Mae? *I* loved Mae.

I wanted to kiss him, but I couldn't. I wouldn't. I didn't want to do that to Mae, and I didn't want *him* to do that to Mae, either.

'I'll take care of Mae and Jolee,' I told him. Don't cry, don't cry, don't cry. 'First thing we'll do is start planning your welcome home party.'

'You stay safe yourself,' he told me.

'I wish I was going with you.' That much I could say with all the emotion in my heart.

He was looking at the bandages on my head again. 'Are you really all right under there?'

I was self-conscious of all that gauze. Although I would have been even more self-conscious if my head *hadn't* been wrapped up. Thanks to the tailgate of the truck, I had a nasty gash a few inches above my hairline. 'They shaved off a chunk of my hair in order to stitch me up.'

'Hair grows back.'

'I hope so.' I had a scrape on my cheek, too, that hadn't completely healed, and I knew it made me look battered. It was hard to meet Walt's eyes – a throwback to the days when I was young and stupid and married to Percy Smith, who'd dinged me up on a regular basis. I hadn't looked anyone in the eye back then. 'I must look awful.'

Walter took my hand. 'You look beautiful, Dorothy – just as you always do.'

I don't know what shocked me more – that he called me beautiful or that he touched me. I do know that the moment his hand touched mine, I clung to him as if my life depended on my never letting go.

And – horrors! – I started to cry.

His hand was so dark and mine was so pale, it was shocking and hypnotizing and heartbreakingly wonderful. And I knew that this was it – even if he came back from this war, he was never going to touch me like this again unless I damn near killed myself again.

'Hey, now,' he said softly, leaning in real close. 'Hush, baby, it's all right.'

He pretended I was crying about the accident, asking me all kinds of questions about how scary it must've been trying to breathe with only half a lung after that truck rolled over and over, and about Betsy Wells, a nurse assigned to the Fifty-fifth, whom I'd just met that night, who died in my arms, and about how I'd climbed back up that incline with a broken ankle to flag down a passing car to go get help.

But he was a smart man, Walter was, and he knew what I was really crying about. He had tears in his own eyes as well.

'I'm sorry,' I told him, as I still clung to his hand, this time with both of mine.

He looked down at those hands of ours and he looked back at me and he opened his mouth to speak, and I stopped him.

'Don't,' I said.

He looked back at our hands and laughed softly before he met my eyes again. 'I wasn't going to,' he said quietly. 'I was just going to say that in a different lifetime . . .'

I nodded as I held his gaze for a long time. It wasn't a kiss, but it was all we could give each other – all we *would* give each other.

Lily Foster was staring now, aghast at the sight of me holding hands with the delivery 'boy'.

Maria, too, was starting toward us.

Walter slipped his hand free from mine and got to his feet. 'I'll give your message to Massah Gaines,' he said in that ridiculous accent.

'Be sure to bring his wife my love,' I told him as I wiped the tears from my face.

'Sho' nuff, Missy Dorothy.'

That one made me laugh, even as I started to cry again. 'Tell him to fly like I'm right on his tail. He flies better when I'm up there with him.'

'You're always with him,' Walter said in his regular voice, meeting my eyes for one last time, for all we knew for *the* last time, as Nurse Maria escorted him out the door.

As if his plaid sports jacket wasn't bad enough, Jon Hopper of Harrison Motors had a comb-over that was distracting as hell.

Sam followed Hopper and Alyssa to the back of the car lot, unable to think of anything except, what the Jesus God did this guy look like in the morning, fresh out of bed? His hair above his left ear probably hung down to his shoulder.

'This is the car,' Hopper said, pointing.

What the . . .? It was Janine's black Honda, not the maroon and light blue POS that Mary Lou had gotten as a permanent loaner when their minivan had been rear-ended and totaled back when they were first married.

Oh, man, that minivan . . . The thought of it still made Sam shudder.

And despite what WildCard and Nils thought, Sam really *hadn't* gotten into that accident on purpose.

The fact that it was the Honda and not the POS was noteworthy. If Mary Lou had been driving her sister's car, that probably meant Janine had been driving Mary Lou's. And lookie who had ended up dead.

And lookie who had called up Mommy dearest, pretending

to be Janine and trying to spread a little disinformation about which sister was in truth still alive – namely Mary Lou.

Which made Sam think a couple of things. One, that someone had been trying to kill Mary Lou in the first place and had goofed. Two, that there was probably more than one player on the killer's team.

Killer A had probably delegated the job to Killer B: Go ice Mary Lou Morrison Starrett. She lives at 462 Camilia Street. She drives a maroon and light blue POS with California plates. Brown hair, kind of short, stacked.

Killer B toddles off to Camilia Street. Janine – brown hair, short of stature, stacked – comes home in the maroon-and-light-blue POS with California plates . . .

It was easy to see how Killer B could've made a mistake that Killer A probably wouldn't have made.

The million-dollar question was, Had Killer A realized Killer B's mistake?

Yes. Why else would Darlene Morrison have been visited by those goons looking for Mary Lou? If they thought Mary Lou was safely dead, their search would've already been over.

The sign on the Honda's windshield said $2000. Hah. Mary Lou would have been lucky to get even an eighth of that from Mr Comb-over.

Sam pulled on the pair of latex gloves that Alyssa had handed him when they arrived at the car lot, and opened the car door.

'Touch as little as you can,' she'd advised him. 'We'll be sending someone out to get fingerprints. Don't mess that up or I'll get yelled at.'

He opened the glove box with a pen and checked under the seats for anything his ex-wife might've left behind.

There was, of course, nothing there.

Alyssa was speaking to Hopper: '—really appreciate it if you could look up the paperwork for this car and tell us who handled this transaction.'

'We got a call on this yesterday,' Hopper said. 'I don't need to look it up again. *I* wrote up this deal.'

That was a stroke of luck in their favor.

'I know it's been a few weeks,' Alyssa said, 'but can you describe the person who sold it to you?'

'Shoot. It was a woman, I remember that much, but . . .'

'Do the best you can, Mr Hopper.'

'Well, she had her kid with her. I remember that. Kids usually make deals like these more of a hassle – everything takes longer, you know, because the parent is being pulled two ways. But this kid was quiet. Cute, too. A little boy with blond hair and big blue eyes.'

A *boy*? That made Sam look up, and Alyssa met his gaze. Still, the hair and eyes were all Haley.

Alyssa looked back at Hopper. 'And the mother?'

He squinted in concentration. 'I remember she was crying, so I didn't really look at her too closely. She was pretending she wasn't – I figured the last thing she'd want was me staring at her red eyes and runny makeup. I think she might've had light hair, too, but I could be wrong. She was, uh, well endowed. I do remember that.'

'Was anyone else with her?'

'Just the little boy.' He said it with such conviction for someone remembering something that had happened three weeks ago.

Sam pulled himself out of the backseat, and Alyssa glanced at him again.

'You're sure of that?' she asked Hopper.

'Like I said, I wasn't really watching her all that closely, but, yeah, I'm sure about it. There was no one else on the lot then or any other time that day. Some days are a ghost town, you know?'

'You have records that confirm that? You know, that there were no other deals made that day?' Sam asked, pulling off the gloves. They left behind a powdery residue on his hands that he wiped on his jeans. 'Just so we're sure you're thinking of the right day.'

'The computer has a record of the day's receipts. That should confirm it.'

'Mind pulling that information up on the screen?'

'Not at all.' Hopper headed toward his office, a single-story former service station dating from the architecturally challenged 1950s.

Alyssa glanced at Sam again as he let her go first. Apparently he looked as freaked out as he was feeling. 'I'm figuring Mary Lou cut Haley's hair, dressed her like a boy. She knew someone was after her and she's trying to hide. This is good news we're getting, Sam.'

'Yeah, I guess.' He shook his head. 'I don't know. Is it really? Can this guy really tell us anything? I keep trying to remember, I don't know, like, the woman who was in front of me in line at the grocery store three weeks ago. I mean, I *know* I went to the grocery store three weeks ago. And I know there was a woman in front of me with a kid in her shopping cart, but I don't remember what color her hair was or what she bought. Or if her husband was waiting for her over by the ATM.'

'Did you talk to her?' Alyssa asked as she opened the door to the office. 'Because unless you talk to someone, it's harder to remember—'

'Yeah, actually I did. I asked her how old her kid was. I don't remember what she said.'

'This is different.' She was trying to reassure him. 'This was a business transaction. A deal was negotiated. That's easier to remember. Even after three weeks.'

'Still . . .'

As they went inside, Alyssa pointed up at the surveillance camera that was mounted in the corner of the room, up by the ceiling. 'Does that work?' she asked Hopper.

Yeah, like this guy would be able to afford a wireless system in a shithole like this.

Hopper glanced up from the computer. 'No, it's just a dummy, to discourage anyone who might be thinking about pulling an armed robbery.'

'You might want to think about putting some kind of dummy power cord up there, then, too,' Sam suggested. 'Make it look more realistic.'

'As long as you're checking records – exactly how much money did you give Mary Lou Starrett for her car?' Alyssa asked.

Hopper actually looked embarrassed. 'It wasn't worth very much. I'm probably going to have to send it out to auction—'

Alyssa cut him off. 'I understand. You're a businessman, not a charity. How much?'

He cleared his throat. 'A hundred and seventy-five dollars.'

Shit. It would have been smarter just to keep the car.

Unless, of course, someone who wanted to kill her was looking for her.

'And that was the only transaction of the day,' Hopper added, swiveling the computer screen so they could see the account file. 'Saturday, May twenty-fourth.'

'Do you know where Mary Lou went after she signed the papers and received payment?' Sam asked.

'Actually, yes,' Hopper said. 'I remember that quite clearly. I drove her to the bus station.'

'You *drove* her?'

'I had a dentist appointment not far from there,' Hopper explained. 'She'd asked me for directions to the terminal, and at first I offered to call her a cab, but she said her bus wasn't till noon, so they'd walk. I think she was probably short on cash.'

You think? After getting only a hundred and seventy-five bucks for her car . . .?

'So I told her if she could wait until ten-thirty, I'd give her a lift over there myself,' Hopper continued. 'I don't usually do that, but I was going that way and I felt bad for her, having to walk with the little boy and those suitcases, so . . .'

Suitcases.

'How long did she wait here?' Alyssa asked. Her cell phone rang, and she reached for it but didn't answer it.

'About an hour,' Hopper said.

Alyssa looked at Sam. She didn't say the words aloud, but he knew what she was thinking. Mary Lou and Haley hadn't been there, held at gunpoint.

And Haley was definitely still alive.

At least as of three weeks ago.

'Excuse me,' she said, and stepped outside to take the call.

'Thank you,' Sam told Hopper.

'So who is she?' the car salesman asked after they'd stood there a moment in uncomfortable silence. 'This Mary Lou Starrett? She didn't look like public enemy number one.'

Alyssa pushed open the door. 'Sam.'

He turned toward her and . . . Whoa.

Whoever had been on the other end of the phone had ratcheted up Alyssa's stress level to about a million. Didn't it figure that just when Sam was relaxing into the relief of knowing that Mary Lou and Haley were still alive, Alyssa would start freaking out?

'Thanks for your cooperation, Mr Hopper,' Alyssa called. 'The folks from the crime lab will be arriving probably within the hour to take fingerprints from the vehicle.' She took Sam's arm and practically dragged him out of there and over to her car. 'Get in.'

He did. And he waited until she was behind the wheel and starting the engine to ask, 'Who called?'

'Max.' She put the car into gear and pulled out of the parking lot, raising a cloud of dust behind them as she got back onto Route 20, heading toward the highway.

'What's going on?' he asked when it became clear that she wasn't going to volunteer more information.

'The fingerprint report from Janine's house came in early this morning.' The glance she gave him was pretty freaking grim. Whatever this was about, it was not good.

'And?'

'The lab analyzed the prints of everyone who'd been in that house,' Alyssa told him. 'And Manny Conseco's team went back to verify it.'

For Christ's sake . . . 'Verify *what*?'

'That Mary Lou's fingerprints are on one of the weapons used in the Coronado attack. Sam, Mary Lou is our missing Lady X.'

Nine

When the door opened, it actually took several seconds for Tom Paoletti to recognize the two enlisted men standing outside his room. It was the combination of dress uniforms and fresh haircuts that made Petty Officers Dan Gillman and Cosmo Richter look nothing like their usual froggish selves. The fact that Cosmo wasn't wearing his sunglasses didn't help, either.

'You better get dressed, sir,' Gillman said, maneuvering his way into the room on crutches.

Tom shook his head. 'No. The leader of the Spanish Inquisition was just here. I'm not needed again for at least a few hours.' And since taking his dress uniform to the dry cleaner didn't seem to be an option while under 'house' arrest, the less time he spent sitting around in it, wrinkling it and making it stink, the better. 'How's the ankle, Danny?'

'It's a pain in the ass, sir.'

'I bet. Look, could you guys do me a favor and give Kelly a call?'

'Excuse me, but you really do need to get dressed, sir,' Cosmo interrupted, shutting the door tightly behind him.

Cosmo Richter's eyes were an unusual shade of pale gray. It definitely had been a while since Tom had seen him without his sunglasses. Or maybe it was the haircut that made him look so different. It actually met military regs.

Or maybe it was just because it had been six months since Tom had been Richter's commanding officer that made the man look like a stranger.

'And you can tell her whatever you need to yourself, Commander. I'm sure you'd prefer that anyway. Kelly'll be up here in—' Cosmo consulted his watch as if he were part of some synchronized plan '—three and a half minutes.' He handed Tom his pants. 'So shake it a little faster, sir.'

Tom pulled them on. Kelly was on her way up, thank God. 'I hate to shock you, Cos, but she *has* seen me in my shorts a time or two.'

Gilligan was already there, holding out Tom's jacket, crutches balanced under his arms. 'Yes sir, but Father Stevenson hasn't.'

Father . . .? 'Who?' Tom asked.

Cosmo and Gilligan exchanged a look.

'Father Stevenson, sir,' Gillian repeated. 'He's like, you know, a Father with a capital F.'

'A *priest*?'

Cosmo cleared his throat. 'Kelly ran into a glitch today, sir. Since she's not legally your wife, they're not letting her visit you. She wasn't too happy about that.'

Son of a bitch. He'd been afraid of that. 'But you said she's on her way up,' Tom pointed out.

Cosmo looked at Gilligan again, who was now straightening Tom's shoulderboards. 'Well, sir, she is, but she isn't,' he said. 'See, the guards aren't going to let her into your room. So we're going to have to do this with her out in the hall and you in here.'

'Do what?' Tom asked.

Cos cleared his throat again. It was probably sore. He'd already spoken more in these past few minutes than he had in all of the years Tom had known him. 'You know that time about a year ago, when we were hanging at the Ladybug Lounge – you, me and the senior chief? Do you remember what you said?'

Tom laughed. 'Try the Sam Adams Summer Ale . . .?'

Cosmo Richter actually gave him a chiding look. Tom hadn't

realized that chiding was in the usually impassive petty officer's arsenal of facial expressions. 'Tommy, this is serious shit.'

'I'm being held under guard in the BOQ,' Tom told him. 'I think I know how serious this shit is.'

Chiding turned to something that was almost eager. 'Say the word, sir, and we'll get you out of here.'

Tom suspected that Cosmo wasn't kidding. He shook his head. 'Just tell me where you're going with this. It sounds like a bad joke. A CO, a senior chief, and a petty officer walk into a bar. And . . .?'

'You told us that one of these days Kelly would be ready to get married, but until then, you were just going to play it cool,' Cosmo reported, and then dropped a bomb. 'Well, Kelly's ready. Today. In fact—' another glance at his watch '—in about thirty seconds, she's going to marry you, Commander.'

'*What?*'

'You need to fix your hair, sir,' Gilligan said as a murmur of voices sounded outside the door.

'You still do want to marry her, don't you, sir?' Cosmo asked, his hand on the doorknob.

Tom smoothed down his hair. 'Yeah, but—'

'You look great, sir,' Gilligan told him.

Not like this.

The door swung open. And there she was. Kelly.

In a freaking wedding gown.

Arguing with the guards.

There was a wide-eyed young man in a priest's collar standing next to her.

'I realize that I'm not allowed in to see him,' she was saying to the two ensigns who stood in front of his door, 'but is there really a problem with my standing here in the hall?'

She was so beautiful, something in Tom's chest snapped. It just broke.

The guards looked very unhappy. One of them said, 'Yes, ma'am. I have to ask you to keep moving.'

She was holding a small bouquet of flowers. 'And I have to ask you to call your commanding officer and verify that I'm not allowed to rest here for a moment after climbing all those stairs. It wasn't easy in this dress, you know.'

It was an amazing dress – a long, sweeping length of some rich-looking shiny fabric that Tom knew would slip coolly beneath his fingers if he touched her. It fell behind her in a glistening, shimmering pool of ivory. But it was the impossibly low-cut neckline that killed him. The entire gown set off the gorgeous smoothness of Kelly's shoulders and the pale voluptuousness of her breasts. And all that creamy skin was a perfect frame for her beautiful face, her incredible eyes.

She caught sight of him and just looked at him, her heart in those eyes. Her heart, and a hint of uncertainty.

'Kelly,' Tom whispered. 'This is insane.'

The other guard glared at him. 'Move back into the room, sir. You must keep this door closed.'

Tom ignored him.

'Isn't it?' Kelly said. 'But I didn't know what else to do.' She turned to the priest. 'Forgive me for rushing things along, but, Father, if you don't mind?'

'Sir,' the guard insisted, 'if you don't move back—'

Tom took a very small step backward. 'Kel, I'm not going to marry you. I'm looking at spending the next thirty years in jail—'

'For something that you didn't do!'

'To hell with that!' Tom winced. 'Excuse me, Father, but would you please tell her that thirty years is thirty years and the fact that it's unjust and unfair isn't going to make it pass more quickly.'

'Sir, this door *must* stay closed.'

Cosmo leaned forward, closer to the guards. 'We need a little air in here, Ensigns,' he said quietly. 'No one's going anywhere. If we were trying to break Tommy out of here, we'd already be gone.' *And you'd be dead.* He didn't say it aloud, but he didn't have to. That message gleamed clearly in his odd-colored eyes. 'This'll be over and done much sooner, sirs, if you put a sock in it.'

'Go ahead, Father,' Kelly said.

Tom shook his head. 'Kelly, I'm sorry, you look incredible. The dress is . . . It's perfect. You take my breath away, but . . . I can't do this.'

'You're not going to jail,' she told him rather fiercely.

'You don't know that.'

'Oh, yes, I do.'

'And if you're wrong?'

'We'll get an annulment,' she said. 'Tom, this is the only way I'll be allowed in to see you. How can I help you if I can't even *talk* to you?'

He shook his head.

'Tom!' She glared at him. 'Are you *giving up*?'

'No!'

'Then marry me, so I can actually stand next to you when I stand by you!'

Tom laughed. It was either that or cry. 'God, I love you.'

'For richer or poorer, for better or worse, in sickness or in health, and even in jail,' Kelly told him. She looked at Stevenson. 'Is that close enough?'

The priest nodded. 'It is. All you really have to do is sign the license.'

'I do,' Kelly said as she gazed at Tom. 'I take you, Tom. For all those things. Forever.'

He nodded, wanting to hold her so badly that his chest ached. 'I do, too.' But forever was going to be godawful long if he had to spend it in prison. And, damn it, he didn't have a ring for her. This was *so* not the way he wanted to do this.

She already had the paper and a pen out and was affixing her name to the document. No doubt she'd torn his den apart searching for the license, God love her.

Cosmo reached out of the doorway and, with a glance at both of the guards, took the paper from Kelly.

Tom couldn't believe he was doing this as he signed his name, as Cosmo and Gillman signed, too, as witnesses.

It was a dream come true – in the middle of a nightmare.

'By the power vested in me . . . I pronounce you husband and wife,' Father Stevenson said.

No rings. No kiss.

No real future.

Except Kelly didn't believe that. And as Tom stood there, looking at her, he didn't believe it, either.

Kelly looked at the guards. 'Thank you,' she said with quiet dignity. 'Now. Please call your CO and tell him that I demand to see my husband.'

'What the . . .?' Sam stared at Alyssa.

When she glanced over at him, she saw that his gaze was out of focus. He wasn't really looking at her. He was merely looking in her direction, thinking hard, no doubt trying to make sense of the stunning news she'd just given him.

Mary Lou Morrison Starrett was Lady X, connected to the terrorists who'd tried to kill the US President at the Coronado naval base six months ago.

Alyssa was having some trouble making sense of it herself.

'Pull over,' Sam said, and when she looked up from the road and over at him again, he was back. Alert, focused, and grim. *Very* grim.

She could relate. This was beyond bad. But she shook her head. 'Sam, we're already late enough as it—'

'Pull over!' he roared. Loudly enough for her hair to move from the force of his voice. 'Jesus Christ, Alyssa. You didn't honestly expect to drop that news flash on me and just keep driving, did you? Pull this car over and at least have the decency to look me in the eye when you tell me the details of—'

'Don't you shout at me!' She gripped the steering wheel and kept driving as she yelled over him. 'I don't *know* the details. Other than the fact that Mary Lou's fingerprints apparently show up quite clearly on one of the terrorists' weapons recovered in Coronado last year. Congratulations. You now know everything I know.'

'Alyssa, I swear to God, if you don't pull this car over, I'm going to grab the steering wheel and—'

He was serious and just crazy enough to try it. Alyssa pulled over, tires squealing as they bounced into the empty parking lot of an abandoned restaurant.

As soon as she hit the brakes, Sam opened the door and got out of the car.

'Whoa,' she yelled. 'Starrett, get your ass back here!'

But he just kept on walking away.

Her tires squealed again as she moved the car into an intercept path. If she could have, she would have slapped him on the rear with the open car door. Instead, she put the vehicle into park and climbed out to face him. 'What are you *doing*?'

He gazed at her, and when he spoke, his voice was soft. Gentle. 'You know what I'm doing, Lys. You know I can't go back to Sarasota with you.'

What? 'You have to. There are a lot of people with a lot of questions—'

'That I can't answer,' he cut her off. 'I have no idea what's going on. Is this a setup? It sure as hell smells like one to me. But why would someone frame Mary Lou? It's absurd – almost as absurd as Mary Lou actually being involved with terrorists. Unless what they're really trying to do is frame *me*.'

Alyssa moved around the car toward him. If he ran, she was in trouble. She was fast, but he was faster. She knew that from experience. 'If she's not involved, then who killed Janine?'

Sam rubbed the back of his neck. 'I don't know. If she is involved with something . . . Still, there's nothing I can tell anyone. I didn't know any of her friends. I didn't even know she *had* any friends. I mean, not outside of AA – and she told me the people she met there were mostly acquaintances. When you're just a few months sober, it's not a good thing to get too close to people who could fall off the wagon any minute – and drag you with them. When she went into rehab, she pretty much dumped all of her drinking buddies – except her sister, who was dabbling in sobriety herself.'

'What about on base?' Alyssa said, wanting to keep him talking as she moved closer. Closer. 'There must've been women she at least associated with?'

He scratched his beard as he thought about that. 'There was a wives group on the base, but it was for everyone on base, not just the SEALs, and I guess that wasn't good enough for Mary Lou. But Team Sixteen doesn't have anything official. We're still a relatively new team, most of the guys aren't married, and the ones who are . . . Mike's and Kenny's wives always go out of town when the team goes wheels up. And these are people who are dealing with a bicoastal relationship. I didn't feel like I could call them up and ask them to form a support group for my wife. Although, shit, Mike and Joan didn't even get married until after Mary Lou left for Florida, so really it was just Ken's wife, but—'

He shook his head. 'I don't know, Lys. Out of the guys in the team who are married, most are enlisted, and, well, I hate to say this, but Mary Lou didn't exactly help people to like her. I know Meg Nilsson – Johnny's wife – and Teri Howe, who's married to the senior chief, they got together with Mary Lou for awhile right after we got married. I think it was weekly or maybe . . . I don't know. But then they stopped coming over, and when I asked why, Mary Lou made all this noise about how Teri's husband was only enlisted so she shouldn't have been invited, and then Meg kept trying to force all this information on counseling down her throat, and she'd done enough of that in rehab, so . . .

'I really don't know what I could tell anyone in an interview. Mary Lou spent all her time taking care of Haley, and doing, jeez, I don't know what. Reading, I thought. She had some bullshit job that she insisted on getting at the McDonald's on base—'

'Which gave her access—'

Sam laughed his disbelief. 'You don't honestly think—'

'I think her prints were on a weapon used in a terrorist attack. I think you need to come to Sarasota with me. I think we need to get there as quickly as possible.' Alyssa moved closer to him, reached into her back pocket, praying he didn't figure out what she intended to do. . . .

'I'm sorry,' he told her.

'I am, too,' she said, and, moving swiftly, handcuffed his left wrist to her right.

'Claire on line one,' Maddy's voice came through on Noah's intercom.

Noah picked up the phone. 'Hey, baby.'

'*What* in the name of heaven has Roger gotten himself into?'

Oh, shit. 'They came to visit you, too?'

'When you say it like that, it sounds almost reasonable. Visit. Right. What they did was come into the nursery school, *right* at drop-off time. I had parents waiting to talk to me. What was I supposed to say? 'Excuse me while I'm questioned by the FBI?' I mean, wouldn't you be a little nervous about putting me in charge of your four-year-old child?'

Claire was the administrator of the nursery school at their church, and they were running a six-week summer program that started this morning. It wasn't a high salary position. In fact, Noah had figured it out once, and, with all the extra time she put in, she was earning well below minimum wage. But Claire loved doing it, that was for sure. And if it made her happy, it made *him* happy.

Although, he really wished that program hadn't started today. She had meetings into the afternoon – no chance for their lunch.

'Believe me, no one's going to fire you for cooperating with the authorities,' Noah told her. 'And if they do, you can finally get a real job.'

'Thanks so much, Noah. That's so comforting and supportive.'

'What did they ask you?'

'A whole bunch of questions about Mary Lou,' she told him. 'Did I know her, were we close, when was the last time I saw her, had we ever visited the Starretts in San Diego. And Roger. My God. They wanted to know his state of mind. Is he violent. Has he ever been violent. And what about his temper. I didn't know what to say. I mean, yes, he does have the tendency to burn hot, but I've got a mean temper, too. And it flared up a bit when they had the audacity to ask if he'd ever expressed any anti-American sentiment. Can you believe that? What kind of question is that to ask about a man who's spent over a dozen years risking his life for his country?'

'It's the same kind of question they asked me,' Noah said. 'Did they tell you to contact them if he calls or shows up?'

'Yes, they did.' Claire paused. 'I may have lied to them a little bit when I told them I would.'

Noah laughed.

'Nos . . .' There was something in her voice that made him stop laughing.

'Yeah?'

'Is it possible that Roger really killed Mary Lou's sister?' she asked him.

He didn't hesitate. 'No.'

'Think about it,' she said.

'I don't have to.'

'Remember that story you told me?' she said. 'About that fight Ringo got into where you thought he was going to kill that kid. What were you – in eighth grade?'

'Yeah. And he didn't kill Lyle. God, what was his last name?'

'Only because you stopped him.'

Noah sighed. 'Claire, I *know* him.'

'I've read about certain kinds of medication that servicemen have to take when they go overseas – pills that prevent malaria – that can sometimes result in psychotic episodes.'

'Morgan,' Noah said. 'Lyle Morgan. What a fool. He thought his being bigger would keep Ringo from swinging at him.' He laughed. 'He didn't know Ringo.'

'Doesn't it creep you out just a little bit that he's been trained as a killer?' Claire asked. 'You know, I read that SEALs can do things like break necks and snap spinal cords. *And* fire shotguns.'

'I know,' Noah said. He'd once wanted to be a SEAL. He'd read all those books, too. 'But lots of people know how to use a shotgun.'

'I don't,' she said. 'And— hold on a sec . . .'

He could hear her muffled voice talking to someone who had come into her office.

'I've got to go,' she told Noah.

'Ringo *didn't* kill Janine,' he said again.

'People change,' she said.

'Not that much.'

Sam couldn't believe it. She'd actually handcuffed them together. 'Oh, for . . . *Come on*, Alyssa.'

'Get in the car,' she told him, pulling him with her as she went in through the passenger's side and climbed over the parking brake.

It was either get in, or resist and end up hurting her.

'Please, *please* don't do this,' he said, hoping quiet begging would get him farther than another temper tantrum. Or than making a pointed comment about exactly how they'd ended up – naked and covered in chocolate syrup – the last time she'd handcuffed herself to him.

But she already had the car in gear and the tires moving before he'd shut his door.

'They just want to ask you questions,' she told him, clearly uncomfortable with the warmth of his arm and hand so close to hers. If she drove with both hands on the top of the steering wheel, his hand was dangling, the weight of it surely making the cuffs cut into her wrist. But if she drove with her right hand down at the bottom of the wheel, that put his hand in her lap.

Which was fine with him.

Or she could put her hand in *his* lap – also fine with him.

She did neither, instead resting her hand on the gear selector between their two seats.

'Just questions,' Sam repeated. 'You want to make a guess at how long it's going to take them to ask me all those questions?'

'I'll do everything in my power to—'

'Four months,' he said. 'If I'm really lucky. Longer – like forever – if they get the idea into their pinheads that I'm somehow involved.'

She was silent because she knew what he was saying was the truth. They already thought that Tom Paoletti was involved.

'Alyssa,' he said. 'Have a heart. If you bring me back, I'm going to be locked in some room, answering those fuckwads' questions, while somewhere out there Mary Lou is hiding from Janine's shooter. Who is probably an al-Qaeda trained terrorist. I need to find her – I need to find Haley. Don't do this to me. Please. I'm begging you.'

She was silent, and he used the time to pray. Please God, if there was ever a time he needed a little divine intervention it was now.

'I'll talk to Max,' she finally said.

'Oh, great. Thanks – this is after you tell me you have absolutely no influence over him. Which I find very hard to believe, by the way.'

Her temper flared, too, as she took the entrance ramp onto Route 75 south. 'Believe what you want, Lieutenant. I'm doing the best I can in an impossible situation.'

He was Lieutenant again. Which meant he was so screwed. Sam or even Roger would have had at least a slim chance of talking her out of bringing him in, but not Lieutenant Starrett.

No, Lieutenant Starrett was going to jail. Directly to jail. No passing Go. No collecting his ex-wife and daughter.

God *damn* it.

'You know, a good blow job can be pretty goddamn influential,' he shot at her. 'And if you're at all uncertain, you could probably get some valuable pointers from Jules.'

Her voice rose. 'Why do you *say* things like that?'

The air-conditioning was cranking, gale forces howling from the vents in the dashboard. But despite the heavy winds inside the car, her words seemed to hang suspended between them, as palpable as the warmth of her arm next to his.

'I don't know,' Sam admitted, his anger suddenly deflated. And he really didn't. What was wrong with him? 'I just . . .' He shook his head. What could he say? 'I'm an asshole. I'm sorry.'

'You purposely antagonize me. You find my buttons and you jump on them with both feet.'

His crack had struck one of her 'buttons.' Was it possible . . . ?

'Whoa. You don't really think I meant that, do you? About getting pointers from – Lys, sex with you was incredible. You could teach a master class. You know, you did things to me with your mouth and tongue that I *still*—'

'Stop,' she shouted. 'You just don't get it, do you? I do not want to talk about sex with you in any way, shape, or form. I do *not* want to reminisce about anyone's mouth or tongue, thank you *so* very much. We did things together that . . . that . . . God, that I'm ashamed of! If I could, I would go back in time and erase it all. Completely.'

Well, *shit*.

Sam almost let that one shut him up. He almost turned away and just sat and stewed in silent misery.

But if stupid things he didn't really mean could come out of *his* mouth, then surely the things that came out of Alyssa's mouth could be things she didn't really mean, too. Right?

Evisceration. It was entirely possible that if Alyssa was ashamed of anything, it was that she'd let herself care enough about him to be eviscerated when he'd said goodbye.

And it took a shitload of caring to warrant an evisceration.

'I want to go back in time, too,' Sam told her quietly. 'I want to walk into your apartment in DC and take you out to dinner.' He wanted to go on that dinner date they'd planned, instead of doing what he'd done – show up to tell her he couldn't see her again, that he was going to have to marry Mary Lou.

Alyssa was silent for a good long while then, just driving, her eyes glued to the road, her mouth a tight line.

Sam waited, silently praying. For what, he didn't really know.

She finally glanced at him, her face and eyes showing signs of fatigue and strain. 'We can't change the past,' she said. 'We both made choices that we can't undo.'

'Mine's been undone.'

That got him another look, this one filled with a crapload of disgust and disdain. 'You think it's that easy? Poof, you're divorced. Poof, you're suddenly back in my apartment, in my *life*? Dinner date with Alyssa, take two? You can show up if you want, Roger, but I won't be home. You're two years too late, and I have moved on.'

This wasn't helping. Getting her all pissed off over the sins of his past wasn't likely to make her want to start over with him.

And, even more important right now, it wasn't going to make her want to give in and set him free.

Although, he *was* back to being Roger.

'How's Nora?' he asked, abruptly changing the subject.

Alyssa narrowed her eyes at him, obviously trying to predict where this new topic was going. 'She's *fine*.'

Jules had told Sam that Alyssa spent a lot of time with her sister, Tyra, and her little niece. The very niece who had been born the very same day he and Alyssa had first made love.

They'd gone together to visit Tyra and the baby in the hospital. And afterward Alyssa had cried from relief and emotional overwhelm. Sam hadn't thought she was capable of that kind of breakdown. She'd always come off as Superwoman, with nerves of steel, and ice water running through her veins.

Ice water. Man, he'd been so wrong about that.

'She must be, what, now? Three?' Sam asked.

'Almost,' Alyssa said.

'Imagine how you'd feel— how Tyra would feel and—' Oh, crap. What was the husband's name? Sam focused hard and pulled it out of his ass. 'Ben.'

Alyssa gave him another look. 'And now am I supposed to be all impressed that you remember my sister's and brother-in-law's names?'

'Yes, ma'am. But it's okay if you're not. I'm impressed enough for both of us.' Sam laughed at the expression on her face. Oh, come on, Lys. She was working every muscle in her face so that she wouldn't smile – just because she was still pissed off at his blow job comment. He really had to learn to keep his mouth shut. 'Imagine how freaked out they'd be if they didn't know where Nora was. Imagine how freaked *you'd* be.'

'Yes, I would be. And unlike you and Haley, I've actually *seen* Nora in the past six months.'

Ouch. She'd cut him in two with that one, but like that robot in *Alien*, he wasn't going to just lie back and die.

But it was time to try another tack. He pulled the conversation and his bloody torso forward with his arms. 'Lys, I swear to you, just let me find Haley and then I'll turn myself in.'

'The entire FBI is searching for her,' she told him. 'Along with local law enforcement agencies. Believe me, by now Mary Lou is the subject of the biggest manhunt of the decade. We *will* find her, and soon. Even without your help.'

'Is that supposed to comfort me? The biggest fucking manhunt of the decade is supposed to *reassure* me?' The implications of that made his head spin. He hadn't even considered . . . 'Holy shit, do the APBs actually list her as armed and dangerous?'

Alyssa clearly realized that she'd only managed to make him more upset. 'I haven't seen them. I don't know—'

'You goddamn well *do* know,' he countered hotly. 'What's SOP for an alleged terrorist?'

'Okay, you're probably right. Since her prints were on an automatic weapon—'

'Fuck!' This was far worse even than he'd first imagined. 'This is insane! Some FBI hotdog is going to spot her and go after her, weapon blazing.' And Haley could well be hit in the cross fire. Jesus, he had to get out of this car. He had to go and find them, now. He had to talk Alyssa into letting him go, or he was going to have to use force or threat of force to get her to release him. Way to get back into her good graces . . . But he had no choice. 'No way is Mary Lou armed *or* dangerous!'

'Maybe she's not, but you know as well as I do that she could very well be with someone who *is*. I know you're probably getting tired of hearing this refrain, Sam, but her prints *are* on that weapon. We know at some point she . . . interacted with someone who wanted the President dead.'

'Why don't you just say what you're thinking?' Sam shot back at her. 'At some point, Mary Lou was screwing around behind my back with some terrorist scumball.'

'That's not what I'm thinking.'

'Well, it should be. It's sure as hell what *I'm* thinking. I find it far easier to believe than the idea that she, I don't know, somehow targeted me from the start. Is that really what you think? Like, she's a *terrorist*? So she picks me up in a bar and purposely gets pregnant so I'll marry her and . . . what? She didn't need *me* to gain access to the Navy base. She just needed that job at the Mickey D's.'

Alyssa glanced at him. 'I think when we get to Sarasota, there *are* going to be a lot of questions about how and where and when you met her,' she said.

'The Ladybug Lounge,' Sam told her flatly. 'During a night of heavy drinking and piss-poor judgment, just about two fucking awful months after you broke my heart.'

Alyssa didn't take his bait. She didn't even blink at the implication of his words. 'So you did pick her up in a bar. Or did she pick *you* up?'

'She definitely hit on me. But it wasn't because she was a terrorist. She was, you know . . . Jesus.' This was embarrassing to admit. 'A groupie.'

SEAL groupies would sleep with anyone in the teams just because they were in the teams. All he'd needed to make Mary Lou want to take him home was a SEAL trident pin and a dick.

Alyssa didn't say anything. She didn't comment, didn't snort, didn't do anything other than drive.

'Why don't you just say it?' Sam said. 'I'm pathetic. I know it.'

She shook her head, laughing slightly. 'Maybe you should just wait and tell this to the task force. You're going to have to tell it again anyway, and I'm not sure I really want to know—'

'Actually, I'd like you to know.' Sam paused. What was the best way to say this? 'She was . . . the exact opposite of you, Alyssa.'

'Okay. Thank you. I'm no longer not sure. I *definitely* don't—'

Sam spoke over her. 'I went home with her that night because I was trying to, I don't know, exorcise you, I guess. I mean, she was drunk. That was maybe kind of similar to that first night you and I got together.'

'Oh, *please*—'

'But everything else about her . . . the way she dressed, her whole attitude . . . was, I don't know, bimbo trash. She actually did this stupid coy thing with her eyelashes that you wouldn't be caught dead doing.'

'Starrett, I *really* don't want to—'

'And, Jesus, she was young. I think she must've used a fake ID to get in there. She wasn't exactly a rocket scientist, either. That's one of the things that I've always found so attractive about you, Alyssa. You're so damn smart.'

That shut her up, but only temporarily.

'Starrett, I really think—'

'I remember thinking that I couldn't compare her to you

because there was clearly no comparison,' he told her. 'I was sick and tired of rejecting everyone I met out of hand, simply because they weren't you. So I went home with her because of that, and also because back then two months seemed like a long time to go without getting laid.'

If someone had told him then that a time would come where he'd be approaching a solid year without sex, he'd have laughed in their face.

Alyssa kept her eyes on the road. 'You're going to tell all this to the investigators?'

Jesus. He was sitting here, baring his soul, trying to make her see how completely messed up he'd been after Alyssa had slept with him and then decided that they should forget about it, just pretend it never happened.

And she was worried about people finding out that they had a past?

'No,' he told her. 'I never told anyone about you and me. I mean, Kenny Karmody knows because he saw us together. Some of the other guys in the team have probably figured out that there was more to what we had going on than a broken dinner date. But they never asked for details, and I never told, and I'm not about to start now.'

Alyssa glanced at him. 'I don't want you to lie about it. It's very important to tell the truth – *whatever* they ask you.'

'I know,' Sam said. 'I just . . . won't volunteer that particular information. I really don't think anyone's going to have a problem believing that I went home with Mary Lou that night for the sex. It was a one-night stand that just kind of kept going for a few weeks.'

He needed her to understand this. 'I was freaking miserable without you, Alyssa. You told me we weren't going to happen again and I believed you. I was looking for, I don't know, a distraction. I honestly thought Mary Lou and I were both on the same page in terms of no strings. As soon as I realized that she wanted a wedding ring and that I was still completely unable to think about anyone but you, I broke it off. And then, Jesus, when you and I *did* get together again . . .'

He'd been so sure he was going to die. It seemed like a good practical joke for God to play on him. Let him sleep with Alyssa Locke again and – finally! – have her agree to have dinner with him, to move their one-night-of-sex-every-six-months relationship into something bigger, like maybe a relationship where they had sex once every two months . . .

It seemed only inevitable that he should be killed during SEAL Team Sixteen's takedown of a hijacked airliner.

But somehow he'd survived. Only to find that God's practical joke was all about Mary Lou. She was pregnant, and guess what? The baby was his. *Really.*

He'd gone charging off to do the right thing because that was the way he'd been raised, and Alyssa had been eviscerated. Silently. If only she had told him . . .

Would it have made a difference? He honestly didn't know.

Right now she was still silent.

'Do you believe me?' he asked.

A glance. 'Yeah.'

He briefly closed his eyes. 'Thank you,' he said.

'It doesn't change anything.'

Sam nodded, letting her believe that.

She moved into the left lane to pass an eighteen wheeler. 'You really don't think it's possible that Mary Lou was part of a terrorist cell – that she specifically targeted Team Sixteen?'

That really cracked him up. 'I do not,' he said. 'You don't know her, Alyssa. She's . . . way too uncomplicated.'

'She's complicated enough to tamper with condoms and get herself pregnant so that you'd marry her.' She shot him a look. 'And apparently she got to know you pretty well during those weeks of one-night stands. It's not every man who would marry a woman just because she was pregnant.'

'I thought it was the right thing,' he tried to explain. 'I was severely mistaken, though. I thought—'

'It doesn't matter,' Alyssa said.

'Yes, it does.' It mattered so much. 'When Noah was seventeen, he got Claire, his girlfriend, pregnant. I was in Sarasota for the summer, and it was extremely intense. Lots of shouting and crying, you know? Claire's parents were talking adoption and even abortion, and Claire had some strong opinions about *that*. And then they announced that they were going to send her to Europe afterward to get her away from Noah, which made *him* completely bullshit. He concocted this scheme to break Claire out of her house, with a ladder to her second-floor bedroom, so they could run away together. They were talking California or Vegas, and . . . I was supposed to create a diversion out front, but it never happened.

'I remember Dot didn't say much of anything other than admonishing Nos for not using birth control. Dot went out and bought me a box of condoms. Can you picture this elderly, practically deaf woman in a wheelchair, rolling up to the pharmacy counter and shouting out that she wanted a box of Trojans, ribbed?'

A smile from Alyssa. Hallelujah.

'Did I tell you she was a WASP, a pilot during World War Two?'

'Really? A black woman?'

'No, she was white. She met Walt during the war. He was a pilot, too a colonel with the Tuskegee Airmen. They were an all-black fighter squadron out of Alabama.'

'I know who the Tuskegee Airmen were,' Alyssa said. 'They had some kind of amazing record, like they never lost a single bomber they were escorting, right? I'm impressed.'

'Finally. I've been working my ass off here, trying to impress you.'

'I meant by Noah,' she countered.

She was actually teasing him. At least he hoped she was teasing. Noah was a very good-looking man.

'He's still married,' Sam pointed out. 'To Claire.'

'And Walt and Dot were his grandparents?'

'Yeah, his father was killed in Vietnam when he was a baby. They pretty much raised Nos from the get go. They were something else, Uncle Walt and Aunt Dot.' Sam hesitated, uncertain of the words to use to try to explain. But he wanted her to know him. And she wouldn't know him without knowing about Walt. 'Walt was, like, the most important person in my life when I was a kid. He was my, you know, hero, I guess. Someday, when we have more time, maybe when you're visiting me in jail, I'll tell you about him and Aunt Dot.'

That one got him an exasperated laugh. 'Sam, don't be ridiculous.'

'Yeah, you're probably not going to visit me, are you?'

She gave him a look. 'You're not going to jail. I'm not going to let that happen.'

Oh, yeah. Good news. If she didn't care about him even just a little bit, she'd just turn him in and let him rot.

'Thanks,' he said. 'You can drop me at the next exit.'

'That's not what I meant.'

'Yeah, I know.' It was worth a try. 'Anyway, Noah came up with this second plan. He would marry Claire, and they would keep the baby. Which was completely insane because they were both only seventeen. I remember thinking that he was nuts and that Walt would never agree to that. But Nos had figured out that he could go to work for Walt to support his wife and child, and get his GED in his spare time. Then he could go to night school to get his college degree. I was like, oh, that's going to be a real fun life.

'But Noah and Walt went into the den and closed the door. They stayed in there a long time, and when they finally came out, Nos went to find Claire without stopping to tell me what had gone down. So I asked Walt, and he said that he was real proud of Noah. That Noah was doing the right thing, and that he and Claire would be married at the end of the month.

'I was like, *shit*. And I figured that Walt had just been waiting for Noah to step up, to take responsibility, you know, to be a man.

'So that's what I tried to do with Mary Lou. I tried to do the thing that would make Walt proud.' Sam shook his head. 'Although I'm pretty sure I've made him roll in his grave.'

They were both silent for several long moments, then Alyssa said, 'I thought you grew up in Texas.'

'I did,' he said. 'Fort Worth. That's where I met Noah. But in sophomore year of high school, Dot had a stroke that was pretty debilitating. And there was this doctor in Sarasota who was getting good results with stroke patients, so Walt and Dot sold the family business to their employees, packed up their house, and moved down to Florida.'

He paused, and when she glanced at him, he added, 'I would have gone with them if I could've. They wanted me to. Their house was always my, well, my sanctuary, I guess. See, my father was this real asshole, and . . . I was wrecked when they left. But I hitched down to visit them every summer, so I guess it was all right.'

Man, he couldn't remember the last time he talked this much. It certainly hadn't been while he was married to Mary Lou. He'd tried talking to her early on in their marriage, thinking that their getting to know each other might be important if they were going to be a real family, but she didn't want to talk to him. She didn't want him to be human. She wanted him to be some kind of superhero. And superheroes were never afraid. They never felt uncertain. They never wrestled with feelings of inadequacy that had been pounded into them when they were children.

And above all, they never, ever cried.

'Alyssa, I really have to find Haley before I can go to Sarasota with you.'

She didn't say anything for a long time. She just drove. She was so beautiful with those ocean-colored eyes that were such a vivid contrast to her mocha-colored skin.

'You're going to have to trust that I'll find her *for* you,' she finally said.

She glanced at him before he could turn his head away. With luck, she'd think that the tears in his eyes were from some emotion other than frustration and disappointment.

'It'll help if you're prepared for all the questions,' she told him. 'They're going to ask about Mary Lou's job at the McDonald's on base. When did she start working there?'

He couldn't remember. 'I think just a few months before she took off for Florida,' he told her. Every minute took them another mile closer to Sarasota. He was going to have to do something pretty damn soon. 'I don't know the exact date, but the manager there would still have those records, wouldn't they?'

'Yeah, probably.' Alyssa frowned, a slight furrow marring the perfection of her brow. 'Let's see, they're surely going to ask if Mary Lou ever questioned you about your work as a SEAL.'

'She only asked about my schedule. When I had to go in and what time was I coming home. She attended an AA meeting almost every night,' Sam explained. 'I made it home on time about three times a week. Sometimes more often, depending on what the team was up to. She would go out, and I would stay home with Haley.' He had to smile, remembering. 'Mary Lou sometimes put her to bed before she left, but Hale, she knew if it was just me and her home alone, I'd let her hang out with me until right before Mary Lou got back. It was weird. She was just a baby, but she was smart. We used to watch ESPN together, and I swear, she knew the Cowboys just from their uniforms.' He looked at Alyssa. 'I know you probably harbor a lot of resentment toward Mary Lou and probably Haley, too. God knows I haven't wrapped my head around Mary Lou's doctored condoms yet. Jesus. But Haley's a treasure, Lys. Don't hold it against her – you know, the fact that Mary Lou's her mother.'

'How could you have stayed away from her for six *months*?'

'I don't know,' he said. 'How could I have stayed away from you for six months?'

'Please let's not start this again.'

'It was because I was scared.' There. He'd said it. 'Scared I'm not goddamn good enough. Scared I'm going to somehow fuck it up and screw her up but good.'

Admitting this, saying it out loud, was damn near making him break into a cold sweat. He'd tried talking to Mary Lou about Haley, telling her that even just holding her terrified him, not because of the physical fears of dropping her or somehow breaking her, but because of the enormous emotional responsibility. His own parents had damaged him so badly, and at least on his mother's part it had been completely without intention. He was scared he'd unknowingly do the same to this tiny, precious baby.

Mary Lou had looked at him as if he were some kind of freak, so he'd shut the fuck up and kept it all inside.

Please, God, don't let Alyssa look at him that same way. . . .

He forced himself to keep talking. 'My own father sucked. I mean, we're talking nightmare scenario. He was a piece of work, Lys. I swear, he was tormented by . . . something, and he took it out on us. All I know about being a father and a husband is to *not* be like him. But even if I do it differently, I can still do it wrong and—'

Sam had to take a deep breath and exhale hard. God damn it, he wished she would say something. But she was definitely listening, so he kept going.

'Except, looking back at my marriage to Mary Lou, I've realized I made some of the same mistakes my father did. I found myself married to a woman I didn't like – a woman I discovered I couldn't love – so I bailed. But only bailed halfway. Just like he did. I actually turned into him in some ways, which is, um . . . pretty sickening to have to admit. Looking back, I can see the transformation, like one of those bad werewolf movies – but I couldn't see it at the time. He traveled for work, so he spent as much time as possible on the road to get away from us. I tried to do the same thing, for different reasons, but whenever the

191

team went wheels up, I was on that plane. And the rest of the time, shit, I was gone, too. I mean, even though I was there in body, the rest of me was out to lunch.' He tried to laugh, but it came out sounding embarrassingly like a sob. 'At least I didn't beat the hell out of Mary Lou and Haley when I was home.'

Shit, that was more than she needed to know. It had just come blurting out. What a loser.

Except, O hosanna, was it possible . . .? Jesus God, it was indeed reward time. Alyssa actually laced their fingers together, holding tightly to his hand.

It was freaking amazing. It was the last thing he'd expected her to do, and it left him breathless and speechless and, God damn, it filled him with hope.

The really stupid part was, he couldn't have manipulated her into doing that if he'd tried. Somehow she knew that what he was saying was the real deal. That it was hard as hell to put what he was feeling into coherent sentences, and harder still to utter them aloud.

They drove past a sign saying SARASOTA, 140 MILES. Alyssa was holding the car at a pretty steady 80 mph. At this rate, he had about ninety minutes left to get himself free.

Ten minutes. He'd give himself ten more minutes of holding Alyssa's hand before he'd tell her he had to take a leak.

That would rattle her, for sure. At the very least, she'd pull over to the side of the highway. Best case scenario, she'd stop at a rest stop. He'd convince her to uncuff him, and the moment she did, he'd ninja out of there. Instant vamoose. One minute he'd be there, and the next . . .

She was going to be mad as hell.

But right now she was actually holding his hand.

Ten

The summer before eighth grade, Roger and Noah both got their growing on in a major way, and by the time school started again, they were neck and neck in a race to see who would hit six feet first.

One of the hardest parts about growing so much so fast was learning to negotiate head room. There'd always been so much of it before, but now every time Roger turned around he was damn near knocking himself unconscious by banging his head into something or another.

The other hard part was recognizing his own strength.

No more fighting, Walt had said to the boys. They were both bigger than most of the bullies by now, and it wouldn't be too long before someone got hurt worse than anyone had intended.

He'd promised them flying lessons. Real lessons, up in the flight school's Cessna. Of course, they had to take and pass the reading and writing part of the class first.

And before they started *that*, Walt had told them that they had to go a solid month without getting into a fight.

When he'd used the word *they* he really meant *he*. Ringo. Roger. Noah didn't get into fights unless Roger was around.

It had been twenty-six days. The past three had been hard, since Noah was home from school with a sore throat. But now there were only four more days to go, and he was damned if he was going to be the one to blow it.

Except Lyle Morgan was following him home from school.

'Hey, *Ringo*, wait up!'

Shoot. Roger picked up his pace and even crossed to the other side of the street.

It didn't slow Morgan down.

Lyle Morgan was one of the few bullies who still had it over him in both height and weight. Of course, he was in high school and played on the football team.

He still hadn't forgiven Roger for grinding his face into the dirt on the elementary school playground a month ago.

Forget about the fact that Morgan had jumped him.

Of course it *had* been after Roger started slinging insults back at the older boy.

Although he did have to admit, in hindsight, that he'd gotten into the self-defense thing maybe a little too enthusiastically, particularly after that bullshit Lyle had spouted about Roger's sister, Elaine.

Nos had had to pull him off, and the look in his eyes was one Roger would always remember.

Afterward, both Noah and Walt had sat him down – separately – and talked to him about something ridiculous called anger management. Noah had gone so far as to present him with the legal definition of manslaughter, as well as an overview of the average number of years spent in prison by a person who killed another person in a fistfight.

Roger had protested. He'd had no intention of killing Lyle Morgan. Although, even as he said the words, he could remember that odd, metallic taste in his mouth and the way his anger seemed to pound through his veins with every beat of his heart.

It had controlled him.

It wasn't just Lyle he was fighting that day. It was his father. And his mother, too. God, why did she take those pills? Pills to sleep. Pills to wake up. Pills that made her drift aimlessly around the house and not really see him.

What she really needed was a pill to make Roger's father go away for good.

'Where you going, *Ringo*?' Lyle asked now. He had a crew cut that didn't work real well with his pumpkin head or his acne. 'Over to your lover's house?'

Yeah, actually, I'm going to your girlfriend's, dickhead. Roger clenched his teeth over the words. Taunting Lyle in return would only escalate the situation.

'Just keep walking,' Walt had advised him when he'd asked the older man for help. 'And say—'

'I'm not going to fight with you, Lyle.' Roger tucked the manila envelope with Noah's school assignments under his left arm, farther away from the older boy.

Unfortunately, his doing that drew Lyle's attention to it.

'What's in the envelope? Pictures of you and Einstein doing it?'

'It's Noah's homework. Mr Gaines called me this morning before school and asked me to pick it up for him.' Roger could have used Nos's steadying support right about now. It was also very likely that if Noah had been with him, Lyle would never have approached. Bullies never liked odds that weren't in their favor.

'Mr Gaines, huh? You his little slave boy? Ain't that a switch.' Lyle laughed at his own joke. What an asshole.

Roger walked a little faster. 'I'm not going to fight with you, Lyle.' *You fricking piece of shit.*

'You know, now that your cousin has come out of the closet, you might as well, too, faggot.' Lyle laughed again.

Jerry Starrett had lived down the street from Lyle and his mother. He was four years older, and back when Roger was in first and second grade, he'd worshiped the ground his cousin had walked on.

Last year, Roger's uncle Frank had kicked Jerry out of the house after he'd been arrested in a gay bar in Dallas. It was old news, but apparently it had just made its way to Lyle's ears.

And now it was going to be all over school tomorrow.

If he was going to make it through these next few days without fighting, he was going to need to come down with that strep throat Noah had contracted. Except Nos had been on antibiotics for so many days, he wasn't contagious anymore.

Roger could always lie and *say* he was sick.

Problem was, Walt disapproved of lying almost as much as he did fighting.

Jesus, it was hard being good.

'I always used to wonder why Jerry would rather play with a stupid first-grader than with me,' Lyle said now. 'Now I know the kind of games you were playing up there in his room.'

Noah's house was in sight. 'I'm not going to fight with you, Lyle.' It was amazing he could speak at all through such tightly clenched teeth.

'You're not even going to deny it, are you, fudge packer?'

Roger didn't know what that meant, but it didn't sound good.

'Stay in control,' Walt had told him. 'Don't let your anger use you. Use your anger. You're smarter than most people. Use your brain to win without violence.'

Lyle's taunts usually came down to homosexuality. Faggot, fairy, homo, queer. That wasn't unusual. Roger himself had found that questioning an opponent's sexuality was usually the fastest way to get a knee-jerk reaction. But he'd also discovered that some people were touchier about it than others. Some kids shrugged it off. But others – like Lyle Morgan – went ballistic at the slightest suggestion that they might enjoy the time they spent in the boys' locker room a little too much.

Maybe because they actually did, and they were terrified someone might find out.

'I'm not going to fight with you,' Roger told Lyle, stopping at the bottom of the Gaines's driveway. 'But you know, now that Jerry has admitted what he's admitted, well, you might want to take care reminding people that you lived down the street from him. I was his cousin – I *had* to go over to his house,' he lied. 'But I seem to recall there were *quite* a few times you and Jerry put a tent at the edge of the backyard and zipped yourselves in together, nice and cozy.'

Lyle lunged for Roger, but he was ready for it, and he sidestepped the rush.

'You so much as *touch* me,' Roger said, 'or spread any rumors about me or any members of my family, and I'll print leaflets about you and Jerry and put 'em on the windshields of cars all over town.'

Lyle stopped cold. 'You wouldn't dare!'

Roger didn't blink. 'I think you know I would. But let's not go there, okay? Let's negotiate a truce. You treat me and Noah with respect, and we'll treat you with respect in return. Does that sound fair?'

'Fuck you!'

'Why don't you sleep on it and let me know in the morning?' Roger said, and went up the steps.

Walt was standing there, behind the screen door. He opened it to let Roger inside, stepping out onto the porch just enough so that Lyle could see him.

Lyle took off at a run.

'That was very impressive, young Ringo,' Walt said.

Roger handed him the manila envelope with hands that were shaking.

'Shoot!' he said. 'I wasn't scared. This isn't 'cause I was scared of him!'

'It *is* okay to be scared,' Walt said. 'I was scared every time I climbed into my plane in Africa and Italy and Germany. I spent a lot of time during the war scared – not so much of the Germans or even of dying, but scared I'd make a mistake and end up killing my men.'

'I *was* scared I'd screw up,' Roger admitted. 'I wanted to rip that smirk off Lyle's fat face just about more than I've ever wanted anything.'

'But you didn't.'

'No, sir. But it sure as hell would've been easier if I could've just killed him.'

Walter laughed and hugged him. Roger had been hugged

more in the months since he'd met Walt and Dot than he had been in the years since his mother had twisted her ankle and had started taking all those pills.

'Maybe yes and maybe no,' Walt told him. 'But remember this, Ringo my dear boy. Anything worth having doesn't come easy.' He headed for the kitchen. 'Let's get you a snack. You must be starving. You appear to have grown another inch since you came in the door.'

Alyssa cursed her bladder.

She could have made the trip from Gainesville to Sarasota without a pit stop quite easily – if she hadn't had all that coffee this morning.

But she'd woken up still weary to the bone, and she'd started chugging it, first getting a cup at the gas station convenience store when she'd filled the tank and bought that map. The sensation of caffeine flowing into her system had been such a good one that she'd bought herself another cup when she'd picked up the doughnuts.

Cup. That was a word that was rapidly becoming obsolete. These days a large coffee came in a container that could not be called a cup. *We have three sizes: barrel, vat or tanker. Would you like milk with that? Is a gallon enough, or would you like a gallon and a half?*

Damn it, she needed to pee.

She glanced over at Sam. He'd gotten really quiet after she'd started holding his hand.

She'd reached for him for a lot of different reasons, and she couldn't deny that high on the list was the fact that his fears about being like his father had moved her.

Who would've thought Sam Starrett had those kinds of insecurities? He came across as so cocky and self-assured, utterly cool and calm under fire, confident and intelligent and just egotistical enough to be the perfect Navy SEAL.

Maybe *egotistical* wasn't the right word. Because Sam truly was faster, stronger, and smarter than most men, with better reflexes and an ability to make well-thought-out command decisions in a heartbeat. The fact that he knew it went with the territory. Navy SEALs were the best of the best, and he was one of the SEALs' best officers. He wasn't smug about it – at least not too often. It was just who he was.

But here she was. Holding his hand. Good thing she was driving, or he probably would have already gotten her naked and into bed with him.

God, she was a fool.

Or she would be if she didn't have that list of additional reasons to be holding on to him – the first and foremost being that she was trying to distract him. Maybe holding his hand for a while would slow him down. Because she knew – without a doubt – that he was going to try to get away.

No way was he going to let her bring him back to Sarasota.

Max had suspected as much, too. Which was why, when he'd called her at the car dealer's, he'd told her in no uncertain terms to tell Starrett that she was taking him to Sarasota, but to instead deliver him to the FBI office in Tampa.

Except Alyssa wasn't going to make it to Tampa without stopping. She was going to have trouble making it to the next exit.

'Sam,' she said.

His hand tightened on hers very slightly. 'Yeah.'

She signaled for the exit. 'I have to stop at this gas station and use the ladies' room.'

'That's a relief. I was just about to tell you that I need to stop, too.'

Oh, crap, how was she going to deal with *that*? She'd figured she could cuff him to the back door handle – a solid piece of plastic – while she ran into the bathroom really fast. But if she took him out of the car, even securely cuffed to her wrist, she knew that somehow he'd manage to get away. And even if he didn't, what was she supposed to do? Go into the men's room with him and stand there, while he . . .?

She looked at the empty enormous coffee cup wedged into the cup holder. Hmm.

She glanced at Sam. 'Don't be offended,' she told him, 'but I'm going to cuff you to the back door while I go in there.'

Both Jules and Max had told her that when she lied, her gaze flicked up and to the right. It was very slight, but it was a classic textbook tell, and right now she worked hard to keep her eyes from moving at all. She just watched the road, taking the exit ramp a little too fast.

'Then I'll come back and take you in,' she continued. Keep those eyes still. 'You're not going to like this, but I'm going to have to go into the men's head with you.'

Sam smiled very slightly as she ran a stale yellow to get to the gas station on the other side of the intersection. 'So that I don't escape through the storm drain?'

She parked at the edge of the lot, away from the other cars, and let herself smile back at him as she released his hand. The smile was mostly to give him incentive to stick around, not really because she liked the way his smile deepened in response.

'Alyssa, I have to tell you—'

'Don't,' she said, digging into her fanny pack for the keys to the cuffs. 'Let's not complicate this more than it already is. Maybe after we're back in Sarasota, after we find Mary Lou and Haley . . .'

'Maybe what?' he said.

There they were, thank goodness. Her key to the handcuffs was on her ring with her house keys. 'I don't know. Just . . . maybe.' She closed her eyes so he wouldn't see that she was lying. *Maybe* she'd use a school bus for target practice. *Maybe* she'd be invited back into the Navy as the first female SEAL.

It was one thing to hold Sam's hand when he told some sad story, but as far as getting involved with this man again, the phrase 'over her dead body' leapt to mind. But 'Maybe's the best I can tell you right now,' she said to him.

'That's, um . . . that's okay,' he said. 'I'm . . . Maybe's okay. Is that leather?' Sam motioned with his chin toward her pack as she zipped it closed.

'Yeah,' she said, tossing it to the floor beneath her legs. 'I upgraded last year.'

'Nice. It's . . . Look, Alyssa, you need to let me go.'

'I *need* to not get fired.'

'Like Max would ever fire you,' he scoffed.

'If you run, I *will* lose my job.'

'If you don't let me go, I'll probably lose my daughter.'

'I said I'd find her,' Alyssa countered.

Sam just sat there, looking at her.

'Climb into the back,' she ordered, putting the armrest down between them, so there was space for him to do just that.

'What do I have to say to make you—'

'Starrett, if you don't climb into the back, I'm going to wet my freaking pants. And you better believe that if that happens, *no* one goes inside. We drive another two hours to Sarasota in a rolling Porta Potti.'

But he still hesitated. 'It's going to be hard to do this while we're cuffed together.'

She spoke through clenched teeth. 'I'm sure you can manage.'

'I don't want to hurt you,' he said, using his free hand to pull himself toward the backseat.

As soon as he wasn't looking, she took out her side arm, stashing it under her seat. There was no way she would shoot him, but she wasn't so sure he wouldn't try to grab it and use it to subdue her.

'I've got these boots on,' he continued. 'I don't want to kick you in the head by accident.'

Was that a threat or . . .? Alyssa took it as a warning and went with him, squeezing between the two front seats while pressed tightly against him, before his feet got anywhere near her head.

She landed in the back, on top of him.

And just as she'd expected, he went for her weapon.

Or maybe she was wrong, and what he was reaching for was really her breast. Because that's what he connected with. And he didn't hesitate or telegraph any surprise at all by the absence of her side arm in her shoulder holster.

He did, however, press his thigh hard between her legs.

As he kissed the hell out of her.

If this was his response to a maybe, what would have happened if she'd actually said yes?

Someone save her.

Kissing Sam Starrett was as world shaking as it had been all those years ago. He clung to her with all the desperation of a drowning man, as if she alone could rescue him.

It was mesmerizing, it was gratifying, it was exciting as hell to be wanted so badly, to be desired with such intense passion.

And, except for the full beard, it was all so heartbreakingly familiar.

He tasted like Sam. He smelled like Sam. He felt like Sam.

But she'd been here, *right* here, before and she still hadn't completely recovered.

His kisses could suck all the air from her lungs, all thoughts from her head.

If she let them.

The dead last thing she needed was to let him get his hands on the keys to the handcuffs. She could just picture that – she would end up handcuffed to the door handle while *he* walked away.

This was *not* going to go down that way. Alyssa pulled back and looked at him. He was breathing as hard as she was, desire making his eyes fierce and incredibly, strikingly blue.

'Lys,' he started to say.

She shut him up by leaning down and kissing him again. Not because she wanted to, but because she suddenly knew how to make him completely compliant. It involved shifting forward and spreading her legs so that she was straddling him and – oh, God. Sam Starrett, man of steel. This was familiar, too.

As she kissed him, she reached between them and started unfastening his jeans, as if they were going to . . . right there in a public parking lot. But then she pulled back, breaking their kiss, laughing and gasping for air. The gasping, at least, wasn't feigned.

'Sam,' she said. '*Sam*. We can't do this here. And I have to pee right *now*. Help me cuff you to the door, and I'll be back in two minutes. We'll find a place a little less populated and—'

He shook his head. 'You don't need to cuff me. I'm not going anywhere.'

She smiled at him as she took the keys from her pocket. 'Oh, but I want to cuff you, baby. And then I want to . . . Do you have any condoms?'

'No, ma'am.' He held out his left hand, Mr Obedient. His right was up under her shirt, underneath her bra, doing things he had no business doing to her breast.

'You trust me to buy some?' Her voice came out breathless and higher pitched than she'd intended, but glory alleluia, she'd gotten the handcuffs off her own arm and locked him securely to the car without his putting up a fight.

'Yes, I do.'

'Then I'll be right back.'

She pulled his hand away and started to back off, but he caught her and drew her down close to him again and kissed her.

It wasn't like those other kisses, those explosions of pure sex.

This time, he kissed her gently. Slowly. He took his time getting there – his gaze dropped to her mouth before he looked into her eyes again.

And then his mouth met hers in a caress that was so sweet, it brought tears to her eyes.

It wasn't without passion. No, she could still taste his need for her as he kissed her longer, deeper, but still tenderly. She could feel it in the way his heart was pounding in his chest. He was just . . . expressing it differently.

God, she was such a liar. He was going to be so hurt when she came back to the car and got back on the highway without uncuffing him. And when he started shouting about the fact that he, too, had to pee, and she'd hand him one of those giant coffee cups.

He'd realize she hadn't really meant a word she'd said, that she hadn't meant a single one of those kisses, either.

And probably right around then, the chances of their ever working things out wouldn't just be over *her* dead body. It would be over his dead body as well.

Which really was just as well.

Wasn't it?

This probably was the last time Alyssa was ever going to kiss him. A man like Sam Starrett wouldn't get fooled like this more than once.

Although, really, she was stupidly assuming that Sam's needs were even remotely like her own. He didn't necessarily want to work things out. What he wanted was to have sex with her again.

All she'd have to do was invite him up to her place. Or drop into the Ladybug Lounge and pick him up at the bar.

Alyssa broke away from him. 'I'll be right back.'

'I'm sorry,' he said.

He let his head fall back against the hard plastic of the door with a solid sounding *thunk* as she climbed into the front seat. She straightened her clothes as she got out of the car, grabbing her fanny pack and neatly pocketing her side arm as well.

'Lys.'

She stopped before closing the door, looking back in at him.

Cuffed to the door, with his pants unfastened and his hair messed, he looked like some kind of fantasy accessory. There was no doubt about it. These cars would sell like crazy if they came equipped with Sam Starrett handcuffed to the back.

He was holding out a twenty-dollar bill. 'Trojans. Extra large.' He waggled his eyebrows at her. 'And will you pick me up some peanut M&M's? I'm all out. Oh, and a razor, too? If you're really taking me in, it's probably better if I don't look like a card-carrying member of al-Qaeda.'

She waved off the money, slammed and locked the doors, and ran for the ladies' room.

Three minutes. It took her three minutes, tops, because of course she didn't buy anything at all.

She rushed back to the door, and the sight of the car, sitting out there under the shade of a tree, relieved her.

It was almost funny. What had she thought? That he was going to be able to get himself free, hot-wire the car, and drive away, all inside of three minutes?

Alyssa took her time walking back to the car, trying to figure out what she was going to say to him. 'I'm sorry' might be a good place to start.

I'm sorry.

That was what *he'd* said to her, right after he'd kissed her so sweetly.

She ran the rest of the way to the car, and shit, *shit, double shit!*

The backseat was empty, the cuffs still hanging from the door handle, the gleaming metal catching and sparking in the morning sunshine.

Sam Starrett, damn him, was gone.

Max didn't say a word as Alyssa Locke told him that Sam Starrett had vanished. He just held onto his cell phone as he looked out the window.

'It's completely my fault,' she said tightly. 'I take full responsibility.'

She sounded upset. Pissed off. Stressed. Pushed beyond the limit.

And he was the one responsible. He shouldn't have sent her to baby-sit Sam Starrett in the first place. What was he thinking? Max silently shook his head, glad he was alone in the private office of the head of the Tampa Bureau. This way no one could see how hard he was gritting his teeth.

'I underestimated him,' she told him.

What he was thinking was that she would take one look at Starrett and see the same selfish, self-absorbed bastard Max saw.

'Please say something,' she said, sounding human and very vulnerable.

Alyssa – vulnerable. He wished they were having this conversation face-to-face. He would have liked to have seen that.

'Did you purposely let him get away?' Max asked. His voice sounded icy even to his own ears. No doubt about it – he was as much of a prick as Starrett.

Her voice practically shook. 'No, sir. I did not. Although I'm not sure if that wouldn't be easier to admit.'

Did you sleep with him? It was one of the top ten questions itemized in that memo listing things male bosses should never ask female subordinates. Particularly subordinates they had the hots for.

But Alyssa had always been able to read his mind. 'I didn't sleep with him.'

'I didn't think you had,' Max lied. She'd been out of reach for quite a few hours late last night and early this morning, and he'd had all that time to speculate. 'Besides, that's none of my business.'

'I had to make a pit stop and I . . . ignored proper procedure. I should have called for backup. I'm at fault. I thought I could control him. I thought . . . Obviously I was wrong.'

Max should have had her hold him in Gainesville. But no. He'd wanted an excuse to go to Tampa.

So here he was. In Tampa.

He'd come up here thinking he would have some time – a lot of time, with plenty left over – to talk to Starrett before members of the investigating committee arrived tonight from Washington.

'I knew he was more concerned about his daughter's safety than he was about how it would look if he didn't come in for questioning—'

'He looks guilty,' Max agreed.

'He's not.'

'You don't know that.'

'Yes,' she said. 'I do.'

'Okay,' he said. 'You know him so well – where'd he go?'

She hesitated only slightly. 'I'm almost positive he'll be heading back to Gainesville. To the bus station. The car dealer told us he gave Mary Lou a lift there around noon on the day she sold him her car. I don't think Starrett's going to find anything, but I think that's where he's going.'

'You were sharing information?' Max asked.

'It was before the news came down about the fingerprints,' Alyssa defended herself. 'Lieutenant Starrett was anxious about the whereabouts of Mary Lou and Haley.'

'So . . . you were just cheerfully helping your lover find his wife and daughter.'

'Ex-wife,' Alyssa said sharply. 'And former lover. And I thought that specific detail was none of your business. Sir.'

Okay, this was definitely personal. If he'd had any doubts about it, they were now gone. And she knew that, because she said, 'I know you're going to pull me off this case, so—'

'Oh, I'm not pulling you,' he interrupted.

She was silent, and he just waited. He was a professional negotiator – he could outwait a dead man.

Alyssa finally spoke. 'If you want me to hand in my resignation—'

'Do you want to resign?' Max the head of the FBI's top counterterrorist team absolutely did not want to lose her. She was that good, despite today's mistake. But Max the man, well, he wanted that letter on his desk three months ago.

'I asked you first,' she said.

If she quit his team, he'd show up at her apartment with

flowers and a bottle of wine that very same night. Hell, he'd bring a diamond ring and drop to his knees and propose marriage right there, the moment she opened the door.

And then, with this extremely attractive, intelligent, very compatible woman he honestly cared about in his life, along with the opportunity to have sex on a regular basis, ending this hellish run of celibacy that had been going on far too long, maybe *then* he'd be able to hold life's chaos at bay.

Maybe then he wouldn't find himself in freaking Tampa for all the wrong reasons.

But when he opened his mouth, 'No, I don't want you to quit' came out. Either the team leader was stronger than the man, or the man was a flipping idiot and didn't really want the chaos to end.

'I want you to go back to Gainesville,' the team leader told her. 'I'm sending Jules up to join you. I want you to make yourself visible as you check out the bus station.' If anyone could find Starrett, it was Alyssa Locke.

Or rather, Sam Starrett would find Alyssa.

And once he found her, the son of a bitch wouldn't be able to stay away.

Kind of the same way Max had ended up in Tampa.

Eleven

Alyssa's cell phone rang as she and Jules Cassidy were leaving the bus station.

'On Saturdays, the only bus to Jacksonville leaves in the morning.'

It was Sam.

Who didn't know what Jules had just told her – that Mary Lou *hadn't* left Gainesville the same evening she'd sold her car, despite the ride to the bus station from used car maven Jon Hopper.

Obviously, just as Alyssa had expected, Sam had come to the bus station before them and had gotten a schedule, too.

She'd expected him to call. She wasn't sure why she was so certain he would, but somehow she'd known that sooner or later, he'd contact her.

If only just to taunt her.

But despite that, she still hadn't managed to prepare for the sound of his voice.

Jules was looking at her, questions in his eyes, as she heard herself ask, 'Where are you?'

Sam didn't bother to answer. 'Next bus out isn't until Sunday morning. But no one remembers a woman with a kid sitting in the bus station all night – not that that necessarily means anything, although it's not like the place is huge. She would've stood out, if anyone was paying attention. Which they probably weren't. Still, I'm thinking that the two nights charged on her Visa at the Day's Inn in Jacksonville was her attempt to lead whoever's following her off her real trail.'

He was probably right, except for the part where Mary Lou and Haley spent the night in the bus station. Jules had reported that Mary Lou's credit card had been checked – but not used – by the manager of the Sunset Motel, a mere seven blocks from the bus station, right there in Gainesville.

That activity hadn't shown up on her regular credit card account. It had taken additional digging by the investigative team, since apparently Mary Lou had settled the bill with cash.

And wasn't *that* interesting? Combined with the fact that that very same night Mary Lou had charged and paid for a motel room in Jacksonville, it seemed to confirm their belief that Sam's ex-wife knew someone was searching for her and was actively attempting to evade them.

'Starrett, there's an APB out for you,' Alyssa told him.

Jules stepped closer, concern on his pretty face. 'Let me talk to him.'

Alyssa shook her partner off, meeting his eyes only briefly.

'I'm guessing that since she wanted Abdul duk Fukkar to think she'd gone to Jacksonville, she probably took, what?' Sam asked. 'The two-fifteen to Tallahassee instead? Or maybe the four-fifteen to Columbia, South Carolina.'

Neither. Mary Lou and Haley had probably taken a bus out on Sunday, which meant they could have gone to Miami, Tampa, Fort Myers, New Orleans, Atlanta, Jacksonville, Savannah . . .

But she wasn't about to tell Sam that. 'I know you think *Abdul duk Fukkar* is really funny, but it's not. It's rude and it's direspectful to all the law-abiding Muslims in the world – of which there are millions. And if you think for even one minute that I'm going to *help* you—'

'But you already have,' he told Alyssa. There was laughter in his voice. On some level he was actually enjoying this. 'Thanks for the tip about the APB.'

Alyssa came close to snapping her cell phone shut. But Max seemed to think she was capable of getting Sam back into custody. And she was much closer to doing that if she had him on the phone.

Besides, Sam was no fool. She hadn't really told him anything new. He had to know she'd called out an APB on his ass ten seconds after he'd gone missing.

He also probably knew that *she* knew that tracing this call was pointless. He knew that *she* knew damn well that he was somewhere close by. She and Jules could set up a dragnet with the local police, but as a SEAL, Sam knew enough E&E – escape and evasion tactics – to turn the whole thing into an embarrassing joke.

Another embarrassing joke.

And one per day was enough for her.

'Look,' she said, taking a deep breath. 'Let's meet somewhere so we can talk. There's a Hardee's down the street—'

'We don't need to meet to talk,' Sam responded. 'We can talk just fine over the phone. And you know it.' He paused. 'Unless you really do want to fuck my brains out. In the bathroom of the Hardee's. Works in a major way for me. Sweet thing.'

'You want to fight with me, Starrett?' Alyssa asked tightly. 'Is that really why you called?'

Jules rolled his eyes and sighed and turned his back on her, giving her as much privacy as he could, considering.

'Yeah,' Sam said, 'maybe I do. Maybe it pissed me off to find out that you actually thought I'd chose sex over my daughter's safety.'

'And you're really in a position to save her now, aren't you?' Alyssa laughed her disgust. 'With every law enforcement agency in the country looking for you?'

'No one's going to find me unless I want to be found. Which won't be until *after* I find Haley.'

'Yeah, and you know how you're going to find Haley, Sam?' Alyssa asked, letting her temper give her voice an edge. 'You're going to find her because you're going to be following *me*. Because *I'm* going to find her. With the help of the rest of the

SUZANNE BROCKMANN

Bureau and the local police. I'm going to do it, even though it would be twice as easy and take only half as long with your help and cooperation. With information that only you can provide through the questioning that you're *not* participating in right this very minute, you selfish, selfish son of a bitch.'

There was silence for a moment, then Sam said, 'It really gives me a hard on when you shout at me and call me names.'

'Can't you be serious for even thirty seconds?'

'I don't know why you're so pissed,' he countered. 'I *told* you I wasn't going to go in with you. What made you think I'd just sit in your car, waiting for you?'

'The fact that you were *locked* there, for one,' she answered. 'Where'd you get the key, Sam? You start carrying one? Learned from past mistakes, maybe?'

At first she'd thought he'd managed to lift her own set of keys. But, no, the key to her cuffs had been right there, still in her pocket.

'Uh,' Sam said. 'Look, just let me talk to Jules, okay?'

He was definitely nearby. He knew Jules was now with her.

'Why?' she asked. It wouldn't surprise her at all if he was watching them right this second. She looked out at the sea of parked cars in the municipal lot. Where are you, Starrett, you invisible son of a bitch?

If he were in a car, it would be at the edge of the lot, near the entrance to the street, parked facing out so he could leave quickly. He'd probably altered his appearance by now, too, either shaving completely or trimming his beard. By cutting his hair or even getting a crew cut. By dressing in something other than blue jeans and a T-shirt.

It didn't matter what he looked like. She'd still be able to recognize him instantly.

'Why do I want to talk to Jules? Because he's a friend of mine,' Sam said with obviously forced patience. 'And I happen to find myself in a situation where I could use a friend.'

Alyssa closed her eyes and took a deep breath. Tried to make

212

her voice sound calm. Calmer, anyway. 'Sam. Come on. *I'm* your friend.'

'No,' he said. 'You know, I've been thinking about that, and although I'm not a hundred percent certain, I'm pretty freaking positive that a friend wouldn't have tried to play me the way you did in the backseat of your car.'

For crying out loud . . . 'Like you weren't playing *me* right from the start?'

'You know, you were good,' Starrett said. 'But the sudden change of heart was a little, I don't know, too abrupt. I mean, it might've been slightly more believable if maybe you'd had a couple of stiff drinks to make the transformation from the FBI ice bitch—'

'You are *such* an asshole.'

His voice hardened. 'Yeah, well, you're not winning a lot of points yourself today, babycakes. You know when I knew for sure, you know, that you were playing me? Honey, sugar . . . sweetheart, *baby*?'

'Oh, shit,' she said.

'Ding ding ding,' he drawled. 'You called me baby, Miss "Terms of endearment make an encounter into something impersonal, something nameless and faceless, so call me Alyssa if you really want to fuck me". It might have worked if I were a stranger and I didn't know you, but . . . You know, right up to that point, I had this wild hope that you were actually . . .' He laughed. 'I'm a fucking fool. No, actually, I'm just a fool. No fucking in sight – which is a crying shame. Although I *do* know where I can get a hand job for a bottle of Scotch. And before you start making those outraged noises that happen to be such a turn-on for me, that was just a joke.'

'Not funny.'

'Yeah, well, life's short, honey. You gotta take your laughs wherever you can get 'em.'

'Okay,' Alyssa said. 'You can stop now with the names.' Her anger had deflated into something bad tasting and depressing.

'The fact that you're pissed at me has been received and noted. But just like you told me you weren't going to Sarasota, I told *you* I wasn't going to sleep with you ever again. I guess we're both guilty of not paying attention.'

Jules had been pretending not to listen, but at that, he sighed.

Alyssa started toward the car. Her partner followed, still shaking his head.

'I guess so,' Sam said, his voice quiet now, too. 'But you can't blame me for trying. There hasn't been a single day that's passed that I haven't thought about you, Lys.'

Oh, God. 'Then, please, Sam, turn yourself in.'

'I can't do that.'

'You said something about respecting me – trusting me to watch your six, to guard your back – but I don't think you really meant it,' she said, the words coming out of her in a rush. 'If you did, you would believe me when I tell you that I'm going to find your daughter. If she's still alive – and from certain information we've received, I'm starting to believe that she still is—' *Certain information.* She probably shouldn't have told him even that much. 'I *will* find her for you, Sam.'

He didn't seem to notice her slip. 'Jesus Christ, if this was about anything but Haley—'

'I just wish you would trust me.'

'Yeah, well, I wish a lot of things, too. I wish you would give us another chance.'

'Okay,' Alyssa said, unlocking the car door.

Sam laughed. 'Yeah, right.'

'No,' she said, opening the door and popping the locks so that Jules could get in the passenger side. 'I'm serious. You surrender yourself to me and Jules. Right now. We'll bring you to the local police, who'll take you to Sarasota while we go and find Haley. And after we find her, we can both go back to DC and take it from my apartment. You turn yourself in, and you'll get to have your do-over, Sam. You pick me up, we'll go have dinner.'

Jules was no longer pretending not to listen. He stared at her across the top of the car. 'Alyssa,' he said.

On the other end of the phone, Sam was silent for a moment, but then he laughed. 'You're a good liar.'

'Jules doesn't think I'm lying,' she told him, looking into her partner's worried face.

'Jules has his own agenda when it comes to you and Max,' Sam said as Alyssa got behind the wheel and closed the car door. 'So where are we going now?'

Yeah, he was definitely someplace where he could see them. 'To rent another car. Jules is going to Tallahassee and I'm going to Birmingham.' This time she *was* lying. Not about the second rental car, though. They had to go check out the Sunset Motel here in Gainesville where Mary Lou and Haley had paid cash to spend the night. 'Which one of us are you going to follow, hot shot?'

She snapped her cell phone shut.

Jules fastened his seat belt as she backed out of the parking spot. 'I hope you know what you're doing.'

Alyssa hoped so, too.

She flipped open her phone again and called Max's assistant, Laronda. She was going to need two agents from the local office to assist at the Sunset Motel, ASAP, as well as George Faulkner from Max's team.

Working together, they were going to help her apprehend Sam Starrett.

She hoped.

January 14, 1944

Dear Walter,

This letter is so very hard to write. I've started it nearly two dozen times, two dozen different ways. But there is no easy or less painful way to impart this sorrowful news.

Early this morning, your beloved wife Mae gave up her fight. She's been ill for so long, dear friend. Please don't blame her for being weak. She fought for so long, but this latest flu was too much for her tired body to take.

Please know that I share your grief and pain. This sad news must be impossibly hard for you to bear, so far away from home and those of us who love you.

But you need to know that, at the end, you were there, with Mae, in spirit. Oh, how she loved you! Her last words were of you – yes, I was with her here in Tuskegee when she passed. She made me promise to watch out for Jolee, and then she said, 'Take care of Walter.'

I confess that I am at a loss as how best to do that while we are a world apart, but I gave her my promise, and I will manage somehow.

I will start by telling you that Mae's mother has come to Alabama to care for Jolee. I, too, will visit as often as I can.

I will be taking care of Mae's burial arrangements. Don't fret about details or payment, I'm handling all of it for now. We'll sort it out after you get back home from the war.

Please allow yourself to weep, dear friend. Grieve deeply for your loss – and what a loss this is! I have already shed enough tears for both of us, but I beg you to feel grief and not anger at your beloved Mae's passing. There's no room for anger in the cockpit of any airplane. You must be cool when you fly. You must be careful and never reckless, or I will be burying you soon, as well.

Now you must become more determined than ever to live. For Jolee, and for Mae, who was taken from this world far too soon. Make your life a good, long, solid, well-lived one.

Of course, you know that if you don't come home from this great conflict, I will take in Jolee and raise her as if she were my own daughter. Rest assured of that, my friend. But that sweet child deserves her father.

And I would hate to lose my dearest friend.

Yours in sorrow, Dot

* * *

Gina Vitagliano really loved Florida's summer weather, especially the daily storms that blew up suddenly, almost out of nowhere. She loved the big, towering, ominous thunderheads, the intensity of the forked lightning that seemed to sizzle the air, the dizzying crash of thunder, and particularly the cloudbursts – the rain that pounded down as if someone in the sky had overturned a giant bucket.

It was absurd how much water could fall in such a short amount of time, capable of giving a thorough underwear soaking to anyone caught out in it for longer than half a second.

But this summer, Florida was having a drought. Day after day after day, it didn't rain. And it didn't rain. And lawns dried up, and flowers didn't bloom. Anyone caught smoking or even so much as lighting a match in a state park was subject to arrest. Barbecuing was outlawed. The entire state felt like one giant tinderbox, ready to go up in flames at any given moment.

But today, finally, it rained the way Gina was used to.

And was she on the beach to see nature's spectacular show?

No, of course she was in her rental car, coming back from the UPS office, when the storm broke, having just shipped the last of the unneeded supplies and equipment back to yacht owner Dennis Mattson's New York base in Cold Spring Harbor.

This kind of bucket-from the-sky rain turned nearly every driver in Tampa into either her great-aunt Lucia or her cousin Mario.

Great-aunt Lucia had been four feet eleven *before* her osteoporosis had shaved a few inches from her height. She was ninety-two years old, but she still insisted on driving Great-uncle Alfonse-may-he-rest-in-peace-the-sainted-man's 1977 Cadillac Cruiseship through the busy streets of East Meadow, Long Island, because even though she might be old, there was nothing wrong with her vision. No, her eyes weren't her problem. It was the fact that she was so short she had to watch the road *through* the steering wheel. And that was *with* her sitting on the pillow.

So naturally, she drove a touch . . . cautiously.

Cousin Mario, Gina's father's fourth youngest brother Arturo's third son, on the other hand, could burn rubber standing still in the driveway, and did so at every opportunity. He had two speeds, motionless but gunning the engine, and wanting to go faster than the car in front of him. Gina's father was convinced his nephew had been permanently warped by too many Mario Andretti jokes when he was a child.

Gina suspected it was the fact that Mario took after Great-aunt Lucia's side of the family when it came to height that had turned him into a motor vehicular madman. Unlike Gina and her pack of hulking brothers, cousin Mario was petite. After he'd failed to bulk up despite joining the local gym and chugging power shakes, he'd turned to cars for his muscle.

But it was a universal truth that the Great-aunt Lucias and the Marios of the world didn't mix well, and particularly not with the added ingredient of pouring rain.

Today when the skies opened, Gina had a Great-aunt Lucia in front of her in an oceanliner, stopped dead, and a Mario in a pickup truck about three cars back.

The smart thing for a sane driver to do in weather like this was to crawl along the road, windshield wipers flapping and slapping ineffectively, until it was possible to pull off to the right, into a parking lot, to wait until the rain let up. And the wait wouldn't be long – it rarely rained for more than ten or fifteen minutes at this time of day.

But the Great-aunt Lucia in front of her was clearly overwhelmed.

The Mario behind Gina was sitting on his horn.

The cars in the oncoming lane of traffic were moving slowly and steadily onward. The Great-aunt Lucia inched her *Queen Mary* forward, then spotted the driveway to the Publix superstore on the left and jumped on her brakes. She put on her left blinker, dooming them all to waiting forever because there was no way in hell she was going to get across the slow stream of traffic in *this* lifetime, and there was no room to pass her on the right without going onto the sidewalk.

The rain was so thick, it almost kept Gina from seeing it happen. But the Mario was in one of those big-wheeled trucks, and his headlights were higher than the other two cars behind her. In her rearview mirror, Gina saw him shift to the right, pulling onto the sidewalk in a classic Mario move.

Just as the Great-aunt Lucia changed her mind and started to pull right instead, into the parking lot for the SwimMart.

Also a classic GAL technique – fake left, go right.

'Oh, shit!' Gina said aloud, because the Mario was clearly fooled by the Lucia's left blinker, still going furiously. She could see that he was actually picking up speed. She leaned on her horn – but it was too late.

Mario hit his brakes, but his truck still slammed into the oceanliner, skidding into Gina's rental car as it fishtailed, and pushing her left, directly – oh, my *God!* – into the oncoming traffic.

Metal on metal on metal on metal – how could it sound so awful? Everyone but the Mario had been going so slowly or not moving at all.

Gina's airbag went off and her seat belt locked down. It was hard to say which was responsible for knocking the air out of her lungs – it all happened so fast.

And then, almost eerily, it was over. There was only the sound of the rain pounding on the roof and the windshield wipers fighting to keep up.

Someone hammered on Gina's window, startling her. The airbag had already deflated, and she reached for the button that would unlock the car.

The door was yanked open.

'Are you all right?'

Gina stared up at Max Bhagat. He was dressed as Max always dressed, in a dark business suit and a white shirt, but he was soaking wet.

Water streamed down his face and his hair was flattened,

making him look about as unlike the impeccable, always well-groomed man as humanly possible.

But it *was* definitely Max.

Her first thought was that somehow, impossibly, the accident had been worse than she'd imagined and that she'd actually been killed. And that this was heaven.

But very real water dripped off of Max's dark hair onto her as he leaned into the car. 'Are you hurt?' he asked, carefully looking her over from her Jekyll Island T-shirt to her cutoff jeans to her flip-flops and her red toenail polish.

He pushed her hair back from her face and his fingers were warm.

Oh, God, he was really here. He'd finally, *finally* come to find her, to tell her he missed her as much as she missed him, to admit that a twenty-year age difference didn't mean all that much in the cosmic scheme of things.

It was not the coolest or most collected response, but Gina couldn't help it. She started to cry.

'Max,' she said, and reached for him.

He was solid and warm and very, very wet. She didn't give a damn about that or the fact that it was raining in as he half sat on the running board, because his arms were around her, holding her, and, for the first time in years, she actually felt safe.

'Hey,' he said, in his incredibly smooth, velvet-perfect, accent-free voice. She still dreamed of his voice, usually a couple times a week – sometimes more, depending on her stress levels at school or at work.

Max Bhagat had been the chief FBI negotiator when the plane Gina'd taken from Athens to Vienna had been hijacked and rerouted to the terrorist hot spot of Kazbekistan. And she'd been the chief hostage when she'd pretended to be a US Senator's daughter – a role she'd assumed to keep the other passengers from being killed by the terrorists who'd taken the plane. For four days, Max's voice over that airliner's radio had been her constant companion.

'Hey,' he said to her now, 'you've got to talk to me, Gina. Are you hurt?'

'Not anymore,' she said into his shoulder.

'Did you hit your head?' Max pulled back from her slightly so that she was forced to look up at him. He was checking her pupils, his own dark brown eyes filled with concern.

'I don't think so,' she said.

Why didn't he kiss her? She'd been waiting for *years* for this man to kiss her.

His arms were still around her and his mouth was right there, right within reach of hers.

And Gina, she was done with the waiting. She'd waited far long enough, so she did what she should have done years ago.

She kissed *him*.

Twelve

Noah answered the phone on the first ring. 'Yeah.'

'Hey, Nos,' Sam said.

There was a brief pause and then, 'Shit, Roger, where are you? What the hell is going on? I'm supposed to call some Agent Winters lady if you so much as pass gas in my direction.'

Which was one of the things Sam had hoped to find out by calling. 'You definitely should call her,' he said. 'Soon as we hang up. I don't want to get you into trouble.'

'Wouldn't be the first time, Cuz.'

'Trust me, you don't need trouble on this scale.'

'Yeah, well, Claire's not too happy with you right now, and when she's not happy with you, she's not happy with me. And me getting arrested for aiding and abetting, well . . . Let's just say if that happened, I'd be very cold and lonely for the rest of my life.'

Sam had to laugh. 'Yeah, like she'd ever leave you. She's loved you since tenth grade.'

'No, I've loved *her* since tenth grade,' Noah corrected him. 'She was just hot for my body.'

'Yeah, right.'

'I'm serious,' Noah said. 'I had to work to talk her into marrying me, you know. She didn't want to do it.'

No way. All this time Sam had thought Noah was just going along for the ride. He'd gotten the girl pregnant, so now this was his life. He'd accepted it graciously, and he *seemed* happy enough, but . . . 'I thought it was her idea. I thought you were just playing out the hand you were dealt, you know?'

'Not even close. I had to *dance* to make that wedding happen. She was like, How do we know this is real? How do we know we're not going to meet someone in a year or two or ten that we're *really* supposed to be with forever?'

'But that's something no one ever knows,' Sam pointed out. 'At some point, you've just got to go on faith.'

'Hey, I knew,' Noah told him. 'I knew she was the only woman I'd ever want. I was freaking seventeen, and I *knew*.' He laughed softly. 'Why do you think Grandpa gave me his blessing? After being so adamant that we *not* get married, that we were too *young* to get married, that it couldn't possibly last?'

Not get married . . .? 'Uncle Walt told me he gave you permission because you were doing the right thing.'

'Yeah, *fuckhead*, I was doing the right thing because I was crazy in love with the girl! I told Grandpa that I knew if we didn't get married right then, if she gave in to her parents' pressure to have an abortion or to give the baby away, that it would be over between us, forever. I knew Claire would never recover from something like that. I knew that she'd break up with me afterward because it would be too hard, you know, being reminded and . . . Jesus, Ringo, I really wanted her to marry me. I told Grandpa I was willing to give up everything I'd ever wanted to be with her. I'd leave school, I'd take a job working for him – the lowest, dirt-eating job – just so I could support Claire and the baby. I'd work my way up, I'd do it all the hard way – GED, night school. Because all those things I thought I'd wanted? They were nothing compared to how badly I wanted to spend the rest of my life with Claire.'

'Holy shit,' Sam said. 'I always thought . . .' That Noah's marriage was a *have to*, not a *want to*.

Noah laughed. 'Yeah, well, Grandpa heard what I was saying, and I guess he knew it was the real deal, too. I remember what he said when he changed his mind. He was like, "What right do

I have to tell you you're too young, that this relationship can't possibly work?" He told me that real love can win over just about any adversity. He said I wouldn't even be alive right now if he had listened to common sense back when Grandma was trying to talk him into marrying her. The entire world said their relationship couldn't possibly work – a black man and white woman. No, *that* wouldn't last. Oh, yeah? Well, how about fifty years?'

'Holy shit,' Sam said. And he'd gone and married Mary Lou, because he'd thought . . .

'Look, man, this conversation isn't helping you. This FBI agent who talked to me was very intense. They want to find you pretty damn badly. You need to think about turning yourself in. I'll go with you, if you want. I'll find you a lawyer, I'll . . . I don't know. *Damn.* Just tell me what you need me to do to help you get this mess straightened out.'

'I need to ask you a favor,' Sam said, pulling his head back from thinking about Walt. 'A huge favor. You and Claire.'

'Yes,' Noah said. 'We'll do it.'

Sam laughed. 'Have you been drinking? Because you can't possibly know what I'm going to—'

'No, I have not been drinking. I had a beer when I got home, is all, and it's about Haley,' Noah said. 'Right? If you and Mary Lou are both taken into custody, we'll take care of her. Roger, man, you didn't even have to ask.'

Sam had to wait several moments before speaking. 'Thank you,' he said quietly. 'When I thought about them putting her into the foster care system—'

'Shhh,' Noah said. 'Don't go there. Claire and I already love her – we can't wait to meet her. We've already talked about this, about her needing to stay here for a while. But you know, I really hope it'll only be for a very short visit.'

'Yeah,' Sam said. 'Me, too.' But if not . . . He couldn't think of anyone better to raise his daughter. 'Hey, Nos?'

'Yeah?'

'Fuck you,' Sam said. It was ninth-graders' code for emotions they couldn't bring themselves to utter aloud.

But they weren't ninth graders anymore. And Noah always had been the more mature one. 'I love you, too, Ringo. Stay safe.'

Those were words Sam had heard so many times. Walter had had no problem at all saying them. In fact, he'd said it nearly every time Roger had left after a visit. 'Thanks, Nos. Don't forget to call the FBI and tell 'em everything we talked about. There are no secrets here.'

'Except where you're calling from,' Noah pointed out.

'Ah,' Sam said, right before he cut the connection. 'But I didn't tell you that.'

Gina Vitagliano's tongue was in his mouth.

Max knew he should back away. The girl was seat belted in – it wouldn't take much effort at all to make her stop kissing him.

He also knew that the dead last thing he should do was kiss her back.

But then again, the dead last thing he should've done in the first place was come to Tampa.

She was sweet and hot and her kiss was twice as mind-blowing as he'd ever imagined, with her fingers in his hair, against his neck and face and God, God, *God* this was exactly what he swore he'd never do.

But her lips were so soft and she kissed him deeper, and he'd wanted this for so long, and suddenly he wasn't just getting kissed, he was kissing her.

And, Christ, it was probably the most selfish moment in his life, which was really saying something since he knew he was a selfish bastard, but he couldn't stop, couldn't stop, couldn't . . .

He had to stop.

He was definitely going to stop now.

But, God damn it, he could taste the salt of her tears and that should've made him want to stop even more, but selfish, twisted son of a bitch that he was, it was actually a turn-on knowing that the mere sight of him made her cry.

She still thought that she wanted him. It had been over a year since he'd last talked to her on the phone, longer than that since he'd seen her. And nothing had changed.

But, God damn it, did that mean that she still had the night-mares, too? Did she still flinch when strangers came too close? Did she still get that distant look in her eyes, remembering what she'd endured at the hands of her captors – a terrorism survivor's version of the battle-weary soldier's thousand-mile stare?

He'd purposely stayed away so that she could heal.

Except he hadn't stayed away, had he? Here he was. In Tampa. With his tongue in Gina's mouth. Screwing up her life even more than it had already been screwed up by the bad guys.

Max Bhagat, emotional terrorist.

He pushed himself away from her.

She was breathing as hard as he was, and the look in her eyes promised paradise. If they hadn't been in the middle of the road, in the heart of downtown Tampa, she would've had her clothes off by now. And wouldn't *that* have been hard to walk away from.

She opened her mouth to tell him God knows what, but he stopped her. He didn't want to hear it.

'That wasn't supposed to happen,' he said, his voice too harsh even to his own ears.

Her face was so expressive, with her wide eyes and generous mouth, and he could read her like a book. Confusion. Amused disbelief. He had to be kidding, right?

Max clarified. 'I shouldn't have let you kiss me, Gina.'

She laughed. Stopped. 'But . . .'

Now the confusion was mixed with disbelief and a glimmer of hurt. God *damn* it. But what did he expect? He'd purposely worded it so that the responsibility for what had just happened fell squarely onto her.

'It was the heat of the moment,' he told her, hating himself. 'It wasn't real.'

Hurt morphed rapidly to anger in her incredible eyes. 'You kiss me back like *that* and . . . that wasn't *real?*' She laughed. 'Maybe you better say it again, Max, because I don't think you've even convinced your*self* that that wasn't *real.*'

'I'm sorry,' he said forcing his face and his voice to be distant. 'But it wasn't—'

Her voice shook as she cut him off. 'There was more truth in that one kiss than in all the hours and *hours* of conversation we've ever had!'

'I can't be more than your friend,' he told her, hearing tinges of desperation in his voice. He took a deep breath, trying to steady himself, realizing as he backed even farther away that the rain had almost completely stopped. 'I've made that very clear.'

'Yeah,' Gina mocked. 'You're a good friend. You don't visit, you don't call, you don't even write. You know, I've considered taking hostages simply to get a chance to talk to you. Although knowing you, you'd send a different negotiator.'

Max didn't say anything. There were times when it was best not to speak at all.

Several police cars had pulled up, and one of the uniformed officers was heading toward them.

'She okay?' the man called.

'She seems to be,' Max responded. He handed the man his ID. 'I still want her taken to the hospital, get her checked out.'

The cop nodded, standing straighter, shoulders back as he realized who Max was. 'Yes, sir. An ambulance is on its way, sir.'

'I don't need to go to the hospital,' Gina said, unbuckling her seat belt and climbing out of the car. Jesus H. Christ, she'd actually gotten a belly button ring. 'I'm fine.'

All of the other drivers seemed fine, too. Thank God for airbags – or cars the size of Texas. The little old man in the 1975 Lincoln Town Car was more worried about his groceries melting in the backseat than any potential damage to his person.

But, 'That's what Princess Grace thought, too,' Max said to her.

'Who?'

Yes, Gina was young. 'Princess Grace of Monaco,' he explained. 'Grace Kelly. She died before you were born so you probably don't—'

'The actress from *Rear Window*,' Gina said. 'Who died of internal injuries after a car accident, in 1982, and I was, too, born. If you'd said Grace Kelly right away, I would have known who you meant. You know, being born in 1980 doesn't automatically make me an idiot, Max.'

But it *did* make him old enough to be her father. In 1980, he was finishing up – two years early – his undergraduate degree at Princeton. Twenty years old, he was already being wooed by the Bureau and was negotiating for a chance to attend the Air Force's legendary Indoc, aka Superman School, without the four-year commitment to the military.

His intention was to go through the Air Force's pararescue jumpers' pipeline – a succession of intensely rigorous training schools – before heading to the relative tameness of the FBI Academy at Quantico.

But the FBI said no can do, so he'd politely thanked them for their time. Instead, he dove into an accelerated master's program at NYU where he took a class given by Professor Glenn Nelson, who was a former FBI negotiator and a lifelong friend of the then-head of the Bureau.

With a little pressure from Nelson, no can do became please, please do, and a year and a half later, when Gina was still practicing walking, Max was finishing up Indoc – earning both a reputation as an unstoppable son of a bitch, and his right to wear that big S on his chest.

He'd slid on down the pipeline as Gina had begun potty training.

By the time she started first grade, he was well on his way to his current position as head of the Bureau's top counterterrorist group.

'So why are you here?' Gina asked. 'No, don't tell me. You just happened to be out for a stroll in the pouring rain and recognized me sitting in my car – through a blurry windshield . . .?'

She was going to figure it out anyway, so he might as well tell her. 'I was in town on other business,' Max said. It was not quite a total lie. 'I knew you were here, too, because . . . I make a point to know everything about everyone. I was just . . . checking up on you.'

She was staring at him.

He cleared his throat. 'I should probably move my car.' His rental was right where he'd left it, two cars behind Gina's, the driver's side door standing open.

Realization was dawning in Gina's eyes as she looked from him to his car and back. 'You were checking up on me, as in watching me to see if I'm okay, as in *stalking* me—' her voice got louder with incredulity '—with no intention of letting me know you're in town?'

Crap. 'Look,' he said. 'I happen to care about you. I know these past few years have been tough—'

'It didn't occur to you that I "happen to care" about you, too?' she said hotly. 'You didn't even once think, "Gee, I bet Gina would like a chance to check up on me, too"?'

'What's to check? I'm not the one who spent four days at the mercy of terrorists. I'm not the one who was—' Gang *raped.* He stopped himself from saying it. Jesus, Jesus, Jesus. Talk about nightmares. He still sometimes woke up sweating and practically gagging, the sound of Gina's cries ringing in his head, echoes of her cries when those bastards hurt her, when he'd sat in the Kazabek airport terminal room that the FBI–SEAL task force was using as a surveillance center and listened to her being attacked in the cockpit of that airliner, powerless to stop them, unable to do a goddamned thing to save her.

'Gee, Max,' Gina said. 'You sound as if you still have a great deal of unresolved anger.'

Max had met Dr Elizabeth Dannowitz, Gina's therapist, a handful of times, so he knew that she was doing a very decent imitation of the woman.

But he answered her as if she were serious. 'Yes, I do.'

She was quiet then, hardly saying much of anything as the police officer approached to check her license and the car rental agreement, as she filled out the accident report, as the paramedics came and checked her blood pressure, as she took her things out of the car so it could be towed away, as Max made arrangements with the local police for them to drive her back to her hotel after taking her to the hospital for a more complete examination.

And then, that was it. She was saying goodbye, still so preoccupied, her dark eyes subdued, and he was standing on the steaming sidewalk, watching the ambulance drive away.

The sun broke through the last of the clouds as he climbed into his car and headed south, for Sarasota.

Tom Paoletti's Navy SEALs had a name for a day like today, the kind of day that started with Sam Starrett escaping from Alyssa Locke and ended with that troubled look in Gina Vitagliano's eyes. A day that had Max's tongue in her mouth somewhere there in the middle.

Clusterfuck.

Today was, indeed, a grade A clusterfuck, no doubt about it.

And it wasn't even over yet.

Mrs Downs handed Mary Lou an enormous ring of keys. 'I'm not sure you're ready for this, Constance,' she said disapprovingly, then got into the waiting taxicab and drove away.

Mary Lou wasn't so sure of that herself.

The house was enormous, and as she went back inside, closing the heavy front door behind her, she didn't feel any pleasure at all. When King Frank had told her she'd be alone here without Mrs Downs breathing down her neck, she had been psyched. It would be a chance to pretend that this was her house. That she was a television star or a supermodel.

But the marble-tiled, two-story foyer seemed cold and lifeless.

She hadn't realized what a huge presence King Frank could be. And the fact that he'd spent quite a bit of time in his shooting range or walking around the house packing this rifle or that revolver had actually made her feel quite safe.

Mary Lou made sure that the door was locked and hurried back toward the wing of the house that held the au pair quarters and Whitney's room.

Haley and Amanda were still napping, so she went into her living room, put the keys down on her kitchenette counter, and picked up the phone.

'You *do* know that all calls into and out of this house are screened.'

Whitney was leaning in the doorway that led to Mary Lou's bedroom.

No matter what Mary Lou said or did, that girl was constantly going through her things.

Mary Lou sighed. 'Whitney, I asked you, just yesterday as a matter of fact, to please respect my privacy.'

'I was putting back something that I borrowed.'

Stolen was more like it. But okay. This new semi-friendship they were developing was a good thing. 'Thank you,' Mary Lou said.

'If you really want to call someone without Daddy finding out about it,' Whitney told her, 'you need to call from a pay phone downtown. That's what I do.'

Mary Lou finished dialing. 'I'm just calling the front gate.'

The younger of the two weekday guards picked up. 'Potter.'

SUZANNE BROCKMANN

'Yes, this is Connie from up at the house,' Mary Lou said. 'I'm a little nervous with both Mr Turlington and Mrs Downs out of town for the next week or so. Please don't let anyone through the gate without calling me first.'

'Yes, ma'am.'

'Will you let the other guards know, too?' she asked.

'Yes, ma'am.'

'Thank you,' Mary Lou said, and hung up the phone. Already, she was starting to feel better. There were guards at the gate and no reason on the planet that anyone at all would be able to find her here.

'Was that Jim Potter?' Whitney asked. 'Was he, like, all "Yes, ma'am, yes, ma'am"?'

Mary Lou had to smile. 'He was exactly like that.'

'He's a dork.' Whitney sat down on one of the stools at the kitchen counter. 'But he's an honest dork. I once snuck in late when I was supposed to be grounded and he caught me. I told him I'd give him a BJ if he didn't tell my father, and he actually said no.'

Oh, Lord.

'You should tell him about your husband,' Whitney said, sliding off the stool. 'At least give him Sam's description. It might make you feel a little less tense.'

Mary Lou doubted it.

Sam sat on the roof of the not-so-beautiful Gainesville Garden Apartments, just across the street from the Sunset Motel.

He'd followed Alyssa here earlier today. She surely knew he was following her and had definitely tried to lose him, but he knew the way her brain worked. He could tell, too, the moment she was certain he wasn't on her tail anymore. Because she headed directly to this motel. No circuitous routes, no delay.

And once she got here, she'd gone inside and stayed inside for a good long time.

A good long conversation's length of time.

It was pretty obvious that Alyssa had gotten some information that led the FBI to believe that this was where Mary Lou and Haley had spent the night after discovering the next bus to Jacksonville didn't leave until 0925 on Sunday morning.

Which was, of course, an option that Sam would've gotten around to considering sooner or later. And once it occurred to him, he would've started checking the local motels, starting with the ones closest to the bus station.

Starting with the Sunset Motel.

Obviously Alyssa expected Sam to show up here sooner or later.

Which was why an FBI agent named George Faulkner – a guy Sam had only seen once or twice in passing – was sitting in room 12A, watching the only public entrance to the motel office through a crack in the faded curtains.

Safely hidden on this roof, Sam had watched George pull up, park his car, go into the office, and then lug what had to be an empty suitcase into the room.

He was wearing a disguise – a wig and a hat and an ill-fitting business suit – but still Sam recognized him.

He'd spotted the other two FBI agents nearly as easily – even without ever having seen them before in his life. A pair of men had pulled up in a truck, pretending to do God knows what to the tiny kidney-shaped pool that was separated from the parking lot by a tired-looking chain-link fence.

A quick surveillance of the area revealed that Alyssa was staked out by the motel's back entrance, near the Dumpster and the access to the laundry rooms.

Sam had no idea where Jules Cassidy was hiding, which was pretty impressive. It kept him glancing over his shoulder, watching his back, and making sure he stayed hidden himself.

Alyssa's setup was pretty good – *if* he were Joe Average Citizen. But he was a SEAL. If she wanted to catch him, she was going to have to do way better than this.

Sam went down the stairs and took the back entrance out of the apartment building. He could've taken the front. He'd altered his own appearance enough so that he could have walked right past Alyssa and she probably wouldn't have recognized him.

But why take that chance? Especially with Jules somewhere out there as potential wild card.

He got into his car and headed back toward the highway. There was a Pizza Hut with a pay phone around toward the back. He pulled into the lot and parked, digging in his pocket for the calling card he'd picked up at the Walgreen's while he was out shopping that afternoon. This way his cell number wouldn't show up on their caller ID.

He dialed the four million required numbers, and then the Sunset Motel. Their phone number had been on a big sign out front, saving him a call to information and serious finger strain.

Whoever answered garbled some kind of greeting. It was hard to make out, but Sam caught the words *Sunset* and *Motel* in there somewhere.

He pitched his voice much higher, doing a pretty damn decent imitation of Jenk – Petty Office Mark Jenkins, SEAL Team Sixteen's version of Radar O'Reilly. By pretending to be calling from Thirsty Toilet Paper Company, it took Sam four seconds to get the name of the motel's manager – Milton Frazier – without rousing any suspicions whatsoever.

He hung up, got into the car and back onto the highway, drove to the next exit, and pulled off at the Taco Bell.

He went through the same routine at that pay phone. The same woman at the Sunset Motel answered. Man, you'd think being able to speak clearly would be a job requirement for a receptionist.

'Milt Frazier, please,' Sam said in his own voice.

'Who's calling?'

'Bill Horowitz, FBI,' Sam lied.

'Please hold.'

Sam was watching his watch, and it wasn't more than seven seconds before the manager picked up.

'Frazier.'

'Hi, Milt,' Sam said. 'I'm Bill Horowitz – Alyssa Locke's personal assistant. I'm actually looking to reach Alyssa. Is she there with you, sir?'

'No, she's not.'

'Darn,' Sam said. 'Well, maybe you can help me. I'm on a deadline to type up these reports – it's pretty important stuff, I'm sure you're aware. But her handwriting is . . . Well, let's just say she's a much better agent than she is a writer. I absolutely cannot make out the name of the desk clerk on duty on the morning of May twenty-fifth. Is it Frank Jackson, Johnson, Josephson—'

'Beth Weiss.'

'Holy cow,' Sam said, writing the name on his arm. 'I really would've gotten that one wrong. That's Weiss, e-i-double-s?'

'Yes, sir.'

'Is it possible Alyssa wrote it as Elizabeth or . . .'

'As far as I know, she's just plain Beth.'

'Thanks. And I have her home address here as – shoot, I'm afraid even to try to guess.'

'Let me look it up again,' Frazier said. He was silent for a moment, then, 'It's 43 Rosewood Drive. Right here in Gainesville.'

'Phone number 352 . . .?'

Frazier obediently filled in the rest of the numbers, and Sam added them to the list on his arm.

'Thank you much,' Sam said. 'Oh, and Milt? Do me a biggie? Don't mention this to Alyssa when she comes back inside. I'd prefer having her think I can actually read her handwriting. Female bosses can be pretty intense – you know what I mean?'

Frazier laughed. 'I can imagine.'

'Thanks again.' Sam hung up the phone and got back into his car. Once more onto the highway, once more going north, this time two exits down.

That one had a BP gas station.

Again, he used the phone card to connect to the Sunset Motel. Marblemouth answered.

Sam put a lot of Texas into his voice. 'Is this Beth Weiss?'

'No, sir.'

'She be in later?'

'No, sir.'

Talkative woman. 'I've got a flower delivery for Beth Weiss. She gonna be in tomorrow?'

'Who's sending *Beth* flowers?' Whoever he was talking to, she didn't sound happy about that.

'Hey, I'm just the delivery service. She gonna be in tomorrow or not?'

'Eight A.M. to two is her regular shift.'

'Thank you, ma'am,' Sam said.

'Assuming she's back from Orlando.'

Uh-oh.

'You know, you could drop the flowers off now. I'll see that she gets them.'

Yeah, after you read the card, you nosy bitch.

'Shoot,' Sam said. 'There's something here on this slip about Orlando. Maybe these flowers are supposed to be sent to her down there. You got an address for her?'

'I have no idea where she's staying. We just work together. I don't really know her that well.'

'Well, if she really is in Orlando, I can put a hold order on the delivery. No point in bringing them out there if she's not going to be back for another week,' Sam said.

'No, I'm certain she'll be in tomorrow.' Marblemouth was suddenly more than willing to provide information. She really wanted to see who was sending Beth flowers. 'The manager was just going over the schedule and I did hear him say Beth would definitely be in in the morning.'

'Well, thanks for the offer,' Sam said. 'I just might take you up on it if I'm in the neighborhood this afternoon. You have a nice day, you hear?'

He got back in the car, back on the highway, and headed back south to Gainesville.

It was time to go over to this Beth Weiss's house on Rosewood Drive for a little sneak and peek.

If she really was out of town, there was a chance – a very slim chance – that Sam could get first access to whatever information she might have about Mary Lou and Haley.

Thirteen

It was after eight-thirty P.M. when Max uncovered the messages on his temporary desk at the Sarasota office.

Kelly Ashton Paoletti had called.

Seven times.

Kelly Ashton *Paoletti*.

In fact, one of the messages actually called her Mrs Lieutenant Commander Thomas Paoletti. No doubt that was in case he'd missed the significance of her new last name.

Max stood up for the first time in what seemed like hours even as his intercom buzzed.

Even though his assistant hated it when he shouted, he crossed the room and pulled open his door. 'Laronda!'

There was really no need to raise his voice, considering her desk was right there, but he was going on five short hours of sleep over three long days, and sometimes shouting and moving quickly fooled his body into releasing a little extra adrenaline. 'Get me Kelly Ashton Paoletti right—'

Away.

Another good reason to stay behind his desk and communicate via the intercom was standing there, looking at him.

'Gina Vitagliano to see you, sir,' Laronda told him, shooting him a look that said *'Now* how am I supposed to tell her that you're in a meeting, fool?'

Jules Cassidy was near Laronda's desk, collecting his phone messages, and the man didn't so much as glance in Max's

238

direction, but he, like everyone else in the room, was suddenly paying very close attention.

Or maybe that was just Max's own paranoid imagination.

Unlike him, Gina hadn't changed her clothes since he'd seen her a few hours ago in Tampa. She was still wearing cutoff jeans. They weren't as short or as low-cut as the styles Max had seen some women wearing today, even in downtown Sarasota, away from the beaches, but despite that, they made her tanned legs look incredibly long. Her funky T-shirt didn't quite meet her shorts, revealing a glimpse of an equally tanned stomach and, yes, that sparkling turquoise belly button ring he'd first been hypnotized by a few hours ago.

It was all Max could do not to break out into a cold sweat.

The sandals, the toenail polish, the leather ankle bracelet, her long dark hair down loose around her shoulders – it all made Gina look as ridiculously young as she actually was.

'Can you give me ten minutes?' she asked him. Her eyes were somber, and she hadn't flashed even a subdued version of her vivacious smile in his direction. She looked tired, with shadows underneath her eyes that he hadn't noticed before. Her makeup didn't hide them so well, here in the land of fluorescent light.

'How'd you get down here?' he asked. It was more than stalling – it was information he needed to know.

One of the big problems caused by her getting into an accident with the rental car was that, technically, she wasn't supposed to be driving. The rental car company, like most in the area, had a 'drivers must be twenty-five years or older' policy. But the vehicle had been rented and insured by Gina's employer, and she hadn't even known about the rule. The company was overlooking the alleged violation, but they had refused to replace the damaged car. Which had left Gina stranded.

Which shouldn't have been a problem if she'd stayed in Tampa until her flight home to New York.

'Bus,' she told Max now. 'Then cab.'

Max nodded as he handed the message slip to Laronda. 'Get

me Kelly Paoletti on the phone in exactly ten minutes.' He knocked on the desk. 'Cassidy.'

Jules looked up as if startled, a question in his eyes, pretending he hadn't been listening to every word. He was a good actor, but Max knew him well and didn't buy it for a second.

'Don't go anywhere,' Max ordered the younger man. He silently held his office door open for Gina, and followed her inside.

He purposely left it ajar, but she went back and closed it tightly as he went to sit behind his desk.

'Thank you for seeing me,' she said.

'I really don't have much time,' he told her. 'I'm in the middle of a situation.'

She sat down across from his desk. Crossed those legs. 'When aren't you?'

'Good point.' Max forced a smile.

She didn't smile back. 'I need to ask you something. I know you're not going to want to talk about this, but . . .'

Well, wasn't this going to be fun? He just waited.

Gina took a deep breath. 'Why did you stop returning my calls?'

It was the question he'd been expecting. The question he was ready for. He'd done everything but rehearse saying it aloud.

'I started seeing someone,' he lied without blinking. Well, it was really only half a lie. 'Someone I'm still very serious about. I don't think it's going to shock you, Gina, if I admit that my relationship with you has always had undercurrents of something more than mere friendship.'

It was a gamble, admitting that, and he could see both surprise and something vaguely triumphant in Gina's eyes. Someone had to teach this girl how to put on a poker face. She just let everything she was feeling and thinking show.

He was a manipulative son of a bitch, which was bad enough, but if he were a truly *evil* manipulative son of a bitch, he could take total advantage of her.

'Under those circumstances, continuing my friendship with you didn't seem right,' he concluded.

She nodded, and then she laughed. 'You're a brilliant liar.'

Max caught himself about to shift in his seat – a basic negotiating blunder. Never let them see you squirm. Instead, he made himself sit still and hold her gaze. 'I'm not lying.'

'Today you said that you were still angry,' Gina told him. 'About what happened to me on that plane.'

Yeah, he *had* said that. Max didn't clear his throat, didn't move. He could still hear the sound her head had made as she had been thrown down onto the cockpit deck. He blinked it away. Nodded. Even managed to smile. 'Of course I'm still angry. Everyone who worked that op is still angry about what happened to you.'

'You said I have no reason to want to check up on you,' Gina persisted. 'That, of course, you were okay. That you weren't the one on that plane.'

'That's right.'

She shook her head. 'No, Max. You're wrong. You were on that plane.'

He smiled again, as condescendingly as he could. 'Gina– '

She leaned forward, her eyes intense. 'You can pretend you weren't, but you were as much a prisoner as I was. You can tell me you walked away, out of that surveillance room, but I know you didn't. I *know* you were listening when it happened. I know you saw at least part of . . . of . . . it . . . with the mini-cameras the SEALs installed.'

He didn't bother denying it.

She laughed in disgust, sitting back a little. 'Listen to me. *It*. When *it* happened. We rarely talk about *it*, and you know, when we do, we always use euphemisms, don't we? When I was *attacked*. When I was *hurt*.' She leaned forward again. 'I was raped and beaten, Max. You were forced to watch and listen while I was *brutally raped* and *beaten*. That happened to me – and it happened to *you*, too.'

241

Max shifted in his seat and cleared his throat. Anything to keep her from looking – God help him – too closely into his eyes.

'I think you stopped calling me because seeing me, talking to me, *thinking* about me, makes you have to think about it, to remember it.'

God damn it, she just wouldn't let up. Max pretended to stare out the window, trying not to think about the way her long hair had fanned out, looking so beautiful, as she'd fallen right in front of the minicamera. Trying not to remember the way her screams had turned from panic to pain to despair.

Gina's voice was quiet now. 'I think that in addition to having to deal with this as something traumatic that happened to *you*, you also have to deal with the fact that you see the entire incident as one of your few failures.'

She was silent then, and when he finally glanced at her, she was watching him, just waiting, with such tenderness in her eyes. Obviously, it was now his turn to say something.

This twenty-three-year-old girl was out-negotiating him.

'What can I possibly say?' His voice was hoarse and he cleared his throat again. 'You asked a question, I gave you an answer. I understand that you don't like my answer, and you can theorize all you want, but that doesn't—'

'You didn't fail,' Gina interrupted him, her husky voice even thicker with emotion. 'Don't you see? You *succeeded*. I'm alive. I'm here!'

Yeah, he'd kind of noticed.

'You saved my life,' she told him. 'You saved the lives of nearly all the people on that plane—'

'Right.' Max stood up. 'This has been fun, but I have to take a phone call—'

She stood up, too, spoke right over him. 'You saved me more times than you'll ever know. You *were* there, *with* me. Every single time I really needed you.'

He laughed aloud at that – he couldn't help it. How could she say that?

Gina knew exactly what he was thinking. 'I didn't need you while they were raping me,' she told him, leaning over his desk, hands braced on the files that held his notes from his meeting with the President of the United States. 'I knew you couldn't stop them. Don't you see? I knew no one could stop them. The best anyone could do was to keep them from killing me. And that's what you did. I heard you talking over the radio, talking to them the entire time, the voice of sanity – reminding them that they were in a better bargaining position if they kept me alive. You didn't fail – you saved my life. And then you saved me again when it was over, when my parents were flying out to be with me in the hospital. You stayed with me. I can't begin to tell you what that meant to me. I'm not your failure, Max. I'm your biggest success!'

The intercom buzzed.

Max looked at the phone, looked at her. 'I have to take this call.'

She straightened up. Nodded. Cleared her throat. 'Well, I said what I came to say. I guess I can't force you to listen, can I?'

'Excuse me for a second.' Max picked up the phone. 'Yeah.'

'Kelly Paoletti on line one, sir.'

'Ask her to hold for a minute, Laronda.'

'Yes, sir.'

'And tell Jules Cassidy to come in.' Max hung up the phone, turned back to Gina. 'I'm going to have one of my agents drive you back to Tampa.'

'I'm not staying in Tampa anymore,' she told him as Jules knocked on the door.

Oh, damn. He waited for her to drop the anvil on his head.

'I'm staying here in Sarasota – out on Siesta Key – for the next few days,' she said. 'At a place right on the beach.'

Boing. The hotel Laronda had found for his team was also on Siesta Key. Please let there be a God and don't let it be the exact same place.

'Come in,' Max called. If that was the case, a solution would be for him just to never leave this office. It wasn't as if it would be the first time. . . .

Jules opened the door, sticking his head in as he looked cautiously from Gina to Max and back.

'Gina Vitagliano, Jules Cassidy.' Max gave them a no-frills introduction. 'Drive her back to her hotel,' he ordered.

Jules recognized it as the dismissal that it was, but Gina didn't move.

'I'm playing tomorrow night at a jazz club,' she said, and at first her words didn't make sense. *Playing?* But then he remembered. She was a musician – a percussionist. She'd been on that plane because she was touring Europe with her college jazz band.

'Fandangos,' she continued, 'on Siesta Key. A friend of a friend needed someone to fill in for his regular Wednesday night gig because his sister's getting married out in Seattle next weekend. I knew I'd be down here, so I agreed to replace him for the night. It's been on my schedule for three months.'

In case he got the idea that she was looking for excuses to stay in Sarasota.

'It's a restaurant, too,' she told him. 'I've heard it's pretty good. So if you're looking for someplace to eat tomorrow night—'

'I've got a situation that I'm in the middle of dealing with,' Max reminded her.

'Right,' Gina said, more hurt than anger in her eyes. 'But in the event that your *situation* gets handled and anything I've said today makes even the teeniest amount of sense . . . I'd really love for you to hear me play.'

Max could do nothing but stand there. If he said anything at all, she'd take it as encouragement. And telling her that he wouldn't go, that he didn't *want* to go, would be too cruel.

Even for him.

'You could sneak in the back,' Gina continued when he didn't respond. 'No one would have to know you were there. *I* wouldn't have to know you were there. That's the way you like to do it, right?'

Max glanced at Jules.

Gina turned to Jules, too. 'Did you know Max likes to follow me – to keep tabs on me? Isn't that kind of creepy?'

Jules looked at Max. 'Uh, actually, it's one of our team's policies to monitor the whereabouts of individuals who have spent considerable amounts of time with known terrorists. It's both for their protection and—'

Gina laughed in disbelief. 'To make sure they haven't crossed to the Dark Side? Yeah, Babur Haiyan and Alojzije Nabulsi were really trying their best to convince me to join their cause. Max witnessed the finesse of their recruitment techniques.' She laughed again – forced joviality. 'Of course, maybe you did, too. Maybe everyone in this office watched.'

And Max realized what it must have taken for Gina to come walking in here. To look Laronda in the eye and announce her name – just in case anyone hadn't already recognized her.

She turned back to Max. 'If you really are wasting taxpayers' dollars stalking me for those reasons, you're in an even worse *situation* than you think.'

'I'm sorry I've upset you,' Max said quietly. 'But—'

'You have to take that call,' she finished for him. 'Right. It's been nice seeing you, Max. But I've got to confess, you look tired. Whoever she is, she's not taking very good care of you.'

She caught the look that Jules flashed in Max's direction, and she laughed. 'I'm almost done. I'm going. I'm not going to flip out. I just want to say, don't worry. I'm a week away from being out of your hair for an entire year. I'm leaving the country. Of course, you probably already know that, right?'

Max didn't. 'You're . . . Going *where*?'

She was going out the door. 'Goodbye, Max.'

'This is not a good time to be an American abroad.' He followed her to Laronda's desk.

She didn't look back.

Jules did. *I'll find out where she's going,* he mouthed to Max.

Laronda was watching him out of the corner of her eye – probably because he was gritting his teeth so hard little pieces of enamel were shooting out of his ass.

'Kelly Paoletti on line one,' she reminded him in a whisper.

Max went into his office to take the call, slamming his door behind him.

'I've just had this incredible epiphanal moment.'

It was Sam Starrett.

Calling her again, from his cell phone.

'Are you ready to surrender?' Alyssa asked.

'Hell, no.'

'Then I don't want to hear it.' She hung up.

Her cell phone rang again.

She opened it and silently put it to her ear.

'Hey,' Sam said. 'I'm serious.'

'I am, too,' she countered. 'I'm not going to play, Starrett. I'm not going to talk to you while you sit somewhere, watching me, jerking off.'

'Jesus, Locke, you really think I'm some kind of deviant, don't you?' It was possible she'd actually offended him.

'I meant that figuratively.' She hadn't. Not really. But she'd said it only because she was pissed off because the earliest this could end was tomorrow.

It was going to be one very long night, and she was tired of sitting here, in her car, near the Dumpster behind the Sunset Motel.

'I'm not going to lie and say that I haven't done my share of thinking about you while I'm ... self-entertaining,' he said, 'but I'd *never* do that while you're on the other end of the phone. God.'

Alyssa sighed. She supposed it was her fault this conversation had turned in this direction. 'You know, I'm just not interested.

I'm tired and I'm hungry and if you really want to talk to me, you can come sit right here, in this car with me.'

She hung up.

Her phone rang again.

'My father was a racist son of a bitch who used to beat the shit out of me just for being friends with Noah.'

'I'm sorry to hear that,' Alyssa said, and hung up.

The phone rang.

'Of course, he used every excuse in the book to beat the shit out of me. After he died, I found this huge collection of child pornography in his house. And suddenly some of those beatings made a little more sense. You know, his belt against my bare ass . . .'

Oh, God! 'You're making that up just to keep me on the phone,' Alyssa accused him. But she couldn't make herself hang up on him again.

'I wish,' he said, and there was something in his voice that made her heart go into her throat. Oh, Sam. 'I was shocked when I saw it – his collection – because he was such a man's man, you know? A rednecked good ol' boy. But it was like, holy fuck, Pop. Some of that stuff he had made me sick to my stomach even just to glance at, and it was clear he'd, um . . .' Sam laughed in disgust. 'He'd worn some of it out, if you know what I mean. Apparently dear old Dad was really into little boys. Who knew?'

'Why are you telling me this?' she asked even though she already knew the answer. He wanted to make it impossible for her to hang up the phone. This was Sam Starrett's version of 1001 Arabian Nights.

'I want you to know me,' he told her quietly. 'I want you to know why I get my back up when you imply that I'm a rednecked good ol' boy – that I'm as narrow-minded as my father was. Because I'm not. You know what it was that I finally figured out tonight?' He didn't wait for her to answer. 'That Roger Starrett Senior was merely my sperm donor. My real father was my uncle Walt. Walter Gaines. I learned all I need to know about being the best father in the world from him. About fucking time I realized that, huh?'

Alyssa closed her eyes. She could tell from his voice that he was sitting, or maybe even lying down. She knew quite well that he wasn't just using this conversation as a means to distract her while he slipped unnoticed into the Sunset Motel.

'With my biological father, love was conditional,' Sam continued. 'If only I could get good grades, if only I could hit a home run, if only I could cut the lawn exactly the way he liked it cut. Of course I never could, and I finally stopped trying.

'But Uncle Walt, he was . . . unswerving in his love for me. He hated when I got into a fight, but he'd patch me up, and he'd give me a hug and he'd tell me how proud he was of me because he knew how hard I'd tried not to hit that other kid. I wish he was still alive so you could meet him.'

'Okay,' Alyssa said. 'I'm talking to you. I didn't hang up. You've won. Now please admit you're making up that stuff about your father.'

Sam rattled off a phone number. She scrambled for her pen. 'Five oh eight, what?'

He repeated it.

Area code 508 was outside of Boston. He'd once told her that was where his sister lived.

'It's Lainey's number,' he told her. 'She was with me when we cleaned out Pop's house. Call me back, okay?'

This time he was the one who cut the connection.

Alyssa glanced at the clock on the dash. Almost 2100. It wasn't too late to call.

Of course, he could be bluffing. He didn't really think she'd call his sister.

Or did he?

She dialed the number.

'Hello?' A man picked up.

'May I please speak to Elaine?'

'Who's calling?'

'Alyssa Locke. I'm a . . . a friend of her brother's.'

She waited while Sam's brother-in-law put his hand over the telephone receiver and had a muffled conversation, probably with Elaine.

Then a woman's voice. 'Do you know where my brother is?' Elaine's Texas drawl was slighter than Sam's. She sounded a little like Holly Hunter.

'Florida,' Alyssa told her. 'Probably somewhere in the Gainesville area.'

'Well, if you see him, will you tell him that the FBI is looking for him? Did you know that? There's some kind of warrant or something out for him. Tell him his sister says to stop being an idiot, to turn himself in before someone gets hurt!'

'He's aware of that,' Alyssa said. 'And I am, too – I'm with the FBI myself. I doubt I'm going to see him, but I *have* been talking to him on the phone. If you want, I'll pass along your message.'

'You're *with* the—'

'I've been friends with Sam for a few years now,' Alyssa said. 'We've been . . .' She cleared her throat. 'Intimate at times and—'

'Oh, my gosh,' Elaine said. 'You're her, aren't you? The one Ringo – Sam – told me about. He wouldn't tell me your name. Just that there was this woman and . . . well. He said something about the FBI and . . . you're her.'

'Yeah,' Alyssa said. Sam had told his older sister about her? 'I guess so.'

'So now you're back, messing with his head some more?'

O-kay. Hostile witness. 'I'm trying to talk him into turning himself in – just as you asked. I've been speaking to him on the phone,' she said again. 'I'm doing the best I can in a bad situation. A terrible situation, if you want to know the truth. This is hard for me, too. Did your brother happen to mention that he stopped seeing me in order to marry Mary Lou?'

Elaine laughed her surprise. 'No.'

'Yeah, well, ask him about *that* next time you see him.'

There was a pause, and then, 'You're not kidding, are you?'

'No,' Alyssa said.

Elaine was silent for longer this time.

'I'm on your side, Elaine. I really don't want Sam to do something stupid and end up getting himself killed. So I need your help. I need to ask you about something that he just told me. It's something you might not be too comfortable talking about, something about your father.'

'Oh, my gosh,' Elaine said. 'He actually told you about Pop?'

'He said when the two of you were cleaning out his house, after your father died, that you found some pictures—'

'Pictures, videos, magazines. Enough to fill an entire trunk,' Elaine told her. 'I can't believe Ringo told you. Shoot, he won't even talk to me about it. What did he say?'

'Just that he found the pictures and . . .' Oh, Sam. Alyssa closed her eyes. 'Do you think there's a chance that your father . . .?'

'Abused him sexually?' Elaine said the words that she couldn't. 'No. I know he didn't. I mean, you should have seen Ringo's face when we found that stuff. He was as stunned as I was. The first thing we did was look at each other and go, "Did Pop ever touch you when we were kids?" But Pop never came near me, and Ringo told me the exact same thing.'

'And you believed him?' Alyssa asked.

'Yes,' Elaine said. 'Although to be honest, in hindsight, knowing what we now know, I really do think Pop got off – really got off, you know, in an icky way – sexually, I mean – on beating the crap out of Roger. Ringo. He was Ringo back then – he started calling himself that around the time he went into eighth grade, although my father never called him that. But he was adamant about being Ringo. He refused to answer if someone called him Roger, which *really* pissed my father off. But the beatings stopped when Ringo got bigger – which happened kind of all at once, one summer. You know the way boys somehow just grow? To tell you the truth, I don't know if Pop backed off because Ringo was big enough to start fighting back, or if it was because he wasn't a little boy anymore, so Pop no longer got off on hitting him.'

'Oh, God,' Alyssa said.

'I know that Ringo's more comfortable classifying Pop's beatings as just plain physical abuse. I think he gives Pop more credit than he's due for keeping his hands off of us – you know, for being strong enough not to do something he was really obviously pulled toward doing? But I also think Ringo knew all along – on some level – that the way Pop treated him was wrong, that there was something, I don't know, sick to it, I guess. I mean, why the name changes? First Ringo and now he calls himself Sam? Who knows who he'll be after he leaves the SEALs. I think he really didn't want to be Roger, you know? He didn't want to be that kid whose father treated him like that.' She paused. 'It probably doesn't help that Roger was Pop's name, too.' Elaine laughed softly. 'I still can't believe he told you about this.'

'I can't, either,' Alyssa said. 'Thank you for being so candid.'

'Do you love him?' Elaine asked. Alyssa was silent, and Elaine laughed again. 'Sorry. Not my business. Please tell him to be safe. Tell him to turn himself in. And tell him I love him.'

'I will.' Alyssa thanked her again and cut the connection.

Did she love him?

Alyssa had so much bad history with Sam. She'd once been right on the verge of loving him more than she'd ever loved any man. But there was so much pain and hurt, so many stupid mistakes made. Could she really let herself get close to him again without bringing all that bad luggage with her? How could a relationship ever survive with all that excess weight?

In all honesty, she was afraid to get too close to Sam.

But Ringo – this Ringo she was hearing about, this former little boy who had been so naturally open-minded to seek out fatherly love from a black man despite the fact that his own father was a racist – Ringo, who had endured his father's sadistic treatment to the point where he'd chosen to change his name, to become someone different . . .

It wouldn't be very hard at all to fall in love with *him*.

Gina closed her eyes as the FBI agent – Jules Cassidy – drove south down Tamiami Trail.

'So where are you going?' he asked. 'To Europe?'

'I really blew it, didn't I?'

She'd done really well in Max's office – right up to the point where Max had ended the conversation. Tried to end the conversation. And then she'd lost the upper hand.

God, she had a stomachache.

'Well, you've got him terrified,' Jules said with a laugh. 'If it's any consolation, I didn't know Max was capable of feeling terror.'

She opened her eyes and looked at him. In the changing light from the streetlamps he looked too young to be an FBI agent. 'How long have you worked with him?'

'A coupla years.' He was incredibly good looking. Like, total male perfection – to the point that he was prettier than she was. Of course, some people didn't think she was pretty at all, with her giant nose that broadcast her Italian roots and a mouth that was too big for her face, which was remarkable since her face was pretty damn big. There wasn't much of her that could be called petite. Her ears, maybe. Yeah, she had little, delicate, feminine ears.

Which were nearly always covered by her hair.

'Were you with him in Kazbekistan?' she asked.

He glanced at her with eyes that were impossibly sensitive, eyes that were surrounded by thick dark lashes. 'I was, but I wasn't in the surveillance room when you were raped.'

Whoa. Someone who actually used the R-word. And without hesitating, flinching or stuttering. The relief was remarkably intense.

'Thank you,' she said.

'It must suck, huh? The way people dance around it. And meanwhile the elephant in the corner of the room gets bigger and bigger. . . .'

'I love you,' Gina said. 'Will you marry me?'

Jules laughed.

If he was perfect in repose, then with that smile he was perfection squared. And still, he didn't hold a candle to Max. Max, with his crooked nose and lines of fatigue and those dark brown eyes that could see inside of her and touch her soul . . .

'I'm tempted,' Jules said, 'if only to piss Max off.'

'Yeah, like he'd care.' Sending her home with this man – handsome, no wedding ring on his left hand, and far younger than Max – was a definite message to her. *Go play with someone your own age.*

Jules gave her another glance. 'Did you know that in K-stan he put his fist through the wall?'

She laughed. 'Max?'

He nodded. 'Yeah. It was the night before the ca-ca hit the fan. He knew trouble was coming and he wanted to go in, take down the plane right then, but Washington said wait. It was a direct order, and he went apeshit, if you'll pardon my French – but there's really no better way to describe it. He completely lost it. Punched the wall.' He gave her another glance. 'He does that sometimes.'

Max. Losing it. It was hard to imagine. Or was it?

'How can *I* make him lose it?'

'Sweetie, I think you probably came pretty damn close today.'

Close wasn't good enough. She wanted . . . She wanted him in her life.

'Do you know his girlfriend?' Gina asked, bracing herself for information she really didn't want to know. Max laughing and talking to someone else, with his arm around her shoulders, his eyes lit with that fire that burned inside of him, 24/7 . . .

For some reason Jules laughed at her question. 'If he told you he's got a girlfriend, he was using a liberal dose of hyperbole.

He's not seeing anyone right now. At least not in the traditional sense.'

Not in the . . . 'Is he gay?'

Jules glanced at her. 'That's not what I meant. But no, he's definitely not gay. You know, I really shouldn't be talking about him.'

'What did you mean, then? By "not in the traditional sense"?'

Jules was silent.

'Please,' she said.

He sighed. 'There *is* someone,' he told her. 'She and Max have been circling each other for a few years now. It hasn't gone anywhere and it's not going to go anywhere because she works for him and Max doesn't have it in him to break the rules like that, and I'm not going to tell you anything more because I hear myself saying this and it sounds like gossip and we don't gossip about our coworkers and we especially don't gossip about our boss. That's kind of like gossiping about God. It's just not done by anyone who wants to stay with him in the Garden of Eden. Which I do. Very much so.'

'People say he's the best negotiator—'

'He's the best, period,' Jules interrupted. 'He's brilliant, he's fair, he's loyal, he's unstoppable. He practically lives in the office because he *cares* about what we do. He's driven, not just by ambition but by conviction. He's the best team leader I've ever worked with because he leads from the front. I would do anything to stay on his team. And I would do anything he asked me to do. Anything. Including die.'

He was actually serious.

They rode in silence for a while. But as they pulled up to a red light, Gina couldn't keep her mouth shut. 'Her name's Alyssa, right?'

Jules looked at her, a blandness in his eyes. It was a case of too little reaction – he was working too hard to hide it, which meant there was definitely something to hide.

'You don't need to answer that. I asked around about a year

ago.' Gina had actually called the older sister of a friend. The sister worked in the Pentagon and had met Max Bhagat several times. Apparently, at the time, there was gossip raging about Max and someone named Alyssa. 'Do you know her? You don't have to say anything. Just nod. Yes or no.'

Jules just laughed as the light turned green.

Gina took that as a yes. 'Is she really as amazing as people say?'

He rolled his eyes. 'Look, if I tell you, will you tell me where you're going overseas?'

Gina made a raspberry sound at that. 'I can't believe Max didn't already have my full itinerary before I even made up my mind to buy the plane ticket.'

'Well, he doesn't, but he *will* get it,' Jules told her. 'It'll just make it that much easier if you give me an idea of which hemisphere you'll be visiting.'

'I'm not going to help him stalk me. If he wants to check up on me, he can do it the way normal people do – by calling me up and asking how I'm doing.'

'Max isn't normal people,' Jules reminded her. 'Which way here? Left or right?'

'Left.' Her motel was just down the road. 'Then on the right-hand side.'

He pulled into the parking lot, leaning forward to look at the place out of the front windshield. He didn't say a word, but she knew what he was thinking as he saw that the access to the rooms were through sliding glass doors. To someone whose world was made up of terrorists and criminals, security here probably looked a little lax. Max, for sure, wasn't going to be happy when Jules gave him his report.

And Gina was certain that, after Jules returned to the FBI office, there *would* be a report.

He held out a business card. 'I'm here if you need anything.'

She looked at him. He'd said he'd do anything Max asked. '*Any*thing?'

He held her gaze. 'Sweetie, I'm adventurous and I like you very much. I could probably force myself to swing your way for a night and make it lots of fun for both of us, but I really doubt that's what either one of us needs.'

Whoa. 'You're . . .' He was looking at her as if he were waiting for something. She said the word. 'Gay.' Most people probably talked around it. And boy, did she know how that felt.

'Thank you.' It was no coincidence that he was echoing her very words to him. 'Although my elephant is different than yours. Mine's bright purple and I like to lead him around on a leash and introduce him to people by name.'

Gina nodded. 'Well, this really sucks. Our marriage is going to need an awful lot of work.'

He laughed.

'Thanks for the lift.' She opened the car door, and he reached over and put his card in her hand, closing her fingers around it. 'I'm not going to need that,' she told him.

'I was thinking that maybe you had a brother you could introduce me to.'

Gina laughed. 'Yeah, I've got three, but you definitely don't want to go near them.'

'You can't be sure. The family's often the last to know.' Jules got out of the car, too, and spoke to her over the top. 'You know, Gina, there are places on the other side of the island that have internal access rooms. You know, like a real hotel? It's much safer for a woman staying alone.'

She fished in her pocket for her key. 'But I like this place. I'm feet from the beach, I can afford it without maxing out my credit card, *and* I'm perfectly safe. But you can tell Max that you tried your best to talk me out of staying here.' She unlocked her hotel room door, slid it open. 'Good night.'

As she closed the door and then shut the curtains, he was still standing there.

But a few minutes later, when she went out to take a walk on the beach, he was gone.

* * *

Sam sat in the car he'd picked up for a buck and a half at one of Jon Hopper's rival used-car dealers on the other side of town, and waited for his cell phone to ring.

He was parked in the Wendy's lot, with a clear view of the exit ramp off the interstate. It was the exit to take when driving from Orlando to the Sunset Motel.

Beth Weiss, the morning desk clerk, wasn't back from her trip to Orlando. As far as her roommate could guess, she was making the drive in the morning and going straight in to work. And no, she didn't know where Beth was staying in Orlando. It wasn't at a hotel – it was with some friend from college.

The straight-to-work thing complicated life a little, considering Alyssa and her gang were still staked out around the Sunset Motel.

If Sam didn't spot Beth's blue Ford Focus – with South Carolina plates, thank you, roommate – before she got to the motel, Alyssa would talk to her first. And warn her not to talk to anyone else – like Sam – about the details of the case.

It wouldn't be long, if it hadn't happened already, before someone – the nosy desk clerk, the motel manager, Beth's roommate – brought to Alyssa's attention the fact that someone had called, looking for Beth.

Alyssa would know instantly that it was Sam. And Beth's lips would be soldered shut.

Although, if she were anything like her roommate, that would be pretty hard to do. The roommate was a talker.

She'd told him that Beth always stopped for coffee and doughnuts on her way into work.

Sam was hoping that this morning would be no exception, and that he'd be able to intercept her there.

Of course, there were two Dunkin' Donuts and a Krispy Kreme to choose from between the interstate and the motel – he'd driven the area until he knew it like the back of his hand – so he'd have to start following her right here at the exit ramp.

Beth wasn't known for arriving to work early, so it was more than likely Sam had a solid seven to eight hours before he had to be watching for her in earnest.

What he really had to do – particularly after a day filled with shopping, not his favorite thing – was to get some sleep.

Problem was, the sound of his phone *not* ringing was keeping him wide awake.

It was entirely possible that Alyssa wasn't going to call him back. Even after everything he'd told her.

He opened his phone, checking to see that he still had service out here, checking to see if the charger he'd just bought and plugged into the cigarette lighter was working.

He did, and it was.

Which meant Alyssa wasn't calling him because she didn't want to call him. Not because she couldn't.

And then, Hallelujah, it rang.

But the number displayed on the screen was . . .

'Donny?' he said into his phone.

'Sam, the game's almost half over.'

Aw, shit, he'd completely forgotten that he'd made tentative plans to watch the Padres get trounced by the Mets tonight with his crazy-ass next-door neighbor back in San Diego.

'Oh, man, Don, I'm so sorry,' he said. 'I should have called you. I'm still in Florida.'

'How are Mary Lou and Haley?'

'Well, I think they're probably just fine.' Sam couldn't tell Donny the truth. The man was quite literally crazy. Seriously mentally ill.

Don DaCosta had missed his friendship with Mary Lou and Haley something fierce when they'd left San Diego. Sam had felt responsible and started bringing the shut-in his mail and dropping off food – little things that Mary Lou had previously done for the guy. Sam had started dropping by Donny's house, too, because despite the fact that he sometimes wore an aluminum foil covered hat to keep the aliens from reading his mind, he was pretty smart, with his own kind of sideways sense of humor.

Sam actually looked forward to seeing Donny a couple of times a week. Watching football, basketball, hockey, and now baseball.

It was ironic, really. Ever since WildCard and Nils had both gotten married and started spending so much of their free time in their own little perfect worlds with their families, Sam's two best friends were a homosexual – Jules – and a nutjob – Donny.

It was pretty freaking amazing.

But tolerance, as Jules would say, was a wonderful thing.

'You remembering to take your medicine, Don?' Sam asked now.

'Yes, but . . .'

But was never a good word to hear from Donny's lips. Sam braced himself.

'I saw him again,' Don admitted. 'The alien.'

Sam's call waiting beeped. Oh, freaking perfect. It figured Alyssa would call right now. But there was no way he could hang up on Donny or even put him on hold when he was using the A-word.

'Which alien is that?' he asked, reaching down deep for the patience he was going to need in order not to sound frustrated. Or, worse, to laugh.

'The one who used to watch me from your driveway. He used to hide behind Mary Lou's car.'

'And he was back? In my driveway?' Jesus God. Sam realized what he was hearing. He'd heard it before, but it suddenly had an entirely new meaning.

His neighbor had seen someone lurking around Mary Lou's car. The car she'd used to get to her job. On the Navy base. Where a weapon with her fingerprints on it had been smuggled in and used to try to kill the President.

Sam worked hard to keep his voice relaxed, light. 'Donny,

how long ago did you first see him? You know, hiding behind Mary Lou's car?'

Time could sometimes be a tough concept for Don. 'Oh, gee . . .'

'I guess it must've been back when Mary Lou was there, since you said he was hiding behind her car, right?'

'Yeah,' Don said, grateful for an easy answer. 'Yeah.'

'How often did you see him?'

'Oh, all the time.'

'Like, every day?' Sam asked. Maybe the guy Donny had seen was hiding so that no one would see him going into and out of Sam's house. Maybe Mary Lou had been stepping out on Sam with some terrorist scum right in his own flipping bed.

'I don't know,' Donny said. He was starting to sound upset, no doubt picking up Sam's sudden tension. 'I'm sorry, Sam.'

'Hey, whoa, no problem,' Sam said as soothingly and as laid-back sounding as he could manage. He took a deep breath, let it out slowly. His call waiting beeped again, but he refused to let his blood pressure rise. 'I was just curious, buddy. If you don't remember, it's no big deal. Here's a question, though, one I bet you can answer easily.' Please God.

'Oh, good.'

'You told me once that the aliens try to look human, right?'

'Right. Right. That's right. Right.'

'Well, that wasn't the question, but that's good, because now we're both on the same page. Here's the question.' Sam paused, trying to figure out the way to get a description of Don's 'alien' without putting too much pressure on the guy. 'What color . . . what color skin does this alien have?'

'White,' Don said. 'Like mine.'

'Excellent. How about – what color hair?'

'Light.'

'Really? I mean, really?' Sam adjusted the tone and inflection of his voice so he didn't sound like he didn't believe Don.

'Yeah, lighter even than Haley's. Very, very light. Shiny at night.'

A blond terrorist.

Well, why the hell not? Just because most of al-Qaeda came from the Middle East didn't mean there wasn't a cell operating out of Stockholm.

Unless this blond 'alien' was simply some random guy Mary Lou was using to two-time – three-time? – both Sam *and* her terrorist boyfriend.

Sam tried another tack. 'When you saw him again – was it today?'

'This morning.' Don said with an unusual amount of decisiveness before adding, 'I think.'

'Do you remember what he was doing?'

'Yes.' Another absolute.

But Sam had been hanging out with Don enough to realize that the mistake was his own, and he shouldn't wait for Don to expound. He hid a laugh inside of a cough. 'Don, I really love you, man.'

Don laughed, clearly pleased. 'Really?'

'Yes,' Sam said, then asked, 'What was the alien doing when you saw him?'

'Oh, he was watching the flower man.'

'The flower man?'

'Yeah,' Don said. 'You know the flower man. Mary Lou's friend.'

Mary Lou was also friends with some flower man. Holy shit. Sam didn't have a clue who the flower man was, but he didn't want to freak out Donny who seemed convinced that he did. 'So what was the, uh, flower man doing?'

'He was ringing your doorbell,' Don said. 'But you weren't home so no one answered the door.'

'So then what'd he do?' Sam asked.

'He came over and rang *my* doorbell,' Don reported. 'But I didn't answer either, because even though he didn't know it, I

261

could see the alien was down the street, watching him.'

'How come he didn't see the alien?' Sam asked.

'Because the alien was in his car. After the flower man left, the alien drove past, really slowly. I got a good look at him. It was definitely him.'

'What color skin does the flower man have?' Sam asked, trying to make sense out of any of this.

'Brown,' Don said.

'And how about *his* hair?'

'Black. Mary Lou told me that he's from Saudi Arabia.'

Well, now, wasn't *that* interesting?

'Did the flower man used to ring my doorbell a lot?' Sam asked. 'You know, back before Mary Lou went to Florida?'

'I don't think he ever did,' Don said.

'You mean, he just walked in the door?'

'No, Mary Lou came outside. I think she saw his truck. Or maybe she heard the lawnmower. He was nice. I wish I could've opened the door.'

Don was talking about . . . 'The flower man used to cut lawns and do yardwork in the neighborhood,' Sam clarified. He had only a vague recollection of a skinny, swarthy man with a beard and a warm smile.

'Yes.'

Oh, man. He had to get this information to Alyssa.

'So are you okay?' Sam asked Don. 'Even though you saw this alien this morning?'

'I guess,' Don said. 'He scared me. He looked right at me, and even pointed his finger at me. He saw me watching from the window.'

Sam had a sudden disturbing image of Don lying facedown in his kitchen, with half of his head blown away. Oh, *fuck* . . .

'Donny, I want you to stay away from the windows and doors, okay?' Shit, this was going to set Don back about ten years in terms of his overcoming his fears of alien invasion. 'Don't answer the door, okay? I'm going to call your sister, see if

Mike – her husband – is back in town. If not, I'll get your grandparents over there. They'll come in with their own keys, Don, so don't answer the door, okay? I'm going to need you to tell everything that you've just told me to someone from the FBI. Do you think you can do that?'

'Can't *you* come over?' Donny asked, sounding very worried.

'I'm in Florida, Don,' Sam said. 'But I promise I'll get there as soon as I can. I'll talk to you later, okay?'

Sam cut the connection and immediately dialed Alyssa's number, pulling out of the Wendy's lot and heading downtown.

Fourteen

Alyssa nearly jumped through the roof when Max knocked on the side window of her car.

'Where did you come from?' she asked as she popped the lock and let him in. She honestly hadn't seen him approach. And she'd been watching.

Her heart was still racing as he sat down next to her and closed the door. She'd thought when he'd first knocked that he was Sam.

No such luck.

'I just walked up,' Max told her.

'Like hell you did.'

'You must've been sleeping.'

'Like hell I was.'

He smiled at her. 'Then I must still be wicked awesome good even though I haven't been in the field in years.'

Alyssa smiled back at him. '*Allegedly* haven't been in the field in years. I work with you, remember? Your interpretation of sitting behind a desk is questionable.'

Max laughed.

'What are you doing here?' she asked.

Despite his laughter – which faded far too quickly – he looked like hell. He looked tired and . . . haunted. She hadn't seen him looking this bad since just after the takedown of that hijacked plane in Kazbekistan.

It was no coincidence, considering . . .

'I took a chopper up from Sarasota,' he told her. 'I wanted to get an update.'

Alyssa held up her cell phone. 'Check out this amazing new technology, boss. It allows you to get that update from the comfort of your hotel room. Right before you fall into bed, unconscious.'

'I've been having a little trouble sleeping lately,' he admitted.

'Lately?' She gave him a look. 'Try the last two years.' Since Kazbekistan.

He sighed.

Were he anyone else, Alyssa would have reached for his hand. But this was Max and there was no touching allowed. 'How can I help you?' she asked as gently as she could.

'Well,' he said. 'Funny you should ask.'

Her cell phone rang, and she quickly glanced at the number. 'That important?' Max asked.

It was Sam. 'No,' she said. It was half a lie. It wasn't important to the case, just important to her. But, 'It can wait.'

Sam wasn't going anywhere tonight. And she wasn't either. He hadn't answered when she'd called him back, and now it was his turn to wonder what she was doing. She switched the ringer over to vibrate, and when she looked up at Max, he was watching her intently.

He looked so serious. 'This is going to sound a little crazy, so don't answer right away. Just think about it, okay?'

Alyssa nodded, suddenly uncertain. Was this something about work or—

He reached over and took her hand, lacing their fingers together. But that wasn't the biggest surprise.

'I was thinking about that night that we, um, very nearly made love,' he said quietly, 'and it occurred to me that I *really* haven't slept since then, and, uh, I think you should marry me.'

Alyssa sat there, completely speechless. Completely unable to move, unable even to think.

She cleared her throat. 'Max—'

'I love you,' he said. 'I'm freaking out at the idea of you and Starrett getting back together. I don't want to lose you.'

To him. Max didn't say the words, but they hung there, unspoken. Alyssa's brain kicked back on and all she could picture was Max, crying in a playground sandbox, because some other kid had stolen his favorite toy truck.

Add that on top of the fact that she knew *she* wasn't the main reason Max was freaking out, as he so accurately put it.

She looked down at their hands, looked back up at Max. 'And?' she prompted him.

He shook his head, not understanding. Or at least pretending not to understand. He was, after all, Max.

'When Jules called,' she told him gently, extracting her hand from his, 'he mentioned that Gina came into the office tonight.'

Max closed his eyes, rubbed his forehead. 'Ah, crap.'

'This is about you running from her, Max. Not about you really wanting to marry me.'

'You're wrong,' he said, but he sounded exhausted. Almost defeated. 'Seeing Gina was a major motivator, yes, but . . . Alyssa, we'd be so good together and you know it.'

She'd put her cell phone between her legs, and it vibrated. Sam. Calling back.

'Our lives would run like a precision automobile,' Max told her.

Alyssa laughed. 'That's supposed to make me want to marry you? We'd bore each other to tears.'

'Oh, yeah?' he said, and he kissed her.

Unlike his approach to the car, she saw it coming. He leaned across the parking brake and gently cupped her cheek, drawing her mouth to his.

And oh, Max could kiss. He could suck her breath right out of her lungs and . . .

She pulled away, angry at him and angry at herself for

momentarily considering that precision automobile thing. Max didn't love her. He said he did but he didn't *love* her. 'You're in love with Gina. You told me you were.'

'That's not love,' he countered. 'That's something else, something possessive, something, Christ, I don't know, greedy and twisted and obsessive and chaotic and . . . I want to own her, Alyssa. I want to wrap her up and keep her safe and put her in . . . in . . . some closet somewhere and take her out when it's convenient for me to . . . to . . . Okay. Yes. Sex. It's about sex and it's about power and control and it's about her looking at me with those Bambi eyes and adoring me when she should God damn *hate* me, and . . . that's not love.'

He pulled her closer to him, so that their faces were mere inches apart. Alyssa could practically smell his desperation.

'Love doesn't have to eviscerate you,' he told her, using that word on purpose, because she'd used it in the past to describe how she'd felt when Sam ended their relationship. 'Love can be something good, something gentle – like what we've got.' He kissed her, so sweetly, again and again, punctuating his words. 'It can be something that *allows* us to sleep at night, instead of torturing us and keeping us awake.'

'And you're just going to forget about Gina?'

He didn't try to be flip and say, 'Gina who?' even as he licked the inside of her mouth.

'I can't have her,' he said instead. 'The same way you know you can't have Starrett. He'll rip you to shreds, Alyssa.'

He kissed her again, harder, deeper this time, and God, it would be so easy to just give in. She knew Max. She trusted Max. She even loved him.

But she didn't want her life to run like a precision automobile. She wanted . . .

Chaos.

She wanted to be with someone who burned for her the way Max burned for Gina. If that meant she would be incinerated – or ripped to shreds – so be it.

Her phone rang again, and she knew Sam was out there, watching her kissing Max.

She pulled back. 'Max—'

'Marry me,' he said, and it wasn't a question but rather such a possessive demand that she wanted to laugh.

But she didn't dare. 'Marry you,' she repeated instead. 'And be forced to leave the team?' Married personnel weren't allowed to work together. It was true in the military and in the Bureau as well.

'No,' he said. 'I've figured out a way to get around that. I'll expand the team. I'll break it down into four separate groups. I'll head one, Peggy'll head one, I'll bring in Manny Conseco from Sarasota for the third – I really like him – and you'll head the fourth. With the unspoken understanding that I've got ultimate control.'

She was breathless at what he was offering her in terms of her career. He was right. Their lives *would* be perfect.

In every way but one.

She would always know that Max loved Gina. And it *was* love, despite his argument otherwise. He just had to figure out a way to flip it around and turn it into something more healthy, something more equal. And maybe then it wouldn't scare the hell out of him quite so much.

But probably not. If Max could get to the place where he'd let her in, Gina was probably going to scare the hell out of him for the entire rest of his life.

And he'd sleep far better because of it.

Alyssa opened her mouth to tell him that she couldn't marry him, that she didn't want perfection, but he cut her off. In true Max fashion, he'd read her mind.

'Don't say no,' he said. 'Just think about it, all right?'

His phone shrilled. Still holding Alyssa's gaze, he pulled it out and answered it. 'Bhagat.' His lips tightened. 'Well, hey, Sam, what a surprise. Ready to turn yourself in?'

There was a longer pause then, and something shifted in

Max's eyes. 'Wait,' he said. 'Hold on. I want Alyssa to hear this, too.'

He pushed the buttons on his phone that would conference her in, and she opened her own phone when it vibrated. 'Locke.'

'Sorry to interrupt.' Sam's voice was tight. 'But I thought I should share this information before you and Max took it into the backseat. You know, that's some interesting stakeout technique you got there, Max.'

'Just tell her what you told me,' Max ordered. 'About your neighbor in San Diego.'

'So I went to the McDonald's here on base, where Mary Lou worked,' Kelly told Tom without so much as a hello as the guards let her into his temporary prison in the BOQ. 'I spoke to the manager on duty, who gave me the phone number of the other managers, too. Everyone agreed that Mary Lou kept to herself while she was at work. She didn't have any friends among her coworkers, and she apparently spent her breaks reading.'

She kicked off her sandals while she talked, and . . .

Slipped her panties off from under her dress?

'Uh, Kel,' Tom said as she hiked up her skirt and straddled his lap, right there at the table where he'd laid out all of his notes. The door was ajar. The guards couldn't see in, but they sure as hell could hear every word they said.

'We have only thirty minutes,' she told him, starting to unfasten his pants.

He caught her hands. 'Kelly.'

'Wow, that was fast. We've only been married a few hours and already you don't want to have sex with me.'

She was just kidding. Wasn't she? 'The door's open,' he said, holding her gaze, trying to make it clear with his eyes that if it was only about what *he* wanted, he'd be inside of her already.

Oh baby, the panties on the floor thing always made him crazy, and she knew it.

Kelly didn't look away from him as she raised her voice. 'Is it going to bother you boys out in the hall if my husband and I have sex on our wedding night?'

There was a pause, then one of the two guards – they couldn't have been much more than twenty years old – said, 'No, ma'am!'

But then the door closed with a definite-sounding *click*.

'Hey!' that first guard said.

'We can take a few steps down the hall,' the other guard said. 'I think it's safe to say he's not going anywhere.'

Kelly laughed.

Tom let go of her hands. 'See, that's not SEAL thinking,' he told her as she . . . oh, *yeah*. 'A SEAL would assume this *is* the time I'm going to try to get away.'

'That's just an excuse to listen at the door.' She kissed him.

'We shouldn't be doing this,' he said, pulling down the front of her dress to discover that she wasn't wearing a bra. 'It's going to make it harder to get an annulment if we need to get—'

'I lied,' she told him. 'I'm not going to let you annul our marriage.'

'If I'm convicted—'

'I'm not going to let you be convicted.'

Tom looked at her as she sat with him buried deeply inside of her, little pieces of her hair falling out of her French braid, her cheeks flushed, her eyes flashing, and her magnificent breasts bare and all but heaving as she breathed hard and fast, unafraid to let him see that he made her pant with desire.

His *wife*.

'God, I love you,' he gasped. She wasn't the only one panting.

'I went to the library,' she said, and he had absolutely no clue as to what she was talking about. She'd started moving, that long, slow slide up off of him, and the even slower slide down that made his eyes roll back in his head. 'And I asked the librarians if they knew Mary Lou.'

Who?

'They said she came in . . . a couple of times a week,' Kelly continued raggedly. 'One of them told me . . . she saw her once with a man. She remembered it because it was so unusual – Mary Lou was always alone. But then . . . there was this one time, with this one guy who was flirting with her . . . and even carried her books out to her car. The librarian thought they maybe knew each other. And – get this – the library has a surveillance camera . . . out in the parking lot because – Oh yes!'

He'd let his mouth take over for his hands, drawing her breast into his mouth and swirling his tongue across the rock-hard pellet of her nipple. What an incredible turn-on, knowing she was so hot for him. But it was hard to say if that was what had elicited her enthusiastic response, or if it was the fact that, at the same time, his hand had slipped lower, touching her lightly between them.

'Don't stop doing that,' she ordered.

And then she was silent for a moment, and it wasn't until she started talking again that he realized she had been collecting her thoughts, which was pretty damned amazing, since his thoughts had been narrowed down to 'Oh God,' and 'Oh yes,' and 'Hold on, hold on, don't come yet . . .'

'There's a camera in the library parking lot,' Kelly told him, 'because there was a . . . a bunch of robberies and vandalism about eight months ago. The librarians told me . . . the camera probably acted as a deterrent . . . because there were no further problems, but they've kept it running. And . . . you're going to love this—'

Yes, he definitely did love this.

'They never recycled the videotapes,' Kelly announced. 'They just labeled them and filed them. Don't you just love librarians? I've got a month and a half of . . . surveillance tapes from the library parking lot in the trunk of the car. To take home and watch. And see if I can't find a picture . . . of Mary Lou with this guy . . .'

'Unh,' Tom said, because although none of what she'd said

seemed to make sense to him, it seemed obvious from the triumphant ring in her voice that she wanted some kind of response.

'I know,' Kelly said. 'It's probably nothing, but I need to do something . . . and finding people who actually knew Mary Lou . . . seems to be a good place to start. I spoke to Max Bhagat on the phone tonight, and he thought that was a good idea, too.'

Max . . .

'Max suggested . . . I talk to the other wives and girlfriends of the guys in Team Sixteen . . . and try to remember the weeks or even months prior to the assassination attempt. If a terrorist targeted Mary Lou as a potential way to get weapons onto the base . . . he had most likely done some surveillance on the rest of us, too. You know, created additional contacts . . . that he might be able to use as a backup plan. Max thought we should compare names and even descriptions of people we'd met during that time . . . see if there's anyone we all knew . . .

'He said to tell you . . . he'll get out here to see you as soon as he can,' Kelly continued.

But then she pulled his head up and kissed him, which was good, because it meant that neither one of them had to talk or listen for a while.

It was long after midnight before Sam's cell phone rang again.

He knew it was Alyssa calling, and he answered by saying, 'What's the situation in San Diego?'

'We've got two agents inside of Donny DaCosta's house,' she reported, 'with him since he's refused to leave, and we're attempting to locate Mary Lou's landscaper friend without tipping off the entire city to the fact that we're looking for him. If someone – Don's "alien" – *is* following him, it could well be in an attempt to locate Mary Lou. If we do it right, we can pull both men in for questioning at the same time.'

'Max go to San Diego?' Sam asked, trying not to think about

that kiss he'd seen. The thought of Alyssa with Max had always been hard to cope with, but *seeing* them together like that had been unbearable.

'No, he sent Peggy and Yashi out there for now. He went back to Sarasota, for—' She paused. '—a number of reasons, one of which has to do with some political bullshit about some Senate investigating committee.'

'It must be tough, having to spend so much time apart from him,' Sam said.

She didn't answer, instead taking a conversational turn to her favorite subject. 'Are you ready to come in yet?'

'Please don't hang up on me,' he said.

'That sounds like a no.'

'Let's not play this game.' He was so freaking tired. 'Please? I just want to talk to you.'

'Okay,' she said. The clarity of their satellite connection was so good, it was almost as if she were sitting right beside him. 'Tell me about Ringo.'

That caught him by surprise. 'What's to tell that you don't already know? It was a nickname.'

'I want to know about Ringo, the person. Your sister said that starting around eighth grade, you stopped answering to Roger – that you became Ringo.'

'You called her.'

'Yes,' Alyssa said. She didn't mention his revelation about his father, although he knew she must've talked about that at length with Elaine, who was always more than willing to discuss her theories on the topic. 'She wanted me to tell you to turn yourself in. She's worried about you.'

'She shouldn't be.'

'She is. She still calls you that – Ringo.'

Back to this again. Sam sighed. 'Yeah. Noah and Claire do, too.'

'Were you into music or something?'

'No,' he told her. 'It was just a nickname Uncle Walt gave me.

273

That was all he ever called me and, you know, I actually thought at one point that he'd forgotten my real name.'

'That's pretty unlikely, considering you spent a lot of time at his house, hanging with his grandson. He probably had a copy of your rap sheet.'

'Yeah, well, I was a stupid kid, what can I say?' Sam laughed softly. 'Shit, I was dumb as a stone. I still am, sometimes. But I didn't have a rap sheet,' he added.

'I was kidding, Starrett. So why did you refuse to be called Roger? And why did you drop Ringo and turn yourself into Sam?'

'I didn't drop Ringo. I just . . . stopped hanging around with the people who called me that. After Walt died, I just . . .' He'd found it hard to keep up their friendship after Noah had married Claire. They suddenly had completely different lives. Sam, in the Navy, working his ass off to achieve what had started out as Noah's dream – to become a SEAL. Then, when he did, it was hard to visit. It seemed almost as if he were rubbing Noah's nose in it.

And yet the few times he had come back, Nos had seemed so happy with his family and his job. Working for Walt . . .

'I'm still Ringo,' Sam told her. Although every time he caught sight of himself in the rearview mirror, he gave himself a scare. With his haircut and clean shave, he looked like a total stranger. And forget about the clothes he'd picked up on sale at the Men's Warehouse. He'd transformed himself into someone completely unrecognizable.

'I don't think you are,' she said. 'I think you took Ringo and packed him up and stuck him in some storage box somewhere – same as you did with Roger back in eighth grade.'

'Okay,' Sam said, trying to pretend that her words hadn't shaken him. Was it possible she was right? Had he really done that? He tried to keep his voice light. 'You now know too much about me.'

'Do you have any pictures?' she asked. 'Of you as a kid?'

Sam leapt upon the tangent eagerly. This was much easier to talk about. 'I think Lainey has a bunch. Probably Noah, too. Walt liked taking snapshots. He had a couple of drawers filled with old photos and letters and all sorts of stuff. Documents. I remember he and Dot got this dog, it was probably back around 1962, and they saved the records from the vet from when he was treated for worms. The dog had been gone for years, but that piece of paper about those worms was in that drawer. I used to love to sift through that stuff. You never knew what you would find. And then one day I found—'

He stopped. Was he actually going to tell Alyssa this story? Yes.

If he told her about this, then she'd understand why he'd purposely packed Roger into a little box – just like she'd said. And maybe she'd also understand why he was still Ringo – why he'd always be Ringo.

At least he hoped he still was.

'One day you found what?' Alyssa asked.

He was going to have to start closer to the beginning.

'Uncle Walt walked with a limp,' he told her, 'because Dot's brother didn't like the idea of her marrying a black man, and the motherfucker went after Walt with a sharpened shovel and damn near cut off his leg. Walt had just come back from the war, and he'd flown God knows how many missions without being injured, and this little racist prick goes and cripples him for life.

'Noah and I hated all of Dot's brothers, but we particularly hated the one who cut him – her younger one. We used to imagine what we would have done if we'd've been there. We used to rant and rave about vengeance and justice, and Uncle Walt would just chuckle and say he'd gotten the ultimate revenge by living a long and happy life. He had the love of a woman he adored and his two boys to look after him in his old age.' Like Walt hadn't been the one who'd looked after Sam and Noah right up to the day he died. 'That's what he called me and Nos. We were *his two boys*.'

Sam had to clear his throat.

'I can't begin to tell you what it meant to me to have Uncle Walter claim me as his own,' he told her. 'Before I met Noah, I was kind of, like, I don't know, this little wild animal, I guess. I mean, in hindsight it's pretty obvious that my father was fucking with my brain – although it sure as hell could have been worse, huh? My mother spent most of the time stoned on Valium and Lainey was great, but she was so much older than me . . .'

How could he explain this? 'See, no one ever touched me,' Sam said, 'and I think little kids really need to be touched. You know, hugged. Even little boys. *Especially* little boys. Walt used to just grab me in a bear hug, and Dot kissed me hello every single time I walked into her house, and even Noah was so comfortable with himself and so at ease with being affectionate that he used to put his arm around me when we were just sitting around and . . .

'For the first time in my life I felt like I had a home. I was safe when I was with them. I could say anything and never be called stupid. I could break shit, you know, and it would be okay. We'd all just work together to glue it back together. It was . . . the first time that happened I was . . .'

He couldn't begin to find the words. So he just plowed ahead. 'I started doing better in school, because if Walt's face could light up like that when I got a C plus, I wanted to see what he would look like if I got a B or, shit, an A. I even stopped fighting.' Sam caught himself. 'Well, I tried to stop fighting. Every now and then some asshole caught me off guard. But I did try.

'In eighth grade, Noah and I started taking flight lessons. Dot and Walt owned a flight school as well as a fleet of small planes, and Walt told us if we passed the written course with a B plus or better, he'd start taking us up in his Cessna. So we had these big books that he gave us, and we spent all our time studying aerodynamics. It wasn't easy. I remember I was taking a break. Noah was on the phone with some kid from his science class about the project they were doing, so I wandered into the dining room and starting poking through the picture drawer, and I noticed there was an old envelope slipped in there, along the side, that I'd never noticed before.

'I took it out and opened it, and it was a bunch of really old pictures. A girl and three boys – two bigger boys and one little tiny one, much younger than the others, like maybe Haley's age. I loved looking at old pictures because it was like staring into a time tunnel. The cars in the street, and the clothes, and even the expressions on the kids' faces was like from a totally different world. So I flip the picture over and on the back it says, "Dick, Frank, Dorothy, and baby Roger, 1934."

'And I realize, holy shit, this is Dot and her brothers, and I turn the picture back over to get a better look at the baby – because he's going to grow up and swing that shovel at Walt, and he's got this goofy smile on his face. He's just a little kid. But there's more pictures, so I look through them, and there's Dot in her uniform with her brothers, and the little one, Roger – God, I hated that he had the same name as me – was about my age, and I'm still looking hard into his eyes, trying to see the evil that's in his heart.

'And then I pull a piece of paper out of that envelope, and it's some kind of official document, and I realize it's a marriage license between some guy named Percy Smith and ... and Dorothy Elizabeth Starrett.'

'What?' Alyssa said.

'Yeah. Dot was married before, too,' Sam said. 'Just like Walt. I knew that. Smith was her first husband's name, and she kept it after he died. I guess it just never occurred to me that she'd once had a maiden name. All the correspondence I'd read had been to and from Lieutenant Dot Smith.

'So I sat there, staring at those pictures, sick to my stomach, because my father was Dot's little brother, Roger. My own *father* had crippled Walt. And I was convinced more than ever that Walt and Dot didn't know my real name. I'd been Ringo to them for so long, I thought . . .'

He had to take a deep breath. 'I thought that they couldn't possibly know who I was, because if they did, I surely would not be welcome in their house. And I was sick about that. Sick about them finding out and sending me away, and sick about deceiving them. I didn't know what to do.'

'Oh, Sam,' Alyssa murmured.

'I went home and I didn't sleep at all that night. The next day was Saturday, and Noah was working on his science project in the morning, and I knew it, so I went over to the Gaineses' house, and I took that big flight textbook and I marched up to Walt and I put it on his desk.

'And I said, *"Thank you for letting me use your book, sir."*

'And he kind of sat back in his chair and said, *"You're not giving up, are you?"*' His voice had been so mild, and his eyes had been so warm. Walt's eyes were always warm. Roger had nearly started to cry right then and there.

'I told him that I couldn't take flying lessons from him,' Sam told Alyssa now, 'because I couldn't afford to pay for them. And I didn't feel right taking them for free. Taking his charity.

'And Walt, he never really got angry, at least not at Noah and me, but he got pretty grim at that. He told me that it sounded like those were my father's words dribbling out of my mouth.

'And I said that my father didn't know about the lessons. And Walt just kind of looked at me. I'm sure he was trying to figure out what was going on. He asked me—' So gently again. So Walt. '—didn't I want to learn to fly? And I kind of scraped my courage together and squared my shoulders and I told him. I told him that he didn't know who I really was, and that he wouldn't want to be so charitable, giving me expensive things like flying lessons, if he knew my last name.

'Walt was completely floored, I'm sure. I was bracing myself to drop the bomb and tell him I was the son of his mortal enemy, Roger Starrett, when he dropped what felt like a bomb on me. He goes, "Roger Starrett, you don't really think I don't know your name, do you? Why do you think I call you Ringo? It's a

on the spelling of Starrett. You know, Ringo Starrett, Ringo
rr . . .?"

'Now it was my turn to be floored. And I told him that I'd just
found out, just yesterday, that Dot was my real aunt, my real
blood relative – not just pretend, the way I'd thought. I told him
that my father was the same brother who'd crippled him, and I
said something like, *"I'm a Starrett, too. You should hate me."'*

It was then that Walter got it. He understood that Roger had
come to him to return that book to make it easier for Walt to kick
him out of the house, out of their lives.

'And Walt said— I'll remember this forever.' Sam's voice
shook but he kept going. 'He said, "Ringo, sweetheart, you are
not your father. You are you, and I will love you until the day I
die. I would love you even if you told me your last name was
Hitler." He told me that Dot was a Starrett, too, and he didn't
have any trouble loving her, either. It was, um . . .'

Sam's voice didn't just shake, it flat-out wobbled, and he
stopped. 'It was the first time I really, truly understood the way
love was supposed to be,' he whispered. 'Unconditional.' Up to
that very moment, the blessed sanctuary he'd found at the
Gaineses' house had always been something that could've been
taken away from him. He'd lived every day knowing that sooner
or later he'd do what he always did and go too far. He'd do
something unforgivable and he'd be cast out of this paradise
he'd found.

'I started to cry,' Sam admitted. 'I mean, not just a quiet manly
tear rolling down my cheek, but you know, a big snotty waterfall
– sobbing and shit. And that embarrassed the hell out of me even
though it wasn't the first time Walt had seen me melt down.

'I was about to flee the scene, but Walt grabbed me and
hugged me and he told me he'd never been more proud of me
than he was right at that moment – especially so because I was
crying. He told me that people with big hearts cried and that
showing emotion was something I should never be ashamed of.
And he told me, um—'

Sam's voice was shaking again – that 'no shame' crying
was something he still couldn't quite manage, so he cleared
throat, but it didn't help, so – fuck it – he just pressed on.

'He told me that even at age twelve I was one of the best men
– one of the most honorable – that he'd ever had the privilege of
knowing, and that I was going to grow up to be a good man, and
that there was no better goal in life than that – to be a good man,
to be honest and forthright, to do the right thing – even when it
was terribly hard to do so.'

Sam took a deep breath. 'That's what I was trying to do by
marrying Mary Lou. The right thing. Only I was stupid, because
marrying someone you don't love isn't the right thing to do, and
if Walt had still been alive, he would've told me that. I've tried
my entire life to be a good man, to be someone Walt would be
proud of, and I think I've probably managed to fail with the
things that matter the most. You and Mary Lou, and now Haley.'

Alyssa was silent.

'You still there?' Sam asked.

'Yeah,' she said. 'I am. Still here.'

Except she wasn't. Not really. His bad choices, his stupid
mistakes had made him lose her a long time ago.

'I'm so sorry I hurt you, Lys,' he said softly. 'I was just trying
to, you know, be a good man, and instead I really fucked the
duck.'

'Yeah,' she said with a soft laugh. 'You've really got to stay
clear of those ducks, Ringo.'

He laughed, too, but then he stopped. 'You really think I
packed up Ringo, the way I did to Roger? And I definitely did
that with Roger. After finding out that my father was the one
who attacked Walt, I didn't want his name. If I had been old
enough, I would have legally changed it. Shit, if I could have, I
would have removed his blood from my veins, I hated him that
much. Although . . .'

'What?' she asked.

'After finding out what I found out after he died, you know, the pictures of little kids.' Sam shook his head. 'It made more sense. His anger and his hatred, you know? He freaking hated himself, probably even back when he was seventeen, when he went after Walt with that shovel. I mean, imagine going through life wanting something that you *know* is wrong. He was raised to be devoutly religious. Even homosexuality was looked upon as something evil in his church, and he didn't just like men – which in his mind would've been enough to doom him to hell – he liked little boys.

'And here comes his sister, announcing that she's going to marry a black man, which at that time, in that part of the country, was nearly as taboo as being a pedophile. And she just didn't give a damn, and all of his anger and frustration and self-loathing pushed him over the edge.' Sam laughed softly. 'Obviously, I've spent a great deal of time trying to understand him. I mean, it's one thing to hate the person who's hurt someone you love and label him evil, you know, the way I did when I was twelve and I saw those pictures of him when he was a baby. But I think it's more likely that he was just a fucked-up man with a shitload of self-hatred.'

He sighed and they sat there for a moment in silence. In two different cars, on two different sides of town.

'Ringo wouldn't have gone six months without seeing Haley,' he said. 'Jesus, Alyssa, do you think she'll ever forgive me?'

'Yes,' Alyssa said. 'She will.'

'You know, I think the only thing worse than her not recognizing me is her actually remembering who I am – and knowing that she probably spent six months wondering where I went.'

'You can make it up to her,' Alyssa said.

'How?'

'Like Walt said, you've got a big heart, Ringo. I'm sure you'll figure out the best way to use it.'

Sam laughed. Then stopped. 'My heart's telling me to find her, Lys. I know you want me to come in and let you be the one to track her down and pick her up, but God damn it, I can't do it that way. Because I know how it would go down. Mary Lou would be grabbed and Haley would be yanked out of her arms and handed off to some stranger, and they'd both freak out. I won't let it happen that way.

'I've made arrangements for Nos and Claire to take care of Haley. But I thought if I could find Mary Lou first, then I could take them both with me to Noah's house and make sure Haley was comfortable there before I turned me and Mary Lou in and . . .'

Alyssa was silent.

'I know that you think it's about me not trusting you, but it's not. I'm sorry I can't do it your way,' Sam said.

'Let me talk to Max,' she said.

'You said you didn't have that kind of influence over him.'

'He asked me to marry him tonight.'

Sam hadn't thought it could get much worse than this. Terrorists – killers – after his ex-wife, his baby daughter God knows where, his former CO accused of treason, an FBI BOLO with his picture on it, and the knowledge that the only woman he'd ever loved really *was* in the habit of soul-kissing Max – the fucker – seemed about as low as it could go.

But no. He'd been wrong.

He knew he was supposed to say something. *No fucking way* was the first thing that came to mind. 'Congratulations.' So this was evisceration. 'Seriously, Lys,' he managed to choke out, 'he's a good man. I know he's going to make you happy.'

And he really did want her to be happy. Really. *Really*. Aw, shit.

'I didn't say yes,' Alyssa told him, and the knife blade stopped moving. But then she twisted it. 'Yet.' She paused. 'I think I might have more influence over him than I'd originally thought. I'll talk to him in the morning.'

'Great,' Sam said.

'You know what really kills me? That Noah's your cousin.' She laughed softly. 'God, Sam, he even *looks* like you, doesn't he? I can't believe I didn't see that.'

'I already have,' he said, his voice tight. 'Gina, you need to get out of there, because it wasn't us.'

'What?'

'Go into the motel lobby,' he ordered her. 'Right now. I'm on my way, and the local police are, too—'

'There's no lobby.' This room was small, but she hadn't checked under the beds or in the closet or the bathroom or . . . She backed toward the sliding door, stretching the curly phone cord as far as it would go, her heart suddenly pounding. 'There's an office, but it's closed and locked at night—'

He swore sharply. 'Is the parking lot well lit?'

'I don't think you could call it *well* lit.' Her voice shook, and she made herself slow down. Don't panic. Don't flip out. 'This is stupid,' she said briskly, as much to convince herself as him. 'I'm just going to look under the beds, because I *know* no one's in here.'

'No. Go out to the parking lot,' Max told her. 'Stand in the middle, away from the parked cars. If you see anyone at all, if you see anything move, start screaming. Wake up the entire island if you have to. I'm two minutes away from you.'

But the parking lot was filled with shadows despite the brightness of the moon, and the fear she was working hard to keep at bay came crashing through her tough-guy facade. A lot of bad stuff could happen in two minutes. She knew that from experience.

'I can't go out there,' she whispered. 'I'm sorry, I can't.'

'Okay,' he said, no argument, just that warm, familiar voice, wrapping around her. 'Just stay on the phone with me then, Gina. Stay as close to the door as you can.'

'I'm there.'

'Good. I'm passing that resort that looks kind of like a castle,' he told her. He was very close. Not two minutes away after all.

'I'm sorry,' Gina said. 'I know you don't need this right now.'

'I'm sorry, too,' he said, and he actually sounded as if he meant it.

And then there he was.

Max.

His headlights swept across her as he pulled in to the parking lot. He got out of his car and ran toward her. He'd thrown a long raincoat over – no way! – plaid pajama pants and a gray T-shirt that had a picture of Snoopy dressed up in an aviator helmet and scarf to fight the Red Baron. He'd jammed his feet into a beat-up pair of sneakers, his hair looked like he'd gone straight from his bed into his car, and he definitely hadn't shaved in the past three or four hours.

It was such a far cry from his usual dress code, she started to laugh. It was either that or burst into tears.

He pocketed his phone as he approached, as he looked at her hard, making sure she really was okay.

'Plaid, Max?' she said.

'If you mention it to anyone,' he said, 'I'll flatly deny it.' He pulled her into his arms and hugged her as hard as he'd looked at her, but it was way too brief. He set her aside and stepped into her room. 'Wait out here.'

He actually had a gun.

Gina hadn't really thought about the fact that as an FBI agent, Max carried and knew how to use a gun. Holding it like that, with that steely look in his eyes, he looked dangerous. Even with the plaid pajama pants and the bed-head.

But a gun was just a gun. Having one in your hand didn't shield you from the other guy's bullets.

'Be careful,' she called, then held her breath as he checked under the beds and in the closet.

He vanished into the bathroom, and she could hear the sound of the shower curtain being pulled back.

And then he was coming toward her, reholstering his weapon. 'All clear.'

'Thank God. Thank *you*.' Gina stepped back into the room, closing the screen behind her as her heart started to beat again.

'Is anything missing?' His Snoopy T-shirt was faded and

worn, clearly a favorite. It hugged a chest that may have been forty-two years old but looked nothing like her father's. Not that it would have mattered to her if it had.

'I don't know. I had my wallet with me. My plane ticket's electronic, so . . .' She looked around. 'Oh, shit. My CDs and my Walkman.'

'Try not to touch anything as you look,' Max told her.

She'd put her laptop into her suitcase and locked it shut. It was still there, thank goodness. But several pieces of jewelry – all inexpensive trinkets with only sentimental value – were gone.

Along with . . . She started to laugh. 'They stole my underwear.' They actually stole *all* of it – her running bras, too. 'Oh, *mum* . . .'.

'Are you sure?'

'Yeah.' She gestured to the drawer that was open and empty. 'See?'

'I meant, are you sure you didn't put it somewhere else?'

'Yes, I am, but feel free to search for it.'

'Why would someone steal underwear?' he asked.

'Because the TV was bolted to the dresser?' Gina countered as he opened the other drawers, using the edge of his raincoat to keep his prints off the knobs.

Outside the door, the police were pulling in to the lot.

'Oh, *this* is going to be fun,' she said. ' "Can you describe your missing underwear, Ms Vitagliano?" "Well, yes, Officer, I could, but I just might give you a heart attack." '

'Is anything else missing?' Max asked. 'Anything of real value?'

'Hey,' Gina said. 'That was two paychecks' worth of goods from Victoria's Secret.'

'I didn't particularly want to know that,' Max muttered as he escaped out the door.

'That's four *weeks* of me going commando before I have the money to buy it back,' she called after him. That wasn't true. She had the money in the bank. But she was determined. Before this night was through, she was going to push Max past his breaking point.

'Any medication or prescription drugs missing?' the young detective who'd introduced himself as Ric Alvarado asked Gina as they stood in her motel room.

Max had stayed silent through most of this, letting the locals do their job. But now Gina glanced over at him. 'I, uh, didn't look.'

'Would you mind checking?' Alvarado asked. He had one of those ridiculous soul patches under his lower lip, and since he'd come in, he'd spent more time looking at Gina than looking around the room.

She went into the bathroom, and the detective turned to Max. Alvarado hadn't missed that look Gina had shot in Max's direction, and knew what it meant. It was possible he was a decent detective after all.

'Would you mind waiting outside, sir?' he said in a low voice. 'Your being in the room might make it hard for your daughter to be forthcoming about whatever prescriptions she might have had stolen – birth-control pills or antidepressants or whatever.'

His *daughter*.

'We've had a rash of break-ins in this area,' Alvarado continued, apparently not noticing that Max was now grinding whatever was left of his teeth into stubs, 'and it's usually always CDs and whatever's in the medicine cabinet. We're pretty sure it's the same group of kids.'

Gina was already coming out of the bathroom.

'She's not my daughter,' Max told Alvarado, making sure that she heard him say it. 'Although I can understand why you might have thought that she was.'

Alvarado was embarrassed. 'Sorry, I—'

'Max is actually my own private stalker,' Gina told him. 'And yes, I'm missing some sleeping pills.' She gave Max a challenging look that said, 'So now you know I have a prescription for sleeping pills.'

As if he hadn't already known that.

Alvarado, boy detective, really didn't like that stalker comment. So Max sighed and pulled out his ID and handed it to the young man, while he shook his head at Gina in a silent reprimand.

The detective recognized his name and nearly crapped his pants as he tried to remember if he'd said anything else that might've offended the Great Max Bhagat, Law Enforcement Legend.

Max let the little bastard squirm. 'You need her for anything else?' he asked as he repocketed his ID wallet. 'Or can I get her moved to a more secure location now?'

'We're done here, sir,' Alvarado said. 'And I'm sorry I didn't realize who you were—'

Gina was looking at Max like he'd grown a second head. 'Excuse me? I'm not going anywhere.'

'Yeah,' he said. 'You are. Pack your stuff. I'm moving you to my hotel.'

'To your room?' she asked.

Their eyes locked, and Max knew with temperature-raising certainty that she wanted to share a room, a bed, bodily fluids. With him. She wanted *him*. Right now. Tonight. All he had to do was say yes. 'No.'

She turned away. 'Then I'm not going.'

He reached down deep for whatever patience he had left. There wasn't much there. 'Gina.'

'Max,' she said with the exact same inflection.

'What do you need to happen?' he asked. 'Your room was broken into.'

'By kids. Right, Ric?'

Alvarado was pretending not to pay attention, but now he turned back to them. 'Uh, yeah. And these doors are easy to jimmy when you're out of the room, but with the night lock on they're—' He saw from Max's face that he wasn't helping. '—safe. I'll go, um . . . Go.' He looked at Gina. 'I'll let you know if we find your CDs or your, uh . . .' He cleared his throat.

'Underwear,' she supplied.

'Yeah, but to be honest, it's not likely you'll get it back. And if you do, you might want to burn it.'

'Interesting.' Gina gave him a smile. 'A man actually suggesting that a woman burn her bras.'

Ric laughed aloud, but his broad grin quickly faded when he glanced at Max. 'Sorry, sir. I'm going now.'

He closed the door behind him.

'Don't you get tired of that?' Gina asked. 'People treating you like you're God?' She sat down on one of the beds. 'Of course it doesn't help when you give them your death glare.'

'Please,' Max said. 'Let me get you a room where I know you'll be safe.'

'I've already paid for *this* room. I don't want to spend more money.'

'I'll pay for it,' he told her.

'But I like it here. And Ric seemed to think I'll be safe.'

'Ric's a fucking child who's been a detective for about two weeks,' Max countered. He closed his eyes. Shit, shit, shit. 'I'm sorry. I'm—'

'Tired?' she supplied. 'I am, too, Max.' She stood up, moved toward him. 'Maybe if you stay here with me, we'll both finally be able to sleep.'

Jesus Christ, she didn't let up. It took every ounce of self-control he had in him not to rip off his raincoat and throw her back down on that bed and—

How could he even *think* of having that kind of rough sex with someone who'd—

Someone he'd *let* get—

They'd had to stitch her back up. He'd seen the hospital reports. Brutal didn't begin to describe it.

'I can't stay, and you God damn know it!' Ah, Christ, he was losing it, transforming totally into Max the raving lunatic. The wall puncher. The asshole. 'Don't you God damn make me sit out in my car, in that parking lot, all night long! If you don't come with me, that's what I'm going to have to do, and I'm too God damn old for that *shit*!'

He was shouting now – although not about what he really wanted to shout about – and she stopped moving closer. Yeah, that's right, honey. Meet the real Max Bhagat.

'You want to know why I don't get tired of people treating me like God?' he told her, practically foaming at the mouth. 'Because when they treat me like God, they *do what I say*! Three hundred million people in this country and everyone treats me like God – except *you*!'

'That's because I'm in love with Max the man,' she told him, her voice shaking – because, Jesus Christ, was she actually afraid of him?

When he got like this, *he* was afraid of him.

He had to get out of here, especially when he paid attention to the words she'd said and not just the tone of her voice. *Love*.

No. No. Love wasn't this crazy, emotional tornado. Love was what he had with Alyssa Locke. Love was a comfortable blend of attraction and friendship and passion. *Controlled* passion.

Not this blinding mix of anger and frustration and howling, gut-wrenching, consuming desire for someone he couldn't have. Someone he would only hurt if he gave in to his desperate, obsessive need to possess her.

'It's not love, it's transference,' he told her harshly as he headed for the door.

She didn't say another word, but the expression on her face nearly brought him to his knees.

'Lock this door,' he ordered, damn near snarling. 'I'll be in the car.'

Mary Lou sat up in her bed, suddenly wide awake.

She sat in the dark, listening, her heart pounding.

Something was wrong.

It was the same feeling she used to get when she left her curling iron on before going to work.

It was a sense of unease. Something had been forgotten or overlooked. She'd slipped up somewhere, and he was going to find her.

At three o'clock in the morning, she was more often convinced than not that he was going to find her.

The man who'd killed her sister.

The man who'd smuggled those weapons into the naval base, in the trunk of her car.

A man she could identify, pick out of a lineup, help convict, and send to jail.

Provided anyone would believe her. After all, she knew her fingerprints were on that gun. She would bet her life his weren't.

He didn't seem to realize that if she came forward, if she called, say, Alyssa Locke, Sam's FBI girlfriend – Lord, she'd probably already moved into the house with Sam. If Mary Lou called the bitch on the phone and said, 'I think you're probably looking for me,' *she* was the one who would go to jail.

And then, while she was in prison, she'd get a knife stuck in her heart, because that's what always happened, at least in the movies. Bad guys always had connections inside the prison, and she'd end up bleeding to death, staring up at the gray ceiling of the prison cafeteria.

But at least Haley would be safe.

Mary Lou's biggest nightmare was that he would find her, and he would pump a bullet into Haley's head first, while Mary Lou was forced to watch.

She reached over and turned on the light on her bedside table. Although what good that did, she didn't really know. All it meant was that she'd see death coming.

Unless he shot her the way he'd shot Janine. In the back of the head.

Mary Lou got up and checked on Haley, who was fast asleep,

holding tightly to her Pooh Bear – as if she'd fight to the death before letting anyone take it from her.

Sam had given her that bear – or at least he'd given her its predecessor. But Haley couldn't tell the difference between New Pooh and Pooh-who-had-been-left-behind, thank the Lord, or there'd be hell to pay.

It was funny – and surely just a coincidence – that Sam should be able to guess so precisely the type of stuffed toy Haley would adore.

She felt a pang of guilt. He'd made plans to come and visit Haley a number of times, but she'd always canceled on him. She'd been terrified even back then that he would be followed by . . .

Bob Schwegel.

It was such a friendly-sounding name for a cold-blooded killer. A sister killer. A presidential assassination conspirator. An insurance salesman impersonator – was that a crime? Surely Bob Schwegel was an alias.

Mary Lou lightly touched her sleeping daughter's cheek before moving to the other bed to check on Amanda.

Both girls were fast asleep.

She turned on the baby monitor that she didn't normally use at night because her own room was nearby, and went back into her own bedroom. Slipping on her robe and slippers, she found the huge ring of keys Mrs Downs had given her that afternoon before she'd left for her niece's wedding.

She took the monitor and headed down the hall, stopping briefly to listen for the sound of Whitney's steady breathing from her bedroom.

Once she was down the stairs, she turned on the lights, leaving them blazing as she went.

Past the dining room.

Past the kitchen.

Past the laundry room.

She turned and went back and into the laundry room, taking

an empty laundry basket from the stack by the door.

Then she went on.

Past the library.

Down the corridor.

King Frank's office was locked, but she and Whitney and the two little girls were the only people here in this great big house, and she had the keys.

It took her a solid ten minutes of trial and error before Mary Lou found the key that opened the door.

She didn't turn on the overhead lamp, she just let the light shine in from the hallway as she crossed the plush carpeting and set down the basket and opened the wall of cabinets behind King Frank's desk.

And there they were. Frank Turlington's vast collection of guns. Firearms, Sam would've called them. Whitney's father had everything from hunting rifles to pre-Revolutionary War flintlocks to teeny little handguns a gangster's moll would hide in her garter to Wild West six-shooters. Not to mention the three racks of assault weapons.

He had everything you could possibly need to keep an invading horde from storming the King's castle.

They were locked behind glass that she'd heard King Frank boast about. It was unbreakable. You could hit it with a tire iron and you still wouldn't get through it.

But Mary Lou didn't need a tire iron.

Because tonight she had the keys.

At three-thirty, Max called Alyssa.

'Oh, good,' she said. 'I needed to talk to you, but I didn't want to wake you up.'

Max laughed, looking at the light still burning behind Gina's window curtain. 'You actually thought I was sleeping?'

'I know how to get Sam to surrender,' she steamrolled over him. 'If you give him forty-eight hours before he needs to come in for questioning, I'll deliver him – and probably Mary Lou, too, because he's extremely motivated to find her – to the Sarasota office.'

'I thought we were working on a plan to apprehend him tomorrow morning.'

'We are,' she said. 'We're ready with that, of course. But there's no guarantee it'll work. This way, you'll have them both in forty-eight hours.'

It was entirely possible Gina slept with the light on.

'He wants to find his daughter,' Alyssa said, 'and get her safely set up with a relative before he and Mary Lou both turn themselves in.'

'He told you that.'

Max hadn't asked it as a question, but she answered it. 'Yes.'

And you believed him. Crap. He'd called her to talk about Gina. He'd called because he was going crazy and he needed her as a friend. But she was so wrapped up in what was going on with Sam Starrett, that she didn't even notice the desperation in his voice.

Gina's curtain moved, and he saw the pale flash of her face as she looked out at him. No, no, no. Don't come outside.

'Marry me,' he said to Alyssa, 'and I'll give him twenty-four hours.'

It was so obviously the wrong thing to say or do – to bring their relationship into this negotiation.

Alyssa made an exasperated sound, and Max's heart sank even farther. She was so personally invested in this negotiation, she didn't even realize that he was messing with her head. 'For someone who tries so hard not to be guilty of sexual harassment, you can be an incredible asshole. Sir.'

'I was kidding.'

'Not completely.'

Yeah. The bitch of it was, she was right.

'Help me,' Max said, 'I'm in over my head.' But he said it without opening his mouth, without making a sound. Please God, let her hear him anyway.

'Sam's not going to agree to this if it's less than forty-eight hours,' Alyssa said.

Sam. Always Sam. 'He's not going to agree to it, period,' Max told her. 'Let's stick with the plan.'

'Max, please,' Alyssa said, and he knew.

She hadn't even realized it herself yet, but Max *knew*. Sam Starrett had won. She was toast, and Starrett was going to gobble her up.

As he watched, Gina pulled aside the curtain, undid the night lock, and slid the door open. She stepped outside.

'You have forty-eight hours,' Max said into his phone, watching Gina move gingerly across the pebbled parking lot in her bare feet. Her feet weren't the only things that were bare. She was wearing a baggy pair of boxer shorts and a tank top that barely covered her – her version of PJs, no doubt. God *damn*, she had an incredible body. A twenty-three-year-old's body, with the kind of curves most twenty-three-year-olds starved themselves to avoid having. 'No, you know what, Alyssa? I'll give you fifty-three. But if you don't deliver Sam Starrett to my office on Friday by eight-thirty a.m., I'll expect your resignation on my desk.'

'Agreed.' God damn it, she didn't even hesitate. 'Thank you, Max.'

'Watch out for his teeth,' he said, but she'd already cut the connection.

He put his phone into the car's cup holder as Gina opened the passenger's side door and slipped her incredible body and her equally incredible, indomitable spirit into the seat next to him.

'I don't sleep too much anymore,' she told him, 'but it doesn't seem fair to make you lose sleep, too.'

'Do the pills help?' he asked. 'Because tomorrow I can help you replace what was stolen.'

Gina looked searchingly into his eyes, and he forced himself to hold her gaze, praying she didn't see his desperation.

'I don't know,' she said. 'I hate taking them, so I hardly ever do. It makes it too hard to wake up in the morning.'

Max nodded. He knew. He'd tried something similar himself, just a few months ago.

'We're really going to be looked at askance if I bring you to my hotel with me in this and you in that,' he said.

'I'm not going to your hotel. But *you* should go.'

Max sighed. 'That's what I was afraid you were going to say. Thanks, but no. I'm fine right here.'

'You're such a liar.'

'I'm not lying. But maybe I should rephrase – I'm just as miserable here as I would be anywhere else,' he told her.

'That's a terrible way to live.'

'Yeah,' he agreed.

They sat in silence for a moment, and then he said, 'I'm sorry about before. I, uh, shouldn't have, uh—'

'You're allowed to be angry,' she interrupted him. 'You don't need to apologize for expressing the way you feel.'

He laughed. 'God, Gina . . .'

More silence.

'What?' she said. 'God, Gina, what?'

'I don't know,' he admitted. 'I don't know anything.'

'I do,' she told him in a voice that was very, very soft. 'I know that when I'm with you, I don't feel so lost.'

Don't look at her. Don't do it. Don't turn your head, Max, you God damn idiot—

He looked. He did more than look. He reached for her, and she went into his arms.

Fortunately sanity prevailed before he kissed her. He kept her head tightly tucked under his chin as he held her.

And Gina seemed to know not to ask for more than he could give. She just clung to him, soft and warm and vulnerable as all hell.

She was trying to hide it, but she was crying. Max stroked her hair and her back and the soft smoothness of her bare arm.

Touching her like that screamed of impropriety, but he was

too tired to make himself stop. Jesus Christ, it was just her arm.

Max closed his eyes, knowing that he had to push her away, that she had to go back into her room.

But it couldn't have been more than ten minutes, fifteen tops, before he realized that she'd stopped crying. She was breathing slowly and steadily.

Gina, who didn't sleep much either anymore, had fallen asleep in his arms.

On the other end of the phone, Sam was silent.

'Are you still there? Still awake?' Alyssa asked him. When she'd called, he hadn't been.

'Yeah, I'm . . .' His voice was rusty from sleep. 'I'm thinking. I'm a little groggy, so . . . So you went to Max and he just *agreed* to give me forty-eight hours?'

'Fifty-three,' Alyssa said.

'And I'm supposed to believe him?'

'You don't have to believe him,' she said. 'You can believe me.'

He was silent again for several long moments. 'Yeah,' he finally said. 'And I want to. I, uh, just don't know if, um . . .'

Sam didn't trust her. That shouldn't matter so much, but it did. 'You know, if you don't agree to do this, I'm going to look really foolish. After going to Max and laying it on the line for you . . .?' Her voice was just a little too sharp.

'I'm sorry,' he said, and he really sounded as if he were. 'Lys, really, it's not you I don't trust. It's Bhagat. Why would he agree to something like this?'

'Your suggestion – you know, the one about the blow job? It really worked.'

'That is so not funny.'

'Neither is you not trusting me,' Alyssa countered.

'Do you trust *me*?' he asked.

'Yes,' she said. 'Enough to promise Max that I'd deliver either you or my resignation to his office by the end of those fifty-three hours.'

'Fuck,' Sam said. 'You shouldn't have promised that. I mean, what if we haven't found Haley by then?'

'We'll just have to work fast.'

'Fuck,' he said again. '*Fuck*. Alyssa, Jesus. I don't know what to say.'

'How about, "Let's meet at the Hardee's in ten minutes"?'

'You're really going to share information with me?' he asked, clearly not believing her at all.

'Yes.' What could she tell him to convince him? 'You'll be part of the team working to find Mary Lou. For fifty-three hours.'

He laughed. 'Yeah, right. And you'll tell me what you found out from the desk clerk at the Sunset Motel, huh? What's her name. Did she actually remember seeing Mary Lou?'

'Beth Weiss,' Alyssa said. This was it. In her attempt to make him believe her, should she tell him about her plan to intercept him, or not? She hadn't considered the possibility that she was going to have to catch him to make him understand that those fifty-three hours Max had granted him were real, but it sure sounded as if that was going to be the case. 'Look, Sam, please trust me. At least enough to meet. Right now. You name the place, I'll be there – alone.'

'And naked?' he asked. 'Because I'm actually considering it, and the naked part would probably push me over the edge.'

Alyssa closed her eyes. 'You know, I'm being serious here and—'

'And I can't do it,' he said. 'Alyssa, there's a part of me that wants to take you up on this offer – if only to prove to you what a bastard Bhagat is. He's messing with you. I know you don't believe that, but as soon as I agree to meet you, he's going to send in the cavalry and have me down on my face on the sidewalk so fast—'

'Max doesn't operate that way.'

'My ex-wife's fingerprints were on a weapon used in a

299

presidential assassination attempt,' Sam said. 'I think he's probably under a great deal of pressure to get *some* kind of answers.'

That much was true. But would Max deliberately lie to her?

After proposing marriage?

Alyssa didn't kid herself. That proposal was a crazy-assed
attempt on Max's part to protect himself from his mixed up
feelings about Gina Vitagliano.

She sighed. 'Shit, Sam . . .'

'Shit is right.'

'Look, I only know what Max told me – that if you surrender
yourself to me, we've got fifty-three hours before I have to bring
you in.'

'I'm sorry,' he said. 'I don't trust him.'

'Sam—'

'I'm *sorry*.' He cut the connection.

The FBI's plan was going to have to work. And wasn't he
going to be surprised when he found out that the fifty-three
hours Max had granted him was real?

Unless . . .

Why *would* Max agree?

If he had a choice between getting Sam Starrett into custody
immediately or in fifty-three hours, wouldn't he pick
immediately?

Maybe Sam *was* right, and Max had an alternate plan that he
hadn't bothered to tell Alyssa about.

She opened her phone and dialed Jules's cell phone number.

Time for her to put into place her own plan B.

Wednesday, June 18, 2003

Gina was roused by the sound of a cell phone ringing. It was
blindingly bright wherever she was, so she kept her eyes tightly
shut. God, her neck and back were stiff from sleeping funny, but,
hey, at least she'd slept.

'I know,' a male voice said. Whoever it was was speaking in hushed tones, probably to keep her from waking up. A pause, and then, 'Alyssa, I'll *be* there.'

Alyssa.

Gina opened her eyes and discovered that she was sleeping in Max Bhagat's rented car, with her head on Jules Cassidy's lap. She had Max's raincoat over her.

Jules looked down at her as he closed his cell phone. 'Damn, I woke you. I'm sorry.'

Gina sat up, rubbing her neck. Maybe it wasn't sleeping funny that made her ache. Maybe it was mild whiplash from yesterday's accident. It was nothing, though, that a hot shower wouldn't fix. 'What time is it?'

'Nearly six,' he told her.

'Where's Max?'

'He has a meeting in about half an hour that he couldn't miss – and couldn't show up for in plaid pajamas and a Snoopy shirt.' Jules smiled. 'Who knew? I think I love him more than ever now.' He handed her a folded piece of paper. 'He asked me to give you this.'

Gina opened it. *Gina, either move to a safer hotel, or Jules Cassidy will be your roommate tonight.* That was it.

'Did you read this?' she asked Jules.

'No,' he said.

She looked at him.

'Of course I read it. I'm an FBI agent. It's a clue.'

'He didn't even sign his name,' Gina said.

'Yeah, I noticed that, too.'

'He's pushing me away because he let me get too close last night,' she said.

'Oh, yeah? Exactly how close did he let you get?'

'Not as close I wanted,' she admitted. She sighed, looking down at Max's neat handwriting again. *Jules Cassidy will be your roommate* . . . 'He's trying to set me up with you, you know.'

Jules laughed at that. 'No, he's not.'

'Yes, he is. Every time I turn around, he's pushing you at me.'

'No, he most certainly is not. He's using me to baby-sit you, which is something else entirely for you to get mad about.'

She waved the letter. 'But—'

'He's using me to baby-sit you because he thinks that because I'm gay, I'm safe. If he knew what I said to you last night, he'd probably have a coronary. And then he'd transfer me to Nebraska.'

'Max knows you're gay? You're positive?'

'Sweetie, either he knows I'm gay or he's an idiot, and I'm pretty sure he's not an idiot. I'm gloriously out of the closet. The entire office knows, even though they don't ask and I don't tell. But there's more than just a discreet gay pride flag in the pencil holder on my desk – there's a signed picture from the cast of *Queer as Folk*. I sing show tunes in the hallway. I use words like *gloriously* when I talk. I smell good all the time. Believe me, Max knows.'

Gina stared at him. She had been so sure . . . But if Max knew . . . 'Oh, man,' she said. 'Just when I'm sure I've got him figured out . . .'

She found out that she was still completely clueless.

Sixteen

One last time, Sam took his car down the roads around all three of the doughnut shops between the highway and the Sunset Motel, driving the potential escape routes.

He'd done it last night, but everything looked a little different now that the sun was up, so he was glad he had the extra time to do it again.

Ninety-eight percent of a successful E&E – escape and evasion – was all about knowing the roads and being familiar with the area. Since it was more than likely he'd be out of his car if and when any bad shit went down, Sam paid close attention to the buildings in those parts of town, too. Places in which to get lost. Stores or medical buildings to enter as one person and exit as someone looking entirely different. He looked long and hard at the alleys and the cut-throughs, too, until he could see them in his mind, with his eyes closed.

He'd gotten out of his car and walked them last night.

He was ready.

Well, almost ready.

Just one more rather important thing to do.

He headed toward the First Unitarian Church, home of the FUC Men's Homeless Shelter.

He'd seen that listing in the phone book last night, and at first his exhausted brain had filled in the missing 'K-E-D'. He'd had to read it twice, thinking, *What the fuck?*, and he'd laughed aloud when he realized what he'd done. It seemed like a sign from God. At the very least, it was a sign that God – or someone who knew Him rather well – had a sense of humor, because surely Sam wasn't the only one who saw that listing and misread it in that particular way.

Sam drove past the church now, slowing down to take a better look. His timing was perfect. All of the FUC-ked men were leaving the shelter, looking as lost and bedraggled as they probably had when they came crawling in late last night.

Up and at 'em, boys. Time to wander the streets. Maybe apply for a job that you have no prayer of getting because you don't have a permanent address and you haven't washed your clothes in four months. Maybe roll a drunk. Maybe earn a few bucks doing something illegal or degrading, and buy a bottle of gin and get drunk, get rolled by kids who are too young and stupid to realize your pockets are emptier than theirs.

The first four men Sam saw were either African-American or Hispanic. The next bunch were white, but all too short.

He went around the block and . . .

Jackpot.

He was too young, barely even twenty, a little too skinny, but he had the right color hair. A jacket would help hide his lack of muscles. He was even wearing jeans and scuffed up cowboy boots.

Sam pulled up alongside of him and leaned over as he opened the passenger's side window. 'Hey. Want to earn an easy twenty bucks?'

The kid scowled at him. 'Fuck you. Go suck your own dick.'

'Whoa,' Sam said. 'That's not what I—'

But he realized that what he must look like with his haircut and shaved face and these new clothes – what he surely looked like from the kid's vantage point – was some casually rich, corporate deviant looking for an early morning jump start to his day.

Not that being gay made you deviant. It was only deviant when you had a wife and kids and pretended to be straight but then went sneaking around, paying street kids like this one to get your rocks off.

Sam got out of the car and followed the kid on foot. 'Hey, junior, you misunderstood.'

The kid turned and looked at him with dead eyes. 'A hundred bucks and you wear a condom.'

Aw, man. 'Fifty bucks,' Sam negotiated, 'for absolutely no sex. You sit in my car with me for an hour, maybe two, tops, while we wait for someone to show up. I don't touch you, you don't touch me, no one even touches themselves. No sex. I'm not into that – you understand?'

The kid didn't even blink.

Sam held up his baseball cap. 'We drive around for a little bit, and you wear *this* into a doughnut shop, buy yourself a cup of coffee. Period. No sex. You walk out of there with fifty bucks in your pocket.'

The kid looked at the hat, looked at him. 'Seventy-five and you wear a condom.'

Sam gave up trying to convince him that he was serious when he said no sex. 'Deal. Get in the car.'

The kid would find out soon enough.

Team Sixteen was back in Coronado.

Tom Paoletti saw his former XO, Jazz Jacquette, as he was being taken back into the BOQ after another extremely early session of questioning.

This time the questions had been all about a blond man and a gardener or landscaper.

The only blond man Tom knew well was Senior Chief Stanley Wolchonok. And as for a gardener . . . He himself spent a lot of time in his own garden. His great-uncle Joe was a gardener, back in Massachusetts.

But neither Stan nor Joe – nor Tom – were terrorists.

Tom didn't mention either of the other men by name. No way was he letting this witch-hunt spread to them.

He pushed open the door and saw that Kelly was waiting for him in his room. No, his *wife* was waiting for him. Just thinking that made him smile, even though he was exhausted from four hours of questioning in a room that was purposely airless and hot. They were trying to make him sweat.

They had succeeded. He now stank.

'The team's back,' Kelly told him, hugging and kissing him anyway, despite his animal odor.

'Yeah, I know.' He held her tightly, hit by a wave of emotion, grateful as hell that she was here for him. With him.

He let her go and took off his jacket. Man, it was damp and it reeked. Just what he needed – to walk into these sessions smelling of fear. 'I need to get this dry-cleaned.'

'I'll get it done right away,' Kelly promised as he unfastened his pants and kicked off his shoes. 'I figured as much. I brought a bunch of your other uniforms over. And some more clean socks and underwear, too.'

Tom kissed her again. 'Thank you.' She was wearing pants today. What a shame. He moved past her into the bathroom, where he splashed cool water on his face and let it run on his hands and wrists before he washed his pits. Jee-zus. He really needed a shower, but that could wait until after Kelly was gone.

'Everyone's been calling,' she said, standing in the doorway, watching as he dried himself with his towel. 'Everyone. Stan. Jazz. Mark Jenkins.' She counted them off on her fingers. 'Izzy, Silverman, Lopez, Muldoon, John Nilsson, Big Mac, the Duke, Kenny . . . They all called, Tommy. They want to know what they can do. They're all willing to resign over this.'

'What? No way!' Resign? 'Call them back and tell them not to. Tell them that's a direct order.'

Kelly backed up as he came out into the main room, probably to avoid the steam coming out of his ears.

'This is exactly what al-Qaeda hoped would happen,' he ranted. 'They don't have the ability to drop a bomb here in

Coronado, but with only three incompetent guys with machine guns, they're on the verge of completely destroying the Navy's top Spec Op team.' It wasn't big enough in there to pace, but he didn't let that stop him. 'Shit! *Shit!*'

'I'll spread the word.' Kelly sat on the bed to stay out of his way. 'No resignations. Although Stan and Jazz were both really interested in your plans for the future. I think they're hoping you'll give them a job.'

He turned to look at her. 'A job doing what?'

'I, uh, may have mentioned something about the security con- sulting group you're thinking of forming, you know, specializing in counterterrorism . . .?'

Tom stopped pacing. *He* was thinking of forming . . .?

She actually looked a little embarrassed. 'I may have referred to it as the equivalent of a civilian SEAL team.' She lifted her chin and dug in. 'It's a good idea, Tom. You and your team could do things you would never be allowed to do as a part of the US military.'

He laughed his amazement. 'I thought you wanted me to join the FBI.'

'I was thinking about it, but why would you want to take orders from Max Bhagat when you're used to being in charge? This way you can make some serious money, too,' she pointed out.

'Working for corporate assholes who risk their employees' lives to get more oil—' He caught himself. 'I can't believe we're having this conversation. I'm being held under guard, about to be officially charged with *treason*—'

'Of which you are not guilty. We're going to beat this, Tom, and then you're going to flip the bird at Admiral Fucker and get back to business kicking terrorist ass. Paoletti International Security and Personal Protection Agency. PISPPA.'

Tom cracked up. 'That's awful. It sounds like piss pot.'

'Yeah, well, Stan and Jazz didn't think so.'

'They both already have jobs,' Tom pointed out. 'Running my

team.' He corrected himself. 'Team Sixteen.' It wasn't his team anymore.

But, God *damn*. Tom could see from Kelly's face that there was bad news coming. 'What?' he asked.

'Jazz told me he isn't going to be your replacement,' Kelly said. 'They're bringing in someone else to be the team's new commanding officer.'

Double damn! 'Who?'

She shook her head. 'I don't know. I asked Jenk to see what he can find out.'

Tom felt sick. He sank down next to her on the bed. 'This is *my* fault. Everyone knows Jazz was my pick. I should've just kept my mouth shut.'

'It's not your fault,' Kelly said, putting her arms around him and holding him tightly. 'None of this is your fault.'

Yeah, right.

She lifted her head and looked up at him. 'Oh, I meant to tell you – there *is* some good news. Now that he's back, I've got Kenny Karmody working on those surveillance videos from the library. He's writing a program so that his computer can search through the tapes, looking for Mary Lou.'

The videos? Of the San Diego library parking lot. It took Tom a moment to figure out what Kelly was talking about. Man, what a long shot that was. And if those videos were their best lead . . .

He was so totally screwed.

'Do you think they're trying to dissolve the team?' he asked her, already knowing the answer.

Kelly didn't try to bullshit him. 'Yeah,' she said. 'I do. If their intention is to tie you into some kind of assassination conspiracy and publicly charge you with treason . . .'

The negative publicity from that would be intense. And anything Tom had ever touched would be suspect. Or, at the very least, tainted.

The idea of Team Sixteen being split up was almost worse than the thought of his spending the next thirty years in jail.

'I spent most of the night on the phone with Meg and Savannah and we contacted every other teammate's wife and girlfriend and ex-wife and former girlfriend we could think of,' Kelly told him as she massaged the muscles in his shoulders and neck. 'We did a bunch of conference calls, trying to figure out if any of us had been targeted by someone who was looking for information about the team, or even a way onto the Navy base. We made lists of people – even acquaintances – that we knew who might also know Mary Lou. But that was hard to do without her participation. I wish we could talk to her.'

'A lot of people want to talk to Mary Lou,' Tom pointed out.

'The only person I'm certain that she and I both knew was Ihbraham Rahman,' Kelly said.

'*Rahman?*' Tom said, turning to look at her.

'Yeah,' she said. 'After they kick me out of here, I'm going to call Max Bhagat to tell him. I mean, it feels uncomfortably like racial profiling to me – Ihbraham was clearly from the Middle East – but—'

'Is he a gardener?' Tom asked. 'You know, like, a landscaper?'

Kelly blinked at him. 'Yeah. Did you . . . I didn't think you ever met him.'

God *damn*. 'How about a man with blond hair?' Tom asked. 'Someone that this Rahman guy might've known. Or maybe not,' he said, thinking aloud. 'Maybe it's just someone that Mary Lou knew, too.'

'A blond man.' Kelly chewed her lip. 'God, I don't know. Ihbraham worked alone, I do know that. Well, at least he was always alone whenever I saw him in our neighborhood. He cut the Jansens' lawn, you know, next door. He came over a few times, to introduce himself and drop off his business card and his rates. He was very nice. And he did a good job at the Jansens'.'

'Call Max,' Tom told her, 'and tell him what you just told me. And call Meg and the others back. Ask them if they remember a man with blond hair. He'd probably be someone they met maybe a month or two before the Coronado attack. Maybe before that, even. He probably disappeared shortly after.'

She nodded, taking his ripe uniform from the closet.

Tom kissed his wife and pushed her out the door. 'Go.'

It wasn't until she was gone that he realized he'd forgotten to tell her that he loved her.

Jules arrived in Gainesville with barely enough time to spare.

Alyssa was on the phone with Max, who was back in Sarasota, thank goodness for small favors. But it meant that she couldn't bitch at Jules for cutting it down to the wire. She could only grimace at him and gesture for him to follow her, grabbing the gym bag she'd taken from the back of her car.

'Everything ready?' Max asked.

'Yes, sir,' Alyssa said. 'Just about. We expect Sam to show up in approximately fifteen minutes.'

'Good,' Max said.

'I'm not entirely sure this rates a *good* just yet,' she told him as she led Jules into the back of the Dunkin' Donuts, into the single seat ladies' room. She set the gym bag down on the floor. 'His showing up isn't the same as my apprehending him. He's no fool.'

'Yes, I'm well aware of that.'

Alyssa locked the door behind them. 'We're going to be waiting for him, here in the store,' she told him. 'When I approach him, I'm going to tell him not to run, that he's not being taken into custody, that he's got those forty-eight hours that I promised him before we bring him in.'

'Alyssa, promise him anything.' He sounded exhausted. 'Just get him in here.'

'In forty-eight hours,' she repeated, but Max had already hung up. 'Take off your clothes,' she ordered Jules.

'Why is it, lately, that only *women* want me to take off my clothes?'

'Please, Jules,' she begged him as she pulled her second-nicest

310

suit out of her bag. 'We have three minutes to do this. I have to get into place before Sam gets here.'

'Sam.' Jules yanked off his jacket and shirt and stripped out of his pants, his eyes sympathetic. 'Sweetie, are you sure you want to do this? I mean, no one's going to blame you if you just get into your car and drive north – all the way back to DC. Take a few weeks off—'

'And for the rest of my life regret not doing something while I had the chance?'

'Why do you want to help Sam Starrett clean up his mess?' Jules countered. 'And you know I love him dearly, Alyssa, but it is *his* mess.'

'You can't blame him for terrorists targeting his wife,' she said.

'Actually, I can,' Jules said. 'Considering if he hadn't had the wrong wife, he wouldn't be in this situation right now.'

Alyssa shook her head. 'I didn't want to marry him. I wouldn't have married him.'

'Yeah, you can pretend that if you want, but I know you. You were so ready to get his name tattooed on your ass.'

'Just hurry up,' she told him.

Jules sighed. 'This is going to be catastrophically bad, isn't it? But what I can't figure out is, which will be worse? If you fail or if you succeed?'

Sam's phone rang just as he saw the blue Ford Focus, with South Carolina plates, coming down the highway exit ramp.

'Don't say a word,' he warned the kid – Kyle – sitting slouched beside him. 'Don't even breathe loudly.'

He opened his cell phone.

It was Alyssa, of course.

'Good morning,' she said.

'Got some information for me?' he asked. 'You know, in the spirit of convincing me to meet you somewhere and take advantage of that fifty-three hours of amnesty?'

'It's forty-eight hours and fifty-two minutes now,' she told him. 'The clock started when I first made the offer.'

'That's fair,' Sam said, pulling out into traffic, about twelve cars behind Beth Weiss's Focus. He could let her get that far ahead, because the nearest traffic light was way down the road. If someone was following her, watching for him, he wanted to be far enough back.

'Sam.' Alyssa's voice was husky with urgency. 'Meet me. Right now. You name the place, I'll be there. We can set it up so that you feel safe. I'm willing to do whatever you want me to do. Your rules. Max isn't a part of this. This is just between you and me. He gave you forty-eight hours – but he didn't say I had to tell him where we are. We'll call in for information. You know that we'll find Mary Lou and Haley much faster if we work together—'

'You remember that motel we stayed in?' he said, cutting her off. 'Go there and get room two-fourteen.'

'Why not just meet in the parking lot?'

'Leave your side arm on your left front tire,' he told her. 'And your keys locked in the car, on the passenger's side floor.'

Up ahead, Beth's blue Focus was signaling to make a left into the Dunkin' Donuts parking lot. Way to go, Beth.

'When you get in the room, take off your clothes and cuff yourself to a chair. They had those chairs with the arms that were attached, remember?'

'Sam—'

'You said my rules.'

Alyssa was silent. He drove past the Dunkin' Donuts, signaling to make a left into the parking lot for a paint store that was two blocks down. He'd drop Kyle here, ditch the car, then head into the parking lot for the twenty-four-hour Wal-Mart that was across the street. He would stand just inside the door of the department store and still have a clear view of the Dunkin' Donuts, while he waited for a cab.

From that vantage point, he could see all the way into the

little doughnut shop. With its big windows, it was like looking into a fish bowl. Last night he'd been able to take an inventory and had noticed that they were running low on glazed doughnuts. He'd be able to see anything that went on in there.

'Yes to the keys, no to the weapon on the wheel,' Alyssa told him. 'You know I can't leave it somewhere where it might fall into the wrong hands. I'll leave the curtains open in the room and my side arm on the bed, where you can see it through the window – and where you can see me, too, in the chair. Clothes on.'

'If you leave your clothes on, I'll have to search you,' he pointed out.

'Yeah,' she said, with what sounded like genuine amusement in her voice. 'That's why you wanted me to take off my clothes. So you wouldn't have to search me.'

'Hey, I figured it was worth a try.'

'It'll take me about fifteen minutes to get there,' she told him.

'You're serious,' he said.

'Yes. Please be there.' She hung up.

No way was she serious. Although, damn, she sounded sincere.

Fifteen minutes . . .

First things first. If Kyle, here, walked into the doughnut shop and back out again without getting arrested, he'd think about taking a spin past that motel.

Sam turned to the kid. 'Show time. Keep the hat pulled down over your face and your hands out of the pockets of your jacket. That's important. Hands in view at all times, all right? Just walk in there and stand in the line at the counter.'

'Is someone going to shoot me?' Kyle asked. 'Thinking that I'm you?'

'No,' Sam said. 'Not if you keep your hands out of the jacket.'

'Who are you?' For the first time all morning there was actually a flicker of life in his eyes.

'One of the good guys,' Sam told him.

The kid snorted. 'Yeah, right.' He pulled the hat down and got out of the car. 'Something tells me it would've been easier just to suck your dick.'

'Maybe for you, but not for me,' Sam said.

* * *

Alyssa was in place.

She'd seen Beth Weiss's car pull into the lot. And now her radio headset crackled.

'Still no sign that Starrett is following.'

Yeah, like they'd be able to spot him. Did they really think finding him was going to be *that* easy?

Sam Starrett was beyond good. He'd told her once that one of the keys to remaining invisible while following someone was to detach emotionally. Emotional energy gave the people being followed that sixth sense tingle at the back of their neck, that feeling that someone was watching them.

She tried to do the same now as she watched for him. No emotional attachment. No emotion at all . . .

Alyssa knew Sam well enough to know he wouldn't look the way she'd expect him to look, and he wouldn't be where she'd expect him to be.

It was a complicated game they were playing. He *knew* she was looking for him. But she knew *he* knew she was looking for him, and likewise, he knew *she* knew *he* knew, etc. etc. etc., ad nauseam.

It came down to both of them trying to second-guess each other. Would he do the obvious, simply because she'd expect him *not* to do the obvious? Or . . .?

Please God, don't let him show up here at all. Please let him already be back at that Motel Six they'd stayed at their first night here in Gainesville. Please let him be ready to trust her.

Surely he'd figured out that both the desk clerk he'd talked to at the Sunset Motel and the roommate had given up information about Beth Weiss far too easily.

Surely he knew that the FBI had found and questioned Beth

in Orlando, that they were using her as bait to reel him in.

'When he shows,' Alyssa said into her radio, '*if* he shows, I'm the one who approaches him, is that clear? No one so much as moves an inch.'

'We've got him,' one of the Gainesville agents said, excitement in his voice. 'Heading across the parking lot.'

Alyssa looked. The height was right and so was the hair, but . . . That wasn't Sam. She opened her mouth to tell them to hold off, to keep out of sight, that this was somebody wearing Sam's baseball cap, someone he'd sent in to test the waters, or maybe even to be a decoy.

He'd pulled that particular hat trick on her before.

He was watching to see what would happen. And what he needed to see was Hat Guy go up to the counter, order a doughnut, and walk back out – unapproached.

Alyssa, after all, was supposed to be over at that motel, cuffing herself to a chair.

After Hat Guy walked away, Sam would wait a few more minutes, and then come out of wherever he was hiding. He'd be far less careful, and she'd finally be able to spot him and—

'Hold off,' she said. 'We don't know that's him. Let's make sure we have a positive ID. And remember, *I* approach him.'

'He's getting closer!'

'Jules, stay out of sight,' Alyssa ordered into her microphone. 'Everyone stay in place. That's not—'

Max's voice cut her off. 'Take him down.'

'*What?*' she said. 'What are you *doing*?'

'I'm sorry, Alyssa. The deal was only good if Starrett took it right away.'

'I'm still negotiating the deal! Max, you're not even here! Shit!' How could he give that order from hundreds of miles away? As Alyssa watched, twenty agents stormed Sam's decoy, taking him down, pressing his face against the asphalt. 'Oh, *shit!*'

'Sorry,' Max said again, sounding anything but.

Alyssa took off the radio headset, flinging it down as she

turned and spotted . . .

Sam's hiding place.

Had to be.

She knew where he was and where he was going to go – out the back door. Now all she had to do was get there first. She ran for her car.

Sam sighed as about twenty agents in FBI windbreakers damn near sat on poor Kyle.

He could see Alyssa over in the Dunkin' Donuts, a scarf over her head and sunglasses on as she tried to be invisible in one of her designer suits. Tried, and failed. It was the curse of being an incredibly beautiful woman. In order to hide herself, she had to go to extremes like the scarf and glasses. Which made her extremely easy to pick out of a crowd.

As he watched, Kyle's baseball cap came off, and Alyssa reacted.

Yeah, that's right, sweet thing. It wasn't him.

They were spending an awful lot of time and energy searching for him, when they should have been looking for Mary Lou and Haley.

Okay, it was definitely time to go, while Alyssa was still caught up asking Kyle all kinds of questions about Sam. He could practically hear the kid's answers. Short hair styled and blown dry, clean shaven, dark pants and a white shirt with the collar open. Tweed sports jacket.

Sam had never owned a tweed sports jacket before, not in his entire life.

Kyle pointed down the street, toward the lot where Sam had left the car.

Good boy.

Of course, Sam didn't own a tweed jacket anymore. It was now sitting, abandoned, in a shopping cart in aisle 14.

He headed for the rear of the store, toward the delivery bays that exited into the back parking lot, purposely taking the aisle that featured hair care products. He grabbed a bottle of goo or gel or what-the-fuck from the shelf and squeezed some into his hand as he walked. He set the bottle down on a shelf with some disposable diapers, rubbed his hands together, and used the goop to slick his hair down and back from his face.

He'd replaced the tweed with the dark suit jacket that matched the pants and put on a rather anemic-looking yellow tie with gray flecks. It was the opposite of a power tie. It was a 'don't notice me' tie.

When he caught sight of himself in a mirror, he realized that he could have walked out the front door. No way, not in a million years, would anyone recognize him.

Not even Alyssa Locke.

He wiped his hands clean on a dish towel as he crossed through housewares, and then there he was, at the door marked EMPLOYEES ONLY.

He slowed down and stopped, pretending to look at a rack of little boys' bathing suits as he made sure there was no one around to challenge him when he went through that door.

There were two shoppers nearby, one an elderly black woman in a housedress that didn't cover her swollen ankles, and the other a woman or maybe even a short man in baggy jeans and an oversized shirt and a knit skull cap. They were together, talking about inflation, so Sam started toward the door, but then the androgynous one turned toward him, and—

Holy fuck, it was Alyssa Locke.

She'd handcuffed him to her before he could even tell his feet to run.

'Hey, Sam. Nice tie,' she said, then yanked him through that back door.

Seventeen

The hallway was empty – Alyssa saw Sam take that in in one swift glance.

Right before he grabbed her and slammed her up against the concrete block wall.

She must've made a sound of pain, because the look on his face was almost comical. That is, if there was anything funny at all about more than two hundred pounds of angry Navy SEAL jamming his arm up underneath her throat, cutting off her air.

'I'm sorry. God, Lys, I'm so sorry,' he told her as he groped her, searching for her side arm.

The one she'd carefully locked in the trunk of her car before coming inside the store.

She tried turning her head aside so she could get some air. She flailed, hitting him as hard as she could, but he just moved his arm, pinning her more completely.

'I'm not going to bring you in, you fool,' she said, although it came out gasped and garbled.

He got the gist of it. 'Damn right you're not.'

'No, Sam—'

She really couldn't breathe. His grip on her tightened, and she knew he was trying to make her black out from lack of air. Whereupon he'd search her for her keys, free himself from the cuffs, and, first making sure she was breathing again, take off for parts unknown.

And then she'd be back to talking to him on the phone.

His face was an inch from hers – the way he'd lifted her off the ground brought them nose to nose – and she stared into his eyes, shaking her head as much as she could, pleading with her eyes. *Don't do this.*

She'd never seen him like this before. He was furious and terrified and remorseful as hell. It was not without possibility that he might actually start to cry. 'I'm sorry,' he just kept saying. 'Don't make me hurt you. Alyssa, I don't want to hurt you . . .'

'Don't—' she managed to gasp as she struggled to get free, or at least get a breath. Just one good breath . . .

So she could beg him to trust her.

So she could tell him she'd locked the keys to these cuffs in the trunk of her car as well. If she blacked out, then he'd be cuffed to dead weight.

Cuffed to . . .

Alyssa stopped fighting him – which wasn't the easiest thing to do when her brain was sending 'no air' panic signals to her body – and went limp.

Sam, however, was ready for her to do that – turning into a dead weight was a basic defense technique from Street Fighting 101 – but he *did* have to adjust his grip on her, which loosened his hold on her arm.

It was the arm with which she was cuffed to him. Which meant she didn't have the reach she needed to hit him in the eye – a blow that didn't need a lot of force behind it to be painful as hell.

Instead, she tried for an elbow to his nose, and – whoa, what a lucky break – to avoid that, he brought his head down and closer to her. Which put his nose well out of range, but made it possible for her to throw her arm – leading with that same elbow – up and over Sam's head. The cuffs and Sam's arm followed, looping around his neck.

That put his own arm into an unnatural position, and now when she went limp, he had to back off fast and duck much farther forward in order to slip their arms back over his head. If he hadn't, she would've wrenched his shoulder damn near out of its socket.

It was then, when he backed off like that, that he finally lost his hold on her.

And there was air. Glorious, wonderful air.

Alyssa took deep gasping breaths as she went down to the floor.

Or at least as close to the floor as she could get while handcuffed to Sam.

She went instantly into a floor fighting position, on her side, one leg bent beneath her, and used the full force of her other leg to kick at him. Hard. She aimed for his knee. He was expecting her to target his groin so she connected and heard him swear.

She kicked him again, but he was a fast learner, and she only managed to hit his thigh.

He grabbed her foot, yanking her off balance before he pulled up hard on the cuffs. He jerked her all the way up onto her feet, obviously expecting her to resist. But she didn't. She pushed herself even farther forward, moving toward him instead of trying to back away.

It put him at a serious disadvantage, especially when she moved even closer – close enough to step between his legs and . . .

She hit him so hard with her knee that his feet left the floor. She herself was knocked off balance as the handcuffs dragged her forward and down with him, and she scrambled to stay on her feet.

He made a sound that was a mix of pain and despair, and God knows a hit to the balls like that would've put another man on the ground for good, whimpering in a fetal position, but Sam was back up and at her instantly, slamming her against that wall again.

But she was ready for him this time, and she tucked her head into him, grabbing him in as much of a bear hug as she could, with her one arm twisted and crushed between them.

She was winning, she realized – if this could even remotely be called *winning* – because he was trying his damnedest not to hurt her.

He could have smashed her head against the wall. He could have broken her arm with very little effort. He could have slapped her or punched her or kicked her to the ground a dozen different times.

But he didn't. And he wouldn't.

She was fighting him as hard and as dirty as she could, and he was being careful.

'I'm not going to turn you in,' she told him again, talking directly to his armpit. All she had to do to stay in this fight was keep him away from her throat. 'If I *was*, my backup would be here by now – twenty FBI agents cleaning this floor with your fancy suit!'

He was breathing hard, each exhale moving her hair, as he pinned her there, as he went through her pockets, searching for her keys.

'Like they did to your friend across the street,' she told him. Once Sam found what he was looking for, he was going to wrestle her to the ground, sit on her, and unlock the cuffs. Except the only keys she was carrying were her car keys and the key to her lockbox in the trunk.

He was going to be very disappointed.

She couldn't move with the full weight of his body against hers, the wall grinding into her backbone. He'd protected himself against another kick to the groin by pushing himself between her legs. She could kick the backs of his legs with her heels, but she couldn't get up enough force that way to do anything but annoy him.

'Forty-eight hours,' she persisted as he attempted to get into the front left pocket of her jeans, as she tried to make it as difficult as possible for him to do so. 'We have forty-eight hours to find Mary Lou and Haley, and you're wasting time!'

Someone was coming.

Sam heard it at the same time she did. A door opening. Voices. Two or three of them. Young women, girls, from the sound of it, heading toward them, about to turn the corner and see . . .

Alyssa wrapped her legs around Sam and lifted her head.

She could taste his surprise as she kissed him.

Kissed him? Hell, she ate him alive. She soul-sucked him so hard, it made those kisses they'd shared in the back of her car seem staid by comparison.

It took him maybe three one-hundreths of a second to catch on and to kiss her back, making it look as if they'd ducked through the 'Employees Only' door to grab a semi-public quickie.

Alyssa heard the girls giggling, felt them hurry past, felt Sam hard between her legs as he ground himself against her, as she tasted blood. . . .

God, at some point in their struggle, she'd hit him so hard he'd cut his lip on his own teeth.

He didn't seem to care. He didn't seem to notice that the girls had gone out the door, that he and Alyssa were alone once more.

He just kept kissing her.

She tried to pull back, but he wouldn't let her go.

'Stop,' she said into his mouth. 'Sam—'

It was hard as hell to talk with his tongue in her mouth. Doubly hard because part of her didn't really want him to remove it.

'Please,' she said, but it probably sounded as if she were begging for more, because he kissed her even more deeply, but slower now. Sweetly.

Oh, dear God . . .

She could feel his heart pounding, or maybe that was hers because the rhythmic way he was rubbing himself against her was enough to make her . . .

Oh, but heavenly Father, if she *did*, then he'd know that it had been years since she'd . . . since *they'd* . . .

'Stop,' she said, but of course he didn't since she hadn't actually managed to say it aloud.

So she bit him.

Not very hard.

But certainly hard enough to get his attention.

'Shit!'

'Stop,' Alyssa ordered him, even though he already had. He was still pressed against her, though, which made her want to scream. 'I kissed you so they wouldn't see that we were fighting, so they wouldn't call the police. But they just might call security, and if the rent-a-cops find us here, cuffed together like this . . .'

But he didn't move. He just stared at her as she looked back at him, at the graceful shape of his mouth, at the smooth, clean lines of his cheeks, at his eyes – startlingly blue eyes he'd kept too often hidden behind all of his hair, or beneath the brim of one of his infernal and always present baseball caps.

'Now,' she said, trying to sound as if her heart wasn't about to pound out of her chest, as if her body wasn't screaming for them to finish what they'd started, 'will you please trust me enough to put me down and walk out of here with me? My car's just outside.

'I'm here alone,' she continued, knowing that if he was still able to stand after that kick she'd given him, then he had a significant amount of adrenaline charging through his system. It was enough to make everything harder – including his ability to comprehend what she was saying. So she brought it down to the bottom line again. 'I'm not here to turn you in. I made a deal with you, even though you were right about Max. Even though he didn't mean it. But *I* did. We have forty-eight hours to find Haley. Let's stop dicking around and go and do it.'

Sam smiled at that – perhaps it was a poor choice of words.

Damn, he was handsome with his hair cut short and his entire face showing. Some women might not agree because there was nothing pretty about this man. His good looks were rugged and he had a smile that was loaded with testosterone. He had the kind of big, lean, man-sized face that was going to get craggier as he got older. But he'd be just as handsome, possibly even more so, at seventy than he was right now.

The suit he had on was not expensive, but it fit as if it had been tailored to his rangy frame. Or at least it had before he'd ripped out the sleeve.

When Alyssa had first spotted him in the store, she'd looked past him. He was so completely the anti-Sam, right down to the shiny black dress shoes.

The embarrassing truth was, she never would have recognized him if she hadn't had sex with him. In the shower. Hungover and sick as a dog from a night of heavy drinking, handcuffed to Sam with the key temporarily lost, stone cold sober and horrified that she'd slept with him the night before, she *still* hadn't been able to keep herself from jumping him one last time.

Yes, it was because she'd seen him before with his hair wet and slicked back from his face almost exactly like this, that she'd realized it was indeed Sam Starrett inside that business suit.

'What can I do to make you trust me?' she asked, well aware that he still hadn't released her.

'Kiss me again,' he said.

'Look, Starrett, this is serious. I didn't kiss you because I wanted to.' *Liar.* 'I also didn't kiss you because I'm trying to play you. I'm done with that. No more games. It's honesty time. I'm not helping you because I want us to have sex again, because I don't.' *Liar.* 'Nothing's changed between us. I'm helping you because your reasons for wanting to find Haley first and put her someplace safe are good ones. I'm helping you because despite what he says now, Max *did* agree to this deal.'

Sam nodded, but he still didn't let go of her. 'Honesty time. Okay. I should probably tell you that if you don't kiss me again, my adrenaline levels are going to drop. Enough so that my body is going to realize that you kicked me so hard that my balls are now lodged near my tonsils. And at that moment of realization,

I will probably drop to my knees and start retching. Oh, Jesus.'

He let go of her, and she slid down him.

'In case you were offended,' he told her raggedly, 'the hard-on didn't really . . . have anything to do with you. At least not . . . at first. It's a . . . male fighting . . . thing. But as long as . . . we're being completely honest, I feel it's fair to tell you that your making love to me . . . would go a long way toward making me trust you.' He sank to his knees and closed his eyes. 'Oh, *fuck*.'

She wanted to sink down beside him, and close her eyes, too, weary from relief, but they had to keep moving. She looked around. There was a machine selling cans of cold soda a little farther down the hall.

'Of course . . . it's entirely . . . possible I'll never . . . have sex . . . or walk . . . again.'

'Do you have your wallet?' Alyssa asked.

'What, are you going to . . . rob me now, too? Right front pocket . . . pants.'

She fished for his wallet as gently as she could, took out a single. Put the wallet back in her own pocket. 'Come on.' She reached under his arms and helped him to his feet. God, there was a lot of him.

'I was serious . . . about the retching.'

'I know,' she said. 'Let's get you into the car. But first . . .'

She stopped at the soda machine and fed it Sam's dollar. A can of soda clunked out. She handed it to him.

'Hey . . . I wanted . . . Dr Pepper.'

'It's an ice-pack alternative, funnyman.'

A wave of hot air hit them as they went through another door and out into the blinding morning light.

There was no one out in the back lot. Alyssa watched as Sam made note of the fact that there were, indeed, no FBI agents staked out and waiting for them to appear.

She'd parked at the end of a row of employees' cars and she led him in that direction.

'Can you hold off on the retching for just a little bit longer?' she asked.

It wasn't a good sign that he didn't speak, that he just nodded.

She held out her car keys to him. 'I need you to get a couple of things out of the trunk.'

He nodded again. He was gritting his teeth, and she knew that he wanted nothing more than to curl up in a ball in the backseat for about twenty minutes. But, as usual, he was determined to be Superman, so he took her keys, and after about three tries, during which he started sweating all over again, he managed to unlock the trunk.

Alyssa purposely stood back, as far away from both him and the car as the handcuffs would allow.

'There's another key on that ring,' she told him. 'It'll unlock the box that my side arm is stored in.'

Sam turned to look at her, surprise and wonder in his eyes. It almost canceled out the haze from his pain.

Almost.

'Thank you for trusting me,' she told him. Although it sure would have been easier if he'd trusted her *before* she damn near killed him. She gestured toward the trunk, toward her handgun. 'This is about me, trusting you, in return.'

He understood. He unlocked the box and took out the weapon. Checking to make sure it was loaded, and then that the safety was on, he stashed it in his jacket pocket. 'Thanks.' It came out as little more than a whisper.

'The keys to the cuffs are in there, too,' she said. 'In my fanny pack.'

He was trying his best to stand up straight, but it was more than clear that he was fighting a losing battle. Of course, he'd never admit that, not in a million years.

Alyssa grabbed her fanny pack, took the car keys from him, and closed the trunk. She led him to the front of the car, unlocked the passenger's side door, and went in first, crawling over the parking brake. Men were entirely too fragile.

Sam got in very gingerly, and when he closed the door it didn't quite latch.

Alyssa reached across him, opened it, and closed it.

He had the can of soda strategically placed, the seat reclined, and his eyes closed as she found the key to the cuffs and unlocked them both.

But he opened his eyes and caught her hand, turning it so he could take a closer look at her wrist, where the cuffs had rubbed her skin raw. 'I'm so sorry I didn't trust you,' he said.

'Yeah, well . . .' Alyssa pulled her hand away from his so she could start the car. 'It's not that big a deal. Especially since I've been wanting to kick you really hard in the balls for a couple of years now.'

Sam's own wrist was equally abraded. But he didn't give it a glance. He just closed his eyes again. 'I don't know which is scarier, thinking you're joking or thinking you're serious.'

'We have to figure out a game plan,' Alyssa said. 'With only forty-eight hours . . .'

'Can I please just have ten minutes to sit here and weep?'

'Can you listen while you do it?'

'You know when you hit your funny bone really hard?' Sam asked, his eyes tightly closed. 'And you're all, "Go away, go away, don't touch me, I just need to be alone so I can scream"? This is like that only much, much worse.'

'So far no retching,' she commented.

'Yes, thanks for noticing. I'm very proud of myself.'

'I have the information that Beth Weiss from the Sunset Motel gave us after we found her in Orlando,' Alyssa told him.

'Okay. I'm listening.'

'She said that Mary Lou and Haley checked out at around twenty to ten. I checked the schedule and the next bus that left Gainesville was at 10:35, which works, but it was going to Sarasota, which doesn't. That's where she was running from, so why would she go back? Next on the schedule was a bus heading for Atlanta. We've questioned the driver, who doesn't remember seeing her, but it's possible she altered her appearance, so—'

Sam's eyes opened. 'Holy fuck,' he said.

'What?'

'Sarasota,' he said, struggling to sit up. He reached along the seat to take it out of its reclined position and ended up smacking himself on the back as it sprang forward. 'Ow! Fuck! Mary Lou went back to Sarasota.'

Alyssa shook her head. 'Why would she do that?'

'*Hide where they've already searched* – I told her that once. We were talking about some movie or some book that she'd read, and I told her if I was the fugitive or public enemy number one or whoever we were talking about, I'd end up back where I'd started. I said, then when everyone's looking for me in Alaska—'

Mary Lou had told her mother that she was going to Alaska. 'Did you really say Alaska?'

'Yeah. Because that's what this was about. I remember now – it was a book she was reading about some guy who went to Anchorage because the mob was after him, and I was like, unless he changes his habits along with his appearance, the mob's going to find him in Anchorage. I mean, sure, he can go out on the tundra and live in a house that's five hundred miles from his nearest neighbors, but the reason the mob won't find him isn't because he's isolated. It's because his isolation keeps him from doing the things that'll allow the mob to catch him. Stealing cars or gambling or fencing hot TVs. When it's just him and the moose, and the moose don't particularly want a great deal on a TV set . . .

'I told her if this stupid ass guy in this book really wanted to get lost, he could get lost just as easily back where he started, in Newark, New Jersey. He just had to hang with a new crowd and stay away from the strip clubs and stop fencing TVs. No gambling, no prostitutes, no strippers, no drugs – he had to cut his ties with all those fun things the mob has its fingers in. He could live two streets down from the mob boss, but if he joined the church choir and volunteered at the old folks' home and really changed his habits completely – you know, along with his appearance – he'd be invisible. And if he left a bunch of clues out there that he was heading for Alaska, he would be even *more* invisible. Because everyone on the mob's payroll has already looked for him in New Jersey. They figure he's long gone, so they're waiting for him to show in Alaska, when in reality, where is he? Back in Newark.' Sam shook his head. 'That's what I told her. I had no idea she was actually listening. She usually didn't want to hear what I had to say.'

'So where did Mary Lou go?' Alyssa asked. 'Is Sarasota back where she started? Or San Diego?'

Sam was silent, staring out the window, wincing slightly as he repositioned the can of soda.

She knew he was thinking about that conversation he'd had with his next door neighbor – Don DaCosta, the mentally challenged man who saw 'aliens' hanging out around Sam's house.

DaCosta had been questioned – gently, per Sam's specific request – by agents who were still staking out the neighborhood and keeping an eye on both his and Sam's houses. DaCosta couldn't remember the name of the dark-skinned man he'd called the 'flower guy'. The man he'd referred to as Mary Lou's friend.

How close had Mary Lou and this 'friend' of hers been?

'I think she'd go to San Diego if she could,' Sam said, glancing over at Alyssa. 'But I don't think she had the money. Knowing how much she got for her car and knowing that she paid cash when she stayed at the Sunset Motel . . . I don't think she could make it as far as California. I think she and Haley are in Sarasota.'

Alyssa nodded. 'Then Sarasota is where we'll start.'

'This is one freaking long shot,' Sam said.

'We have to start somewhere,' she told him.

He was quiet as she took the entrance ramp to 75 south. In fact, he was quiet for so long that when she glanced over at him, she expected to find him asleep.

Instead, he was watching her with those intensely blue eyes, his hair still slicked back from his face in that style Alyssa would forever associate with raw, screaming sex.

'I wish we had more than forty-eight hours,' he said quietly, and she knew he wasn't just talking about the time they had left to find Mary Lou and Haley.

It was best to be honest, best not to leave him hoping for something that she'd be crazy to let happen.

'I'm doing this to help you find Haley,' she told him. 'As far as you and I are concerned, I'm still feeling like we've been there, done that.'

'I hear you,' he said, but she knew he didn't believe her.

And when he looked at her like that, with his heart in his eyes, she wasn't sure she believed herself.

Eighteen

'Jules Cassidy to see you, sir.'

Max sighed and leaned forward to push the button on his intercom. 'Send him in, Laronda.'

The team had returned from Gainesville, pissed as hell that Sam Starrett had slipped through their fingers. Max was betting that they'd drawn straws to decide who would come and confront him – and lay the blame for this goatfuck squarely on his desk.

Which was exactly where it belonged.

Jules Cassidy opened the door and came in, a modern-day Oliver Twist. *Please, sir, may I have some more?*

Interestingly, there was no sign of recrimination or even anger in his eyes. Just cool curiosity.

Max looked at him over the top of his reading glasses. It was a 'this better be good' look, and since they both knew damn well that it *wasn't* good, that Jules had no business coming in here in the first place, the kid should have been shitting bricks.

But Jules gazed back at him, pretending to be unperturbed. 'May I sit?'

'No. Whatever this is, it's not going to take long enough for you to sit.'

Jules actually laughed. 'I really have to learn to do that,' he said. 'That icy stare thing. It's very effective.'

'I'm busy,' Max said tersely. 'If you have some kind of complaint—'

'I'm not here to complain, sir,' Jules cut him off. 'I just wanted to make sure that today's little exercise went down the way you planned.'

Max kept his face expressionless. The office was filled with angry people who were sure that his interference had created a giant snafu. And yet somehow Jules Cassidy, a man most people didn't want working for them because – horrors! – he was gay, had figured it all out.

'So what was it?' Jules asked. 'The committee from Politicians R Us breathing down your neck? This way you could tell the senators and congressmen, "Well, we almost had Starrett. Unfortunately, he got away. But see how hard we're trying?" This way Alyssa finds him and gives him those forty-eight hours you promised, without *you* getting reamed for it.

'What I'd like to know,' he continued, 'is how you knew Alyssa was going to position herself outside of the doughnut shop, when she didn't even let anyone on the team there in Gainesville know. I'd also like to know if she's called in yet. She vanished right after we found out we had the wrong man. I can only assume she's with Sam right now.'

Max nodded as he took off his glasses and tossed them down on his desk. 'So what do you want, Cassidy? A promotion for being so smart?'

Surprise, and then something very like hurt, flashed in the younger man's eyes. 'That's not why I'm here. Sir.'

'I know. Sit down,' Max said more gently than he'd ever spoken to Jules before, trying to make up for being such a bastard.

As he watched, Jules sat on the edge of a chair. This kid was the real deal. He was not only smart, he was also extremely loyal. And Max really had to stop thinking of him as a kid. He only looked ridiculously young. In truth Jules was rapidly approaching thirty.

'You're worried about your partner,' Max said. He sighed. 'Well, I'm worried about her, too. She hasn't called in. I don't know if she's thinking clearly enough to piece it together the way you did. I may have made her so angry at me that . . .'

He could see the words he'd left unspoken in Jules's eyes. *That I've lost her forever.* But, Christ, maybe that was part of his plan, too. Maybe he had some subconscious desire to push Alyssa away. He thought of Gina, sleeping in his arms last night . . .

'If Alyssa calls me,' Jules said, leaning forward in his seat, 'I'll tell her—'

Max shook his head. 'No. Not over her cell phone. Someone might start monitoring that. I don't want word to get out – in fact this conversation doesn't leave this room.'

'Of course, sir.'

'But you have my permission to give her whatever information she asks for. Don't ask her if she's with Starrett, though. And don't let her tell you, either. Keep her from saying it. You and I aren't going to know anything about that, all right? As far as we're concerned, she's on her own, following a lead.'

Jules nodded. 'Yes, sir. Don't ask, don't tell. I'm familiar with the concept.'

Max forced a smile. 'But if you do see her in person, go wild in my defense, would you?'

'I don't think I'm going to see her. At least not for forty-eight hours.'

'Yeah,' Max said. 'I don't think so either.'

Jules got to his feet. 'How *did* you know what she was going to do? You know, put me in the doughnut shop in her place, with one of her scarves on my head?'

'I didn't know. But when you headed toward Gainesville . . .' Max smiled. 'I trusted she had something good up her sleeve.'

Jules nodded. 'Thank you for taking the time to see me, sir.'

'Yeah,' Max said. 'Oh, and Jules?'

Cassidy stopped, his hand on the doorknob.

Max cleared his throat and picked up his glasses. 'Gina Vitagliano's apparently checked out of her motel room. Did she, uh, give you any idea where she was going?'

'No, sir. But there are dozens of other little places to stay right there on the beach.'

'Yeah, I'm aware of that,' Max said. There were 155, to be exact.

'The info came in, you know, regarding her trip overseas,' Jules told him. 'Did that cross your desk yet?'

Ah, Christ. 'No,' Max said. 'What have you heard?'

Jules made a cringing face. 'Oh, sweetie, you're going to hate this, but Gina's going to Africa. I believe her final destination is Kenya.'

Max kept a whole string of expletives from escaping by closing his mouth and gritting his teeth. But somewhere in his brain, a vein definitely popped. *Kenya.*

'What I *really* hate,' Max somehow managed to say without sounding apoplectic, 'is you calling me sweetie.'

Jules actually blushed as he went out the door. 'Sorry, sir.'

Sam was driving even though his balls still ached. There was no doubt about it, he was going to be feeling Alyssa's mighty wrath for days, if not weeks, to come.

Every time he caught a glimpse of the scrapes and bruising on her wrist from the handcuffs, his queasiness returned. He suspected those weren't the only bruises he'd given her, because God knows he was feeling pretty tender in various places himself.

Every time he'd tried to bring it up, to talk about it, to apologize again, she'd shrugged it off. *Forget it, it's over.*

But it was kind of hard to forget, considering that she wouldn't have a single mark on her if he'd only trusted her.

She was talking to Jules on the phone, making notes on a pad on her lap.

The stretch of road they were on was straight, so Sam took his eyes off it to glance down and read what she'd written.

Publix supermarket, she'd scribbled, along with an address, and a date – *May 24th – and Mary Lou never shows up for work, no phone call, never returns.*

So they knew where Mary Lou had worked. It was worth going over there, talking to her coworkers, as well as checking the Alcoholics Anonymous blue book to see where the meetings were in that area – meetings Mary Lou had gone to on a nightly basis in San Diego. They could try to figure out which meetings were close to her Sarasota home, too. Or – better yet – which meetings were close to the house that she and Janine had shared with Clyde. The two addresses weren't so far apart that Mary Lou would necessarily want to change meeting locations after a move.

The AA meetings were support groups. Drunks who didn't want to drink, leaning on each other. It seemed like a shaky way to rebuild a life, but it really could work.

It had for Sam's mother.

'Uh-huh,' Alyssa said to Jules, as she wrote down what looked like a name. *Ihbraham Rahman*, a dash and then the words *gardener, also currently AWOL*.

Hoo-yah! That had to be the name of Donny DaCosta's so-called flower guy. The man Mary Lou was probably screwing on the side. Except, maybe it couldn't really be called on the side, since by the end of their marriage, Sam hadn't been sleeping with her at all. She was just living in his house, using his last name, taking care of his daughter, and probably getting it on with the neighborhood gardener.

Except there was something really wrong with this picture.

Ihbraham Rahman was an Arab-American with very dark skin.

And Mary Lou was a racist – something Sam hadn't found out until months after they were married. She wasn't a vicious racist, the way his father had been. And she probably would have been offended if someone had called her a racist to her face. She never used obviously derogatory words – she would never dream of it. But she had a real 'us' and 'them' attitude that only worked to perpetuate the racial divide.

Instead of trying to find similarities between different races and cultures – a philosophy that Walt and Dot had preached at Sam and Noah endlessly – Mary Lou focused on differences.

No, no matter how Sam tried to view the situation, he just couldn't see Mary Lou hooking up with a man who wasn't Wonder Bread white.

Unless she'd somehow had her eyes opened, had her archaic way of thinking overhauled . . .

Yeah, and maybe she'd also learned to fly by flapping her arms.

He glanced down Alyssa's pad.

Kelly Paoletti, she had written, *knew Rahman, too.*

Holy shit. Wasn't *that* one hell of a coincidence? Except for the fact that Sam didn't believe in coincidences. It was a variation on Occam's razor. If you're looking for a terrorist, and you've got a likely suspect, chances are he's the terrorist you're looking for.

Maybe he was wrong about Mary Lou and this Rahman. But no. He just couldn't see it.

It was possible that Rahman had a light-skinned associate, though, that Mary Lou was involved with. And of course, there was always Donny's blond alien.

'So Rahman's already been investigated – six months ago, while he was in the hospital with a head injury – and he's believed not to be connected,' Alyssa said to Jules, obviously for Sam's benefit. Wasn't *that* interesting? She paused, listening. 'So let me get this straight. We have a guy – Rahman – who gets his skull fractured during the Coronado assassination attempt. We've placed him there, in the crowd at the Navy base, during the terrorist attack, but he's *not* connected?'

She paused. 'No . . . No, wait, let me finish with Rahman first. So as of just a few days ago he allegedly comes knocking on Starrett's door, possibly looking for Mary Lou – this coming from a neighbor who's mentally challenged, who also gives us reports of some light-haired man, his alien, who's following Rahman. Okay, yeah, you're right, if Rahman's part of the terrorist cell behind the Coronado attack, he's probably *not* going to march right up to the front door of Mary Lou's house and ring the bell. But still . . . Her prints are on that weapon. They got there somehow.' Pause. 'So Rahman's being checked out again, except now he's vanished.' She shot Sam a hard look. 'And vanishing when the authorities want to ask questions never looks good.'

Yeah, yeah. Point taken.

'So Tom Paoletti's wife—'

'She's not his wife,' Sam whispered, and got another sharp look from Alyssa. No talking while she was on the phone with Jules.

'So Kelly Ashton, who just married Tom Paoletti—' she said.

No kidding. Kelly finally married the commander. About freaking time.

'—has no recollection of Ihbraham being associated with this mystery man with blond hair. Although hair is only about *the* easiest characteristic to alter.' Alyssa sighed, jotting the words *library* and AA *meetings* on her pad.

Yeah, that, along with work, about summed it up as far as what Sam knew about Mary Lou's activities outside of the house. There were no meetings supporting extremist Islamic jihad on the FBI's list, either.

Of course it was entirely likely that the terrorist fucking had been an in-house activity.

'Okay, let me know if anything more comes up on Rahman,' Alyssa continued. 'So tell me now about this thing that just came in.' She listened for a moment, but then froze, pen above paper. 'Oh, dear God . . .'

'What?' Sam asked. Her tone was enough to strike terror in his heart. His biggest fear was that the FBI investigation would uncover Mary Lou's and Haley's bodies.

Alyssa glanced at him as she shook her head. Yeah, he knew. He was supposed to stay quiet so Jules wouldn't know they were together. But come on . . .

'How long were they in there?' she asked.

They wasn't a good word.

Frustration and exasperation rang in her voice. 'Well, what's their guess? They do know how to guess?' She listened, then, 'Shit.'

It was a quiet *shit*. A very, *very* bad news *shit*. As if the look on her face wasn't enough of a clue that whatever Jules was telling her was really going to hurt.

Sam had a strong feeling that crushed balls had nothing on the pain that was coming.

'Please,' she said. 'Keep me updated. Anything that comes in. No matter how little.' Pause. 'Thanks, Jules.'

'Tell me,' Sam ordered as she hung up her phone.

'It's not conclusive,' she said. 'There's been no positive ID.'

Oh, no . . .

Alyssa actually touched him, her hand on his arm. 'Maybe you should pull over.'

Sam nodded. 'Yeah.' The nearest exit wasn't for another six miles, so he just pulled to the right on to the shoulder of the highway.

It took forever to get there, to brake to a full stop, to put the car into park, to turn and face Alyssa and see the sympathy in her eyes. Oh, Jesus . . .

'This isn't conclusive,' she said.

'You said that.'

'I wanted to make sure you understood—'

'Alyssa, *tell* me.'

She nodded. 'Bodies have been found. A woman. And a child who looks to be about Haley's age.'

No. 'Where?'

'Just west of Sarasota,' she said. 'In the trunk of a car. The car's been burned, and the bodies are . . . well, hard to identify. As far as anyone can tell, they've been there somewhere between two and three weeks.'

Sam sat in silence, just looking at her.

'I'm so sorry,' she whispered.

'No,' he said. His stomach was churning. 'Don't be. Because it's not them.'

She nodded, even forced a smile. 'You're probably right.' Yeah, she didn't believe *that* for one second. 'Let me drive now, okay?'

Sam nodded, opened the door, and pulled himself out, forgetting to be extra careful. Holy fucking shit, these stupid pants were too freaking tight, and they really probably only brushed against him, but that was enough, and he was on the ground, on his knees, by the back of the car, fighting nausea all over again.

Alyssa was there, her hands cool against his face. 'Oh, Sam.'

She probably thought he was going to get sick because the thought of Haley burned to death in the trunk of a car was so fucking awful.

'It's not them in that trunk,' he said through gritted teeth. 'I know it's not. I just . . . whacked myself getting out of the car. Hypersensitive today.' He forced himself to look at her. 'Which is good, actually. It gives me something else to focus on.'

Alyssa laughed at that, as he'd hoped she would. 'Well, shoot, I'll be happy to kick you again, whenever you want.'

Sam laughed then, too, but allowing himself to do that was a mistake, because it opened the door to everything else he was trying not to feel. His eyes almost instantly filled with tears.

No, no, no . . .

Oh, please, don't let her notice . . .

But he knew she did. Alyssa noticed everything. She pushed back a chunk of his hair that had fallen over his forehead, and her touch was heartbreakingly gentle.

'You do get through it, you know,' she told him quietly. 'Losing someone you love. You may never get over it, but you *do* get through it.'

'Yeah, well, I haven't lost Haley yet.' He forced himself to his feet. They had to get back in the car before some state trooper came to check them out. 'Let's get to Sarasota, go to that Publix, and talk to some people who might know Mary Lou.'

His use of present tense was not lost on Alyssa, who nodded. But she also touched his arm, her hand warm against his elbow. 'Careful getting in the car.'

'Yeah.'

Gina called from a pay phone, giving her name and asking to speak to Max.

He picked up almost immediately. 'Kenya?'

'I'm fine, thanks,' she said. 'And how are you? Did you sleep at all last night?'

'No. Why Kenya?'

His voice was so cold, she almost faltered. But she'd made up her mind. The worst he could do was hang up on her.

'Because I've made friends with some people who are doing good things there, and I need to do *some*thing worthwhile. Look, that's not what I called to talk about. I called because I have a favor to ask you.'

He was silent. Max was capable of the loudest silences in the world.

But he'd taught her everything she knew about negotiating during all those days she'd spent on the hijacked airliner, and she ignored it. She knew it was only meant to rattle her.

Of course, it was working.

'It's a big favor,' she said, resisting the urge to ask him if he were still there. He was. She knew he was. 'I have this problem. It's about sex.'

There should have been a response here, even if it was a growl of anger or disbelieving laughter, but Max's silence just stretched on.

'I'm all jammed up about it,' she continued. 'I haven't been with someone since, well, you know.'

'Since you were raped.' His voice was so cold. 'I thought we decided to put that word back into our working vocabulary.'

340

'Yeah,' she said. 'Thank you. We did. Since I was raped.'

'No,' Max said. 'I can't help you.'

'Maybe you should wait to hear what I'm asking.'

'I know exactly what you're asking, and I'm telling you no.'

He only sounded so glacial because he was freaking out. She knew that. She *knew* that. Still, it took everything she had not to mumble an apology and run from the phone.

'Guys my age are afraid to get close to me,' she told him, and her voice only shook a little. 'I completely wig them out.'

She heard him draw in a breath – ragged proof that he was human and not some relentlessly calm, cold robot. 'I'm very sorry to hear that, but—'

'I'm not asking for a relationship, Max. I'm asking for one night. *One.*' Gina closed her eyes and prayed that he wouldn't know she was lying, that he wouldn't be able to hear it in her voice. In truth, she was hoping that one night would lead to another, and another and . . .

'I'm sorry—'

'I need you,' she pleaded, laying as much of it on the line as she dared. 'I know you'll make me feel safe. I *trust* you.'

'Which is exactly why—'

'I want that part of my life back again,' she told him.

'—I can't.'

'I need it back! God damn it, they *stole* that from me!'

His silence wasn't silent anymore. She definitely could hear him breathing, hear him sigh. And when he spoke, there was finally emotion in his voice. 'I'm so sorry.'

'Please,' she whispered.

'Gina, I can't help you. I have to take another call.'

'Okay,' she said, no longer caring whether or not he knew that she was crying. 'I understand. And it's, you know, okay. Really. I'm disappointed, but . . . I've got that gig tonight.' She played her last card. 'I'm sure I'll find *some*one in the bar who's willing to—'

'Don't do this.'

'Someone old enough to be gentle—'

He finally raised his voice. 'Gina, for the love of God—'

'What are you going to do about it?' She wiped her face. This wasn't over yet. 'Send Jules over to arrest me? Except last I heard, picking someone up in a bar wasn't a crime.'

'No, it's just insanity!'

'No, Max,' Gina said. 'Insanity is you saying no when we both know you want to say yes.'

She hung up the phone with a hand that was shaking. She stood there for a moment with her eyes closed, praying that this would work, that she'd see him tonight, that he'd give himself permission not just to confront her in person, but to take her home.

And stay.

Alyssa's cell phone rang while they were in the Publix supermarket.

None of the cashiers in the store knew Mary Lou well enough even to speculate on where she might have gone. The store managers were just as spectacularly lacking in information.

Apparently, while she was employed there, Mary Lou showed up, did her job, kept to herself, read a book during her breaks, and went home. She was responsible and reliable. She always showed up on time. Until the day that she didn't show up at all.

Sam looked exhausted. He was standing and staring at a community bulletin board, at a brightly colored sign advertising a church nursery-school fun fair. It was right next to a help wanted poster for a nanny. A live-in position, the sign said. Room and board plus a generous monthly salary. Single mothers welcome to apply.

Sam interrupted the store manager midsentence. 'That sign been up there for very long?'

The man blinked at him and then at the poster. 'I doubt it.

Anything that's been up for more than two weeks automatically gets taken down.'

'Too bad,' Sam said. 'Because if I were Mary Lou...' He pointed to the poster.

And it was then that her phone rang.

'Thank you for your time,' Alyssa said to the manager.

Sam went from completely exhausted to completely wired in the space of a heartbeat, and all of that intense energy was suddenly focused on Alyssa and her phone.

She went out into the early evening heat and started for the car as she checked her caller ID. 'It's Jules,' she told Sam, and pressed the Talk button. 'Locke.'

Sam caught her around the waist, pulling her close and lowering his head so that his ear was next to hers, so that he could hear, too.

'Yo, it's me,' Jules said. 'I've got thirty seconds to tell you some really bad news. I know you're going to have questions, but I swear, I'm telling you everything I know, and I'll call you again as soon as I hear anything else.'

Sam's arm tightened around her waist, and Alyssa spoke for him. 'Just tell, uh, me.' She'd almost said us. Sam wasn't the only one who was exhausted.

'There's been a car bombing in San Diego.' Jules gave it to them point blank. 'Someone parked a car in Don DaCosta's – you know, Sam's neighbor's – driveway, ran like hell, and the thing blew.'

'Oh, fuck,' Sam said. 'Is Donny okay?'

'I'm really sorry, *Alyssa*, but I don't think so, although the reports coming in are still pretty garbled.' Jules didn't seem fazed by the sound of Sam's voice, but his message made it clear that she shouldn't start broadcasting the fact that the SEAL was in her company. 'We've gotten conflicting casualty reports, although Don seems to be on both of them. Apparently he refused to leave his house, and the fire that started was too intense and ... Okay, yeah, I'm getting something new here that . . . Thanks, George. Yeah, God damn it, it's bad news. I'm sorry, we've confirmed DaCosta's death. One of the agents and at least one firefighter died, too, trying to save him.'

Sam had his eyes closed and the muscles in his jaw were jumping. Don DaCosta had been a friend of his.

Alyssa put her arm around him, but he kept his eyes tightly shut.

But Jules wasn't done. 'That's not all of it, I'm afraid. Kelly Paoletti and Cosmo Richter were apparently there, too, when that bomb went off.'

'What?' Alyssa said. Sam's eyes opened. 'Why? What were they doing there?'

'I don't know. Maybe it was take tea with the town lunatic day.'

'Show a little respect for the dead,' Sam growled. 'He was a good guy.'

Jules was instantly contrite. 'Forgive me. That was insensitive. I didn't realize you knew him that well—'

'I didn't know *they* knew DaCosta,' Alyssa interrupted. She couldn't figure out what Lt Commander Tom Paoletti's perky little blond cheerleader of a wife and Cosmo Richter, a quiet man with freaky-colored eyes and the whispered reputation on the Spec Op grapevine of being a remorseless killing machine when the need arose, were doing together, let alone with DaCosta.

'I didn't either, but I guess they did,' Jules said. 'I don't know their status. One list has them wounded, another has them down as dead. I don't know details. I don't know dick. This just happened – we're still in chaos mode. Again, I apologize for my inappropriate—'

'It's all right,' Sam said. 'I know what it's like. It's so fucking awful, you try to find whatever humor in the situation that you possibly can, with no disrespect intended.'

'Thank you, sweetie. That's very generous of you to say.' Jules cleared his throat. 'I'll call, I promise, as soon as I find out anything else.'

'Any word on the bodies in the trunk?' Alyssa asked. She wasn't sure whether to hope that there was or that there wasn't. The news they'd just received was bad enough. And yet not knowing whether his ex-wife and daughter were dead was taking its toll on Sam.

'I'm not expecting the preliminary forensics report until the morning,' Jules told her. 'But, unofficially, I have to tell you that it doesn't look good. Cause of death is gunshot, not burning. Both bodies have a bullet in the back of their heads.'

Just like Mary Lou's sister. Alyssa didn't dare glance at Sam.

'I'll call you later – I've got to go,' Jules told her. And he was gone.

Sam was, too. He was already getting into the car. 'Let's hit the library,' he said. 'See if anyone there knew Mary Lou. At the same time we can get the information we need about the AA meetings in this area. Actually, maybe we should do that first, since most meetings are in the evening – they'll be starting pretty soon. We can always talk to the librarians in the morning and—'

'Sam.'

He wouldn't look up at her, instead flipping through the pad of notes they'd made during the drive down from Gainesville. 'I'd also like to pay a visit to Haley's day care provider.'

'Sam.'

He glanced at her, but only briefly.

He was terribly upset by the news they'd just received. Alyssa crouched next to the open car door.

'Maybe we should take a break,' she said as gently as she could. 'We're both tired, and you've just found out that some good friends are dead.'

'We don't know that Kelly and Cosmo are—'

'You're right,' she said. 'We don't. But even if it's just Donny, that's bad enough. Why don't we find a motel so we can sleep for a few hours and . . .'

And be more prepared, at least physically if not emotionally, to receive the bad news that was surely coming from that forensics report in the morning.

But Sam was shaking his head. 'If Mary Lou and Haley are still alive—' He broke off, and the expression on his face made her want to cry. 'I can't believe I said *if*.'

Alyssa took his hand. 'Maybe that's a good thing. You know, to be prepared for the worst case scenario.'

'No.' He shook his head, tightly gripping her hand. 'There's no preparing for that. Jules is going to call, and you're going to say, *Oh, no*, and then you're going to have to look me in the eye and tell me that my daughter was murdered by some *fuck* who I'm then going to find and kill.' He finally looked at her, finally held her gaze, and she knew he wasn't kidding. If someone had killed Haley, Sam was going to rip him to pieces.

'But until then, I'm not going to live in the land of *if*,' he continued. 'I can't do that, Lys. Haley's alive until she's dead – no *if*, no *maybe*. And since I haven't heard you say she's dead, I'm going with she's alive. And since she's alive, the same people who killed Janine and Donny DaCosta and maybe Cosmo and Kelly – Jesus God! Tom must be going nuts! You think that was a coincidence she was at Donny's when that bomb went off? Think about it. She and Don both knew Ihbraham Rahman – who also knew Mary Lou. This son of a bitch and the rest of his cell are cleaning up after themselves. This guy is removing anyone who can ID him from the playing field, and if—' He caught himself. '*Since* Mary Lou and Haley are still alive, he's going to be coming after them next. I have to find them first.'

Alyssa nodded. 'Okay. Let's hit some of those AA meetings. But you know it's a long shot, right? Everywhere else she goes, Mary Lou keeps to herself. And if she *was* paying attention to what you told her about changing habits to stay hidden . . .'

'I know,' Sam said. 'But we've got to try.'

She understood. 'After that, we're going to have some down time.' Alyssa told him this. She didn't ask. 'I mean, unless we get an obvious lead.' She didn't think that was going to happen. She thought Mary Lou and Haley were in the forensics lab right now, having autopsies done on their dead bodies. 'I know we'll both be able to think a little more clearly if we get some sleep. If you don't want to get a room, we can park somewhere and just shut our eyes for a few hours.'

'A room?' Sam asked, but it was obvious that he had to try very hard to be his usual obnoxious self.

'Yeah.' She tried hard to pretend, too, that this was business as usual between them. 'As in you get a room and I get *a* room.'

He drew her hand up to his mouth and kissed her fingers. 'Rats. And here I thought my luck was going to change.' He smiled at her, but it was clear that his heart wasn't in it.

Because he had to know that luck didn't play a part in whether or not those bodies belonged to his ex-wife and daughter. It had to do with Mary Lou getting involved, more than six months ago, in something deadly with someone dangerous who she never should have trusted.

And it was already too late for luck to play any part in that.

Tom was making tremendously slow progress through the first of a stack of books about the judicial process when someone actually knocked on his door.

'Come in,' he called.

The door swung open to reveal a squad of SEALs from Team Sixteen. Nearly all of them were wearing BDUs – battle dress uniforms – which was nothing new. It was the way they dressed most of their time on base.

There was nothing unusual about them at all – except for the fact that Duke Jefferson and Izzy Zanella were down on the deck, just finishing tying knots in the ropes that bound the wrists and ankles of the two guards who'd been posted in front of Tom's door.

'Oh, come on,' Tom said. This couldn't happen.

Jay Lopez and Billy Silverman helped Duke and Izzy carry

SUZANNE BROCKMANN

the guards into Tom's room, as Ensigns MacInnough and Collins
– both resplendent in summer whites – shouldered the former
guards' weapons and took their places at the door.

'Time to go, sir,' Chief Karmody told Tom. Figures Karmody
– also known as WildCard – would be part of something like
this.

Tom sighed as Lopez, who was carrying his medical kit, put
several syringes in a container marked SHARPS – BIOHAZARD, and
removed a pair of latex gloves from his hands with a snap.

Whatever Lopez had given the guards – and Tom really
didn't want to know – had knocked them out.

Izzy arranged one of the guards on Tom's bunk, positioning
the man so that his back was to the door. He covered him with a
blanket. 'Sleep tight.'

The other guard had been safely stashed in the bathroom.

'I appreciate the effort, men,' Tom said, 'but I'm not going
anywhere.'

'Begging your pardon, sir,' apologized Ensign MacInnough
– a monster of a young man who'd been appropriately nicknamed
Big Mac. 'But we're under direct orders from Lieutenant
Jacquette to test base security. Our assignment is to take you
off the base and to deliver you to an as-yet-undisclosed location. Our orders, sir, are to do this with or without your
cooperation.'

This was a hell of a time for Jazz Jacquette to be war-gaming.
But the look in Big Mac's eyes was unmistakable. Tom could say
no. He could refuse to leave. And Mac would give Lopez a nod,
Tom would get a needle of his own in his ass, and they'd end up
carrying him out of here.

Tom sighed again as he looked around at his men. His *former*
men. They were deadly serious, to the point of downright grim.
No one so much as cracked a smile. Was this really what they
were like these days on an op? 'I'd like you all to know that I'm
leaving under protest.'

'Duly noted, sir,' said Ens. Joel Collins – Tom still thought of

348

him as 'the new guy.' He'd joined the team just a few weeks before Tom had been relieved of his command.

Petty Officer First Class Mark Jenkins was standing watch at the top of the stairs. 'Sir.' He nodded a greeting, then led the way down, leaving Big Mac and Collins in place.

If anyone came onto the floor, they'd never know that Tom wasn't securely in his room.

'If your plan is to just walk me out the door – which, by the way is brilliant,' Tom pointed out as they moved in a group down the stairs, 'you might want to consider the fact that I don't think I've ever seen you guys walking around the base dead silent like this. Karmody, don't you have any bad jokes to share?'

'Sorry, Tommy, I'm not quite in the mood today.'

'Have you guys had a chance to talk to Cosmo or Gilligan?' Tom asked.

'Yes, sir,' Duke said.

'So aren't you going to congratulate me?' Tom asked. 'Kelly finally married me. If I'd known it would do the trick, I'd've gotten myself locked up a long time ago.'

No one laughed, probably because it wasn't very funny.

'Congratulations, Commander,' Silverman said. But he wouldn't meet Tom's eyes.

'Congratulations, sir,' the other men echoed. But Zanella and Duke, too, seemed fascinated by the tiles on the floor.

And Jenk and Lopez exchanged what was definitely a worried look.

Tom was pretty sure he knew why. 'Hell of a time to get married, huh?'

'Come on, sir,' WildCard Karmody said, with something that looked a lot like sympathy in his eyes. 'We really do need to hurry.'

Nineteen

'Something's been bugging me,' Sam said as they bent over the street map of Sarasota that Alyssa had spread out on the hood of the car. They were attempting to locate the AA meetings in the area, to figure out which one Mary Lou might have attended on a Wednesday night.

Alyssa glanced up and into his eyes. 'Oh, yeah?' she said. 'That's funny, because something's been bugging me, too.' The look on his face became one of pure guilt – as if he already knew what she was going to say. 'About my handcuffs?'

Back at that rest stop, he'd unlocked himself – somehow – from a pair of cuffs with a lock that was allegedly pick-proof. It was the exact same pair of cuffs that had kept them locked together – naked – that dreadful morning after, more than two years ago, when she'd woken up hungover and sick as a dog. She'd been unable to locate the handcuff key, and he hadn't volunteered to pick the lock then.

'Oh,' Sam said now, 'yeah. I was, uh, wondering when we'd get around to that.' He forced a weak smile. 'Look, mind if I go first? Because it's going to be difficult to discuss why this Ihbraham Rahman guy is bugging me after you get so mad you won't ever talk to me again.'

She laughed her outrage. Holy God. He *had* been able to pick the lock. This wasn't a skill he'd learned in the past few months. She *knew* it. She knew it. He'd purposely allowed her to be humiliated and mortified and . . . 'You are *such* an un- believable *jerk*.'

Sam looked at her with eyes that were the same color as the early evening sky.

'Yeah,' he said. 'Maybe I am. I mean, you can definitely look at it from that perspective. And, yeah, I can see where you'd think I was being a jerk not to tell you I could open the lock without a key, but at the time you didn't exactly ask me and . . .' He glanced away from her, down at the map, as he shook his head. He looked back up and this time held her gaze. 'Maybe you could try to see this from *my* perspective. I was looking for a way to stay close to you. If I'd've unlocked those cuffs, I'd've had to leave. I guess I was hoping maybe you'd . . . I don't know. Get used to me? I mean, there I was, right? Attached to your arm. Maybe if I stayed there long enough, I'd grow on you. Shit, I really don't know what I was thinking, Alyssa. All I knew was I was crazy about you. That I'd just had the best night of my life, and you . . . you had nothing but regrets.'

Alyssa didn't know what to say, so she didn't say anything at all. But she couldn't hold his gaze, so she pretended to look down at the map. She'd been so sure on that awful morning that he was going to brag about what they'd done the night before to all his friends and teammates – people she worked closely with. She had been terrified. Of so many things. Of getting too close. Of appearing too vulnerable. Of *being* too vulnerable.

She still was.

Sam cleared his throat, but his voice came out as barely more than a whisper. 'I guess I was hoping that after you got all that out of your system, you know, after you calmed down a little, you'd realize that maybe I wasn't so bad after all. I mean, you sure seemed to like me a hell of a lot the night before. I guess I didn't want to believe it was only because of the alcohol. And you know, I still don't believe that.'

She couldn't look at him, and she forced herself to focus on the map. 'It wasn't,' she admitted. 'I think I probably made that pretty clear in Kazbekistan.'

Six months later, on the other side of the world, she'd actually gone back to his room, and they'd had a replay of their one-night stand.

He was silent then, and she could feel him watching her.

She was looking for Beneva Road. 'Here's the Lutheran church.'

He bent over the map, too, his head close to hers as she circled the intersection with her pen. 'That's a good one,' he said. 'It's right between both her old house and the newer one.'

'Yeah.' She risked a glance up at him. 'So are you going to apologize?'

'Nah,' he said, without even the slightest hesitation.

She stared at him, and he shrugged, pure Sam Starrett. 'Why should I apologize for doing what I thought was the best thing for both of us? You, however, should probably apologize to me.'

'What? Yeah, right.' She laughed. When hell froze.

'No, I'm serious,' he said. 'You fuck me like there's no tomorrow, make me start rhyming sappy verses that end with words like *love* and *stars* above, and then you wake up and treat me like shit on a stick. I'm still carrying the scars.' He put his finger on the map. 'Here's the Baptist church.'

Alyssa made another circle on the map. 'Yeah, you really suffered that night. Poor baby.'

'No, but I suffered the next day, and a whole Christload of days after, when I realized that you didn't love me even a little. You were just using me for sex. I was crushed.'

Alyssa put her pen down. 'This is a perfect example of revisionist history,' she said hotly. 'You were using me, too, Starrett, or have you forgotten that you got me drunk that night? You not only used me, you *planned* to use me—'

'No,' he said. 'No way. I didn't get you drunk so I could sleep with you. I got you drunk because you were strung so tight, I thought you were going to shatter. I was trying to help.'

'You definitely took advantage of my inebriation,' she countered.

'Yes. Okay. I'll cop to that. But you can't deny that your

"inebriation",' he mimicked, 'was pretty damn hard to resist. But I guess I should have said, "No, no, no, don't do that," when you took off your clothes and sat on my *face*.'

Alyssa felt her cheeks heat. Was that really what she'd done? She remembered him . . . Oh, God. But she wasn't sure how she'd gotten there. It was all such a blur.

'Alyssa, I'm only human,' Sam continued. 'And congratulations. I found out that night that you are, too. It's not such a bad thing to be, you know.'

'You're not a woman – a black woman – trying to compete in a white man's world,' she said quietly.

'I don't understand what that has to do with any of this,' he said just as quietly. 'If anything, I would think that would make you even more eager to have someone who loves you by your side.'

Love. There he went, using that word again.

'You know what your problem is?' she asked him.

Sam exhaled a laugh. 'No, but why do I have a feeling that you're about to tell me?'

'You're guilty of making the same mistake most people make. You say, "I love you," but what you really mean is, "I want you." You think it's the same thing, but it's not. You don't fall in love with someone just because they fuck you like there's no tomorrow.' Alyssa purposely used his words. 'I don't doubt that you wanted me, Sam. That you still do. Because on that really primitive, physical level, yeah, I still want you, too. But that's not love. That's about possessing, about being possessed. It's not real – it can't possibly last. Love is something you give. It's not about taking, or possessing.'

Sam found the last location on the map, and he picked up the pen and marked the spot. And then he wrote a one, two, three, and four next to the locations. 'And what you've found with Max? *That's* real love?'

'I don't know,' she admitted. 'Max and I . . .' She shook her head. 'It's way more complicated than you think.'

'Yeah, I bet. Mind if I drive?' Sam asked, folding the map so that their first destination was facing up.

'No.' But she made sure she got into the car before handing him the keys.

He smiled at that, scooping up the M&M's wrappers he'd left on the floor of the passenger's side and stuffing them into an empty McDonald's bag. 'Still think I'm going to drive off without you, huh?'

'I don't just think it,' she told him. 'I know it. If I'm not careful, sometime in the next—' She looked at her watch. '—approximately forty-one hours and seven minutes, if we don't find Haley, I am definitely going to be eating your dust.'

He glanced at her as he started the car. 'Who knows? One of these days, maybe I'll surprise you.'

Whitney was acting weird.

She'd been hanging around all day. Every time Mary Lou looked up, there she was.

She even asked if she could help when Mary Lou got out the fingerpaints and spread newspaper on the playroom table.

It was a little nerve-wracking, to be honest. Especially when, as Mary Lou got ready to put Haley and Amanda down for their naps, Whitney picked up a magazine and settled into one of the easy chairs in Mary Lou's little living room.

Mary Lou had been counting on having this time, while the girls were sleeping, to put those guns back in King Frank's office.

In the light of day, having unlocked weapons around two-year-olds seemed to be a greater danger than terrorist assassins.

But Whitney – who usually spent most of her time looking for ways to escape her father's house – wasn't going anywhere today.

As Mary Lou closed the door to the girls' room, Whitney put down the magazine and said, 'Don't you think it was romantic in *Castaway*, when Tom Hanks came back from being ship-wrecked and went to see Helen Hunt?'

'It was really sad,' Mary Lou said, 'because she was married to someone else.'

'Yeah,' Whitney said. 'I keep thinking there should be a sequel. You know, where her husband starts beating her up and she runs away because she knows he's going to kill her, and then Tom Hanks comes to the rescue. Don't you think that would be really romantic?'

'Don't you want to go to the mall?' Mary Lou asked her. She'd put those weapons in her bedroom closet and locked the door, but that wasn't safe, especially with Whitney's habit of poking around where she didn't belong. And what if King Frank changed his mind and came home early?

He'd fire her so fast . . .

If Mary Lou couldn't put them back now, during the girls' nap, she'd have to wait until after they were asleep tonight.

'I think it would be really romantic.' Whitney went back to reading her magazine, clearly not moving from her chair.

Mary Lou sighed and picked up her own book.

Tonight couldn't get here soon enough.

Once they left the confines of the naval base, and after receiving a call on his cell phone, WildCard Karmody drove like a man possessed.

Tom was wedged in the middle of the backseat, between Lopez and Jenk. It was not a backseat that was designed to hold three Navy SEALs, even when one of them was as vertically challenged as Mark Jenkins.

Izzy was riding shotgun, up with WildCard. Usually the pair of them could keep the mock insults and banter flowing in a steady stream, but today they were dead silent.

'So where are we going?' Tom asked the Card.

'We'll be there soon, sir' was all he would say.

If they hadn't been so damn grim, Tom would've guessed that his former team had broken him out of the BOQ to take him to the Ritz, or some other fancy hotel, so that he and Kelly could have a proper wedding night.

But the pucker factor in the car was way too high, and when WildCard's *there* proved to be Sharp Memorial Hospital, the buzz of uncertainty he was feeling turned into a flicker of real fear.

'What the fuck is going on?' Tom asked as WildCard ignored the speed bumps and pulled up right at the front doors. 'Someone God damn better answer me. That's a direct order. I still outrank you bastards.'

'Sir, we were ordered to deliver you here to Lieutenant Jacquette and the senior chief,' WildCard told him.

Sure enough, the XO and senior of Team Sixteen had come out of the hospital's lobby and were approaching the car.

Lopez slid out, and Tom followed.

Jazz Jacquette's default expression was grim. It was the look on Senior Chief Stan Wolchonok's face that turned that flicker Tom was feeling into an icy stab of fear.

Sweet Jesus, Stan actually had tears in his eyes.

'No,' Tom said. No, not Kelly.

Stan took him by one arm, Jazz by the other, and together they hustled him into the hospital.

'Tommy, she's alive,' Stan said, 'but the doctors don't think—' His voice broke. 'But they're wrong. Those fuckers are always wrong. She's a fighter. She *is* going to make it.'

'She's got a lot of internal damage, sir,' Jazz told him as they pulled him into an elevator. 'They've been trying to get her stabilized before they take her into surgery, but she's just not responding. The doctor thought it would be best for you to be here before—' He cleared his throat. 'We didn't have time to go through channels, so I ordered a training op to test base security.'

Kelly was dying. Neither of them said it directly, but that was what they'd just told him.

This was unreal. This couldn't be happening. This was just part of the godawful nightmare he'd been trapped in for the past few days. It had, however, just been ramped up to a new, more terrifying level.

'What happened?' he asked as the doors opened onto a floor marked ICU. 'How did she get hurt?'

'Car bomb,' Jazz reported.

'*What?*' Tom stopped walking, but they kept carrying him forward.

'Cosmo was with her, Tommy,' Stan told him. 'He's injured, too, but not as bad as Kelly. It's probably best if you get the whole story from him.'

Damn it, this was his own fault. Kelly had been digging around, looking for ways to help prove Tom's innocence, and it never even occurred to him that she might actually stir up real trouble. A fucking *car bomb*.

'Was the bomb in her car?' he asked. Dear God, how badly had she been hurt?

'No,' Stan said, but then Tom stopped listening, because there she was.

Kelly.

In the middle of a hospital bed, hooked up to all sorts of machines with wires and tubes and, oh, God . . .

Her face was scraped and her hair was singed. She still had all her arms and legs. But *internal injuries*, Jazz had said.

Stan or maybe Jazz pushed a chair up behind him, and he sat, holding on to her hand. It was scraped. She had little nicks and cuts on her wrist and all the way up her arm. Flying glass could do that to you.

'Hey, Kel,' he said to her, even though she was unconscious. Maybe, just maybe, she could hear him. 'It's me. Tom.'

His voice shook, and he stopped, took a deep breath. He didn't want her to hear his fear. No fear. No doubt. No letting her think there were any options besides getting through this.

'Here's what we're going to do, all right?' He leaned close. 'I'm going to stay here with you. Every step of the way. You're not alone. Whatever you do, don't forget that. And what *you're*

SUZANNE BROCKMANN

going to do is stay alive. Keep fighting. Don't quit on me, okay? Keep breathing. Inhale and then exhale. Remember when I told you about going through BUD/S training? Well, this is just like BUD/S, Kel. So stay in the moment, and stay in the game. One breath, one heartbeat at a time. Don't think beyond that. Don't think about how much it hurts or how tired you are. Don't think. Just breathe. Just stay alive. I'm counting on you to do that.'

'Sir.'

He looked up to find a nurse standing beside him, a clipboard in her hands.

'I'm sorry to interrupt, but the surgeon's ready,' she told him, and hope was in her voice, her eyes, her body language. 'If you'll just sign these forms . . .'

'Who's the doctor?' Tom asked.

Jazz was there behind him. 'Anne Marie Kenyon's the head of the trauma team. She's the best, Tom. I made sure of it.'

The nurse explained the procedure, but the words flew past Tom, only a few standing out. *Stop the internal bleeding at the source . . . force of the blast . . . multisystem trauma . . . damaged kidneys and liver . . . spleen . . . a risk to operate . . . Dr Kenyon's opinion . . . Kelly's only real chance.*

Jazz leaned closer. 'I spoke to Dr Kenyon before you arrived, and I made some phone calls and talked to the other doctors about her, too. She knows what she's doing. Sign the releases, sir.'

Tom let go of Kelly's hand and signed the forms. 'May I walk with her?' he asked the nurse.

She smiled at him. 'I'm sure Kelly would like it if you did. But only to the double doors, I'm afraid.'

It was maybe twenty-five feet, but Tom took Kelly's hand and held it the entire way.

But then he had to let her go. 'Don't forget what I said,' he told her. Please don't let this be the last time he saw Kelly alive. Please . . . 'I love you,' he called as they wheeled her away, as the doors swung shut behind her.

358

He sensed more than saw Stan and Jazz beside him. 'Take me to Cosmo,' he ordered them. *'Now.'*

Recovering alcoholics had privacy issues.

Alyssa had always thought Alcoholics Anonymous meetings were open to the public – places where people stood up and said loudly and proudly, 'My name is Joe and I'm an alcoholic. I've been sober for three years.'

Apparently that was only a small part of the program. Some meetings were twelve-step meetings, some were women-only meetings, some were meetings that focused on reading from a special book, and most were closed to everyone but recovering alcoholics.

Walking in and flashing a picture and asking if anyone knew Mary Lou Starrett was not getting the response she'd hoped for.

It wasn't getting any kind of response at all. Except for being asked to leave by two very large men wearing motorcycle leather.

But Sam spoke their language. He pulled them aside and in very short order had them looking at the picture of Mary Lou and Haley that Jules had sent to Alyssa, thanks to the Internet and a brief stop at Kinko's.

But they both shook their heads no.

And then Sam was walking back toward her, shaking his head, too.

He'd taken off his suit jacket because of the heat. He'd actually sewn the sleeve back on with neat, tiny stitches as they drove down from Gainesville, using a needle and thread they'd picked up at a convenience store during a stop for gas and coffee and peanut M&M's.

His pants were a little dusty – he'd never managed to brush them off completely after wrestling with her in the back hallway of the Wal-Mart. His sleeves were rolled up, but one was higher than the other, and his tie was loosened to the point of ridiculousness.

Aside from the dust and disarray, his clothes weren't that different from those of men who worked in offices all over this city. But were he and a businessman to stand side by side, Alyssa would have had no problem identifying the Navy SEAL.

It was evident in the way Sam stood, the way he moved, the way he breathed.

'Hank and Roy have been running this particular meeting for the past four years,' he told her now. 'They don't remember seeing her. And they would have. They're protective of the women in their group. They keep an eye out for thirteen-Steppers.' At her blank look, he explained. 'Men who pretend to be part of the program but are really just trolling for vulnerable women.'

'Wow, that's a shitty thing to do.'

'No kidding.' He led the way out of the building, back toward the car. 'I don't know if we're on the right track here. It's possible Mary Lou stopped attending meetings after she moved in with her sister. It's possible she was already lying low back then. I mean, think about it. She left California the day after the Coronado attack. She must've known her prints were on that weapon.' He shook his head. 'I just hope wherever she is, she's not drinking again.'

Alyssa suspected Mary Lou wasn't – because dead people couldn't drink. But she kept that to herself as she unlocked the car and they got in.

Sam glanced briefly at the map, finding their next location, before he started the car. 'So you want to hear what's been bugging me about the Ihbraham Rahman thing?'

'Okay.'

He shot her a look. 'You think this is a waste of time, don't you?'

'Sam, I said okay.'

'You think they're dead,' he accused her.

'I'm trying to be supportive, but . . .' She sighed. 'I'm sorry. I'm . . . Look, just tell me.'

'Two things,' Sam said. 'First is that I don't believe Mary Lou would get involved with a man who wasn't white. So whatever her connection to Rahman was, it wasn't romantic or sexual. I'm virtually certain of that. She had strong opinions about racial separation.' He laughed in disgust. 'I don't know why I just don't say it. She was racist, all right? I didn't find out until a couple of months after we were married.'

Alyssa laughed softly as she looked at him in the light from the dashboard. 'Oh, Sam. That must've hurt, huh?'

'It made her completely unattractive to me,' he admitted. 'I couldn't get past it. I tried talking to her about it, tried to widen her narrow-minded view – it just came from ignorance – but she just never wanted to talk to me about anything.' He sighed. '*That* was when our marriage ended. I swear, I should've filed for divorce right then and there, but I was too stupid to realize it. Instead, I just stopped trying. It wasn't conscious. I didn't even know I gave up. I was so freaking depressed and . . . I *thought* I was still trying, but I was just kidding myself. Like I'm really going to be able to make a relationship with this woman work?'

'That would have been a hard one for me, too,' Alyssa told him. 'I mean, flip flop it around a little. I've dated black men who are really vocal about how much they dislike interracial relationships. They start in on how their little sister better never date a white man, and I'm thinking, *Hello*. My mother was someone's little sister, and she *married* a white man, and if she hadn't, she never would have had me.' She shook her head. 'Needless to say, there's usually no second date.' She shot him a look. 'See how smart it is to have a policy about never having sex with strangers? You never wind up married to someone you don't want to talk to, let alone live with.'

'Yeah, well, I don't need any policies like that anymore,' he said. 'Because until I have the operation to remove my testicles from my sinuses, I won't be able to have sex again. Which really isn't that big a deal since it's been so long since I've had sex, I've forgotten what it's like.'

Alyssa snorted. 'If you're looking for sympathy, Starrett, you're looking in the wrong place.'

'I'm not,' he said. 'I'm just trying to be funny and failing. But there was nothing funny about my marriage. I mean, shit, the whole thing was a tragedy from the start. I didn't love her, but I honestly did try to like her. But after finding out that . . .'

Sam stopped at a red light and turned to look at her. 'She said something about Jazz, about how hard it must be for me to take orders from him, and I'm telling you, I didn't get it at first,' he told her. 'I honestly thought she had a problem with him because his demeanor is so, you know, grim and serious. I thought she was talking about the fact that it seems like he never smiles, but when I realized that it was because he's black, I was blown away.'

The car in front of him was moving, but much too slowly. Sam signaled to move into the left lane so he could pass.

He glanced at Alyssa after that. 'I didn't mean to go off on a rant. I just wanted you to know why I'm having such trouble with her alleged connection to Rahman.'

'Don DaCosta did call him Mary Lou's *friend*,' Alyssa pointed out. 'And he was obviously looking for her.'

'Well, I don't think she'd be unfriendly to him,' Sam said. 'She wasn't like my father.'

He was silent for a moment as he drove. But then he said, 'You know, I've been thinking about the fact that Rahman was nearly killed in Coronado. That he got jumped by people in the crowd who were afraid he was armed. There were plenty of other people of Middle Eastern descent who got tackled during that attack. But they were sat on. They weren't beaten nearly to death.'

'It happens sometimes in a crowd,' Alyssa said. 'People lose control. Mob mentality, you know?'

'Yeah, okay, maybe,' Sam said. 'But what if it wasn't an accident that *he* was the one to get beaten nearly to death? One possibility is that he really was involved with the attack, and the FBI just hasn't found the connection yet. But maybe someone set him up to be killed there, in Coronado. Because what if Rahman can ID the *real* terrorists – just like Donny and Mary Lou? Maybe Rahman knows this light-haired guy Donny mentioned – this alien that Don saw all the time in my driveway. You know, the same guy he saw following Rahman yesterday. Jesus, I don't—'

He stopped. Cleared his throat. Kept his eyes on the road. 'Donny never hurt anyone. He was—' He stopped again. 'He was a good guy. God, his family must be devastated.'

Alyssa didn't dare touch him. 'We don't have to talk about this right now.'

'Yeah,' Sam said. 'We do. Because I want to catch this fucker and watch him fry.' He was holding tightly to the steering wheel. 'Lys, what if Rahman's not the tango? What if it's Donny's alien, the blond man – a white guy, right, so Mary Lou's okay with sleeping with him – who brought that weapon onto the base in Mary Lou's car?

'Maybe Rahman's not AWOL,' Sam continued. 'Maybe he's dead. Maybe he's in the trunk of some car somewhere, with a bullet in his head.'

Alyssa already had her phone out and open and was speed-dialing Jules.

She needed Max to hear Sam's latest theory about Ihbraham Rahman, but she was still too angry to call him herself.

Fort Worth, Texas
1987

'We'll still have Sundays to fly,' Noah pointed out as Ringo followed him up the stairs and onto the front porch.

'I don't think Coach MacGreggor is going to want me to try out,' Ringo said. They went through the screen door, closing it behind them with a bang.

'Why not?'

'Well, to start, he hates my freaking guts.'

363

The baseball coach also taught history, and Noah knew that he and Ringo had clashed many times over what Ringo insisted were simplified, rich white men's propagandistic versions of the past.

Noah set his backpack down by the stairs. 'He's not going to bring that with him onto the baseball field.'

'Want to bet?' Ringo muttered.

'You're just paranoid.' Noah raised his voice. 'Hey, we're home!' He turned back. 'Or scared.' He did a quick shuffle to get well out of Ringo's reach. 'You're a girly man,' he said, imitating Hans and Franz from *Saturday Night Live*. 'Too scared to try out for the high school baseball team, girly man?'

Roger cracked up. 'Shut up, fuckhead!'

'Grandma!' Noah pretended to shout, knowing full well that Dot wasn't wearing her hated hearing aid. 'Ringo called me a *fuckhead*!' Laughing, he escaped Ringo's skull duster by dashing down the hall to the kitchen.

'Don't gallop in the house, young sir.' Ringo mimicked Walt's deep voice as he followed.

'Seriously, Ringo,' Noah started to say, but then he stopped short, just in the doorway to the kitchen.

What the . . .?

'Seriously, Nos.' Ringo was behind him and didn't see it. 'If you honestly want to, I'll go to the tryouts with you. God help us both, though.'

'Grampa?' Nos shouted, pushing past Ringo and bolting back toward the stairs.

'Holy fuck,' Ringo said as he saw it – an entire pot of bloodred tomato sauce spilled on the kitchen floor. Walt's stool was overturned, as well as one of the kitchen chairs.

Noah took the stairs three at a time, heading for the upstairs bathroom, praying that Grandpa had burned himself cooking and that Grandma was with him in the bathroom, searching the medicine cabinet and cussing because she couldn't find the aloe vera gel.

He could hear Ringo running through the first floor of the big house, shouting for Walt and Dot.

The bathroom was empty. All the bedrooms were, too.

Noah didn't think of them as old, but they were. They were old, and old people died. Johnny Radford's father had just had a fatal heart attack. And he had been younger than Walt.

Panic made his chest tight, but he forced it away as he clattered back down the stairs and pushed his way out the screen door.

Walt's blue station wagon was still parked in the driveway.

Ringo was thinking along the same lines as Noah, and he'd already hopped the fence into the Leonards' yard – an impressive feat that usually brought Mrs L out of her house to chase them with her broom. She said she was tired of big boot prints in her flower bed, but that wasn't Ringo's fault, that was all Noah. It had been months since Ringo had failed to clear the garden.

As Noah took the long way around, Mrs L met Ringo on the porch, wiping her hands on a dish towel.

'Please, ma'am, do you know where Walt and Dot went?' he asked.

'You missed the excitement by just half an hour,' she said, as Noah got to the gate. 'Two ambulances, a firetruck, and three police cars.'

No.

'What happened?' Ringo asked. 'Where are they?'

'Harris Methodist Hospital,' she told him. 'I'm not really sure of the details. I think Mrs Gaines fell or collapsed or something, and I guess Mr Gaines called 911. I don't know if it was a heart attack or what. But they got her out of here pretty fast. He went with her in the ambulance.'

Grandma. Don't let her be dead.

'Please, ma'am,' Noah called to Mrs Leonard from the gate, 'I know we're not your favorite people in the world, but we really need to get to that hospital right away. Please, will you drive us?'

'I would if I could,' she said, 'but Sherman has the car. He'll be back around five-thirty. If you still need a ride then, just give me a shout.' She narrowed her eyes at Ringo. 'But from now on use the gate.'

Noah looked at his watch. Five-thirty. It was barely even three.

'Thank you, ma'am,' Ringo said. 'But I think we'll try to find another ride.'

He headed for Noah and the gate at a dead run, and vaulted clear over the damn thing.

'*Use* the gate!' Mrs L shouted after him. 'Unlatch it. Walk through it. Like a human!'

'Let's call the hospital,' Ringo said as they ran back to the house. 'Find out what the hell's going on.' He was trying to be reassuring, but Noah knew he was scared, too. 'It's probably nothing big. You know how sometimes old people fall and break a wrist or a hip? I'm sure she's all right.'

'Breaking a hip is pretty big.' Noah grabbed the phone book from the shelf.

'Well, I don't know that's what happened.' Ringo picked up the phone. 'What's the number?'

Noah read it to him, then started cleaning up the tomato sauce while Ringo went through verbal contortions, trying to find out who he should talk to to learn Dot's fate.

They needed to get to the hospital now. Not at five-thirty. *Now.*

They could call Jolee, but it would take her just as long to get up here. Although, they needed to call her anyway to tell her Grandma was in the hospital. Noah grabbed a pencil from the cup on the kitchen desk and started one of Walt's lists. *You can't forget to do something if you write it down.* 'Call Jolee.'

Who else could they call for a ride?

Ringo hung up the phone with a crash. 'Those dickheads won't give out any information about Aunt Dot over the telephone.'

They stared at each other.

Noah voiced what they both were wondering. 'Do you think that means she's dead?'

'Fuck, no!' Ringo said, but it was so obvious he was lying, Noah couldn't help it. He started to cry.

'Hey, come on, Nos.' Ringo put his arms around him. 'She probably just twisted her ankle.'

'Then why wouldn't they just tell us that?'

'I don't know! It's probably some stupidass hospital policy. You know what Uncle Walt always says about bureaucracy. Let's figure out a way to get to the hospital, okay? Then we can stop guessing.'

'I don't know who to call,' Noah said. All the other neighbors were at work, except elderly Mrs Jurgens, who had cataracts in both eyes.

'I'll find us a ride.' Ringo had a look of sheer determination all over him. He pushed Noah toward the kitchen door. 'Why don't you go upstairs and get a bag and pack some of Walt and Dot's stuff in it. You know, things they might need. Get Uncle Walter a change of clothes, in case he spilled that sauce on himself. And ... and pack, you know, their toothbrushes and ... and Walt's razor. A warm pair of socks and a sweater for Dot, 'cause she's always cold. And whatever book's on her bedside table. Stuff like that.'

Noah nodded and went upstairs. Grandpa's leather overnight bag was in the closet, and he quickly packed it and started back down the stairs.

He heard Ringo hang up the phone with a crash, heard him curse over and over. 'Fuck, fuck, *fuck*! Why aren't you home?'

Ringo picked up the phone again and dialed. 'Be home, be home, be home ...' he said. And then his next words made Noah freeze there on the bottom step of the stairs.

'Pop. It's me. Roger.'

Ringo had actually called his father, to ask for a ride.

Noah sat down on the stairs. He hadn't even realized that son of a bitch was in town this week. He should have recognized it, though. All of the signs were there. Ringo had disappeared during lunch – no doubt running home to make sure his mother was okay.

Roger Starrett Senior had stopped beating the crap out of Ringo about a year ago, but Noah suspected that hunting season on his wife was still open.

Ringo's father was so loud that, when combined with the extra-powerful speaker Walt had installed on the kitchen phone for Dot, his voice easily carried to where Noah sat.

'Well, now, I thought you was calling yourself Ringo or something equally foolish these days,' Starrett drawled.

'Noah and I need a ride to the hospital, sir,' Ringo told him. 'You know I wouldn't ask you if it wasn't a matter of life or death—'

'You hurt?'

'No, sir. But Noah's grandmother was taken to the hospital by an ambulance right before we got home from school—'

'You haven't *come* home from school yet,' he said.

Unbelievable. Roger Starrett Senior knew good and god-damned well that Noah's grandmother was his very own sister. Ringo had just told him she was in the hospital, and he was messing around with semantics.

'Excuse me, sir,' Ringo said instead of *Fuck you, you mean-spirited prick*. Noah couldn't believe what he was hearing. He couldn't believe Ringo was doing this for him. And it was for him. To get him a ride to that hospital, Ringo was willing to ask this man that he hated for a favor.

'I meant to say,' Ringo continued, 'before we got to *Noah's* house.'

'I thought I made it clear that I didn't want you going over there.'

'Pop,' Ringo said, desperation making his voice crack. 'Didn't you hear what I told you? Aunt Dot might be *dying*.'

There was silence on the line, then, 'Considering she's been dead to me for forty years, it's about time she was put in her grave – end the embarrassment she's brought to her family. Get yourself on home, boy. *Now.*'

'I *am* home,' Ringo said quietly. 'I won't be bothering you anymore.'

He hung up the phone, and Noah heard him start to cry. He was trying not to, trying to hide it – typical of Roger.

Noah dried his own eyes on his sleeve, stood up, and went into the kitchen.

Ringo heard him coming and stuck his head under the kitchen faucet, letting the water run on his face and into his mouth.

'You okay?' Noah asked.

'Yeah.' Ringo pretended to be all right as he dried his face on the kitchen towel. 'Lookit, I just had an idea. If I cut my hand open with one of Uncle Walt's cooking knives, you could call an ambulance, and they'd take us to the hospital.'

He was serious.

Noah's mouth was hanging open. 'Roger, that's completely insane.'

'So what? It'll get us there. Fast.'

'I'm not going to let you do that,' Noah told him. '*Cut yourself?* It's bad enough that you went and called your father—'

'Aw, shit, you heard that?' Ringo was beyond embarrassed.

'You shouldn't have called him.'

'I thought . . .' He worked hard to keep from crying again. 'Maybe he'd do something decent for once, you know?'

Noah did know. He knew that Roger was almost unbearably ashamed of his father, ashamed to be the man's son.

'I mean, Jesus,' Ringo continued. 'Even Darth Vader apologized to Luke for being such a dickhead.'

'Darth never gave Luke a ride to the hospital.'

'Luke wouldn't have asked,' Ringo pointed out. 'He didn't need a ride anywhere. He had a speeder.' He stopped. 'That's it!'

'We'll blow up the Death Star,' Noah mocked him, 'and then when the ambulances come, we'll get a ride to the hospital.'

Ringo laughed, which had been Noah's intention. 'Shut up, fuckhead, and help me find Uncle Walt's car keys.'

They were, of course, in the key box.

Ringo held out his hand for them, but Noah didn't hand them over. 'This, too, is insane.'

'Everyone always says that we both look much older than fifteen.'

'Driving in a parking lot's different than driving on the street,' Noah told him. 'I wouldn't want to do it.'

'Well, I would,' Ringo said with complete conviction. 'I want to. If you want, I can go by myself and then call you from the hospital once I find out if Dot's okay.'

Noah handed him the keys. 'Like I'm going to let you do that.'

'I would,' Ringo said, heading for the door.

'Yeah, I know,' Noah said, hefting Walt's bag and locking the door behind them.

They got into the car, and Ringo adjusted the seat and the mirrors, the way Walt had showed them.

He had to be scared shitless, just like Noah. But he put the key in the ignition, and turned it, and the engine roared to life. Ringo was going to get them to the hospital if it was the last thing he did.

'Luke Skywalker's proof that paternity amounts to squat,' Noah told him. 'And you are too my brother.'

'Fasten your seat belt,' Ringo said, and pulled out of the driveway.

The band had started playing early, at seven, so by nine-thirty, Gina was more than ready for another break.

Fandangos was filled, and she had to squeeze her way through the crowd to get to the bar.

Max wasn't there.

The musicians were set up on a platform with a direct view of the front door. As she'd played, she'd been able to see everyone who came in or left.

Max had done neither.

Unless he'd come in through the kitchen.

There was this one spot, back by the rest rooms, where it was really dark. She was sure she'd seen an extra shadow there while she was playing. But when she looked now, no one was there.

'Hey. How're you doing? Gina, right?'

She found herself staring up at Detective Soul Patch.

He was holding a beer in his left hand and he held out his right for her to shake. 'Ric Alvarado.'

'Ric. Right.'

'I didn't know you were a musician.'

Yeah, sure. As if Max hadn't sent him over here. All of her hopes crashed and burned. He was never going to give in. He'd gone so far as actually to send over a replacement . . . a *real* replacement this time – not just Jules Cassidy.

'You okay?' Ric asked.

Gina forced a smile. 'Yeah, it's just a little too crowded in here. I get claustrophobic sometimes.'

'I know what you mean. Hey, so far no luck in my search for your underwear,' he said, and then laughed and rolled his eyes. It was too dark in there to tell for sure, but it was possible he blushed. 'Oh, man, I'm such an asshole. I can't believe I actually said that.' He looked around the room. 'It is crowded tonight. Wow. Hot, too.' Another eye roll. 'Look, can I buy you a drink? Something frozen, maybe?'

'Actually, because I'm in the band, I drink for free.'

'Oh. Well, that's . . . sweet.'

'Yeah,' she said. 'I guess.'

Sweet. Her last college boyfriend, Trent Engelman, used to call everything sweet.

Ric Alvarado himself was pretty damn sweet – at least as far as replacements for Max went. Dark hair, heavily lidded brown eyes, killer cheekbones, broad shoulders, trim waist. Younger than Max, but older than Gina. She'd bet that he was a good dancer, too.

'Well.' Ric looked embarrassed, as if he were about to back away, as if she'd given him a brush-off instead of an honest response about that drink. So she grabbed him by the shirt and pulled him closer to the bar.

'Hey, Jenn,' she called to the bartender. 'This is Ric. He's going to make sure my wineglass is never empty during the next set, okay?'

Jenn pushed a refill in Gina's direction.

'I think we can take that as an affirmative,' Gina said to Ric, whose embarrassment had turned to nearly palpable hope. Oh, come on. Didn't Max mention she was a sure thing? She made herself smile back at him as she took a healthy sip of her wine. 'You don't mind being my slave tonight, do you, Ric?'

Someone bumped into her, and she had to hold her glass out to keep it from spilling. Ric steadied her with a hand at her waist. A hand he didn't bother taking away again. 'Absolutely not,' he said.

'So tell me,' Gina said, determined to play this through. If this was really what Max wanted . . . 'How far are you willing to go in your search for my underwear?'

Cosmo Richter's right leg was in traction.

As Tom went into the SEAL's hospital room, a tight-lipped nurse was coming out. 'Tell him he doesn't have to be a superhero,' she snapped, before marching off down the hall.

Cosmo's face was almost the same color as his eyes. Kind of pale bluish-gray.

'He's refused to take any pain meds until he's talked to you,' the senior chief said quietly into Tom's ear.

'Sir,' Cosmo said to Tom. 'I'm at fault. Chief Karmody ordered me to stay with Kelly, to keep her safe. I should have—'

'You should have expected a *car* bomb? In suburban San

Diego?' Tom shook his head. 'No, Cos. You got her out of the house.' Stan had told him that Don DaCosta, the man who lived there, hadn't fared so well. 'On a broken leg,' he added. Man, there was a cast on Cosmo's left ankle, too. 'Two broken legs.'

Once again, Stan and Jazz had a chair for him. Tom sat, part of him still upstairs, in surgery with Kelly.

'Can you start at the beginning?' Tom asked. 'Why were you over there in the first place?' Stan had also told him that this Don DaCosta lived next door to the house Sam Starrett had shared with Mary Lou before they separated. DaCosta was mentally ill – a shut-in who never left his house.

'Kelly had these videotapes from somewhere, I don't know exactly—'

'The library parking lot?' Tom asked.

'Yeah, that's right,' Cos said. 'Card wrote a computer program to help her check to see if Mary Lou Starrett appeared in any of the tapes, and she did.'

Chief WildCard Karmody could do things with a computer that would have made him filthy rich, were he not employed by the US Navy.

'He printed out a bunch of pictures of Mary Lou with this guy some guy Kelly recognized.'

'Sweet Jesus.' Tom hadn't thought she'd actually find anything from the information gathering she had been doing.

'She said he came into her office a coupla times. He was selling drugs. You know, not the illegal kind, but—'

'A pharmaceuticals rep,' Tom said. Kelly had told him that salesmen and women from drug companies came into the clinic on a daily basis, pushing various antibiotics and prescription medications, encouraging doctors to prescribe their company's brand of pills.

'Yeah, that's it,' Cosmo said. 'This was about six weeks before the Coronado attack.'

'And Kelly found a picture of this same man talking to Mary Lou Starrett,' Tom clarified.

'Yes, sir.'

'Mother of God.'

'Yes, sir.'

'Where's the picture?' Tom asked.

'Card's making copies right now – he's sending it as a download to everyone on the team to share with girlfriends and family and such,' Cosmo reported. 'He was in here just about a half hour ago, and we suddenly realized if this guy *is* one of our tangos—' He used the radio-code word for the letter T, which stood for this decade's version of trouble – *terrorists*. '—he may have contacted other people close to the team, and they may be in danger, too.'

Tom looked at Stan and Jazz. 'I want a copy of that picture,' he ordered. 'ASAP. And we need to get this information to the FBI.'

Stan left the room as Jazz said, 'Cosmo's already spoken to Peggy Ryan. She's XO of Max Bhagat's CT team.'

Tom nodded. 'Good.' He knew Peggy. She was no Max, but she was good. He turned back to Cos. 'So what the hell were you doing at DaCosta's house?'

'Kelly was in touch with the other wives and girlfriends,' Cosmo told him, 'looking for someone just like this guy – someone who'd maybe been sniffing around, looking for access to the base. You know, so he could smuggle those weapons in.

'Lieutenant Muldoon's wife, Joan, is Don DaCosta's sister. Joan told Kelly that her brother had some FBI agents camping out in his house. He's in the habit of seeing aliens in the shadows, and he told Lieutenant Starrett that an "alien" he used to see lurking around Starrett's house had come back. From what I understand – and I'm not sure I've got it entirely straight, sir, it's pretty freaking confusing – DaCosta recently saw this same alien following some Middle Eastern gardener who used to work in their neighborhood—'

'Ihbraham Rahman?' Tom asked. God *damn*, Kelly really had been on the right track.

'That sounds right, sir, but, it's been a hell of a day, and I was paying more attention to the other guy. The guy in Kelly's picture. That's why we were at DaCosta's – because Kelly wanted to show him the picture, to see if this guy was his alien.' Cosmo nodded. 'And sure enough, DaCosta IDed him. I mean, as much as someone who's mentally challenged can make a positive ID. But as far as I'm concerned, the words, "That's him, that's the alien", makes me think we probably have a photo of a man who may have helped set up the Coronado attack.'

Tom ran his hands down his face. He'd never thought . . . It had never occurred to him that Kelly might be in danger – that she'd actually get close enough to the truth . . . He looked at Cosmo. 'What happened? You got there, you went inside, Kelly showed DaCosta the photo, and then what?'

'One of the agents got right on the phone – this picture is a very major deal as far as the investigation goes,' Cosmo said. 'We got what we came for, so I wanted to get out of there. I was spooked. I don't really know why. I was just . . . The hair on the back of my neck was standing up – you know how that sometimes happens? But Kelly was trying to calm down DaCosta. The picture got him really worked up and she didn't want to leave him like that.

'She was telling him he was safe, because the FBI was there, and I was there, and I was a SEAL. He's got this hero worship thing about SEALs. And he was telling us about how Lieutenant Starrett always came over to watch the game on TV, and I was thinking, Shit, he's a better man than I am. I was thinking that it was the closed windows that were freaking me out.

'And the second FBI agent – the one who wasn't on the phone – suddenly goes, "Are we expecting more visitors?" I look up and he's over by the window, and he's got the blinds open, and I can see there's a car pulling up, right out there. And someone gets out and starts running, and Christ, Commander, I *knew*. Kelly was sitting across the room, on the sofa, next to DaCosta, much closer to that side of the house than I was. I should have been right next to her. But I wasn't, and I shouted to get down. But she didn't and aw, fuck, it blew, and the force just picked her up and I couldn't do a fucking thing.'

'Except carry her outside on two broken legs,' Tom reminded Cosmo quietly.

'I didn't know they were broken, sir. I just knew they didn't work the way I needed them to.' He shook his head. 'I tried to go back in there for DaCosta and the others, but I couldn't do more than crawl, and then the fire truck was there and they pulled me back. I had to hit some dumbfuck in the face to make him stop dicking around with me. Kelly obviously needed more immediate attention. Those guys got there fast, but I'm telling you, they need a refresher course in triage.' Cosmo's eyes were red.

Tom knew his own eyes must've looked the same. 'She's going to be okay, you know,' he told the petty officer. 'She's going to pull through.'

Cosmo nodded. 'I'm praying for that, sir.' He paused, his face working as he tried not to cry. 'But oh my holy God, sir, you need to know . . . I saw the way she hit that wall, and . . .'

Cosmo Richter, the man with the reputation of being one of the coolest, most deadliest operators in SEAL Team Sixteen, covered his eyes with his hand and cried.

Twenty

Sam stared up at the patterns of light on the ceiling, light that had sneaked in past the heavy motel room curtains.

Alyssa had talked him into coming here after they'd run out of AA meetings to visit.

That was kind of funny – Alyssa having to talk him into going to a motel. Of course, they did get separate rooms, which made it considerably less funny.

If this had been a Hollywood movie, every motel and hotel in the city would have been filled up – except for one last place that had one last room with one king-sized bed. Real-life people didn't have the same kind of luck as people did in the movies.

Real-life people also didn't have the kind of luck that would make them walk into the one AA meeting attended by someone who actually knew Mary Lou well enough to know where she was hiding.

Sam hadn't even had any luck finding someone who admitted just to *seeing* Mary Lou at one of these meetings.

He didn't know whether to feel panic because she wasn't attending meetings, or admiration. If she truly had listened to what he'd told her about hiding, she would have changed her regular habits upon coming to Sarasota, and he might never find her. Of course, the people who were looking for her wouldn't find her, either.

But could she really stick to it? Hiding like that meant never returning to old ways, never calling or visiting old friends, never letting Haley see her father.

Never could last a hell of a long time.

Besides, Mary Lou had obviously slipped up somewhere, since someone *had* found her and killed Janine.

Sam stared at the ceiling. Checking AA meetings was getting them nowhere. They had exactly zero leads. They could start over again tomorrow, because, hey, it was possible that Wednesdays were the days Mary Lou was always too busy to go out.

But maybe they should back up, put this investigation into a mental reverse.

Maybe, instead of trying to find Mary Lou, they should focus on finding the fuckers who were trying to kill her.

The end result would be the same – Mary Lou and Haley would be safe.

So okay. Sam should try to figure out who, besides him, had had Mary Lou and Janine's address after they moved out of Clyde's house.

Clyde hadn't had it, that was for sure. Although wasn't it interesting that right after he tracked down Janine, possibly even that same night, she'd been killed?

Holy fuck. Sam sat up in bed. Maybe someone had been watching Clyde, knowing that sooner or later he'd lead them to Janine, and therefore to Mary Lou.

But how had they found Clyde?

He grabbed the phone and dialed Alyssa's room.

She picked it up after one ring. 'Sam, please go to sleep.'

'Yeah,' he said. 'I'm trying. But—' He told her his theories about Clyde as concisely as he could.

Alyssa sighed. 'Sam, if I were looking for Mary Lou, *you're* where I'd go to find her, not Clyde Wrigley. *You* know where she is. Your *lawyers* know where she is—'

'Yeah, but I don't have an address book,' he told her. 'My entire address book is in my head – if I write it down, I lose it. So I memorize it, and it's always there. I also don't keep important papers in my house. My entire file for the divorce was at my office, on base. We're not supposed to do that, but I've always been paperwork challenged.'

She laughed. 'Who, *you*? No way.'

Sam smiled. She was actually teasing him.

'So, okay,' she said. 'Say I'm a member of a San Diego terror cell. I'm looking to stay active and to stay in the area, so I need to make sure Mary Lou disappears, because she can ID me. I don't know you're paperwork challenged and that you don't have an address book by your telephone. The only thing I know about you is that you're a SEAL. Isn't it likely I'd break into your house to find out where Mary Lou's gone?'

Sam turned on the light. 'There was a break-in. It was about two weeks after Mary Lou left. Someone came in through the kitchen window. The cops thought it was kids because nothing was taken. They just made a mess.'

Alyssa didn't sound happy at that news. In fact, she sounded pissed. 'You know, Starrett, this is why you need to go in for questioning.'

He was back to being Starrett, which wasn't quite as bad as Lieutenant. 'I don't think whoever broke in found anything at all.'

'Okay, if I'm the terrorist and I found nothing in your house, my next step would be to get Mary Lou's phone number by waiting for your mail and stealing your long distance bill.'

'I don't get phone bills,' Sam countered. 'Not through the mail. I pay my bills online. My system's secure, too. Hacker proof. Kenny Karmody set it up for me.' He was liking this theory more and more. 'And if you're the terrorist, you probably know if you watch me – and try to follow me – I'd make you within the first day.'

She snorted. 'More like the first *hour*.'

He paused. She really thought that highly of him. 'Well, shoot. Thanks. That's really—'

'Sam, let's sleep on this, okay? My brain's mush. I know I must be missing something here—'

'Just wait. Just two more seconds, okay? You're the terrorist, you know I'm a SEAL, so you're not going to follow me because I'll see you. Who *are* you going to follow?'

'Not Clyde,' she said. 'Because I don't know anything about Janine or Clyde. I just know I'm looking for a woman with a child, a woman who likes to read and attends AA meetings and gets jobs in the service industry because she never finished high school.' Alyssa sighed. 'Sam, look, I'm a really stupid terrorist right now because I'm so, *so* tired—'

'You'd follow her close friends.'

'You said she didn't have any close friends,' Alyssa pointed out.

'From what Donny said, someone sure as shit was watching Ihbraham Rahman.'

Which would make a hell of a lot more sense if Rahman were Mary Lou's lover.

Which just wasn't possible.

Okay, open mind, Starrett . . .

No, he just didn't see it. Rahman was Arab American and Mary Lou was Mary Lou.

Shit.

'Ihbraham Rahman,' Alyssa said through a yawn. 'Why is that name so familiar? Wasn't he my first husband?'

Sam settled back in his bed. 'Okay. I'm done annoying you. I'm hanging up.' But he wasn't going to do much sleeping over here.

He didn't tell her that. He didn't say, *Alyssa, I'm too scared to sleep. Please help me survive this godawful night.*

Instead, he said, 'See you in the morning, Lys,' and hung up the phone.

'You don't have a car here, do you?' Ric asked Gina. 'Because, as a police officer, I really can't let you drive home.'

It was the moment of truth.

Gina had said her farewells to the guys in the band. She'd

thanked the wait staff and the bartender, and she'd gathered up her jacket and her leather bag with her sticks and brushes. The drum kit belonged to the drummer she'd replaced, and he was coming by the club to pick it up some time next week.

It was, without a doubt, the easiest gig she'd ever done.

As well as the hardest.

The shadow had been back again, in the dark corner by the rest rooms, for the last set of the evening.

It *had* been Max. She was sure of it.

And knowing him, he was probably still watching her right now.

As she was talking to Ric Alvarado in the parking lot.

'I'm walking back to my motel,' she told Ric. 'It's not far.'

He had his key ring on his finger, and he flipped it so that his keys landed in the palm of his hand with a smack. 'Can I give you a lift?'

He was a nice guy. He was an incredibly nice guy. In a different lifetime, Gina would have really liked him.

'Or, if you want, I could walk you,' he said. He was trying so hard to be casual about the fact that he was hoping to go home with her.

'How much did Max tell you?' she asked.

'How much did . . . what?' He pretended not to know what she was talking about. It was an Oscar-worthy performance.

'Max,' she said, resisting the urge to applaud. 'He asked you to come here tonight, right?'

'Max *Bhagat*?' Ric said. 'From the FBI?' He shook his head. 'No. Are you . . . Is he . . .' He stopped and started over. 'Did I make a mistake, Gina? I thought maybe there was something going on with you two the other night, but then he wasn't here at the club, and you were being so, um, friendly . . .'

Oh, he was good. 'Max didn't call you and ask you to let me pick you up here tonight?'

Ric laughed. 'Did you pick me up? Because I thought I was trying to pick you up.'

'Is that what he told you to do?' Gina asked.

'Nobody called me and told me to do anything.' He was definitely getting uncomfortable with this conversation. 'I came here because it was my night off and I love jazz. Do you have something kinky going with this guy? Because I'm absolutely not into that.'

'No!' Gina said. 'God, no!'

Ric was serious and had been from the start. Max *hadn't* contacted him.

But that still didn't mean that Max hadn't somehow manipulated him into being here tonight.

Gina caught herself. Come on. Max was powerful and an extremely magnetic leader, but he wasn't Obi-Wan Kenobi. He couldn't use mind control or the Force or whatever to make Ric bend to his will. *You want to go to Fandangos* ... That was ridiculous.

Wasn't it?

She sat down on the curb, definitely feeling every ounce of wine she'd had tonight. 'Max saved my life a couple of years ago. I was on a plane that was hijacked by terrorists and . . .' She shrugged.

'Oh, man. Really?' He sat down next to her.

'Really.' She sighed, chin on her knees, arms wrapped around her legs. 'I'm in love with him.' She turned her head so that she could look up at him. 'Want to sleep with me?'

Ric laughed. But then he looked at her closely. 'Are you really drunk?'

Gina sighed again. 'No.'

'Did you maybe take something mind altering tonight that I don't know about?'

She sat up straight, indignant. 'No!'

Ric held up both hands in a gesture that said *easy there*. 'Hey, I'm not asking you this as Detective Alvarado. I'm asking as a man who likes you. You're not going to get in trouble or anything. I just want to know the truth.'

'The truth is I don't do drugs,' Gina told him. 'And I'm really not drunk. I'm just . . .' She rolled her eyes. 'Pathetic.'

'I don't think you're pathetic,' he said. 'I think you're really hot and . . . yeah, I really want to sleep with you. Your being in love with this other guy is probably going to make it suck, but, you know, I'll suffer through somehow.'

Gina looked up at him and laughed.

He was looking at her with half-closed eyes and a crooked smile on his handsome face. He reached up to push her hair back, and his fingers were warm against her face. 'I bet I can make you forget about him tonight.'

Wouldn't that be nice – if she really *could* forget everything. Max, the airplane, the way it had felt to be so certain she was going to die . . .

Ric leaned toward her as he pulled her chin up to meet him. His lips were soft and his mouth tasted sweet, like Fandangos's coffee, rich and strong and laced with cinnamon.

His hand was in her hair. Gina closed her eyes and let him kiss her and tried to imagine his hands all over her, his body on top of hers, and . . .

She pulled away, scrambling to her feet.

'Hey!' He followed, catching her as she tripped in her haste to get away. 'Whoa, whoa! You okay?'

'I can't do this,' she said. 'Oh, God, I'm so sorry.' She tried to pull free. 'Please let go of me.'

He didn't. 'Gina—'

'I *said*, let *go* of me!'

He let her go, both hands in the air. 'Okay, now you're *really* freaking me out.'

She walked away from him, toward her motel, as fast as she could without it being called running. But when she got to the corner, she stopped. And turned and went back. Because she owed him at least an explanation.

He was still standing there looking at her as if she was insane.

She was. She was definitely insane.

'You don't really want to sleep with me,' she told him, trying her hardest not to cry. 'You don't know this yet, but I do. So I'm just skipping ahead to the part where you say, "Oh, gee, Gina, all your baggage is a little too heavy for me. I mean, wow, the responsibility's just too intense. I think we should just be friends."'

'All what baggage?' he asked. His eyes were open a little wider now, and his smile was gone.

Gina couldn't bear to watch his warm brown eyes change from wary to horrified to filled with embarrassed discomfort. So she closed her own eyes and told him. 'I haven't had sex since before I was gang raped on that hijacked plane.'

'Oh, shit, you were . . .?' Like most people, he couldn't say the R-word. 'Oh, Gina, oh, baby . . .'

Ric put his arms around her and held her tightly, but it wasn't with passion anymore, it was only with kindness, and she wanted to cry.

'I wasn't going to tell you,' she said, 'but that's not fair to you, because I really don't know if I'm going to flip out, or if I'm going to need to slow down or even stop, and it's just not fair *not* to tell. But as soon as I tell, no one wants to touch me!'

'Shh,' he said. 'It's all right. It's okay, baby. It's going to be okay.'

She smacked his arms, pushing him away from her. 'That's such a stupid thing to say! Maybe it's going to be okay for you, but it's not going to be okay for me!'

He took a step toward her. 'Gina—'

She took a step back. 'Just go home!'

He kept coming. 'I'd rather go with you. Back to your place.'

Yeah, right.

'Don't touch me,' she warned him. He probably thought she wouldn't know that he was lying.

He held out his hand to her. 'Come on. I'll drive.'

Gina looked at him. It had finally happened. She'd finally met a guy who was too nice to say no.

But she suddenly knew that rejection really hadn't been her problem all these months. She had actually been relieved that Elliot hadn't wanted to sleep with her.

Because she wasn't ready for this. It was possible that she'd never be ready for this kind of casual 'I like you, let's do it' sex again.

Her body had been used. Viciously, brutally. Sex had been forced on her as an expression of terrible violence and hatred.

She'd told Max that she wanted that part of her life back, but she really didn't.

She didn't want to experience sex ever again as anything less than a meaningful demonstration of real, deep love.

And as nice as Ric was, she didn't love him.

'I'm sorry,' she said. 'I really am.' And she turned and ran away.

Here he was. Lying alone in a bed in a cheap motel room, balls still aching from being flattened by 120 pounds of angry woman, buzzing from all the caffeine in his system. Exhausted as hell, weary from worry and grief, but too freaking scared to fall asleep.

Sam had taken a warm shower in an attempt to relax, but even that hadn't helped.

He wanted to reach for the phone again, to call Alyssa, who was on the other side of the wall just behind his head, in the next room over.

And say what?

Please, I don't want to be alone tonight. I keep thinking about kind-hearted Donny burning to death in that fire, and Tom losing Kelly, and Janine on the kitchen floor, and how terrified Haley must've been right before she died . . .

No. Haley wasn't dead and he wasn't going to call Alyssa.

Because if he called her, she might come over. And if she came over, they'd end up in bed together and . . .

And Sam wasn't going to sleep with her. He'd made that

decision today while they were talking about love, about the differences between 'I want you' and 'I love you'. He'd realized, with remarkable clarity considering how tired he was, that sex – as much as he desperately wanted it – would only complicate the shit out of their relationship.

Their relationship. Sam found himself smiling wanly at the ceiling. As bad as this situation was, it *had* brought about something good.

Whether she liked it or not, he and Alyssa Locke were in a relationship again.

Yes, it was freaking mixed up and about the farthest thing from normal that a relationship could be, but it *was* a relationship.

True, neither one of them had completely figured out how Mary Lou and Haley and, yeah, even Max Bhagat fit into the equation, but what the hell.

Sam was determined to take this embryonic, misshapen, ugly lump of a relationship and grow it into something beautiful. Something honest. Something permanent. Something real.

Something like the relationship Walt had shared with Dot.

That one had started out nearly as screwed up as this was.

Well, maybe not quite. Because Walt and Dot had been careful to keep sex out of things until their feelings for each other had grown into real, rock-solid love.

Sam looked at the phone again. Don't do it, idiot. Don't call her again.

Of course, there were definitely a lot of missing steps in the dance that would start with his picking up the phone and end with her over here, in his bed. Assuming it would automatically go there was arrogant and egotistical.

She could say no. She *would* say no.

But then Sam closed his eyes, remembering the way Alyssa had kissed him in the back hallway of the Wal-Mart. Holy, holy Jesus. She was fire in his arms. For a few minutes there, he'd been convinced that she was going to come. Just from a dry hump in a public corridor.

He'd almost lost it himself, but his excuse was that he'd been celibate now for nearly a year.

Sam squinted at the ceiling. Was it possible . . .?

Nah. He'd seen the way she'd kissed Max. The fucker.

Still . . . Maybe it meant that Max wasn't so great in bed after all.

Yeah, wouldn't *that* be nice? Sam wasn't any closer to sleep, but thinking about Max being unable to keep it up, or maybe just boring Alyssa to tears, was definitely better than thinking about Donny burning to death or Mary Lou and Haley jammed into some trunk.

But even better than the thought of Max, impotent, was the idea of Alyssa maybe being as desperate for Sam's touch as he was for hers, not because she missed great sex, but because she missed *him*.

In which case, if he called her on that phone, she might say yes.

Which was why he couldn't call. Because if she said yes, then in order to stick to his plan about growing something real, Sam would have to be the one to say no. And he did not have a good history with that particular word. At least not when it came to Alyssa Locke and sexual intercourse.

Sam heard Alyssa's cell phone ringing through the thin motel walls. He sat up.

Was that Jules calling her? Or Max?

Either way, it was probably news.

He could hear the murmur of her voice through the wall, but try as he might, he couldn't make out the words. Probably because his heart was pounding too freaking loudly.

Please God, let her come hammering on his door to tell him that those bodies in the trunk were definitely not Mary Lou and Haley.

He heard her stop talking, heard only silence.

Then the sound of water running, a toilet flushing.

Then nothing.

Until she knocked, softly, on his door.

Oh, no.

That was not a jubilant knock, and Sam knew that the news was not going to be good.

Please God . . .

'Still nothing absolutely conclusive,' she said before he even got the door all the way open. 'Jules said they're having some trouble with the dental records. The fire was . . . apparently very hot.'

Sam nodded, just looking at her.

She'd had an overnight bag in the back of her car, and unlike him, she had a change of clothes. She either slept naked or her pajamas were too revealing, because she'd thrown her jeans and that baggy T-shirt back on.

She'd splashed water on her face before coming over here – part of her hair was still wet – but despite that, her eyes looked red, as if she'd just been crying.

As she looked back at him, tears welled in her eyes. She covered her mouth with her hand as, Jesus, her face contorted and she started to cry.

Nothing *absolutely* conclusive, she'd said.

Sam's ears roared as he pulled her into the room, into his arms, closing the door behind her.

'What did Jules tell you?' Sam asked, even though he knew. Mary Lou's driver's license or something else that could identify them had been found near the car.

'I'm sorry,' she said as she cried into his chest, this tough-as-nails woman who fought so hard never to be seen as weak.

He clung to her as tightly as she was holding him. God, give him the strength to endure this. 'Please, Lys, tell me.'

She looked up at him. 'They were killed by a shotgun, at close range, same as Janine.'

That was it? *That* was the bad news?

Sam nearly fainted from the relief.

'I'm so sorry,' Alyssa said, holding him even tighter.

It was beyond nice that she was in his arms. And he was definitely blown away by her tears, but . . .

'You do know that you can't match slugs from a shotgun,' he told her. 'Forensics can't know for sure it was the same weapon. That's why people use shotguns to kill other people. And come on, Lys, there must be thousands of shotguns in this part of Florida alone.'

She lifted her head to look at him again, wonder in her eyes. 'You still don't think it's them.'

'I'm trying hard not to,' he told her. 'I'm scared to death that it is, but . . . What you just told me isn't good news, yeah, but it's not bad enough to make me quit hoping.'

She was so beautiful, gazing up at him with streaks of tears on her face and such emotion in her eyes. It was hard to believe he'd once thought she was cold and unfeeling.

'You stopped hoping they were still alive as soon as the news came out that those bodies were found, didn't you?' he asked her gently.

She nodded, fresh tears escaping. 'I'm sorry.'

'No,' Sam said. 'Don't. Don't apologize.' He touched her face, but trying to wipe her tears away was futile because they were still pouring down her face. God, she was crying and she wasn't trying to hide it from him. 'It's just . . . I don't get it. I mean, maybe I'm the one who's being overly optimistic, but—'

'Bad things happen,' she told him earnestly. 'It's just part of life. I guess I think it's easier to assume that when the . . . the *piano* falls from the sky, it's going to fall on you. Otherwise, you're blindsided. And if that happens, you may never get back up.'

When the piano falls, not *if*. Oh, Alyssa. What a way to live. With potential pain and heartbreak lurking around every corner.

And the only way to effectively counter it was to prepare for the worst to happen.

Or maybe even to run away from the good things – like love. If you didn't let yourself love someone, you couldn't lose them.

No wonder Alyssa had fought so hard for so long to keep Sam out of her life. And when she'd finally opened up, finally agreed to give him a chance, to give their relationship a try, he'd gone and dropped a piano named Mary Lou squarely on top of her.

'I guess that makes me a pessimist, huh?' she told him, pulling out of his arms. As he watched, she crossed the room, heading to the mirror and sink by the bathroom, pulling several tissues from the slot in the counter. 'I wish I wasn't. It's not something I particularly like about myself. But—' She blew her nose. 'I was only thirteen when my mother died. I think a lot of kids who lose a parent become pessimistic. And those numbers probably increase among the kids who lose a parent to violent crime.'

'Oh, man.' Sam sat on the edge of the bed. 'I didn't realize . . .'

'I don't talk about it much,' she admitted. 'It's still . . .' She looked around the room. Anywhere but directly into his eyes. But then she did. She made herself hold his gaze. 'It's hard to talk about. I still miss her so much.'

Sam nodded. 'I'd really like you to tell me,' he said quietly. 'I want to know you, Alyssa.'

She started to cry again. 'Shit,' she swore. 'I'm a mess tonight.' She got another tissue from the counter, and then came over and sat down on the bed, next to Sam.

Not right next to him, but close enough.

She looked at him, and her eyes were watery and her nose was red, and she said, 'You know, I think that was probably the nicest thing any man has ever said to me – that you want to know me. So if you just said it because you were looking for some play—'

'No.' Sam cut her off. 'I said it because I meant it.' He moved back, away from her. 'And I'm not sleeping with you again until you really get to know *me*.'

She laughed at that. 'Yeah, like you wouldn't be all over me if I gave you the least little encouragement.'

'You sat on the bed, and I just backed away,' he pointed out.

He watched her realize that that was true.

'You said something day before yesterday about hiding in a closet,' he told her. 'Did you actually see your mother get killed?' He braced himself for her answer, praying that he'd gotten it wrong.

'No,' she said. 'It was ...' She closed her eyes, shook her head. 'It was Lanora in the closet.'

Lanora, her niece? No, Lanora was also Alyssa's youngest sister's name. Lanora, who had died several years ago from complications from a pregnancy.

And how often did *that* happen in these modern times? Talk about pianos falling from the sky ...

'Can you tell me about it?' Sam asked her.

Alyssa nodded. 'I'd like to,' she said quietly – three little words that filled his heart with so much hope he was sure for a minute that he was going to start to cry, too.

But she didn't notice. She was back to looking at the floor.

'I was at school,' she told him. 'My mother stayed home from work that day because Lanora had a stomach virus. I guess my mother was tired because Lanora had been up all night. They were both taking a nap when someone broke in. You know, any other day, the apartment would have been empty.' Her voice shook.

'Aw, Jesus,' Sam said.

She glanced back at him. 'Yeah, Lanora told me that Mommy woke her up by putting her hand over her mouth. She told her to get in the bedroom closet, to hide. I guess they were lying down together, in our bedroom, and my mother heard a noise out in the other room. We didn't have a phone in there – she had to get to her room to call 911. I don't really know exactly what happened. She must've surprised whoever was in there – some addict looking for things to sell for drugs. They caught him when he sold our stereo to a pawn shop for ten dollars.' She made a sound that was something like laughter but had nothing to do with humor.

'He killed my mother for ten *dollars*,' Alyssa told him. The tears that were now in her eyes were from anger, and she brusquely pushed them away.

Sam didn't know what to say. 'I'm so sorry.'

'The police report said she was struck in the head with a blunt instrument,' she continued. 'The injury wasn't bad enough to kill her, except it did. There was swelling and hemorrhaging, and she never regained consciousness.'

Alyssa had been only thirteen. 'Where was your father?' Sam asked. She hadn't mentioned her father before today.

'He and my mother split up when I was eight – after Lanora was born. He just dropped off the map. He completely disappeared, except he sent a check every month. And then the checks stopped coming, and we found out he'd died in a car accident.' She looked at him. 'I think right until then my mother hadn't given up hope that he'd come back.'

Sam nodded. 'Hope can be a pretty powerful thing.' He knew all about that.

Alyssa nodded, too. 'We had a rough couple of years. But things were actually starting to turn around. We had plans to move out of that neighborhood.'

She was silent for a moment, and then she looked at him again and said, 'To this day, I do not understand why she didn't just hide in the closet with Lanora.'

'She wanted to protect her,' Sam said. 'She had no idea that whoever was out there wasn't going to harm your sister, that he wasn't going to search the closets and—'

'I know,' she said. 'I just wish . . .' She shook her head, wiping her eyes again. 'I came home from school and the street was crawling with emergency vehicles. Tyra – my other sister – had gone over to a friend's house after school. I remember being glad about that when I realized the ambulance was there for Mommy. Oh, God, Sam, all that blood on the kitchen floor . . .'

Sam closed his eyes, flooded by a memory of tomato sauce, bright against the kitchen tile in Walt and Dot's house. Jesus, imagine if that had been blood. It had been bad enough as it was.

'I really want to put my arms around you, Lys, but I'm afraid you'd take it the wrong way.'

'I think I'd like it,' she said, barely loud enough for him to hear, 'whichever way you meant it.'

He reached for her, and she met him halfway, which was *such* a freaking mistake, because there they were, smack in the middle of his bed, holding on to each other.

But okay. He was a grown-up. Embracing a woman he craved more than oxygen while in the middle of a bed didn't mean that he *had* to take off her clothes and bury himself inside her.

Even if *she* took off her clothes, he could leave his pants zipped. Well, except for the fact that he wasn't wearing pants and his boxers didn't have a zipper.

It was entirely possible that if he could keep this from turning sexual, he might succeed in impressing her. She might realize that he was serious. Then when he finally got up the courage again to tell her that he loved her, she'd realize he meant *I love you* instead of *I want you*.

But, oh, Jesus. Jesus . . .

'The police didn't realize that Lanora was in the closet,' Alyssa said into his neck. 'They'd searched the apartment, but they weren't looking for a little kid. At first I thought whoever had hurt my mother had taken Lanora. But then I went into the bedroom and heard her crying. She was in the closet – Mommy had told her to stay there, not come out.'

Sam closed his eyes as he stroked Alyssa's hair.

'By the time I found her, she was completely traumatized. I'm sure she heard whatever happened, but she blocked it. She used to have these nightmares and I'd wake her up and she'd say that Mommy was screaming. She never got over it,' Alyssa said. 'All her life she was running from all that fear and pain. She tried to shut down the noise in her head with drugs and alcohol and stupid, empty sex.'

And Alyssa had tried to take control of her own emotions.

Don't get too close to someone who might leave you. And always, always expect the next piano to drop directly on your head.

'So now you know,' Alyssa whispered. She pulled back to look into his eyes.

Oh, man, that look on her face meant . . . Sam knew this woman well enough to know that she craved physical intimacy right now for a lot of different reasons.

The first being comfort.

The second was that she was unbelievably hot, and she just plain flat-out loved having sex.

But the other reasons were more complicated. They had to do with her expectations when it came to him, and the way she'd defined their relationship in the past as one of pure sex.

He didn't want her to look back on this moment and be able to discount their solid emotional connection. He couldn't risk letting it be overshadowed by the physical, by the lightning bolts that were going to shoot around the room if he let himself so much as kiss her.

'I'm not going to kiss you,' Sam told her.

Alyssa didn't believe him. He could see it in her eyes, and then he could taste it as his lips brushed hers.

'Ah, fuck,' he said, completely disgusted with himself, and kissed her again.

Twenty-one

Alyssa put her arms around Sam's neck and kissed him back.

This was a mistake. She knew it was a mistake. Every other time she had let herself fall under this man's spell had been a bona fide, screaming, full-throttle, hit-the-wall-going-a-hundred-miles-an-hour mistake.

But while it was happening, while she was here in the denial phase, making love to him was, without doubt, the best idea she'd ever had in her entire life.

It had been too long since she'd been in his arms, in his bed, but every kiss, every touch was so familiar. She recognized the way she fit against him so perfectly, his taste, his scent, the heat in his eyes.

Sam was wearing only his boxer shorts and she let herself run her hands across his back – all that smooth skin, satin over rock-solid muscles.

His hair was short and darker brown than she remembered, all his golden, sun-bleached ends on some hairdresser's floor back in Gainesville. She was used to it being much longer, down around his shoulders. She'd loved running her fingers through it.

But even cut short this way it was still nice to touch, so soft and thick, and without it in his face, his eyes weren't hidden from her. She could watch him watching her as he kissed her, touched her.

She kicked her legs free from her jeans and yanked off her shirt and pushed off her panties.

SUZANNE BROCKMANN

Sam groaned, letting go of her and lying back on the bed, one arm up over his eyes. 'Oh, Jesus, you're naked.'

Alyssa laughed. 'Is that really a problem for you?' She pulled off his boxers so that his erection sprang free. Oh, yes. Oh, *yes*. Praise the Lord for his magnificent creations . . . 'It sure doesn't seem to be.'

But he stopped her before she could take him in her mouth, pulling her up with him so that they were both kneeling on the bed. 'Just tell me that you honestly know what you're doing. Promise me this isn't just a reaction to stress, or high emotion, or Jesus, I don't know what . . .'

His eyes were so blue. He was looking at her so searchingly, as if he were trying to see inside of her head.

Alyssa looked back at him. Was it possible that he was seriously going to stop them from . . .

She spread her legs apart, and he swallowed, his eyes following her movement. But he didn't touch her, and when he looked back at her, he shook his head slightly, desperation in his eyes, even as he laughed. She could read *his* mind very clearly. *Don't do that to me.*

But she was determined to do that – and more. She reached to touch him, and he caught her hand.

'Please,' he said. 'This is important to me.'

He *was* serious. And she couldn't lie to him.

'I have absolutely no idea what I'm doing,' she admitted. 'I just know that right now I want you so much.'

It was not the correct answer. She could see his disappointment.

'I'm sorry if that's not enough,' she said. She brought his hand down, between her legs. 'Are you sure it can't be enough for tonight?'

There was no way he could miss the fact that she was completely ready for him. He didn't pull his hand back, so she rocked against him, pushing his fingers slightly inside of her. Oh, yes.

'I'm not going to do this,' he said on an exhale, as if he'd been

396

holding his breath. But just like before, when he told her he wasn't going to kiss her, he began touching her, his fingers moving on their own, exploring. . . . He shifted closer.

And this time, when she reached for him, he didn't stop her.

'Alyssa,' he breathed as her hand closed around him.

Oh, *yes* . . .

'I need you,' she told him, and kissed him.

His surrender couldn't have been more obvious if he'd pulled out a pen and paper and signed it right in front of her.

He kissed her as feverishly as he touched her, all of her, skimming his hands down and across her body, then kissing and licking and, oh, *yes* . . .

He made a sound that made her laugh because it expressed so exactly all that she was feeling.

'Please tell me you have a condom,' she lifted her head to gasp.

'God,' he said, 'I don't.'

'I do,' she said. 'In my fanny pack.' She carried them with her. Smart women did these days. 'In my room.'

Not that she'd had the opportunity in the past few years to actually use one . . .

Sam picked her up, throwing her over his shoulder in a fireman's hold. 'Oh, my *God*,' Alyssa laughed. 'Sam!'

He grabbed her jeans from the floor that was where she'd stashed both her room key and her cell phone – and his room key from the top of the TV.

'Wait!' she shouted, but he just went on out the door.

They were both completely naked.

No, Sam was *more* than naked. He was extra-specially naked, considering his body was standing at full, proud attention.

'Whoops, 'scuse me, ma'am,' she heard him say, and she squeaked and closed her eyes. Oh, *no*.

But as he opened the door to her room and went inside, she opened her eyes to look back and to apologize, but there was no one there. She smacked him, hard, on the butt. 'Sam, you nearly gave me a heart attack—'

He was laughing as he tossed her down on her bed. 'No one saw us. Besides, I used a special ninja technique to make myself invisible.'

'You maybe,' she said. 'But not me.' She scrambled for her fanny pack sitting on the bedside table. It was jammed full of all kinds of stuff, so she took it and dumped its contents on the floor.

'You have to work very hard to be invisible,' he agreed. 'You're too beautiful. Although you did a great job of it back in the Wal-Mart, you know.'

She looked up from her search, feeling almost ridiculously glad at his compliment. 'You think?'

'Yeah,' he said, coming over to help. 'I didn't know it was you, so you caught me. You won.'

'I like to win,' she said.

He smiled at her. 'I noticed.'

And there they were. Two little red packages, attached to each other by a perforated connection that hadn't yet been torn.

She tore them apart and turned to Sam, who had a funny look on his face.

Oh, no. No, no. She was *not* going to let him put the brakes on. Not now.

'Are those—' He stopped. Shook his head. 'Never mind. I'm just paranoid, I guess, when it comes to condoms.' He held out his hand, and she gave the package to him. 'You still sure you want to do this?' he asked as he covered himself.

'What do you think?' she said, purposely lying back on the bed in an extremely provocative pose.

Sam laughed as he looked at her, as he took his time looking at her.

She'd always loved the way he looked at her.

And she loved looking at him, too. His body was sculpted by hard work and the SEALs' constant training. He'd put on muscle since she'd last seen him without his clothes. Every time she saw him naked, he was more filled out, more of a full grown man.

It seemed impossible that he could be more gorgeous, but somehow he managed to pull it off.

And the haircut really worked with that body. Dear Lord, he was an amazing-looking man.

'I think,' he said slowly, as he sat down on the edge of the bed, far enough away so that he couldn't touch her and she couldn't touch him, 'that if I try to negotiate with you right now, I won't stand a chance. But I know that I've sold myself way short in the past when it comes to me and you, so I'm going to give it a try. Okay?'

He was serious.

She was here on the bed, dying for him, and he wanted to *talk*? Alyssa laughed.

'At least nod your head yes,' he told her.

He wanted yes? She'd give him a yes.

Alyssa ran her hand from her breasts to her stomach, and then lower. She caught her lower lip in her teeth as she looked up at him.

Heat sparked in his eyes, as he laughed, too.

But to her total surprise, he still kept his distance. 'Well, okay *then*. I'll take that as an affirmative.' He cleared his throat, but when he spoke again, his voice was still hoarse. 'Here's the deal, Lys. If you want me, you need to promise, right now, that you'll have dinner with me when this mess is over. You don't promise – I turn around, right now, and go back to my room.' He laughed again. 'Yeah, we both know there's only one place I'm going, but I said it like I really meant it, didn't I?' He closed his eyes. 'I hate myself. I'm so fucking weak.'

He wasn't completely kidding.

Oh, Sam . . . 'Come here,' she told him, holding out her arms for him.

He came, crawling across the bed to her, all blue eyes and

tanned skin and hard, male muscles in motion, and she kissed him.

'I didn't mean to make light of what you're saying,' she told him, unable to keep from touching him now that he was close enough to touch. 'I appreciate your being honest with me, I really do. I think that I probably need to be honest with you, too, because you don't seem to realize what a major event this is – my being here with you like this.'

'Yeah, actually, I do,' he said.

She touched his face. He had such a beautiful face, with those beautiful, beautiful eyes. 'No, you don't. I know you think I've spent the past few years with Max, and I have to confess that I purposely let you think that, even to the point of giving you—' She cleared her throat. '—misinformation about it when you asked me directly. But the fact is, I went out with him only a handful of times. And I never slept with him. Not even once.'

'But I went to your hotel room and Max was there,' he said. 'In San Diego. It was that night Jules was shot—'

'And Carla Ramirez died?' she asked.

'Yeah.'

'I think he sat in my room all night. I was a mess after—' Alyssa shook her head. 'But we didn't sleep together. Sam, I haven't been with anyone since I was with you.'

There was wonder in his eyes now. 'Holy shit, Alyssa . . .'

She caught herself. 'To be *completely* honest, I probably would have hooked up with Max, but he didn't want to. . . . No, that's not completely true either. He wanted to, but he *wouldn't*. Not while I was working for him.'

'He's insane. He's got to be completely—'

'He's principled,' she corrected him. 'He's amazing. He really is a good man, Sam. I think if you didn't spend so much energy hating him, you might actually like him.'

The wonder was replaced by worry. 'Do you, um . . . Shit, I know I've asked you this before, but he makes me so jealous. . . . Do you love him?'

Alyssa looked at him. 'Yes, Roger,' she said. 'I love him. That's why I took off your clothes. That's why I'm dying to make love to *you*.'

He kissed her then, and kissed her and kissed her, pushing her back on the bed, his weight heavy between her legs. He kissed his way down her throat, licking her breasts, drawing her into his mouth.

'Oh, God!' She arched against him, searching for him, needing him inside of her, but he'd shifted back.

'Hey, Lys?' he said, and as she looked up at him, she saw that his eyes were luminous. 'Could you maybe say that to me again?'

She knew what he meant, what he wanted to hear. Make love. Not sex. *Love*. The idea that hearing her say those words could mean so much to him took her breath away. She almost couldn't say it. She had to whisper. 'I'm dying to make love to you, Sam.'

He held her gaze as he shifted his position and . . .

Oh, it felt so good.

'Sam,' she breathed, realizing that she hadn't told him what she'd wanted to tell him, and needing him to know. 'I know a really great restaurant, not far from my apartment in DC. They don't chase you out after you finish dinner. You can just sit there and talk all night if you want.'

If you really, honestly wanted to get to know someone.

He understood what she was saying. She could see it in his eyes.

He kissed her then, the sweetest, deepest, most perfect kiss of her entire life.

He remembered exactly how to touch her, how to move to make her crazy. Slowly. So slowly.

Oh, the things he was doing to her . . .

It was too good. Nothing could possibly be this good, but it was, because it was *Sam*, and it scared her to death that she was back here, right here again, like this, with him.

He was breathing her name. 'Alyssa . . .'

It might've been a question. He seemed to want an answer. She gave him one, although it wasn't quite a word.

'Tell me what you want,' he breathed in her ear.

'Please,' she managed.

'Tell me . . .'

'You,' she gasped. 'I want *you*.'

And, oh, that got the right response, the response she'd hoped for. He knew damn well that she liked sex – making love – hard and fast, that she loved driving *him* crazy.

This would do it.

Oh, yes. Oh, *yes* . . .

'Lys . . .'

She heard the tension in his voice and she opened her eyes to look up at him, and she saw it in his face, in the corded muscles of his shoulders and arms. She watched his eyes as he fought his release, as she fought hers, too. This was too good to end, too good, too—

'Come on!' He half growled, half laughed his frustration, because he somehow knew what she was doing, knew she was holding back. Sam knew her, knew her . . .

He *knew* her.

Alyssa exploded.

There was no other way to describe it. One moment she was looking into his eyes, and the next she was shattering.

He was right with her, all the way, shouting something she couldn't hear because she didn't have ears anymore.

And then she was in little fragments, floating around him, settling back down so that her arms that were holding him so tightly were once again attached to her shoulders.

'It's good to know,' Sam murmured into her re-formed ear, 'that we're finally both on the same page.'

Max watched Gina as she ran away from that young detective.

Enrique Alvarado. Born here in Sarasota. Father originally from Cuba, mother a Valdez, as in Valdez Imports of Miami.

After seeing Gina with him, Max had come back to his car to make a few quick investigative phone calls.

Detective Ric Alvarado had attended Dartmouth College, graduating at the top of his class. Went on to Harvard Law School but left after less than a year to focus on law enforcement. He'd apparently wanted to help put the scumbags of the world behind bars rather than get them out. And he'd done just that. His record with the Sarasota Police Department was beyond exemplary.

And Max had been wrong – how often did *that* happen? – about both his age and his status as a brand-new detective.

Alvarado had been a detective for seven long years. The man was thirty-one years old.

Either he was like Jules Cassidy and had a baby face, or as Max got older, anyone under thirty-five was starting to look like a child.

Max had watched as Gina and Ric came out into the parking lot.

He'd watched them talk, watched Gina smile and laugh, watched Alvarado kiss her.

He should have left. He should have driven away right then.

Instead, he sat there. Torturing himself. Hating the idea of her taking Alvarado home with her.

That wasn't what she needed – casual sex with some near stranger.

Except, as he sat there, watching Gina, he had to face the honest truth.

Max really hated the idea of her taking Alvarado home not because it wasn't what *she* needed, but because it wasn't what *he* wanted.

He could pretend that he'd come here tonight – a night when he should have been flying to San Diego – to protect Gina from herself. To make sure she didn't put herself into any real danger.

But that wasn't the only reason he was here.

Out on the sidewalk, Alvarado had his arms around Gina,

and damn it, now she pushed him away and started running, this time in earnest.

Alvarado gave chase, but Gina just ran faster.

All right, this bullshit wasn't going any farther. Max switched on his headlights and pulled out of the shadows, driving swiftly toward them.

Alvarado caught Gina's arm, and she pulled hard to get away, only, son of a bitch, he tripped and they both went down onto somebody's lawn.

Max screeched to a stop with his front tires on the sidewalk and jumped out of the car.

Gina was scrambling away from Alvarado. It was to his credit that he didn't try to stop her, didn't try to hang on to her or pin her down.

'That's enough,' Max said. 'Gina, get in the car.' He looked at Alvarado. 'Thanks for your help. I'll take it from here.'

The detective pulled himself to his feet. 'I wasn't trying to—'

'Note that you're still alive,' Max said. 'If I thought your intention was to hurt her, that wouldn't be the case. Go home, Detective.'

Alvarado looked past him to Gina, who was standing now, breathing hard, one arm wrapped around herself as she wiped tears from her face with the heel of her other hand.

'Are you going to be all right with him?' he asked her, refusing to be bullied, gaining another point or two in Max's scorebook.

Gina nodded. 'I'm so sorry, Ric.'

He nodded, too, as he brushed off his pants, giving its torn knee barely a glance. 'She needs some serious help, man,' he told Max in a low voice as he walked back toward the parking lot.

Max looked at Gina. She was watching him, her eyes huge, her pale face eerily lit by the streetlight. 'I think he's probably right,' he said.

She didn't say anything. She just looked at him.

'Get in the car,' he said again, adding, 'Please.'

Gina did. Her eyes still on him, she moved around to the passenger's side and opened the door. And climbed in.

Max got behind the wheel, extremely aware that she was still watching him, extremely aware of the hope that was in her eyes.

Oh, no, Gina, that was *not* why he was here.

'Did you like the music tonight?' she asked.

It didn't seem worth the effort to lie and say he wasn't there. He'd seen her looking in the corner where he'd stood. 'It was . . . Well, I've never paid much attention to jazz, but it was . . . interesting.'

'That good, huh?'

'It's not my thing,' he admitted. 'It's so chaotic and out there.'

'You know, it's not that different from Hendrix,' she said.

She remembered that he'd once told her that Jimi Hendrix was one of his guilty pleasures.

'I think there's actually *more* chaos in Hendrix's music,' Gina continued. 'I mean, he's always on the verge of a meltdown. There's such wildness and, I don't know, a desperation to his guitar playing. The big difference is that, for you, it's familiar desperation.'

'Yeah, maybe.' God *damn* it. Wildness and desperation. No wonder he loved Hendrix. He could relate so completely. He put the car into gear. 'Where are you staying?'

'It's not far,' she said. 'You can drop me at the corner.'

Max just looked at her.

'So even though jazz isn't your thing, didn't you think I was good?' she asked.

She was sitting there with her nose red, with her makeup smudged and smeared around eyes that still looked as if she might start crying again any second, looking impossibly beautiful. She was wearing some kind of sports top, in a style that Alyssa had once told him was called a racerback. It had really showed off her incredible body as she'd played.

There was something about a healthy woman playing the

drums that was a total turn-on. The few times she'd really cut loose, hair and arms flying, legs working, breasts moving, he'd had a definite physical reaction.

Except, *Yeah, you gave me a real hard-on,* was probably not the response she was looking for.

Max smiled despite himself. Although, knowing Gina, she would probably laugh. And then she would be all over him. His smile faded. *All* over him.

'What were you thinking just then?' she asked softly.

'I was thinking that you're as talented as you are beautiful, and that I wish I'd never had to meet you.'

She understood what he meant. 'Well, you did,' she said. 'And here we are. Sitting in your car again, in the middle of the night.' She laughed, but it was only to cover up the fact that she had tears back in her eyes. 'If I tell you where I'm staying, will you come in for a little while?'

He started to protest, but Gina cut him off.

'Just to talk,' she said. 'Please, Max. You don't know how much I miss talking to you.'

Oh yes, he did. It was probably just about as much as he missed talking to her. Sometimes it manifested itself in a physical ache in his chest or his throat.

'I'm at the Siesta Beach House,' she told him. 'Take a right at the stop sign, fourth driveway on the left. My room is down by the water. Number 21.'

It *was* close.

It was so close, Max hadn't yet figured out what the hell he was going to do before he was there and putting the car into park.

He couldn't go into her room with her. That would be a huge mistake.

'Please come in,' she whispered.

'I can't,' he said just as quietly.

'Just to talk.'

'Really.' He looked at her.

'Yes.' She was lying. If he went in there, he wasn't coming out until morning.

Some of his frustration escaped. 'Are you going to tell me what happened tonight? Why you ended up running down the street, with some stranger you *picked up in a bar* chasing you?'

'Ric's a police detective and you know it,' she responded just as hotly. 'He's not just some stranger.'

Max nodded. 'Great. So you got lucky. *This* time.'

'You want to know what happened?' she said. 'I got scared. He was all ready to come home with me, and I got *scared*. So I told him. Everything. And then he got . . . you know. The way guys get when it's too heavy and they'd rather go home and watch Comedy Central. But he was going to do it anyway. I was going to be his pity fuck for the month – I'm real *lucky*, huh? But it felt really, *really* wrong, and I knew that it's always going to feel wrong, unless you change your mind, because the only time *any*thing feels right is when you're with me. But I know you're not going to, so God! Why do I even bother?'

Max felt his insides ripping open as she started to cry, as she got out of the car.

'Gina, wait—'

But she slammed the door and hurried toward the building.

Don't follow. He couldn't follow. But he also couldn't let her go. He couldn't leave her like this. He got out of the car, too, and followed her, because it seemed like the lesser of two evils. 'Gina.'

'I'm sorry,' she cried. 'I'm so sorry, Max.' She was standing there, trying to unlock the door to her room, fumbling with the key. She dropped it, and he cracked heads with her as he tried to pick it up.

'Sorry!' He moved her aside. 'Let me get it.'

He picked up the key, unlocked the door, and pushed it open. Her room was dark, and he stepped inside, looking for the light switch.

He found it, but when he flipped it, only one lamp went on.

It must've had a twenty-five watt bulb in it, because it barely lit the shabby room. Which was probably just as well, since the last time this place had been redecorated was back in 1975, and seeing it in bright light would have been too awful.

'Oh, Christ, Gina,' he said. 'You sure know how to pick 'em.'

'I *am* sorry, Max,' she said. 'Because I do understand. I *do*.'

The door closed behind her, and Max realized that he'd somehow ended up exactly the last place he should be. In Gina's room.

He had to get out of here.

'I know you blame yourself for what happened to me,' she told him, 'and I wish you wouldn't, because, really, the fault was mine. I pushed them – Babur and Al – on the plane. You told me not to. You told me to be careful, not to go too far. But I was trying to be Wonder Woman. I was trying to save the day.'

'No,' Max said. Damn it, did she really think . . .?

'I was trying to give you as much information about them as I could,' Gina told him, tears running down her face. 'I thought they were asleep, but they weren't and they heard me, and I gave away the fact that there were microphones planted and that you didn't need the radio to hear me. It was my fault—'

'*No*.' He reached for her, but she pulled back.

'*Yes*. You told me not to provoke them, but I did. I *provoked* them, so they raped me, and the captain tried to stop them, so they killed him and it was *my fault*.'

She sank to the floor, and he followed her there, afraid to touch her, afraid not to. 'No, Gina, you can't think that way!'

'You told me,' she said, looking at him with such heartbreaking grief in her eyes. 'You warned me. But I didn't listen. And now you can't even look at me without being haunted by it, by *my* mistake. It was *my* mistake, my fault, Max, not yours.'

Oh, God. Oh, almighty, vengeful, terrible God. Had she really been carrying this around for *years*?

'Gina, it was *not* your fault. Do you honestly think that?'

She did. She honestly did.

He put his arms around her and this time she didn't resist. This time she clung to him, still sobbing that she was sorry.

She was *sorry* for *provoking* her *rape*.

It was all Max could do not to cry, too.

But he'd wait and do that later. Right now, as quickly as possible, he had to correct this terrible misconception Gina had been living with for so long.

'Listen to me,' he said, working hard to make his voice calm. Soothing. Christ, he'd managed to sound matter-of-fact and unperturbed when he'd talked to the terrorists on the plane while they were raping her. Surely he could do it again now. But his voice broke. 'Gina, you *need* to listen to me.'

'Don't leave me,' she sobbed. 'Please, Max . . .'

He would have promised her anything. 'I'm not going anywhere,' he told her, holding her tightly, his cheek against the top of her head. 'I'll stay as long as you need me.'

He heard the words leaving his lips, and part of him stood off to the side and lifted his eyebrows at such an obvious error in judgment.

But the rest of him took note in the fact that his promise seemed to work quite well in calming Gina down, and he actually said it again. 'I'll stay as long as you want me to. You just have to take a couple of deep breaths and listen to me. Really listen, okay?'

She nodded and breathed.

'Okay,' he said, smoothing her hair back from her face. 'I'm going to tell you something that I've learned from years of negotiating and from years of dealing with people who are as desperate as the terrorists were who hijacked flight 232. I need you to listen carefully, and I need you to believe me. You trust me, right?'

Gina nodded again.

'I was straight with you about the jazz, right?'

Another nod. This one came with half of a laugh, too. Okay, good. She was listening.

'Can you sit up a little?' he asked. 'I want you to look into my eyes when I tell you what I'm going to tell you. Can you do that?'

She lifted her head, and the sight of her face, pale and tear-streaked and weary with grief and the weight of responsibility she'd been carrying for so long, broke his heart.

She was much too close, dangerously close, her mouth only inches from his, but he was the one who was unwilling to let her move back any farther. He wanted his arms around her.

'When Babur Haiyan gave the order to Nabulsi to attack you,' Max told her, 'he said, among other things, "You know what to do." Your attack, your rape, was something that they planned before they even got onto the plane. They thought you were the senator's daughter, remember? Your rape was symbolic as well as a literal retaliation. It was a political statement, believe it or not. It was going to happen, Gina, no matter *what* you did.'

He could see her listening, see her struggling to understand what he was saying. He held her gaze, willing her to believe him.

'And it was also their means of provoking *us*,' he continued. 'They wanted our troops to rush the plane. They had a bomb on board that was set to blow *after* the Navy SEALs had come into the plane, after the hijackers were dead, after we thought we'd won. You know this. They were tired of waiting – they were ready to die for their cause. So they attacked you, knowing that if they did, we'd probably stop stalling and send in our men.

'They knew we'd put those microphones and cameras in place. It was SOP – standard operating procedure – for a hijacking. You didn't give *any*thing away, I swear it. And if you really want to know the reason that you're alive today, it's because that pilot rushed to save you. Because they killed him, they had a body to throw off the plane. If no one had tried to help you, they probably would have killed you.'

He could still see a glimmer of disbelief in her eyes. She trusted him completely. He could see that, too, but she'd been living with another truth for so long. 'But Haiyan was so angry when he caught me telling you about their machine gun clips.'

Okay. How could he make her understand? 'I'm going to tell you what would have happened that morning if he *hadn't* caught you feeding us that information,' Max told her. 'You ready for this?'

She nodded.

'They would have said something like, "Don't look at me when you speak to me. Don't you know it's disrespectful in our country for a woman to meet a man's eyes?" And you would have looked down at the floor and said you were sorry. And they would have said, "Are you smiling? Do you think the way our people have been murdered is funny?" And you would have said no, and maybe you would have glanced up at them when you said that, and Haiyan would have hit you across the face for your disrespect, and you would have apologized, and it really wouldn't matter what you said or what you did, because Haiyan would eventually have said to Nabulsi, "*You know what to do.*" '

Max pushed her hair back from her face. 'You provoked none of that, Gina. Do you understand?'

If it was anyone's fault, it was his for not insisting that the SEALs take down the plane the night before.

She nodded, and then, as if she could read his mind, she said, 'If it wasn't my fault, if it was destined to happen the way you said, then it can't be your fault, either.'

It was Max's turn to nod. 'Yeah.' Right.

Gina settled deeper into his arms, her eyes distant, lost in her own thoughts, processing everything he'd told her.

'You should go back to that doctor,' Max told her, resting his cheek against the top of her head. 'Talk it out some more.'

'I will.' She lifted her head to look up at him. 'Do *you* have someone to talk to about it?'

SUZANNE BROCKMANN

He thought of Alyssa. He'd talked more to her than to anyone. But there was still so much he couldn't say to her. Wouldn't say.

And he'd just practically wrapped her up and put a bow on her and thrust her into Sam Starrett's eager hands.

'You should find someone,' Gina said softly. 'Someone you can be absolutely honest with. About everything.'

'Yeah, I should,' Max said, even though he knew damn well he'd never do it. Because before he could be honest with someone else – a friend or even a shrink – he first had to be honest with himself.

Jazz Jacquette touched Tom's knee.

Tom looked up to see the nurse who had helped take Kelly to surgery coming into the hospital waiting room.

He got to his feet. This was good, right? They wouldn't send the nurse down to tell him that Kelly had died in surgery.

Would they?

He searched the woman's face but saw only fatigue.

Stan was sitting to his right, and he stood, too, putting his hand on Tom's shoulder. It was the cosmic equivalent of a full body embrace from the nondemonstrative senior chief.

'The doctor would like you to come upstairs,' the nurse told him.

She's out of surgery.

So far so good.

She's going to be okay.

That's what Tom had wanted to hear. Instead, he'd been summoned because . . . *why*? The possibilities that leapt to mind were all bad. Kelly was dying. Kelly was already dead.

Fear hit him so hard, the room spun and blackened, and he nearly hit the deck.

Jazz and Stan pushed him back into his seat, jammed his head down between his knees.

'Is she alive?' he heard Jazz ask through the roaring in his ears.

412

Please God, please . . .

'You haven't gotten a status report?' The nurse's distant voice got only slightly louder as she knelt next to him. 'Oh, Commander, I'm so sorry—'

That was it. *Sorry.* The word he was praying that he wouldn't hear. Kelly was dead.

Tom stopped fighting the tunnel vision and checked out.

Twenty-two

'Yo, sleeping beauty.'

Tom opened his eyes to see Stan Wolchonok frowning down at him. 'Your wife's out of surgery, sir,' the senior chief chided him, 'the doctor needs you upstairs to hold her hand, and you decide it's time to take a nap?'

'Kelly's alive?' Tom sat up too fast, and his head spun.

Jazz was there, too, and he helped steady him. 'See, I told you he didn't hear that,' the XO said. 'Nurse Sunshine over here goes, "I'm sorry", and Tom didn't stick around long enough to hear the part that went, "that no one came to tell you that Kelly's out of surgery".'

The nurse was actually crying and laughing, both at the same time.

'She's alive?' Tom asked again, needing to hear it from her. 'Is she all right?'

She nodded, wiping her eyes. 'Dr Kenyon stopped the bleeding. The first twenty-four hours after surgery can be touch and go, but we're very hopeful. I'm so sorry, I thought you knew.' She laughed, covering her mouth with her hand. 'I can't believe you fainted.'

'He didn't faint,' Jazz said. 'He was just a little dizzy.'

'It happens to the best of us,' Stan chimed in. 'A shortage of oxygen to the brain.'

Tom closed his eyes. Kelly's bleeding had stopped. *Thank God*. 'Thank you,' he told the nurse.

'A little uneven on his feet,' Jazz said.

414

'Lack of sleep combined with excess stress.' Stan nodded. 'A big guy like the commander stands up too fast, he's gonna get a little dizzy.'

'I fainted,' Tom told them.

'Passed out,' Jazz corrected him at the same time Stan said, 'Blacked out, sir.'

Tom started to get up, and his former XO and senior chief helped him to his feet.

'Take me to her,' Tom ordered.

'This way, gentlemen,' the nurse said.

'Hey, Sam?'

He didn't lift his face out of the pillow, too happily exhausted and perfectly relaxed to move. 'Mmph?'

'I need you to tell me something.' Alyssa was lazily running her fingers up and down his back, which was just about the nicest feeling in the world. 'About Mary Lou.'

Sam sighed and lifted his head, propping himself up on one elbow, chin in his hand so he could look down at her. 'Do we really have to bring her into the room right now?'

Alyssa nodded, her eyes so serious. 'She's already here. I was kind of hoping to kick her out, once and for all.'

'What do you need to know?' Sam asked. He'd already told her a great deal about his marriage, about why he'd picked up Mary Lou in that bar in the first place – because she was so different from Alyssa in so many ways.

'I need you to tell me that you had sex with her only once – that one time you got her pregnant – and that you were drunk when it happened and you ejaculated prematurely and then passed out so she didn't get to come.'

Sam laughed and kissed her. 'I wish I could, Lys, but I'm not going to lie to you. Not ever.'

Alyssa nodded and touched his hair, pushing it back from his face, combing it and arranging it with her fingers, making him look like Elvis or Mickey Mouse or the devil or God knows what.

He let her play – it kept her from having to look into his eyes. He knew this conversation had to be hard for her.

'Did you sleep with her every night?' she asked.

Ah, boy. 'I was away an awful lot,' Sam said, 'so no. We didn't have sex very often. And not at all during the last few months before she left. And when we did . . . it was just sex, Alyssa.'

'Yeah, well, I've had 'just sex' with you,' she said. 'So I'm afraid that doesn't make me any less jealous.'

She was jealous. Sam kissed her again. Maybe this was a good time to say it. Maybe it wasn't too soon. He could start by saying, *Well, I never had 'just sex' with you* . . . and go from there.

'I have to confess that my feelings about Haley are pretty mixed,' Alyssa told him. 'If Mary Lou goes to jail, you'll get custody. I don't know how you'll manage that with your career—'

'What career?' Sam said. She knew as well as he did that his career with the SEALs had ended when Mary Lou's fingerprints showed up on that automatic weapon used in the Coronado attack. There was no one up the chain of command who would let him continue to work in Spec Ops after something like that. It might seem unfair for him to lose his job and his status over his wife's – ex-wife's – mistake, but that was the way it worked. SEALs had to be careful who they married, who they let into their lives.

And he hadn't been. Chances were that he'd walk away from all of his years of service with a dishonorable discharge. Man, the idea of that really hurt. And not just because it would affect his future employment.

'I was thinking maybe I could work for Noah,' Sam told her. 'Move back to Sarasota, be near Haley . . .' He cleared his throat. 'Maybe you could, I don't know, transfer down?'

She was very silent. He was pushing too hard, as usual.

She finally spoke. 'That would be a solid step backward in my career.'

Jesus. He wasn't even thinking about *that*. 'Oh,' he said. 'Yeah, I guess it would be. Sorry, I'm an idiot sometimes—'

'Maybe we're moving a little too fast,' Alyssa said. 'I mean, Sarasota to DC – that's not that far.'

Yes, it was. It was close to a thousand miles. But Sam kept his mouth shut. He didn't want to scare her. She was clearly feeling discomfort at the turn this conversation had taken.

What was he actually hoping? That she'd agree to marry him?

After a comfort fuck in a cheap motel?

Marriage *so* wasn't on her agenda.

Sam had to keep his eye on his goal. Dinner. Lots of dinners. A *real* relationship, based on real emotions.

He had a bazillion options – or at least he would after he got kicked out of Team Sixteen – including moving to DC, if that was what he needed to do.

Telling Alyssa that the mere thought of her continuing to work for Max – who, last he'd heard, wanted to marry her – was driving Sam out of his flipping mind, wasn't going to help right now, either. *Honey, give up your career with the best CI team in the Bureau, because I'm screamin' jealous of your boss, despite the fact that you never actually slept with him.*

Not the way to make her love him.

'Sam.' Alyssa was shifting beneath him. 'Oh, God, I think . . . Is the condom leaking?'

Holy shit. He reached between them. But it was still on, and it wasn't leaking. 'No, it's okay.' Just to be sure, he held it in place as he pulled out of her, and . . .

'Oh, fuck,' he whispered.

Alyssa stared at the very broken rubber he was wearing. Or rather, at the extremely useless piece of latex that was doing little more than decorating his dick.

It had split. Completely.

'Dear Lord,' she said. 'You do have terrible luck, don't you?' She stood up and went into the bathroom.

Sam followed. 'You know, maybe this time the bad luck's yours.'

She turned on the shower. 'Yeah, no kidding, Roger. Hey, I know. Maybe Mary Lou and I can form a *support group*!'

She was seriously unhappy and laughing was the last thing he should do. Instead, he cleared his throat and thought about what it would mean if she were to stay pissed off at him for another six months.

That sobered him up good and fast.

'No,' Sam said. 'You see, I meant, it was *your* condom and—'

'So it's *my* fault?' She grabbed at him. 'Will you please take that thing off of you?'

'Ow,' he said. 'Jesus! I'm still recovering from— Be gentle!'

'I'm exactly at the wrong place in my cycle,' she said through clenched teeth as she flung the useless thing into the garbage. 'If I were *trying* to get pregnant, I would have had unprotected sex tonight.'

'Were you trying?' he asked before he had the chance to think.

The expression of outrage on her face was one for the photo album. Too bad he didn't have a camera. Or maybe good thing.

'Nice, Sam,' she said. 'Yeah, that's what I was *trying* to do. Because women everywhere want to get pregnant on purpose when they have sex with you. They want to marry you because you have the reputation of being such a great husband and a *wonderful* father.'

Aw, *fuck. That* hurt.

Sam closed his mouth, biting back everything equally nasty that otherwise might've escaped. He was *not* going to do this again. He was not going to fight with Alyssa until one or both of them lay bleeding on the floor. Not, not, *not*.

Instead, he had to figure out what to say before he said it. Come on, Starrett. You've got a fairly large brain. *Use* it.

He also had to remember what he knew about this woman.

She'd let him get close, and now she was probably pretty fricking scared.

'I guess I must deserve that,' he said quietly. 'I didn't mean to ask that, you know, "Were you trying?" and make it sound like an attack, the way it must've. I just . . . I know you're an intelligent woman, and the condoms in your pack . . . You know, I saw them, and I thought, Are those from the same box that we used back in Kazbekistan? That was years ago. Those were your condoms that night, too. You brought them with you, and they're definitely the same brand, which doesn't necessarily mean anything. But I know *you* know these things have a shelf life and—'

'Oh, dear God.' Alyssa sat on the edge of the tub. 'I knew they were old, so I bought a new box just a few months ago, and I switched them. Didn't I? I thought I had, but . . .' She looked up at him, self-recrimination in her eyes. 'It *is* my fault. Totally.'

Sam sat down next to her. 'It doesn't matter whose fault it is. If you have sex – make love – with someone, you've got to be prepared for the consequences. That's just the way it goes.'

'So what are you saying?' she asked. 'If I'm pregnant, you'll marry me? Thanks, but no. I'm not doing that. No sir.'

Yeah, she'd made it pretty clear that marriage to him – husband of the year – was the last thing she wanted. Sam sighed. 'I'm *saying* that I wouldn't've made love to you tonight if the idea of marrying you and having babies with you made me run screaming for the hills,' he told her.

Alyssa looked at him. 'That's . . . very mature.'

He shrugged, looking back at her. 'I hope I've learned something from the past few years.' He looked down at the bathroom floor, because he didn't want her to see the hurt he knew would be in his eyes when he said, 'I guess I still need to learn to ask whether the person I'm making love to feels the same.'

The steam from the shower was heating up the bathroom.

He stood up. 'You better get in there. Although the way I

SUZANNE BROCKMANN

understand it, showering's not going to help. I've heard of something called a morning-after pill, though. It gives some kind of hormone boost that knocks your system out of whack and keeps you from getting pregnant. Any chance of your getting hold of one of those?'

He turned to look at her, still sitting there on the edge of the tub. 'Yeah,' she said. 'That's a good idea. I'll call my doctor in the morning.'

'Great.' He started for the other room.

'Sam.'

He turned back.

Alyssa had stood up. She was dazzlingly naked and he made himself keep his eyes on her face. There was no point torturing himself. He was not sleeping with her again. Not until she was ready to spend her life with him.

'I didn't mean what I said about you, you know, as a husband and father,' she told him.

'Well, yeah,' Sam said. 'I kind of think you did.'

'I didn't, and I'm sorry,' she said. 'I was just really freaked out and—'

'It's okay,' he said. 'Really. I can't imagine being a woman and having something like this happen. It must be . . . extremely stressful.'

She nodded. She was looking at him and she was making absolutely no effort to keep her eyes on *his* face.

Idiot that he was, he just stood there, staring back at her, as his body betrayed him. Apparently the message that he wasn't sleeping with her again hadn't made it through his central nervous system to his various appendages.

Alyssa cleared her throat. 'So. Since I'm going to be taking one of those pills tomorrow, um . . .' She glanced at the shower, looked back at him. 'You want to . . .?'

This was where he had to say no and walk away. Stick to his principles, damn it.

'You mean, without a condom?' he heard himself ask.

420

Alyssa shrugged and rolled her eyes. 'Considering the damage is already done and we're already completely screwed . . .' She held out her hand to him and gave him a smile that was half pure sweetness and half pure sin. 'Come on.'

Sam imagined how surprised she was going to be when he said no. But imagining it was as close as he was going to get.

'Fucking A,' he said, and picked her up and carried her with him into the shower.

'Is it really so awful to be here with me like this?' Gina whispered, breaking the silence they'd fallen into. She pulled back slightly to look up into Max's eyes.

He couldn't lie to her. 'Yes, it is.' To his continuing despair, he felt his eyes fill with tears. 'It makes me want . . .' *You.*

He knew she didn't understand and he tried to explain. 'I know you think that I have trouble with the fact that I'm older than you, and yeah, I confess that makes me uncomfortable. But if that was it, Gina, I'd learn to deal with it. But that's not it.'

'Transference,' she said flatly.

'Yes,' he said. 'Transference. We met in an extreme situation. I became your only link back to safety. You didn't have a choice about trusting me. You had to do what I said, you had to listen to me – I became *every*thing to you. Your father, your savior, your God.'

'My *friend*,' Gina countered. 'My lover, if we both could only just relax and let it happen.' She laughed softly. 'Although what's the likelihood of that? Between the two of us, our tension level is off the charts. Can you imagine us in bed together? I'm not sure whose head would explode first. Still, I'm not going to pretend that I don't want to try.'

Max resisted the urge to scream. His voice came out sounding strangled. 'How can I go from a situation where I'm everything to you, where of course you love me because you depend on me for your very *life*, into a sexual relationship, without wondering – *constantly* – if I'm taking advantage of your trust?'

'Stop wondering,' she told him. 'Because you're not. Max, seriously. How could this still be transference? It's been years.'

'I don't know,' he confessed.

'It's not,' she said. 'And you're not taking advantage of me. I want this.' And then she kissed him.

He should have been expecting it. He was all but inviting it, sitting on the floor with Gina nearly in his lap.

Still, she managed to take him by surprise with her sweet mouth and her arms up around his neck and the softness of her breasts against his chest.

She caught him off balance, too. Because he never would intentionally have pulled her back onto the floor like that . . .

Would he?

Except his arms were around her, and his tongue was in her mouth, and he was angling his head to kiss her even more deeply.

This was insanity.

It was double insanity because he recognized it as such and yet did nothing to stop it.

Max held her loosely, afraid to hold her too tight, afraid he'd scare her, afraid she'd get overwhelmed and pull away.

But then he realized that that was the solution. He needed to stop this, and since he couldn't seem to do it himself . . .

He rolled them over, so that he was on top of her as he kissed her harder. He wasn't overly rough, but he wasn't particularly gentle either as he pushed his way between her legs, as he ran one hand down her body, his palm overflowing with the fullness of her breast.

Oh, Christ. Gina arched against him, her body pressing up against his as she clung to him even more tightly.

He kissed her harder, and she moaned and reached between them to slip her hand inside his pants and . . .

And gave him about the farthest thing from a *please stop* message that he'd ever gotten in his entire life.

Particularly when she used her other hand to unfasten his belt and unzip his fly.

He pulled back from her, out of the softness of her hands. 'Whoa . . .'

She took the opportunity to pull her top over her head, and she was so abundantly twenty-three years old that he was stupefied – there was no other word for it – by the sight of her.

She had her shorts and panties off before he could form a coherent thought let alone a single word of protest. And then she started removing his clothes.

His jacket, his shirt, his shoes, his pants. Was it possible he was actually helping her?

No, he was too busy kissing her, her mouth, her neck, her delicate collarbone, her shoulders. Those incredible breasts.

Then, finally, when he was naked, too, she hesitated. 'Max . . .'

He didn't want to stop, but he knew that he had to.

I'm sorry, he was about to say. *Oh, damn it, I'm sorry*, but he never got the chance.

'We need a condom,' Gina told him, in her sexy as hell, husky voice, and he realized she was, by no means, stopping anything. In fact, the way she was touching and then kissing him was a definite full speed ahead.

'I don't have one,' he gasped. And there it was. Finally. The reason to put their clothes back on.

But, 'I do,' she told him. She untangled herself from him and vanished into the bathroom.

Max pushed himself onto his hands and knees. If there was ever a time to run away, it was now.

But he'd only made it up to his feet, his shorts in his hands, before Gina returned.

She stopped in the bathroom doorway. 'You're gorgeous,' she breathed.

'I think that's supposed to be my line,' he said, looking at her standing there. Her legs were incredibly long and her hair spilled down around her shoulders. Her skin gleamed, and those breasts . . . With the exception of her belly button ring that sparked as it caught the light, she looked like a movie star from the days when movie stars were allowed to have hips and breasts and smooth, slightly rounded, marvelously female stomachs.

Raquel Welch. Sophia Loren.

Gina Vitagliano.

She came toward him, looking at him as if he were something special. Yeah, he kept in excellent shape, but it didn't warrant that look.

Of course, it didn't mean he didn't like it.

A lot.

'This is a bonus,' she said, taking his shorts out of his hand and dropping them on the floor, 'because I always pictured you as kind of lazy and overweight – you always sounded so laid-back over the radio.'

'That's not really me,' he told her.

'Yes, it is,' she said. 'It's one of you. You've got this Dr Jekyll and Mr Hyde thing going—' She took him by the hand and pulled him toward the bed. '—that I happen to think is very sexy.'

He had no choice but to follow. 'I have to work hard to sound that way. Laid-back. I'm really a maniac. Gina, this is—'

She didn't let him finish. She pressed that body up against him and kissed him.

Max opened his eyes to discover that they were on the bed. How the hell did they get on the bed? 'Gina . . .'

She handed him the condom and kissed him again. He was on top of her, and she wrapped her legs around him, pressing him down on her, sliding her slick heat against him.

Yeah, okay, if she was going to do that, they definitely needed to get this condom working. But . . .

'This feels so right,' she whispered. 'It finally feels right. . . .'

He barely had the condom on – God *damn*, had he put it on himself? He must have – before she pushed herself up and he slid inside of her.

And oh, Christ, reality slapped him hard in the face and he was instantly terrified. And not just because he was breaking every rule he'd ever made about his job, about sex, about his responsibility as a man who held a great deal more power than nearly all of the people he'd encountered in his life.

He didn't want to hurt her, he didn't want to scare her, he didn't want to move.

And, to make matters even more complicated – or maybe, quite possibly *less* complicated – he was losing his erection.

Very rapidly.

She moved against him and ... So much for keeping *that* a secret.

'Bang,' Gina whispered into his ear. 'I think I just heard your head explode.'

'Yeah.' So this was what complete mortification felt like. 'I think you did.'

She wouldn't let him pull away. 'I'm okay, you know,' she said, looking up at him, touching his face, tracing his nose, his eyebrows, his jaw, his lips with one finger. The light from the room's one lamp was so dim, it was possible that she couldn't tell he was actually blushing, but he doubted it. 'And I think it's really incredibly sweet. That you care so much that ... you know.'

'Well, *there's* a new spin on it,' he said.

She started to move again, but just a tiny bit so that he didn't slip out of her. 'I love knowing that you really are human,' she whispered. 'And I also love knowing that I have this much power over you. I bet this has happened to you ... what? Never before?'

'What would you say if I told you that this happens all the time?' Max asked. 'You know, I am pretty old. As far as sex goes, I'm way past my peak.'

She knew he wasn't serious. He could read it quite clearly in her eyes. But she answered as if he were. 'I would say, "So what?" I would say I'm not in love with your ability to get it up. I'm in love with *you*.'

Oh, man, hearing her say *that* wasn't going to help. But the way she kissed him after she said it ...

Gina kissed him and just kept on kissing him. Slowly and sweetly, and then deeper, longer, harder.

Harder . . .

When she broke off to whisper, 'Let me be on top,' he pulled out of her and rolled over. And he was actually back in the game, with something there for her to climb on top of.

Still, she took her time, stroking him as she straddled his thighs, smiling down into his eyes.

You don't really love me, Max wanted to tell her. And it wasn't just because of transference. It was because he wasn't that guy she thought she liked so much, on the other end of the radio. Mr Smooth, Mr Cool, laid-back and comfortable inside his own body, inside his own head.

In truth, he was flipping crazy. He had constant chaotic noise jangling inside of his brain, and he couldn't remember the last time he'd actually been content. He spent too much time thinking, second-guessing and outmaneuvering everyone and everything. And he spent *all* of his time keeping his internal lunatic in check.

You don't know me at all, Max wanted to shout at her.

But her smile and her eyes had turned dreamy as she touched him, as she rubbed him against herself. Watching her, feeling her touching him was such a turn-on, he kept his mouth tightly shut.

She brought his hand up to her breast, and that, combined with what she was doing with her hands, nearly made him come. God *damn* it, one extreme to the other. He had to stop her, to physically move her hands and her body away from him. He touched her instead with his thumb.

The sound she made was unbelievably sexy, and she lifted herself up and slid down on top of him, pushing him deeply inside of her.

Max tried to hold himself still, tried to let her have total control over everything, but when she leaned forward and began to move on top of him, her breasts close to his face, he completely lost it. He licked one taut, perfect nipple into his mouth and suckled her harder than he should have, moving with her, driving himself more deeply than he should have inside of her.

'Max,' she was saying as he felt her release. 'Oh, Max!'

He came in a hot, blinding rush of sheer pleasure that he couldn't have postponed even if his life had depended on it.

It consumed him with noise and light and total, exhilarating, mind-blowing chaos, and he didn't want it ever to end.

But when it did, he could hear Gina laughing. There were tears on her face, and when she kissed him, he could taste the salt.

'Thank you,' she told him. 'I needed that. I really, *really* needed that.'

He didn't say anything. He couldn't. The reality of what they'd just done – *he'd* just done – was crashing around him. He touched her face, praying that in her happiness she wouldn't notice that he was so completely shaken he couldn't even speak.

But this was Gina, and as she looked down at him, her gaze softened.

'Bang,' she whispered. 'Right?'

He nodded, closing his eyes. What had he done?

And, maybe more important, what was he going to do now that he'd done it?

'Sleep,' Gina whispered as if she could read his mind, climbing off of him and out of the bed.

She was back almost instantly, with a hand towel from the bathroom. She gave it to him as she carefully took off the condom he was still wearing, vanishing again into the bathroom to dispose of it.

He knew he should get up, get dressed, get the hell out of there, but then she was back, moving across the room with her naked movie-star body. Leaving would require a discussion and probably more tears – maybe even from him this time – and he was too exhausted for that.

He'd wait, and leave after she'd fallen asleep.

She turned off the light, plunging the room into darkness,

which was a shame because then he couldn't see her walk back across the room. But she climbed into the bed again, pulling up the covers and settling warm and soft against him, her head on his shoulder, one smooth, cool leg possessively draped across his.

Don't leave. She did everything but say the words out loud.

Max stared into the darkness as she sighed.

'Thank you,' she whispered again.

He kept his mouth shut, because he knew if he opened it, he'd say nothing that would help either of them.

He just lay there and waited and tried to figure out what the fuck he was supposed to do now.

It took a little while, but her breathing evened out. She shifted, curling closer to him as she fell asleep – the softness of her breast against his ribs, her hand on his chest, the heat between her legs against his hip, the soft inside of her thigh across his already returning erection.

Didn't it figure? Now he couldn't keep the damn thing down.

Max waited, counting minutes – until he realized that he'd closed his eyes and lost track of how long it had been since she'd fallen asleep.

Her hand on his chest was warm and solid and oddly soothing.

But then she shifted again, and her hand slid south and found him.

'Mmmmm,' Gina said, and slipped back to sleep, still holding him.

This wasn't going to work at all, Max thought, and instantly fell asleep.

* * *

February 20, 1945

Dear Dot,

Not much time to write more than a sentence or two. I figure that's better than no word. I live for the letters you and Jolee send. Please forgive me for not giving as good as I receive.

Forgive me also for my last letter – filled as it was with complaints. I am honored to fly for my country. Please don't ever think that's not true. But the lack of respect my men and I receive from American servicemen – white servicemen – continues to irk me.

The Germans treat us better, with higher regard. It's not unusual for women here to date the Negro pilots from my squadron. In fact, one of my officers has asked permission to marry a girl from Munich. A white girl. Both she and her family seem not to care for differences such as skin color. Perhaps it is a German thing. But from what I've heard, if Captain Johnson were Jewish – now, that would be intolerable.

I don't understand such thinking. If it's not race, it's religion. I don't understand why people look for each other's differences, instead of the ways in which we are all the same.

We all want to be loved.

That's what it comes down to, I think.

God forgive me, but I'm tired and I want nothing more than to come home.

Your friend,
Walter

March 18, 1945

Dear Walt,

I, too, want you to come home.

By the way, I am at least one quarter German, from my mother's side.

However, I would not give a flying fig if you were Buddhist or Muslim or Catholic or pagan or Jewish or Baptist or . . .

Oh, you are Baptist. Do I care? Not a whit. Jolee and I visit the Baptist church each Sunday, since she is Baptist, too. The music is much better than that which the Unitarians provide. The congregation is always warm and welcoming. It's a good church, a joyful church where God is praised – loudly – and people pray for peace and harmony.

I hope to be married – someday soon – in that very church.

With all my love,
Dot

April 17, 1945

Dear Dot,

Word has come down the chain of command that the Russians are closing in on Berlin. The Reich's days are numbered. I pray each day that this war moves even more swiftly to its end.

I have before me your letter, dated March 18th. You've written hundreds before it and at least three others after that I've already received.

I must confess that of all the letters you've sent, I've read this one, this very shortest of them all, so many times that the paper is starting to tear.

At times, your message seems so clear. At others, I'm sure you're only making a joke, as you are prone to do.

And yet I remember my visit to you in the hospital.

I remember your eyes.

You and I have been friends for years. I know you loved Mae nearly as much as I did. I know you miss her as much as I do. You have been there for us, for Mae, for Jolee, for me, right from the start.

My love for you, dearest friend, has grown deeper over time. And I carry your love for me in my heart. At all times you are with me, and because of that I am a better man.

But my love for you is a curse as well as a blessing.

Much has happened since the hospital. Mae has passed on. We have both known hardship and pain and much sacrifice. I *have seen the atrocities that we humans wreak upon ourselves, and I am forever changed.*

Yes, much has changed, but in truth, nothing's really changed at all.

Because just as it was then, this cannot be.

We cannot be.

The reasons seem different. There's no longer a danger of betraying someone we both love. Mae lives on inside me, and I hear her voice, rich with affection, calling me a fool and urging me to follow my heart.

Oh, how I burn to do just that.

But Texas is far from Germany. You know as well as I that your family would not welcome me with the same joy and celebration that Hilde Gruen's parents greeted my Captain Johnson.

I remember the day we met, and how you moved to the colored bench so we both could sit as we waited for the bus.

I cannot ask you to make such a move permanent. I am outraged that I must sit there. I am incensed that Jolee must sit there. And I will be damned if you – you who do not have to – will be forced to sit there, too.

This cannot be.

Please, I beg you, let us never mention this again.

Forever and always your friend,
Walter

Twenty-three

Thursday, June 19, 2003

'So there we are,' Sam said, 'me and Nos, in Walt's car, and we realize the only way we know how to get to the hospital is via the interstate. I'd done some unauthorized neighborhood driving before – when my father was out of town and while my mother was . . . sleeping – but I'd never gone onto the freeway. But I figure what the hell. There's a first time for everything, right?'

He was touching Alyssa, sliding his hand from her shoulder down past the curve of her waist to her hip and back up again as she lay against him, her head on his shoulder, his arm around her, their legs intertwined.

It felt impossibly good, and she tried not to worry about the future's harsh reality – the forensics report that was probably going to tell them that Mary Lou and Haley were dead, the call she was going to have to make to her doctor about last night's incredibly stupid broken condom. What was she going to do if she couldn't get a prescription for a morning-after pill? And what was she going to do if it didn't work?

That wasn't even taking into consideration the other dangers of unprotected sex. If Mary Lou *had* been sleeping around on Sam, that put him at risk.

'We had boys like you in our school,' she told him now. 'Wild boys who pushed the edge of every envelope they could find. I stayed far away from them.'

Sam laughed. 'Yeah, most of the girls in my school stayed away from me, too. At least the ones I was interested in.'

Alyssa lifted her head. 'Really?' She'd always pictured him with women falling all over him from about the time he'd turned twelve.

'Really.' He smiled at her. 'Even back then I liked girls like you. Smart, bossy girls who knew better than to mess around with someone like me.'

'Someone like you – an arrogant, egotistical male chauvinist – or someone like you – a kid whose father kicked the hell out of him on a regular basis?'

Something shifted in his eyes. 'That's not what defines me anymore,' he said, all teasing gone.

'I know,' she said, serious, too. 'But it's still where you came from, Roger.' She used his real name on purpose, and he knew it. 'You can't really make it go away.'

He kissed her, and she closed her eyes and kissed him back, wishing that this night would never end, that they could simply stay here forever.

His hand wandered between her legs, and she shifted out of reach. 'Hey. Aren't you going to tell me the rest of this story?'

'We made it to the hospital without getting arrested, the end,' he said, pulling her back to him and kissing her again.

'The end.' She moved away from him and, holding his hands, kept him at arm's length. 'Except your aunt had had a stroke.'

'Yeah,' Sam said. 'That sucked. It was pretty massive. She never walked again, although not because she didn't try. That was hard for her – hard for Walt, too.'

'And that was when they moved here to Sarasota?' she asked.

'Yeah. Walt heard about this doctor who was getting really good results with stroke patients. He sold the company – the airfield, the crop dusters, everything. He claimed he was retiring, although it wasn't six months after he was down here that he opened a new flight school. He just couldn't not do it, you know? Teach kids to fly. Although at that point, I think all of the proceeds from the school went toward scholarships for under-privileged students. Noah still struggles to keep the business afloat.' He laughed. 'Or maybe I should say *aloft*.'

'But you didn't go with them,' Alyssa said.

'Nah.' He shook his head. 'They wanted me to. It was hard watching them leave, but . . .'

Alyssa looked into his eyes, knowing why he'd stayed in Fort Worth when the people he'd considered his true family had moved south. 'Your mother,' she said.

'I don't like it when you're so far away from me,' he said.

'I know,' she said. 'Believe me, I know all the tricks. This way you can't avoid eye contact by kissing me.'

'That's not why I want to kiss you.'

'Am I right?' Alyssa asked. 'You stayed behind because you knew if you weren't there, your father would start using your mother as his personal punching bag?'

Sam was actually embarrassed. 'It wasn't that big a deal. I knew Lainey would be home in the summer. She had a job teaching at a private school, and she needed someplace to live from June to the end of August. As long as one of us was there, Pop seemed to keep it under control, so . . .' He shrugged. 'I came down here each summer.'

'And went back each fall.' Alyssa wanted to shake him. 'You gave up a chance to live with people who loved you in order to take care of someone who'd never been able to protect or take care of you?'

'Yeah,' Sam said. 'She had a name – it was *Mom*.'

'Sam—'

'I'm a fucking hero.' He clearly didn't believe that at all. 'Come here and kiss me.'

Alyssa did.

And her phone finally rang.

Whitney read Amanda and Haley another chapter in *Alice's Adventures in Wonderland* while Mary Lou got their breakfast.

It was bizarre. It was amazing. It was a miracle of sorts. Without Mrs Downs and her father around to torment, Whitney was actually capable of being a helpful, contributing human being.

Mary Lou yawned as she added an extra scoop of grounds to the coffee. Lord, she hadn't slept at all last night.

And she was suffering – badly – from light of day syndrome. By the time Whitney had gone to sleep after hanging out in Mary Lou's living room all evening, watching *Moulin Rouge* nearly twice in a row – Ewan McGregor *was* a God, but come on – all of Mary Lou's demons had returned. They'd whispered their urgent warnings in her ear and made her unwilling to return the arsenal of weapons she'd taken from King Frank's office.

In fact, she'd locked her bedroom door and taken a closer look at one of the rifles, trying to get a sense of where she was supposed to put in the bullets.

She still wasn't exactly sure.

This morning, with the dawn, her fears had subsided enough to make her feel foolish for not returning the guns to their proper locked place while she'd had the chance.

'What are your plans for today?' she asked Whitney.

'I thought I'd hang around here. What are you guys doing?'

'We're cleaning out my refrigerator this morning,' Mary Lou said, even though that wasn't the case.

The look on Whitney's face was comical. 'Oh.' And here came the excuses. Except, 'Can I, um, help?' the girl asked.

Curiouser and curiouser.

'I was kidding,' Mary Lou said. 'We're just going to stay inside, because it's so hot out.' And because she was spooked, even in the light of day, about being a potential sniper target. 'Maybe do some puzzles, play some games. I think it's Amanda's choice this morning. You're always welcome, of course, to join us.'

Whitney smiled, all sweetness and light. 'Thank you. I will.'

* * *

Alyssa untangled herself from Sam and opened her phone. 'It's Jules,' she reported and hit Talk. 'Any news?'

'Nothing from forensics yet,' Jules said.

'Nothing from forensics yet,' Alyssa repeated for Sam.

'Oh, my God,' Jules said. 'He's in your *room* at this hour of the morning?'

'Who is?' Alyssa closed her eyes, wincing. *Shit*. She definitely gave that one away. Sam rolled out of bed and went into the bathroom, closing the door behind him.

'Right,' Jules said. 'Right. No one is in your room with you, and you are *such a fool*. But take heart – you're not the only fool, sweetie. Apparently last night was International Fuck the Wrong Person Night – for everyone on earth but those of us too pathetic to leave the office before dawn.'

What was he talking about? 'Jules, will you please translate that into something I can understand?'

'I'm calling to see if you've heard from Max in the past, oh, eight to twelve hours.'

And Alyssa understood. Holy God. 'Max didn't call in all night?'

'That might be exactly what I just said, girlfriend. He's not in his room, and he's not answering his cell.'

Alyssa couldn't believe it. But then she *could* believe it.

'Peggy thinks he's dead, and she wants to call the President and put out an alert,' Jules continued. 'But she doesn't know about—'

'Gina,' Alyssa said in unison with him. Oh, Max . . .

'What do I do?' Jules asked. 'If Max hasn't told Peggy or the rest of the team anything about this girl, I sure as hell don't want to be the one to do it. And yet Peg's genuinely worried.'

'Be vague,' Alyssa recommended. 'Tell her you have reason to believe he's fine, that he's got a female friend here in town. No names, okay? Just tell her she needs to stand down, to give him a few more hours to extract himself from, uh . . . Wow. I never thought he'd actually—'

'Have you met her?' Jules asked.

'No.' Alyssa had been placed on the roof in a sniper position during the takedown of the hijacked plane where Gina had been held captive. As the SEALs stormed the plane, she and Chief Wayne Jefferson had used sniper rifles to take out the two terrorists in the cockpit. They'd fired through the aircraft's windshield, putting bullets into the heads of the men who'd raped Gina and killed the airliner's pilot.

But when Gina had asked to meet the team of SEALs and FBI agents who had saved her life, Alyssa had managed to be out of town.

It was just too hard. Alyssa had taken out a target, eliminated a terrorist. She knew that her target had lost the right to his identity and his life when he'd stepped onto that plane with his intention of killing everyone on board.

But meeting Gina, putting a face to her name, shaking her hand, looking into her eyes and letting her become a real, living person, meant that the hijackers who hurt her were real, too.

And real people had mothers and families to mourn them.

No, it was just too hard.

'Max never stood a chance.' Jules laughed. 'Although it is possible he spent the night parked outside of her motel room, again, in his car.'

'Again?' she asked. Oh, *Max* . . .

'Jealous?' Jules said.

'Not even a little. Call the second you get that forensics report.'

'I will,' he promised. 'Hey, you know those bikers who jumped Ihbraham Rahman in Coronado? In their initial report, they said that some guy told them to keep an eye on Rahman because he was supposedly acting suspiciously. This guy said he was going back to the gate to get help from the Secret Service, but they never saw him again. Their conversation went down well before the shooting started – which seems noteworthy, huh? Anyway, we sent someone over to talk to them again, to try to get a description of this mystery guy. And guess what?'

'Blond hair?'

'Give the woman a prize. Oh, wait, she already got hers last night—'

'No need to be a jerk, sweetie.'

'We showed our biker dudes that nifty little photo taken of our suspect with Mary Lou Starrett in the San Diego library parking lot, and we got ourselves another positive ID. It's definitely our man. Dudes one through three have been moved into protective custody. Tell Sam – when you see him that is, cough, snort – that his theory about the gardener also being a target of the terrorists sure seems to be a good one. However, there's still no sign of Rahman – either dead or alive.'

'Any word on Kelly Paoletti and Cosmo Richter?' Alyssa asked, as Sam came back out of the bathroom.

'Mrs Paoletti's still in ICU. Say a prayer when you get a minute. Richter got some broken bones, but he's going to be fine,' Jules reported. 'Whoops, Laronda's waving at me. Peggy's on the line two. I've got to go tell her – without really telling her – that Max isn't dead, just really, really happy.'

An odd, persistent buzzing woke Gina from a sound sleep.

Her first thought, upon opening her eyes, was that she must still be sleeping. But then she knew she wasn't, because she never in a million years would have even dreamed that Max would still be here this morning, boneless and unconscious in her bed.

The buzzing was Max's cell phone, set on vibrate. It was actually rattling against whatever was in the pocket of his suit, on the floor where they'd thrown it last night.

Last night . . .

Max looked exhausted – she hoped whoever was calling had given up.

But it began rattling again, and his eyes opened and he looked directly at her.

'Someone wants you,' Gina told him as it kept on shaking.

He stared at her, and she watched last night play in super-fast-forward in his eyes as he remembered where he was and what he was doing there.

'Do you want me to find your phone for you?' she asked.

He swallowed, lifting his head and wiping his mouth, grimacing as he realized he'd been so totally unconscious that he'd actually been drooling. 'No. Thanks.' He flipped the pillow over as he cleared his throat. 'What time is it?'

His phone stopped its dance.

'Nearly seven-thirty.'

Gina watched his eyes as he realized that he'd not only slept, but he'd slept for nearly seven hours.

'Hooray for sex,' she said.

'Yeah.' He met her gaze only very briefly again before rolling onto his back, his arm up over his eyes. It was remarkable how quickly his beard grew. She'd always thought he was just being meticulously anal retentive to shave every few hours throughout the day, but he really did get a total *GQ* look with very little effort.

'Christ, I have to go,' he said on an exhale, definitely not moving at all. 'I should've been in the office an hour ago. Manny Conseco's probably sitting behind my desk. Of course it was his desk up until a few days ago.'

Gina propped her head on her elbow. 'I guess this means you don't have time to take me to breakfast.'

'Breakfast?' he asked. 'What's that?'

Hey, a joke. That was a good sign.

She put her hand on his chest, but his phone started shaking again, so she didn't really know which it was that made him push himself up so that he was sitting on the edge of the bed.

'God,' he said. 'You know, this is why I don't sleep – because once I start, I don't ever want to stop.'

'If you do it every night, it makes it a little easier to wake up in the morning.'

'Oh, yeah,' Max said, rubbing his face. 'That makes sense.'

He reached for the remote control on the bedside table and turned on the TV, flipping until he reached CNN. There was a news report about the increase in gun sales over the past year, and he put it on mute.

'It's always good when I turn on the TV and nothing's blowing up or on fire,' he told her.

Despite the fact that he didn't seem to want her to touch him, this morning-after thing was going okay. They were talking, and it wasn't too weird.

But his phone was still buzzing.

'Aren't you going to answer that?' she asked.

'No. It does that all the time.'

She sat up, and the covers slipped off of her, and Max turned away, fast.

Okay. Now the mood in the room was definitely weird.

'You know, you saw me naked last night,' she pointed out.

'Yeah, I'm very much aware of that.' He stood up and staggered toward the bathroom, keeping his back toward her, as if she wouldn't notice that his body was far more awake than he was.

The phone was silent for only a few minutes. It started to buzz again after he flushed the toilet.

'God *damn* it,' he said, and came out of the bathroom with a towel around his waist to dig through the pile of clothes they'd left on the floor. He opened his phone. 'Bhagat. This better be good.'

Max listened for a moment, letting himself look at Gina before apparently remembering that he didn't want to let himself look at her while she was naked, and turning away.

'Yeah,' he said. 'Thanks. Oh, and Laronda? I'm going to need access to a computer and a printer today.' Another pause. 'Because I need to write a letter.' Pause. 'Yeah, I've kind of caught on to the concept of dictation after eighteen years. But this is one I have to do myself.' A sigh. 'I don't know. Thirty minutes?' He glanced at Gina again, turned his back on her again. 'Give or take a few.'

He hung up his phone and picked up his wrinkled suit and sighed. 'You think anyone will notice if I wear this into work again today?'

Gina laughed at the picture of Max going to work, looking like he'd slept in his clothes. 'Only if you don't shave.'

He laughed, too, letting himself look at her out of the corner of his eyes. 'Yeah, I better call Laronda back. I need to stop at my hotel. Thirty minutes. What was I thinking?'

'Give or take a few,' Gina reminded him, hoping that glance meant he was going to climb back in bed with her and get into work *really* late.

'Did I tell you last night that I find you incredibly beautiful?' he asked. 'I've been trying to remember, but the entire night's a little sketchy. If I didn't say it, I should have, because it's . . . You are. Amazingly beautiful.'

'Yeah,' she said, somehow managing to talk around her heart, now permanently lodged in her throat. 'Actually, you told me that right before you asked me to marry you.'

He froze.

Oh, man, did he actually think . . .?

'Max, I'm kidding,' she said. 'That was a joke.'

But congratulations, she'd managed to freak him out even more than he was already freaked out. *And* she'd completely blown any chance that she had of talking him back to bed. It was her fault completely for trying to be funny. Idiot. *Idiot.*

She half expected to need to do CPR on him.

But Max went into the bathroom and splashed water onto his face instead of clutching his chest and falling onto the rug.

'I'm going to shower back at my hotel,' he told her, coming back out and pulling on his clothes. He was trying to sound casual, but his voice was tight as he tossed his towel onto the back of the desk chair. 'What time does your flight leave tonight?'

'Seven forty-five,' she told him, wishing she could go back in time and start this morning over. She should have grabbed him and kissed him before his eyes even opened. 'I have to check out of here at noon.'

He didn't look happy at that news as he sat down on the edge of the bed to put on his socks and shoes. 'I'm not sure I'm going to be able to take you to the airport.'

'That's okay. I didn't expect you to.' This was where she was absolutely not going to offer to stay a few extra days. If he asked, that was fine, but she *had* told him again and again that she only wanted one night. Now wasn't the time to tell him she'd been lying.

'Call me,' he ordered her so fiercely that her heart lightened. 'When you leave here. And let me know where you're going. I want to know where you are today.'

Of course, maybe he didn't want her to call so he could see her again. Maybe this was just more of that protective crap he was so good at.

'I'm just going to the beach for a couple of hours,' she told him. 'And then I'm taking the bus to the airport.' Play it cool, play it cool. She watched as he stood up and slipped his arms into his jacket, stashed his tie in his pocket. 'In case I don't see you before I leave – thank you for everything.'

Max looked at her, but he kept his eyes above her neck. 'You'll see me.'

'That would be nice,' she said.

Come on, Max. How about a lunch date? Or they could meet in his hotel room for a different kind of midday refreshment.

But he headed for the door, already starting to dial his phone.

'But just in case I don't see you,' she called, 'I want you to know how much last night meant to me. I really do think you're wonderful and—'

'*Stop.*' He turned back to her with a trace of that wildness – a trace of Mr Hyde – in his eyes. After last night, he fascinated her more than ever. 'Jesus Christ, I'm not wonderful. I'm not even close. I'm a total *asshole.*'

What? 'No, you're not.'

'Yes,' he said through clenched teeth. 'I am. Gina, look, I have to go. I'll talk to you later, all right?'

'All right.'

He returned his attention to his phone as he opened the door. 'Alyssa, it's Max,' she heard him say as he shut it behind him. 'Call me, damn it. I need to talk to you *now*.'

Gina sank back into the bed, wishing she hadn't heard that, wishing he'd bothered to take an extra five seconds to kiss her goodbye, wishing she'd understood why he'd run, practically screaming, for the door, just because she'd made a bad joke about getting married.

Towel around his waist, Sam went back to his own room to get his clothes.

Alyssa was on her cell phone, leaving a message for her doctor in an attempt to rectify last night's condom horror show. It had seemed like a good time to give her some privacy.

Sam didn't want to hear about it, didn't want to think about it. There was no room in his head for what her taking that pill meant, both in the cosmic scheme of things and in regards to their budding relationship.

Obviously he had his work cut out for him if he was going to convince her to take a chance on him – on *them*.

He got dressed in the same suit he'd worn for the past few days. It was far longer than he'd ever worn a suit before, and he thought wistfully of his jeans and boots. Between clothes shopping and his haircut, he'd put them in a big box at a Mail Boxes Etc. in Gainesville and shipped them back to himself in San Diego.

It was one thing to ditch a sports jacket, but those jeans were broken in. And the boots . . . He'd once sent a pair of boots home from Pakistan. Took 'em four months to get to San Diego, because he'd sent them to a friend in Indonesia first. At the time, and in that part of Pakistan, it would have been bad for his health to ship a package directly to the United States.

He put on his tie, adjusting it in the mirror, and stared at himself. He hadn't given it much thought when he'd bought the damn thing, but really, when was the last time he'd worn a civilian business suit?

Ever since high school, since joining the Navy, whenever he'd needed to look nice, he'd worn his dress uniform.

But that wasn't going to be an option anymore, thanks to Mary Lou.

No, be a man about it, Starrett. It was thanks to his own carelessness.

Sam closed his eyes. He could give up his job, his career. He would even accept a dishonorable discharge without complaint. But please God, let Haley and Mary Lou be alive and safe.

His cell phone rang.

Sam searched for it in his jacket pockets, first finding Alyssa's side arm. Whoops. Forgot he had that.

He opened his phone.

'If you hurt Alyssa again, I will make you sorry you were born.'

'Good morning, Jules,' Sam said.

'I am so, *so* serious, Starrett!'

'I hear you,' Sam said. 'And I have no intention of—'

'That's what you say now. And in four hours, we'll find Mary Lou and she'll tell you that she has a brain tumor so if you divorce her she won't have the medical insurance necessary to pay for her lifesaving series of operations, which will take fifteen years—'

'Jules,' Sam said. 'Breathe.'

Jules took a breath.

'The divorce papers are already signed,' Sam said. 'It's just a matter of the lawyers filing them. Nothing like that's going to happen.'

'I know. And I hate you,' Jules said. 'You're going to take away the best partner I ever had, aren't you?'

'Alyssa's not leaving the Bureau.'

'That's what you say now. But I know that you're going to have to leave Team Sixteen, which, by the way, is a crying shame. But there are already rumblings on the Spec Op grapevine, speculating that if Tom Paoletti can prove his innocence – which isn't going to be as easy as it sounds – he's going to be forming some kind of civilian superhero team, and you, my handsome friend, are a shoo-in for some kind of executive officer position.'

'No shit?' Now *there* was a job he wouldn't turn down.

'Of course, Alyssa's admired Paoletti for years,' Jules told him. 'That XO spot would probably be something she wouldn't refuse if it was offered to her.'

Ah, Jules, Jules, Jules. The little *gâteau de fruit* hated the idea of losing Alyssa as his partner, and yet he'd told Sam exactly how to steal her away from the FBI. 'If I were gay,' Sam started, 'I'd—'

Jules cut him off. 'Say no more. And these are just rumors, remember. But I do love you, too, angel cake.'

'I don't think I'm quite at the point yet where I'm comfortable with you saying that to me.'

'Are you a happy, happy man this morning?' Jules asked. 'Are you ready for me to make you even happier? Because gorgeous George just came over to my desk bringing tidings of great joy – at least from your perspective. The forensic report's in. The bodies are those of a migrant worker and her daughter, gone missing in April.'

Sam's knees stopped holding him up, and he sat down heavily on the bed. 'Oh, thank God.'

Jules was saying something more, but Sam couldn't hear it.

It *hadn't* been Haley, shot in the head and burned to a crisp.

The rush of relief turned his muscles to rubber and his brain to oatmeal. It made it hard to breathe, made his vision swim, made his throat tight and his head light.

'Thank you,' Sam whispered. It was the best he could manage. 'I have to . . . go now. Thank you. God.'

'Hey, are you okay?' Jules asked.

Sam closed his phone.

He wasn't sure how long he sat there, waiting for the roaring in his ears to ease up, waiting for the light-headedness to go away.

But he knew that he had to share this news with Alyssa.

Somehow he stood up. He only had to make it as far as the door though, because when he opened it, Alyssa was already standing there.

She had tears on her face. 'Jules just called me. You really freaked him out.' She reached up to touch his cheek, and he realized that he was crying, too. 'Oh, Sam.'

He reached for her and she went into his arms, holding him as tightly as he held her.

'I was so sure,' she whispered. 'I'm so glad I was wrong.'

He didn't bother to pretend he wasn't crying. 'Thank God,' she murmured, as he just hung on to her and wept.

'I was so scared,' he finally said.

He'd slept maybe a total of an hour last night, and it had been a fitful sleep, filled with ominous, threatening dreams. With the relief, there now came an incredible wave of fatigue.

Somehow Alyssa knew. 'You want to take a nap or you want to get some coffee?'

'Coffee,' he said.

She laughed softly and kissed him, her eyes filled with tenderness. 'How did I know you were going to say that?'

'Let's find Haley today,' he said.

Alyssa kissed him again. 'That would be nice.'

Tom Paoletti sat holding Kelly's hand as she lay in the hospital bed, listening to the machine that monitored her heartbeat.

It was beeping steadily, solidly, reassuringly.

There were voices in the hall, and he looked up. God *damn*.

Admiral Tucker and the shore patrol had made the scene.

He'd spent most of the night wondering when they were going to show up.

Out in the hall Jazz and Stan intercepted them, standing up and making a very large wall between this room and the admiral.

He could hear the senior chief. 'I'm sorry, sir. Only immediate family are allowed inside the ICU.'

Nice try, Stan. Tom squeezed Kelly's hand.

'I think I'm getting more out of my being here than you are,' he told her even though her eyes were closed. 'So maybe it's okay if I have to go. I love you so much, Kel. I need you to fight for me. Whether I'm here or not, I'm with you. Just listen to that monitor, okay? Because that's my heart, too.' His voice broke. 'Every beep, that's me saying that I love you. God damn it, I don't want to have to leave you, but Tucker's here, and—'

Her fingers moved.

Her fingers *moved* and her eyelids fluttered.

'Nurse!' Tom shouted. 'I need a nurse in here!'

Jay Lopez, the hospital corpsman from Team Sixteen, was beside him in a flash. Where the hell had *he* come from?

The ICU nurse, an African-American woman who was nearly as tall as Tom, was just a few steps behind.

'She's waking up,' Lopez said. 'Man, you scared me, sir. I thought I was going to have to use the defibrillator.'

Mother of God, nearly the entire team, and their wives and girlfriends, too, were out there. They were standing back to give the medical staff room to maneuver, but they were all there.

'She's okay,' Lopez called to them.

'She certainly is.' The nurse pulled the curtain around Kelly's bed, giving her some privacy. 'Good morning, Mrs Paoletti,' she said as she adjusted the oxygen tube that fed into Kelly's nose, as she checked the IV. 'We're very glad to see you today.'

'Tom,' Kelly whispered. 'Don't leave.'

'I won't,' he promised her. 'I won't.'

'No, he's not going anywhere,' the nurse told her. 'We've got an entire SEAL team guarding this door. And me, as well. I may not be a SEAL, but I am not afraid to call security to remove an admiral who has no business being here.' She glanced at Tom, then leaned closer to Kelly. 'Oh, honey, don't you love a man who's not afraid to cry?'

By nine o'clock, Whitney was positively antsy. She made the two-year-olds seem staid as they sat at the table in the playroom and colored.

She hopped up. She sat down. She sang bits and pieces of top forty songs. She talked nonstop about movies she'd seen, like some kind of mad version of Chris Farley on speed. '*It was awesome . . .*'

'Maybe you should call that friend of yours – Ashley – and the two of you can go for a swim,' Mary Lou finally suggested.

'No,' Whitney said. 'I'm having fun with you guys. Besides, Ashley's a bitch.'

The phone rang, and the girl rocketed out of her seat. 'I'll get it.' She picked it up. 'Hello?' A pause, and then a shriek. 'Finally! Yes, send him up. *Definitely.* Front door. Thank you, Jim, I looove you!' She hung up the phone.

'Was that Jim from the gate?' Mary Lou asked.

'Yes, it was.' Whitney danced toward the door. 'I'll be right back. There's a . . . a package I've been expecting, and it's finally here. Don't go anywhere, okay?'

She ran out of the room.

A package.

They colored in silence for a while. In blessed, blessed silence. Even Amanda and Haley didn't make any noise.

Please, dear Lord, don't let Whitney's package be firecrackers. Or a case of whiskey. Or a new powerboat. Or—

'What's a bitch?' Amanda asked.

'That's not a very nice word, honey,' Mary Lou told her as mildly as she could manage. She smiled at Haley, who was all eyes – and ears. 'So we won't use that one again, okay?'

'Mrs Downs is a bitch,' Amanda said.

'No, she's not,' Mary Lou said, even though she was thinking, Oh, yes, she is. 'Mrs Downs is just a little grumpy sometimes. If we smile at her, maybe she won't be so grumpy.'

'And maybe the sky will fall.' Whitney was back. 'Look who's here, *Mary Lou.*'

What did Whitney just call her?

Mary Lou looked up, and, dear Lord God in heaven, Ihbraham Rahman was standing just inside the playroom door.

Twenty-four

Max heard a click as Alyssa answered her cell phone. 'Locke.'

'Surprise,' he said, closing his office door, 'it's me.'

'How did you—'

'It's this new device that sends a signal that messes with the receiving cell phone. The last number you dialed shows up on your screen instead of my real incoming number. Slick, huh?'

'Very.'

'So who'd you think I was?'

'None of your business,' she said much too sweetly. She was definitely still pissed at him.

'I wish you'd called me back. I really have to talk to you.' Max didn't sit down at the desk, knowing if he did, he'd automatically start reading files. This conversation deserved 100 percent of his attention. He looked out the window, instead.

Florida's sky was its own special shade of blue. He could see the water from here, sparkling in the sunlight.

'I'm a little too busy right now to return phone calls to jerks,' Alyssa told him. 'Can't it wait?'

'No,' he said. 'But I'll make it quick. I can't marry you because I'm more of a jerk than you think. I'm sorry. I, um, really screwed up last night and—'

'Oh, Max,' she said. 'I already know. You don't really think you could stop answering your phone for all those hours and not have anyone notice?'

'Yeah,' he said. 'I figured there'd be rumors. I just wanted you to hear it from me first. And I wanted you to hear the truth.'

He took a deep breath. 'God, Alyssa, I slept with her.'

She laughed, a low, warm sound. 'About time. Are you okay?'

'No,' Max admitted. It was possible he was never going to be okay again. 'There's something else I need to tell you.'

'Uh-oh, I don't like the sound of that.'

'I've handed in my letter of resignation.'

'Max—'

Max rested his head against the warm glass of the window. 'Effective as soon as this mess is over or by the end of the month, whichever comes first.'

'My God—'

'I've recommended that Peggy Ryan take over as team leader,' he said, 'and that you be moved into the position she'll be vacating.'

'You can't do this!'

'I screwed up, Alyssa,' he told her. 'I shouldn't have slept with her. She's still so vulnerable and . . . and that's not even taking into consideration that not even forty-eight hours earlier I'd asked you to marry me, which, by the way, was also completely inappropriate.'

'I said no,' Alyssa reminded him.

'You said you'd think about it.'

'Yeah, but I was going to say no, and you knew it. Come on, Max, we both knew you weren't serious.'

'Yeah,' he said. 'I was.'

'Please don't quit,' Alyssa said. 'How can you quit? We *need* you.'

'How can I *not* quit?' he asked. 'Look, I have to go. I just wanted you to hear it from me first.'

'Running away is not the answer,' she told him. '*Damn* it, Max—'

'You get an update this morning from Jules?'

'Yes. Max—'

'Be careful,' he said. 'The threat is very real. This is not just a terrorist cell we're dealing with, with their two weeks of terror-camp training. This is a professional, a high-level operative – I'm guessing a mercenary – who doesn't want his identity known.'

'Max,' she said. 'Please listen to—'

'I'm terribly sorry if I hurt you—'

'You *didn't*.'

'I'm still sorry,' he said. 'And I do have to go.' He hung up the phone.

Florida's sky was still its own special shade of blue. He could still see the water from here, sparkling in the sunlight. He could see pelicans gliding effortlessly along on the air currents. He could see the causeway over to Siesta Key.

Where Gina was getting ready to check out of her room.

Max turned away from the window. 'Laronda!' he shouted. 'I need my car!'

By the time he opened his office door, his assistant was already off the phone. 'It's waiting for you out front,' she told him, giving him absolutely zero crap for shouting.

He hadn't told her about the letter yet, but she knew something big was up and she was worried. He could see it in her eyes.

'I don't know how long this is going to take,' Max said. 'Field my calls, will you? I don't want my cell to ring unless it's the President or someone calling to tell me we've located Mary Lou Starrett.'

'Yes, sir.'

He headed for the elevator.

Mary Lou stood up so fast her chair fell over backward.

'Hello, Mary Lou.' Ihbraham Rahman. Alive and well and looking at her with tears in his beautiful brown eyes. He smiled at Haley, too. 'How are you, Haley?'

'How did you find me?' Mary Lou breathed. But she looked at Whitney, and she knew.

Yesterday – probably after she'd called Ihbraham – Whitney

had referred to Mary Lou's ex-husband as Sam, even though Mary Lou had never used his real name.

That was what had been gnawing at her, making her anxious.

'Whitney called me,' Ihbraham told her in that musical, faintly British accent that was so familiar to her. 'It didn't make much sense at first – I didn't know who she was talking about – but then I realized that it must be you. She said Sam is trying to kill you? I don't understand this. When you spoke of him before you said he'd never hurt you. But she said you were here and that he was after you, and that you needed me, so I got in my truck and . . . here I am.'

Oh, Lord, oh, *Lord* . . .

'I found him by calling information. There was only one Ihbraham Rahman in San Diego.' Whitney smiled, proud of herself. 'Aren't you going to kiss him?'

Mary Lou nearly slapped her. 'Do you realize what you've done? You've killed us all!' Keeping her voice low so Haley and Amanda wouldn't freak out, she pulled Ihbraham with her out the door and into the hall. 'What I *needed* was for you to stay *away* from me!' She couldn't believe this was happening. 'I needed you not to get killed, like Janine!'

'Your sister is dead?' he asked.

'Yes, they killed her. Oh, my God, Ihbraham! My *God*! We have to get out of here. Right *now*!' Whitney was standing in the doorway, her eyes wide. 'Get Haley and Amanda,' she ordered the girl. 'Take them to their room, and get Pooh and Dinosaur and sweatshirts for everyone. I have to get something out of my apartment, then we're heading for the garage. We are leaving here. Now.'

'*Who* killed Janine?' Ihbraham asked, catching her arm. 'Sam? Mary Lou, you need to tell me what's going on.'

It was his hand, with his long, graceful, dark brown fingers, so warm on her arm, that made her start to cry. She grabbed for him, holding him tightly as she kissed him, her arms around his neck.

'Ah, Mary Lou,' he breathed. He held her just as close as he kissed her, too, just the way she remembered, the way she'd dreamed about for months and *months*, with real love – his lips so gentle, his mouth so soft. 'I prayed for you to call me. I thought you changed your mind.'

'I didn't call because I love you,' she told him through her tears. 'I was afraid they'd kill you, too.'

'Who?' he said, pulling back to look at her.

Whitney, of course, was still standing there, gaping, along with the girls.

Mary Lou wiped her face. She'd promised herself she'd never cry in front of Haley. 'Run ahead and get Pooh Bear and Dinosaur,' Mary Lou told the two little girls as cheerfully as she could.

Then she told Ihbraham, and Whitney, too, as she led the way down the hall to her apartment.

About the gun she'd found in the trunk of her car. About the way it disappeared before she could show it to Sam. About seeing Bob Schwegel, Insurance Sales, again, outside Janine's house. About Janine lying dead in the kitchen. About Mary Lou's frantic flight and her attempt to hide.

About the fact that Bob knew of her relationship with Ihbraham, and that he'd surely followed him here.

'Get sweatshirts,' Mary Lou told Whitney again as she went into her bedroom, went into the closet, and started loading all those guns she'd taken from King Frank's office into her beach bag.

She'd never heard Ihbraham curse before, and she wasn't quite sure she'd heard him curse now, because whatever he said, it wasn't in English. She suspected, though, that it was the Arabic version of *holy shit*.

'Wait,' he said, kneeling down next to her on the floor. 'Mary Lou. Wait. This is . . . No, this is not the answer. If you are so certain we're in this much danger, we need help. We need to call the police.'

'They'll arrest me,' she told him.

He caught her hands. 'If they do, they will quickly see you're innocent of any wrongdoing. This is not the answer. Running and hiding and living in such terrible fear.' He pushed her hair back from her face. 'Please listen and trust me. It's time to ask someone in authority for help.'

'This is a wild goose chase,' Sam said as they pulled into the Publix parking lot.

They were going back after that help-wanted poster for a live-in nanny that he'd seen there yesterday. Maybe what they should do was go back to the library, look at the want ads from three weeks ago, see what other live-in positions Mary Lou might've tried for.

Alyssa glanced at him. 'We could head back to San Diego,' she said. 'Try a completely different approach. See if we can't track down this Ihbraham Rahman that Mary Lou was friends with. Maybe he can lead us to her.'

'It'll take more than twenty-four hours to drive to San Diego,' Sam pointed out. 'There's no way we could get on a plane with the FBI looking for me.'

She nodded. 'I know.'

What was she telling him?

She glanced at him again after she parked beneath a tiny, thirsty-looking palm tree that provided only a scrap of shade. 'I think it's probably going to take us more than twenty-four hours to find them,' she told him. 'I think we should stop thinking in terms of that particular time limitation.'

'But you said you had to deliver either me or your resignation,' Sam said. 'Or has Max changed his mind about that?'

He'd tried not to listen when she'd gotten that phone call from Max. He'd gone into the bathroom and turned on the water and tried to respect her privacy.

She'd said nothing about it when he came back out, which had worried him. Sure, he'd given her privacy, but that didn't mean she had to take it, did it?

He took a deep breath. Maybe if he silently chanted, *I will not be an asshole*, he'd start to believe it and behave accordingly.

'No,' she said. 'I'm sure he hasn't.'

Holy fuck, Alyssa was willing to give up her career for him. Sam cleared his throat. 'I've heard rumors that Tom Paoletti's going to need an XO for a civilian team he's maybe thinking of starting.'

'Whoa.' That caught her attention. 'Sam, that's great. You're a good choice for that.'

'You're a better one,' he told her.

It was his turn to surprise her.

'A lot of the consultant-type work that would come to a group like that would be handed off from the Bureau or the CIA,' Sam said. 'It makes more sense to have a second in command who came out of one of those agencies.' He smiled at her. 'You could be my boss. Order me around. Be honest now. Wouldn't that be a dream come true for you?'

She laughed, but there were tears in her eyes. 'I thought you were against the idea of women in the teams.'

'I was and I am,' he told her. 'But this isn't a SEAL team. This is something else. And I'd love to work with you. A shooter like you, guarding my six?'

Alyssa grabbed him by the tie and pulled him close enough to kiss. Which she did, quite thoroughly.

'Go get that phone number from that help-wanted poster,' she told him. 'I'm running in to the drug store.'

Sam couldn't keep his mouth shut any longer. 'Alyssa, what if you don't take that pill?'

She let go of his tie, her eyes suddenly wary.

'I can't pretend that it doesn't bother me,' he said. 'I mean, what's the difference between that pill and an abortion? I'm sorry, I know it was my idea, but—'

'It's my body,' she said quietly. 'Shouldn't the choice be mine?'

'Yes. It should,' he told her. 'And it is. I'm not saying it's not. But it's also *our* baby, and . . . I know you think I'm a jerk, but I really do want to have a family with you. I know it's way too early for me to tell you that, but it's true and I think you need to know it before you go taking some pill, just in case you were maybe thinking that it was something I didn't want. I just think it's fair – and important – for you to know how I feel.'

Alyssa was quiet for a long time.

So Sam kept going. He'd completely jumped the gun anyway. Might as well go big. 'I am going to marry you, Alyssa. And if not now, then someday we *will* have a baby together. I'm determined. You might want to start bracing yourself for the inevitability of that.'

She was looking at him, but he had absolutely no idea what she was thinking.

And of course, just as she took a breath to speak, her phone rang.

She opened it, frowning slightly as she glanced down at the number. 'Alyssa Locke.' She listened for a moment, then laughed. 'Where are you? Are you all right? Oh, my God. There're a lot of people looking for you, worried about you.'

She motioned for a pen and paper, and Sam grabbed the pad that they'd been making notes on. There was a pen sticking out of one of the cup holders and Alyssa already had it uncapped.

'Repeat that, please.' She wrote down an address as he held the pad in place.

'It's Mary Lou,' Alyssa told Sam. 'She said she had my cell number and—'

No fucking way.

'She's fine,' Alyssa said as he opened up their street map of Sarasota. 'Haley's with her. Along with – get this – Ihbraham Rahman. He talked her into calling. Apparently she's very worried for their safety.'

No *fucking* way.

'Mary Lou, can you describe the man you saw outside of your sister's house on the night she was killed? Blond hair? You saw him? You could ID him in a lineup? Wait, hang on a sec, will you?' Alyssa leaned over the map, too. 'She described it as a compound, Sam. She said it's a main house and two guest cottages on a lake, about twenty miles south and west of Sarasota. There's a gatehouse and guards – not for a development, but for this individual piece of property.'

'Got it.' Sam found the street on the map, angling it so Alyssa could see. 'Man, it's in the middle of nowhere.'

'We're about twenty-five minutes away from you, Mary Lou.'

'That's pretty optimistic,' he said.

Alyssa looked at him. 'Not if you drive.'

He was out the door and sliding over the hood of the car as she scrambled over the parking brake.

'What's your phone number?' she asked Mary Lou. 'In case we get cut off?'

Sam backed out of the parking spot and headed for Route 41 south as Alyssa wrote the number down.

'We're on our way,' she told Mary Lou.

The maid knocked, and Gina adjusted her robe more tightly around her as she went to the door.

'I'm still in here,' she said. 'I won't be out until—'

It was Max.

'Hi,' he said. He'd showered and was wearing a very crisp white shirt with a suit that had nary a wrinkle.

His dark hair was neatly combed and his cheeks were so smooth and clean, he must've shaved on the way over, in the car. He smelled delicious, and his eyes were so richly brown that just looking into them made her knees weak. He looked so good, so solidly, intensely male, Gina's mouth went dry.

'I didn't expect to see you again,' she said. 'Today,' she amended when he frowned.

'May I come in?'

'Of course.' She stepped back, opening the door wider, then closing it behind him.

He looked at her suitcase open on the bed. Looked at the

clothes she'd worn last night, still lying on the floor where she'd thrown them.

Gina picked them up, jammed them into her laundry bag. 'I hate packing.'

'Yeah,' he said. 'I do, too.'

He was looking at her now, at her hair, still damp from her shower, at her thin cotton robe. It was kind of obvious she had nothing on beneath it.

Still, he let himself look. Gina allowed herself to hope that that was a good thing.

But then he said, 'Gina, how do I fix this? I've been trying to figure it out and—'

'What's to fix?' she asked, turning away so he wouldn't see the way his words made her heart sink. She forced herself to laugh. 'Max, we had sex. It was good sex. It was something I *really* needed. I was under the impression that you maybe enjoyed it a little bit, too.'

'I'm not quite sure *enjoyed* is the right word.'

'Oh,' she said. Now she really didn't want to look at him. 'I thought . . .' But then she had to face him. She had to know. 'Are you embarrassed because you—'

'No,' he said. 'Yes.' He closed his eyes. 'Gina, no, the sex was great. The sex was . . .' He looked at her and held her gaze. 'You know it was incredible. It was unbelievable. And it shouldn't have happened.'

'Says who?'

'Me.'

'Why? And if you say *transference*, I swear, I'm going to scream.'

'Because a day and a half ago, I asked Alyssa Locke to marry me.'

'Mary Lou, I'm going to call you back in a few minutes, okay?' Alyssa hung up the phone and turned to Sam. 'She seems to think there's a serious and immediate threat, and I have to agree.

Ihbraham Rahman drove from San Diego, where we know he was being followed. It stands to reason that he was followed all the way here.'

Sam nodded. 'I agree.' He glanced at her. 'Go ahead. Call for backup – that's what you want to do, right?' It wasn't the way he'd wanted it to go down, but he'd rather have Haley frightened than dead. He dug for his own phone.

Alyssa was already dialing hers. 'Praise God for his creation of intelligent, reasonable men.'

He had to laugh. 'Are you talking about *moi*? Fuck me, I wish you could time travel and say those very words to yourself, oh, about three years ago.'

'Well, I can't time travel, but I can – Yeah, Jules. Big news. We've found Mary Lou. Or rather, she found us. We need heavy backup at this address.'

As she rattled the info off, Sam dialed his phone.

'Who are you calling?' Alyssa asked. 'Better not be CNN.'

'Noah and Claire,' he told her. 'I'm going to ask them to meet us over there, to take custody of Haley.'

Jesus, he was going to see his daughter again in just a few minutes.

Alyssa was back on with Jules. 'We're about twenty-two minutes away. It's going to take you longer to get there – you're much farther north. Can you get choppers?' Pause. 'What do you mean no? I don't *care* who's in town! Get Max on the phone. He'll get us the choppers.'

Claire was waiting outside as Noah pulled in to the nursery school parking lot.

'I brought a map,' she said as she climbed in and fastened her seat belt. 'What's the address?'

He held out his left hand – he'd written the street address Ringo had given him on his palm.

'And the deal is we connect with Ringo,' Claire said, leafing through the map book, 'we take a little time – just a little – for

Haley to get comfortable with us, and then SEAL-boy and Mary Lou turn themselves in to the authorities?'

'That's right.' Noah backed out of the spot.

'And we don't find ourselves slapped with aiding and abetting charges when Ringo changes his mind?'

'He's going to turn himself in.'

'Just like that?'

'Just like that.'

She snorted. 'Why do I find that hard to believe? I don't think he's ever done *anything* the easy way. And that sounds way too easy for Ringo.'

'High adventure does seem to follow him around,' Noah agreed. 'I think it's because he's always operated at full speed and a hundred and fifty percent effort. He may get into trouble faster than some people, but once he gets there, he works his butt off to get out of it.' He laughed. 'His life is never boring, that's for sure.'

Claire shot him a look. 'And yours is?'

He didn't think he'd sounded even the slightest bit envious – he really was just making a statement about Ringo. 'No, no,' he said. 'Trust me, I don't need to be on the FBI's wanted list to feel fulfilled.'

'Wait,' Claire said. 'Go back. I forgot. If we're going to take that little girl home with us, we're going to need a car seat. I've got an extra inside the church.'

Noah went around the block and pulled back in to the church parking lot. 'Hurry,' he told her.

Gina stared at Max. He'd asked Alyssa Locke to *marry* him. There was absolutely nothing she could say in response to that. Except, 'Oh, wow.'

'Yeah,' he said. 'I didn't think of her once last night. I mean, I just didn't even *think* of her. It was like she didn't exist.'

She sat down on the edge of the bed, unable to stop her eyes from filling with tears. She, too, hadn't thought even once last night of anyone but herself and Max. And not even so much of Max. Oh, God . . . 'Maybe if you explain, she'll understand.'

'Yeah,' Max said. 'Well. She's known about you for a while. And she *does* understand, maybe a little too well. She says she wasn't going to marry me anyway, so . . .'

Oh, *God*. 'I'm so sorry,' Gina said.

'I don't know. She's probably right, that the reason I asked her in the first place was to force myself to stay away from you – yeah, that worked, huh? But I wouldn't have asked her if I didn't honestly want her to . . .' He shook his head. 'I want you to know that I didn't intentionally set out to hurt her or you or . . . I should have slowed down, because obviously I was unable to think clearly, and I should have. I *should* have thought it through. What kind of excuse is "I didn't stop and think"? A God damn lame one. And the truth is, there's *no* excuse good enough. What I did was absolutely unforgivable.'

He really believed that. He was wrecked about this. Gina had used him to try to repair herself and had ended up hurting him more than she could have imagined. 'I seduced you, Max. I kissed you first.'

He laughed. 'Yeah, excuse me, but I had a choice. I chose to stay.'

'Why?' she asked him, forcing herself to look up at him. She suspected she already knew the answer, and sure enough, there it was in his eyes. She answered for him: 'Because I needed you.'

'No,' Max said. 'Because I wanted to.'

He was *so* lying. Even his being here right now had *obligation* written all over it. Or maybe he wasn't technically lying. Maybe he wanted to stay because he knew how much she'd needed him.

Which wasn't a good enough reason, when it came down to it. She'd thought it would be, but it wasn't. Especially knowing that he really was in love with Alyssa, enough to want to *marry* her . . . Oh, God. Her heart was breaking for him, for Alyssa . . .

For herself.

'So where do we go from here?' Max asked quietly.

He was serious. He honestly didn't know that the answer was *nowhere*.

They went absolutely nowhere.

'I'm going home to New York tonight,' Gina said, 'and you're in the middle of a situation.'

'I'm going to have some, uh, time off,' he said, 'starting somewhere between now and the end of the month. Is there any chance we can get together then?'

He was serious. But then again, with his need to take care of and protect everyone he'd ever met, he probably meticulously followed up on all of his one-night stands. A phone call. A lunch date. Periodic check-ins.

This was so not the way she'd imagined this would happen. She'd fairy-taled it completely in her personal fantasy version. Max should have come pounding on her door to tell her that he couldn't live without her, that he loved her.

Not that he was in love with Alyssa and that since sleeping with Gina had completely blown his chances with her, he might as well make plans to see Gina again.

'Get together?' she asked, one part of her wanting to torment him. 'You mean, like, hook up? Have sex again?' She knew damn well that he meant have lunch.

And he knew it, too. He just looked at her.

'You mean in Africa?' she asked. Now that she'd started, she was unable to stop. She'd wanted him to love her. 'Because I'm leaving for Kenya next week.'

Max looked stunned. It was remarkable. She didn't think he did *stunned* to that extreme. 'You're not . . . You're still planning to go?'

'Uh, *yeah*.' she said, more anger creeping in around the hurt. 'What did you think, Max? I'd spend one night with you and then change my plans for the next *year* of my life, so I could rush home and stay by the phone, hoping you'll call when you have some time off? In between your meetings with your wedding planner?' That last comment was a little too sharp, and she stood up, hating the idea of dissolving into jealousy. All she really had right now was her dignity. Well, what little of it there was left. 'Max, I don't know why you're here with me. You should be talking to Alyssa. I mean, if you really wanted to *marry* her . . .'

'Gina—'

'Talk to her. Make her change her mind.' Gina opened her door and he took it as the invitation it was. Time for him to leave. 'Tell her I'm sorry. Because I am. I'm *really* sorry.'

'She's not going to change her mind. I don't want her to change her mind.'

Oh, the hope that crashed through her at those words was remarkable. She almost threw herself into his arms, until he added, 'I want to fix this, between us. I need to make sure you're all right. Some of the things you said last night—'

She cut him off. 'I said I'd go back into therapy.'

'You're going to find a therapist in *Africa*?'

'Yeah, you know, I'm betting there actually *are* one or two people with degrees in Kenya.'

'This isn't a good time for you to leave the country,' Max told her grimly, as his cell phone started ringing. It was amazing it had gone that long without making any noise.

'Thank you for your concern,' she said. 'I have to finish packing now and you need to take that call.'

He moved toward the door, but stopped right next to her, inches from her. And he waited until she looked up, into his eyes.

'The bitch of it is, I still want you,' he whispered. 'I've screwed everything up, but nothing's changed at all. I'm still dying for you, Gina.'

The heat in his eyes was incredible, and Gina was sure he was going to kiss her. Kiss her and strip her robe from her and . . .

But he went out the door and headed for his car, phone still ringing, without looking back.

'Hey,' she called, since it seemed as if he wasn't intending to answer his phone.

He stopped, turning around only slightly, so that he couldn't quite see her, but so that she knew he was listening.

'If you still feel that way next year, when I get back,' she said, her voice shaking only a little, 'maybe you should give me a call.' She cleared her throat. 'You know, provided you haven't proposed marriage to anyone else in the meantime.'

He turned all the way around. 'Gina, I'm so sorry.'

'I am, too,' she said. She wished he would kiss her goodbye, but she knew it was too much to ask – of herself as well as him. 'Thank you for last night.'

He obviously couldn't deal with her thanking him, so he got into his car, finally answering his phone.

Gina watched him back out of his parking spot and pull out of the lot, tires squealing. She watched until he was out of sight, which didn't take long at all.

Wherever Max was going, he sure was in a hurry to get there.

Or maybe he was just in a hurry to leave.

'My heart is pounding out of my chest,' Sam said, 'at the thought of seeing Haley again.'

Heavy traffic had them stopped. He was trying to pull right so he could take a side street, but the cars in front of them just weren't moving.

'Don't expect too much,' Alyssa warned him.

'I won't but, ah, Lys, what if she hates me?'

Oh, Sam. 'I don't think kids that little have been taught how to hate yet.'

'What do I say to her?'

'Well,' she said, 'before you even open your mouth, you need to do an immediate fuck-ectomy of your vocabulary.'

He laughed. 'Fuck-ectomy. I like that. Okay. Fuck-ectomy in progress.'

'Part of doing it means you can't say *fuck-ectomy* anymore.'

'I have a feeling I'm not going to say much of anything anymore,' he pointed out dryly. 'So the you-know-what's complete. What do I say? "Hi, Haley, I'm your daddy. Boy, have I missed you."'

'That's good. Don't ask her if she remembers you – you'll both feel bad when she says no.'

'When,' he said. 'Yeah. Yeah. I don't remember the last time I've been this nervous.' He glanced at her. 'I'm nervous, too, about you meeting her. I know you said your feelings for Haley were mixed—'

'Not about loving her,' Alyssa told him. 'I'm going to love her. That's why babies are so cute. So everyone automatically loves them.' She laughed. 'Everyone with a heart, that is.'

'Why do I get the feeling there's a story there?'

Because he'd spent the past few days talking to her, and listening while she talked. Because he knew her.

'Yeah,' she said. 'Well . . .'

'Let's have it.'

'Well, it was after my mother died,' Alyssa told him.

'Why do I already have the urge to kill someone?' he asked.

'We went to live with my father's sister – Tyra, Lanora, and I,' she said. 'It was a pretty stressful time – on top of the grief and loss – because my aunt Joyce kept saying that she was going to take only Tyra and me. That Lanora had to go live with my mother's cousin. I practically had to go to court to keep us together.'

'Mmph,' Sam said.

Alyssa looked at him.

'I can't say anything,' he told her, 'because I want to say what the *fuck* was wrong with her?'

'Lanora wasn't my father's child,' Alyssa told him. 'That was what was wrong with Aunt Joyce. Apparently this was why my parents broke up. My mother was unfaithful, she got pregnant, and when my father found out, he left her. Us, too, though, you know? Which was kind of unfair. I didn't know anything about any of this at the time. I just knew that one day he was there, and the next he was gone. But Aunt Joyce, well, she was a little too happy to fill me in. She told me Lanora couldn't live with us because of that, because she felt no responsibility toward her.'

'Grphh,' Sam said.

'I remember I just kind of looked at her, and said, "But she's still my sister."

'And Aunt Joyce said – I remember this as clear as yesterday – she said, "When you're older, you'll understand."' Alyssa shook her head. 'Joyce ended up taking Lanora, too, because Tyra and I weren't going *any*where without her, but she never gave her any affection. That sweet little baby . . . My mother's transgressions were not her fault, but Joyce constantly held it against her. I'm much older now, and the only thing I fully understand is how completely wrong Joyce was. She shouldn't have taken us in if she couldn't love us all. And believe me, it wouldn't have been hard for her to love Lanora. It must've been a lot of work to stay that hard and cold. But she cared more about blaming my mother – for everything from my parents splitting up to my father's death – than she cared about the welfare of an innocent child.'

Sam had managed to make the right turn and was now barreling down side streets, trying to make up for lost time. But he still glanced over at her. 'Thank you for telling me that.'

'So I'm going to love Haley,' Alyssa said. 'Because she's not responsible for Mary Lou's mistakes, or your mistakes, or my mistakes. And I'm going to love her twice as much because she's yours. But you need to know, Sam – I'm not going to take care of her for you. When she's with you, she's with *you*. I'll help, and I'll be her favorite aunt Alyssa. I'm good at that. But if you really want her in your life, you're going to have to be her father for real.'

'That's, um, some of the best news I've had all day – the fact that you seem okay with the idea of spending time with me and Haley.' He glanced at her again. And then, almost as an afterthought, he matter-of-factly added, 'I love you so much, Lys, sometimes it takes my breath away.'

Twenty-five

Mary Lou took comfort in the fact that this house was a fortress.

The security system was on. Windows and doors were all locked. The blinds and shades were pulled. Jim Potter and Eddie Bowen were on guard at the gate, and they'd been told to let no one else in.

The man she knew as Bob Schwegel wasn't getting anywhere near them.

At least that was what Alyssa Locke had told her when Mary Lou had called and explained what was going on.

'Don't leave the house,' her ex-husband's girlfriend had said in her melodious voice. She sounded like someone who reported the news, with a cool authority to her voice that actually helped calm Mary Lou. 'You'll be much safer there than in a motor vehicle.'

Why was it FBI agents didn't just say car?

Mary Lou had met the woman only a few times. Alyssa Locke was unbelievably beautiful with flawless brown skin and slender hips and big green eyes and sleek, dark hair with reddish tints that just *had* to come from a bottle. Either that or God deserved to be bitch-slapped for His almighty unfairness to all other women on earth.

It was bad enough that Alyssa had that mouth, with the kind of lush, full lips that white women everywhere tried to copy by getting collagen injections.

And yet Alyssa walked around dressed like a man saying things like 'motor vehicle'.

Mary Lou had to wonder if Alyssa's entire cool, reserved, professional demeanor was some kind of twisted turn-on for Sam. She'd spent a lot of sleepless nights wondering about that, jealous as hell.

She'd even found out Alyssa's cell phone number, but she'd never gotten up the nerve to call her.

Until today.

Who would've thought, even just six or seven months ago, that she'd ever call up Alyssa Locke to ask for her help?

There was probably only one person in the world who could've talked her into doing that. And she was sitting here, holding his hand, watching Whitney read another chapter of *Alice* to Haley and Amanda.

Talk about Wonderland . . .

'It's going to be all right,' Ihbraham told her quietly.

'I'm scared they're going to put me in jail,' she admitted. 'Alyssa told me that Sam's cousin and his wife are meeting us over here, that they'll make sure Haley's okay while I'm being questioned, but . . . Could you go with them? Be with her, too?'

His smile was apologetic. 'I'm certain they will wish to question me, as well.'

Because he'd been born in Saudi Arabia. Because he looked the way a terrorist was supposed to look.

'That's not fair. This doesn't have anything to do with you.'

'Perhaps I can help give them a description of this man you believe is behind all this trouble. I met him once, you know.'

'I remember,' she said. 'But maybe if you left now, they wouldn't—'

'I'm happy to stay right here,' he said. 'More than happy.'

Mary Lou leaned against him. He smelled so good – spicy and warm. 'I missed you so much.'

He put his arm around her. 'I'm sorry I wasn't able to get here faster. All those months in the hospital, I lost clients and it's taken longer than I'd hoped to get my business back up to speed. I'm ashamed to admit I didn't even have enough room on my credit card to get a plane ticket.'

'I can't believe you drove all that way.'

'I'm pretty tired.' His fingers were in her hair. His touch was gentle but extremely sensuous. 'I find I'm most eager to retire tonight.'

She looked up at him, and although he was smiling, the look in his eyes told her that she'd read his innuendo quite correctly.

'Unless you'd prefer we wait for our first night together until after we're married,' he murmured.

After . . .? Mary Lou's heart nearly stopped. 'Did you just ask me to marry you?'

He laughed, but his eyes were so serious. 'I thought I wouldn't ask – just tell. I thought perhaps if I didn't give you a choice, you wouldn't think about all your reasons not to marry me. Wherever I go, if there's trouble, people *will* look to me.'

Mary Lou felt her eyes fill with tears. 'Because they'll say, Look at that man with his incredibly beautiful wife. Trouble must just follow them around.'

'Did you just tell me yes?'

She nodded.

And the lights went out.

'Hey!' Whitney said. It wasn't dark in there by any means, because sunlight was still coming in from behind the blinds, but she was trying to read.

There was a sound in the distance, like ripping fabric, that Mary Lou had heard before. It was a sound a person could hear only once but then never forget.

'Those are gunshots,' Whitney said, her eyes wide.

The phone rang, lighting up the button that was a direct line to the guardhouse at the gate.

Whitney lunged for it. 'Jim! What was that?' She listened. 'Who is this? Where's Jim?' Her face contorted. 'Oh, shit.' She held the phone out to Mary Lou. 'He says Jim's dead. He wants to talk to you.'

Mary Lou stood up. Took the phone. 'Who is this?' she asked, even though she already knew. It was the man she knew as Bob Schwegel.

'Well, hello, Mary Lou,' he said in his slightly nasal voice.

It was the man who had smuggled guns into the Coronado naval base in the trunk of her car, the man who had murdered her sister.

Mary Lou hung up the phone, punched an outside line, and dialed 911.

'Check the map, would you?' Sam asked Alyssa as they continued to drive along side roads. 'Make sure we're not going too far east.'

'No, we're okay,' she said, head bent over the map.

She had said exactly nothing in response to his declaration of love.

Sam took it as a good sign, even though 'I love you, too' had been noticeably absent. Truth was, he hadn't really expected to hear her say that. The real thrill came from the fact that he'd said 'love' and she hadn't said, 'No way.' She hadn't accused him of misinterpreting what this was he was feeling.

And she was the one who was talking about Haley as if the three of them would be spending lots of time together.

Alyssa looked up from the map. 'You know, it just occurred to me that I never told you that I got my period this morning. We started talking about having a choice and . . . But that's what I needed to pick up from the drug store. Tampons. Not that prescription.'

What? 'But you said you were right at the point in your cycle—'

'I am,' she said. 'I was. But I started bleeding, so—'

Holy fuck. But it was fear that gripped him, not relief. 'Are you all right? I didn't, like, hurt you or something, did I?'

'No.' Alyssa smiled, as if there was something funny about the idea that he might've been too rough. 'God, no. This actually happened to me before. I go a real long time without having sex, then I have a lot of sex, and my cycle gets all out of whack. I think it's the result of a hormone overload.' She laughed. 'You know, I've always kind of thought of you as a hormone overload.'

He wasn't sure, but it was possible she'd just insulted him. Except her smile was very warm, and that look in her eyes . . . 'Wow,' Sam said. 'I'm . . . man, that's, um . . .'

'An enormous relief,' she filled in for him.

But his fear had turned into something else entirely and it wasn't relief. He glanced at her. 'Is it?'

She looked away first, no longer laughing. 'Sam, you're insane if you— '

Her cell phone rang.

'If I what?' he asked.

She shook her head as she answered her phone. 'Locke.' She sat forward, her body language shifting to high tension as she listened intently.

'No,' she said, 'but call me right back.' She closed her phone, but opened it right away. 'We're getting reports of shots fired in the vicinity of the Turlington estate, and the local police have gotten notification from the security company. Someone inside the house has triggered a silent alarm.'

Fuck! Sam floored it as Alyssa dialed the phone number Mary Lou had given her.

'How could you lose your cell phone?' Mary Lou asked Whitney. She couldn't believe this was happening.

All of the phone lines from the house had been cut – with exception of the line to the front gate, which was ringing and ringing and ringing.

She'd run down to the front door and pushed the panic button on the alarm system the way Mrs Downs had shown her when she'd first arrived. The housekeeper had said in her know-it-all manner, 'Here's something that you need to know, but you'll never need to use.'

Mrs Downs apparently didn't know everything.

'I didn't *lose* it,' Whitney said. 'It's somewhere in my room. It doesn't work half the time anyway. Cell service out here sucks dick.'

'Find it anyway!' Mary Lou said. Ihbraham had brought Haley and Amanda into the bathroom, where whatever he was doing was keeping them giggling. Mary Lou had sent them in there. She'd read lots of books where the characters climbed into the bathtub for protection when the shooting started.

When the shooting started . . .

Lord, that incessantly ringing phone was starting to drive her mad.

Whitney went into Mary Lou's bedroom instead of down the hall to her own.

'You need to find that phone!' Mary Lou followed her. 'If we don't call and warn them, Alyssa and Sam are going to drive right up to the gate and then they're going to be just as dead as Jim Potter and – What are you doing?'

Whitney dumped the guns and ammunition from Mary Lou's beach bag onto the bed. She was lining them up and . . .

Loading them?

'I'm not going to let terrorists walk in here and just shoot us,' the girl said.

'You know how to use those things?'

Whitney gave Mary Lou a teenager's 'shit, you're stupid' look as she attached one of those clips to a very deadly looking, very large weapon. 'Daddy took me to his firing range for the first time when I was five. I qualified as an expert marksman when I was eleven. In case you haven't exactly noticed, in this house we worship at the altar of Smith and Wesson.'

'Keep those things away from the girls,' Mary Lou ordered. 'But show Ihbraham how to use one. I'll be back in a sec.'

She was going to find Whitney's phone if it was the last thing she did.

Noah looked at Claire. 'You know, I'm not jealous of Ringo.'

'Really?' she asked. 'Not even the ten-year-old in you?'

'Really,' he said. 'I wanted to be a SEAL more than anything in the world – right up until the moment I walked into Mrs Fucci's English class and started listening to you arguing with her about the importance of rap music in the American cultural experience.'

She laughed, her face lighting up. 'You remember that?'

'Yeah. You and Calvin Graham got up and did that rap version of that scene from *Romeo and Juliet* that was, um—'

'It was pretty awful.'

'No,' he said. 'I went home and read the play that night, and I got to the part where Romeo sees Juliet for the first time, and I'm sitting there thinking, *Damn. I've got the same affliction Romeo's got. And what am I going to do about this Calvin guy?*'

'He was so gay.'

'I didn't know that then.' It had been Noah's first day in a new school – his first day in years that Ringo hadn't been by his side. He'd spent a lot of time those first few weeks worrying about Ringo alone back in Texas, without Noah, without Dot and Walt.

Please God, don't let Ringo get blindsided by the loss of his family. Don't let him let Lyle Morgan piss him off. Don't let him kill Lyle and spend the rest of his life in jail . . .

Noah should have had more faith. Just the fact that Ringo had opted to remain behind with his mother was proof he was capable of thinking things through and not always reaching for the easiest, most instantly gratifying solution.

He hadn't realized just how difficult a sacrifice it had been

475

for Ringo to stay in Texas until the summer he came down to visit.

Ringo had hitchhiked the entire way because his father not only wouldn't give him the money for a bus ticket, but he also wouldn't let him touch the money Ringo himself had earned, loading trucks after school. That money was for college, or so Roger Senior had insisted.

So Ringo had packed a duffel and walked to the truck stop off Route 20, with only seven dollars in his pocket.

Every year after, Walt sent him the money for a bus ticket. Ringo pretended he took the bus, but Noah knew he still hitched. He used the money to buy presents for them, because he hated showing up empty-handed.

That summer had been wonderful. It was Ringo who had walked up to Claire and said, 'My cousin Noah, here, thinks you're incredibly hot. He's too much of a fuckhead to tell you that himself. Want to help me drive him crazy and go to a movie with me?'

Noah was standing there, embarrassed as hell, ready to drag Ringo off and beat the crap out of him – right after he cleared up a thing or two. 'I didn't say you were hot,' he told her.

Claire looked at him, her eyebrows raised, like, *no?*

'I said you were beautiful and smart and funny,' he said, going into freefall just from looking into her eyes, part of himself completely unable to believe he was standing there and talking to her, let alone saying what he was saying, '. . . *and* hot.'

Claire didn't look away from Noah as she'd answered Ringo's question. 'I think I'd rather drive him crazy in other ways.'

Instant hard-on. Of course, he'd been sixteen and it didn't take much. Still, it was something of a miracle that he and Claire had kept their clothes on – at least most of them – for a full year.

By the end of that first summer Noah was so wrapped up in Claire, he almost didn't notice when Ringo left.

Except for the fact that Ringo got really quiet those last few days of his visit.

And when Walt and Noah took him to the bus station, he broke down and cried.

All three of them did. People gave them a wide berth – three guys all well over six feet tall, weeping like babies.

'Do you think Ringo and Mary Lou will get back together after this?' Claire asked. 'That happens sometimes. People go through a traumatic experience and they try again.'

Noah glanced at her. 'You know, I might be tempted to agree, but . . . I didn't tell you this before, but this woman – an FBI agent – a sister – she showed up after you left Janine's house. Alyssa Locke. Ringo introduced her to me as a friend. I almost told her, "My cousin thinks you're hot."'

Claire laughed. '"But he's too much of a fuckhead to tell you that himself"?'

'Yeah. You should have seen the way he looked at her,' Noah said, pulling up to a stop sign at the end of the road. 'And she was looking back at him, too. Do I go right or left here?'

Claire studied the map. 'Left. If we're where I think we are.' She looked up. 'Either way, I don't think it's too much farther.'

'Mary Lou's not answering,' Alyssa reported.

'Dial it again,' Sam said.

She did. 'Still nothing.

'What's the status of those choppers? What's Max's ETA? What's *our* ETA?'

'I'm working on reaching Max,' she reported, juggling the phone and the map. 'We've got another ten minutes as far as I can tell.'

'Shit-fuck! Noah! Use my cell and call him,' Sam ordered her. 'Now, Alyssa, *please!*' The way he was driving, it was good he was keeping both hands on the wheel. 'Tell him not to approach the gate. Jesus, *Jesus* . . .'

She took his cell phone from between his legs and hit Redial. Come on, Noah. 'Sam, he's not picking up.' She looked at the phone. 'Oh, shit . . .'

'No,' Sam said. 'Don't say that.'

Alyssa tried her own phone. It, too, was giving her an out-of-range signal.

Sam glanced at her, and she shook her head. 'We've lost our cell phones.'

'This is Max Bhagat. Connect me to the President.'

'I'm sorry, sir—'

'Wrong answer.' Max didn't have time for this. He had more than twenty agents – himself included – driving like bats out of hell for the address Alyssa had given them, and another twenty heading toward MacDill Air Force Base, up in Tampa, ETA two minutes, where there were three Navy Seahawks waiting to take them the forty miles they needed to go in about fifteen minutes.

Provided they had the President's permission to assist in this FBI operation.

'He's in a meeting with the—'

'Do you know who I am?'

'I'm sorry, I'm new. This is my first day, sir. I'm trying—'

'Connect me to someone who is not new, *right now*,' Max said, 'or this will be your last day.' On earth.

Someone else picked up. 'Peterson.'

'This is Max Bhagat—'

'I'll connect you to the President right away, sir.'

Two seconds, maybe even less, and Allen Bryant picked up. 'Max. What's going on?'

'Sir. I need three Seahawks at MacDill—'

His cell phone beeped and died.

No signal.

Perfect. He'd just hung up on the President of the United States.

Max reached for the radio even as he hit the brakes and skidded to a stop. 'This is Max Bhagat. I need trucks with satellite towers moved into this area immediately, over!'

He put his car into reverse and drove backward as fast as he could, engine whining, while he watched his phone, waiting for the signal to return.

'Sir.' Laronda's voice came over the radio. 'We just got a call from Deb Peterson at the White House. Three Seahawk helicopters are standing by, at our disposal.'

Max hit the brakes again, and shifted back into drive. He'd worked hard to establish that kind of trust with the country's commander in chief. It was gratifying to know all he had to say was 'I need . . .' and President Bryant would deliver.

'We're working on setting up a direct connection between you and the Army commander,' she continued. 'Until we do, do you have any orders for me to relay? Come back.'

'Yeah, tell them to haul ass. And get communications up and working. Alyssa Locke is at least twenty minutes in front of all of us, but that won't do us any good if she can't talk to us, over.'

'She's in a rental car, no radio,' Laronda came back. 'We've ordered local police to set up roadblocks in the area, but otherwise to wait for us to arrive. I'll get an unmarked car with a police radio into the vicinity, over.'

'Locke needs to be told to do surveillance, to report, and then to wait for backup. Repeat, tell her to wait for backup. Over.'

'Dream on, sir,' Laronda told him. 'Over.'

Mary Lou found Whitney's cell phone in a pair of jeans at the bottom of her closet.

Thank God, thank God. She pulled it out, opened it, and . . .

Low battery.

No!

Okay, maybe there was enough to make one call . . .

Except Mary Lou couldn't even tell if there was service available. She dialed anyway, but the screen went dark.

Low battery had become no battery.

Whitney's car had a charger – the kind that could be plugged into the cigarette lighter. The kind that would let the phone be used even while it was charging.

Mary Lou ran back to her apartment, where that frigging phone had finally stopped ringing.

'I found it,' she announced. 'I'm going down to the garage to see if—'

Boom!

An explosion rocked the entire house, pushing Mary Lou down onto her butt and breaking the glass in her kitchen windows.

She scrambled to her feet, ran for the bathroom.

Ihbraham was shielding Haley and Amanda with his body. The two little girls were wide-eyed.

'Whitney,' Mary Lou shouted. 'Are you all right?'

'I'm fine,' came a return shout. 'What the hell was that?'

Out in the living room, the phone started ringing again.

All over the house, the fire alarms started shrieking.

'Okay,' Sam said. 'Okay. Here's what we're going to do. We're going to stop at one of these houses, and you're going to get out and use their phone and call Noah while—'

'You go on without me?' Alyssa said. 'I don't *think* so.'

'I know it's not what you want to do,' he said. 'But I'm begging you, Lys. This man is my brother. He has no training, no reason to believe he can't just drive up to that gate. They are going to kill him—'

'How am I going to call him?' she asked. 'If we can't use our cell phones, he can't use his, either.'

'Maybe there's coverage down where he is.'

'We're moving farther away from civilization,' Alyssa told him. 'Just *drive*.'

* * *

Whitney went down to the control panel and turned off the fire alarm, and Mary Lou could once again hear the phone ringing.

'There was some kind of bomb,' Whitney reported as she ran back up the stairs. 'The main kitchen's completely destroyed. If we'd been in the north wing instead of the south . . .' She looked like Lara Croft Junior, the way she was loaded down with weaponry. For the first time in all of the weeks Mary Lou had lived there, she saw the girl's resemblance to her father in the hard light in her eyes. 'The entire back of the house is on fire.'

Sure enough, thick smoke was already curling through the air.

Lord God, everything was so dry, it was going to go up like a tinderbox.

Whatever a tinderbox was.

'There's one man out front with a sniper rifle,' Whitney said, 'and two in the back, one with an AK-47, one with something else, I can't tell what. Looks like they're putting gasoline on the parts of the house that aren't burning yet. These asswipes want us dead.'

As if a fire would need any kind of help at all in this dry heat. Mary Lou picked up the phone.

'Here's the deal,' the man she knew as Bob said before she could even say hello. 'You and Rahman walk out the front door right now, and everyone else in the house – including Haley – stays alive.'

Oh, Lord.

'The FBI is on its way,' she said. 'If you don't want them to kill you, you better leave right now!'

'Thanks for the tip, honey,' he said. 'I'll put my men here at the gate on alert.'

No!

'They're going to be here,' Mary Lou said, praying she was right. 'Lots of them. Any minute.'

'Any minute,' he said. 'That would be about how long it's going to take for that house to become completely inescapable. If you and Rahman walk out now—'

Bile burned her throat. 'So you can shoot us.'

'Better than burning. Better than watching your daughter burn.'

Mary Lou might've done it. If it were just her and Haley, she *would* have done it. But she would not let him kill Ihbraham. No, sir.

'Go to hell,' she told him, and hung up the phone.

'Perhaps we should move downstairs,' Ihbraham said. He was carrying both Haley and Amanda, and watching her from the door to the bathroom.

Whitney was watching her, too. Everyone was looking to her for what they should do next.

'Yeah,' Mary Lou said. The smoke was thick at the ceiling. 'Let's move downstairs.'

Sam didn't slow as they went past the drive that led to the Turlingtons' gatehouse.

'There's no physical gate, just a guardhouse with one of those flimsy arms blocking the driveway. I saw no cars stopped,' Alyssa reported. 'No sign of Noah and Claire, no sign that anything is wrong at all.'

The brush at the side of the road already concealed them from the gatehouse. It was jungle-thick growth, typical of this part of Florida but definitely suffering from the recent lack of rain.

Sam pulled off the road and got out of the car. Jesus, he was wearing a freaking white shirt. He yanked it over his head. Better to be half naked than a flipping neon target. He kicked off his shoes and stripped off his socks, too, preferring bare feet to slipping around in the underbrush.

Alyssa, too, was attempting to cammy-up. She'd opened the trunk and pulled a green T-shirt out of her bag, changing into it right there by the side of the road.

482

They had one little handgun between them. Sam handed it to Alyssa. It was hers, after all. She gave him a Swiss Army knife in exchange.

'Gee, thanks.'

Was that smoke he smelled? He started through the brush. The ground was soggy, parts of it brackish puddles of stinking mud. If not for the drought, this entire area would have been a knee-deep or even hip-deep swamp.

Alyssa followed, slipping her shoulder holster on and securing the weapon. Yeah, jeez, don't drop that thing here.

But she wanted her hands free for a different reason. She reached down into the thick mud and grabbed several handfuls, smearing the tar-colored substance down his back and arms. 'Hold up, white boy,' she said. 'I need to get your front.'

'I'm tan,' he said.

'Not tan enough,' she told him, streaking his chest with black and rubbing both his face and hers with the dirt, too. 'I like your body just fine without any bullet holes in it, thanks.'

Then they were moving again, this time with her in the front, weapon back in her hand.

'Alyssa—'

'I've got the weapon that can do the most damage,' she told him. 'I'm on point, unless you can throw that Girl Scout knife faster and farther than a bullet.'

'No,' Sam said. 'I wasn't going to . . . I just wanted to tell you that I'm glad you're here.'

They'd reached a chain-link fence.

'And to be careful,' he added as he quickly plucked what looked like a long strand of grass from the surrounding vegetation. He held it against the fence to see if the thing was electrified. But there was no jolt.

'Aha,' she said. 'Well, you be careful, too.'

'Always am.'

It was just a regular old fence with a little barbed wire at the top. Pretty flipping ineffective in terms of security.

Both he and Alyssa were over it in a matter of seconds.

And, in moments, there they were. Within sight of the gatehouse.

From this angle, things didn't look quite so normal. Two bodies – the guards, Sam presumed – had been dragged outside the door. He could see bullet holes in the windows.

The entire building was about the size of a one-car garage. There were windows all around, so you could see clear through it, almost like a ranger station or an air traffic control tower. Anyone inside had a 360-degree view of the surrounding area. And not a whole hell of a lot of cover should an army of terrorists attack.

Sam needed to have a serious talk with the owner of this compound about the clown who had designed his security.

Two men were inside the structure, both of them armed with what looked like some kind of room brooms.

The range on that type of little semiautomatic wasn't that extensive, but up close it was deadly.

There were quite a few yards of clearing between the brush and the guardhouse – enough so that they would have to step out of hiding in order to get close enough to make Alyssa's little popgun anything more than an annoyance.

'We need a diversion,' she whispered.

Sam nodded. 'Okay. I'll go back and get the car—'

But she'd started running forward, because – holy fuck – a car already was approaching the gatehouse.

It was – Jesus, no – Noah and Claire.

The smoke was just as bad down on the ground floor.

Both Amanda and Haley were coughing and crying. The heat was incredible.

Ihbraham had filled the bathtub with water and had soaked towels that they all draped over their heads.

'If we opened a window,' he said, 'we can get some fresh air.'

'They're not going to let us anywhere near the windows,' Whitney said.

All three of the men with the guns were out front. Mary Lou hadn't seen Bob's golden hair, though. Wherever he was, he was keeping out of sight.

'Let's get to the garage,' Mary Lou decided. The phone charger was there, in Whitney's car. Like the girl said, there was no guarantee there would be cell service, but, Lord, they had to try.

Alyssa was up on her feet, weapon out, moving swiftly toward the gatehouse.

She heard more than saw Sam follow – he angled away from her, running hard, shouting at the top of his lungs.

He was trying to draw the gunmen's fire away from Noah's car, away from Alyssa, trying to buy her the time she needed to get within range, to aim and shoot.

She kept her eyes on her targets as she squeezed off one shot and then another, but she heard the gunfire and she knew she'd been just a heartbeat too late.

She saw Noah and Claire ducking, she saw her targets punched back and falling.

She saw Sam get hit, too, saw the force of a bullet spin him full around before he slammed into the ground.

'No!' The word was ripped from her, even as she did her job the way she'd been trained and moved toward the gunmen to make sure they weren't going to pop back up. But she'd taken head shots and no one was going anywhere.

Noah was out of the car, running toward Sam.

Alyssa beat him over there.

'Fuck,' Sam said.

She had never heard a more wonderful word in her entire life. All she could think was, *Thank God*. Thank God he was alive, thank God he was talking, thank God.

'*Fuck!*' he said again through clenched teeth.

'Ringo!' Noah said, down on his knees beside them. 'Holy shit! Holy *shit*!'

'Give me your shirt,' Alyssa ordered Sam's cousin, and he stripped off his jacket and his white dress shirt. He had a T-shirt on underneath, and she pointed to it. 'That's even better.'

Sam had been hit in the side of his abdomen. He was bleeding badly, but the entry wound was clean and small, and there was no gaping exit wound in his back. Which was either good news or bad news. Either the bullet that hit him was spent, or it had ricocheted around inside of him, doing serious damage to his internal organs, possibly even hitting his spine.

'Can you move your legs?' Alyssa asked him as Noah gave her his T-shirt. She folded it up and was hesitating to press it against Sam's wound. She knew from experience how much that was going to hurt.

He answered her by pushing himself onto his hands and knees and then standing up. 'Fire,' he said.

She looked up. Whatever was burning was huge. Thick black smoke rolled up into the sky.

Sam took the T-shirt from her and pressed it against himself.

'Fuck!' He staggered slightly, and Alyssa put her arm around him on one side, Noah on the other.

'We need to get him to the hospital,' she said.

'Like hell we do,' Sam countered, shaking them both off. Noah had put his dress shirt back on and draped his tie around his neck, and Sam now pulled the tie off of him. He used it to bind the makeshift bandage into place. 'We need to get up to that house. Haley's probably in there.'

Claire was out of the car now, too.

'That's not going to stop the bleeding,' Alyssa told Sam.

'It'll do for now' was his terse reply.

'What the fuck is going on?' Noah asked, sounding remarkably like Sam.

'Are those men *dead*?' Claire asked.

Noah was staring after Sam, who was heading toward the

gatehouse. 'And, Jesus, what's with the bare feet?'

'The bad guys got here first,' Alyssa told them. 'Yes, they're dead, and Sam didn't want to wear dress shoes in the woods – he was afraid he'd slip.'

'Hey,' Sam shouted from inside the guardhouse, and she dashed over to join him. He had a phone handset to his ear. 'There's a direct phone line to the house. At least that's what the little label says this is. Everything else is out but . . . Hey, Mary Lou. Halle-fucking-lujah. It's Sam. We've taken back the gate. What's your status up there? Where's the fire? Is Haley all right?'

'There's no phone line going out?' Alyssa asked as she picked the semiautomatics up off the floor. 'Ask if they have a working phone up at the house.'

'Mary Lou, do you have a phone with an outside line?' Sam looked at Alyssa and shook his head no.

'Okay,' she said to Noah and Claire as she went outside, 'here's what we need you to do. Find the nearest neighbor and use their telephone. Call and ask for Max Bhagat or Jules Cassidy. Give them a status report. Tell them we've taken the gate, but we're going to have to leave it unattended so there might be trouble again when they arrive. Tell them there's a fire at the house – my guess is the tangos are trying to smoke Mary Lou out. Tell them that Sam and I can't wait for backup.'

She took a pen from her pocket and, using Sam's technique, took hold of Noah's arm, writing both Max's and Jules's names and phone numbers right on his forearm. He already had this address on his hand, and Alyssa had to smile. 'Guess you are Sam's cousin.'

'We really should take Ringo to the hospital,' Claire said in a very no-nonsense voice as Noah sat down on the ground and took off his shoes.

Alyssa glanced at her. Noah's wife could have passed as her own sister. Wasn't *that* interesting? She wondered inanely if Noah liked chocolate.

'Sam'll go when he's ready to go,' she told them. 'Wait by the phone for an all clear before you return. Do not come back here until you know it's safe. You've got to promise me that.'

Noah nodded, back on his feet. 'That's not a hard promise to make. Give these to Ringo. They've got rubber soles. And promise *me* you'll take care of him.'

'If he dies,' Alyssa told them as she took Noah's shoes, 'it's only going to be because I've died, too.'

Twenty-six

'Alyssa, I could use your brain over here,' Sam shouted, and she came running into the gatehouse.

Outside, Noah and Claire were getting into their car and backing out, onto the street.

'They're going to find a phone,' Alyssa reported as she set Nos's shoes – he still wore Hush Puppies – on the table. 'And then they're going to stay where it's safe.'

'Thank you,' he said. Good thing someone here was thinking clearly.

Throughout his life, pain and Sam had never stayed strangers for any great length of time. He was always walking around dinged up, as Dot had called it, one way or another. Twisted ankles, sprained knees, black eyes, split lips, broken collarbones, and cracked ribs.

They all hurt to some degree.

Getting shot, however, *fucking* hurt.

It made it a little hard to concentrate.

And Alyssa had been right about the bleeding. It wasn't stopping. He had to apply pressure, which he hadn't been able to do with one hand holding the phone and the other drawing a layout of the house and the yard as Mary Lou described it to him.

'Thank you for taking care of them,' Sam told Alyssa.

She didn't even glance at the bodies on the floor – her whole attention was on his little pencil drawing. 'What's the situation?'

'We've got two shooters, formerly three, up at the house.

One's been taken out, if you can believe that. Mary Lou's boss is a gun collector, and his teenage daughter's up there with Mary Lou and Rahman. They're all hunkered down over here—' He tapped on the right side of the drawing. '—in the garage right now. Rahman went to open the window because the smoke's thick, and he got shot for his trouble. Whitney – the daughter – actually returned fire. She's some kind of marksman, and Mary Lou thinks that shooter is dead. And they did manage to get a little air. But just a little.

'Rahman's alive,' Sam told her, 'but he's bleeding and immobile. Whitney's daughter, Amanda, is also with them, and she and Haley are having trouble breathing. The heat's getting intense.

'Mary Lou says the two other shooters faded back into the trees. She doesn't know where they are, but they're definitely still there because she stuck a rake up in front of the window and it was shot at.'

'Good thinking,' Alyssa said, looking up at him.

'Yeah,' Sam said.

'So what's the plan?'

'We go up there,' he said, 'and we do the same thing. Only this time we make them shoot at the rake in the window with you in position on the second floor, ready to snipe the snipers.'

'Okay,' she said. 'And there's a rifle and ammunition up there? Because the weapons we have here won't get that job done.'

'As far as I can tell,' Sam said. 'Yeah. We just have to get there. I'm thinking we'll just drive like hell, right through the front door.'

Alyssa nodded again. 'I'll get the car. You call Mary Lou back and make sure Annie Oakley is told to hold her fire.'

'Lys.'

She turned back, her concern for him in her eyes.

'There's a variable here that you need to know about. Mary Lou spoke to someone she called Bob, on this very telephone.

He's the man from the photo – Donny's light-haired alien. She says he's definitely here, but she hasn't seen him.'

She started to look, maybe for the first time, into the faces of the men she'd killed just moments earlier, while she was saving Noah's and Claire's and his lives. Knowing Alyssa, that had to be hard. Sam knew she didn't want to think of them as people with faces and names, so he stopped her.

'I already checked,' he told her. 'No one here is even remotely blond.'

'So he's out there, too, somewhere,' she said.

'Yeah,' he said. It made her own risk in this so much greater.

Alyssa didn't even blink. 'I'll get the car.' She handed him one of the room brooms. 'Keep your eyes open.'

'Yes, ma'am.'

'Ready for this, bossman?' Jules sounded really excited about whatever he was going to report over the radio, and Max had a moment of deep regret.

As good as Peggy Ryan was – and she was a solid choice for his replacement – she didn't have any kind of a relationship with Jules Cassidy. His sexual orientation was a problem for a lot of people, though – not just Peggy. And it wasn't that she disliked him. He just made her uncomfortable. Because of that, she tried not to notice him, which meant he wouldn't go far on her team.

And that was a real shame, because Jules had genuine talent.

Of course, if the frustration got too intense for him, he could always resign and join that civilian team of Tom Paoletti's that everyone in the Spec Op dungeons was speculating wildly about.

Max had to laugh. He wondered if Paoletti even knew about it yet. Damn, the man was still facing treason charges.

'We've identified the man in the picture from the San Diego library – the one with Mary Lou Starrett – as Warren Canton,' Jules said. 'He was born in Kansas, moved to Saudi Arabia when he was two years old. His father worked for an oil company, had a heart attack and died, and his mother remarried a Saudi national when he was five. He came back to America about once a year to visit grandparents, then came to attend college at Harvard but left after three semesters. In 1990, he completely dropped off the map.

'Except we have some really good people in intel who dug harder and found out that after Harvard, the golden boy took a Grand Tour with a lot of very interesting destinations. Afghanistan, Algeria, Libya, Azerbaijan, Iraq. It's possible Warren forsook his Ivy League education in favor of Terrorist School.

'Then, hey ho. Meet Husaam Abdul-Fataah, who's been on our most wanted list since he sprang to life full-grown in 1995. We have no photos and no real information on this guy, just a couple of stray fingerprints and this whispered name – oh, and his nickname, too: the Ghost. Everyone's afraid of him – we are, they are. He's got connections with most of the brand-name terrorist organizations, although his interest appears to be purely monetary. But he's got a devoted following and an almost mystical reputation for being able to access targets on American soil and at military installations around the world. We thought it might be a supernatural thing – you know, the Ghost – but intel just tossed out a groovy new theory for us to chew on.

'They think that Husaam Abdul-Fataah is an aka for Warren Canton. Blond hair, blue eyes, boy-next-door smile, he can travel in the West and not get looked at twice.

'He's believed to be behind a number of attacks in addition to Coronado. If we could get Canton to hold still long enough for us to take his fingerprints and prove he *is* Abdul-Fataah, we would gain huge strides in this war on terrorism. But dude's pretty slippery. If he is Abdul-Fataah, this is the first photo anyone anywhere has of him – I'm telling you, this is major.

'We've got some analysts who are speculating that his MO is to walk away from an attack, in full view of anyone who might be looking for someone named Abdul-Fataah. Which really pisses me off, by the way. This is the flip side of racial profiling. This bastard is taking advantage of our fine, Western propensity for assumption. We hear a name like Abdul-Fataah, and we automatically think terrorist, we think Arab, we think Muslim extremist – forget about the fact that there are only a handful of extremists, as opposed to the millions and millions of law-abiding Muslims who would never harm another human being. And when we hear Abdul-Fataah, we *certainly* don't think white American using an alias.' Jules stopped. Cleared his throat. 'Forgive me, sir, I, um, just wanted to add a heads-up in case you get there before the rest of us, over.'

'Good work,' Max said. 'Over.'

'I'm just relaying information, sir,' Jules said. 'But I'll definitely pass your praise along to both intel and analysis. Over.'

'Any word on those sat tower trucks?' Max asked. 'I'm getting tired of saying over. Over.'

'I'll work on it a little harder, sir. Out.'

Mary Lou couldn't breathe.

Ihbraham was sitting inside the Explorer with Haley and Amanda. He'd gotten a bullet in his leg while opening one of the garage windows, but the air outside the house was almost as smoky as that inside.

When she saw him fall, pushed back by the force of the bullet, her heart had nearly stopped. But he was alive, thank God, although his leg was broken and bleeding badly.

It was driving him crazy to be packed off to the relative safety of the car, but someone had to stay with the children, and not being able to walk put him at a serious disadvantage.

Lord, this was all her fault. She should have called Alyssa Locke months ago. She should have turned herself in right from the start.

Her fears of being wrongfully convicted were nothing

compared to her fears of Haley and Ihbraham and Amanda and even Whitney dying.

Save them, Lord. Mary Lou closed her eyes and prayed. She would give up anything. Her life. Her freedom. She would willingly spend the rest of her days in jail if that would insure their safety.

'Here comes the cavalry!' Whitney shouted. The bloodthirsty girl was lurking near the windows, hoping to get another shot at the men who wanted to kill them.

Lord, it was getting hard to hear over the sound of the fire. Who knew fires could be this loud?

She *could* hear the ripping sound of gunfire, though, and then an enormous crash as a car came right through the locked front door.

It was like something out of a movie. The car's engine was smoking and the front end was crumpled, but there it was. In the Italian marble tiled foyer. Mrs Downs would've shit pumpkins.

There was more of that automatic gunfire, and then Alyssa Locke came scrambling out of the driver's seat.

Sam followed, looking like a savage, with something that looked like war paint streaking his naked torso and face.

And wearing a blood-soaked bandage held in place by a necktie just above the waistband of his pants?

Obviously, since she'd left, no one had been doing his laundry.

They were both carrying big, deadly-looking guns that looked like the one Mary Lou had found in the trunk of her car, all those fateful months ago.

They also both started to cough from the inescapable, throat-burning smoke.

Sam – some things never changed – started to curse.

'Are you all right?' Alyssa asked him.

He was bleeding from more than his side, Mary Lou realized. His forearm had what looked like a deep four-inch scrape, and blood was dripping down his hand.

He barely glanced at it. 'I'm fine. Jesus, it's hot as hell in here.' He spotted Mary Lou. 'Hey! Are you okay? Is Haley safe?'

'Yes,' she said, bringing them both towels to drape over their heads. 'It's a little less smoky in the garage. She's there. Down this way. She's—'

'I don't want to see her,' Sam said. 'Not looking like this. I don't want to scare her. Just keep your head down and make sure she's safe and she's got enough air, okay, Mary Lou?'

'Where's this Whitney?' Alyssa asked. She had dirt on her face, too, but she still managed to look beautiful.

'Here.' Whitney stepped forward, completely unable to keep her eyes off Sam. Mary Lou knew what that was like.

Alyssa's attention, however, was on that rifle. 'I'm going to need that,' she said.

Whitney stopped staring at Sam's abs and went into selfish mode. 'It's mine. I've got another upstairs you can use.'

'Okay,' Alyssa said. 'Show me.' She looked at Sam. 'Give me ninety seconds to get into place.'

'Be careful.' He touched her arm.

'You, too.' She glanced at Mary Lou.

Six months ago, seeing that exchange would have made Mary Lou crazy with jealousy. Now it just made her wistful. There was more love in that one little touch than there had been in her entire farce of a marriage to Sam Starrett.

She knew that for a fact, because that was the very same way Ihbraham touched her. She didn't just know what it looked like -- she knew what it felt like.

'I need that rake, fast,' Sam said, still watching Alyssa as Whitney led her up the stairs. It was even smokier up there. 'And maybe an extra shirt to hang from it, if you've got one.'

He was practically choking, and it was clear that each cough jarred his injury and hurt him badly.

Mary Lou led him down the hall to the garage, where she grabbed the rake and her sweatshirt from the pile.

'Stay here,' Sam ordered her.

'Are we going to die?' she asked him. 'Because if we're going to die . . . oh, Sam, I owe you such an apology.'

'Only if we die?' he asked as he walked away.

Mary Lou followed him. 'I got pregnant on purpose,' she said. 'I thought I could make you love me. I didn't understand that love's not something you can force someone to feel.'

'I owe you an apology, too,' Sam told her. 'But I'm going to do it later. After this is over. Now go take care of Haley.'

'If we don't die, I'm getting remarried,' she told him. 'His name's Ihbraham Rahman.'

Sam actually stopped walking. 'No shit?'

She shook her head. 'He's a gardener.'

'I know.' He was moving again.

'He's a good man. He loves me and I love him.'

'I'm happy for you. I really am.' Sam looked at his watch. 'But you need to go now and let me do this.'

Mary Lou went.

It was all too likely that they were going to die.

Alyssa hadn't quite considered that possibility as she drove her rental car into a burning building.

But this fire was spreading fast, and the smoke made her lungs feel sunburned.

The shades up here hadn't been pulled down, and she had to position herself far enough back from the windows so as not to become a potential target herself, which meant she could see only a portion of the yard and the brush. But she knew where she'd place herself if she were a shooter looking to pick off the people hiding inside of this inferno.

And sure enough, she saw the movement of the shot and aimed and squeezed and then dropped to the floor.

Because if someone else was watching the house, knowing the people inside were armed and prepared to fire back, he'd be looking to take her out, too.

'You got him,' Whitney reported from another room down the hall. 'Shit, you're good!'

But Alyssa was already running down the hall to the other side of the house, crouching low to try to escape the smoke. 'Go tell Sam to give me another minute to get into place. We're going to do this again.'

Max keyed his radio microphone. 'Where the hell is this place? Over.'

Laronda answered. 'Noah and Claire Gaines were just there, sir, and they said it was farther than they thought, from looking at the map. They said to watch for the smoke. Come back.'

'Whoa.' Max caught sight of it, way in the distance. 'Tell the choppers they've got one hell of a signal flare. Over.'

'They've spotted it, sir. Over.'

'What's their ETA? Over.'

'They're still a good five minutes north. Over.'

No one was shooting.

Sam even threw down the rake and put his body in front of the window, but no one took the bait.

It was possible that whoever had been out there was now gone.

But it was probable that the bad guys had realized that within the next five minutes, the smoke was going to push everyone inside the house out and onto the driveway, where there was absolutely no cover.

They could run for it, sure, but a shooter of even moderate skill could easily pick them off without any fear of being a target himself.

Unless, of course, Alyssa stayed up on that second floor.

Then only one of the good guys would get shot.

Of course only one of the good guys would get shot if only one of them went out there.

Alyssa was coming down the stairs, coughing and choking.

'Do you have it in you to give it one more try?' Sam asked.

'Absolutely,' she said. But what was she going to say, no?

'Change of plans, though. I'm going to take one of the cars in the garage,' he told her, 'and I'm going to make it look like we're all inside. We'll pile blankets on the seats, and it'll seem like everyone's keeping their heads down. That'll get this guy to start shooting – and maybe it'll even bring the blond alien out of hiding, too.'

Alyssa didn't look happy. 'They'll be shooting at you.'

'Yeah,' he said. 'That's the tricky part.'

Alyssa couldn't believe it. 'You're using yourself as bait?'

'Someone's got to.'

Sam was in serious pain, but he was pretending he wasn't. She could practically feel it radiating from him.

'No,' she said. 'Let's just do it. Let's actually get everyone in the car and—'

'And they'll cut loose with whatever they've got,' Sam told her. 'For all we know, they've got a grenade launcher out there.'

'If they did, wouldn't they be taking shots at the house with it right now?'

'Yeah, unless they've got a limited supply of ammunition.'

He had an answer for everything.

'Just get into place,' Sam said again.

'You're asking me to do the impossible,' she argued. 'There are two shooters out there. I'll get one. The other will get you.'

'We don't know there're two,' he countered.

She couldn't believe this. 'Yes, Sam, we do.'

'Okay,' he said. 'So it's going to be a little harder for you to do this, to shoot them both. Get Whitney to help. I'll make myself a difficult target. Get into place.' He started for the garage, as if it were decided.

Alyssa followed him. 'You're willing to trust a sixteen-year-old girl with your life?'

'No, I'm trusting *you* with my life.'

'I don't want you to die!'

'Good,' he said. 'You've got motivation to succeed.'

She caught his arm. 'Sam, I'm serious.'

He turned and kissed her, hard. 'I am, too. Now go upstairs and save my ass.'

'What if I can't do it?' she asked.

He kissed her again, sweetly this time. 'What if you can?'

She looked at him, and even though his smile was laced with pain, it was still such a typical Sam Starrett smile. 'You don't ever give up hope, do you?'

He shook his head. 'Not anymore. You know, I gave up too early on you and me, after that first night we spent together. I should have chased you back to Washington. I should have kept knocking on your door. I should've let myself hold on to that hope that you would change your mind. It's the biggest regret of my entire life, because I *did* love you, even back then.' He kissed her again. 'I love you twice as much now, and I need you to get into place. You got ninety seconds. Make it count.'

'No,' Alyssa said. 'Wait. Listen. Here's what I need *you* to do. When you pull out of the garage, head first for the row of hedges, and then the line of trees directly behind that. That's where I think they're hiding. If you can make them scramble, I can plug these motherfuckers.'

Sam smiled and kissed her again. 'I can make them scramble.'

She nodded. 'I'll get into place. Give me an extra fifteen seconds. I want to go up to the third floor.'

She ran for the stairs. God, it was smoky up there, but maybe that was good. It would conceal her as she moved into position. 'Whitney, where are you? I want you downstairs in the garage with Mary Lou. Be ready to get the hell out of here!'

Mary Lou gave Sam the keys to the Town Car. 'Are you sure you don't want to see Haley? She's right in the Explorer—'

'Yes,' he said. 'God damn it. I do want to see her. But I don't want to scare her.'

His ex-wife used the towel she had draped over her head to wipe off his face. 'Just cover your arm so she can't see the blood.'

'I'm not going to open that car door,' Sam said. 'If the air in there is cleaner than it is out here . . .'

But Mary Lou was already tapping on the glass, pulling him closer.

The light was on inside the car, and . . . Oh, Jesus. There she was.

Haley's eyes looked back at him from a face that was half baby, half little girl. 'My God,' Sam breathed. 'She's so big.' He glanced at Mary Lou. 'Is she talking more now?'

'Not a whole lot, but some. She's a thinker, not a talker.'

Ihbraham was in there, too, sitting in the backseat with Haley and another little girl, reading to them. Sam met his eyes, and the man nodded.

But Haley, she was down on the floor, looking for something. Sam laughed as she pushed her Pooh Bear up against the window for him to see. 'Oh, man,' he said. 'I gave that to her. Do you think she remembers that?'

'Yeah. I'm sure she does.' Mary Lou had always been a lousy liar.

Inside the car, Haley was now starting to cry. Ihbraham tried to comfort her, but it was clear she wanted Mary Lou. Sam wasn't foolish or stupid enough to try to convince himself he was the one she was crying over.

'Get in there with her,' Sam ordered his ex-wife. 'Tell her everything's going to be okay.' He headed for the Town Car. 'And if . . .' He couldn't say it.

'If this doesn't work,' Mary Lou started.

'Oh, it's going to work,' Sam said. Alyssa was going to make those shots. That he knew for a fact. But while hope was good to have, it was also important to keep a firm grip on reality. And the truth was . . . 'I just might not walk away from it.' He was feeling the loss of blood, and that, combined with the smoke . . . 'If

I don't,' he told Mary Lou, 'make sure Haley grows up knowing that I loved her.'

Max heard them before he saw them.

Three Seahawk helicopters racing overhead and past him, toward that pillar of smoke.

He keyed his radio. 'I have visual contact with the Seahawks. I want those fire trucks and ambulances ready to move in on my command!'

Alyssa lay on her stomach in the attic, practically melting from the heat, eyes watering from the smoke.

The window up here was an improvement over the second floor. She could see the entire yard, and it was possible, too, that she'd IDed the location of one of the shooters. She kept that dark lump in her sites, waiting . . .

Waiting . . .

Come on, Sam.

Stay alive.

She needed him to stay alive.

She was good enough to make these shots, and he was good enough to stay alive.

The hope he'd kissed into her filled her throat, her chest, her lungs, her heart, and she wanted – more than she'd ever wanted anything – for this to be over. For Sam to get out of that car, for her to run down the stairs and out of the house and . . .

Don't let him die. Don't let them get off a lucky shot that crashes through his skull and shuts off his incredible light and life. Don't let him slump over that steering wheel and have her run down those stairs to find that her life was cold and colorless without his spark.

Don't make her have to learn how to live without him all over again.

Stop that. Don't think about that. Think about the way he was going to smile and high-five her as Mary Lou and Haley and the

501

others were taken to a hospital, to safety. Think about sitting with him in the emergency room, too. About the doctor smiling as he came out of surgery, to tell her that the bullet that went into Sam didn't do very much damage at all. Think about him telling her that Sam could go home in just a few days. Think about her taking him home.

Yeah.

Alyssa Locke lay on the attic floor of a burning house and, with the part of her brain that wasn't watching the yard, she thought about what she was going to wear to her wedding.

Sam got into the car. Checked his watch.

He started the engine, gesturing for Mary Lou to move back.

He put the car into reverse, taking another glance back at the construction of that garage door he was about to blast through, and then . . .

Show time.

Mary Lou held tightly to Amanda and Haley as Sam plowed Frank Turlington's favorite Town Car through the garage door.

She could feel Ihbraham's hand on her head. Steady. Comforting.

One way or another, this was all going to be over soon.

Sam kept his head down as the windshield shattered, as he threw the car into drive and stomped on the gas.

He spun the wheel hard and headed straight toward the shrubs.

He saw the shooter diving out of the way, heard the shot, saw him fall, boneless.

Way to go, Alyssa!

He saw the second man, too, standing up and taking aim, right before he hit the tree, right before his world went black.

* * *

Sam wasn't moving.

The car was stopped, its entire right front mangled.

Come on, Sam. Get out of the car. Make sure those shooters are down.

Alyssa couldn't see the second man she'd hit – the one who'd been farther back in the woods. She aimed and put another bullet into the first one, just for safety's sake.

But still Sam didn't move.

Please don't let him be dead. Please God, please *God* . . .

And then – as if in answer to her prayers – God appeared.

In the form of three Seahawks, coming from up above. One of them landed directly in the center of the circular driveway.

It was deus ex machina.

Two minutes too late.

Alyssa started toward the attic stairs, and the entire back roof of the house caved in.

As Mary Lou watched, the helicopters landed, and what looked like FBI agents as well as soldiers swarmed out and toward the house.

Whitney was out of the car. 'Hey, over here!'

And then a man in a windbreaker with 'FBI' in big white letters on the back was getting into the car. He drove them out of the garage, out through the hole Sam had made in the doors, and right over to the nearest helicopter.

They were in time. They were *just* in time, because as soon as they pulled outside, the house groaned and shook, and sparks and flames flew way up into the sky.

About seven men and women, all wearing those FBI jackets or T-shirts, helped them out of the car and up into the helicopter.

Other people were there, giving oxygen to the babies first, then to the rest of them, gently lowering Ihbraham to the floor and giving him first aid.

Someone closed the doors.

They were up. In the air. Flying faster than Mary Lou had dreamed it was possible for a helicopter to fly.

They were safe. They were *safe*.

But . . . 'Sam's still down there,' she shouted over the noise of the blades to the nearest FBI jacket. 'And Alyssa Locke is still inside that house!'

Sam used Alyssa's Swiss Army knife to deflate the airbag that had punched him directly in his bullet wound.

Holy Jesus God. That had hurt so much he'd actually passed out.

And now look. He'd opened his eyes to a pair of Seahawks on the lawn and a third one heading back to wherever they'd come from.

It was, no doubt, an early birthday present from Max Bhagat.

Sam pulled himself out of the car.

The yard was filled with agents and – hoo-yah! – what looked like special forces soldiers. Way to go, Max.

Several cars and vans had pulled up, too, and it was only Jules Cassidy's timely arrival that kept Sam from being tackled or, shit, even shot, since he was dressed more like a tango than one of the good guys.

'Where's Alyssa?' Sam shouted to Jules.

'We took everyone out of the house on that chopper that just left – express for a safe hospital,' he shouted back.

'No,' Sam said. 'There's no way she would have gotten on that thing without me.'

Jules looked at the burning house, no doubt thinking the same thing Sam was thinking.

Alyssa was still inside.

Sam ran for the house with Jules on his heels.

Max pulled over to the side of the driveway so that the emergency vehicles and fire trucks would be able to get through.

'I want a body count,' he shouted as he got out of his car. 'Are all the shooters accounted for? Let's find 'em and bag 'em and get IDs started. I want to know who these bastards were yesterday! And someone get me Alyssa Locke!'

Okay, so the stairs were gone.

She was going to have to jump down from the third to the second floor, which was kind of scary since she didn't know whether or not she would go right through those floorboards when she landed.

The heat and smoke were so intense, Alyssa's lungs felt as if they were going to burst.

Okay, God. Favor time. Keep Sam alive and keep those floorboards intact. Oh, and it would be nice to have the stairs from the second to the ground floor still intact too.

And a cool glass of lemonade waiting for her outside this hellmouth.

A lottery win for her sister's family.

Peace on earth, goodwill toward men.

A sunny day for her wedding . . .

Nah. That was not at all necessary. It didn't matter if it rained or shined as long as Sam was smiling at her.

Alyssa jumped.

'Jesus,' Jules shouted, coughing up what sounded like an entire lung. 'Stay low.'

'She was upstairs,' Sam shouted back. 'Third floor.'

A beam fell, showering them with embers.

'We're not going to make it without masks and oxygen!'

No kidding. There was no point in both of them dying. 'Go get some,' Sam yelled, grabbing the little bastard and throwing him back out of the house.

He ran for the stairs – if you could really call the half-assed staggering he was barely capable of doing *running* – but then fell on his face as a piece of falling ceiling hit him hard on the back of his head.

SUZANNE BROCKMANN

* * *

Alyssa found him on the stairs.

Sam.

Rushing to rescue her.

The blood from his bullet wound had completely soaked through Noah's T-shirt. He had plaster in his hair and on his back, and as she rushed toward him, he was already pushing himself up onto his hands and knees, ready to keep climbing, ready to walk into hell, if need be, to find her.

She helped him up, slipping his arm around her shoulders, pulling him down the stairs, no longer trying to stay low to avoid the smoke, trying instead for speed. But, God, there was so much of him. She was lucky he was helping. Carrying him on her own would have been a real challenge. 'You are *such* a jerk. Running into a burning building with a gunshot wound?'

'Are you all right?' he gasped.

And then, alleluia! They were out in the air.

Twenty-seven

Twelve different people rushed to help them move farther from the house, but Sam wouldn't let go of her. Jules was there, too, with oxygen.

Alyssa put her mask over Sam's mouth and nose, and realized he was doing the same for her.

She pushed it away. 'I need a medic!' she shouted in a voice that was harsh from the smoke. 'Right now! *Right* now!' She looked at Sam. 'I can't believe you came in there after me!'

'I think you taste perfect just the way you are,' he told her, his voice raspy. 'I didn't want you to get overcooked.'

He was grinning at her – *grinning* – as a team of paramedics swarmed around them, tending to his injuries, pushing her back.

Jules was there, next to her. He gently placed the oxygen mask back onto her face. 'He's going to be okay.'

She took a couple of deep breaths before she took it off. 'Did I get that last shooter? Is the area secure?'

'We have seven dead,' a familiar voice said from behind her. She turned around to see Max. 'Four at the gate,' he told her, 'two are the guards who were on duty – and three up here by the house.' He looked at Jules. 'None are Warren Canton.'

'Yeah, I noticed that,' Jules said.

'Warren *who*?' Alyssa asked.

Sam floated.

The really nice guy in the EMT uniform had started an IV and added something special to the saline drip.

507

'I'm okay,' Sam told them as he and another guy took Noah's necktie off his waist.

'You're not quite,' the first guy said. 'But you definitely will be.'

He could see Alyssa. She was listening intently to something Max was telling her.

Jesus, they looked good together.

Something Max said made Alyssa smile up into his eyes, and Sam knew with a sickening certainty that Max Bhagat was the better man for her. He was a good man, a principled man, a man who was able to keep sex out of a relationship until the time was good and right. Max wouldn't drive her crazy and piss her off all the time. Max was the kind of guy Alyssa could be seen with, feel proud of, rise alongside of in the political arena of Washington, DC.

If that was really the life she wanted, then Sam should close his eyes and just quietly float away. He should do the right thing and fade back, let her have a chance at happiness.

As Sam watched, they embraced.

Fuck!

Fuck doing the right thing. And whose right thing was it, anyway? Max's? Fuck that. Letting Max waltz away with Alyssa wasn't the right thing for Sam, and it *sure* as hell wasn't the right thing for Alyssa, whether she knew it or not.

He sat up. 'Hey! Tell him you can't marry him because you're marrying me!'

The EMT guys were not happy about this, but Sam pushed them away. He would've stood up, if Alyssa hadn't come running over to him.

'Lie down,' she said. 'And behave.'

'I love you,' he said. 'You have to marry me. Tell that fucker to keep his hands off of you. You're mine.'

The look she gave him probably would have terrified him without the medication flowing into his veins. 'I'm *yours*?'

'Yes. Fuck it if it's not politically correct,' he said, laboring to get the words out. The top of his head was floating way above his mouth. 'You are mine. You are my heart and my soul and the . . . the very breath from my lungs. And I'm yours. I'm totally yours. You own me. Tell me what you want, Lys, and I'll do it.'

She was laughing. Or maybe she was crying. He couldn't tell.

'I want you to lie down.' She looked at the EMT. 'What did you give him?'

'Max,' Sam yelled. 'You *fucker*! You—'

Alyssa kissed him, and he completely forgot whatever it was that he was going to say.

Max stepped back as the chopper carrying Sam and Alyssa to the hospital left the yard.

The fire was still burning out of control, and the place was swarming with firefighters, FBI, local police and EMTs.

'Cell tower trucks are in place,' Jules reported.

Max opened his phone. Sure enough. Just when they no longer needed them.

'Do me a favor,' Max said, 'and call Noah Gaines. Alyssa asked me to call and see if he and his wife will meet Mary Lou and Haley at the hospital. Apparently Sam's afraid we're going to drag his ex-wife by her hair into a questioning session – first ripping her terrified baby out of her arms.'

Jules was already dialing his phone. 'Oh, yeah, why would he think that?' He looked up at Max. 'Oh, because it sounds like something we might actually do. Hey, I meant to tell you, we've got roadblocks in place in this entire area. Unless Warren Canton can dematerialize, we have a good chance at picking him up.'

Max wasn't quite so optimistic, but there was no point bursting Jules's bubble. The younger man was unbelievably happy at the outcome of this. And why shouldn't he be? Sam and Alyssa were his friends. Sam's ex-wife and daughter were safe. Jules had no doubt been extremely worried about them.

Max looked at his watch. Debriefings and interviews would continue on until late tonight. There was no way he was going to make it over to the airport to apologize to Gina yet one more time before her flight left for New York.

Yeah, that's why he wanted to go there and see her. To apologize again. Right.

Jules waved as he climbed into his car, parked at the side of the driveway. 'See you back there.'

Max's car had been moved out onto the street. As he rounded the corner to the guardhouse, he could see a team of people hard at work on the crime scene.

As he watched, one of the men approached a sawhorse that had been set up and deftly removed an FBI windbreaker that someone had tossed there.

There was something about his movement that struck Max as off. As he watched, the man slipped on the jacket – despite the fact that it was a billion degrees in the shade.

He was wearing a baseball cap and jeans and sneakers – not so different from every one else, but . . .

His left sneaker was stained with blood. It was harder to see it on his jeans. Yeah, he was definitely walking as if he were injured and trying to hide it.

'Hey!' Max shouted as he reached for his side arm. He knew as soon as he opened his mouth that he'd made a mistake.

His cell phone was working. He was surrounded by agents. It would have taken very little effort to set up a dragnet around this son of a bitch.

Instead, he gave away the upper hand by shouting 'Hey.'

It was possible that he deserved to die.

The man turned around, weapon firing. Max moved and would've dodged it, but somehow this guy knew where he was going to go, and instead he moved right into the bullet. It smashed into Max's chest and it threw him back, but he rolled with it and aimed and plugged the son of a bitch, not once but twice and then three times, because he didn't just want him dead, he wanted him fucking dead.

'Man down!' He could hear Jules, shouting, running. 'Max!'

And there Jules was, kneeling over him, tearing at his shirt, looking at the damage.

Max didn't need to look. He knew it was bad.

'One step behind,' he said to Jules in a voice that didn't even qualify as a whisper. This entire op, he'd been one lousy step behind.

Chaos was around him now. EMTs shouting, moving him, pain.

'Gina . . .' Max let himself slide away from the noise into blackness, remembering Gina's smile as she leaned forward to kiss him. Remembering Gina's eyes.

Remembering . . .

Still one step behind.

September 8, 1945
From the journal of Dorothy S. Smith

I really didn't have a choice in the matter. I brought Jolee with me to meet Walter's ship in New York City. How could I leave her home?

I knew there was no one he'd rather see than that little girl. And as much as I would have liked to be the first one to fall into his arms, I knew this entire homecoming would be strange for him.

And there was the not inconsequential fact that he was determined to ignore the romantic love that had bloomed between us after Mae's untimely death.

So our first embrace was one with Jolee between us, which was better than fine with me, since I loved them both so much.

We went to dinner, and it was Jolee, chattering on and on to this tall, quiet stranger – whom she'd recognized the moment he stepped onto the pier, because we kept photos of him everywhere in the house – who said it first.

'—when you and Mama Dot get married.'

Walt looked at me. I just smiled at him as I ate my pie.

I'd gotten us a suite in a hotel in a colored neighborhood. It wasn't quite the Ritz, but it was nice and clean and the people were friendly. Jolee and I had stayed there the night before and were made to feel nothing but welcome.

'Jolee and I will share the bedroom,' I told Walt as I unlocked the door. 'The couch opens out. That's yours.'

He looked at the supplies, the tents and such, that I'd brought inside – not feeling it was safe to leave them in the back of the pickup truck while we were in the big, bad city.

'We're going to camp on our way back to Texas,' I informed him. 'I know you've probably had enough of camping for a lifetime and a half, but Jolee and I, we don't get a chance too often.'

It would remove the discomfort of attempting to stay in motels in which Walter and Jolee would not be welcome. As far as I was concerned, I had no desire to give the people who owned those places *my* hard-earned dollars, anyway.

Jolee got ready for bed, and Walter pretended not to cry as he read her a story. I sat by the window and also pretended not to cry. Jolee must've thought we were nuts. She was just so happy her daddy was home – what were the tears for?

Five-year-olds rarely cry from happiness.

Walter put his daughter into bed, while I went into the bathroom and changed into my nightgown and robe. I knew Jolee well – so I knew she'd be asleep almost immediately upon hitting that pillow.

Walt was standing at the window as I came out.

'Bathroom's yours,' I told him.

He turned to look at me.

'This isn't that bad, is it?' I asked.

He knew what I was talking about. However, my gown and robe were designed to confuse and they were indeed doing the trick. It took him a moment or two to answer. 'It'll be different in Texas.'

'I hope so,' I said. 'In Texas I'll be sharing a bed with you instead of Jolee.'

He shook his head. 'Dot . . .'

'I know how strange this must seem to you, to be back in the States. Your daughter's so big – and I know you must still miss Mae. I will not rush you into anything, Walter, but you do need to know that I will not take no. You said that this – that we – cannot be? Well, I am responding by telling you that there are no acceptable alternatives. I love you, and I do believe you love me. Take all the time you need to get used to the fact that you, Jolee, and I already are a family. I'll be here when you're ready. Good night.'

And then I went into the bedroom where Jolee was sleeping, and I closed the door.

I'm not sure who was more surprised, him or me. I'm pretty sure we both expected me to jump him the moment Jolee was asleep!

September 18, 1945
From the journal of Dorothy S. Smith

We are back in Texas.

Our camping trip was a huge success.

We came home via Alabama, where Walter and Jolee spent some time at Mae's grave. It was good for Walt to see it, even though that day and the next were quiet ones, with little conversation between any of us.

But we took our time, spending two days along a river in Mississippi, where the sky was so blue you'd swear you were in heaven.

It was there that we let ourselves laugh again.

Yes, it was a most successful trip.

As was my campaign. As we brought our luggage in from the truck, Walter didn't say a word as I carried his bag into my bedroom. He just stood there, giving me that look.

'Yes? No?' I asked.

And he nodded. 'Yes.'

And, oh, *that's* when I jumped him. Such willpower I'd had up to that very moment and it all crumbled. I kissed him, and Lord Almighty, he kissed me and we were both crying.

'This is going to be hard,' he said. 'This life we're choosing.'

'Maybe so,' I said, kissing him again, 'but I'd prefer hard and wonderful any day over easy and run of the mill.'

And then, of course, Jolee came running in. Walt told her we were getting married and she just looked at him. This was not news to her. Of course we were.

This afternoon and evening has seemed to last forever.

Walter's in with Jolee right now, reading her a story. It's become his tradition – that bedtime story. I love that it's been only ten days and we already have traditions.

We truly are a family now.

I'm writing this while I wait for him to join me here. I'm nervous and excited and, oh dear Lord—

He's here.

September 19, 1945
From the journal of Dorothy S. Smith

I've written in this journal almost every night for the past five years.

I may never find the time or inclination to write in here ag—

* * *

Gina was at the airport five hours early.

That was the trouble with traveling by public transportation. The one time she didn't allow an extra five hours to get somewhere would be the one time the bus would be five hours late.

She wandered through the bookstores and strolled through the terminal, checking out the restaurants, trying to guess from the way the food smelled if it would give her indigestion.

Although it was probably getting on an airplane that gave her indigestion, regardless of what she ate.

For a while after the hijacking, she'd traveled only by train or car. But that became inconvenient – especially when she decided to take that trip to Hawaii.

So she flew.

And got indigestion.

Gina settled into a seat near the terminal windows and tried to look forward to getting home, to seeing her parents and her brothers.

She had to smile at the idea of setting up one of her brothers with Jules Cassidy. Leo and Rob were married, so count them out. Victor dated ferociously – a new woman every other week. It was almost as if he were trying to prove something.

Hmmm.

She settled back and opened her book and tried not to think about Max.

This was where he'd show up. If her life were a movie, this was the scene where he'd come looking for her, running through the airport, after having searched his soul and realizing that he didn't really love Alyssa, that it was Gina who'd owned his heart all along.

'Gina!'

She didn't look up. That was just a coincidence. Had to be. She was completely losing her mind if she actually thought –

'*Gina!*'

That definitely wasn't Max's voice. Was it?

She stood up.

And there he was. Pushing his way through the crowd. Shouting her name. *'Gina!'*

Only it wasn't Max, it was Jules Cassidy.

He spotted her, ran toward her. 'You gotta come with me,' he said. 'It's Max. He's been shot.'

'What? Where? Oh, my *God* . . .' Gina dropped her book as she grabbed her bag, her purse. The book went skittering under the row of seats and she left it there.

'He took a bullet to the chest,' Jules said as she ran with him, back to the terminal entrance. He had blood on his shirt. 'He's in the OR right now. He was asking for you.'

Oh, my *God*.

'Well, no,' Jules corrected himself as he took her bag for her. 'He didn't actually ask for you, but it wasn't like he was able to talk much with a hole in his . . . He *did* say your name, though.'

Oh, God. Oh, *Max* . . . 'That's close enough for me,' Gina said.

Sam was out of the operating room but still under from the anesthesia when Mary Lou came into the room.

'Is he going to be okay?' she asked.

Alyssa didn't let go of his hand. 'Yes. He's doing really well. The doctors were optimistic. They thought that I'll be able to take him home in just a few days. He's very healthy to start with, so . . .'

Mary Lou nodded. 'Ihbraham's okay, too. His leg's broken, but he's okay.'

'I'm glad he's all right,' Alyssa said.

'I can't stay,' Mary Lou said. 'Haley's with Noah and Claire. Did you know Sam's cousin is . . .'

'Black?' Alyssa supplied. 'Yeah. He kind of looks like Sam, doesn't he?'

Mary Lou stared at her.

'You don't see it, huh?' Alyssa said.

'Haley likes them,' Mary Lou said. 'That's good. Because I

don't know how long the questioning is going to last, or even if I'm going to have charges against me. My prints were on that gun, but it was only because I found it in the trunk of my car. I thought it was Sam's and I went to tell him about it and make him take it out, but then it was gone and—'

'You'll get a chance to explain all that,' Alyssa told her. 'Don't be afraid to get advice from a lawyer, though.'

'I know. I am.' She glanced back toward the door. 'I have to go. I just wanted to thank you again.'

'You'll be seeing me around,' Alyssa said.

'Are you going to marry him?' Mary Lou asked. 'Sam?'

'Yeah,' Alyssa said. 'I am.'

'He's loved you for forever.'

That couldn't have been easy for her to admit.

'Those papers were filed,' Mary Lou added. 'My lawyer let me know that the divorce is final. Will you tell Sam?'

'Yeah,' Alyssa said.

'I'm getting remarried, too,' Mary Lou told her with a smile that could only be described as genuinely delighted. 'To Ihbraham.'

Ihbraham Rahman? *'Really?'*

Mary Lou looked at her. 'That's pretty much what Sam said, too. I guess that's kind of hard to believe, huh?'

'No,' Alyssa lied. 'It's not. It's . . . I think it's wonderful.' And *that* was no lie.

'I know it's going to be hard,' Mary Lou said, 'but I really love him.'

'Then it won't be harder than being without him, will it?' Alyssa told her.

Mary Lou smiled. 'No.'

'I hope you'll live somewhere near San Diego,' Alyssa said. 'Sam really wants Haley in his life.'

'I'm not sure what we're going to do,' Mary Lou admitted. 'I seem to have just burned down my employer's house.' She started to laugh. 'That's not funny.' She covered her mouth, unable to stop her laughter. 'Can you imagine him coming home . . .?'

Alyssa grinned, too. 'Way to get that promotion.'

Mary Lou giggled. 'Yeah. It's really not funny, though. Those two security guards were killed.' She sobered up fast. 'I thank the Lord we're all still here. And I thank *you* for all you did. We're alive today because of you and Sam. I'll never be able to thank you enough.'

'Just let Sam be a part of Haley's life,' Alyssa said, but then Sam stirred and she turned to give him her full attention.

She didn't notice when Mary Lou slipped out of the room.

Max was out of surgery by the time they reached the hospital, and his prognosis was good.

Gina didn't know what Jules did or said to get her into the ICU. She didn't care. Just as long as she was there.

He looked so pale in that bed. So fragile . . .

She wanted to touch him, but she didn't dare.

'Where's Alyssa?' she asked Jules. 'Does she know? You should tell her.'

'She's with Sam,' he told her. 'Here in this same hospital. He was shot, too.'

'Who's Sam?' Gina asked.

It was possible that Jules told her, but it didn't matter, she wasn't listening.

Twenty-eight

Friday, June 20, 2003

'I hate it here. I want to leave,' Sam said for the godzillionth
time. It was amazing that Alyssa was still there in his hospital
room, still sitting by his bed. He would have either driven his
own self crazy or bored himself to tears a long time ago.

'I know,' Alyssa said with patience that was admirable. She
took his hand, which was very nice. 'But the doctors say you've
got to wait until—'

'How do they know how I'm feeling?'

'Well, I think they know because they ask you and they take
your vital signs and—'

Something about the way she was sitting or talking or
something reminded him of . . .

'Did I dream Mary Lou coming in here and having a
conversation with you?' he interrupted her.

'No,' she said. 'She was in here. Yesterday afternoon. You
were still completely out of it.'

'Maybe not completely. Did you . . .?' Sam laughed. 'I'm sure
I dreamed this.' He looked hard at her. 'Mary Lou asked if you
were going to marry me, and you said—'

'Yes.'

She was looking back at him, a little smiling playing about
the edges of her mouth.

Holy fuck.

Sam was having trouble breathing, but it had nothing to do

with his medical condition. 'Does this mean I asked you to . . .?'

Alyssa nodded. 'Oh, yeah.' She narrowed her eyes at him. 'You don't remember?'

He laughed. 'No. Jesus.' He put his hand over his heart. It was pounding so hard, he was surprised the nurse wasn't in here, making sure he wasn't about to die. 'And you actually said . . . *yes*?'

'Well, I haven't exactly said yes directly to you, since you pretty much lost consciousness,' she told him. 'So . . . *yes*.'

Sam reached for her, and she sat on the edge of his bed so he could kiss her.

He definitely wasn't bored anymore.

She pulled back. 'Easy there. Did the doctor say you could kiss me like that?'

'What did I say?' Sam really wanted to know. 'I mean, how'd I talk you into it? I was sure I was going to have to talk for hours.'

Alyssa was trying her damnedest not to laugh. 'What do you think you said?'

Uh-oh.

'I don't know,' he confessed. 'I was planning to give you this speech about how much I love you and want you in my life, and that I was willing to wait until you were ready, that I was more than willing to do this entire relationship thing your way. Your call. Your rules. If you wanted us to date for a few years before we even thought about getting married, well, I'd do it. Gladly. And if you wanted to get married tomorrow, I'd do that, too. The only thing I wasn't going to do was take no for an answer. I didn't need a yes right away, but I would not take a no.' He looked at her hopefully. 'Is that what I said?'

Alyssa nodded, and he could've sworn she was still trying not to laugh. 'Pretty much.' She leaned forward and kissed him. 'I really love you, Sam.'

Well, that brought tears to his eyes.

He couldn't believe he'd finally managed to say the right thing.

Monday, June 23, 2003

Max woke up to find Jules Cassidy sitting by his hospital bed.

'Hey,' Jules said. 'Welcome back, nap boy.'

Nap boy? 'Are you here to break me out?' Max asked.

'No, sir, just to provide a thrilling mix of entertainment and information – to keep you updated as to what's going on in the real world. As opposed to this hideous alternate reality where they serve orange Jell-O every day with lunch.'

'Sam Starrett went home two days ago,' Max complained.

'Two *fucking* days ago,' Jules said in something that was supposed to be a Texas drawl. 'Where's Gina, boss?'

'I don't know,' Max said. 'Maybe she went back to New York.' He glared at Jules, who was responsible for bringing her here. 'Where she belongs.'

One of the nurses stepped into the room. 'Are you looking for your daughter?'

Jules laughed. 'Gina's actually *my* daughter.'

She blinked at him. 'Oh, I'm sorry, I thought . . .'

Max just shook his head and closed his eyes.

'She went downstairs to get some coffee,' the nurse said.

'Let's start with the stuff you might not want Gina to hear,' Jules said. 'Like this letter that came today from Allen Bryant?'

Max opened his eyes to look at the piece of paper Jules was holding out.

'You might recognize the seal of the United States President on his letterhead,' Jules continued. 'Apparently he has rejected your letter of *resignation*.'

Max would've sighed, but sighing hurt too much. 'That was private.'

'*Was* private,' Jules agreed. 'Not so much anymore, seeing how since you've been laid up, Laronda is opening your mail. She's madder than hell that you didn't tell her about this—'

'I was going to.'

'She's planning to shoot you again when you get out of the hospital. So you might want to take your time with the whole recovery thing. And then go into hiding.'

Max took the letter and read it. While discretion was always appreciated, there was no problem for an unmarried team leader to have a relationship with a woman – also unmarried – well over the age of consent. Yada yada yada, this woman's experiences as a hostage took place years ago, yada yada yada, no need for discipline of any kind.

In other words, Max's boss, and his boss's boss, which would be President Bryant, saw no wrongdoing in Max's actions.

Swell.

Except for the fact that Max didn't see it the same way.

But okay. 'You think I should stay on? As team leader?' he asked Jules.

'I think this letter says you don't have a choice.'

'What am I going to do about Gina?'

'Well, you could decide to forsake women altogether.' Jules was actually fluttering his eyelashes at him. But then he grinned. 'Have you been suitably entertained yet?'

'Yeah,' Max said. 'You can stop.'

'You want to hear the latest on Warren Canton, also known as Husaam Abdul-Fataah, also known as the terrorist who shot your ass?' Jules asked.

Max just waited. Jules would tell him sooner or later. And Max sure as hell wasn't going anywhere.

'Here's how all this went down, according to the information we've gathered from the various interviews.

'Fact: Warren Canton, aka Abdul-Fataah, has been linked to an Afghanistan military officer – forgive me for mentally misplacing his name, but it's a mouthful – who had access to weapons that were allegedly placed on a US Army Black Hawk helicopter before it crashed in January 2002. Allegedly placed, but not in reality. There was an entire crate that never made it on board thanks to Abdul-Fataah and his friend.

'Fact: The chopper crashed and was submerged in a mountain lake. SEAL Team Sixteen stepped in either to salvage the weapons or to make sure they were destroyed. The area was hot, there were time pressures, so SEAL commander Paoletti opted to scuttle both the Black Hawk and the weapons, and he signed off that all was destroyed without taking a week to do an inventory of equipment. This is done all the time in front line conditions.

'Fact: Three of those weapons that were signed off as destroyed by Commander Paoletti were used in the Coronado attack.

'Theory: Canton used those weapons on purpose, as a genuine attempt to throw suspicion on a Spec Ops team that had an excellent combat record against Taliban and al-Qaeda forces.

'Fact: Mary Lou Starrett and Kelly Ashton Paoletti were both targeted by Canton one to two months before the terrorist attack in Coronado. Mary Lou knew him as Bob Schwegel, an insurance salesman, Kelly as Doug Fisk, pharmaceutical salesman.

'Theory: Canton discovered that the trunk of Mary Lou's car was broken and that she worked at the McDonald's that was on the Navy base. When he decided Mary Lou would be his way to smuggle in the weapons he needed, he – fact – broke off contact with Kelly.

'Fact: Mary Lou found and touched – hence her fingerprints – an automatic weapon in the trunk of her car and believed that weapon belonged to her husband, Sam Starrett, a member of SEAL Team Sixteen. Because of their marital problems, she never actually questioned him about it, and the weapon mysteriously disappeared.

'Fact: Canton met Ihbraham Rahman, an Arab-American, while in Mary Lou Starrett's company. Rahman could – and did – identify him.

'Fact: Mary Lou Starrett put two and two together incorrectly on the morning of the attack and called 911, believing that her friend Ihbraham Rahman and his brothers were involved in the assassination attempt. She didn't identify herself to the operator when she made that phone call.

'Fact: Mary Lou Starrett filed for divorce and fled to Florida the day after the Coronado attack. She did not come forward with her information, because she feared repercussion.

'Fact: During their relationship, Mary Lou told Canton about finding the gun in the trunk of her car, blaming its presence there on her husband.

'Theory: Canton realized that Mary Lou's fingerprints were on that weapon, and knew that sooner or later, she would be apprehended. She could – and did – identify him.

'Fact: Sam Starrett's house was broken into two weeks after the Coronado attack. Nothing was stolen. A police report was filed.

'Theory: Canton was looking for Mary Lou's whereabouts but didn't find any leads because Starrett kept all of his personal files in his office on base.

'Fact: Ihbraham Rahman's phone was altered to allow Canton to have a record of all calls he made and received. It wasn't a tap – conversations couldn't be overheard – but phone numbers could be traced.

'Theory: Instead of killing Ihbraham Rahman, who could identify him, too, Canton monitored his telephone calls, assuming that sooner or later, Mary Lou would get in touch with him.

'Fact: Mary Lou's sister Janine *did* call Rahman, from the house they shared with Janine's soon-to-be ex-husband, Clyde Wrigley. Janine spoke to Rahman, who urged Mary Lou to call him. Mary Lou, now believing Rahman wasn't involved, was afraid to contact him, fearing such contact would be dangerous for him.

'Fact: The next day, Mary Lou, Haley, and Janine moved out of Clyde's house, without telling Clyde where they were going.

'Theory: Canton used the information from Rahman's phone to get Mary Lou's phone number and address, and sent someone to Sarasota, to find her and kill her. But there was no sign of her at Clyde's – she'd moved out. One of Canton's men watched Clyde, following him in the hope that he'd lead them to Mary Lou, while Canton continued to monitor Ihbraham's phone.

'Fact: Clyde bumped into a friend of Janine's who knew where Janine was working. Clyde went to her place of employment, followed her home.

'Theory: Canton's man was following Clyde, saw Janine, who fit the description of Mary Lou and who was also driving Mary Lou's car – fact. After Clyde slinks off, Canton's man goes to the back door and blows away Janine, thinking he's wasted Mary Lou.

'Canton's man reports in. Mary Lou is dead. Canton asks, what about the kid and the sister? The man is like, what kid, what sister? Canton comes to Sarasota to make sure his guy killed the right sister.

'Fact: Mary Lou is on her way home and sees Canton outside of her house – she keeps driving, but later goes back and finds Janine, dead.

'Theory: Canton went inside, saw Janine, and knew Mary Lou was still alive. The hunt continues – including the monitoring of Ihbraham's telephone.

'Fact: Mary Lou's car – the vehicle Janine was driving on the day she was killed – has turned up abandoned and stripped.

'Theory: Canton moved it out of the driveway for some reason – possibly because his fingerprints may still have been in or on the trunk, possibly to throw off friends and neighbors who might otherwise have come looking for Janine. We're not really sure, but the car did turn up just a few days ago, in Orlando.

'Fact: Mary Lou tells her employer's daughter, Whitney Turlington, that she had a romantic relationship with Ihbraham Rahman, and Whitney plays matchmaker, calling Ihbraham and telling him that Mary Lou needs him, that her ex-husband is trying to kill her.

'Fact: She makes that call from a pay phone, so Canton doesn't have the Turlingtons' address.

'Fact: Ihbraham is curious, because in past conversations, Mary Lou has told him that Sam Starrett would never hit a woman. He goes to Starrett's house, but no one's home. Donny DaCosta, Starrett's neighbor, sees Rahman and also sees Canton following Rahman.

'Theory: Canton realizes that DaCosta can identify him and puts him on his list of people to remove – which includes Kelly Ashton Paoletti.

'Fact: Ihbraham Rahman drives from San Diego to Sarasota in about thirty-six hours – which is extremely impressive – with Canton's men on his tail.

'Fact: Canton, using the alias Doug Fisk, takes an airline flight from San Diego to Sarasota, approximately one hour before a car bomb destroys half of Don DaCosta's house, killing DaCosta and injuring Kelly Paoletti.

'Fact: Mere minutes after Rahman arrives at the Turlington estate, Canton arrives, too, with five of his men. They kill the guards and cut the phone lines and call the main house.

'Theory: Canton was attempting to walk out of the area, in full view of everyone, when you stopped him. Which was pretty fucking unbelievable, boss. Very James Bond of you – going one on one with the villain. You know, if you hadn't done that, we probably wouldn't have apprehended him and gotten his fingerprints and a crapload of additional information, as well as the pleasure of knowing this guy's never going to hurt anyone again.

'This is huge,' Jules told Max, and for once he was dead serious. 'If I were the President, I wouldn't let you quit, either. It's an honor, sir, to be on your team.'

Max didn't know what to say. 'Thank you, but . . .' But what the hell was he going to do about Gina?

She chose that moment to breeze into the room. 'Hey, you're awake.'

Max found it impossible not to smile back at her. When she was in the room, he was undeniably glad that she was here with him. It was the other times that he began to panic.

Jules stood up. 'I've got to go.' He headed toward the door, but then did a U-turn. 'You understand that Canton's connection to Afghanistan clears Tom Paoletti, right?'

Max nodded, watching Gina settle into the chair that Jules had just vacated, the book she was reading aloud to him in her hands. 'Yeah. I'm glad about that.'

Jules nodded. 'About that other thing we discussed . . . I think you can probably cut yourself a little slack.'

Max knew Jules was talking about Gina.

'See you, boss,' he said, then leaned over to kiss Gina right on the mouth. 'Later, gorgeous.'

The room was significantly quieter without Jules in it.

Max looked at Gina. 'You know, the nurse thinks you're my daughter.'

She laughed. 'No, she doesn't. I told her to say that,' she said. 'Your blood pressure was a little low this morning.'

'It's not anymore.'

'Good,' she said. She opened the book and started to read, her hand warm on his leg.

It felt good there. Too good.

But the rest of him hurt, so Max closed his eyes and took Jules's advice and cut himself some slack.

Tuesday, June 24, 2003

'The guards are gone,' Kelly said as Tom came into her hospital room.

'The charges have been dropped,' he said. 'Well, I'm not sure charges were ever officially made, but you know what I mean.'

'That is *such* good news.' She was looking terrific this morning. She actually had a little color in her cheeks. But she had total bed-head.

He got her brush from her drawer.

'You're not wearing your uniform,' she also noted.

'Yeah,' he said, looking down at his jeans and sneakers. He forced a smile. 'Weird, huh?'

'Did you . . .?'

'Yeah,' he said as he started brushing her hair. 'I'm out. I'm done. As of this morning, it's official. They offered a desk job, but—'

'You don't need to explain.'

But there was something he needed to talk about. Tom cleared his throat. 'I, uh, got a call about thirty minutes ago from the CIA.'

Her eyes widened as she looked up at him. 'They want you to work for them? I'm not sure I want you to—'

'Not exactly. They want to, um, *hire* my *team*.'

Kelly didn't get it. He just braided her hair, waiting for her to understand.

She laughed when the light went on. 'Really?'

'Those rumors you started have turned into something a little more solid than I'd anticipated. Apparently, Alyssa Locke is going to be my executive officer.'

And Kelly wasn't too happy about that. 'I'm not sure she's such a good choice—'

He leaned over and kissed her. 'Yeah, you're just jealous. I love it.'

'Well, yeah, because she's gorgeous and she adores you and—'

Tom fished in the drawer for a ponytail holder. 'And she's marrying Sam Starrett – who's also apparently part of my team.'

'Wait a minute,' Kelly said. 'Is that the rumor or . . .?'

'No, she's really marrying Starrett.'

'I thought he just got a divorce.'

Tom poked her. 'Some people don't need to take years and years before they remarry.'

'Hey, be nice to me, I'm in the hospital.'

'I noticed. You want some lotion?'

'No, thanks, I'm okay,' she said. 'Thanks for the braid.'

'Anytime. I'm good with hair. Mine used to be about that long in high school, remember?'

'Oh, yeah.' Kelly smiled at him.

She swore she'd always had a thing for Jean-Luc Picard. Good thing, because she was now married to a man who was on the verge of being very bald.

'So what did you tell the CIA?' she asked.

He laughed. 'What do you think? I told them I don't really have a team together.'

'Yet,' Kelly added.

'Yet,' Tom agreed.

His cell phone rang, and he glanced at the screen and laughed.

'Who is it?' Kelly asked.

'Sam Starrett,' he told her. 'Probably wondering where he can put his desk.'

Twenty-nine

Alyssa sat in Noah and Claire's den and looked through a scrapbook Walter Gaines had made several months before he'd died.

It was filled with school papers – one of them a terribly poignant and sensitive poem Sam must've written when he was about fourteen – and clippings from the local paper of Sam's enlistment in the Navy, of his admittance to BUD/S training, of his acceptance first into the SEAL teams and then to Officers Training School when he made the leap from enlisted to officer.

There were photos in the book, too. Pictures of Sam when he was just a skinny little kid. There was one of him with Walter's arms around him, where he had the traces of what looked like a terrible black eye. But both Walt and Sam – Ringo – were laughing, and the boy's face was completely lit up.

There were photos of Ringo and Noah, and in some of them the expression on Ringo's face was so totally Sam, Alyssa laughed aloud.

There was a picture of Sam, barely eighteen, holding Noah and Claire's infant daughter, Dora.

And another picture had Sam in his Navy uniform, standing with his mother and Noah and Claire outside of a church. There was a caption under that one, reading: 'Suellen Starrett gets her one-year chip'.

From Alcoholics Anonymous, Alyssa realized. Sam's mother had finally dumped his father and gotten her life together.

The very last photo in the book was a picture of Sam and

Noah, taken when Sam received his SEAL pin.

Wow, he'd been young when he first became a SEAL. Pride radiated from him with an intensity that was so strong it seemed to reach out in time to touch her through that photograph. He looked ready to take on the world, as one of the very best of the best.

SEAL Team Sixteen had lost a lot with Sam's recent resignation.

But there was no way he could have stayed in, not after everything that had happened.

Still, Alyssa's mother had been fond of saying, *When someone shuts a door, a window always opens.*

Tom Paoletti had called both Sam and Alyssa this morning, asking if they were interested in meeting with him to discuss potential opportunities working in the public sector.

Paoletti was legendary, and Alyssa suspected that even though Sam was no longer a Navy SEAL, his days of being the best of the best had not yet come to an end.

Beneath that final photo, in Walt's own hand, was a message to Sam. 'My two boys,' he'd written. 'May they find the same joy and happiness in their lives that I found in mine, dear Lord. Guide them and let them be blessed with a life filled with love and adventure.'

'I wish you could have known him,' Sam had said to her about Walter Gaines.

Alyssa had the feeling that she did – just by knowing Sam.

As she put down the book, she realized that the house was extremely still. Claire was working up in her office, and Noah had taken Devin and Dora to the movies. The idea was to give Sam a little one-on-one time with Haley, who was spending her days with Noah and Claire until all of the endless questioning and interviews and debriefings ended.

It looked as if charges would not be filed against Mary Lou, which was a very good thing, for all their sakes.

Alyssa stood up and stretched. When she first came into this den, over two hours ago, Haley had Sam down on the living-room floor, playing with a set of plastic dolls.

She went down the hall to the living room now, wondering if they'd gone outside. It was so quiet.

And then she saw why.

Sam was lying on his back on the floor. Haley was on his chest, and they were both fast asleep. He looked so at peace, so content. And Alyssa knew Roger/Ringo/Sam had finally found a name that was going to stick. *Daddy*.

She stood there, watching them, with so much love in her heart it nearly took her breath away.

Let them be blessed with a life filled with love – and adventure.

Between Alyssa and Haley, the love part was handled.

As for the adventure – well, the biggest adventure of all was only just beginning.

21st–
CENTURY
SMALLHOLDER

How to get back to the land without leaving home

Paul Waddington

Paul Waddington is the author of **Seasonal Food: a guide** [...........]n, **when and why** as well as a professional writer. He takes a deep i[....]d and environmental issues, and lives as sustainably as possible with his wife and two children.

Also by Paul Waddington

Seasonal Food

Shades of Green

TRANSWORLD PUBLISHERS
61–63 Uxbridge Road, London W5 5SA
A Random House Group Company
www.rbooks.co.uk

First published in Great Britain in 2006 by Eden Project Books
an imprint of Transworld Publishers

This paperback edition published in 2008

Copyright © Paul Waddington 2006, 2008

Paul Waddington has asserted his right under the Copyright, Designs
and Patents Act 1988 to be identified as the author of this work.

A CIP catalogue record for this book
is available from the British Library.

ISBN 9781905811168

Addresses for Random House Group Ltd companies outside the UK
can be found at: www.randomhouse.co.uk
The Random House Group Ltd Reg. No. 954009

The Random House Group Limited supports The Forest Stewardship Council (FSC), the leading international forest certification organization. All our titles that are printed on Greenpeace-approved, FSC-certified paper carry the FSC logo.
Our paper procurement policy can be found at:
www.rbooks.co.uk/environment

Art direction & design by Fiona Andreanelli (www.andreanelli.com)
Design assistance by Vanessa Bowerman (www.foliotypo.co.uk)
Illustrations by Gillian Blease (www.gillianblease.co.uk)
Garden designs pp. 32, 37, 41 by Simon Saggers
Table on p. 207 courtesy of Simon Fairlie
Typeset in Gill Sans
Printed and bound in Great Britain by Cox & Wyman Ltd, Reading, Berkshire

2 4 6 8 10 9 7 5 3 1

21st-CENTURY SMALLHOLDER

Paul Waddington

Acknowledgements

I would like to thank Susanna Wadeson, who decided that this book's time had come, and the rest of the team at Transworld and Eden who also made it happen: Sarah Emsley, Mike Petty, Gavin Morris and Brenda Updegraff. Thank you too to Gillian Blease for the beautiful illustrations. Being a complete novice in so many of the subjects covered by the book, I have many experts to thank: Simon Saggers, whose beautiful smallholding is an inspiration and whose garden designs in this book will hopefully inspire others; Simon Fairlie for his expert advice on smallholding; Michael and Julia Guerra, who show how to create abundance from small spaces; John Chapple, a bee guru; Tony York for his pig expertise; and Caroline Muir for letting me get to know her urban chickens. Adrian Evans and Helen Stuffins were inspirational and instrumental in shaping my views on sustainability. Peter Harper from the Centre for Alternative Technology provided a pragmatic corrective to the less practical extremes of 'green' thinking. Biologist David Perkins showed how beautiful biodiversity can be created in the most urban of spaces; Penney Poyzer and Gil Schalom demonstrated how a Victorian house can become an eco-home; and Will Anderson shared his experience of creating an eco-friendly house from scratch. Thanks are due, as always, to my agent Sappho Clissitt; and to my wife and sons, Fiona, Finn and Fergus, who were a source of joy and support throughout.

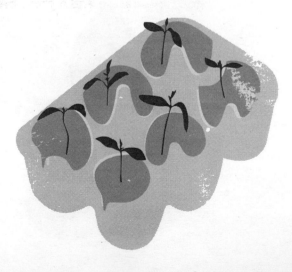

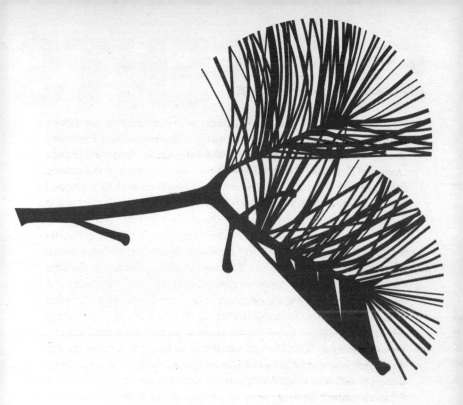

In memory of Helen Stuffins,
a great inspiration and a great friend

CONTENTS

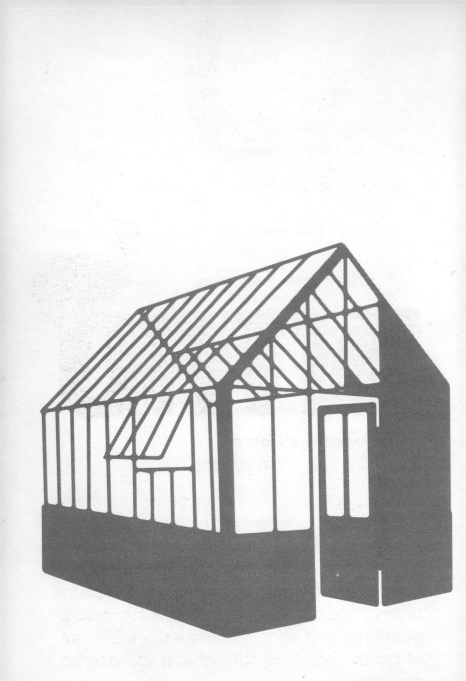

INTRO

Who wants to be a
21st-Century Smallholder?

Many of us dream of 'four acres and freedom' the idyllic, self-sufficient life in which we flee the city to live in harmony with the land, dependent on no-one. For all but a fortunate few, this is now an impossible dream. Absurd property prices have put four acres and a farmhouse out of reach of anyone lacking a six-figure sum of capital. Today, only the rich can afford to be peasants.

But a way of life that reduces our impact on the planet whilst also improving our quality of life has never been more sorely needed. Look at any aspect of modern living and there's a very good reason for doing things differently.

The food we eat now comes from a handful of gigantic retailers. Their demand for an uninterrupted, year-round supply of cosmetically perfect produce is turning our countryside into an agribusiness factory. Our food chain is now entirely dependent on fossil fuels: first, to manufacture the pesticides and artificial fertilizers without which industrial agriculture fails; and second, to power agricultural machinery and the enormous, road-based transport infrastructure that delivers food from farmer to warehouse to supermarket. As Felicity Lawrence points out in the food industry exposé *Not on the Label*, just a few days without fuel would bring this country's food supply to a standstill.

So the modern food chain is insecure. It's also killing us: polluting the environment with runoff and residues, decimating biodiversity and – as we are now beginning to learn – giving us produce that is depleted in the minerals and micronutrients that make it worth eating in the first place. Is a lettuce that is grown with artificial fertilizer, slathered with pesticides, then chilled and trucked around the place for a few days before spending a week in the fridge going to be as good as the one just picked from your garden? The evidence suggests not; and intuition screams it. Growing your own is more than just a nice idea.

Then there's the way we use energy and resources. Our homes are responsible for a third of Britain's CO_2 emissions. Almost all are highly dependent on energy sources that are not only insecure and non-renewable but whose use is also – the evidence is now overwhelming – transforming our climate into something that could even become hostile to much of humanity in our lifetimes. It would take three planet Earths to support the entire world's population living as the British do. Thinking about reducing energy and resource dependence is no longer the preserve of the thrifty smallholder; it's something we could all benefit from, now and in the future.

Many of us dream of living differently because we can see what our Western lifestyles are doing to the environment. But I think we also aspire to peasantry because we instinctively feel that there is deep satisfaction to be gained from tasks that the consumer society would file under 'drudgery': growing and preserving food, animal husbandry, or managing your own water and energy resources. Our national fondness for gardening and pet ownership – scorned by nations that are closer to their pre-industrial pasts – surely points to a longing to be closer to nature. We have become 'de-skilled' since we industrialized, losing our ability to live off the land. Today, that de-skilling has accelerated as our needs have become provided for by corporations. Even being a parent can be outsourced today. In a generation, we've forgotten how to grow things, fix things, even cook from scratch. And we are all having to relearn about what food is in season when. If society collapsed tomorrow, only Ray Mears would survive. Skills that were once effortlessly handed down from generation to generation now have to be learnt through piles of books, lengthy courses or painful trial and error. But – as I have learnt – it's worth it. Few things beat the satisfaction of picking your own produce or knocking together your first beehive.

So perhaps we should all attempt to be self-sufficient at home in order to be healthy and happy and save the planet? I don't think so. Genuine self-sufficiency, in which you provide all your own material needs, is very, very tough. As the two case studies at the end of this book show, it requires a vast amount of learning, planning, investment and time, as well as a good-sized plot of land. If you had an immense garden, an iron will, accommodating neighbours and a complicit family, it might just be possible to emulate Tom and Barbara Good. Most of us aren't like this, though. And even if it were practical, I doubt whether widespread self-sufficiency is really desirable. For a start, it would put out of business the small-scale farmers who are finding new outlets for seasonal, local and often organic produce through farmers' markets and box schemes.

In between the Goods and the people who rampage from shopping mall to ready meal in a monster 4x4 is the 21st-Century Smallholder. You don't need four acres to be one; nor do you need vast amounts of capital and time. You won't be self-sufficient; but you'll grow and do the things that suit your home and your life. If you have a small flat, then maybe your window boxes could keep you in salads and herbs. If you have a small garden, perhaps you'll use part of it to grow gourmet fruit and veg that are best when just picked, and maybe have some chickens scratching around the place. And if you're fortunate enough to have a lot of outside space, then you may well be eating your own produce for much of the growing season; there might be bees ... or even pigs. And wherever you live, you could be harvesting rainwater, making your own compost, saving – even generating – energy and turning your home into a wildlife haven.

Why be a 21st-Century Smallholder? There's a long list of good reasons: here are just a few. It's deeply satisfying. Whether it's your first home-grown salad, home-laid egg or solar-heated shower, there's a great sense of achievement to be had. Being a 21st-Century Smallholder also makes your house and garden look beautiful and attract wildlife. A productive fruit and veg garden is a nicer place to be than a desert of decking, both for you and for the countless bugs and creatures that run our ecosystem. If you grow and raise some of your own food and manage some of your own resources (like water and energy), it reduces your dependence on our damaging consumer culture. It may only be a token reduction – cutting yourself off from the mains, for example, is not something to be undertaken lightly – but it feels good; it feels like taking control in a world where the power to run one's day-to-day life is being reduced to nothing more than consumer choice. Finally, it's good to feel like part of the solution. Your water butt may not solve the world's freshwater crisis; your home-made compost may not save the peat bogs; and your solar panels might not stop the glaciers melting; but big changes start with lots of grassroots actions.

It doesn't have to take much time, or cost much money, to be a 21st-Century Smallholder. You can start growing fruit and veg on a shoestring budget; and many of the actions that most reduce your environmental 'footprint' are free and will save money. Solar electricity, big food growing operations, 'eco-retrofitting' your house: these things do cost money. But there's something for everyone in the 21st-Century Smallholder's lifestyle. However far you want to go, this book is designed to help you along the way.

So how much of a 21st-Century Smallholder is the author? At the time of writing, not much at all, I'm afraid. Being on the verge of a long-distance house move, I've handed the allotment plot on to the next eager person on the enormous waiting list and donated the bees, which are unlikely to enjoy the journey, to another beekeeper. We still have a minor fruit and veg operation in the back garden and are still happily composting away. We should be at our next destination for a good few years so there will be a productive garden, possibly bees and chickens, and a house with every eco-modification we can afford. And the car, on the relatively rare occasions it gets used, still runs happily on filtered waste-vegetable oil.

Why grow your own food?

It's a very good question. After all, growing food is what farmers are for. Unless we have lots of land and lots of time, why should we bother? Glossy utopian gardening books and self-sufficiency manuals rarely point out the downsides of growing your own food, so let's start by being practical and looking at the pitfalls as well as the pleasures.

GROWING YOUR OWN FOOD

Five reasons not to grow your own food

It can cost a lot to get started

In the past, nobody started growing from scratch. Our peasant ancestors inherited everything from their forebears. They didn't really need to buy land or equipment or go on gardening courses: all the kit and the skills they needed were handed down from generation to generation. Today's aspirant grower, hemmed as she or he often is into a small house and garden, usually has a lot of stuff to buy, from garden tools and propagating gear to soil improvers, sheds, water butts – the list is endless.

You won't save much money

In Victorian times, the price of food meant that growing your own would have saved up to 50 per cent of your annual expenditure. Today, we spend only around 10–15 per cent of our income on food and only a fraction of this goes on the stuff you could grow in your garden. If you really want to save money on food and drink, be a teetotal vegetarian.

You will not achieve self-sufficiency in anything other than salads and herbs

Even if we adopt the 'Mediterranean food pyramid' – a diet in which cereals, pulses and vegetables predominate and animal protein forms only a small part – it is very tough to be truly self-sufficient in food, particularly from a small space in a temperate climate. If you give up meat, accept that all your carbohydrates will come from potatoes (which store well and can give bulk yields in small spaces), and brace yourself for lean times and preserved or frozen food in the April–June 'hungry gap', then it's maybe do-able. But desirable? Probably not.

It takes time, particularly when you want to go on holiday

Peasants who learnt to grow as they grew up did not have to invest much time in getting started; and strong social and family networks meant that an equally skilled person was always around to help. Leave your veg garden alone at the wrong time of year, though, and weed apocalypse could greet your return from holiday. Growing food does need an investment of time, often when you least have it.

Children aren't always compatible with horticulture

Few things are more distressing than watching a small child innocently upend a module tray full of carefully tended seedlings. A garden largely given over to growing is not always somewhere in which you can relax with offspring. Compromise is needed to keep parents, kids, fruit and veg happy.

But if you can cope with these downsides, there are of course many, many good reasons for growing your own which far outweigh the disadvantages.

Five reasons to grow your own food

It is deeply satisfying ...

Even if it's just the one radish that escaped the slugs, the satisfaction of eating your own produce is enormous and hard to communicate to those who haven't given it a go. And the more time and effort you invest in raising a particular plant, the better it feels when you finally eat its produce. Knowing how much effort it can take to get, say, a humble sprouting broccoli plant from seed to plate (propagating, transplanting, protecting – over maybe ten months) also gives a deep appreciation of the value of food.

... and very healthy

More is being discovered all the time about the true nutritional value of food. And the evidence suggests that modern, industrial agricultural techniques not only damage the land and expose us to pesticides and herbicides: they have also depleted both the mineral and micronutrient content of vegetables and fruit in the last fifty or so years. Buying seasonal, local organic food helps avoid this; but growing your own gives you total control over what goes into your food. The nutrient content of fruit and vegetables is optimal when they have just been picked. Plus, of course, you get to spend time exercising in the fresh air.

You will have new gourmet experiences

We are accustomed to buying food, refrigerating it and then eating it when we're ready. And if it's from a supermarket, it has already spent far too much time on the road and in a fridge. For many vegetables and fruit, this does terrible things to their nutritional value and to their gourmet appeal. The garden, however, keeps fruit and veg in perfect condition, so if you get into the habit of picking and eating straight away, the quality is streets ahead of anything you could buy in the shops. For particular produce: herbs, salads, tomatoes, soft fruit (see pp. 24–7 for a table with a 'gourmet value' rating) this is absolutely crucial.

You can stick two fingers up at the modern food industry

Every time I pick a sprig of thyme from the garden I think of over-packaged herbs grown in a monster high-tech greenhouse somewhere and sold for a ludicrous price by supermarkets. And I rejoice in the small victory of depriving these undeserving behemoths of a tiny bit of revenue. If you hate the modern food chain and what it's doing to the land and to communities, then growing your own is a small, maybe insignificant, but satisfying political act.

You will learn a great deal and develop new skills

In learning to grow food, you inevitably find out a great deal of fascinating stuff about nature, from soil composition to the role of flora and fauna to weather and seasons. This is satisfying in itself; and it also brings you closer to the seasons and the cycle of life in a way that introduces constant variety and interest into your life. And of course you learn a whole range of skills – composting, planting, amateur weather forecasting – that enrich your life and can be passed on to others.

What are vegetables and fruit?

Before I started growing fruit and vegetables I knew very little about how, why and when they grew. And I found that many gardening books seemed to skip this fundamental information and dive straight into gardening techniques and principles.

If, as I was (and still feel!), you are a complete newcomer to edible gardening, then I think it's worth going right back to first principles and taking a quick look at what fruit and vegetables are, and how they behave through the year. It's not essential to help you plan your time; but it's useful and perhaps interesting background.

Most of the vegetables that we grow are 'annuals', which means that the plants die off every year, having put all their energy into setting (producing) seed. We eat this energy (which is contained in different parts of these vegetables) at different points in their seed-setting cycles, depending on what's best. So with 'leaf vegetables', like lettuce and cabbages, we eat the leaves because these are good and the seeds are tiny. (However, rapeseed oil – made from the seeds of a cabbage relative – forms a huge part of the modern food chain.) With peas and beans we eat the immature seeds. Sometimes we eat the unopened flowers (as in broccoli); or the stems (celery); or the root (parsnip, carrot). And sometimes we eat the 'fruit' that contains the seeds, as with tomatoes, cucumber or pumpkins.

Temperature and day length are the main factors that affect when things grow. Below 6°C, plants are dormant and nothing grows: so in the depths of winter in Britain the growing season grinds to a halt. (Global warming is, however, rapidly bringing a year-round growing season to much of Britain.) Increasing day length from January onwards kicks off the growth of a small number of plants (such as rhubarb) that respond to this. And then increasing warmth prompts more natural growth and eventually heats the soil enough for planting many things outside. By May, weeds are in aggressive competition with your young vegetables. The first, early outdoor crops are ready by May and June, and then, as the summer warms up, more and more produce becomes available. By August and September, peak harvest season, sowing and planting activity starts to tail off, and into the autumn the business of preparing the soil for the next year's growing season starts up.

Over the centuries we have selectively bred different types of vegetables – and taken advantage of their different characteristics – to provide us, as much as possible, with a year-round supply within the constraints of our temperate, four-season climate.

Root vegetables such as carrots, parsnips, swede and turnips store goodness in their roots over the winter to power a vibrant flowering in the spring. We take advantage of this concentrated nutrition, either lifting and storing the roots when they are ready or leaving them in the ground until we want to eat them. The same principle applies to leaf vegetables: we take the energy stored in their leaves before they flower and turn it to seed. For fast-growing salads, this means a quick meal, early on in the growing season. And for hardy, slow-growing winter cabbages, it means fresh greens in the coldest months. Pea and bean plants, well-adapted to our climate, flower and set seed early in the growing season, enabling us to eat their immature seeds in the early summer; whilst non-native 'fruiting' vegetables like tomatoes need more heat and light to come to fruition.

Fruit, on the other hand, is perennial, growing on trees and shrubs over many years, depending on the species. So because fruit has to complete a cycle of growth, flowering and fruiting before it's ready to eat, it tends to have a short season, during – and mostly towards the end of – the warmest months in our climate (unless we cheat nature with greenhouses and heating).

There are also perennial vegetables, which present the edible gardener with a low-effort (if sometimes space-intensive) food-growing option. Artichokes, asparagus, sorrel and rhubarb (botanically a vegetable) are just four examples of plants which, once established, will continue cropping in their seasons with minimal intervention from the gardener.

It's not essential to know all this background information in order to plan your edible gardening time. But it's helpful. If, for example, you have very little time to spare through the year and spend lots of time away, then the best strategy would be to concentrate on fruit trees and bushes and perennial vegetables. Such a food-growing operation can take a long time to establish itself (the trees have to grow and mature) and its yields are lower and concentrated more on fruit. But there's much less need to worry about maintenance and, crucially, no need for sowing, propagating and planting once it's established.

Grow annual vegetables and you will need more time, depending on what you want to eat. A simple balcony-based salads and herbs operation won't take much time at all. But growing annuals to get a constant year-round supply of fresh food does take a little more effort; and there are times when it's good not to go away.

The 21st-Century Smallholder's year planner (pp. 144–157) gives a full run-down of the edible gardening year and the time taken by other related things – such as beekeeping or pond-building – that you may or may not wish to explore. Read through this and you will quickly build up a picture of when different things happen, and which are the busiest and quietest months.

The table below summarizes in brief how the growing year pans out. In reality, many of these tasks go on all the time. But this gives a picture of how the intensity of work needed follows the growing season.

SOWING, PLANTING AND HARVESTING												
	J	F	M	A	M	J	J	A	S	O	N	D
Soil preparation	♦♦♦♦	♦♦♦									♦♦♦♦	♦♦♦♦
Sowing/ planting		♦♦	♦♦♦	♦♦♦	♦♦♦♦	♦♦♦	♦♦♦	♦♦	♦	♦	♦	♦
Propagating		♦♦♦♦	♦♦♦♦	♦♦♦♦								
Weeding		♦	♦♦	♦♦♦	♦♦♦♦	♦♦♦♦	♦♦♦♦	♦♦♦	♦♦	♦	♦	♦
Harvesting	♦	♦	♦	♦♦	♦♦♦	♦♦♦	♦♦♦	♦♦♦♦	♦♦♦♦	♦♦♦	♦♦	♦
Watering						♦♦♦	♦♦♦	♦				
Days per month*	1	1	1	2	2	2	2	2	2	2	1	1

*Very rough estimate for a large vegetable plot of, say, 100 square metres.

♦♦♦♦ = lots of work needed   ♦ = little work needed

Where to start?

Fruit- and veg-growing often seems like a huge and daunting subject and it is the subject of many huge and daunting books. Perhaps the easiest way to start is to consider your space. Do you have a window box, a balcony, a small garden or a big garden? Or maybe an allotment too? Does it get lots of sun? Lots of wind? Lots of rain? What's the soil like? Is there any? Even if it's just a window box, you'll be able to grow things all year round; but the size and nature of your space will help determine what to grow.

Then there's the question of what you want to eat. Perhaps it's things like tomatoes and strawberries that never taste as good as when picked and eaten straight off the plant. Or maybe you're after maximum yield, for example growing potatoes in a tub to get a huge supply from just a few square feet.

Finally there's the question of your time. How much do you have? Will it be a snatched fifteen minutes every evening, or an afternoon a week? Or more? And on the subject of time, how long can you wait? Six weeks for some salads to grow, or six years for a 'forest garden' to start establishing itself?

There are, of course, other variables to worry about: how much hassle a particular plant is to grow, how long its season is, how good it looks… but space, time and what you want to eat will help you to make some practical choices to get started.

The table on pp. 24–7 'scores' fruit and veg according to these factors: browsing through it will give you an idea of what things will suit you and help you to decide where to start with growing your own food.

VEGETABLE	COMMENTS
Artichoke, globe	Easy to grow (it's a thistle), tastes great, looks good too, but each plant takes up a great deal of space.
Artichoke, Jerusalem	Very space-hungry but highly nutritious and a good crop for breaking up the ground.
Asparagus	Needs permanent, dedicated space and lots of time to mature. But perennial and with unmatched gourmet value.
Aubergine	Needs greenhouse, preferably heated. Not a natural for the British climate.
Beans, broad	Tough plant, easy to grow, great gourmet value, provides different delicacies throughout its season (pods, fresh beans, dried beans).
Beans, French	Slightly more finicky than broad beans, but great gourmet value and yield.
Beans, runner	A garden favourite, but there are things that taste better . . .
Beetroot	Easy to grow and can be eaten at various stages; also stores well.
Broccoli, Calabrese	The nutritional value of your own broccoli is (just about) worth the hassle of growing it.
Broccoli, sprouting	Space-hungry and with a long growing season, but provides a superb delicacy in late winter when little else is fresh.
Brussels sprouts	Need a lot of room, but taste great and stand through the winter.
Cabbage	The huge variety of cabbages can provide fresh veg all year round, but plants can be space-hungry.
Cardoon	A gourmet treat, but only for those with room to spare.
Carrots	Can be tricky to grow and prefer lighter soils.
Cauliflower	Pest-prone like all brassicas and needs a lot of water. Long growing season.

Key: Space Time Gourmet Season Hassle Beauty

VEGETABLE		COMMENTS
Celeriac		Long growing season and hard to produce a big bulb.
Celery		'Trench' celery is hard work, self-blanching type is easier.
Chard		Easy to grow, looks lovely, tastes great and stands through the winter.
Chicory		Complex range of varieties; can be labour-intensive but fine eating.
Courgettes		Take up some space but very easy to grow and crops heavily.
Cucumber		Ideally needs to be grown in a greenhouse or polytunnel.
Endive		The taste of chicory without the hassle. A good year-round, small-space crop.
Fennel		Works best in warm areas.
Garlic		Hardy, space-efficient and very healthy.
Kale		A great standby through the winter: hardy and easy to grow.
Kohlrabi		Beautiful, tasty, not demanding of space and can be grown nearly all year round.
Leeks		A 21st-Century Smallholder's essential. Lots of tasty produce through the winter from small space.
Lettuce		Everyone should grow it: a cold frame or greenhouse extends the season nearly all year round.
Onions		Store well and give a good yield for the space they occupy.
Onions, spring		Tasty, handy and useful for small spaces.
Parsnips		Very long growing season. Needs same conditions as carrots. Magnet for insects if left to flower.

Key: ■ 3 (excellent)   ■ 2   □ 1 (not so good)

VEGETABLE		COMMENTS
Peas		Nothing beats your own peas. Don't take up too much space but do need support. Also add to soil fertility.
Peppers and chillies		A greenhouse or windowsill proposition.
Potatoes		Vast yield available from small spaces; great tastes, too.
Radishes		Fast growing and fiery-flavoured: a salad essential.
Rhubarb		Needs its own (large) space but looks after itself once established.
Rocket		Easy and quick to grow, tastes great, an edible gardening must.
Sorrel		Perennial, hassle-free and one of the first interesting flavours of the growing year.
Spinach		Easy to grow, versatile, long season.
Squash (winter) and pumpkins		Needs space but can be 'trailed' between other plants. Great late summer/autumn treat and can store well.
Swede		Slow growing, likes cool conditions, a good winter standby.
Sweetcorn		Needs a good summer, but worth it for the unparalleled gourmet experience.
Tomatoes		Easy to grow but need feeding and watering, especially if in containers. Gourmet value makes it all worthwhile.
Turnips		Very tasty and the leaves can be eaten too. Reasonably space-efficient.

Key: Space • Time • Gourmet • Season • Hassle • Beauty

FRUIT		COMMENTS
Apple and crabapple		Obviously not a window-box proposition, but worth it for delightful blossom and the endless possibilities of apples.
Blackberry		Vigorous is an understatement: they'll have your whole garden given a chance.
Blackcurrant		Needs netting but tastes great and fruit is hugely nutritious. Plants not too big.
Blueberry		Tremendously good for you. But needs acid soil.
Cherry		Different types can fit into different parts of the garden.
Elderberry		Abundant in the wild, but why not have your own supply?
Gooseberry		Hardy, easy to grow and a superb seasonal treat.
Medlar		Almost impossible to find this quirky fruit in the shops; trees are beautiful too.
Mulberry		Superb summer treat, unobtainable commercially. Takes a long time to crop.
Pear		Not as hardy as apples, but still beautiful and tasty.
Plum (and relatives)		Essential summer fruit. Plums don't like cooler springs but damsons grow well further north.
Quince		Very attractive tree and unusual fruit.
Raspberry		An essential fruit for the edible garden.
Red and white currants		Good for jellies and summer pudding.
Strawberry		Nothing tastes better than your own.

Key: ■ 3 (excellent)   ■ 2   □ 1 (not so good)

How are you going to garden?

Another important starting point is to decide how you are going to garden. If you are planning to do things organically, then you will need less money – because there is no need to buy pesticides, herbicides and artificial fertilizer – but more time, because, for example, you will need to do more weeding and crop protection.

Conventional

Applied to cultivation, this term somewhat ironically refers to the less than sixty-year-old technique of growing food crops with a reliance on 'scientific' intervention: artificial fertilizers, pesticides and herbicides. It's an adversarial way of tackling the land: man vs. nature. Growing food this way may bring quick results, but its downsides are numerous. It will cost more in the short term, because the inputs you need are expensive; and it will cost more in the long term, because growing food this way depletes biodiversity, puts toxic substances into the food chain and exhausts your soil. To find out more about conventional growing, buy a different book!

Organic

Going organic means growing food with an absolute minimum of scientific intervention and with a focus on improving the soil. It is ideally suited to the 21st-Century Smallholder's edible gardening efforts because it's cheap, makes your garden more fertile over time and encourages a biodiversity that helps to protect what you grow as well as making your garden beautiful. Rather than fighting nature, organic growing seeks to recruit natural predators to deal with pests, uses natural barriers such as mulches to deal with weeds and natural fertilizers like home-made compost to enrich the soil. 'Biodynamic' growing adds further techniques to organic principles, using an astronomical calendar to determine auspicious planting times and treating compost with special preparations.

Permaculture

Edible gardening according to permaculture principles means working organically, but taking natural ecosystems as a model for what you do. So the ultimate permaculture food-growing operation is a managed 'forest garden' in which the careful choice and siting of trees and mainly perennial plants provides an ultra low-maintenance, sustainable food source. This can be hard to achieve in practice, particularly in temperate climates. However, the permaculture principles of careful planning and of maximizing the beneficial relationships between people, plants and animals are very useful, particularly when gardening in small spaces.

The recommended ways of growing in this book are based on a combination of organic and permaculture principles.

Planning your space

The next step is to plan your growing space. It is enormously tempting to get carried away and see the entire garden or outside space as nothing more than a food-growing operation – after all, there's so much good stuff to grow! However, the obvious pitfall of this is that the garden ceases to be a space for leisure, or even for biodiversity. Children and a gardening-enthusiast wife soon made me realize that our meagre outside space needed to be more than just a mini market garden. And organic gardening dictates that there should be some space for wildlife habitats, including maybe a pond to encourage slug-eating frogs, as well as room for a decent compost heap and a rainwater butt. (See also Chapter 4 for more on building biodiversity.)

Answering the following set of questions will help you to plan your food-growing operation.

What do I want to do with my outside space? If it's going to be used exclusively for food-growing, then fine: but bear in mind that, in gardening organically, you will need room for plants and features that encourage pest predators; crops will need to be rotated (see pp. 55–6) and you will benefit hugely from a compost heap, rainwater collection and even a small greenhouse. Most of us will want our garden or outside space to be several things: a playground for the kids, somewhere to eat, a wildlife haven, a retreat – maybe all of these. The sample 21st-

Century Smallholder's garden designs on pp. 32–41 are based on a balance between food-growing, leisure and creating the biodiversity that is essential to organic gardening (and also fascinating for children and adults alike).

How big is it? Size matters when it comes to edible gardening. There's little point, for example, in growing space-hungry Brussels sprouts on a balcony. You can produce an awful lot in a small space (see example on pp. 32–3), but choosing space-efficient plants and trees is the most sensible way to do it. (It is surprising how many different fruit and vegetables are appropriate for small spaces – see table on pp. 24–7.) As your space gets bigger, you have more room for luxuries like greenhouses, chickens, bigger ponds; and the choice of vegetables you can grow widens to include really space-hungry gourmet crops like asparagus and artichokes.

What's there already? If it's all paved or decked then you have work to do: but this could involve using containers or building raised beds (see pp. 46–7) rather than digging the whole lot up. There's maybe stuff you could use: trees and shrubs that provide great wildlife habitat, for example. And you'll also have to consider the soil (see pp. 42–5), which will probably need some form of improvement to support greedy fruit and vegetables.

Which way does it point? North or south, up or down? Orientation is another factor to consider. Tomatoes would delight in a south-facing wall; a small morello cherry tree won't mind the shade. If it's steep, some terracing might be necessary to create viable vegetable beds.

What's the climate like? Whether you live in Bristol or Braemar will affect the things you can grow. Latitude and elevation will determine, for example, whether certain fruit trees really are viable; or whether you'll get a decent crop of sweetcorn. 'Microclimate' should also be considered: if you have, say, particularly windy, wet, sunny, shady or frost-prone spots, these should all be taken into account when planning your food-growing.

The 'Meet the fruit and veg' section on pp. 64–95 will help you to decide which plants will work in your outside space. And the three sample designs which follow will illustrate how these can integrate into an outside space that provides for food, leisure and wildlife whether it's a small balcony, average-sized garden or large garden.

Three garden designs

The balcony

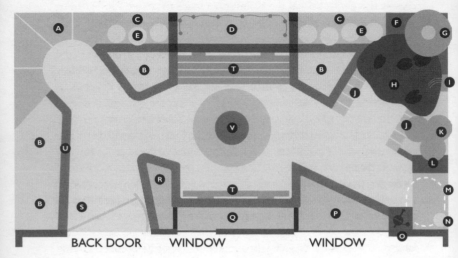

BACK DOOR   WINDOW   WINDOW

A Greenhouse for toms/
   cucumbers and all-year cropping
   of salads etc.

B Annual rotational veg beds

C Fruit tree against wall

D Head board and small (40cm)
   covered trellis and pagoda for
   vines & soft fruit

E Summer salads

F 'Wild' area under tree

G Standard fruit tree

H Raised pond

I Fountain

J Raised brick seats

K Permanent bed (rhubarb etc.)

L Compost bin, against the wall

M Storage shed

N Filter-in downpipe to
   underground water tank

O Watering can fed by hand pump
   bringing water up from the tank

P Permanent bed (strawberries
   and asparagus)

Q Raised 'head board' bed for
   herbs & flowers

R Herbs at ground level (20cm)

S Permanent reclaimed brick path

T Folding benches

U 'New' sleeper edging

V Solid table with permanent
   central herb buffet!

Lack of a garden needn't stop you being a 21st-Century Smallholder. You may not get vast yields from tiny spaces but, as this illustration shows, even a small balcony can provide a huge amount of variety for the committed flat-dweller. This design ticks all the boxes: it is a space for leisure, food-growing and biodiversity, all crammed into a mere 4m × 2m (13ft × 6.5ft).

In this example, as in many of our homes, the orientation isn't perfect: the balcony faces east and slightly to the north, so this has influenced where things go. On a south-facing balcony, the back wall would be the obvious place to put plants that love heat and sun. Here, the growing activity is arranged so that different plants get maximum benefit from the balcony's orientation. On the north (left) side, two half-metre-wide beds (raised about 40cm from the ground) will expose annual vegetables to the best light; and next to these, a small customized greenhouse will provide excellent summer crops of tomatoes and cucumbers as well as a year-round supply of small salad plants and leaves. A third bed to the right of the greenhouse provides more space for annual vegetables. Behind this is a small salad bed. As we move round the design clockwise we come to the centrepiece: two folding benches and a table at whose centre is a living herb 'buffet'. On the north side of this, behind one of the benches, there is room for vines and soft fruit to grow up and over a small trellis and pagoda. To the right of this is room for more salads and a fourth annual vegetable bed – even in such a small space, there is room for the classic crop rotation of organic cultivation (see pp. 55–6 for more on crop rotation).

The south-east (top right) corner of this balcony is a riot of activity. There's a tiny wilderness area underneath a small fruit tree. A raised pond with a fountain will provide beauty, relaxation and a haven for all manner of beneficial bugs and creatures. Small seats next to the pond provide a restful spot in your own 'wild' space.

As we move into the shadier part of the design, permanent beds for rhubarb, asparagus and strawberries flank a small compost bin and shed: and for those with a ground-floor balcony and the appropriate permission, there's space here for an underground water butt too. Behind the east-facing bench on the back wall, there's a raised bed for herbs and flowers; and another herb bed right by the back door, where you need it.

The average garden

It's not easy to get a fix on how big the 'average' garden in Britain is. Research from a major DIY chain suggests as much as 300 square metres, which at around 30 by 100 feet (in old money) is a pretty big space. A Royal Horticultural Society/Wildlife Trusts survey reckons that there are fifteen million gardens in Britain covering 270,000 hectares, which makes the average a more modest 180 square metres. But this still seems a lot for the houses in which most of us live today and is probably skewed by a few very big gardens. So based on some more sources and a bit of educated guesswork, I've chosen 100 square metres as an area to represent what those of us who live in houses or garden flats are most likely to have available.

Obviously, every space is different in terms of shape, orientation, climate and what's there already. But whatever it's like, unless your garden has really extreme environmental constraints – far too much shade, a very severe slope – there's a lot you can do with it. And most constraints can be dealt with: terracing to deal with slopes, sheltering barriers to deal with wind.

This 'average' garden measures 12.5m × 7.5m (41ft × 25ft) and faces east (which is not ideal: south-facing is best). It illustrates how a still-modest space can be productive, diverse, beautiful and practical. The pathways and area nearest the house are all paved (perhaps with old bricks) for ease of maintenance and to control weeds. Gravel or mulched paths might not be as sturdy and grass pathways would be prone to muddiness and impossible to mow. Nearest the house is all the stuff to which you need easy access: a lean-to store for garden kit, a pump from an underground rainwater tank (which, at maybe 1,000-litre capacity, will be all the irrigation water you will ever need), a window box of herbs and a dining area, sheltered with an edible canopy of vines.

Then there's a children's play area and flower/veg bed for them to experiment with, and a flower-bordered lawn with a fruit tree. The vegetable-growing operation starts in earnest about halfway down the garden, with four beds to accommodate the traditional rotation of annual vegetables, for example legumes (peas and beans), brassicas (cabbages, kale), alliums (onions, leeks) and potatoes. There are also permanent beds for useful gourmet perennials like rhubarb, artichoke and asparagus. Using the available space to the maximum – whilst at the same time creating natural beauty – fruit trees are trained along the south-facing wall and also over arches that form a 'living walkway' between the vegetable beds.

At the bottom of the garden is a lot of practical stuff that also provides another relaxing haven. The greenhouse will take care of all the seed trays and potting activity in the spring and summer whilst providing a supply of fresh salads through the autumn and winter. A bench provides a restful spot in a small, fragrant niche of herbs. And then, slightly concealed by a fruit tree, are the compost bins and comfrey patch that are an essential feature of any organic garden. Next to that, shaded by the north-facing wall, is a chicken house and fenced-off run, with room for two hens (giving you a supply of 200–600 eggs per year, depending on breed). The hens also get access to a small 'orchard' of cobnut and hazel bushes. This is permanently enclosed on the north side by a fence along which soft fruit like raspberries can be trained; and in the middle, a fence of wattle hurdles allows the chickens to be 'rotated' on each side of the orchard to avoid too much damage to the ground and to prevent the build-up of parasites. Alternatively, the chickens' space could be occupied by beehives and the ground in the orchard left to develop as a small wildflower meadow around the bushes.

The pond, which will play host to pest predators such as frogs as well as being decorative, is bordered with fences and a bench to discourage small children, but also has a shallow 'beach' area to help its amphibious inhabitants get in and out. And to the south and west of the pond is a wild space of long grass and native hedging which will provide food and habitat for insects and birds.

So this garden will provide the 21st-Century Smallholder with a great deal in the way of food, leisure, beauty and biodiversity. Such an area won't make you self-sufficient in vegetables – far from it – but, carefully managed, it will provide fresh, local vegetables and herbs all year round, a good supply of fruit in season, fresh eggs or more honey than you need. Despite the compost heaps, you will probably need to import fertility in the form of compost or manure, but with a bed system (see pp. 46–7) this can simply be applied to the surface rather than dug in, for a low-effort, 'no-dig' approach to gardening. The eating and relaxation spaces, the lawn and the pond make sure that the space is a haven and not just a market garden; and the wilderness areas will encourage wildlife that the children will enjoy and the crop predators will fear.

Such a garden won't be expensive. With the exception, perhaps, of the proposed bridge over the pond, much of the structural stuff can be DIY: compost bins, pergola, fencing, raised beds, even the chicken-house. The pond can be built easily using a butyl liner (see p. 138). The most expensive items are likely to be the greenhouse and the purchase of the fruit trees: but these are investments that pay back dividends over a long time.

The average garden

A Greenhouse against wall 1.5m x 2.25m
B Potting bench
C Raised herb bed and planter
D Bench
E Herbs
F Comfrey bed
G Compost bins
H Fruit tree
I Cosy 2 x chicken house
J Soft fruit along fence
K Fenced chicken run
L Cobnut and hazel bushes
M Wattle hurdles
N Raised brick gourmet beds
O Wooden bridge over the pond
P Wild space
Q Flow form fountain
R Native hedge

S Paved pathway
T Hand-pump water from tank
U Lean-to storage shed (forks, spades, etc.)
V Wall-trained fruit trees
W Underground water storage tank
X Downpipe with in-line filter
Y Vine-covered seating
Z Bark chips
0 Sand pit
2 Wendy house
3 Kids' garden veg etc.
4 Annual rotational veg beds
5 Trained fruit arches/tunnels
6 Shallow 'beach' area
7 Flower bed
8 Permanent bed
9 Solid bench

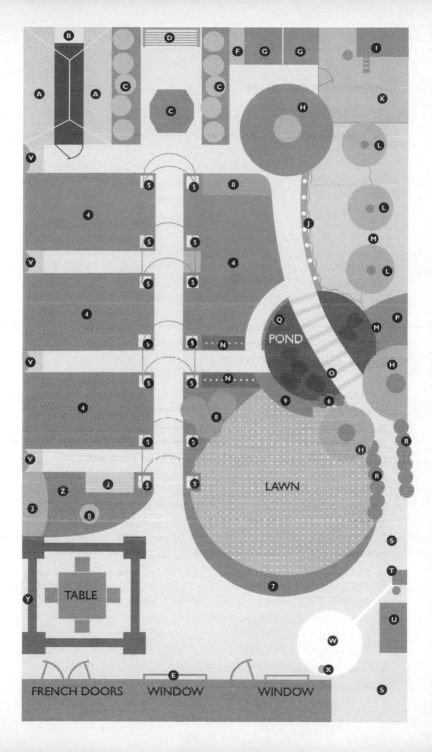

POND

LAWN

TABLE

FRENCH DOORS   WINDOW   WINDOW

The substantial space

For those blessed with big gardens, 21st-Century Smallholding options expand yet further. This example measures approximately 300 square metres: it's about 23m (74ft) from the back of the house to the end of the garden and about 19m (62ft) across at the widest point. This may be big, but it's still only 0.07 of an acre (0.03 hectares) and it's amazing just how much activity can happen in a space that is still a great deal smaller than a real smallholding.

As with all these examples, the orientation isn't perfect: this is a north-facing garden so space has to be left to allow for the shade cast by the house on the food-growing operation. This design has plenty of space for leisure: a kids' garden, generous seating area and a lawn; as well as plenty of growing space. The four rotational vegetable beds of 1.2m x 5m (4ft x 16ft) will provide a large supply of annual vegetables through the year; and two-and-a-half permanent beds will provide low-maintenance gourmet perennial crops like rhubarb, asparagus, artichokes and strawberries. All the beds are arranged north–south to minimize shading and flower beds at the south end of each one provide interest and attract insects. A lavender and herb 'walk' between the two groups of beds will provide scent, flavouring and another reason for beneficial insects to visit.

Like all these designs, this garden uses the permaculture principle of 'zoning', in which things are placed not only according to orientation and microclimate but also according to how much attention they need and how much use they get. So herbs, salads, the greenhouse and annual vegetables are near the house, making it easy to nip out and pick something (or shortening the trip for a night-time slug hunt). The orchard, undersown with a wildflower meadow, needs much less maintenance and is therefore further away. OK, so the chickens and compost bins will need daily visits, but it's hardly an onerous walk. Five full-sized fruit trees will give you a serious crop of fine seasonal fruit; and the orchard also doubles as a chicken run for up to eight birds, who can be rotated on either side of a central fence to make sure they don't damage the ground

and always have a good surface to scratch on. In a garden this size, there's ample space for a couple of beehives too, which in a good year will provide far more honey than a family could eat.

On the east (right-hand) side of the garden are some small cobnut trees, providing another seasonal crop as long as you can get to them before the squirrels do. And there's a pond for wildlife and aesthetic interest: in this example it has a solar-powered fountain. Next to this is another benefit of the large garden: a permanently covered soft-fruit cage. Netting fruits such as blackcurrants, raspberries and gooseberries is labour-intensive and having a permanent cage gets rid of the bird problem for good.

A friend of mine once said, 'You can never have too many sheds.' There will be a lot of paraphernalia associated with a garden like this, from hand tools to beekeeping gear and chicken feed. There's only one shed here, but it's big: and it doubles as a space for growing soft fruit.

Finally, to the west (left) of the house, there's space for a good-sized greenhouse, which can be used for raising and potting seedlings as well as growing heat-loving summer crops and keeping a winter supply of salads going. Just next to this, the wall space behind the herb and salads beds is used for 'trained' fruit trees.

The substantial space

A Chicken house for
   8 chickens
   & rotational runs
B Wild-flower meadow
C Beehives
D Bench
E Herbs
F Cobnuts
G Compost bins
H Fruit trees
I Comfrey beds
J Covered soft-fruit cage
K Greenhouse
L Pond and fountain fed by
   batteries and solar panel
   on fruit cage
M Solar panel
N Permanent beds for
   asparagus, strawberries,
   rhubarb and Jerusalem
   globe artichokes etc.
O Kids' garden
P Wall garden for herbs
Q Annual rotational veg beds
R Native hedge
S Paved pathway
T Thyme and marjoram in cracks
   of the walk
U Soft fruit over door
V Flower beds
W Pump
X Downpipe with in-line filter
Y Seating
Z Salads
2 Wendy house

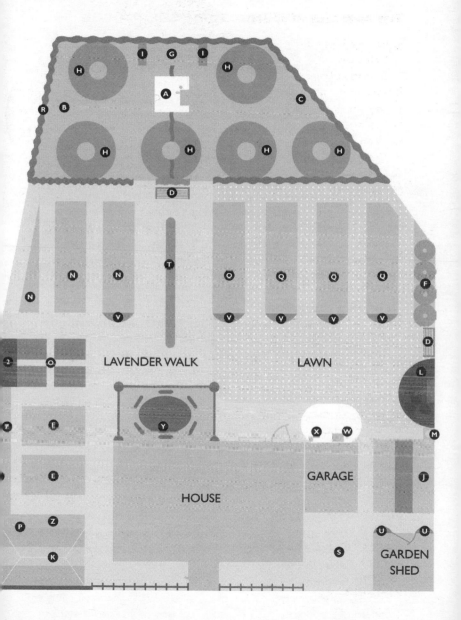

Preparing and managing the ground

'You are what you eat' is a maxim that applies to fruit and vegetables as well as people. If plants eat 'junk food' like artificial fertilizer, then they may grow fast but won't necessarily contain the good stuff that makes them worth eating in the first place. 'Chemical' agriculture depletes the soil, rather than building its fertility. This is supported not only by evidence in the 'developed' world of topsoil loss and erosion but also by studies which show sharp declines in the mineral and micronutrient content of vegetables since the advent of industrial farming. Growing your own food gives you total control over (at least part of) your diet. And it all starts with the soil, a gramme of which can contain more than a billion organisms of ten thousand species. Plants take up nutrients from the soil and pass them on to us when we eat them: our job as edible gardeners is to make sure we replace and build this fertility so the soil, the plants and those who eat them stay healthy. So the ultimate aim of a 21st-Century Smallholder who wants to get healthy plants is to build good soil.

Clearing the ground

If you are lucky and have bare soil all ready for planting, then you won't have to worry about this first step. But for many of us, starting out with growing fruit and veg involves clearing away what's there already. Once you've got rid of major obstructions like paving slabs or unwanted trees and roots, there are a couple of ways of doing this:

Mulching: minimum effort but lots of time. If you have a lawn or an overgrown patch of ground, simply covering it up with light-excluding material will kill off the existing growth and get the ground ready for planting. The thicker the material the better: I learned the hard way that big sheets of plastic can get blown around, punctured and generally messed up. Old carpet or heavier-gauge materials are best. Six to nine months is recommended; leaving the mulch for a whole growing season will get rid of most weeds, but perennials such as bindweed may remain a problem if present. A more immediately useful alternative is a 'grow-through' mulch: a layer of newspaper (several pages thick) is covered by a layer of well-rotted organic matter (manure or compost), then a layer of cardboard, then another layer of compost. You can start planting into this after six months. It is not recommended for heavy clay soils because it might inhibit aeration.

Digging or rotovating: hard work but much quicker. If you want to get going straight away, then more effort is called for. Digging will loosen up the soil and enable you to incorporate organic material into it. It does not, however, have to be an ongoing, onerous part of the gardening year: in many cases, once the ground is dug, you need never do it again (see 'To dig or not to dig' on p. 45). Soil in new housing developments or that has been uncovered beneath paving may well be compacted and denuded of fertility, so digging will be essential to aerate and 'open up' the soil as well as to incorporate organic matter. A rotovator will make faster work of larger areas. 'Double digging' may be necessary if the subsoil is deeply compacted: it involves digging sections of ground to two spades' depth (turning over both topsoil and subsoil) and incorporating organic matter as you go. Turf can also be 'dug in' in this way, if an area of grassland or lawn is being cleared: it needs to be buried at the subsoil level (to stop it re-growing) in a practice delightfully known as 'bastard trenching'.

Testing the soil

Clay or sand? Acid or alkali? It's worth checking before you start sowing. Very sandy soils are easy to work but drain quickly, so need lots of organic matter adding to them, whilst at the other end of the scale, soils with a lot of clay hold moisture and fertility well but can be heavy and hard to work (see 'Improvement strategies') on p. 44. At my London allotment, the heavy clay soil is rock-hard in summer and a gluey bog in winter: choosing the right time to work it is vital. The quick and easy way to check your soil type is to pick some up, moisten it and try to roll it into a ball. If it won't cohere at all, it's probably sand; if it forms a gritty ball it's loam; and if it forms a sticky ball, it's likely to be clay or silt.

As to the pH, this determines what will thrive. As a rule, the wetter the local climate in this country, the more acid the soil is likely to be. The ideal is a neutral pH of 6–7, which suits most things. You may, however, want to create a soil 'microclimate' for acid-loving edible plants such as blueberries: containers (see pp. 46–7) are one way of doing this. Soil testing kits are cheap and easily available from garden equipment retailers.

Improvement strategies

To get soil in the best shape for edible gardening, it needs a good structure and a balance of the major elements – nitrogen, phosphorous and potassium (often referred to as NPK) – that plants need. Artificial fertilizers will provide a 'fix' of these but won't build soil fertility. The best materials to add are:

Compost: garden compost (see p. 48) is an excellent all-round source of fertility and improves soil structure. However, if you're just starting out, your own home-made stuff is unlikely to be ready for a while. You can buy in compost cheaply from some local authorities; and, of course, there's a huge range of commercial compost available. Be sure to avoid anything containing peat: it's good stuff, but comes from an unsustainable source. 'Eco-friendly' compost can be found at good garden centres and from mail-order suppliers.

Manure: horse, cow and pig manure are great sources of nitrogen. Most of the goodness comes from the straw, which contains the animals' urine and also conditions the soil. It is essential that manure is well rotted, or composted over several months, to stabilize the nutrients in it. Farms and stables are the best sources of manure: buying it in bags from garden centres is ruinously expensive as I discovered when two tiny veg beds effortlessly swallowed up fifty quid's worth of bagged manure.

Leafmould: (see p. 50) won't add much in the way of fertility but is very good for improving the structure of hard-to-work soils like clay.

STRATEGIES FOR DIFFERENT SOILS	
Clay	Dig in grit, fork in or mulch with well-rotted manure or compost, leafmould.
Sand	Add copious organic matter and mulch with regular quantities of it.
Acid soils	Add ground lime (but not at the same time as manure – leave a few months after liming before manuring).
Alkaline soils	Add compost and manure.

In organic gardening, soil fertility is also maintained by rotating crops (see p. 55) and by using 'green manures' (see p. 56). These can be particularly useful in smaller spaces as a way of keeping bare ground covered during the autumn and winter. When the crop is mature it can simply be hoed off and left as a mulch, where the worms will do the hard work of incorporating it into the soil. Nitrogen-fixing legumes (such as field beans or winter tares) and grasses such as grazing rye are the most common green manures.

'No-dig' gardening

The traditional image of vegetable gardening is of an annual cycle which involves regular, laborious digging. However, once the soil is prepared it is not always necessary to submit yourself to this drudgery, which can harm the soil as well as your back. As long as your soil is in reasonable shape and not compacted, it is possible simply to keep adding a mulch of well-rotted organic matter to the surface and to let the worms do the digging for you. As well as being hard work, digging can damage soil structure and bring weed seeds to the surface so they can germinate. An essential tenet of 'no-dig' gardening is not to tread on the soil, so it is particularly appropriate for bed systems and raised beds (see pp. 46–7).

To dig or not to dig?

DIGGING	NO DIGGING
Advantages	**Advantages**
Breaks up compacted soil Exposes soil pests to predators and cold weather Kills annual weeds	Reduces the loss of water and organic matter Preserves and enhances soil structure Encourages earthworms, microbes and mycorrhizzas Takes minimum effort Doesn't bring weed seeds to the surface
Disadvantages	**Disadvantages**
Increases loss of moisture and organic matter Reduces earthworm, microbe and mycorrhizza populations Adversely affects soil structure Brings weed seeds to the surface Takes lots of hard work *	Can take longer to improve soil Doesn't expose soil pests to predators and cold Only appropriate for very heavy soils once they have been thoroughly improved

* Some may, however, see this as an advantage: my late friend Helen Stuffins (to whom this book is dedicated) was a highly accomplished organic allotment gardener and confessed to enjoying 'just mindless digging' more than almost any other task on her plot.

Beds and containers

Go to any allotment site and you will see 'row cropping' – the traditional veg-growing practice of cultivating the entire area of the plot, leaving spaces between rows of plants for access to the plants for watering, weeding and harvesting. This technique maximizes use of the space available but inevitably results in some soil compaction, which increases the need for digging.

Far better suited to low-effort, organic vegetable gardening in small spaces is a bed system. If vegetables are grown in narrow beds, the soil need never be trodden on, meaning that, once it is in good shape, it need never be dug and its structure and fertility can improve gradually over time. Because there is no need to allow space for walking between rows of plants, it is also possible to get better yields from beds by having less space between plants. Close growth of plant foliage in beds also helps to exclude weeds; and beds are much easier to cover, for example with netting against pests or with films or fleeces to encourage growth.

The optimum width for a bed is around 1.2m (4ft). If only I'd read up on this before setting out my allotment beds at 1.7m (5.6ft), which is just too far to plant, weed, water and harvest comfortably in the middle of the bed. At 1.2m, anything you need to do can be done from the path.

Beds can either simply be marked out or raised, enclosed with the edging material of your choice: wood, bricks, even inverted wine bottles. Raised beds are useful if you have sloping land, or no soil at all and want to start growing on, say, a concrete surface. However, bear in mind that if you live in a damp, slug-prone area, the edges of raised beds make superb slug habitat. So having edgeless beds (which will become 'raised' anyway as you add compost) removes a potential hiding place for the gardener's arch-foe. In this case all the soil and soil improver needs to be brought in, but this gives you complete control over your growing medium.

The paths between beds (which should be around 0.5m/2ft wide) need to be low-maintenance and able to support plenty of foot traffic. Weeds will rapidly grow on any exposed ground and will invade even raised beds, so paths need to be protected from them. A mulch of chipped wood or straw on top of a base of newspaper looks attractive, but will need renewing from time to time because the weeds will always find a way through. Gravel is a more permanent but slightly less pretty option; and brick paving is sturdier still but needs more in the way of time and resources to build. Grass is fine, too, should your beds have been carved out of a lawn. But the mowing will be fiddly if the beds are raised.

A final factor to consider with beds is orientation: ideally this should be north–south in order to minimize the shading effect of taller plants.

If you don't have room for beds, then anything edible can be grown in a container – whether it's a yoghurt pot with some basil in it, a posh terracotta planter from the garden centre or a stack of tyres being used for growing potatoes. There are two things to bear in mind when using containers: one is that the soil will need to be renewed every year. Containers don't have enough space to keep worms happy – they need a larger range – and therefore they won't be there to do their customary job of incorporating and transforming organic matter and improving soil structure. So the soil in a container will just become depleted over time if it is not renewed. The second issue with containers is watering. Plants in containers need three times as much water than if they were planted out in deep soil, where moisture is retained better and their roots can reach down for water. But if containers are all you have room for, then chances are you'll be close at hand to watch and water regularly. Ideally, though, if you have room to build a few proper beds, they will provide more hassle-free growing than lots of containers.

Compost

Compost inspires great passion, and much discussion. I once couldn't resist buying a T-shirt with the slogan 'make compost not war', partly because it elevated such an ostensibly humble subject to geopolitical heights. I think people get excited about compost because there is a certain alchemy about it. Throw veg scraps and garden waste onto a heap and, in time, all is transformed by bugs and worms into sweet, dark crumbly stuff that does wonders for your soil and thus your plants. Compost also gets people going because it is such a blindingly obvious thing to do if you are growing organically and trying to do things sustainably: with a minimum of effort, it turns waste that would otherwise be burnt or landfilled into free soil improver, produced exactly where it needs to be applied.

Composting is rarely a complete solution to soil fertility, though: it is unlikely that most of us will be able to produce enough to keep all our soil in perfect shape. Unless you have a big acreage and some manure-producing livestock, you will most likely have to 'import' soil fertility by buying in compost or manure from outside (see also p. 42, 'Preparing and managing the ground'). However, there are so many plus points to composting that everyone who is growing anything should have a heap.

How composting works

In essence, composting is the liberation of nutrients from decaying matter. It is a managed process of natural recycling: a similar process, for example, happens completely naturally on a forest floor, where decaying leaves return fertility to the soil. A compost heap teems with life and activity: macro-organisms like worms, beetles and centipedes break the materials down and micro-organisms – bacteria and fungi – digest the composting materials, releasing the nutrients and completing the transformation to compost.

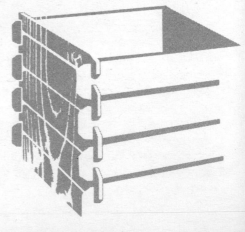

How to make compost

There are three main types of composting – the type you choose depends on what sort of 21st-Century Smallholder you are.

Cool composting

This is composting for most of us. It suits people with a garden or outside space who produce a bit of vegetable waste, grow some plants and read a few newspapers. The heap can be built up gradually and needs little attention. The downside is that it takes a while – usable compost is ready in about a year – and cool composting does not kill weed seeds. The key is to build a decent bin (see p. 50) and to get a good balance of 'greens' and 'browns' (see table on p. 51) to provide the right balance of elements that the decomposer organisms need. 'Greens' provide the nitrogen and 'browns' provide the carbon. Material should either be added in layers, or just mixed as you add it: so, for example, add some shredded newspaper with each handful of vegetable scraps. You can also add nitrogen-rich materials to 'activate' the heap: nettles, comfrey and human urine are particularly good. Peeing on newspaper gives the heap a carbon/nitrogen hit in one go, as well as perhaps providing some ideological satisfaction. Once the heap is full, and sufficient time has elapsed, you can either take off finished compost from the bottom of the heap or – with a multi-chambered heap – cover up the full heap to let it 'mature' and start a new one.

Hot composting

Hot composting is more labour-intensive and it also requires that you start with a cubic metre or so of fresh, mixed greens and browns, which is a lot. But it will provide finished compost much more quickly (in just a couple of months in summer) and the heat – generated by intense bacterial action – will kill weed seeds and disease organisms. So hot composting suits those who are doing a lot of growing or have generated a great deal of waste organic matter. The trick is to mix everything together – browns, greens, activators – cover the heap and then turn it after two weeks or so (or when it has cooled down). This makes sure that everything gets treated to the hot composting process and it also re-supplies the aerobic bacteria with air. The heap will need to be turned every two weeks or so; and care must be taken to make sure it's neither too dry nor too wet. Commercially available compost 'tumblers' can make it easier to turn and manage a hot heap.

Worm composting

If you have only a minimal outside space or none at all, worm composting might be the answer. Worms can eat half their own body weight in vegetable waste every day and turn it into worm casts (which are, in effect, excellent compost) and a liquid that can be turned into plant food. So if all you have to compost is veg scraps and the odd bit of window-box plant, a wormery could be the answer. To get started you can either buy complete kits (which include worms) or go the DIY route by modifying a small plastic bin and scoring some worms from a muck heap or fishing tackle shop. The worms you want are called 'brandling' or 'tiger' worms and they are smaller than earthworms with a distinctive striped appearance. For a home-made wormery, use a plastic bin with a lid and start with a layer of gravel topped with a board drilled with drainage holes. The bin should also have a few drainage holes drilled in the bottom. Then add some 'bedding' for the worms, such as shredded card or paper. Throw in the worms, then add veg scraps (little and often to start with) and keep the heap covered with damp card or paper to stop it drying out. You can empty the heap maybe once or twice a year, taking off the uncomposted layer and the worms (which then go back in the bin) to get at the good stuff. Commercial worm bins have multiple chambers that make it easier to get at the compost and the valuable liquid the worms create.

Finally, leafmould should get a mention. Anyone who lives under trees will have the annual problem of gathering and disposing of the leaves. There are usually too many to add to a standard cool compost heap, but fortunately there's a perfect way of dealing with them. Piling the leaves up in a square enclosure made of wire netting attached to strong poles, and compressing the leaves when they are added, eventually creates leafmould. The process takes around two years but the resulting material is an excellent soil conditioner.

Getting a compost bin

There is a bewildering array of heap-building options for the novice composter. The best rule of thumb is to aim for a main composting space of around 1m x 1m x 1m and if possible, have a multi-chambered heap. So the optimum heap with three chambers might take up, say, a 4m x 1m (13ft x 3.25ft) space in your garden. This is a lot for a small garden, so for many of us a single heap will do the trick. You can buy all manner of posh compost bins (there's even one that looks like a beehive, for goodness' sake) but this is one area where DIY really is within reach of all of us. As I discovered, three scavenged pallets held together with cable ties will make an excellent heap, as will a low structure made of straw bales (which can themselves be composted afterwards). A compost heap also needs a lid (old carpet held down with bricks is fine) and a bit of drainage: if it's standing on an impermeable surface it should be built on a mesh base laid on top of bricks or stones. You can make compost in wheelie bins or stacks of tyres; however, tall heaps made of impermeable materials like this need aeration at the bottom to stop everything going anaerobic and smelly.

Composting materials

ACTIVATORS	GREENS	BROWNS	DON'T COMPOST
Urine	Fruit and veg scraps	Cardboard	Perennial weeds (e.g. dock, bindweed, couch grass, ground elder)
Nettles	Grass clippings	Newspaper	
Comfrey leaves	Young weeds	Straw	Thorny or woody material*
Poultry manure	Old plants	Egg boxes	
	Teabags	Paper bags	Fat, oil or meat
	Coffee grounds	Chopped brassica stems	Cat and dog faeces
	Hair	Autumn leaves	Diseased vegetables
	Vacuum cleaner contents	Sawdust	Glossy magazines
	Herbivore manures	Bracken	

* Although such material will eventually produce excellent compost in very tall bins if left for several years.

Sowing, planting and propagation

So now you have beds full of beautiful soil: time to throw in some seeds and see what happens! You can do that, and stuff will happen – but a few pointers will help you to be more successful.

Most things can be sown in situ (where they are going to grow to full size), but many species benefit from spending their formative weeks either in a dedicated seedbed or in a protected environment where tender seedlings can be kept safe from the ravages of weather and pests.

What this means for the 21st-Century Smallholder is that a bit of planning is necessary, because you need somewhere to put seedlings before they go into their final 'planted out' position. In an ideal world, we would all have a greenhouse which, once it has finished housing your seedlings in the spring, can also be home to summer and winter crops for which our climate is just too harsh. However, we don't all have the money or the space. I found out that a small 'lean-to' greenhouse just a few feet high will house enough seed trays for an allotment-scale veg-gardening operation; failing that, an improvised 'cold frame' (maybe an old window frame on a wooden box) or even a few windowsills inside your house will do the trick.

There are no hard-and-fast rules about what should be sown directly and what should be raised before planting out. Some gardeners prefer to raise everything up to a good size before planting out; others are more flexible. Some general guidelines:

Sow in situ: root vegetables, such as carrots, parsnips, radishes and turnips, because they don't transplant easily; or 'cut-and-come-again' crops like lettuce, whose leaves can be cut when the plants are young.
Sow in seedbeds or trays: leeks and brassicas, because the seedlings mature slowly and take up valuable space in your vegetable beds.
Sow under cover: frost-tender, 'half-hardy' plants such as tomatoes and cucumbers.

Sowing in situ

Sowing techniques vary enormously according to the type of plant. A 'tilth' of fine, light soil is important.

Small seeds (e.g. lettuce, brassicas) generally need only around 2cm/0.5in of soil covering them once sown. These should be sown 'thinly' (not too many seeds together), then 'thinned' as they grow to create the final spacing. Thinning is an unsettling business: it feels strange to uproot and discard your carefully nurtured seedlings. However, the good news is that most thinnings make excellent eating and can provide intensely tasty, early salads.

Bigger seeds (e.g. beans, peas, courgettes, sweetcorn) can be planted out at their final spacing, usually at a greater depth than small seeds.

It is worth noting at this point that the spacings on seed packets are often designed for traditional row cultivation and sometimes for 'competition' size, rather than optimum eating size, which is often smaller. Joy Larkcom, the author of *Grow Your Own Vegetables*, the bible of vegetable-growing, recommends equidistant spacing (which is also ideal for bed systems). Many seed packets suggest a spacing between seeds and a further, often larger, spacing between rows. Larkcom suggests adding these two figures together and halving them to create the ideal space between plants. So if a packet suggests that the final position is 20cm/8in apart in rows 30cm/12in apart, the equidistant spacing between plants will be 25cm/10in.

Seedbeds and trays

Seedbeds can be difficult for the small-space gardener because they hog valuable growing space; and because they are outside, the seedlings in them are vulnerable to the weather and pests. Seed trays (which can be used indoors or in a greenhouse) are more flexible; and module trays (seed-tray inserts with individual cells) are even better, because they allow seedlings to be transplanted without disturbing their roots and with a ready-made 'plug' of soil to put in the ground. Egg boxes make good, cheap module trays. The individual compartments can be torn out and planted when the seedling is ready; its roots will grow through the cardboard as it rots away. Module trays will need regular, attentive watering because they dry out quickly. Some plants (e.g. tomatoes) will benefit from 'potting on' into larger pots, giving them a chance to develop further before being planted out.

Under cover

Some plants will need to be started under cover, either indoors/heated or just protected. Guidelines can be found in 'Meet the fruit and veg' on pp. 64–95. If they are indoors, good access to natural light is essential: seedlings with insufficient light will strain towards it and become 'leggy' (too long) and weak. As they grow – and as the season progresses – seedlings can be 'hardened off', which means gradually exposing them to the elements so they don't get a fatal shock when planted out in the open. In practice, this either means putting seed trays outside in the daytime as the weather warms up; or opening the doors or vents of a greenhouse or cold frame.

Growing media

If you're not using a seedbed, then you'll need something to fill the seed and module trays. An issue for the environmentally conscious gardener is that many commercial 'potting' composts contain peat (a non-renewable resource) and artificial fertilizer. So it's worth looking around for eco-friendly composts, which tend to be made from coir or from peat filtered from natural moorland rainwater runoff. Your own garden compost, mixed with a bit of sand and soil, will ultimately make an excellent growing medium for seedlings.

Successional sowing

It's worth thinking about this from the outset (I didn't). If you sow all your seeds at once you'll get a glut of produce; and if you save some seeds, they might not last until the next season and may therefore go to waste. Sowing little and often, however, means that you get a longer, more reliable supply of produce. This technique is particularly important for fast-growing vegetables that are best eaten young: lettuces, radishes, salad rocket, dwarf French beans, spinach. The trick is to wait until the first sowing has germinated before putting in the next.

Organic gardening practices

Everything discussed about growing in this chapter – natural soil improvement, using a bed system, no-dig gardening, making compost – could be described as an 'organic' practice. However, there are some specific practices that are essential to successful edible gardening without artificial fertilizers, pesticides and herbicides.

Rotation

At the heart of organic farming as well as just edible gardening is crop rotation. Different crops make different demands on the soil, and if they are planted in the same place year after year, the soil becomes exhausted and 'sick'. So the classic crop rotation order of legumes→brassicas→roots→ onions takes advantage of each group's feeding habits (see table below).

The other key reason for rotating is to avoid the build-up of diseases that attack specific crops. Clubroot, for example, which attacks brassicas, can stay in the ground for twenty years; onion white rot can remain in the ground for eight years. To avoid these diseases, as a general rule there should be a three-year gap before returning one of the main rotation groups to the same bed. These are summed up in the table below, together with the other main vegetable groups.

FAMILY	VEGETABLES	FEEDING HABITS
Main rotation groups (most important to rotate)		
Legumes	Beans, clover, peas	'Fixes' atmospheric nitrogen in root nodules, providing nutrition for following crops.
Brassicas	Broccoli, Brussels sprouts, cabbage, cauliflower, kale, rocket, swede, turnip	Hungry feeders.
Umbellifers	Carrots, celeriac, celery, parsley, parsnips	Take nutrients from deeper in the soil.
Alliums	Garlic, leeks, onions	Hardy, need little feeding.
Nightshades (*Solanaceae*)	Aubergines, peppers, potatoes, tomatoes	Hungry feeders.

FAMILY	VEGETABLES	FEEDING HABITS
Other groups		
Cucurbits	Courgettes, cucumbers, pumpkins, squash	Hungry feeders.
Beet family (*Chenopodiaceae*)	Beetroot, chard, spinach	Need fertile soil, can be rotated with carrots and parsnips.
Lettuce family (*Asteraceae*)	Cardoon, chicory, globe and Jerusalem artichokes, lettuce, salsify and scorzonera	Like well-drained soils. Perennial cardoon and globe artichoke can be planted in own space; Jerusalem artichoke, salsify and scorzonera can be grouped with roots; lettuce can go anywhere.

So it is ideal to have at least four vegetable beds to allow for the main rotation groups to be moved around from year to year: having five would give potatoes their own dedicated space, and six would give even more flexibility. However, crops with similar habits can be grouped together, for example potatoes and cucurbits, both of which are heavy feeders.

Green manures

This is the practice of growing a crop whose sole purpose is to help the soil. Green manures can be added into a crop rotation, conditioning the ground between plantings. They add fertility with either their foliage or nitrogen fixed at their roots; and they also provide cover and structure that prevents nutrients being leached out of the soil by rain. When required, they are either dug into the soil or hoed off and left on the surface for the worms to deal with: this should be done up to four weeks before planting the next crop. Green manures won't provide all the fertility the following crop needs: but having something growing in your vacant veg bed is much better than having bare soil. Many of the crops will stay in the ground through the winter, protecting and conditioning the soil. Others work as 'catch crops' to fill the gaps between a crop being cleared and another sown.

Some of the main green manures and their uses are summarized in the table below:

PLANT	USES
Clover	Fixes nitrogen. Sow from early spring to late summer – prefers light soil.
Field beans	Fixes nitrogen. Sow in autumn to overwinter – prefers heavy soil.
Winter tares	Fixes nitrogen. Sow in late summer/autumn to overwinter – avoid dry soils.
Grazing rye	Improves soil structure and boosts organic matter. Sow in late summer and autumn to overwinter – suits most soils.
Mustard	Adds nitrogen when foliage is dug in. Sow in early spring/late summer. Suits most soils.

Mulching

Mulching simply describes the practice of covering the ground with a layer of material: it can be anything from gravel to cardboard, comfrey to compost. The main purpose of mulching is to control weeds by excluding light; it also helps conserve moisture in the soil and can also release nutrients into it; and mulches can keep crops clean and are also an important feature of 'no-dig' gardening (see p. 45). Some mulches and their uses:

MATERIAL	USE
Compost	Apply around established vegetable crops in the growing season to provide nutrients and suppress weeds.
Well-rotted manure	Use around hungry feeding plants when they are putting on growth.
Straw	Around fruit (e.g. strawberries) to keep the fruit clean; or under squash and pumpkins.
Hay	Controls weeds and keeps in moisture around fruit trees and bushes.
Plastic film	Controls weeds, keeps in moisture: crops can be planted through the film for maximum weed control.
Wilted comfrey leaves	Release nutrients.
Cardboard, old carpet, thick newspaper, chipped wood	Control weeds and keep in moisture.

More advanced techniques

Pests thrive in vegetable gardens because they have a large supply of their favourite food in the same place. A big brassica patch, for example, is heaven for the cabbage white butterfly. However, simply putting in plants known to attract pest predators will not necessarily solve the problem; and trying to attract precisely the right kind of predator at precisely the right time is a complex business. It's easier to seek to get a healthy biodiversity going in the garden (see Chapter 4) and to make sure you grow a good range of food crops. 'Intercropping' has more proven pest-control value: alternating carrots with four rows of onions will deter carrot root fly whilst the onion leaves are growing. And intercropping can also be used to get more productivity out of the edible garden, for example by planting fast-growing spring onions amongst slow-maturing leeks. Undercropping works with tall plants that don't exclude too much light: a classic combination is to train trailing pumpkins around blocks of sweetcorn plants.

Weed, pest and disease control

After the different approach to soil fertility (natural fertilizer and soil improvement vs. artificial fertilizer), the next most obvious difference between organic and 'conventional' gardening (and agriculture) is the attitude to weed and pest control. The 'conventional' approach uses herbicides and pesticides to control weeds and insect pests. This gets instant results, which is great, but brings with it a range of problems. Pesticides will kill pest predators as well as the pests themselves, bringing the possibility of even bigger pest populations in the coming year and therefore creating an escalating cycle of pesticide use. Then there is the question of potential residues in food: there seems to me to be little point in growing your own produce for its gourmet and nutritional value if it is going to be doused in poisons through the growing season.

Weed control

Unlike fragile, over-bred annual vegetables, weeds need no pampering and tender loving care: they are perfectly adapted to their soil and climate. As such, they have a major head start on your crops. It is, of course, seriously tempting to zap them with some high-tech concoction when you see them colonizing your edible garden during the frenzied growing season of late spring. However, the most sustainable way to deal with them is by doing strategic things to deny them habitat or by physical control (see tables on pp. 59–60).

A crucial piece of weed intelligence is the difference between annual and biennial weeds, and perennial weeds. The former grow, flower and set seed either within a year or two years. Because their roots are shallower than perennials, they are easier to control by hoeing and therefore your focus should be on catching them before they set seed. (Nothing is more disheartening than dislodging a big weed plant only to watch hundreds of seeds spill all over your vegetable beds.) Perennial weeds persist for longer and have impressive survival strategies that make them very difficult to eradicate. Hedge bindweed, for example, can regenerate from the tiniest fragment of root buried in the soil. To eradicate perennial weeds completely needs either long-term mulching, persistent effort to remove every bit of root or rhizome, or just resigned acceptance and plenty of hoeing and hand-weeding.

Common weeds

NAME	TYPE	COMMENTS
Chickweed, fat hen, groundsel, hairy bittercress	Annual	Relatively easy to control. Hoeing, mulching, close spacing of crops will do the job. Weeds can be composted as long as they have not gone to seed.
Burdock, hogweed	Biennial	Strategies as above.
Couch grass, ground elder, bindweed	Perennial	Harder to control. Dig out and remove all roots; mulch over a full growing season or more; or simply hoe and weed regularly. Avoid composting these perennial weeds: burn them instead.
Dandelion, bramble, nettle	Perennial	Also hard to control. However, these three are edible and useful: nettles are a good compost activator and plant food source and dandelions attract insects as well as making good salads.

Weed strategies

PREVENTION	
Don't dig	Digging brings weed seeds to the surface, where they germinate. A 'no-dig' system (see p. 45) avoids this problem.
Rotate	Some crops (potatoes, squashes) suppress weeds well; others (alliums) are susceptible to them. Crop rotation prevents a uniform build-up of weeds in your vegetable-growing area.
Use a 'stale seedbed'	This involves preparing a seedbed two or three weeks before sowing: exposed weed seeds germinate and can be easily hoed off before the crop goes in.
Space plants closely	Closer spacing of leafy crops excludes the light that many weeds need.
Start plants off in modules	Planting vegetables out when they are better established gives them a stronger chance of competing with weeds.
Mulching	From the extreme strategy of growing everything through black plastic film to applying a covering of organic matter, mulching is an effective way to control weeds.
CURE	
Mulching	If you are able to 'set aside' a patch of ground, a light-excluding mulch will clear all annual weeds in around six months in the growing season and even perennials after 2–3 years.
Hand weeding	The most painstaking but effective way to get weeds out from amongst your crops; made easier by a narrow-bed system (see p. 46). Using a hand tool is essential to remove deep-rooting perennials like dandelion.
Hoeing	Quick and easy way to chop down annual weeds, which can then be left to wither on the soil surface or can be composted. Will also weaken (but not remove) perennials.
Flame weeding	Highly targeted but rather high-tech way of dealing with annuals and perennials.
Permanent war	A regular combination of mulching, hand weeding and hoeing is the only non-chemical way to deal with established weeds during the growing season: however, good prevention strategies and mulching will keep the effort needed to a minimum.

Pests and diseases

There is a bewildering and potentially depressing array of bugs and illnesses that can scupper your edible gardening plans. However, they will only be truly devastating if you're just growing one thing: a garden monoculture of nothing but potatoes, for example. Organic and permaculture growing techniques focus strongly on prevention, by creating the healthiest possible environment for both flora and fauna. They try, as much as possible, to create a diverse, balanced ecosystem in which pests are dealt with by natural predators and diseases prevented by good husbandry. Chapter 4 outlines the broad techniques for creating such a balanced ecosystem and it also lists some of the predatory creatures that should be encouraged.

It is not necessary to know every single pest and disease in detail; however, it's worth being familiar with the most common ones. The table below lists common pests and diseases, while the table on p. 63 outlines the main techniques for preventing and curing pest and disease problems. In 'Meet the fruit and veg' (pp. 64–95), plant-specific pests and diseases – and strategies to deal with them – are outlined.

COMMON EDIBLE-GARDENING PESTS	
What they are	**What they do**
Caterpillar and insect larvae	Eat leaves, particularly of brassica plants (cabbage white); also eat roots and tubers (carrot root fly).
Slugs and snails	Eat leaves, young plants, fruit.
Aphids	Suck the sap from plants.
Beetles and weevils	Eat young plants, flowerheads, buds.
Birds	Eat seedlings, fruit and fruit buds, green veg.
Mammals	Rabbits eat veg; foxes, dogs, cats disturb ground; moles cause structural mayhem (but denote a healthy earthworm population).
COMMON DISEASES	
Potato blight	Destroys foliage and rots tubers.
Clubroot	Deforms roots and causes poor growth in brassicas.
Cucumber mosaic virus	Kills cucurbits.

Slugs

A special mention must go to slugs, every organic gardener's arch-foe. They delight in the organic matter-rich environment that we create, eat almost anything we grow and there is no non-chemical strategy that will stop them completely. The most damaging slugs are the small ones that live just below the soil surface; most slugs also feed at night, making control even more difficult. Here are some slug strategies:

Hunting	Go out at night with a headtorch and tongs, then put them in a bucket and fill it with boiling water. Compost the dead slugs. Doing this on several consecutive nights will severely deplete a garden's slug population but it is hard work.
Trapping	Bowls full of beer sunk into your veg beds will soon fill with happily expiring slugs, who have a taste for the stuff (their only endearing characteristic). The bowls (or commercial slug traps) need to be refreshed regularly, otherwise they will become too horrific to approach. Another trapping technique is to leave a long, heavy piece of wood or slate somewhere on the veg bed: slugs will congregate underneath this in the daytime and can be removed and dispatched.
Biowarfare	Commercially available parasitic nematode worms can be applied to slug-infested areas. This can be expensive for big areas but is good for raised beds (but not for heavy clay soils). The encouragement of frogs and ducks, both slug gourmets, can help control populations, although frogs will not thrive where there are cats.
Barriers	Rough material around susceptible plants can impede slugs' progress. Eggshells, special slime-sucking grits and ground ash from fires are all used. Cloches made from sawn-off plastic bottles can protect young plants.
Disruption	Slugs and snails pick up trails they have used before: hoeing around plants disrupts these and makes life harder for the slugs.

Pest and disease strategies

PREVENTION	
Encourage nature	Planting and creating habitats that encourage beneficial creatures (see Chapter 4) will go a long way towards creating an environment in which pest control happens naturally.
Rotate	Crop rotation (see p. 55) prevents the build-up of soil-borne diseases.
Build good soil	Building good, healthy soil will create healthy plants that are more resistant to disease.
Put things in the right place	Putting plants where they will get the balance of nutrients, sunlight, shelter and water they need will also help them to fight disease.
Be there	'The best fertilizer is the farmer's footprint': this traditional saying can be adapted to pest and disease prevention. Regular attention helps in catching problems early on.
Timing	Planting some crops at particular times can help them to avoid pest and disease problems (for specific crops see 'Meet the fruit and veg', pp. 64–95).
Interplanting	A mix of vegetables and flowers can deter or confuse some pests.
Hygiene	Keeping gardening kit clean reduces the risk of disease transmission.
Cultivar choice	Buy disease-resistant cultivars; be wary of plants from unknown sources.
Deterrents	Bird-scarers work if changed from time to time. Human hair and male urine will deter foxes.
Barriers	Cloches – protect from slugs and birds. Netting – keeps birds off fruit (although make sure gaps are big enough for pollinating insects); also keeps cabbage white butterflies off brassicas. Fences – low barriers keep out carrot root fly; bigger fences necessary for mammals.
CURE	
Physical removal	Removing pests individually (see slugs, p. 62) can be effective; and clearing diseased or infested plants can prevent problems spreading.
Biological control	Insects and invertebrates – a range of predators can be deliberately introduced to deal with specific pest species. Bigger creatures – chickens will clear pests from the ground; frogs, ducks and slow-worms will eat slugs.
Chemical control	There is a small range of 'natural' pesticides permitted under organic rules. See the Soil Association website to find a listing of these.

Meet the fruit and veg

This section gives basic cultivation information for more than sixty fruits and vegetables. At the end of each entry are ratings which score the produce against a number of criteria relevant to the 21st-Century Smallholder looking to grow things at home or in a small space. These ratings are also summarized in an at-a-glance table on pp. 24–7.

Vegetables

ARTICHOKE, GLOBE

This plant has advantages and disadvantages for the 21st-Century Smallholder. It's perennial (and therefore low-maintenance), beautiful to look at and it's a gourmet vegetable, expensive to buy. But it takes up a vast amount of space, with a single plant growing up to 1.5m (5ft) tall and spreading up to nearly a metre (40in). So this is a crop for those blessed with a lot of space, or those who value aesthetics over yield.

Soil, position, climate: doesn't like heavy, wet soils. Needs a sunny site, ideally sheltered.

Cultivation: planting from seed is difficult: it is best to grow from offsets (sections of shoot and root from an established plant). Plants crop for around three years so it is best to keep taking offsets to guarantee continuity. Mulch to control weeds.

Sow/plant: plant offsets in April.
Spacing: 1.25m (4ft) each way.
Harvest: July–September.
Pests and diseases: few problems.

Key: ▥ Space ◷ Time ♟ Gourmet ◆ Season ↓ Hassle ✿ Beauty

ARTICHOKE, JERUSALEM

Very different to the globe artichoke (you eat the tuber rather than the flower head); but Jerusalem artichokes offer similar advantages and disadvantages in that they take up a lot of space but are excellent to eat. The plants additionally make a good windbreak, suppress weeds and, like potatoes, condition the soil well because of their fibrous roots. You will, however, need a lot of room to get a worthwhile yield out of this crop.

Soil, position, climate: tolerates most soils and will manage in partial shade.
Cultivation: plant tubers. Earth up stems in summer for more support, remove flower buds and water in summer to increase yield. Cut stems down to 15cm (6in) when leaves wither in the autumn.
Sow/plant: February–March; plant tubers 15cm (6in) deep.
Spacing: 45cm (18in) each way.
Harvest: October–February; tubers don't store well so should be eaten straight away. Save good ones for replanting.
Pests and diseases: few problems.

ASPARAGUS

This is the ultimate gourmet vegetable, providing a superb eating experience in a short early-summer season. It's perennial, needing little attention once established, and will crop for up to twenty years, but it will take at least two years from planting before you get your first harvest. Asparagus also needs a dedicated bed, making it suited to larger gardens (although it can be grown in large containers or raised beds).

Soil, position, climate: needs free-draining, slightly alkaline soil; doesn't like cold and wet climates. The soil must be clear of perennial weeds.
Cultivation: it can be raised from seed but buying one-year-old crowns reduces the time to harvest from 3 to 2 years.
Sow/plant: March–April (crowns). Work organic matter into the soil before planting crowns 20cm (8in) deep, 45cm (18in) apart, in a mound of soil in the bottom of the hole or trench.
Spacing: 30cm (12in) each way.
Pests and diseases: asparagus beetle, slugs.
Harvest: April–June. Cut spears 5cm (2in) below soil level when 15cm (6in) tall.
Pests and diseases: asparagus beetle, slugs.

Key: ■ 3 (excellent) ■ 2 □ 1 (not so good)

AUBERGINE

Strictly speaking, aubergines have no place in a book largely concerned with outdoor produce for temperate climates. Tropical plants, they grow best indoors or under glass, unless you live somewhere exceptionally warm and sunny. However, this makes them ideal for people with little space, because the compact plants can provide an interesting crop from a windowsill.

Soil, position, climate: need rich compost if in containers, reasonably fertile soil. Very warm, sheltered site needed for growth outdoors: temperatures of 25–30°C give the best yield and aubergines also like humidity.

Cultivation: sow indoors or in a heated greenhouse in spring at 20°C. Pot on into small pots then move into growbags, beds under cover or 20cm (8in) pots when first flowers appear. Allow only 4–6 fruits to grow on each plant.

Sow/plant: March–April (indoors or heated greenhouse).

Spacing: 40cm (16in) each way if in beds.

Harvest: August–September.

Pests and diseases: whitefly, aphids.

BEANS, BROAD

Broad beans are a perfect crop for the home-based, novice grower. They do need a bit of space, but they are hardy, easy to grow, fix nitrogen in the soil and provide a copious, delicious crop that changes through its season. The pods can be eaten when very young; thereafter the beans are great raw or briefy boiled; and end-of-season, tougher beans can be dried or used in soups and stews. It is very hard to match the freshness of your own crop, even at the best farmers' markets.

Soil, position, climate: likes well-dug, fertile soil; thrives in cool climate.

Cultivation: plant direct, 4–5cm (1.5–2in) deep in either autumn or spring. Autumn or early spring sowings can avoid blackfly attack. Pinch out the tops when plants are in full flower to reduce the attraction to blackfly.

Sow/plant: October–December (outside, autumn-sown); February–April (outside, spring-sown). Plant seeds 5cm (2in) deep.

Spacing: 23cm (9in) each way.

Harvest: May–September.

Pests and diseases: blackfly (black bean aphid), pea and bean weevil, chocolate spot, mice.

Key: ▓ Space 🕐 Time 🍴 Gourmet 🍃 Season ⬇ Hassle 🌸 Beauty

BEANS, FRENCH

This is a crop that can provide very good yields from small spaces. Dwarf and climbing varieties are available; and climbing varieties in particular, with their attractive flowers, can be trained well over 2m (6ft) high to add colour to the garden in summer. French beans are not as hardy as broad or runner beans, so need to be planted later or started off under cover.

Soil, position, climate: reasonably fertile soil and a warm, sunny, sheltered spot.
Cultivation: sow under cover in spring or outdoors in early summer. Never sow in cold weather or wet soil. Climbing cultivars need to be trained up tall canes or wigwams.
Sow/plant: April–June (outside). Plant seeds 5cm (2in) deep.
Spacing: 23cm (9in) each way.
Harvest: June–October. Keep picking to ensure a heavy crop.
Pests and diseases: blackfly (black bean aphid), bean seed fly, slugs.

BEANS, RUNNER

A staple of edible gardening in Britain, runner beans are hardier than French beans and provide the same floral beauty in the summer as well as a tasty and copious crop. They will climb over 3m (10ft) and provide a useful screen at the height of their growing season. The pods are eaten before the seeds develop. As with all legumes, freshness is crucial so your own crop is likely to provide the best possible eating experience.

Soil, position, climate: need fertile, moisture-retentive soil (that also allows the plants to root deeply) in a sheltered, sunny spot.
Cultivation: sow direct late spring to early summer. Train up double rows of canes, cane wigwams, trellises.
Sow/plant: May–July (outside). Plant seeds 5cm (2in) deep.
Spacing: 15cm (6in) each way or in rows 30cm (12in) apart.
Harvest: July–October. Keep picking to ensure a heavy crop.
Pests and diseases: blackfly (black bean aphid), bean seed fly, slugs.

Key: ■ 3 (excellent)   ■ 2   ☐ 1 (not so good)

BEETROOT

With a good cropping season and the ability to store well, beetroot is a handy feature of the edible garden. Also on the plus side are its good looks, the fact that it can be eaten at any stage of growth and that the first tasty, nutritious beetroot of the year really is a harbinger of summer. Beetroot is relatively easy to grow and puts up with cooler climates. A large range of cultivars is available.

Soil, position, climate: likes an open sunny site and prefers lighter soil, although this is not essential.
Cultivation: can be sown in modules under cover in late winter or outside from spring to summer. Needs watering in hot, dry weather.
Sow/plant: February–March (under cover); March/April–June (outside).
Spacing: 15cm (6in) each way. Spacing options vary for different cultivars.
Harvest: June–October.
Pests and diseases: few problems.

BROCCOLI, CALABRESE

Calabrese is what most of us call broccoli and it offers the edible gardener the chance of a valuable crop with a long summer season. Freshness is of paramount importance with calabrese, as its many nutrients decline rapidly after picking, so growing your own gives the best guarantee of goodness. However, like all brassicas, calabrese is victim to an army of potential pests and will need to be well protected (with fine netting) and cared for to ensure a successful crop.

Soil, position, climate: will manage on less fertile soils than other brassicas and likes high nitrogen content (so a good crop to follow nitrogen-fixing legumes). Needs an open but sheltered site.
Cultivation: sow in modules under cover (resents root disturbance so doesn't transfer well) or sow direct from April onwards. Water in hot weather.
Sow/plant: March–April (under cover); April–July (outside).
Spacing: 15cm (6in) each way. Spacing options vary for different cultivars.
Harvest: June–October. Pick main head before flowers open; then pick side shoots.
Pests and diseases: slugs and snails, cabbage white fly, mealy cabbage aphids, cabbage root fly, birds, caterpillars, flea beetle, clubroot.

Key: ▦ Space ⏱ Time 🍴 Gourmet ❦ Season ⚓ Hassle ❀ Beauty

BROCCOLI, SPROUTING

This is a vegetable of tremendous gourmet value that has the extra advantage of providing a fresh crop at a lean time in the growing year. The downside to sprouting broccoli is that it takes up a lot of space and its growing season is very long, so small-space gardeners will find it hogs too much of their valuable growing space. However, for those of us fortunate to have big gardens or allotments, this is a great crop for the food enthusiast.

Soil, position, climate: likes rich soil, lots of nitrogen and protection from strong winds.
Cultivation: sow in modules under cover (resents root disturbance so doesn't transfer well) or sow direct from April onwards.
Sow/plant: March–April (under cover); Apri–May (outside).
Spacing: 60cm (24in) each way.
Harvest: January–April. Pick shoots regularly to ensure a good crop.
Pests and diseases: slugs and snails, cabbage white fly, mealy cabbage aphids, cabbage root fly, birds, caterpillars, flea beetle, clubroot.

BRUSSELS SPROUTS

The Brussels sprout is a very hardy winter vegetable that provides a crop over a long season. Like many in the brassica family it has excellent nutritional and gourmet value; Brussels sprouts also offer an end-of-season treat: the sprout 'tops' can be eaten after the last sprouts have been picked. This crop is really only suitable for large gardens or allotments, because the plants are slow-growing and take up a great deal of space.

Soil, position, climate: likes fertile soil with lots of nitrogen.
Cultivation: sow in deep modules under cover or sow direct from March–April. Mulch with grass mowings if not growing well in mid summer; remove yellowing leaves in winter. May need staking in the winter.
Sow/plant: March (under cover); May (outside). Plant out late May–June.
Spacing: 45–90cm (18in–3ft) apart each way, depending on cultivars.
Harvest: September–March. Early-, mid- and late-season cultivars available.
Pests and diseases: slugs and snails, cabbage white fly, mealy cabbage aphids, cabbage root fly, birds, caterpillars, flea beetle, clubroot.

Key: ■ 3 (excellent)   ■ 2   □ 1 (not so good)

CABBAGES

It hardly does justice to the cabbage to have just one entry. There's a cabbage for every season and each has its culinary delights. For the 21st-Century Smallholder, there are a few things worth bearing in mind: some cabbages, particularly the winter varieties, grow slowly and take up a lot of space. However, the more tender spring cabbages are smaller and can grow over winter. Certain varieties can be stored or pickled, if you're going for serious food independence.

Soil, position, climate: likes an open site with rich fertile soil and lots of nitrogen. A cool-climate crop.
Cultivation: varies according to variety; however, starting in module trays before planting out works well for most. Needs watering in dry weather. Cabbages will also need netting against their many flying predators.
Sow/plant: August–September (spring varieties); February–March (under cover, summer varieties); May (autumn/winter varieties).
Spacing: 30–50cm (12–20in) apart, depending on cultivars.
Harvest: all year round, depending on variety.

Pests and diseases: slugs and snails, cabbage white fly, mealy cabbage aphids, cabbage root fly, birds, caterpillars, flea beetle, clubroot.

CARDOON

Strictly for the committed edible gardener, cardoon cultivation takes a lot of space and quite a bit of time. It may be a perennial – closely related to the globe artichoke – but it's the stems of the cardoon rather than the flower heads that are eaten, so it is grown as an annual for eating. The plant is beautiful but very space-hungry: it grows to 1.5m (5ft) high and spreads to 90cm (3ft). And it needs lots of watering and then blanching to create an edible crop.

Soil, position, climate: doesn't like heavy or wet soils and needs shelter and sunlight.
Cultivation: can be raised and transplanted, or sown direct in spring. Needs regular watering. In the autumn, stems are blanched to make them tender for eating with a tight collar of cardboard or thick newspaper.
Sow/plant: April.
Spacing: 1.5m (5ft) each way.
Harvest: October–December.
Pests and diseases: few problems.

Key: ▓ Space ◕ Time ¶ Gourmet ♦ Season ⵏ Hassle ❀ Beauty

CARROTS

They can provide a fresh, home-grown crop nearly all year round and their long, narrow shape means big yields from small spaces. But carrots can be tricky to grow and don't like heavy soils, which can prevent the roots from growing properly. Early varieties mature more quickly and are eaten fresh in spring and summer; maincrops take longer and can be stored once lifted in the late summer and autumn.

Soil, position, climate: light–medium, fertile soils, free of stones. Shelter needed for earlies.
Cultivation: sow and thin to required spacing. Careful weeding needed in early stages, not too much water. Need barrier protection or careful timing of sowing to avoid carrot fly problems.
Sow/plant: February–March (earlies); April–June (maincrop).
Spacing: 7–15cm (3–6in) each way.
Harvest: May–October. Store well too.
Pests and diseases: carrot fly.

CAULIFLOWER

They may be terribly good for you but cauliflowers can be hard to grow and many varieties grow to sizes that are not suitable for the small-space gardener. They need steady growth through a long growing season in order for the 'curds' to develop properly, which means careful attention to watering, mulching and pest control. Summer and 'mini' varieties are best for small spaces.

Soil, position, climate: reasonably fertile soil.
Cultivation: start off in modules as they don't transplant well. Need watering and mulching in dry weather. Protect curds in autumn by tying up leaves.
Sow/plant: October/February (earlies, under cover); March–May (summer–autumn varieties, under cover); May (winter varieties, outside).
Spacing: 12.5cm (5in) each way for mini cauliflowers; 50–70cm (20–28in) for other varieties.
Harvest: all year, depending on variety.
Pests and diseases: slugs and snails, cabbage white fly, mealy cabbage aphids, cabbage root fly, birds, caterpillars, flea beetle, clubroot.

Key: ■ 3 (excellent)   ■ 2   □ 1 (not so good)

CELERIAC

Close to celery both botanically and in terms of flavour, celeriac can also be quite hard to grow well, because it needs a long period of uninterrupted growth. This means attentive watering and mulching during the growing season so the plant can develop a good-sized 'corm' (the plant's swollen stem-base).

Soil, position, climate: likes an open site with rich, fertile soil. Will tolerate some shade.
Cultivation: start in modules, pot on then harden off before planting out in May. Needs watering in dry spells; lower leaves should be removed in mid-summer to expose the corm.
Sow/plant: April–May (under cover); plant out in June.
Spacing: 30cm (12in) each way.
Harvest: September–May. Will survive through the winter.
Pests and diseases: slugs, celery leaf miner, celery leaf spot.

CELERY

There are three options for the gourmet celery gardener. 'Trench' celery, the traditional English variety, offers better eating quality but is demanding of soil quality and needs labour-intensive earthing up or blanching. 'Self-blanching' celery – the type most commonly sold commercially – is less effort but not quite as tasty. 'Leaf' celery is hardy, vigorous and provides the celery flavour with less gardening effort than the other varieties.

Soil, position, climate: needs rich, fertile soil that drains well and retains moisture.
Cultivation: start out in modules under cover then plant out, retaining cover if there is a danger of frost. Slug protection measures are essential, as is regular watering. Blanch trench celery with collars or by earthing up in the autumn.
Sow/plant: April (under cover); plant out in June.
Spacing: 30cm (12in) each way.
Harvest: August–November.
Pests and diseases: slugs, celery leaf miner, celery leaf spot.

CHARD

This is one of the 21st-Century Smallholder's ideal crops. It is easy to grow, good to eat, doesn't take up much space, looks great and crops for ages, even through the winter. Related to beetroot, and also known as Swiss chard or seakale beet, it has varieties in a range of striking colours for good ornamental value.

Soil, position, climate: will manage on most soils, likes heavy ones best. Doesn't mind a bit of shade and tolerates drought.
Cultivation: sow direct from late spring to early autumn, water and mulch if necessary.
Sow/plant: April–August.
Spacing: 30cm (12in) each way.
Harvest: all year round. Cut leaves as needed.
Pests and diseases: few problems.

CHICORY

Chicory is a complicated business. There is a range of varieties grown for eating in different ways: 'Witloof' and some red chicories (radicchio) are 'forced' in darkness for tender and tasty winter crops; 'Sugarloaf' chicories grow outside and make autumn crops of either whole plants or cut-and-come-again leaves.

Soil, position, climate: reasonably fertile, deep soil.
Cultivation: varies according to cultivar. Forcing process needs attention in the winter.
Sow/plant: all year round, depending on variety.
Spacing: 20–35cm (8–14in) each way.
Harvest: all year round, depending on variety.
Pests and diseases: few problems.

COURGETTE

We used to let them grow into huge, bland marrows: now we eat them smaller and call them courgettes. They are easy to grow and a good late-summer crop with many culinary uses. 'Bush' cultivars, suitable for containers and small spaces, make the vigorous, prolific plants viable for most gardens. The flowers are also edible.

Soil, position, climate: reasonably fertile, well-drained soil.
Cultivation: sow in pots under cover in late spring and transplant carefully when established; or sow direct in early summer. Very susceptible to frost. Water until established; mulch with hay or straw.
Sow/plant: April–May (under cover) and plant out in June; June (outside).
Spacing: 90cm (36in) (bush); 1.5m (4–6ft) (trailing).
Harvest: July–October.
Pests and diseases: slugs, cucumber mosaic virus.

CUCUMBER

Related to courgettes and pumpkins but less hardy, cucumbers are largely a greenhouse proposition unless you grow the spiny (and tastier) 'ridge' outdoor varieties. The business of indoor cucumber growing is complicated and tricky, so the directions below are for outdoor varieties.

Soil, position, climate: reasonably fertile, well-drained soil.
Cultivation: sow in pots or modules indoors or in a heated greenhouse in spring, or under cover in late spring. Harden off then transplant when at three-leaf stage. Can be sown direct under cloches. Need watering and mulching.
Sow/plant: April–May (inside or heated greenhouse); May (under cover); June (direct, outside under cloches).
Spacing: 75cm (30in) each way.
Harvest: July–September.
Pests and diseases: slugs, cucumber mosaic virus.

ENDIVE

If you want the distinctive bitter note of flavour without the hassle of chicory cultivation, endive is an easier proposition. It is a cool-season plant that can provide a year-round crop; and it offers versatile eating because the seedlings, cut-and-come-again leaves, or whole plants can be eaten. There are curled (frisée) or broad-leaved varieties.

Soil, position, climate: reasonably fertile soil; summer varieties tolerate light shade, winter varieties need shelter and relatively infertile soil.

Cultivation: raise in modules under cover in spring and autumn or sow direct in summer. Can be grown under cover or cloched to provide a winter crop.

Sow/plant: April–May/August (under cover); June–July (outside).

Spacing: 30cm (12in).

Harvest: almost all year round, depending on variety.

Pests and diseases: slugs, aphids.

FENNEL

The type of fennel we find in the shops and eat for its aniseed-flavoured bulb is Florence fennel. It grows quickly but can bolt (go to seed) rather than form a bulb if sown too early. Florence fennel needs warm, moist conditions to thrive; however, it works well in small spaces and is a very attractive plant. The perennial herb fennel offers similar flavours for less effort (see p. 87).

Soil, position, climate: rich, well-drained, moisture-retentive soil.

Cultivation: sow bolt-resistant cultivars in spring under cover, or sow direct in mid-summer. Needs mulching, watering and earthing up when the bulbs are egg-sized.

Sow/plant: April–May (under cover); May–July (outside).

Spacing: 30cm (12in) each way.

Harvest: July–October.

Pests and diseases: slugs, bolting.

Key: ■ 3 (excellent)   ■ 2   ☐ 1 (not so good)

GARLIC

Although commercial garlic cultivation tends to happen only in the south of Britain, garlic is a hardy plant that needs a sustained period of cool weather to do well. It fits into the vegetable rotation along with onions and leeks and can provide copious yields from small spaces: in *The Edible Container Garden*, author Michael Guerra reports that a raised bed of one square metre can produce fifty-two bulbs.

Soil, position, climate: light, well-drained soil on an open site.
Cultivation: garlic is grown from cloves rather than seed: these are planted in the autumn or winter, flat end downwards, 2.5–10cm (1–4in) under the soil. Only minor watering and weeding needed.
Sow/plant: November–February.
Spacing: 18cm (7in) each way.
Harvest: July–August (bulbs can be dried and stored, depending on variety).
Pests and diseases: few problems.

KALE

Kale should be high on the first-time vegetable gardener's list of choices. It is easy to grow, highly nutritious, extremely hardy – providing a fresh crop right through the winter – and many varieties look delightful too. It also works better in small spaces than its brassica relative, cabbage, because the plants can stand in good condition for a long time, providing a constant 'cut-and-come-again' harvest from the leaves.

Soil, position, climate: rich, well-drained soil; however, kale is less demanding than other brassicas.
Cultivation: sow in modules in spring and plant out in mid-summer, water until established.
Sow/plant: April–May (outside or under cover); June (plant out).
Spacing: 30–70cm (12–28in) each way, depending on cultivar.
Harvest: August–April (cut leaves as needed. Flavour improved by frost).
Pests and diseases: all the usual brassica suspects – slugs and snails, cabbage white fly, mealy cabbage aphids, cabbage root fly, birds, caterpillars, flea beetle, clubroot – but kale is less susceptible to them.

Key: ▌ Space ● Time ▓ Gourmet ● Season ↓ Hassle ● Beauty

KOHLRABI

A weirdly beautiful brassica that provides both gourmet and aesthetic interest and works well in small spaces. Kohlrabi also grows fast, is highly nutritious and less finicky and pest-prone than other brassicas. Its tennis ball-sized swollen stem – like an exceptionally tasty turnip – is eaten, as are the leaves.

Soil, position, climate: fertile, light soil (will tolerate heavy soil) and an open site.
Cultivation: sow in modules or direct; successional sowing is recommended for a longer crop as the plants do not last long when ready to eat.
Sow/plant: March–August (under cover or outside).
Spacing: 25cm (10in) each way.
Harvest: May–November (can also be stored).
Pests and diseases: slugs and snails, cabbage root fly, birds, flea beetle, clubroot.

LEEKS

No edible garden should be without leeks. They provide superb flavour for the kitchen, stand through the winter and give a good yield from a relatively small area. Growing them takes a bit of effort but it's worth it for the reward of a reliable cold-season crop.

Soil, position, climate: fertile, moisture-retentive, free-draining soil.
Cultivation: sow in modules and plant out in mid-summer when 15–20cm (6–8in) tall, 'watering' each plant in to a 15–20cm (6–8in) deep hole. Water until established and weed as required.
Sow/plant: March–May (outside); June (plant out).
Spacing: 10–23cm (4–9in) each way. (As with onions, spacing influences size: smallest spacing will give a bigger yield of smaller leeks.)
Harvest: September–May.
Pests and diseases: few problems, however can be affected by slugs, leek moth, leek rust and cutworm.

Key: ■ 3 (excellent)　■ 2　□ 1 (not so good)

LETTUCE

There's a lettuce for every garden and for every gardener. Lettuce is easy to grow and the huge range of varieties available means it can provide a fresh harvest almost all year round, as long as the plants can be protected in winter. 'Hearting' types such as Little Gem can be picked whole, whilst leaves of 'loose-leaf' varieties such as Catalogna can be picked as needed.

Soil, position, climate: most soils OK as long as not too dry or poorly drained.
Cultivation: sow under cover in spring for early crops or autumn for winter crops, sow successively outside for constant summer supply. Use thinnings as transplants if needed.
Sow/plant: February–July (under cover); April–September (outside).
Spacing: 15–35cm (6–14in) each way, depending on variety.
Harvest: all year.
Pests and diseases: lettuces are subject to a wide range of pests and diseases and problems, from slugs and snails to birds, aphids, fungal diseases, and bolting in summer heat.

ONIONS

This culinary staple is extremely easy to grow, albeit over a fairly long growing season. 'Maincrop' onions are not worth growing in the smallest spaces as it's hard to get a worthwhile crop and they tie up a vegetable bed for a long time. However, if you have a little more room they provide a good yield of high-quality produce for minimal effort; and if dried properly will keep for a long time in good condition.

Soil, position, climate: reasonably fertile soil on an open site.
Cultivation: can be grown from seed or 'sets' (small bulbs); latter is easier. Netting is needed in early stages if birds are a problem: onions must be weeded carefully.
Sow/plant: February–March (seed, under cover); March–April (sets, outside). Or sow in August (plant sets in September–November) for overwintering early summer harvest.
Spacing: 10–15cm (4–6in) each way. Spacing determines bulb size.
Harvest: July–October (can be dried and stored thereafter).
Pests and diseases: onion fly, onion white rot.

Key: ▦ Space ● Time ♟ Gourmet ♠ Season ↓ Hassle ✿ Beauty

ONIONS, SPRING

The onion option for the small-space gardener. Spring onions are selected varieties of bulb onion that are harvested early for their aromatic leaves and small bulbs. Like other salad crops, they are well-suited to containers and raised beds and can be grown closely together or amongst other crops.

Soil, position, climate: reasonably fertile soil on an open site.
Cultivation: successional sowings every 2–3 weeks in spring and summer give a long-lasting crop. Water and weed as needed.
Sow/plant: March–June (outside, for summer/autumn crop); July–September (overwintering/early spring crop).
Spacing: 1–2.5cm (0.5–1in) between seeds; sow in rows 10cm (4in) apart.
Harvest: all year.
Pests and diseases: onion fly, onion white rot.

PARSNIP

Parsnips give a guarantee of fresh produce in the cold months and seem to have been designed for winter dishes. However, they are not appropriate for small spaces as the roots grow large and deep and their lengthy growing season ties up valuable space for a long time. Leaving a few parsnips to go to seed does, however, produce flowers that are hugely attractive to beneficial insects such as hoverflies.

Soil, position, climate: well-cultivated soil, free of stones, in a sunny position.
Cultivation: parsnip seeds are slow to germinate. One suggestion is to sow with radishes: when these are ready, the parsnips will be starting to show. Need careful weeding.
Sow/plant: April–May.
Spacing: 15–20cm (6–8in) each way.
Harvest: September–April. (Parsnips are best after frost; and can either stay in the ground or be lifted and stored.)
Pests and diseases: carrot fly, parsnip canker.

Key: ■ 3 (excellent) ■ 2 □ 1 (not so good)

PEAS

Once a staple food in Britain, peas are well suited to our climate and are one of the earlier crops in the growing year. Because the sugars in peas start turning to starch immediately after picking, it is impossible to match the quality of your own home-grown peas, no matter what the frozen-pea people say. Growing them takes a bit of effort, as most varieties need staking and support to provide a decent yield.

Soil, position, climate: fertile soil with good drainage.
Cultivation: sow direct. Peas need to be staked as they grow and provided with netting or mesh to climb up (although 'semi-leafless' types need little staking).
Sow/plant: March–June (using early, second early and maincrop varieties).
Spacing: 5cm (2in) apart, in broad drills.
Harvest: June–October.
Pests and diseases: birds, mice, pea and bean weevil.

PEPPERS AND CHILLIES

These tropical plants need heat and protection to thrive in our climate, which means being indoors, or in a greenhouse or polytunnel. However, they grow well in pots and small spaces and can provide a productive and ornamental crop for a sunny windowsill. Chillies grown here will still be hot; however, the hotter the variety, the longer the growing season.

Soil, position, climate: reasonably fertile soil; ideally grown under cover.
Cultivation: need 21°C to germinate. Grow in modules and then pot on into 10cm (4in) pots, then plant in final position when first flowers are showing.
Sow/plant: March–April (indoors); plant out under cover around June.
Spacing: 30–45cm (12–18in) apart.
Harvest: August–October.
Pests and diseases: aphids, red spider mite, whitefly.

Key: ▦ Space ● Time ♟ Gourmet ♦ Season ↓ Hassle ❀ Beauty

POTATOES

If you ever want to attempt self-sufficiency in food from a small space, then potatoes will be your staple carbohydrate in the British climate. They can be grown in deep containers giving big yields; however, grown thus they need much watering and feeding. For anyone with a reasonable amount of space, potatoes can provide either a fresh early crop or a main crop for storage later in the season. Potatoes are also good for conditioning the soil.

Soil, position, climate: fertile, deep, slightly acid soil.
Cultivation: seed potatoes are 'chitted' (sprouted) indoors (egg boxes are good for this) in late winter then planted out in spring, 5cm (2in) below soil surface. Mulch or earth up as the plants grow to stop tubers being exposed to light (which makes them green and poisonous). Water when flowering.
Sow/plant: February (chitting); March–May (planting out).
Spacing: 30–35cm (12–16in) each way.
Harvest: June–August (earlies); September (maincrop – can be stored).
Pests and diseases: slugs, potato blight, potato cyst eelworm.

RADISH (SALAD OR SUMMER)

Radishes can provide a fresh home-grown crop over a long season. Easy and quick to grow, they are a favourite with children (at least until they try to eat them and find the strong peppery flavour offputting!). Radishes are ideally suited to small containers and window boxes. They are best eaten when very fresh; another good reason for growing your own.

Soil, position, climate: rich, light soil; need shade in summer to avoid bolting.
Cultivation: sow in succession throughout the growing season. Don't over-water. Thin early (the thinnings are good to eat) and harvest as soon as mature.
Sow/plant: February–September (outside, in succession, at two-week intervals); October–January (under cover, in succession as before).
Spacing: 2.5–5cm (1–2in) apart.
Harvest: all year.
Pests and diseases: slugs, brassica pests.

Key: ■ 3 (excellent)   ■ 2   □ 1 (not so good)

RHUBARB

It may be eaten as a fruit, but it's classed as a vegetable. Rhubarb is a low-maintenance, high-yield perennial crop, perfect for the lazy or novice gardener. The plants take up a great deal of space, but one is usually enough to keep a family in rhubarb through its season. Responding to increasing day length rather than heat, it is the first 'fruit' of the British growing season.

Soil, position, climate: will manage on most soils but doesn't like shade.
Cultivation: easiest to grow from 'sets' or crowns. Plant these in autumn or late winter and water until established. Plants can be divided once established, allowing for some to be 'forced' with a pot or bucket in February to create more tender shoots. Forced crowns should be left for two years.
Sow/plant: October–November/February–March (plant crowns).
Spacing: 90cm (3ft) each way.
Harvest: January–March (forced), January–July. (Don't harvest until second year after planting.)
Pests and diseases: few problems.

ROCKET

This is a 'no-brainer' for the first-time edible gardener. Rocket is easy and fast to grow, perfect for small spaces and containers and extremely tasty, pepping up the dullest of salads. Salad rocket is faster-growing, whilst the perennial wild rocket grows more slowly but has a more pungent flavour. If rocket is left to flower, the small blooms attract bees and are also edible.

Soil, position, climate: will manage on most soils.
Cultivation: can be sown almost all year round, under cover in the coldest months. Ready to cut leaves in 3–4 weeks. Rocket bolts quickly in hot weather – and the leaves become bitter – so avoid sowing (or cut quickly).
Sow/plant: February–June/late August–September (outside); December–January (under cover).
Spacing: 15cm (6in) each way.
Harvest: all year round.
Pests and diseases: few problems; include in the brassica rotation.

Key: █ Space ◷ Time ♵ Gourmet ◆ Season ↓ Hassle ✿ Beauty

SORREL

As a perennial, sorrel is perfect for the low/no-effort edible gardener. Its value – apart from easy maintenance – is that it provides one of the first fresh crops of the growing season. Its sharp flavour goes well with eggs and creamy sauces. Leaves cut earlier in the year taste best.

Soil, position, climate: will manage on most soils.
Cultivation: sow direct in autumn and spring, remove flower spikes to get more leaves (or let it self-seed). Renew plants after 3–4 years.
Sow/plant: October–November/ March–April.
Spacing: 30cm (12in) each way.
Harvest: March–November (cut leaves).
Pests and diseases: slugs, aphids.

SPINACH

Popeye was right – it's good stuff. And perfectly suited to window boxes and containers as well as bigger gardens. Spinach grows fast and is a versatile and nutritious leafy vegetable, best by far when fresh out of the ground. It prefers cool temperatures and has a tendency to run to seed in hot weather.

Soil, position, climate: fertile, moisture-retentive soil on an open site (but tolerates some shade in summer).
Cultivation: sow direct in spring and early autumn. Can be intercropped in summer between beans, peas or sweetcorn. Needs water in dry weather.
Sow/plant: March–May/late August–September (outside); March/September (under cover).
Spacing: 15cm (6in) each way.
Harvest: all year round, using different cultivars.
Pests and diseases: slugs, birds (eat seedlings), downy mildew.

Key: ■ 3 (excellent) ■ 2 □ 1 (not so good)

SQUASH (WINTER) AND PUMPKIN

In the same family as courgettes, pumpkins and hardier winter squashes provide an interesting and tasty crop into the autumn – one which suits perfectly the warming dishes of the cooling season.

They are space-hungry, however. 'Bush' cultivars can be contained a little but more common 'trailing' varieties head off at great speed (and length) and need to be trained, even in big gardens.

Soil, position, climate: reasonably fertile, well-drained soil.

Cultivation: sow in pots or modules indoors or in a heated greenhouse in spring, or under cover in late spring. Harden off then transplant when at three-leaf stage. Can be sown direct under cloches. Need watering and mulching. Train trailing varieties with pegs: in amongst sweetcorn works well. Cut wilting leaves at the end of the season to help the plants mature.

Sow/plant: April–May (inside or heated greenhouse); May (under cover); June (direct, outside under cloches).

Spacing: 90cm (35in) bush varieties; 1.5m (60in) trailing.

Harvest: July–October. Leave on the plant as long as possible: they feel hard and sound hollow when mature. 'Cure' outside for 10 days to complete ripening and ensure long storage.

Pests and diseases: slugs, downy mildew.

Key: ▦ Space ◉ Time ▟ Gourmet ◆ Season ▼ Hassle ✿ Beauty

SWEDE

This hardy winter vegetable is best suited to those with larger gardens, because it grows slowly and takes up a bit of space. Swede likes cooler climates – hence its historic popularity in Scotland – and can stay in the ground in the winter and be stored thereafter, providing a very tasty and nutritious crop that suits the season's dishes well.

Soil, position, climate: fertile, moisture-retentive soil. Doesn't mind the cold.
Cultivation: sow outside in late spring. Needs regular watering in dry weather to stop roots becoming woody.
Sow/plant: May (outside, cooler areas), late May–June (outside, warmer areas).
Spacing: 90cm (35in) bush varieties; 1.5m (60in) trailing.
Harvest: October–December (lift beyond December and store – see p. 126).
Pests and diseases: slugs, downy mildew.

SWEETCORN

Freshness is more important with sweetcorn than with almost any other vegetable. It deteriorates rapidly after picking, so growing your own is the only way to experience it at its absolute best. Even though the plants grow to great heights (up to 2m/6ft), they can still work in smaller gardens, as long as you're content with a modest crop.

Soil, position, climate: fertile, moisture-retentive soil, preferably on a sheltered site. Needs a warm summer to do well.
Cultivation: sow in modules in late spring or direct in June (warmer areas). It is important to plant in blocks rather than rows, because sweetcorn is wind-pollinated. Planting through black plastic mulch, which warms the soil, speeds growth. To control weeds, hand weed to avoid damaging shallow roots.
Sow/plant: April (under cover); May (outside, with cloches); June (outside, warmer areas).
Spacing: 35cm (14in) each way.
Harvest: August–October. Eat immediately.
Pests and diseases: slugs, downy mildew.

Key: ■ 3 (excellent) ▨ 2 ☐ 1 (not so good)

TOMATOES

If you only grow one thing …
Tomatoes are relatively easy to
grow, your own crop will taste
infinitely better than almost
anything you can buy, and the
plants can thrive indoors, making
them an edible crop suitable for
the most space-constrained edible
gardener. A vast range of varieties
is available and there are types to
suit containers and pots as well as
bigger spaces.

Soil, position, climate: fertile,
well-drained soil in a warm,
sheltered, sunny spot. South-facing
walls are good.

Cultivation: start off indoors
in modules then move into
progressively bigger pots, hardening
off when all danger of frost is
passed. Can also start under
cover. Cordon (or indeterminate)
tomatoes grow tall and the side
shoots must be 'pinched out'.
These also need support. Bush or
'determinate' varieties are better
for outdoor growing and there
are dwarf varieties for containers.
Plants in containers need
careful, regular watering.
Greenhouse growing
extends season but can
adversely affect flavour.
Sow/plant: March–
April (indoors or
heated greenhouse);
plant out May–June.
Spacing: 45cm (18in)
each way.
Harvest: July–October.
Pests and diseases:
potato and tomato blight;
slugs on mature fruit.

Key: ▥ Space 🕐 Time 🍴 Gourmet 🍃 Season ↓ Hassle ❀ Beauty

TURNIPS

A close relative of the swede, turnips need not be the dull agricultural fodder crop of reputation. Small, tasty, fast-growing varieties are useful in smaller spaces and they can provide an extra crop from their leaves or 'tops'. Turnips suit cool climates and different varieties can provide an almost year-round supply.

Soil, position, climate: fertile soil with plenty of organic matter on an open site.
Cultivation: early, fast-growing cultivars can be sown under cover or outside in early–mid spring; maincrop varieties are sown direct later in the summer. Need regular watering in hot, dry weather to prevent bolting.
Sow/plant: March–August (outside, depending on variety).
Spacing: 15cm (6in) each way.
Harvest: June–December (maincrops can be stored thereafter).
Pests and diseases: potato and tomato blight, slugs.

Herbs

All herbs are viable in small spaces, priced ludicrously in supermarkets and of great value in the kitchen. Most can be bought as small plants (albeit at more expense than seeds) and most are very easy to look after. Many herbs tolerate poor soils. Here is a list with brief comments:

Basil	Great for south-facing windowsill, greenhouses.
Bay	Evergreen shrub, very low-maintenance. Protect from frost.
Borage	Easy to grow, self-seeds, good in fruit punches.
Coriander	Needs warmth and sunshine.
Dill	Self-seeds, great with fish.
Fennel	Attractive perennial, leaves, stems and seeds all used. Attracts insects.
Horseradish	Needs to be contained as it is very invasive.
Lavender	Attracts beneficial insects, drought tolerant, aromatic.
Marjoram	Hardy perennial shrub, low-maintenance.
Mint	Plant in containers as it is very invasive.
Parsley	Pick the heads regularly for a continual supply.
Rosemary	Drought-tolerant evergreen. Needs pruning in spring.
Sage	Evergreen shrub, needs pruning in spring.
Thyme	Hardy, evergreen shrub. Likes poor, free-draining soil.

Key: ■ 3 (excellent) ■ 2 ☐ 1 (not so good)

Fruit

This is not an exhaustive list of fruit that can be grown in the British climate. It omits warmer-climate fruits such as grapes, figs and apricots that grow successfully only in certain parts of Britain, and focuses on those that will grow in most areas.

Tree fruit

Compared to vegetable growing, which – depending on how you approach it – can demand regular time and attention, growing fruit on trees is relatively easy. And perhaps surprisingly, fruit trees can be grown in very small spaces or trained up and over walls and trellises to provide an edible framework or boundary in the garden. It's getting started with fruit trees that's the tricky bit. You need to know a little bit about four subjects:

Rootstocks: fruit trees are usually grafted on to a 'rootstock' (the root of a compatible tree) which has a particular characteristic. This is done so that the height and productivity of the trees can, to an extent, be predetermined. Rootstocks are also said to make the trees sturdier and more resistant to disease. However, there is a school of thought that prefers 'own-root' trees, which have strong roots, take longer to crop but grow more vigorously. Examples of apple rootstocks include 'M27' (very dwarfing – to 1.8m/6ft) or MM106 (semi-dwarfing – to 5.5m/18ft). So choose your rootstock according to your space and preference. It is possible to buy trees with different varieties on the same rootstock (for diversity and successful pollination); and there are even 'fruit and nut' trees available.

Pollination: the reproductive habits of fruit trees are complex. Some can pollinate themselves (with the help of insects such as bees) but others need similar, compatible trees nearby in order to set fruit. So depending on the reproductive habits of the tree you buy, you may need to plant several trees, buy two varieties on the same rootstock, or have a neighbour with compatible trees.

Pruning: fruit trees need pruning, usually in winter, to create a tree shape that optimises fruit production (and doesn't fall over). Pruning is best learnt by 'apprenticeship'—watching an expert at work—but can also be learnt from books and diagrams.

Training: fruit trees don't need big open spaces to grow successfully. Many can be trained against walls and over garden structures in flat 'fans', 'espaliers' (branches following horizontal wires) or 'cordons' (straight lines). This dramatically increases your fruit-growing options if your outside space is very limited: the lawn can be kept free for the kids and the walls can become an orchard.

Fruit trees should be bought and planted in autumn and winter.

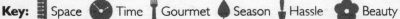

Key: ▓ Space 🕐 Time 🍴 Gourmet 🍃 Season ↓ Hassle 🌸 Beauty

APPLE AND CRABAPPLE

This quintessentially British fruit
can be grown successfully in
containers and small spaces as well
as big orchards. Growing your own
apples gives you access to the vast
range of delicious varieties that
are now so hard to get hold of in
the shops. Crabapples are worth
growing because they are rarely
sold commercially, make great jelly
and have superb spring blossom.
Choose a self-fertile variety of apple
if you only have room for one tree.
Soil, position, climate: rich,
well-drained soil; an altitude
of less than 120m (400ft) is
recommended.
Care: hang up codling moth traps
in spring; remove fallen fruitlets
in the summer and leaves in the
autumn to reduce chances of
disease, prune in winter. Apply
greasebands to control aphids.
Control weeds around the tree
with mulch in late spring; remove
the mulch in the autumn.
Harvest: July–November,
depending on variety. Some later
varieties store well.
Pests and diseases: aphids,
codling moth larvae, canker.

CHERRY

There are two types of cherry:
sweet ones, which are eaten straight
from the tree; and acid cherries,
used in cooking. Acid cherries such
as 'Morello' can handle cooler, shady
spots and are a good use for a
north-facing wall. Sweet cherries
need the opposite spot: a sunny,
south-facing wall is recommended.
Soil, position, climate: rich, free-
draining soil; lots of sun for sweet
cherries.
Care: prune in spring, net against
birds when fruit sets. Need regular
watering in dry periods. Keep 1m
(3ft) weed-free area around the
base of the tree.
Harvest: June–August.
Pests and diseases: birds, aphids,
cherry blackfly.

ELDERBERRY

More bush or shrub than tree, elders
are so prolific in the wild
(at least in England and Wales) that it
would seem daft to plant one.
But they provide two crops – elderflower in the spring and elderberries
in the late autumn – and as a native
tree are great for wildlife (see p. 140).
Elders are available commercially
and provide a low-maintenance – if
rather vigorous – edible tree.

Key: ■ 3 (excellent)   ■ 2   ☐ 1 (not so good)

MEDLAR

You'll rarely find medlars on the shelves; they're an unusual fruit, picked late in the season (November) then left to 'blet' (decay) for a few days until edible. Medlars can be eaten as a delicacy in their own right or made into jellies. The trees are attractive and a medlar tree extends your fruit-growing season as far as it can go in the British climate.

MULBERRY

Mulberries don't turn up in the shops either, because they are impossible to transport and need to be eaten straight off the tree. The trees are slow-growing and it will be up to a decade before you get a crop off a newly planted one. However, the fruits are superb, the trees crop for many years and provide good shade too.

Soil, position, climate: free-draining, fertile soil. Frost-sensitive and need a warm and sheltered position.
Care: prune in winter.
Harvest: August–September.
Pests and diseases: few problems.

PEAR

Pears are a little more hassle than apples in that they are less hardy, therefore less suited to cooler parts of the country. And the fruits don't store so well. Still, if you have good sunshine and shelter in your space, growing your own is the best way to get hold of a perfectly ripe pear. Pears respond well to being trained but do not work as well as apples in containers.

Soil, position, climate: rich, free-draining soil; warm, sheltered location.
Care: hang up codling moth traps in spring, apply greasebands to control aphids. Control weeds around the tree with mulch in late spring; remove the mulch in the autumn. Remove fallen fruit. Prune in winter.
Harvest: August–December.
Pests and diseases: aphids, codling moth larvae, canker.

Key: Space · Time · Gourmet · Season · Hassle · Beauty

PLUM (AND RELATIVES)

Plums are a fine summer crop with a season that can be maximized by choosing different varieties. Gages tend to prefer warmer climates, whilst damsons and bullaces can be grown successfully further north. All types flower early and are therefore susceptible to late spring frosts.

Soil, position, climate: rich, free-draining soil; avoid growing where cool springs are likely.
Care: prune in spring after the last frost, unlike other fruit trees. Otherwise mulch in spring and remove mulch in autumn; protect against aphids; collect fallen fruit.
Harvest: August–October.
Pests and diseases: aphids, silver leaf, canker.

QUINCE

These trees are worth considering for their aromatic blossom and interesting fruit. Quinces make superb jellies and 'cheeses' and desserts. The trees are easy to grow and can be planted in containers as well as developing into large trees.

Soil, position, climate: rich, free-draining soil; doesn't have a problem with frost.
Care: prune in winter, mulch in spring and remove mulch in autumn.
Harvest: November.
Pests and diseases: few problems.

Key: ■ 3 (excellent) ■ 2 □ 1 (not so good)

Berry and soft fruit

Berry fruit takes up less space than tree fruit and can always be grown in containers, making it an option for the space-constrained gardener. Birds can be a problem, however, and if you have the luxury of enough space for a fruit cage, it's a garden structure worth building.

BLACKBERRY

Is it worth growing blackberries? The reason they are so abundant in the wild is that they are rampantly invasive: your garden could quickly become a bramble patch. However, the fruits are superb; and carefully trained and tamed, blackberries can provide an abundant crop, to which you have exclusive access.

Soil, position, climate: blackberries aren't fussy.
Care: train regularly during the growing season.
Harvest: July–October.
Pests and diseases: few problems.

BLACKCURRANT

Most of Britain's commercial blackcurrants end up in Ribena, leaving little for the jam-makers and summer-pudding enthusiasts among us. A new bush takes around three years to come into full production so your blackcurrant crop is a long-term prospect.

Soil, position, climate: rich, free-draining soil.
Care: feed with garden compost or manure every other year; mulch in spring with straw or hay. Prune in winter. Net against birds.
Harvest: June–September.
Pests and diseases: aphids, birds.

Key: Space ● Time ¶ Gourmet ♦ Season ↓ Hassle ❀ Beauty

BLUEBERRY

Much touted as a 'super food' for their various nutritional benefits, blueberries will fit into most gardens, but with one important caveat: they need acid soil. For most of us, this means that container growing is the only option. Two or more bushes are recommended to achieve good cross-pollination and a full crop takes 5–6 years to develop.

Soil, position, climate: damp, acid soil with a pH of 4–5.5.
Care: mulch with composted bark or pine needles, water with rainwater (not tap water) and net against birds.
Harvest: July–September.
Pests and diseases: few problems.

GOOSEBERRY

Gooseberries are the first berry fruit of the British produce year and not always easy to find in the shops, so growing your own is worth consideration. They cook beautifully and their famous seasonal pairing with elderflower should not be missed. The plants are very hardy and can manage in shade, although berries without full sun will remain sharp in flavour. Like all berry fruits, they are well suited to small spaces.

Soil, position, climate: rich, free-draining soil; suitable for cooler climates.
Care: mulch in late spring with hay or straw; prune in winter and summer.
Harvest: June–July.
Pests and diseases: aphids, mildew, gooseberry sawfly larvae.

Key: ■ 3 (excellent) ■ 2 □ I (not so good)

RASPBERRY

There's a long list of good reasons for growing raspberries. Here are just a few: they tolerate cool conditions and grow successfully almost anywhere in the country; the range of varieties gives you a potentially lengthy season; they crop abundantly and, most importantly, they are a gourmet delight either fresh or preserved. Autumn-fruiting varieties take up less space and will crop in the first year after planting; summer varieties will give fruit in the second year.

Soil, position, climate: plenty of compost or well-rotted manure; will tolerate some shade and cool conditions.
Care: always buy healthy stock, never plant where there has been cane fruit or strawberries in the last six years. Provide support for canes as they grow. Cut back canes that have fruited down to ground level after harvest.
Harvest: June–October.
Pests and diseases: aphids, raspberry beetle, birds, viruses.

REDCURRANT AND WHITECURRANT

Related to blackcurrant, these fruits are an essential ingredient of summer pudding and make good astringent jellies: being high in pectin they also help other jams to set. They crop on branches that are two years old, so this should be borne in mind when buying plants.

Soil, position, climate: rich, free-draining soil.
Care: feed with garden compost or manure every other year; mulch in the spring with straw or hay. Prune in winter. Net against birds.
Harvest: June–September.
Pests and diseases: aphids, birds.

Key: Space ● Time ❚ Gourmet ◆ Season ↓ Hassle ✿ Beauty

STRAWBERRY

The British strawberry industry is proud of the fact that, thanks to more and more high-tech growing methods, we now have a fresh strawberry season that stretches from March to December. But outside their natural summer season, strawberries taste tough and bland. Your own sun-kissed crop will provide a gourmet experience that far exceeds anything you can buy in the shops. Strawberries are ideal for small spaces and container growing and can provide a crop throughout the summer. They will provide a small crop in the first year then be productive for around three years.

Soil, position, climate: not too fussy about soil; slightly acid is OK. An open site in full sun is best.
Care: plant pot-grown plants in autumn or spring. Strawberries send out stems that root to form new plants and most of these should be removed, leaving around three to create new plants. Strawberries need to be kept clean and dry so a mulch of black plastic or straw is recommended. The crop will need netting against birds. Start a new strawberry bed somewhere else after three years to avoid disease build-up.
Harvest: June–September.
Pests and diseases: birds, slugs, viruses.

Fruit and veg top five

Top five fruit and veg for the

Complete novice, small garden	Complete novice, bigger garden	Gourmet	Aesthete	Self-sufficiency enthusiast
Garlic	Broad beans	Asparagus	Artichoke (globe)	Apples
Lettuce	Chard	Broccoli, sprouting	Beans (French)	Cabbage
Rocket	Leeks	Fennel	Crabapples	Carrots
Tomatoes	Kale	Quince	Kohlrabi	Onions
Strawberries	Raspberries	Sweetcorn	Medlar	Potatoes

Key: ■ 3 (excellent) ▥ 2 ☐ 1 (not so good)

Vegans and vegetarians, look away now. This chapter deals with raising different kinds of creatures for the food they can provide or produce. The 21st-Century Smallholder will, however, get much more than meat, eggs, milk and honey from his or her livestock. Bees will pollinate plants and improve fruit and vegetable yields; pigs will clear and fertilize ground for planting; chickens will eat pests and weed seeds; and ducks will eat your slugs.

RAISING YOUR OWN FOOD

Throughout history, sustainable agriculture has relied on a kind of 'managed symbiosis' between farmed creatures and crop growing. And it is for precisely this reason that modern agriculture is unsustainable. Rather than coming from animals, fertility is often provided by fossil-fuel-dependent artificial fertilizers that give the crops a quick fix but don't build the fertility of the soil. And such is our appetite for meat in the Western world that two-thirds of our arable agriculture is given over to providing feed for animals. The planet cannot provide for this carnivorous appetite to be extended globally.

Perhaps we should all just give up meat and stop fantasizing about keeping our own chickens, pigs or bees? If we did eschew all animal products, however, organic agriculture would become unsustainable and smallholding impossible. A fully self-sufficient smallholding of the type championed in John Seymour's *Complete Book of Self-Sufficiency* is a 'managed ecosystem', in which everything is recycled and animals are essential to build soil fertility. Take the pigs, cows and chickens out of the equation and fertility has to be imported from somewhere else: the smallholding loses its independence.

What you end up with in such 'closed-loop' farming, however, is, arguably, a perfect diet. It is no accident that the cuisine frequently touted as the world's healthiest – the peasant food of the Mediterranean – is rooted in small-scale, sustainable agriculture. A true smallholder is unlikely to eat too much meat, because the inputs needed to sustain, say, the levels of chicken or beef consumption common in the Western diet are impossible to produce on a self-sufficient smallholding. Try to keep chickens for food in an average suburban garden and you will have to recreate precisely the unpleasant, intensive conditions that put you off chicken in the first place.

It is extremely unlikely that a 21st-Century Smallholder is going to become completely self-sufficient. (If, however, you are interested in the implications and economics of this, read Chapter 7, 'Going all the way', for a practical introduction.) Growing food on balconies or in back gardens means that we will almost always have to 'import' fertility in the form of, say, manure from the local stables, or municipal or commercial compost. Most of us don't have enough space to grow the food to feed the animals so they can provide the fertility that ultimately feeds us.

And yet – assuming it is compatible with your beliefs – there is great value in considering raising your own food, albeit in a way that suits your circumstances. Bees and chickens, for example, will provide superb, healthy natural food in the form of honey and eggs whilst either pollinating or helping to fertilize your garden. And you don't need acres of outside space to keep them happy. For those lucky enough to have more space, pigs can provide great service to the 21st-Century Smallholder before providing great food; ducks can do slug patrol and goats provide home-made milk and cheese. And for those with the space and so inclined, there's even the possibility of a home supply of fish from sustainable aquaculture.

Bees

It is our duty to keep bees. In one of many examples of unfortunate human interference in natural systems, we imported a pest from Asia – the varroa destructor mite – that means honeybees can no longer survive in the wild in Britain. Because our bees have no defence against varroa, the only way to ensure a continuing supply of honey is to keep bees ourselves, managing both them and the pest. But bees are about a lot more than honey: they are central to our ecosystem, because many plants rely on pollination by bees in order to reproduce. As Albert Einstein is reported to have said, without bees, there is no life. It is also said that every third mouthful of food we eat depends on bees. Fortunately, there are many species of bee that can survive in the wild without human management (bumblebees, for example), but only *Apis mellifera*, the rather dowdy, small brown honeybee, can provide us with good supplies of honey as well.

But what is honey? Honeybees are social insects, living in complex and sophisticated communities. What distinguishes them from other bees is the fact that these communities are perennial, surviving from year to year rather than dying out in the winter. Key to their survival is honey, a food source gathered from the nectar of plants and processed within the bee into the delightfully sweet and sticky substance that is so good on toast. As well as being a great source of energy, honeybees' honey also stores indefinitely, so the overwintering colony has a valuable, non-perishable larder to keep it going until plants start to flower again in the spring.

Humankind has been exploiting this resource for around 5,000 years. Initially, we just took the honey from wild bees' nests. Although this resulted in the destruction of their home, it wasn't as bad for the bees as it sounds, because they could go and start a new nest somewhere else. The problem, of course, was guaranteeing a regular supply. 'Farming' bees – providing them with an ideal habitat (a hive) in return for a regular supply of honey – was the answer. The big advance in beekeeping was the introduction in the nineteenth century of movable frames within beehives that enabled honey to be removed – and the bees to be inspected – without destroying any part of the nest. Today, beekeeping is big business (for example, honeybees' value in North American crop pollination is estimated at $14 billion) as well as a productive pastime for the hobbyist or smallholder.

So is it worth having your own honey supply? It's not hard to get hold of high-quality honey these days; and while it isn't cheap, it's not something that tends to get consumed in large volumes. But there are some strong arguments for making (or, rather, letting your own bees make) your own. It's good for your garden: a honeybee colony contains tens of thousands of worker bees who will help pollinate your plants and food crops. If you have a sweet tooth, honey is a relatively healthy way to satisfy it, and can be used as a substitute for sugar in almost all cases.

The medicinal properties of honey have been known for millennia – it has antibacterial and antimicrobial qualities – but these are often lost in commercial honey production. Making your own (or giving the bees the optimum environment in which to make it for you) is the best way to guarantee that all the good bits stay in. The 'cappings' of wax that seal each cell of honey, for example, are most likely to contain traces of pollen and propolis (an adhesive substance produced by bees, with healing qualities). The pollen content of cappings and of unprocessed honey can help counter hayfever; for sufferers, eating locally produced honey is said to be the best way to build defences against local pollen.

And whilst the 21st-Century Smallholder is unlikely to strike it rich from honey production, it is one of the few foodstuffs in which you can rapidly become self-sufficient. A well-managed hive can produce 10–35 kilos (25–80lb) of honey each year, which will give you at least a jar a fortnight!

Finally, it's a satisfying pastime that – like growing your own food – brings you closer to the natural rhythms of the year.

Keeping bees – what it takes

Skill

As with so many aspects of being a 21st-Century Smallholder (or indeed a full-time smallholder), beekeeping is something best learnt by 'apprenticeship' to someone who knows what they are doing. You need to know quite a lot about bees and their habits in order to understand about honey production; and foreknowledge is essential before diving into a hive for the first time.

However, few of us have beekeeping friends or relatives living nearby and the days when households routinely had hives are, of course, long gone. The next best thing, then, is to join your local beekeeping association and get on a course. This will not only equip you with the essential background knowledge about bees and beekeeping: it will also introduce you to local beekeepers who will often be happy to help a novice along. See p. 218 for beekeeping organizations, contacts and background reading.

There's no 'innate' skill needed in beekeeping: everything you need to know can be learnt by observation and practice. However, a relaxed approach to the bees is always good. Working with the bees gently and restraining one's desire constantly to pester them is important and it is for this reason that women are said to make particularly good beekeepers.

It is also useful in beekeeping if you are not frightened of hammers and nails. You don't have to build the hive yourself – they can be bought ready-made (at extra cost) and second-hand ones will of course be already made up. However, making the hive yourself does save some money. I was assured by a supplier that this was a 'therapeutic' activity, something not reflected in my first swearing-laden attempt: there are scant instructions in a flat-packed beehive and all the measurements are imperial. However, it is ultimately very satisfying, not too tricky and, whatever happens, you are likely to have to build the frames (on which bees build honeycomb) yourself. So a bit of (very) basic woodworking skill is helpful.

Equipment

Beekeeping does involve a lot of gear. To get kitted out for your first colony will cost in the region of £300 if you are buying everything new, although most beekeeping requisites can be had second-hand on the internet or through beekeeping associations. New beekeepers are, however, recommended to buy new hives to minimize the risk of disease.

At a minimum, you will need:

Some bees: these can be had for free during the swarming season, or you can buy a 'nucleus' of bees (a queen and some workers) from beekeeping suppliers or specialist beekeepers. The latter option gives a better guarantee of well-behaved and disease-free bees, but may add around £130 to your set-up costs.

Hive: this is the single most expensive item and, ideally, you should ultimately have two in order to manage your bees more effectively (and get more honey). The traditional sloping-walled, white-painted beehive that we most readily think of is in fact the most expensive and least efficient. The WBC hive, as it is called, is heavy and has room for fewer bees and honey that the National hive, less visually alluring but most commonly used in Britain.

Hive tool: a simple tool to prise apart the hive and remove frames, needed because the bees tend to glue everything together with propolis.

Smoker: this pacifies the bees whilst you are working on the hive. The smoke triggers an ancient instinct, making the bees think there is a fire nearby: it causes them to gorge on honey (in readiness for an escape flight) so they become more placid.

Protective clothing: opinions differ on this. Some recommend nothing less than an all-in-one bee suit for beginners, others are less prescriptive. The bare minimum is a veil: a sting on the face is not alluring and a sting in the eye can cause blindness. You can get away with standard overalls (but not blue ones, which bees apparently hate). Or just wear a jacket, long trousers and a pair of Marigolds and make sure everything is well tucked in.

Bee brush: something that gently persuades the bees to get off whatever it is you want to look at. A long feather works well.

If you are building a hive, you will also need a ruler with imperial measurements, a decent hammer and a try square. To extract honey you will need a honey extractor, which removes the honey from the comb by centrifugal force. Even the simplest of these is costly (£100+), so the new beekeeper is recommended to borrow the use of one from a local beekeeping association or experienced beekeeper.

Resources

Bees are clever enough to get all their resources themselves, finding food and water wherever they are. However, if you take their honey in September, they will be left with little for the winter, so you will need to feed them with sugar solution in the autumn so they can build up stores to survive the cold months.

Space

You do not need a big garden to keep bees. The main problem is likely to be neighbours, who may not appreciate that bees are not particularly interested in stinging people, and that even if they do, their stings are largely preferable to those delivered by wasps, mosquitoes and horseflies. The trick is therefore to site the hive(s) discreetly if possible, perhaps building a simple 1.8m (6ft) mesh barrier around it so that the bees are forced to fly off above head height. Such a barrier may also be useful if there are children around, whose curiosity may be annoying for the bees and therefore distressing for the infants. Flat roofs and balconies are also ideal for bees (assuming they are not too exposed) and cities abound with discreet rooftop beekeepers.

Time

Beekeeping is not particularly time-consuming: there is virtually nothing to do during the winter apart from check that the bees have enough food and make sure the hive is OK; and during the peak season of May to July around six hours a month is the maximum you should need to dedicate. An important caveat is that a colony of bees is likely to swarm (duplicate itself) in May/June if the swarming process is not dealt with: although, paradoxically, they are at their most mellow when swarming, a big buzzing clump of thousands of bees can be very unsettling for neighbours. And if the swarm is not captured it may decide to go and live in someone's chimney. So planning for the swarming season – which involves careful observation of the bees and a strategy for managing the swarm – is an important consideration in beekeeping. May is probably not the best time for the unprepared beekeeper to go on holiday.

See also Chapter 5, 'The 21st-Century Smallholder's year planner'.

Money

Once the initial set-up costs are out of the way, the main cost in beekeeping is your time.

SET-UP COSTS (COSTS ARE ALL FOR NEW EQUIPMENT)	
Bees (if commercial nucleus bought):	£130
Hive, including frames + 2 supers (new):	£220
Second hive (not needed straight away, but recommended by year two):	£150
Smoker:	£30
Hive tool:	£10
Bee suit:	£70

Legal considerations, paperwork

There is no law to prevent you keeping bees on your own property; and by arrangement you may well be able to have additional hives in local parks or on allotments (where honeybees' pollination skills are always welcomed). Bees don't need any paperwork (unless they are being imported or exported). However, if you discover that your colony has varroa, or the more serious American Foul Brood or European Foul Brood diseases, then your nearest Bee Inspector from the National Bee Unit must be notified.

Chickens

Chickens provide the obvious entry into livestock for the 21st-Century Smallholder. They'll be happy in back gardens and, as well as producing a regular supply of eggs, will perform weeding, manuring and pest-control duties. Chicken-keeping is, however, worth it for the eggs alone. It's widely known now that 'free range' on an egg box means little more than the fact that there is a tiny door somewhere in the dingy barn in which thousands of such birds may be kept. Organic eggs mean a happier life for the chicken and a healthier egg for the consumer, but even most of these are not a patch on the real thing: a just-laid, still-warm egg heading to your kitchen from the henhouse. Eggs keep reasonably well, but the quality starts to decline as soon as they are laid. So as with so many foods, the longer they spend on the road or in the shops, the less good they'll be to eat. The gastronomic argument for keeping your own supply is very strong indeed. You may have fewer eggs in the winter – or no eggs – depending on the breed of chicken you choose and whether you use artificial light. But maybe this becomes a seasonal event rather than a problem.

Could you also keep chickens to eat? Of course; but if you are an average British consumer of chicken, supplying your own needs will be a major undertaking. We eat around a third of our body weight in chicken each year. So a family of four could need as many as sixty-two chickens a year to feed their habit. Which is a serious flock (given that you'll also want eggs, breeding stock and a cockerel, which the neighbours won't like) and another indicator of the unsustainability of modern eating habits. For most people, eggs and maybe the odd older bird for the pot is probably the most practical chicken operation.

If you're getting into food-growing, chickens have a strong role to play. Using a movable chicken ark, they can be 'tractored' over ground that you want to prepare for sowing. They will scratch away at the ground, breaking it up a little, and, most importantly, will go pecking for weeds, weed seeds and pests, as well as applying a light dressing of nitrogen-rich fertilizer. So if you're a lazy 21st-Century Smallholder, chickens are a very good idea. Practitioners of permaculture, which seeks to create beneficial natural relationships to productive ends, take the chicken symbiosis thing one step further. They suggest building a combined 'chicken-greenhouse' in which the chickens keep the greenhouse warmer at night and the greenhouse warms up the chickens in the morning: if you have a good few chickens and a decent greenhouse, this might be worth a try.

And whilst it's difficult for most of us to get captivated by the personalities of bees, chickens can be much more alluring. Children can make friends with them; they can defuse (or detonate!) family rows; and they bring the fresh dimension of animal husbandry into your life.

It's not all a rosy bucolic glow with chickens, though. At the time of writing a fox attacks our tiny new-laid lawn every night unless I use the celebrated and effective 'male urine' deterrent. I live in central London, in the middle of back-to-back terraced houses, all of which have chicken-free gardens with good-sized garden walls. The fact that Mr Fox is prepared to overcome all of this just to mess with our grass, when all around us are parks and fast-food outlets, suggests that there are more than a few of him in my street alone. Put some chickens in your garden and wherever you live, particularly if it's in a city, the fox will come calling. Unless you assiduously lock the birds up at dusk and take them out at dawn, he'll have the lot. (He may even attack during the day.) So be prepared to lose a few; rats are a problem too.

Making chicken-keeping a little more complicated is the fact that not all chickens are the same. There are around a hundred breeds in the UK, each with its own characteristics and specialization. The broad choice is between hybrids, which are cheaper and offer higher egg yields (up to 300+ per year); and pure breeds, which are more expensive, lay fewer eggs (around 100 per year) but will be hardier and better at the alfresco scratching and foraging side of things. The easiest route for a 21st-Century Smallholder looking for an egg supply is to buy hens at 'point of lay', which means 16–18 weeks old and ready to start laying in around four weeks.

Some popular breeds:

PURE BREEDS	HYBRIDS
Welsummer	Black Rock
Cuckoo Maran	Calder Ranger (Columbian Blacktail)
Light Sussex	Speckledy
Rhode Island Red	White Star
White Leghorn	

Keeping chickens – what it takes

Skill

Chicken-keeping needs no specialist skills beyond an ability to empathize with other creatures. *Secret Life of Cows* author and organic farmer Rosamund Young points out that hens are inquisitive, playful and sociable. If you interact with them at feeding time they will come to see you as being at the head of the pecking order, which makes for a harmonious flock.

Equipment

Another reason for chickens' suitability to the 21st-Century Smallholder is that you don't need specialist equipment to keep them. Your chicken infrastructure could be anything from a home-made henhouse and chickenwire run, through to a top-of-the range poultry ark costing several hundred pounds. You will also need a feeder and a drinker; these can either be created with a bit of DIY or bought cheaply.

Resources

Food: chickens need a varied diet. Most require a 'compound feed' to meet their protein requirements and this will need to be organic if you are worried about GMOs potentially creeping into your food chain. Chickens will also get nutrients from grass and the soil and will benefit from the odd bit of grain. They need grit in order to digest properly and will also enjoy brassicas and greens to peck at.
Water: chickens need a constant supply of clean, fresh water.
Grass: this is what they most like to be on.
Wood shavings, sawdust or clean, chopped straw: to line nest boxes.

Space

What is the minimum space for a chicken? It depends on how 'free range' you want to be. Chickens can live in an ark that takes up only 2m x 1m (6.5ft x 3.25ft) of space; however, this will have to be moved around so that pests and diseases don't build up in the ground. So a grassy space twice this big could theoretically support a few chickens. More room is, however, preferable: ideally they should be able to run and stretch when outside the henhouse. But this still means that most gardens are viable for chicken-keeping. Grass is ideal: it provides them with extra nutrition and is their preferred surface. Bark chippings or similar can substitute if you have no grass. Chickens also need somewhere to have a dust bath.

Time

Chickens won't take up much of your time, but like any animal in your care, they are a tie. They need to be let out first thing and shut up at dusk, fed, watered, cleaned out regularly, talked to and maybe tractored around the garden. Although they can in theory be left to their own devices for a couple of days, ideally you will need friends or neighbours to look after them whenever you go away.

Money

Keeping chickens can be done on a shoestring budget, depending on how smart you want the birds and their housing to be.

SET-UP COSTS	
Chickens:	
Ex-battery layers:	25p each
Hybrids:	£5 each
Pure breeds:	£15–20 each
Housing:	
Home-made ark:	free
Basic wooden ark for a few hens:	£200
Posh wooden ark for 10+ chickens:	£300–500
Feeders/drinkers:	either home-made or £5–40 depending on materials
ONGOING COSTS	
Food:	roughly £12 per chicken per year for organic feed, less for non-organic

An honourable mention must go to the Eglu, a trendy plastic henhouse and run that can be bought complete with two hybrid layers, feed and all necessary equipment for £365.

Legal considerations, paperwork

Chickens are pretty much an admin-free zone. Small, movable chicken housing doesn't need planning permission, and there is no need to register a flock under 250 birds. The only time you are likely to encounter problems is if you keep a cockerel, which will inevitably upset nearby neighbours, or if local by-laws, deeds or tenancy agreements forbid chicken-keeping. Eggs can be sold to friends, from your house or at a market stall, but only to retailers if you are a registered producer.

Pigs

'The hogs are the great stay of the whole concern,' wrote William Cobbett in *Cottage Economy*, a handbook for 19th-Century Smallholders. Cobbett was referring to the ability of pigs not only to provide superb meat that could be preserved for the rest of the year as bacon and ham; but also to the value of their manure, which, when properly rotted down, is vastly superior to both horse and cow dung as a fertilizer. For these reasons pigs have long been central to smallholding life. But what value do they have to the 21st-Century Smallholder? Won't you simply be arrested for having one in your back garden?

The short answer is no (and a more detailed answer is on p. 114). It is possible to keep a pig, or even several pigs, at home. Should you choose to do so, then there is the potential to do anything from fattening some bought-in pigs to turn into pork or bacon for yourself or for sale, to breeding pigs for fun and profit. Pigs also have many uses before being abruptly transformed into delicacies. They are excellent rotovators, turning rough ground into something ready for planting whilst at the same time applying fine fertilizer to it. Properly managed, pigs – originally woodland creatures – have a fine symbiosis with orchards. In return for shade and food they provide fertility and clear up the windfalls. Pigs will also recycle all your vegetable and dairy waste.

And, of course, once they have completed these tasks, pigs provide an amazing range of fine meat. Your own will be better than almost anything commercially available. Intensively reared pigs have a short, nasty life and an unnatural diet; and the resulting meat – flabby, waterlogged and bland – reflects this. Really high-quality, rare-breed pork and bacon are completely different, a taste many of us will have almost forgotten. It's also a good deal more expensive than intensively reared meat, so what with all the other good things pigs can do – and the fine company they make – pigs can make financial as well as gastronomic sense as part of a 21st-Century Smallholder's set-up.

However, once you take on even one pig you enter the 21st-Century Smallholding 'big league'. Pigs need paperwork, veterinary care, lots of food and plenty of time and attention from their keepers.

Two types of pig-keeping:

Weaners for pork or bacon. Pig-keeping doesn't have to be a year-round commitment. Fattening 'weaners' (eight-week-old pigs just weaned from their mothers) is the easiest route. Even slow-growing rare breeds are ready to be turned into succulent pork at twenty-six weeks, meaning that you need to devote only around four and a half months to keeping them and feeding them up. Keeping them for bacon takes longer – about ten months. Taking on two pigs as a minimum is often advised (as they love company) and if you can sell one and a half to family and friends and keep a half for yourself, you could even make a profit. And you'll also get free fertilizer and rotovation services and a fulfilling (if fleeting) relationship with intelligent and sociable creatures.

Pigs for breeding. Moving up the scale of pig husbandry, you could get into small-scale pig breeding. There is a good demand for rare breed weaners for fattening, so keeping a sow, who could produce two litters of at least ten piglets a year, would provide income as well as 'free' weaners. The downside is that this is a year-round commitment, and altogether more involved than merely fattening a pair of pigs.

Breeds of pig and their uses

'Rare breed' pigs are the best option for any smallholder because they are hardier and provide higher-quality meat. Each has its characteristics and its uses, summed up in the table below:

BREED	CHARACTERISTICS	USES
Tamworth	Red-haired, athletic, good 'rotovators'	'Dual purpose': pork and bacon
Gloucestershire Old Spot	Pink-white with distinctive black spots, good in orchards	Dual purpose
British Lop	Hardy, make good mothers, lop ears	Dual purpose
British Saddleback	Black with white saddle, hardy, make good mothers	Dual purpose
Oxford Sandy & Black *	Colours as in the name; hardy, docile, pleasant personality	Dual purpose
Large Black	Black, lop-eared	Bacon
Berkshire	Black with a white face, good temperament	Pork
Middle white	Hairy white pig with rather ugly flattened face	Pork

* Not a true rare breed.

Keeping pigs – what it takes

Skill

You do not need to be an expert livestock farmer to keep pigs: the skills needed are within reach of everyone. The key – as with all animal husbandry – is in keeping them happy. Pigs can grow to daunting sizes but it is said that only badly treated pigs behave badly: the rest, as long as they have good food, company, water and shelter, are very easy to be around. You will, however, need some awareness of the illnesses of pigs and a more in-depth knowledge of pig behaviour and biology is essential if you are going into breeding. It also helps to be able to administer injections, as pigs need to be wormed regularly and injections are the most reliable way of getting the drug into the beast.

Equipment

Getting set up for pig-keeping does need a bit of investment and thought. But most of the kit lasts a long time so pigs become cheaper over the years.

 Housing: although most rare breeds are hardy and happy to be outside in all weathers, pigs need somewhere dry and warm to sleep. A wooden pig ark is the best option for the 21st-Century Smallholder: these are relatively cheap (or easy to build), don't need planning permission and can be moved around.

Fencing: pigs can cause chaos if they get into the wrong places. Wire-net fencing with barbed wire at the bottom is ideal; electric fences also work and have the added advantage of being more easily movable.

Feeding and drinking troughs: these need to be very heavy or set into concrete so that the pigs don't knock them over: cheap alternatives are old butler's sinks or buckets set in cement.

Resources

Pigs get through a lot of resources. If you are trying to turn your garden or smallholding into an 'ecosystem' which manages itself with minimum input, then pigs are probably inappropriate because they need a lot of 'input' in the form of a good supply of high-protein, grain-based feed. Only the much larger smallholding is likely to be able to grow and process this sort of stuff itself.

 Straw: pigs need a supply of dry straw for bedding. They never soil their bedding, but it is good to keep it clean and fresh.

Water: pigs drink a lot, so a supply near to where they feed is essential.
Food: a pig will get through 0.5kg (1lb) of pig nuts (grain-based pig food) per day for every month of their age up to a maximum of 3kg (6lb) a day. They will also need fruit and vegetables and, ideally, access to soil and grass, from which they extract vital nutrients.

Space

Whilst it is theoretically possible to keep pigs in poky urban gardens, in my view it is only really appropriate to keep them if you have a very generous outside space: a field, or a garden of, say, 300+ square metres. Pigs will simply trash a small garden (albeit in an ultimately constructive and fertile way) unless they are tightly confined; and doing that would defeat the object of rearing 'free-range' pork. Space for an ark or sty is essential and the ability to shift the fencing so that the pigs move around on the space (perhaps as part of a crop rotation) is ideal.

Time

Pigs need to be fed twice a day, in a visit that will inevitably take longer than the 10 minutes it needs. Pig-keeping is only a year-round tie if you are breeding; otherwise rearing weaners for pork could be timed to fit around other commitments. So, for example, you could keep weaners and still go on holiday without needing other smallholders on standby.

Money*

SET-UP COSTS	
Pigs:	£50–80 each
Housing:	£250+
Fencing:	£0–500
Troughs, bits and pieces of kit (if bought new):	£200
ONGOING COSTS	
Food:	£100 per year (porkers); £200 per year (baconers)
Straw:	£30 per year
Vet:	£50 per year
Butchery:	£25 per pig

* This doesn't include the cost of the smallholder's labour, by far the biggest item if accounted for.

Legal considerations, paperwork

To keep pigs you need to apply for a CPH (County Parish Holding) number from your local Rural Development Service Office. If you are planning to keep them in a garden, then this may need to be assessed for suitability; and getting the neighbours on side, perhaps with the offer of a few juicy rashers, is recommended. You also need a herd number, which will be supplied along with the CPH number, which must be tagged or marked on pigs sent to slaughter or over twelve months of age. Joining the British Pig Association is essential if you want to sell your meat as 'rare breed' (which of course commands a price premium). You must also keep an Animal Medicine Record Book and complete an Animal Movement Licence whenever the pigs are moved. And you can't kill them at home: pigs need to be dispatched at an approved abattoir.

Ducks

Domestic ducks fit nicely into the 21st-Century Smallholder's set-up. They produce good quantities of eggs, are superb at slug control and are themselves edible. Ducks are also hardier and less disease-prone than chickens. However, ducks have a complication that all aspirant domestic waterfowl-keepers should consider. They need a pond, which is fine, because every garden should have one. The problem is that garden ponds exist largely to promote biodiversity and encourage amphibians; and ducks will munch their way through most of the flora and fauna in a garden pond. So the first rule for integrating ducks into your food-producing ecosystem is to give them their own pond and also limit their access to the rest of the garden, otherwise they'll eat all your veg, too. Like chickens, their housing can be moved around the garden in rotation so they don't completely destroy the grassy surface they love. Also like chickens, ducks are prone to fox attack, so their housing needs to be made safe against this devious predator.

Your choice of duck is determined by what you are keeping them for. There are many types available – here is a short list of popular breeds:

Indian Runner – egg-laying, slug control
Khaki Campbell – egg-laying, slug control
Aylesbury – 'table' (eating)
Pekin – table
Rouen – table
Muscovy – table

Keeping ducks – what it takes

Skill

No need to take a degree in duck-keeping: they are relatively easy to look after. As with all animal husbandry, it's about their welfare and happiness.

Equipment

Ducks need similar accommodation to chickens, with a different door that takes into account their size and walking style. Fancy, bespoke stuff isn't necessary and home-made duck-housing will keep them perfectly happy. The pond is the main bit of 'equipment' needed for ducks: clean water is essential for them to keep their feathers in good condition and water is, of course, their favoured environment. A natural pond with a flow of water is ideal; however, ducks will be content with small, static ponds (made, say, from a small plastic tub) as long as they can get in and out easily and the water is refreshed regularly. It is, however, only fair to give them the biggest, most natural pond possible.

Resources

Food: ducks need food to supplement what they will find whilst foraging, particularly in winter. They need a pelleted feed, and in winter will need fresh greens to make up for the lack of natural forage. Like chickens, they also need grit to aid digestion.

Water: ducks need a constant supply of clean, fresh water for drinking.

Grass: provides grazing as well as comfort.

Wood shavings, sawdust or clean, chopped straw: to line nest boxes.

Space

Confined to a small space, ducks will make a boggy mess of the ground they are on. A minimum recommended outside space per duck is around 2 square metres (6.5 square feet) and the ideal is about 4 (13). This is in addition to the space the pond and the duck-house take up.

Time

As for chickens: ducks are quite low-maintenance. There is a minor difference in routine, in that ducks will lay eggs anywhere if left to their own devices. As they tend to lay between 8 and 9 a.m. it is advised to wait until then before letting them out of their house for the day, so the business of egg-collection is made easier.

Money

SET-UP COSTS	
Ducks:	
Hybrids:	£5 each
Pure breeds:	£15–20 each
Housing:	
Home-made house:	free
Basic wooden house for a few ducks:	£200
ONGOING-UP COSTS	
Food:	roughly £12 per duck per year for organic feed, less for non-organic

Legal considerations, paperwork

No hassles with ducks, as long as your pond doesn't abstract water in a big way or produce effluent, and as long as your duck-housing is not a large, permanent structure.

Fish

Can one be self-sufficient in fish? Is domestic aquaculture for food viable, affordable or ecologically sustainable? Despite the fact that fish farming is not something that the majority of 21st-Century Smallholders are likely to be inclined to undertake, it's worth a look for the interest value alone. After all, centuries ago, monasteries provided themselves with fish from ponds stocked with carp in a form of fish aquaculture which fitted into the rest of their agricultural practices. Despite the emergence of a few enlightened practitioners, modern fish farming is, in general, a ghastly business. Like other contemporary monocultures, it demands unsustainable inputs (pesticides, additives and the fact that it takes 3–5kg of wild or other fish to raise 1kg of farmed carnivorous fish such as salmon) and it creates unpleasant outputs in the form of pollution and animal cruelty.

However, there is another way. See a fish farm as an ecosystem, rather than a resource to be worked to exhaustion, and it is possible to create a sustainable supply of healthy food. Water is much more productive than land as a resource, particularly as a source of protein, because fish – being cold blooded and supported by water – don't waste energy keeping warm or building big bone structures: they're mostly food. The trick is to make sure that this food can be produced in a way that is both economic and ecologically sound; and the key is to use herbivorous fish, which are highly efficient at converting food into flesh. As John Seymour points out in *The Complete Book of Self-Sufficiency*, carp can yield 1 ton per acre without feeding, given the right pond.

Keeping fish – what it takes

Skill
Sustainable fish farming involves a lot more than just feeding fish. It demands high levels of skill and understanding because you need to create a balanced ecosystem in which, for example, animal wastes are used to provide nutrients for creatures upon which the fish then feed. You also need to be an accomplished pond-builder.

Equipment
Surprisingly, ecological aquaculture doesn't demand much in the way of kit once the ponds are designed, built and stocked. If all has been done properly, the main piece of equipment you will need is a large net.

Resources

Food: if you're raising carnivorous fish such as trout, then they will need feeding. Even organic farmed trout – which feed on prawns introduced into watercress beds – need some supplementary protein and this will, of course, cost money. Vegetarian fish such as carp can get by with no feeding at all.

Water: goes without saying really: carp will manage in a pond but trout will demand a constant supply of fresh water from a stream to provide the oxygen levels and low temperatures they need.

Heat: common carp can manage without it but other carp species need a small heated pond in which to breed.

Space

This is the big one with aquaculture. Unless you're content with snacking on the odd goldfish, getting a serious amount of food from fish demands a big pond, or maybe a couple of big ponds that can be used in rotation. This means at least a spare 200 square metres (or about twice the size of an average British garden) just to keep the fish in. So aquaculture ideally suits those of us with a good amount of land.

Time

Assuming you're going for the low-maintenance common carp option, time input is likely to be minimal once the operation is established.

Money

The sums involved in domestic aquaculture will vary hugely depending on whether you have ponds or need to build them, and how low- or high-tech your approach to building them is. The fish themselves are not ruinously expensive: young carp can be had for less than £40 per hundred, although they then take several years to grow to edible age.

Legal considerations, paperwork

If your ponds abstract water or discharge effluents, then you will need to seek permissions from the Environment Agency; a permit is needed from the same organization to introduce fish into any body of water bigger than a garden pond.

Other livestock

Raising your own food works on a sort of sliding scale. It starts with bees, which need the least space and time, then moves on to chickens, which need at least a garden and daily attention. Then perhaps ducks, which have similar demands to chickens but also need a decent pond; and then pigs, easy to care for but requiring a generous outside space. Serious edible aquaculture, whilst very low-maintenance once established, demands even more space.

With the exception of aquaculture, these are the livestock options that are most practical for the 21st-Century Smallholder, who is looking to fit the growing and raising of food into a normal domestic situation. As long as you have a little time and money to spare and some space, ranging from a rooftop to a large garden, then some or all of the above could provide you with food, fulfilment and fertility to varying degrees. Move beyond bees, chickens, ducks and pigs, however, and you get inexorably closer to the world of real smallholding or even small farming. There will be people happy to keep, say, goats or sheep in small places; there are doubtless 'house cows' that live up to their name; but for most of us, getting more involved with livestock brings a commitment that probably won't fit easily into our lifestyles or, indeed, our gardens.

If your property includes several acres of land, however, then there are obvious arguments for going further with livestock. Cows will convert grass into milk, cream and butter whose quality will exceed anything you can buy and they provide fertility in the form of manure. Sheep will turn marginal land into fine meat. And a 'polyculture' of animals creates relationships that are beneficial for the land, the animals and thus the smallholder. Clearing woodland, for example, could be started by goats (which love woody stuff) and then continued by pigs, which will root and turn the soil. Cattle will graze the long grass, leaving the shorter stuff for sheep. And a combination of animals will help to reduce the build-up of pests and diseases. So for those 21st-Century Smallholders thinking about 'going all the way' (see Chapter 7), here's a brief summary of some of the issues involved in getting into more serious livestock.

● **Geese:** their eggs taste good, and so does their meat; and they are additionally famed for their role as 'guard dogs'. But their size and the noise they make means geese are less compatible with 21st-Century Smallholding.

● **Goats:** they're small and produce superb dairy products (goat's milk and cheese does not seem to provoke the same intolerances and allergies as cow's milk). Goats would seem the perfect choice for the 21st-Century Smallholder. It's their eating habits that let them down. If allowed, goats will rapidly lay waste to your edible (and ornamental) gardening efforts. As John Seymour, speaking of the goat enthusiast, puts it in *The Complete Book of Self-Sufficiency*: 'What he forgets about is that goats have 24 hours a day to plan to get into his garden, and he doesn't.' Your choices for restraint are either serious fencing, or tethering: which means either expense or a certain unkindness to an animal. Goats also need housing and, of course, milking.

● **Sheep:** the main thing sheep bring to the party is their ability to graze on marginal land and turn its meagre output into high-quality meat as well as wool, enabling you to be self-sufficient in cardigans as well as

RAISING FOOD: SUMMARY

	Skill	Equipment	Resources	Space	Time	Money
Bees	2	2	1	1	1	2
Chickens	1	2	2	2	2	1
Pigs	1	2	3	3	3	2
Ducks	1	2	2	3	2	2
Fish	4	1	3	4	2	3
Geese	1	2	2	3	2	2
Goats	2	2	2	3	3	2
Sheep	2	2	2	4	2	2
Cows	4	3	4	4	4	4

Key: 4 = lots, 1 = minimum

protein. The reason sheep need more space than most 21st-Century Smallholders can provide is that they are susceptible to parasites that build up in the soil and are therefore best rotated with other animals. Also – and this applies to geese too – the ease with which you can buy superb organic and free-range produce (and thus encourage better agriculture) outweighs the hassle of growing your own in most situations.

Cows: there is a school of thought that says pasteurization removes much of the goodness from milk and may be at the heart of some of the health problems (such as intolerance) ascribed to dairy products. With 'green-top' (unpasteurized) milk hard to get hold of and under assault from legislators who would have its sale banned completely, a 'house cow' is the best way to get your own supply. This is just one of the many reasons for keeping cows: but this level of animal husbandry requires a very great deal of commitment. Cows must have a calf in order to produce milk, need careful and copious winter feeding, daily milking, much paperwork and lots of space for grazing. Only for the committed smallholder with plenty of land.

Legal, Admin.	Comments
🪶	The easiest way into raising food. Need some expertise and apprenticeship and maybe a few hundred quid to set up.
🪶	Cheap, easy, useful and happy in all but the smallest gardens. Need daily, year-round attention, though.
🪶🪶🪶	Very useful and productive, but for big gardens only. Daily attention essential, as is (some) paperwork. Not expensive to keep, but need housing, feeding and fencing.
🪶	Need similar attention to chickens, but also require a dedicated pond, so a bigger overall space is best.
🪶🪶	Vast outside space needed to accommodate worthwhile aquaculture. Low-maintenance once set up, though.
🪶	Noisy and bad-tempered. How much goose do you want to eat?
🪶🪶	Useful, but hard to contain destructive eating habits.
🪶🪶	Best if you have your own hillside.
🪶🪶🪶🪶	The centrepiece of a self-sufficient smallholding, but exact a heavy price in time and effort.

It's all very well growing and raising all this food, but what happens when it's ready? Many crops can be picked through a long growing season: winter leeks and cabbages, for example, will stay in the ground until you want them, and salads can be picked for the leaves if they are 'cut-and-come-again' varieties, or as whole plants over a long period if you sow in succession (see p. 54). Some crops will, however, present you with a glut, providing you with a big yield in a short season. There would be no point in growing just enough tomatoes or potatoes to eat when they are ready: you wouldn't be eating them for very long and it would be a criminal waste of a lot of growing effort!

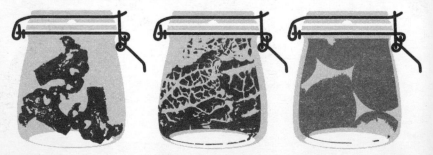

GETTING
THE MOST FROM YOUR
HOME
HARVEST

Complete your first, tentative fruit- and vegetable-growing season and the remarkable skills of our peasant forebears become apparent. You need not only to be able to plan, sow and manage crops, but also to know how to deal effectively with the surplus your efforts inevitably create. Our ancestors mastered both of these out of necessity, creating a year-round food supply with no recourse to freezers, high technology or air-freighting. And the same applies to (some of) your livestock activities. You've killed your pigs – so now what?

Unless you 'go all the way' to a life of fully self-sufficient smallholding, you are never going to be dependent on your own stored or preserved produce for survival. Professional farmers and growers take care of this for us, ensuring that there is always something available. But there's little point in getting into growing and raising your own food if you're not also going to consider how to spin out your harvest. Not for survival, but for the sheer pleasure of having your own stuff available for as long as possible. And also for pride: there's nothing worse than watching all that effort of sowing, propagating, potting, planting out, protecting, feeding, watering and harvesting disappear in a mushy, rotting mess. It's a lot of work if all you get for your efforts is some extra compost!

Storing and preserving fruit and vegetables

Although careful planning and sowing can provide a near year-round harvest for pretty much all fruit and for many vegetables, the harvest is over quickly. If you are growing on an allotment or large-garden scale, there may simply be too much to eat.

What you do with your cornucopia depends on what it is. Different produce responds to different treatments – and some things just need to be eaten. The table below gives a (slightly subjective) summary of this and may also help in planning your edible gardening year.

For example, it illustrates that there's no need to be worried about a cabbage glut: not only do most cabbages stay happily in the ground until you are ready to eat them, they can also be stored or pickled (say, as sauerkraut or the fiery Korean staple kimchi). On the other hand, an excess of sweetcorn should be the subject of a large barbecue or party. Sweetcorn can be dried and stored, but the real pleasure is in cooking the sun-kissed cob as soon as it has been picked.

	FRUIT	VEG
Stores well	Apples, Pears (not early varieties)	Beetroot, Cabbage, Carrot, Garlic, Kohlrabi, Onion, Parsnip, Potato, Pumpkin, Swede, Turnip
Good for bottling	All fruits	Tomato
Makes delightful things (e.g. pickles, preserves, wine*)	All fruits	Aubergine, Cabbage, Cauliflower, Courgette, Cucumber, Onion, Tomato
Can be dried	Apples, Damsons, Plums	Beans, Peas, Tomato
Freezes well	Berry fruits, Apples and Pears (if puréed)	Broad beans, Broccoli, Calabrese, French beans, Peas, Runner beans
Lasts well on the plant or in the ground	Rhubarb	Artichoke (Jerusalem), Beetroot, Broccoli (sprouting), Brussels sprouts, Cabbage, Carrot, Cauliflower, Celeriac, Celery, Chard, Chicory, Kale, Leeks, Lettuce and Salads, Parsnip, Swede, Turnip
Eat when ready: few or no good storage or preservation options		Artichoke (globe), Asparagus, Cardoon, Radish, Sweetcorn

* Almost any fruit or vegetable can be turned into wine. Parsnip, anyone?

Storage

A problem with many traditional ways of preserving the harvest is that techniques like bottling, pickling and drying take a bit of time and effort. Storage, on the other hand, is much easier, but it does demand that you have some space and the right kind of environment to keep your produce happy. Start thinking about where to put all those apples or onions and you rapidly realize that most houses were not designed with long-term vegetable storage in mind.

Ideally, you need somewhere dark, well ventilated and with a reasonably cool and constant temperature. Owners of cellars or large pantries are in luck. Attics are OK, but only during the coldest months because they are prone to heating up too much. Otherwise it is possible to build some storage space if you have the room outside. At the simplest level this could a clamp (see below). Or if you have more space, time and a bit of budget, a shed or, even better, a modest straw-bale outbuilding (secured against mice and rats) could be the thing. If there's nowhere cool and dark in the house, then it's probably best to look to more labour-intensive (but very rewarding) ways of spinning out your harvest, such as bottling or preserving.

The key to good storage is to make sure your crops are unblemished and disease-free before being laid down. Many will last until early spring before the desire to rot or sprout finally takes over.

 Clamping: this works for potatoes and root vegetables and involves letting the crop dry out after lifting before creating a pyramidal pile which is then covered with straw followed by a thick layer of earth. Such enclosure makes the picked crop 'respire', which increases the concentration of carbon dioxide and reduces the oxygen level in the clamp, slowing decay. Roots and spuds can alternatively be stored in earth, in boxes in a cellar or a cool, dark place.

Storing on racks or shelves: slatted containers that allow good air circulation are best for things like apples, onions and squashes. Apples and pears should be individually wrapped in paper before storing.

Bottling

This needs some equipment but is worth considering if you simply don't have the time or energy to make vast quantities of jam or chutney or don't have a big freezer. Bottling involves sterilizing the produce by cooking it in sealed jars from which air is also expelled by the process to create a vacuum. All fruit can be bottled; and tomatoes bottle particularly well. If vegetables are to be bottled it should be in a pressure cooker, which really does sound too complicated to bother with. To do bottling you will need:

'Kilner' or equivalent thick glass storage jars with rubber seals and tight-fitting lids.

A sterilizer or large pan (like a preserving pan) in which the jars can be boiled.

The process involves boiling the (sterilized) jars of prepared produce for a specific period of time. It is quite labour-intensive; and many with good-sized freezers will probably use them instead. However, if you have lots of shelves, lots of produce and don't fancy freezing, bottling is a practical (and good-looking) option.

Making delightful things

Before the advent of canning and freezers, we had to be inventive about storing food. And the big difference between modern and traditional methods is that the latter often transformed food into something new. Jams, chutneys, pickles (and even wine) not only preserve your harvest for years to come: they create delightful things in their own right. And there's no neighbourhood currency like a good jar of your own jam or chutney, or a bottle of successful country wine. Bookshops and the internet are overflowing with jam- and wine-making guides, so here is just a brief overview:

- **Pickling:** this preserves food by using acid to prevent the enzyme action that spoils food. In chutneys and pickles, vinegar is the active agent, whilst in, say, sauerkraut, fermentation by lactic acid-producing bacteria works on the enzymes. Both methods are easy; but the products (and smells) of the latter are not to everyone's taste.
- **Jams and jellies:** these work by cooking the food to destroy enzymes; the sugar stops the work of bacteria and other micro-organisms.
- **Wine:** wine (and cider and perry) are fine homes for seasonal surpluses – the alcohol does the job of preserving.

Making pickles and jam is an easy, satisfying ritual that fills the house with seasonal smells and the shelves with long-lasting produce. It's not particularly cost-effective, as both products are commercially cheap to buy and you'll need a lot of sugar and a bit of time to make your own; but your own is somehow always best. Wine-making is a slightly bigger commitment, needing a minor investment in demijohns and fermentation locks, but simple country wines are easy to make.

Drying

This is a technique that used to sustain peasant Britain many hundreds of years ago: dried peas were what kept the people going through the winter. Is it worth it today? The legumes (beans and peas) that store so well are also at their best when utterly fresh, and it seems a lot of effort to dry them unless it is a matter of survival or hard-core gourmet behaviour. Apples, cored and sliced, can be strung up over heat until crisp and dry, whereafter they will store well and taste great. You can even make your own prunes or sun-dried tomatoes, although the temptation of fresh produce and fine jams and pickles seems to me at least to outweigh the hassle involved.

Freezing

Smallholding purists may eschew the freezer on financial, philosophical and ecological grounds; but the fact is that most of us have one and they are very effective at preserving some fruit and veg, crucially with most of their nutrients intact. And I bet our ancestors would have jumped at the possibility of raspberries in the depths of winter. Beyond the purist's concerns, there are a couple of other issues with freezing: there isn't much room in many freezers and, also, some are prone to breaking down. But if you have a big, reliable freezer and a huge berry-fruit harvest, for example, it's hard to resist stocking up for winter. Some tips for freezing:

- Blanch vegetables first in boiling water for 1–2 minutes to destroy enzymes.
- Freeze separated fruit and veg on a tray first to stop them forming a solid block, then transfer to bags or tubs.
- Use well-sealed bags and tubs to avoid 'freezer burn'.
- Purée orchard fruits before freezing.

Preserving Livestock

The vast majority of 21st-Century Smallholders will not be concerned with how to store or preserve their livestock. If you are lucky enough to have enough chickens to be able to eat the odd one, then you'll probably want to eat it straight away. Ditto ducks; and any fish farmers among us will be able to take what they need, when they want it. No need to worry about curing carp.

Pigs are where you will need to worry about storage and preserving. Kill a pig and you get enough meat to last a long time (up to 74 kg/165lb for a 'baconer'). If it's a porker (grown for fresh meat rather than bacon) then there's no complication: once slaughtered and butchered, the animal goes straight into the (big) freezer, giving you a long-term supply of home-grown meat.

If, however, you've raised your pigs for bacon, then there is work to do. This was the traditional smallholding practice in the days before freezers: pigs were fattened through the year and then slaughtered in November, providing fleeting treats of black pudding, offal and pork before the bulk of the animal turned into bacon and ham to last through the winter and beyond. Learn about the ghastly industrial process in which the majority of bacon and ham is produced these days and you will be highly motivated either to seek out traditionally prepared meat or even to grow and prepare your own. Preservation techniques for pork include:

◆ **Dry-curing:** traditionally used for bacon, this involves rubbing a salt/sugar mix into the meat repeatedly, over a period of up to three weeks, depending on the size of the cut. The salt and sugar suppress enzyme action and bacterial activity. The resulting bacon must then be hung in a cool, dry place and can additionally be smoked (see below).

◆ **Brine-curing:** hams can be cured by being submerged in a brine solution, then hung as for bacon before the optional smoking.

◆ **Air-drying:** more commonly associated with continental Europe, for hams this involves salt-curing then lengthy hanging (up to six months) in a cool and well-ventilated space. For salami-style sausages, salt is mixed with the meat mixture then the sausages are hung for a minimum of a month (but can also be eaten raw).

◆ **'Cold'-smoking:** this alone doesn't preserve the meat; it simply adds an antiseptic coating to it, as well, of course, as creating excellent flavour.

So smoking is a technique that can be used in addition to any of the others. To do it yourself, you will need to build a smoker (perhaps above a stove or fireplace): this is a box big enough for the meat (or fish) into which smoke is diverted. If you have a large fireplace and high, wide chimney, then you could hang it in there and smoke it the old-fashioned way. The temperature must be less than 50°C to stop the meat cooking, and the fire needs to be going for about a week.

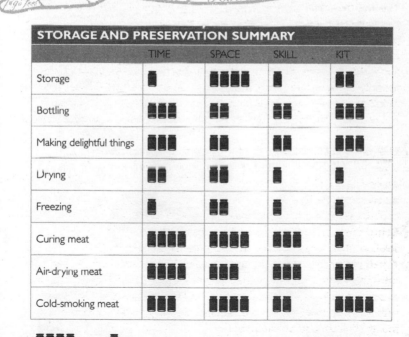

STORAGE AND PRESERVATION SUMMARY				
	TIME	SPACE	SKILL	KIT
Storage	▮	▮▮▮▮	▮	▮▮
Bottling	▮▮▮	▮▮	▮▮	▮▮▮
Making delightful things	▮▮▮	▮▮	▮▮	▮▮▮
Drying	▮▮	▮▮	▮	▮
Freezing	▮	▮▮	▮	▮
Curing meat	▮▮▮▮	▮▮▮▮	▮▮▮	▮
Air-drying meat	▮▮▮▮	▮▮▮	▮▮▮	▮▮
Cold-smoking meat	▮▮▮	▮▮▮▮	▮▮	▮▮▮▮

▮▮▮▮ = lots   ▮ = not much

'Gardens are England's most important nature reserve'

Professor Kevin Gaston and Dr Ken Thompson, University of Sheffield

BUILDING
BIODIVERSITY

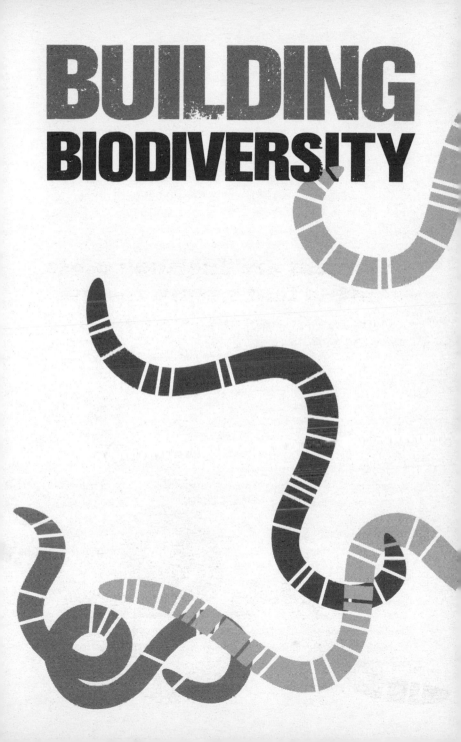

It is now over forty years since Rachel Carson wrote *Silent Spring*, a seminal book which first drew the world's attention to the destructiveness of industrial agriculture and, in doing so, kick-started the modern environmental movement. If we had heeded Carson's warnings, the British countryside would today be a very different place, bustling with a vast variety of wildlife. As it is, the agricultural heartlands of Britain are little more than a desert of monocultural, intensive food production. Look at the arable fields as you pass through these places in the growing season and most sport the tell-tale 'tramlines' used by boom sprayers to deliver herbicides, pesticides and fungicides to the crops. The popular image of the countryside – a gentle arcadia of small farms, swathed in flowers and buzzing with life – exists only in memory and in tiny pockets of Britain.

The industrialization of farming since the Second World War has had many consequences: it has given us food with potentially harmful residues, degraded our topsoil, polluted watercourses and transformed once-attractive rural Britain into an identikit wasteland of vast, prairie fields. But most of all, it has been largely responsible for decimating the country's biodiversity. Farmland species such as hare and partridge have declined by up to 85 per cent since the Second World War. As many as 54 per cent of our native bird species and 28 per cent of native plant species have declined in the last forty years. Tree sparrows are down by 89 per cent in the past twenty-five years; skylarks down by 58 per cent. Since the 1930s, 97 per cent of semi-natural lowland grassland (the flower meadows of our rural imaginings) has gone. I could go on.

Industrial farming affects species because it destroys or disrupts ecosystems. Herbicides kill the weeds on which many insects thrive. Insects that survive are killed by pesticides. As a result, birds and creatures further up the food chain have nothing to eat. Even if there was any food left for them, there's nowhere for birds and mammals to live in intensively cultivated fields without hedgerows or wild boundaries. And the flower meadows? Chemical fertilizers have largely turned these into monocultures, dominated by a single species of grass that crowds out all the others.

So how is the 21st-Century Smallholder's garden going to change all this? It can't, of course, have a direct effect. For the decline in the countryside's biodiversity to be properly reversed, agriculture has to change. And in my view this doesn't mean 'sticking-plaster' solutions like leaving little strips of uncultivated land at the edge of the farmland deserts for supposedly grateful creatures to live in. Doesn't that sound a bit like decimating an indigenous population and forcing the survivors to live in reservations? I thought we'd stopped doing that. I personally believe that Britain could feed itself (as it has before) with a more ecologically benign agriculture based on local production and consumption, mixed farming and organic principles.

But until the agricultural revolution happens – which it surely must, because apart from being highly destructive, today's practices are entirely dependent on oil – biodiversity begins at home, as the quote at the beginning of this chapter implies. Covering a total of one million acres, Britain's gardens are a final refuge for some of the creatures driven from the countryside. Our gardens, balconies and backyards can't provide a haven for everything: hare and partridge, for example, require much larger ecosystems. But they can still be home to an astounding variety of wildlife, from the microscopic to the big and furry.

There are reasons for doing something about biodiversity beyond just being nice to species under pressure and helping to counter the depredations of industrial farming. A garden (or even just a balcony) designed to attract wildlife is a beautiful place to be. There's deep satisfaction in observing the fruits of your labours: following birds through the nesting season or knowing that the frogs in the pond you built are on slug patrol tonight. Finally – and crucially for the 21st-Century Smallholder – building biodiversity is great for your edible gardening efforts. A garden with the right balance of bugs and creatures is less likely to suffer pest problems than an intensive food-producing space in which there's only room for crops.

How to design for biodiversity

It isn't hard to attract wildlife to your garden. Abandon it completely to nature and it will provide cover, habitat and food for wild species as the grasses grow and the brambles invade. Leave a big enough garden for long enough and you could end up with woodland. But in a completely wild state, your garden or outside space won't necessarily have too much room for its human occupants. And whilst you can make a food-producing 'forest garden', the untended wild garden is unlikely to yield as much edible stuff as you might like.

If you manage your garden according to organic principles, then biodiversity will automatically be boosted because a good mix of species is essential to pest control. A combination of laziness and lack of pesticides has turned my allotment plot into a nature reserve. Ironically, destroying biodiversity takes the most effort; an effort that must be sustained in order to resist the relentless fight-back of nature. Bare-soil, chemical vegetable cultivation combined with a neatly clipped lawn and ultra-tidy flower beds will certainly keep the bugs at bay. The problem, of course, is that such an approach just creates more work, and more of the wrong sort of bugs: spray an infestation of pests and chances are that next year they will come back redoubled in force because the spray will also have killed their predators. Once you've started down the 'adversarial', man-vs.-nature garden path, the struggle is constant.

Gardening for biodiversity does, however, present the 21st-Century Smallholder with a dilemma. It can be tempting to think of every bit of outside space as somewhere to grow food. However, treating the whole space as nothing more than a market garden can mean neglecting creatures that might make the process of growing food easier. And missing out on the 'wildlife' bit arguably reduces the aesthetic appeal of your outside space too. As Patrick Whitefield says in *The Earth Care Manual*, 'Anything which adds diversity is likely to add to the health of the garden and to the aesthetic enjoyment of its human inhabitants.'

So the key is to try to strike a balance between the three main functions of a garden or outside space: recreation, food production and providing a haven for wildlife. The good news is that the wildlife side of things is easy, needn't take up too much space and is entirely complementary to the other two.

Five steps to a biodiverse garden

Creating a biodiverse outside space is all about providing both food and shelter for insects, birds, mammals and invertebrates and you can achieve this through a combination of planting and landscaping. In *How to Make a Wildlife Garden*, author Chris Baines notes that many of our native flora and fauna originally lived in a woodland environment and that a 'woodland glade' – with a balance between shaded and open space and a rich variety of habitats – is a good analogy for what an outside space built for biodiversity should be aiming to emulate. So here are five steps towards turning your outside space into a wildlife haven.

1. Be untidy

This is the easiest bit of all. I haven't yet met the people who live downstairs on the north side of my house, partly because they never use their garden. If they did, in high summer they would need a machete to get from one side to the other. The main 6 × 4.5-metre space contains a fantastic variety of flora: buddleia, bramble, elder, thistles, to name but a few. Two doors to the south in a similarly unvisited garden, a sycamore is growing fast and, in summer, foxgloves reach for the sky. Unwittingly, my neighbours are providing excellent habitat and food for inner-city wildlife. Their approach is a little too untidy for most; and a completely unmanaged space won't always develop a great diversity of species. But as a general rule, a garden or outside space will develop much more biodiversity if we resist the urge to, say, tidy up piles of wood or mow all the lawn to within an inch of its life at all times.

Untidiness tips:

- **Don't burn or throw away old logs and prunings:** piled up in a shady corner they will provide refuge for insects that will feed birds, solitary bees and wasps that will control pests and pollinate your plants, and small mammals like mice, voles and hedgehogs.
- **If you have a lawn, take a more relaxed attitude to mowing:** a closely mown lawn may be good for croquet but it doesn't provide much in the way of habitat or floral diversity. Either mowing less frequently, or using a strimmer or even a scythe instead of the mower will allow plants to flower and more insects to live in the lawn. Even better for wildlife of all kinds is to create a meadow: but this takes a bit of management (see p. 141).
- **Let things go to seed:** dead stems and seedheads provide habitat for bugs.

⬤ **Leave the soil alone:** disturbing the ground under plants can disrupt the habitats of useful insects like mining bees.

2. Build a pond

Every outside space or garden should have a pond if possible. It needn't be big: a pond little bigger than a bucket can provide a useful habitat for all sorts of creatures. For the 21st-Century Smallholder's food-producing activities, a pond holds out the promise of an answer to every edibles gardener's prayer: slug control. Even the smallest ponds can attract frogs: and frogs love to eat slugs. Beyond amphibians, a pressured class of creature for whom garden ponds are an essential habitat today, ponds can attract fascinating insects like damselflies and dragonflies, give birds somewhere to bathe and the insects that hover over their surface provide food for birds and bats. And if you keep honeybees (see pp. 100–105) a pond will provide them with valuable drinking water: a single hive can get through 25 litres in a year.

Ponds can also play host to the ultimate slug controller, ducks (see pp. 114–16), but these will eat the frogs and pretty much everything else in the pond before starting on your vegetable patch. So to keep everyone happy, ducks ideally need a separate, fenced-off pond, making them a practical proposition only for those with a larger garden or maybe serious aquaculture aspirations (see pp. 117–18).

Pond tips:
⬤ **Make your pond in the spring:** this is the best time to stock it with plants and frogspawn.
⬤ **Site it in a sunny spot, away from trees:** leaves falling on a pond are not only a pain to clear, they also remove oxygen from it and create a foul-smelling layer at the bottom. Pond creatures also tend to prefer direct sunlight.
⬤ **Give it shallow, sloping edges and a maximum depth of at least 60cm:** the shallows make a good birdbath, provide space for marginal plants and the slope makes it easier for the pond's larger inhabitants to get in and out. The depth stops it freezing solid in winter.
⬤ **Use a pond liner:** if you have clay soil, you can create an impermeable base for the pond by 'puddling' it with plenty of energetic stamping. Otherwise, a butyl rubber pond liner gives the maximum

flexibility, because pre-formed plastic or fibreglass pond liners rarely give the shallow edges that amphibians need. The base of the pond should be free of sharp stones and lined with sand or damp cardboard before the liner goes in. A layer of sandy soil on top then provides somewhere for plants to root. Make sure the liner isn't exposed when the pond is full, as sunlight can damage it.

● **Fill and top it up with rainwater if possible:** whilst you can get rid of the chlorine in tap water by leaving it to stand for a while, it's not possible to remove its often high mineral content, which can lead to excessive build-ups of algae. Rainwater is better, but in short supply when it's most needed in the summer. All of which is another good argument for serious rainwater harvesting (see p. 187).

● **Add a bucketful of water from an existing pond:** this will contain eggs, spores and seeds that will help creatures to colonize your pond.

● **Stock it quickly with oxygenating plants:** small ponds may not naturally be colonized by the right plants quickly enough, so a trip to the garden centre or a friend's pond will be necessary. Water milfoil and water starwort are well-known native oxygenators. Otherwise, the pond should have a mixture of submerged plants, 'emergents' that grow in the shallows and floating plants such as water lilies. You may need initially to 'anchor' submerged plants with stones to stop them floating to the surface.

● **Avoid fish:** they will eat the amphibians, ruining your slug-control plans

● **Keep an eye on it:** whilst a golden rule of wildlife gardening is minimum interference, the pond will need some maintenance: to shift excessive algae, maintain the water level or maybe remove duckweed so there is always some clear water showing.

3. Plant natural habitats

A little untidiness and a pond create incredibly rich habitats. But there are many more steps you can take towards providing shelter for creatures that will make the garden lovely and keep the vegetable pests at bay.

Habitat-planting tips:

- **Go for 'maximum edge':** the point where one ecosystem meets another is often the most productive – estuaries or the edges of woodland, for example, are extremely biodiverse. A garden, usually bordered on three sides, is ideal for achieving 'edge'. Low-growing shrubs can provide shelter and food for wildlife and be planted in front of trees, which provide yet more habitat. This 'multi-level' approach suits a broader range of fauna: for example, blue tits prefer to forage higher up than great tits. Hedges are also superb wildlife habitats.

- **Plant native trees and shrubs:** these are often considered best as they support more insect species and are less likely to be uncontrollably invasive. Hawthorn, for example, supports over two hundred insect species whilst sycamore manages only forty-three. Mulching between the shrubs whilst they grow will suppress weeds.

  - **Some useful native shrubs for gardens:** wild roses, elder, honeysuckle, holly, bramble.
  - **Some useful native trees for gardens:** crabapple, silver birch, hawthorn, rowan.

◉ **Make a meadow:** you won't find idyllic wildflower meadows in the countryside any more, so why not make one at home? If you have enough space, allowing the grass to grow tall and possibly seeding it with wildflowers will attract butterflies, small mammals and, as a result, maybe even birds of prey. Meadow essentials:

◉ **Planting** – it is unlikely that wildflower seeds will survive the competition of the grass in an established lawn, so they ideally need to be in 'plugs' that enable them to survive until germination. A more labour-intensive alternative is to strip the existing turf and sow a mixture of grass and flower seeds on it.

◉ **Mowing** – meadows are not entirely 'natural': it is annual cutting that allows the wildflowers to flourish. So a late-summer/autumn mowing is all a meadow needs. The lawnmower will not be up to this task: it's strimmer or scythe, depending on your attitude to manual labour, fossil fuels, etc. Remove the mown grass, otherwise the soil will gain fertility and favour grass over wildflowers.

◉ **Use climbing plants:** crawling up the side of your house, all over your giant water butt, or up trellises and pergolas, climbing plants can provide shelter and food for birds and insects. Some top climbers: ivy (perfect for nesting blackbirds), honeysuckle, bramble (if you can keep it under control).

4. Make artificial habitats

Depending on where you live, man-made habitats may help to encourage useful garden wildlife. Our contemporary tendency to tidiness in the countryside and in parks and gardens has reduced the living space for many creatures, who like hollowed-out dead trees and rotting wood.

Artificial-habitat tips:

- **Put up some nest boxes:** it is possible to provide alternative shelter for a huge range of birds, from blue tits to barn owls. Nesting-box design is key, for the size of the entrance hole determines which types of bird can fit in. Nesting boxes can be bought at garden centres or through the RSPB; or their designs can be copied and knocked up at home: most nest boxes are easy to make. Bats, another useful species increasingly denied habitat, can also be persuaded to take up residence in nest boxes, as can hedgehogs.

- **Make insect habitats:** an untidy wildlife garden will most likely provide excellent habitats for insects, but there are a few steps you can take to be sure of attracting useful species. Solitary bees, which are excellent pollinators, like to live in tunnels: you can buy pretty 'bee hotels' for this purpose or simply drill holes from 2–10mm in diameter in a thick piece of wood and fix it to a sheltered wall. Lacewing larvae and adults are prodigious consumers of aphids and can be encouraged to overwinter in rolled-up corrugated cardboard stuffed into a plastic bottle and hung from a tree. Compost heaps (see pp. 48–51) harbour a vast amount of insect life too.

- **Build a stone wall:** rough walls with lots of nooks and crannies are ideal for spiders, toads, beetles and bumblebees.

- **Pile up some logs:** logpiles provide a home for insects, hence food for birds and for small mammals who might also live there.

5. Provide food

From a bird table to plants chosen for their value to wild creatures, the 21st-Century Smallholder's outside space or garden can easily entice a variety of species.

Food-providing tips:
- **Plant things that will provide food all year round:** the garden can provide a source of food when it might be scarce elsewhere. By choosing early- and late-flowering plants you can help insects like bumblebees that have just emerged for the spring or those which are just about to retire for the winter. Leaving flowerheads to form seed will provide food for birds.
- **Put up a bird table:** which could be the main source of food for some birds in a hard winter. Take care to site it away from any cover behind which cats could lurk.

TOP TEN CREATURES TO ATTRACT TO THE EDIBLE GARDEN

	WHAT THEY DO	HOW TO ENCOURAGE THEM
Frogs and newts	Eat small slugs and young snails	Build a pond.
Hoverflies	Larvae eat aphids	Plant daisies or let umbelliferous plants flower (fennels, parsley, carrots).
Lacewings	Adults and larvae eat aphids	Make a lacewing hotel.
Ladybirds	Eat aphids	Difficult – but they like crevices to hibernate in.
Bumblebees	Crucial pollinators	Provide shaded cover for hibernation and sunny cover for nest sites.
Solitary bees	Pollinators; and their presence indicates a healthy ecosystem	Make a bee hotel.
Wasps	Eat caterpillars and grubs	Provide a nest site – an air-brick in the side of the house is ideal. Encouraging wasps may not suit everyone.
Starlings	Eat leatherjackets, which damage plant roots	Provide nest boxes.
Wrens and robins	Control caterpillars like gooseberry sawfly	Provide nest boxes.
Song thrushes	Eat snails	Difficult to attract: provide lots of 'edge' habitat.

THE 21st-CENTURY CENTURY SMALLHOLDER'S YEAR PLANNER

January

It's the depths of winter and there's not a lot to do if you don't have much land. Winter vegetables are still cropping well but it's too cold to put much in the ground.

Growing your own food

SOWING, PLANTING AND HARVESTING	
Sow	Under cover: lettuce, salads
Plant	Garlic, rhubarb sets
Harvest	Artichoke (Jerusalem), sprouting broccoli, Brussels sprouts, cabbage (winter), cauliflower (winter), celeriac, chard, chicory, endive, kale, leeks, indoor lettuce, parsnip, rhubarb, spinach

Other food-growing tasks
Force established rhubarb crowns
Order seeds
Prune autumn raspberry canes

Raising your own food
Make sure pigs and chickens are warm and well-fed

Storage and preserving
Enjoy your stored produce

Building biodiversity
Keep feeding wild birds

February

The produce year slowly starts to wake up in February. This is the time to begin giving attention to some of the main crops: acquiring and chitting seed potatoes is a priority, and onions and garlic can go in.

Growing your own food

SOWING, PLANTING AND HARVESTING	
Sow	Under cover: Brussels sprouts, cabbages, kale, lettuce, salads Outside: broad beans, onions, parsnip, peas, radish, spinach
Plant	Cabbage (spring), garlic, onion sets, rhubarb sets
Harvest	Artichoke (Jerusalem), sprouting broccoli, Brussels sprouts, cabbage (winter), cauliflower (winter), celeriac, chard, chicory, endive, kale, leeks, indoor lettuce, parsnip, rhubarb, spinach

Other food-growing tasks
Put seed potatoes out to sprout (chit)
Start to prepare ground for sowing; add organic matter to vegetable beds
Dig up over-wintering brassicas when they are finished

Raising your own food
Make sure pigs and chickens are warm and well-fed

Storage and preserving
Enjoy your stored produce
Perhaps a time to consider preserves made from forced rhubarb

Building biodiversity
Keep feeding wild birds

March

If you haven't already pruned your fruit trees and bushes, this is the last chance to do it before growth really starts to kick in. It's time to have a first look at the bees, do a lot more sowing and maybe consider acquiring some pigs if you have the space and the inclination.

Growing your own food

SOWING, PLANTING AND HARVESTING	
Sow	Under cover: beetroot, Brussels sprouts, cabbages, celeriac, celery, kale, leeks, lettuce, salads Indoors, or heated greenhouse: aubergines, peppers, tomatoes Outside: beet (leaf), broad beans, cabbages, carrots (early), onions, parsnip, peas, radish, spinach, turnips
Plant	Artichokes (Jerusalem), asparagus crowns, garlic, lettuce, onion sets, potatoes (maincrop and early), rhubarb sets
Harvest	Artichokes (Jerusalem), sprouting broccoli, Brussels sprouts, cabbage (winter), cauliflower (winter), celeriac, chard, chicory, endive, kale, leeks, indoor lettuce, parsnip, rhubarb, sorrel, spinach

● Other food-growing tasks
Last opportunity to prune apples, pears and soft fruit
Cover land that will not be used until summer by sowing fast-growing green manures
Cut back shrubby herbs like lavender and thyme

● Raising your own food
Bees: check the hive for food stores by 'hefting' or brief inspection and feed if necessary
Pigs: a good time to buy weaners for autumn bacon

● Storage and preserving
Enjoy your stored produce

● Building biodiversity
Keep feeding wild birds

April

The business of food-growing really gets into gear in April. There's a lot to sow under cover and outside, growing seedlings to harden off and pot up and emerging weeds to deal with. The bees will need a little more attention; and now is the time to get started with chickens if you don't already have some.

Growing your own food

SOWING, PLANTING AND HARVESTING	
Sow	Under cover: beans (dwarf and runner), celeriac, celery, courgettes, cucumber, tomatoes Outside: artichokes (globe), beetroot, broad beans, broccoli (sprouting and calabrese), Brussels sprouts, cabbages, carrots, chard, chicory, endive, kale, kohlrabi, leeks, lettuce, parsnip, peas, radish, salad rocket, spinach, spring onions, turnips
Plant	Artichoke (globe) offsets, asparagus crowns, Brussels sprouts, cabbage (spring), lettuce, onion sets, potatoes (maincrop)
Harvest	Asparagus (end April), sprouting broccoli, cabbage (spring), cauliflower (spring), celeriac, chard, chicory, endive, leeks, indoor lettuce, radishes, rhubarb, rocket, sorrel, spinach, spring onions

● Other food-growing tasks
Feed plants in containers with liquid feed or worm compost
Weeding
Earth up early potatoes
Harden off seedlings started under cover
Support peas
Pot on seedlings raised under cover such as
    aubergines, cucumbers, marrows, peppers, tomatoes
Enjoy apple blossom . . ,

● Raising your own food
Bees: find and mark the queen; put on a queen excluder and honey
    super if necessary; check for varroa
Chickens: best time to start chicken-keeping; watch out for broody hens

● Storage and preserving
Enjoy your stored produce

● Building biodiversity
This is a good time to build a pond or stock it with frogspawn or maybe
    a bucket of water from a good established pond

May

This is not the best time for the 21st-Century Smallholder to go on holiday. The weeds are growing much faster than your produce and the bees need close attention.

Growing your own food

SOWING, PLANTING AND HARVESTING	
Sow	Under cover: courgettes, cucumber, sweetcorn Outside: Beans (broad, French and runner), beetroot, broccoli (sprouting and calabrese), cabbages, carrots, chard, chicory, endive, fennel, kohlrabi, leeks, lettuce, parsnip, peas, radish, salad rocket, spinach, spring onions, turnips
Plant	cabbage, lettuce, onion sets, potatoes (maincrop and early)
Harvest	Asparagus, cabbage (spring), cauliflower (spring), celeriac, chard, chicory, elderflower, leeks, lettuce, radishes, rhubarb, rocket, sorrel, spinach, spring onions

Other food-growing tasks
Mulch fruit trees and soft fruit
Harden off seedlings started under cover
Lots of weeding
Mulch established vegetable crops
Pinch out tomatoes
Earth up potatoes
Support peas
Thin out beet, carrots, lettuce, parsnip, radish, spinach, turnip if sown direct
'Pot on' seedlings of aubergine, celeriac, celery, courgettes, cucumbers, peppers, tomatoes
Keep an eye out for pests

Raising your own food
Pigs: a good time to buy weaners for early autumn pork
Bees: probably the busiest month in the beekeeping year. Inspect the hive weekly. Add honey supers as required; take an early honey harvest if appropriate (if oilseed rape is nearby, honey must be removed immediately because it crystallizes in the comb). Check for signs of swarming and artificially swarm if necessary. Ideally, have a spare hive available.

Storage and preserving
Do anything possible to extend the elderflower season: making elderflower champagne or syrup is best

June

For our forebears, who were utterly reliant on their own produce, this was one of the hungriest times of year, with the winter crops gone and the summer maincrops still not ready. However, today it's a time to start enjoying your produce in a big way, as early fruit and veg crops start to kick in.

Growing your own food

SOWING, PLANTING AND HARVESTING	
Sow	Outside: Beans (French and runner), beetroot, broccoli (sprouting and calabrese), cabbages, carrots, chard, chicory, courgettes, cucumber, endive, kohlrabi, lettuce, parsnip, peas, radish, salad rocket, spinach, spring onions, winter squash and pumpkins, swedes, sweetcorn, turnips
Plant	Sprouting broccoli, cabbages, cauliflowers, celeriac, celery, courgettes, fennel, kale, leeks, winter squash and pumpkins, sweetcorn, tomatoes
Harvest	Asparagus, broad beans, beetroot, blackcurrants, broccoli (calabrese), cabbage (early summer), carrots (earlies), cauliflower (early summer), chard, cherries, chicory, elderflower, gooseberries, kohlrabi, lettuce, peas (earlies), potatoes (earlies), radishes, raspberries, redcurrants, rhubarb, sorrel, spinach, spring onions, strawberries

🌿 Other food-growing tasks
Prune plums and cherries
Net fruit bushes, raspberries and maincrop strawberries
Weed, hoe and mulch
Pinch out and stake tomatoes
Thin out beet, carrots, lettuce, parsnip, radish, spinach, turnip if sown direct
Stay vigilant against garden pests

🌿 Raising your own food
Bees: continue weekly inspections if the colony has not swarmed. Remove honey if oilseed rape is nearby and make sure bees have sufficient food.
Chickens: check them for parasites as the weather warms up

🌿 Storage and preserving
Dry out and string up onions and garlic for storage
Freeze broad beans and peas if you have a glut
Time to start preserving gluts of fruit

July

The first mad flush of spring growth calms down, making weeding a little easier; and the bees need less vigilance. Drying a substantial onion crop now will give you a long-term supply of this culinary staple.

Growing your own food

SOWING, PLANTING AND HARVESTING	
Sow	Outside: beetroot, chard, chicory, courgettes, cucumber, endive, kohlrabi, lettuce, parsnip, radish, salad rocket, spinach, spring onions, winter squash and pumpkins, swedes, turnips
Plant	Broccoli (sprouting and calabrese), Brussels sprouts, cabbages, kale, leeks
Harvest	Apples, artichokes (globe), beans (broad, French and runner), beetroot, blackberries, blackcurrants, blueberries, broccoli (calabrese), cabbage (summer), carrots (maincrop), cauliflower (early summer), celery, chard, cherries, chicory, courgettes, cucumber, elderflower, fennel, garlic, gooseberries, kohlrabi, lettuce, onions, peas (maincrop), potatoes (earlies), radishes, raspberries, redcurrants, rhubarb, sorrel, spinach, spring onions, winter squash and pumpkins, strawberries, turnip

● Other food-growing tasks
Pinch out and stake tomatoes
Water and feed celeriac, celery, courgette, cucumbers, leeks and potatoes and tomatoes in containers
More weeding, hoeing and mulching

● Raising your own food
Bees: harvest honey (if you want to let them build up their own supplies for the winter)
Chickens: pay special attention to protein in their diet if they are moulting

● Storage and preserving
Dry harvested onions for storage
Jam- and wine-making

● Building biodiversity
Cut spring wildflower meadows

August

The planting tails off rapidly: August is all about enjoying your produce and preserving it when you have a glut (or just fancy some jam).

Growing your own food

SOWING, PLANTING AND HARVESTING	
Sow	Outside: chard, kale, lettuce, spring onions
Plant	Leeks
Harvest	Apples, artichokes (globe), aubergines, beans (broad, French and runner), blackberries, blackcurrants, blueberries, broccoli (calabrese), beetroot, cabbage (summer), carrots (earlies and maincrop), cauliflower (summer), celery, chard, cherries, chicory, courgettes, cucumber, garlic, kohlrabi, lettuce, mulberries, onions, pears, peas (maincrop), peppers, plums, potatoes (maincrop), radishes, raspberries, redcurrants, sorrel, spinach, spring onions, winter squash and pumpkins, strawberries, sweetcorn, tomatoes, turnip

● Other food-growing tasks
Keep watering and feeding
Stake tall brassicas
Prune apples and pears that are fan-trained or in cordons or espaliers
'Stop' cordon tomatoes from further growth to encourage more fruiting
Thin spinach, turnips
Cut old leaves of pumpkins and squash to help ripening

● Raising your own food
Leave the bees alone unless you want to get stung

● Storage and preserving
Even more preserving activity as courgettes and tomatoes start
   cropping in earnest

● Building biodiversity
Last chance to put up a lacewing hotel
Cut hedges when birds have finished nesting

September

The peak of the produce year, with more fresh produce available than at any other time. It's also the traditional time for harvesting honey – a labour-intensive but satisfying task.

Growing your own food

SOWING, PLANTING AND HARVESTING	
Sow	Under cover: chicory, radishes, salad rocket Outside: cabbage (spring), endive, kohlrabi
Plant	Garlic, autumn onion sets
Harvest	Apples, artichoke (globe), aubergines, beans (French and runner), beetroot, blackberries, blackcurrants, blueberries, broccoli (calabrese), Brussels sprouts, cabbage (summer), carrots (earlies and maincrop), cauliflower (autumn), celeriac, celery, chard, chicory, fennel, kohlrabi, lettuce, mulberries, onions, pears, peas (maincrop), peppers, plums, potatoes (maincrop), radishes, raspberries, redcurrants, rhubarb, sorrel, spinach, spring onions, winter squash and pumpkins, strawberries, sweetcorn, tomatoes, turnip

● Other food-growing tasks
Sow overwintering green manures
Take nets off fruit so birds can get at overwintering pests

● Raising your own food
Pigs: take porkers to slaughter if bought in late spring
Bees: harvest honey (if you're going to take the lot and feed them on sugar); start winter feeding, put mouse guards on hive

● Storage and preserving
Put maincrop potatoes into a clamp or root cellar for storage
Furious bottling and preserving activity for fruit and veg

● Building biodiversity
Sow new wildflower meadows
Sow hardy annual attractant plants for early flowering
Net ponds to keep leaves out if necessary

October

Many crops are still in full flow and now is the time to get into serious pickling and preserving mode to get maximum value from your edible-gardening efforts.

Growing your own food

SOWING, PLANTING AND HARVESTING	
Sow	Under cover: lettuce (winter), salad rocket Outside: cabbage (spring), endive, kohlrabi
Plant	Autumn-sown broad beans and peas
Harvest	Apples, blackberries, beans (French and runner), beetroot, Brussels sprouts, cabbage (autumn), cardoon, carrots (maincrop), cauliflower (autumn), celeriac, celery, chard, chicory, fennel, kohlrabi, lettuce, onions, parsnip, pears, peas (maincrop), peppers, potatoes (maincrop), quince, radishes, raspberries, sorrel, spinach, spring onions, winter squash and pumpkins, swede, tomatoes, turnip

● Other food-growing tasks

Last chance to sow many green manures

Make a muck heap

Collect leaves for leafmould

Prune blackcurrant, blackberry bushes

Apply greasebands to apple, plum and pear trees to control winter moths

● Raising your own food

Pigs: introduce baconers to your established orchard

Bees: finish winter feeding; put mouse guards on hive entrances

● Storage and preserving

Drying apples, making cider, jam, chutney, jellies . . .

● Building biodiversity

Cut summer wildflower meadows

November

It's the end of the road for anything that isn't frost-hardy; but the beginning for crops that are improved by frost such as parsnips and kale.

Growing your own food

SOWING, PLANTING AND HARVESTING	
Plant	Autumn-sown broad beans and peas, garlic, rhubarb sets
Harvest	Apples, artichokes (Jerusalem), Brussels sprouts, cabbage (summer), cardoon, carrots (earlies and maincrop), cauliflower (winter), celeriac, chard, chicory, kale, kohlrabi, lettuce, medlar, parsnips, pears, radishes, sorrel, spinach, swede, turnip

❯ Other food-growing tasks
Fork over heavy soils to 'weather' over winter
Prune red- and whitecurrant bushes

❯ Raising your own food
Pigs: take baconers to slaughter if bought in early spring
Chickens: make sure their accommodation is well-insulated, water supplies don't freeze and they have a good supply of food

❯ Building biodiversity
Put out bird feeders

December

A perfect time to plan the next year's activity, December is also a good time to attend to fruit, planting new bushes and trees and pruning existing ones.

Growing your own food

SOWING, PLANTING AND HARVESTING	
Plant	Autumn-sown broad beans and peas, garlic, rhubarb sets
Harvest	Artichokes (Jerusalem), Brussels sprouts, cabbage (summer), cardoon, carrots (earlies and maincrop), cauliflower (winter), celeriac, chard, chicory, kale, kohlrabi, lettuce, parsnips, sorrel, spinach, swede, turnip

◗ Other food-growing tasks
Remove dead fruit from trees
Best time to plant fruit bushes and trees
Prune apple and pear trees, gooseberry bushes

◗ Raising your own food
Make sure the pigs and chickens are warm and well fed

◗ Storage and preserving
Lift and store parsnips and swede

◗ Building biodiversity
Keep feeding wild birds

Our homes are not sustainable. That is not to suggest that they are all going to fall down any time soon; but they consume more energy and water than the planet can provide and produce more greenhouse emissions and waste than it can cope with. Perhaps surprisingly, only 10 per cent of a building's environmental impact happens in its construction; most of it is during its lifetime, mainly through energy use. The house contributes around one-third of a family's CO_2 emissions (food and transport take the other two-thirds) and domestic energy use accounts for 27 per cent of Britain's overall CO_2 emissions.

MAKING YOUR HOME MORE SELF-RELIANT

The main reason houses are so hungry for energy is that they are, on the whole, badly insulated, so when the weather gets cold, the fossil fuel demand rises sharply. Culturally, thanks to cheap fossil energy and efficient central heating, we've become accustomed to houses that are warm and cosy throughout. Our homes today are on average ten degrees warmer inside than they were in the early 1900s, when costlier and more cumbersome coal fires meant that only the occupied rooms were heated.

But any energy efficiency brought about by the slow spread of better heating systems, insulation or glazing through our housing stock – or by better-performing appliances – has been cancelled out by our fondness for heat, light and gadgetry. Since 1990, domestic energy use has gone up by 19 per cent, thanks to more electrical appliances, fancy lighting and the ever-rising central heating thermostat.

What with global warming, peaking oil supplies and the UK's increasing reliance on vulnerable gas supplies for power and heating, domestic energy use makes me nervous.

Our Western lives also guzzle water like it was going out of fashion (which, thanks to climate change and usage patterns, it may well be). The average UK citizen uses 150 litres of fresh drinking water per day, of which nearly half is used by toilet-flushing, laundry, washing and bathing. With the average toilet flush at around 8 litres, one trip to the loo uses nearly twice as much drinking water as an inhabitant of Saharan Africa might use each day, for all their needs.

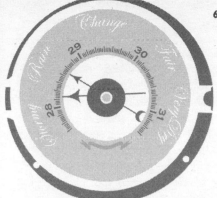

And we could use our waste products more efficiently too. The thought may make you squirm with disgust; or you may simply see it as a retrograde step to a filthy, old-fashioned way of doing things, but wee and poo are valuable commodities. Urine can activate compost and feed plants; and faeces, properly treated by lengthy composting, can, for example, fertilize your fruit bushes with no risk to health.

Anyone reeling at the thought of a composting toilet should simply answer this question: do you want to live next to a sewage farm? Thought not. But, thanks to the way our systems are currently ordered, someone's got to, whether they like it or not. I want to live next to a sewage farm like I want to live next to a landfill site, waste incinerator or power station, which is not at all. But my current lifestyle demands that these places exist.

In *The Earth Care Manual*, author Patrick Whitefield notes, simply and trenchantly, that 'In ecological systems, there is no such place as "away"'. Nature has no cesspits, no middens, no slag heaps. It is instead characterized by re-use and recycling: it is full of 'closed-loop' systems that take care of themselves; human society is not.

This question brings us to the whole point of why a 21st-Century Smallholder should be worrying about energy and water. As with food, it's about taking control, taking responsibility and doing things that are more sustainable. It's not necessarily about achieving self-sufficiency – although in certain circumstances, energy and water autonomy is possible – but about reducing your reliance on unsustainable sources. And it's also about making a contribution: one solar hot-water panel won't make a difference, but a panel on every house will shut down a few power stations.

Our smallholding forebears had no choice but to take responsibility for their own energy, water and waste. In their time, it was a question of survival. In our time, many people will quite legitimately question the sanity of taking such responsibility, say by installing a costly solar electric system or a composting toilet, when there's already an electricity grid and a sewage network. It might seem like affectation; like a bit of green grandstanding. But most of the people who invest in such systems do so out of a deeply held conviction that they want to be part of the solution, not part of the problem; and that they want others to see what's possible too.

There are people out there generating more power than they use, slashing their heating bills or even becoming completely 'carbon neutral'. And many of them are doing this from normal, boring, existing houses, not from dream 'eco-houses' that only a fortunate few of us will ever get to build or live in.

It's not hard to make moves to a more 'self-reliant' home; many of the actions you can take are quick, cheap and effective. Sure, many of them are also ridiculously expensive and have payback times that stretch into decades. But most of them are satisfying and some are even fun. And as with any aspect of being a 21st-Century Smallholder, there will be something in this chapter that works for you.

Saving energy

The arguments for saving energy are difficult. We currently live in a world of energy abundance and, on average, just 3.5 per cent of our total household expenditure goes on heat and power. On average that's about £800 per year. Such is the affordability of power that by 1994 we used 50 per cent more electricity for lighting and appliances than we did in 1970. If it's about saving money, then we can do it much more quickly and effectively by buying fewer clothes, holidays, cans of beer or tankfuls of petrol. If money is tight, however, then there are a few energy-saving actions that will save money straight away, albeit at the cost of some comfort, for example turning down the thermostat and putting on some extra jumpers. But many energy-saving measures involve investment: loft insulation may not be particularly expensive, but it still costs money and the payback is long and gradual. And big, serious energy-saving measures like cladding your house in a layer of insulating material cost big, serious money: an investment you may never recoup.

So until fuel costs go through the roof, you have to care about saving energy – to think it's worth the (fuel-efficient!) candle – before you take steps to do it. I think there are two reasons for caring: the altruistic and the personal. The former is predicated on a belief that there is an energy problem. And there is a vast weight of evidence to suggest that there are two big energy problems. The first is that the supply of fossil fuels, in particular oil, has peaked. Britain is fast losing any autonomy in fossil fuels it had; and our move to gas-fired power stations means that in a few years' time we will be dependent on dwindling supplies piped from unstable regions of the world. Renewables are developing slowly and even if it didn't terrify many of us, a nuclear renaissance won't happen in time. The other big energy problem is of course 'anthropogenic' (human-generated) climate change, seen now by all but a few self-interested nay-sayers in the fossil-fuel industry as the defining crisis of this century. In a world that likes grandiose technical fixes: 'The hydrogen economy!' 'Windfarms everywhere!' 'Nuclear power, yes please!' the boring, prosaic fact is that energy efficiency could go a long way to solving both the power problem and the carbon dioxide problem.

The altruistic reason for saving energy is therefore all about seeing yourself and your household as part of the solution to these twin energy crises, for it is certain that in the future energy will not only cost more, but we will be forced to use less by the demands for CO_2 reduction. In the short term, therefore, there's little in it for you; but your energy-saving actions are making a contribution to solving a future problem.

The personal reason is all about reducing dependence. Personally, I don't like the idea of being beholden to an energy network that has a deeply uncertain future; and I'm uncomfortable that my home belches more greenhouse gases than it should. For purely selfish reasons, I'd like to lessen my feeling of dependence by making my home use as little energy as possible.

Living a more 'sustainable' life, being less dependent: taking control of energy use is all part of being a 21st-Century Smallholder.

As this chapter shows, there are a lot of ways to make a difference, some cheap and easy, some costly and complex. But they're all worth a look; and, in my view, many of them will be standard practice before too long.

Changing behaviour

This is the cheap and easy bit. We keep our houses at 20°C because unless we're poor (or worse, old and poor), energy is relatively cheap and we don't notice the cost. The humble central-heating thermostat could, however, make a big difference to our energy consumption. Every degree centigrade you turn it down reduces your bill by around 10 per cent. As the Energy Saving Trust (EST) points out, if we all dropped our thermostats by one degree during the heating season, we would save over £650 million worth of energy and 9 million tonnes of CO_2 emissions every year. Rather that than a new nuclear power station or windfarm at the end of the garden. Peter Harper of the Centre for Alternative Technology ran an experiment to see how his family reacted to thermostat changes; and in a week, people had become accustomed to 16°C, setting his heating bill up for a 50 per cent reduction straight away. Any lower than 16°C, though, as Peter pointed out, you're into thermal-underwear territory, which is not everyone's thing; but for those really committed to this quick, cheap and highly effective way of saving energy, there are a lot of cheap and cosy fleeces on the market these days.

The thermostat is the biggie, but there are other cheap and easy energy-saving measures:

🔥 Turn off the lights – unless you need them.

🔥 Drop the hot water cylinder thermostat to 60°C.

🔥 Switch off appliances on sleep or standby – a single TV that spends its downtime on standby consumes 30kWh per year of electricity.

Buying efficient stuff

And this is where you have to spend in order to save. Some energy-efficient appliances are comparable in cost to the energy-guzzlers: fridges, for example. Others, like compact fluorescent lightbulbs, cost more but last up to twelve times longer and – suggests the Energy Saving Trust – can save up to £7 per bulb per year on your electricity. A list of products carrying the EST's 'Recommended' stamp can be found at www.est.org.uk

Improving your house

The next step to take is to help the place in which you live use energy more efficiently. This is difficult for those in rented accommodation, who may lack both the permission and (quite rightly) the motivation to spend money making their flat or house more energy efficient. But for those who are willing and able to tamper freely with their house, here, in ascending order of cost, are the 'basic' steps (i.e. those that don't need changes to its structure).

🔥 **Draught-strip the place.** The older your house, the leakier it's likely to be, with heat escaping between floorboards and around doors and windows. Plugging these gaps is a cheap and effective (if a little labour-intensive) way of helping the house to retain heat. From plugging floorboard gaps with a glue/wood dust mix to using sophisticated draught strips on internal and external doors, and on windows, draught-stripping is an essential part of an energy-efficient refurbishment. Average cost less than £200.

🔥 **Get a high-performance boiler.** If your gas boiler needs replacing, then a modern gas-condensing boiler should replace it. These make use of the heat created when water vapour in the flue gases condenses. With an operating efficiency of 85–95 per cent (as against 65 per cent for standard systems), such boilers can cut bills by up to 40 per cent and pay back in a single year. Average cost £400–£800.

■■■ **Fit effective loft insulation.** About 20 per cent of heat escapes through the roof. According to the Government's English House Condition survey 2001, 95 per cent of dwellings with lofts have some insulation, so chances are yours has. But whereas serious green builders suggest a minimum depth of 300mm in order to get a worthwhile effect, the Building Regulations (which dictate how houses should be built) stipulate only 150mm of insulation, or 200mm in less energy-efficient buildings. So most lofts are unlikely to have all the insulation they need. The cheapest way to achieve this with an environmentally friendly, renewable material is to use Warmcel, which is made of recycled paper and can be pumped quickly into your loft by a specialist installer (or installed at great length by hand). Easier to install but much more expensive to buy is sheep's-wool-based Thermafleece. Average cost £150–200.

■■■ **Have your cavity walls insulated.** With up to 50 per cent of heat escaping through the walls, having them insulated is well worth doing. This is much more of an issue for detached houses than it is for terraced houses and flats, where adjoining dwellings insulate each other (up to a point). Most houses built after the 1930s have a cavity wall that was originally intended to deal with damp: filling this with a waterproof insulating material is an effective energy-saving measure. Today, however, only 36 per cent of cavity walls are insulated. As a rule, the newer your house, the more likely it is to have insulated cavity walls. If you're worried about potential health and environmental issues, then choose mineral wool or polystyrene beads over urea formaldehyde insulation. Average cost £200–400 (with grant, depending on house size).

■■■ **Fit high-performance glazing.** Half of all modern houses are completely double-glazed, meaning there are plenty more to go. If your house needs new windows, then double- or even triple-glazed systems can help to retain the 20 per cent of heat that escapes through the windows. Serious, top-of-the-range gas-filled triple-glazing offers better insulation value than a cavity brick wall. Average cost £500+.

Grants for energy-saving measures in the home are available from the government, energy suppliers and local authorities. The Energy Saving Trust (www.est.org.uk) has good information on these.

Serious steps

If you've done all this and are still not satisfied that your house is as energy-efficient as it could be, then it's possible to go a great deal further, albeit at more significant cost and effort. It will always be difficult for a 'standard' house (whether new or old) to achieve the efficiency of a purpose-built 'eco-house'. But it is possible to get pretty close, as long as you are prepared to make some serious investment and possibly some structural changes. Again in order of ascending cost, here are the options.

Build a conservatory. Not one of those rather fraught, fiddly designs that goes jutting out into the garden, but a simple 'lean-to' greenhouse style, with an emphasis on width across the house. This provides a 'passive solar' gain and has many advantages, as long as it is separated from the heated house. By creating a pre-heated buffer between part of the house and the outside world, it acts as a layer of insulation. It also warms fresh air entering the house and conducts heat into the place. The house repays the compliment by warming the conservatory in the evening. All of which is also a reminder that conservatories are nice places to be and very good for growing and propagating fruit and vegetables. A south-facing wall is ideal. Average cost £10,000.

Fit solar hot-water panels. This can be a cheap option, if you choose the DIY approach of, say, building a glass-fronted frame around an old black-painted radiator. It's certainly satisfying to know that you get hot water when the sun shines (and even a bit when it doesn't – solar systems can provide 50–70 per cent of your hot water through the year). But solar hot water (whilst nowhere near as expensive as solar electric – see p. 172) is not cheap and has a payback time likely to run to more than ten years. You won't, as for solar electric, need a south-facing roof: panels on west- and east-facing sides will do. But you will need some plumbing and possibly a new boiler. Solar hot water systems mostly work by pre-heating water in the tank so that the existing fuel source has less work to do. Average cost £1,000–£2,000, including grants but excluding extra plumbing work.

Fit exterior or interior insulation. If you don't have cavity walls, then the only way to get better thermal efficiency out of them (apart from the extreme but often appealing option of demolition and reconstruction) is to add insulation, either to the inside or outside of the building. Each approach has its advantages and disadvantages.

Insulating the outside of the building avoids 'cold bridging', when outside temperatures are transferred to inside walls. And it doesn't affect the size of the rooms. But it won't be ideal in a conservation area, where cladding a nice brick-built house in, say, 200mm of rendered insulation is unlikely to find favour with the planning authorities. Adding insulation on the inside means slightly smaller rooms and potential 'cold-bridge' problems, but is the only wall-insulation option for those of us fortunate enough to live in old listed buildings. Cost range £1,000–£15,000.

Ultimately, the measures you take depend on your budget and beliefs. As specialist architect Gil Schalom says, doing something is always better than doing nothing; any of these measures will have an effect on your home's energy performance. Gil and his partner, green activist Penney Poyzer, have, however, taken energy-efficiency measures to extremes in their own home, which they claim is the most comprehensive eco-friendly 'retrofit' in Britain of an existing house. Their project is based on the premise that there will never be enough 'eco-newbuilds' to address the problem of Britain's energy-inefficient housing stock: they wanted to demonstrate what could be done with their Victorian end-terrace house, described by Gil as 'the worst example of a thermal slum'.

See p. 194 for a case study of this house, which also incorporates many other 'green' upgrades (e.g. heating, water harvesting) covered in this chapter.

And the case study on p. 196 illustrates what sort of energy-saving measures are possible when you build from scratch.

Energy saving at a glance

	Cost/hassle	Payback time	'Green' value	Things you need to know
Behaviour changes	∿	∿	∿∿ ∿∿	Anyone can do these and payback is quick.
Buying efficient stuff	∿∿ ∿∿	∿∿ ∿∿	∿∿ ∿∿	Worth doing if you are replacing or buying new appliances. Low-energy lightbulbs can have a big impact on energy use. Not worth investing in renewable energy like solar PV until you've done this.
Draught stripping	∿∿ ∿∿ ∿	∿∿ ∿∿	∿∿ ∿∿	Can be hard work in older houses but essential if you are aiming for maximum energy efficiency.
Better boiler	∿∿ ∿∿ ∿∿ ∿∿	∿∿ ∿∿ ∿∿ ∿∿	∿∿ ∿∿ ∿	Worth doing if you are replacing or buying new.
Loft insulation	∿∿ ∿∿	∿∿ ∿∿ ∿∿ ∿∿	∿∿ ∿∿ ∿∿	Essential to achieve decent energy efficiency in the home. Needs to be at least 300mm thick to be worthwhile.
Cavity wall insulation	∿∿ ∿∿	∿∿ ∿∿ ∿∿ ∿∿	∿∿ ∿∿ ∿∿	If you've got cavities, fill 'em. 50% of the heat goes out of the walls.
High-spec glazing	∿∿ ∿∿ ∿∿ ∿∿	∿∿ ∿∿	∿∿ ∿∿ ∿∿	Costly but worthwhile if you are building new or replacing and looking for absolute maximum energy savings.
Conservatory	∿∿ ∿∿ ∿∿ ∿∿ ∿	∿∿ ∿∿ ∿	∿∿ ∿∿ ∿∿ ∿	Again, costly but brings many extra practical benefits: propagating fruit and veg, socializing ... South-facing is best.
Solar hot water	∿∿ ∿∿ ∿∿ ∿∿	∿∿ ∿∿ ∿	∿∿ ∿∿ ∿∿ ∿	Needs a few square metres of roof space, preferably south (or SW/SE)-facing. Doesn't work with combination or mains pressure hot water systems.
External or internal insulation	∿∿ ∿∿ ∿∿ ∿∿ ∿	∿∿ ∿∿ ∿∿ ∿∿	∿∿ ∿∿ ∿∿ ∿∿	A big, expensive step with a long payback time. May have planning implications on conservation areas or on listed buildings. However, essential for high levels of energy efficiency in older buildings.

Cost/hassle: ∿ = free and easy or as near as dammit; ∿∿ ∿∿ ∿∿ ∿∿ ∿∿ = possible five-figure sum and professional help needed

Payback time: ∿ = less than 1 year; ∿∿ ∿∿ ∿∿ ∿∿ ∿∿ = more than 10 years

'Green' value – subjective score rating overall environmental benefit: ∿ = none; ∿∿ ∿∿ ∿∿ ∿∿ ∿∿ = maximum

Generating energy

There is something innately appealing about the idea of being 'off-grid', totally self-sufficient in heat and power. Apart from not getting any bills, there's the sense of security and independence in knowing that power cuts won't affect you. And, if your energy and power generation is from a renewable source, there's the satisfaction of knowing that it's having the lightest possible impact on the environment.

But is such 'unplugging' possible? Or affordable? Or even desirable? The picture is more complex than it seems. Wind and solar power, for example, do not provide 'on-demand' electricity; they only generate when the conditions are right. Switch on the kettle on a cloudy, windless day and your wind turbine and solar panels will not make you a cup of tea. Such systems need storage; storage means batteries; and batteries – particularly of the size that might keep domestic appliances ticking over – bring environmental problems of their own, being made of hazardous, toxic materials. To get over the storage problems, you could install a diesel generator, but that's hardly an eco-friendly option. Going 'off-grid', therefore, has environmental issues of its own; and the relatively small amounts of electricity that often result mean that it is best suited to the 'hardcore greenie' who is prepared to face a life with a bare minimum of electrical appliances: low-energy lighting, or a laptop or two. If you want to use 'green' power, then buying renewable energy from the grid via someone like Ecotricity is by far the simplest way.

So should the 21st-Century Smallholder give up on the idea of generating power at home? Not necessarily. But there's little environmental or economic point in doing so unless you are at the same time taking serious steps to make your home as energy-efficient as possible. Powering electricity-guzzling tungsten filament lightbulbs with a photovoltaic (PV) solar panel would, for example, just be plain silly. At present, there isn't really an economic case for generating your own power. By putting solar PV panels on your roof or installing a micro-wind or micro-hydro system, at the moment you are substituting cheap electricity from the grid for more expensive electricity from your own systems. Without a grant, for example, you won't get your money back from a solar PV system for a hundred years. However, renewable-energy technologies are developing fast and some – particularly wind – can pay back reasonably quickly. And it seems unlikely that fossil fuel prices will be falling in the future.

There may not yet be an economic case but, depending on your views and your means, there is a philosophical case for domestic power generation. You may see it as a way of 'doing your bit' to create a more sustainable energy future. Indeed there is a school of thought that suggests that 'micro-generation' – small, domestic-scale power generation – is the only route to a sustainable power grid, because even renewables cause problems when implemented on a large scale. Witness, for example, the ecological devastation caused by large-scale hydroelectric projects or the nimbyism generated by major wind-power projects. A power grid of the future could consist of thousands of devices built into the fabric of our homes and communities, rather than vast wind-turbine arrays or mighty, CO_2-belching power stations with their accompanying armies of pylons.

If you want to generate your own heat and power, whether for a sense of independence, out of conscience, or even as a building block of a future power grid, the technologies for doing it are all out there. And whilst many are not cheap, they are rapidly becoming more affordable and more efficient.

Solar electric

The natural world runs on solar power: all living organisms are ultimately dependent on the sun as a source of energy. Human society also, in effect, runs on solar power, because the fossil energy on which 'developed' economies depend is nothing more than captured solar energy from millions of years ago. In *The Whole House Book*, authors Pat Borer and Cindy Harris put the sun's power into perspective by pointing out that the amount of solar energy hitting the Earth in one hour is equivalent to the world's annual demand for fossil fuels.

We hugely under-use the power of the sun to help power our modern British lifestyles. Good building design and the use of a simple technology like solar hot-water generation can go a long way to dealing with our heating and hot-water needs (see p. 167). Solar-generated electricity is a less efficient, more expensive and more high-tech way of capturing and converting the sun's energy. But as long as you're prepared for it not to make financial sense in anything but the very long term, solar PV has a lot going for it. It can, for example, generate as much electricity as a family uses in a year. It looks good – the deep blue of PV panels or tiles combines with their eco-friendliness to create a very benign aura indeed. And it's very low-maintenance and reasonably long-lived. It's 'free' electricity, just sitting on your roof. But it's not for everyone: before getting too excited about the promise of PV, take a look at the 'reality check' list opposite.

How solar electric works

Solar photovoltaic panels work by using thin layers of semiconducting materials (in most cases silicon) which are adapted to release electrons when exposed to light. The resulting flow of electricity (which increases with the intensity of light) is conducted away by metal contacts as direct current (DC) then carried to an inverter (a small box that will most likely live in your roof space) which converts it to alternating current (AC).

Solar PV systems can either be backed up by battery arrays (for an 'off-grid' system) or, more commonly, they are 'grid-connected': plugged into the mains. This, in effect, uses the electricity grid as a giant battery. It also has the advantage of turning the householder into a potential vendor of electricity, as any surplus can be sold back to the grid. You will need to contact your Distribution Network Operator (DNO) in order to set this up.

What you need for solar electric

☀ **A south-facing roof.** It's not strictly necessary – within 45° of south facing is OK – but this will give you the best possible PV performance. The roof should also be pitched, at an angle from 15–50°, but ideally at around 35–40°. It should also not be shaded in any way.

Solar panels or tiles can be put up in other places: on conservatory roofs or façades, or even as free-standing arrays, but these options (particularly the latter one) may have extra cost and even planning implications.

☀ **At least 10 square metres of free space.** The ideal south-facing roof or sloping space needs to have at least this area free to make a PV installation viable. To generate as much energy as an average family uses in a year (3,300kWh*) would need around 40 square metres.

☀ **Preferably not to be living in a listed building or conservation area.** Although there are unlikely to be planning restrictions on most PV installations, permission may be needed in some cases: check with your local authority.

☀ **Upwards of £5,000 to spare.** A 2kWp** system (which will generate half of an average household's annual electricity requirements) will cost in the region of £8,000-£18,000. The DTI's Low Carbon Buildings Programme offers grants for solar PV.

Is it worth it?

In pure economic terms, domestic solar electricity is madness. But I'd wager that most people considering PV are not thinking about making a fast buck. They're probably thinking about the other potential 'yields' from solar electricity. There's the feelgood factor; the aesthetics; and the possibility that such a system may add value to your property. There's also a certain element of 'demonstration', too: conspicuous solar panels show others that renewable energy is happening. And who is to say that the payback time won't reduce radically as fossil energy becomes more expensive in the future?

*kWh – a unit of electrical energy (equal to the work done by one kilowatt acting for one hour)

**kWp – the theoretical maximum output for a given area of PV installation

Wind

Britain is windy. We have 40 per cent of the total wind resource in Europe and this could, according to the British Wind Energy Association, meet our electricity needs eight times over. However, wind energy is a highly emotive subject, splitting even members of the green movement, who tussle over the aesthetics vs. sustainability arguments. Perhaps our thinking about wind is going in the wrong direction. Stick hundreds of turbines in an Area of Outstanding Natural Beauty and even without the powerful, covert goading of the nuclear lobby, people are going to be upset.

Maybe 'micro-generation' is the way forward for wind? It's certainly becoming more accessible. Until quite recently, even small-scale wind turbines were pretty big, meaning that domestic wind-power generation was really only viable for those in possession of a few acres. Today, however, turbines have been developed that are little bigger and arguably a great deal less ugly than satellite dishes, and prices are heading down to levels that make domestic wind-power generation a more practical proposition.

Like solar PV, wind power is an intermittent source, needing either to be grid-connected or backed up by batteries; and it's certainly not suitable for every household. It's cheaper than solar PV, though, so if you have the ideal conditions, it offers a cost-effective and low-maintenance source of clean energy.

How wind power works

Unlike solar PV, there's no real mystery here. The turbine turns a generator which produces a DC current: this is then switched to AC by an inverter and then stored or fed directly into the grid. The power output varies according to the cube of wind speed, so increases in wind make a big difference. Overall, wind turbines will produce an average output over the year of 30 per cent of their rated capacity.

What you need for wind power

❋ **A windy site.** Goes without saying, really; but the energy yield of wind turbines is radically affected not only by the amount of wind, but also by its quality: if the wind is made turbulent by buildings or mitigated by trees, then a turbine is unlikely to be viable. So in Britain, this means clear exposure to the south-west, from where our prevailing wind blows, preferably uninterrupted by buildings, hills or trees. The presence of anything higher than your turbine site within 100 metres is likely to make it unviable. For house-mounted turbines, a south-west-facing gable end is ideal. Being high up, in the north or west of England, or preferably Scotland, Wales or the Pennines is also a distinct advantage.
In practice, all this means that many houses in both urban and rural areas will not be suitable for domestic wind generation. However, there are a good few that will be, and the benefits for such houses are likely to improve, as the technologies are developing fast.

❋ **Planning permission.** For all but the tiniest battery-charging toy turbines, you are likely to need permission from your local authority. This currently applies to the new generation of 'house mounted' small turbines as well as the more serious 'stand-alone' machines. There are, however, moves to ensure that small-scale wind generation is readily granted permission, so this hurdle should become easier to clear over time.

❋ **Upwards of £1,000 to spare.** The smallest turbines, designed to be fitted directly to a house, are now heading down towards the £1,000 mark, installed. For this price, you get a 1kW system. The cost rises with power, with systems in the 1.5kW to 6kW range costing between £4,000–8,000 installed. The costs are, of course, higher for stand-alone, off-grid systems that need battery or diesel-generator backup. Grants are available as for solar electric.

Is it worth it?

It is only worth looking at micro-wind generation if you have an absolutely ideal site. Whilst a 1kW turbine could, in theory, knock one third off your electricity bills, in practice, few urban homes will get the strength and quality of wind needed. And some manufacturers' claims are based on the fantasy of an optimum wind blowing twenty-four hours a day, 365 days a year and should therefore be scrutinized with great care.

Micro-hydro

Domestic hydroelectricity? Are you serious? Well yes, it can be done. 'Micro-hydro' systems (those that generate less than 100kW) are indeed available for the householder. And there's nothing new about this: small-scale hydroelectric schemes were once common in areas such as Wales in the early twentieth century, before the arrival of the National Grid put them out of business. But this particular form of renewable energy generation is highly location-specific. Few of us are fortunate enough to live next to a stream that would be just right for a bit of home hydropower. For those of us that are, however, this is a technology worth investigating. Although the capital costs are high, good micro-hydro systems are long-lived, easy to maintain and provide a more reliable flow of electricity than the wind or sun.

How hydro-electricity works

As with wind power, no great complication here: water turns a turbine, which drives a generator, which produces electricity. Assuming the stream flows all year round, hydro systems produce electricity all the time, albeit at a rate that varies with the flow of water. Micro-hydro schemes are likely to work at about 50 per cent efficiency.

What you need for micro-hydro

A good stream. To get a viable micro-hydro system, you need to be close to the right kind of stream. It should ideally be one that flows all year round and it needs a good enough rate of flow and sufficient 'head' (height) to power a turbine. To generate around 1kW from a micro-hydro turbine, you would, for example, need a flow rate of 15 litres per second and a head of 15 metres. The minimum head requirement is 2.4 metres; but the lower the head, the higher the flow rate needed.

Professional help. You could go down the DIY route, but only if you're an engineer or seriously talented hobbyist. You will need help to assess the site, choose the right type of equipment and build the infrastructure (intake, powerhouse, outflow, cables).

Permission. Micro-hydro schemes are likely to need permission from both the local water company and the Environment Agency (SEPA in Scotland), who will assess them for environmental impact. Building weirs and dams necessitates further permissions.

Around £20,000+. Capital costs for micro-hydro are high, with the 5kW needed to power a house costing around £10,000 in fixed costs and around £2,500 per kW. Grants are available as for solar electric.

Is it worth it?

Bizarrely, yes, in the long term and if you have the right site. If you are grid-connected, then sales back to the grid (combined with savings) could bring payback in under a decade. And if you are in a remote location, then the cost of a grid connection could make the prospect of even such a significant investment in renewable energy attractive.

Combined heat and power (CHP)

CHP differs from wind, solar and hydro in that it doesn't use renewable energy. The systems that are becoming available for home use are powered by natural gas: although CHP systems using biofuels (organic matter of recent origin) are being developed, these are not currently viable for the householder. However, domestic CHP is an interesting energy-saving technology: a unit similar in size and appearance to a conventional gas boiler generates heat and also produces electricity. Whilst fossil-fuel-powered CHP is not a 'sustainable' source of electricity, it does bring about efficiencies, with a claimed reduction in CO_2 emissions of 1.5 tonnes per household per annum.

How CHP works

Domestic CHP units use Stirling engines, in which pistons are powered by the repeated heating and cooling of gas in a cylinder and move through an alternator in order to produce electricity. The heat output of this process is then used to heat water in the same way as a conventional boiler.

What you need for domestic CHP

A reasonably well-insulated house. The heat output of a typical CHP unit means that it works best in a house with a heat loss of around 8kW, which generally means a new five-bed detached house, a 1990s four-bed detached house or a 1970s three-bed semi.

About £3,000. Domestic CHP units cost more than even the fanciest energy-efficient boilers.

Is it worth it?

If the cost of solar electricity is too scary, wind isn't viable and you don't live next to a powerful stream, then a CHP unit is the next best way of generating electricity at home. Its proponents claim savings of £150 per year, including the proceeds of your sales back to the grid.

Biofuels

You won't generate electricity with biofuels, but you could heat your house with them. The term 'biofuels' covers everything from 'energy crops' like corn fermented and turned into ethanol to power cars, to methane; from sewage and landfill, to burning agricultural wastes and wood. On a domestic level, biofuels basically means wood. Even the hardest of hardcore environmentalists is unlikely to have the stomach for a home-based methane digester, producing gas for cooking from a foul-smelling slurry of anaerobically decomposing organic matter. Wood does count as renewable energy; and it is 'carbon-neutral', because it absorbs the same amount of CO_2 whilst growing as it does when burnt. However, burning ancient woodland to heat your house is clearly not ideal, so finding a sustainable source of fuel is important, as is finding the most efficient way of burning it. Fortunately, both fuel supplies and wood-burning technology have come a long way in recent years, so, surprising though it may seem, a good old-fashioned fire can heat your home efficiently and sustainably. The options are either to have a stove for simple space heating, or to have a boiler connected to your hot water and central-heating system.

How biofuels work

They burn and make either you or some water warm. There is a little more to it, in that modern stoves and boilers can achieve very high efficiencies (of over 80 per cent) and with good design and dry fuel can burn with a minimum of pollution. (That crackling, spitting pine log found in the woods and thrown onto a jolly campfire is in fact emitting a worse cocktail of pollutants than any fossil fuel.)

What you need for biofuels

● **Ideally, not to live in a Smoke Control Area.** Smokeless Zones, as they were once called, cover most urban areas in Britain. You can burn fuel in these areas, but it must be of an exempt type and none of the exempt fuels could be described as completely sustainable. However, there is also a list of 'exempted appliances' that can burn wood, so with a little research it is possible to have a sustainable stove in a smokeless zone.

⬤ **A sustainable source of fuel and somewhere to put it.** There's more and more choice for sustainable sources of wood-based fuel. At the high-tech end, wood pellets made of compressed sawmill waste can be used with stoves that feed in the pellets with computerized controls to ensure maximum efficiency. Woodchips from tree surgery and forestry waste can also be used in this high-tech way, although mainly with bigger 'community-sized' stoves. Logs, correctly seasoned for between one and four years to remove moisture, are the most 'natural' option. But it's worth pointing out that for heating, cooking and hot water, even a low-energy household would need around 3 tonnes a year, which takes up a lot of space. And to produce this for your own needs would take a hectare of coppice woodland and a lot of effort. Otherwise, there's the no-cost option: scavenged pallets burn very well indeed.

⬤ **Compliance with Building Regulations and planning requirements.** Heating appliances need to be installed in accordance with Building Regulations (something a professional installer will take care of) and chimneys/flues may need planning permission in listed buildings or areas of outstanding natural beauty.

⬤ **Upwards of £1,500.** Which is about the minimum installed cost for a stand-alone stove for room heating. Pellet- or log-burning systems for water and central heating might cost around £5,000 installed for a typical 15–20kW system. Grants are available. It's worth remembering as well that unless you manage your own coppice woodland or find the wood for free, this is the one renewable energy source that does cost money on an ongoing basis.

Are they worth it?

If you're away from mains gas, it is worth considering wood-burning for both space and water heating. Together with high-spec insulation it can work very efficiently, and for space heating you can't beat the cosiness of a wood-burning stove. If you happen to have a smallish house with a good space for solar water heating (see p. 167), then this, combined with a wood-burning stove with a back boiler and excellent insulation, could be all the heating you need.

Ground-source heat pumps

Not to be confused with geothermal energy, in which heat is extracted from geological heat sources, ground-source heat pumps work in a mysterious way. Using the fact that the ground just a few metres deep stays at a constant 11–12°C all year round, they concentrate this heat into something that can be used for space heating or even to pre-heat domestic hot water. It's not strictly renewable energy, because some power is needed to make this mystery happen, but it uses less power and emits considerably less CO_2 than fossil-fuel heat sources.

How ground-source heat pumps work

There is in fact nothing particularly fancy about this technology: a ground-source heat pump is just a fridge working backwards. Heat taken from the embedded pipes is compressed and concentrated, then pumped around the house via heat exchangers and the chosen heating method. Heat pumps can be used to cool buildings as well, with the ground loop being used to store, rather than generate heat, but this is not efficient for domestic installations. Ground-source heat pumps generate around 4kW of heat energy for every 1kW of power needed to run the heat exchanger and compressor.

What you need for ground source heat

Space or depth. The key component of a ground-source heat pump is a 'ground loop': a long length of thin pipe that is a closed circuit of water mixed with antifreeze. This either goes into deep boreholes, or into trenches around your property as a straight pipe or 'slinky' coil. Around 80 metres of trench length would be needed for a typical 8kW installation using slinky coil, so if boreholes are impossible, a big garden (that you are prepared to dig up) is essential.

Ideally, underfloor heating. Ground source heat works with radiators, but these need to be of the right size to deal with lower temperatures of 45–55°C. It works best with underfloor heating, which is effective at lower temperatures. This can be retrofitted to homes but it's not an insignificant task.

A very energy-efficient home. The lower temperatures at which these systems work are not suited to older, 'leaky' buildings. Your home needs to be insulated to high standards before a ground-source heat pump becomes viable.

At least £6,000. Installation is expensive and the distribution system will cost more.

Are they worth it?

Ground-source heat pumps are most viable for houses that don't have mains gas: thanks to the capital costs and the electricity needed to power them, the overall cost is currently slightly higher than gas, although this is likely to change over time. It is possible to run the electrical equipment with battery-supported solar PV for a completely carbon-free system, but this raises the capital costs yet higher. In general, if you have a well-insulated house with a big garden (or the ability to have deep boreholes drilled), and either don't have mains gas or aren't bothered by the higher cost, this is a good alternative, with a long lifespan.

Generating energy at a glance

	Cost/ hassle	Payback time	'Green' value	Things you need to know
Solar electric	◊◊◊◊◊	◊◊◊◊◊	◊◊◊◊	Unshaded south-facing roof with 10m² free is essential. May be planning implications if listed or in a conservation area.
Wind	◊◊◊◊	◊◊◊◊◊	◊◊◊◊◊	Need planning consent and the perfect windy location.
Micro-hydro	◊◊◊◊◊	◊◊◊◊	◊◊◊◊	Strictly for those with a handy stream nearby.
Domestic CHP	◊◊◊◊	◊◊◊	◊◊	Need an energy-efficient house. Not renewable energy.
Biofuels	◊◊◊	◊◊◊◊◊	◊◊◊	Best not to live in a smokeless zone. Gets very costly for big houses.
Ground-source heat pumps	◊◊◊◊◊	◊◊◊◊◊	◊◊◊◊◊	Dig garden or deep boreholes essential. Only works with energy-efficient houses.

Cost/hassle: ◊ = free and easy or as near as dammit; ◊◊◊◊◊ = possible five-figure sum and professional help needed

Payback time: ◊ = less than 1 year; ◊◊◊◊◊ = more than 10 years

'Green' value: Subjective score rating overall environmental benefit: ◊ = none; ◊◊◊◊◊ = maximum

Dealing with water and waste

It is just daft that we use on average around 8 litres of purified drinking water each time we flush away our bodily wastes. This is but one of the many absurdities of the way in which we deal with water and waste. The problem is not that we are all evil, uncaring and profligate. Our attitudes to water and waste – and many of the technologies through which we deal with them – were conceived when water was not considered to be a finite resource and improving sanitation was of primary importance. Today, we know fresh water to be a dwindling resource, abstracted excessively around the world for everything from agriculture to golf courses. And whilst, in the developed world at least, we have solved the sanitation problem, we've done so at the cost of enormous water profligacy. It is ironic that hosepipe bans are the first response to drought in Britain: hosepipes account for a mere 3 per cent of domestic water use, whilst toilet-flushing accounts for over 30 per cent. Being less heavy-handed in the loo does much more to keep water poverty at bay than letting the plants wilt.

However, dealing with water and waste differently is not just about helping to solve a pressing environmental problem: both represent an under-used resource for the 21st-Century Smallholder. Rain, for example, falls mainly down the drain when we could be capturing some of it to water plants (who prefer it to treated drinking water), flush our toilets or even wash our clothes. And although years of social conditioning make it seem unthinkable, our own by-products have their uses too. Urine, when diluted, makes great plant food and can boost fruit and vegetable yields; and composted faeces can provide an effective, free fertilizer. Anyone squeamish about this should know that 54 per cent of the 1.1 million tonnes (dry weight) of sewage sludge we produce each year in Britain is currently used in 'agricultural applications' after treatment. Yum.

There are strong and sensible arguments on both sides of the water and waste debate. For example – as with renewable energy – why go to the trouble of investing in your own system if there's an existing one to plug into? Why invest in an expensive and potentially unnerving composting toilet if you're connected to a perfectly good sewage network? There are ways of being 'green' about water and waste that don't involve going to extremes. But equally, some might feel that the 'extremes' are appropriate: that, for example, dealing with one's own bodily waste should be a household rather than a municipal duty. Whichever side of the debate you're on, changing your relationship with water and waste is worthwhile.

Saving water

Changing behaviour
As with saving energy (see pp. 163–4), simple and easy actions can make a huge difference to your water use. Locking up the hosepipe won't make much of a difference; using the toilet differently will. Pre-1993 toilets use around 9 litres of water per flush; new ones are required to use no more than 6 litres; however, there are dual-flush models available that can do the job with 2–4 litres (depending on what the job is). So simply not routinely flushing away urine is one way: it's pretty benign stuff (unless you've been eating asparagus, in which case it gets a bit whiffy). If this isn't acceptable, putting a device in the cistern to displace water can save up to 3 litres per flush in an older style toilet. You could try a brick or a plastic bottle full of water, but I couldn't work out how to do this without almost dismantling the toilet. The 'Hippo' is easier: basically a bag made of stout but flexible plastic, it forms a reservoir that confines and saves flush water.

Then there's a long and fairly familiar litany of behavioural changes, all of which will save more than giving up the hosepipe: sorting out any water leaks or dripping taps; taking showers instead of baths; using the dishwasher and washing machine less frequently. As an incentive to these, it's worth getting a water meter fitted, because then these behavioural changes will salve your wallet as well as your conscience. The makers of the Hippo, for example, claim a saving of £20 per year if their devices are used in a metered household.

Gardening differently can also make a difference to water use, although if all your garden watering is from harvested rainwater (see pp. 187–9), then it's less of an issue. Some tips for a water-efficient garden:

- **Don't water too often:** so roots will search deeper for water, strengthening the plant.
- **Let the grass grow:** it won't dry out so readily.
- **Make good soil:** soil rich in organic matter retains moisture better (see also p. 57).

🌢 **Use mulches:** which reduce evaporation (see also p. 57).
🌢 **Plant in beds rather than containers:** pots or tubs always need more water.
🌢 **Consider perennial plants:** which often make better use of available moisture.
🌢 **Use targeted watering systems:** like seep hoses or 'leaky pipes'.

More serious steps

If you want to get really serious about saving water, then harvesting rainwater and recycling greywater (see pp. 187–9) can make a big difference. Investing in more water-efficient appliances is also worth considering, particularly as and when existing ones need replacing.

Washing machines and dishwashers account for over 20 per cent of domestic water use. Modern dishwashers now use around 16 litres per cycle, compared to 25 for older machines: as long as they are used only when fully loaded, this makes them more water-efficient than washing up by hand. The latest washing machines now use 50 litres per load rather than older appliances' 100 litres. And all such appliances now carry energy labelling (from 'A' for best to 'G' for worst) that details water as well as electricity use. Even with a metered supply, converting to modern appliances won't necessarily pay back financially over the average eight-year life of an appliance, but this may change over time.

Targeting the toilet and the taps can also make a big difference. Replacing a perfectly good bog is a needless expense, however, so using something like a Hippo (see p. 185) is the best way if you don't need a new one. It is also possible to fit an 'Ecoflush' device to some toilets to control the amount of water used. If, however, you are refurbishing or building a house, a low-flush toilet such as the Ifö Cera costs a little more to buy, but with half the water use of a standard loo it will pay back a metered household over time. More extreme sanitation solutions are dealt with in 'Sewage alternatives' (pp. 190–3). Spray taps and low-flow shower heads can also be fitted to reduce water use.

Harvesting water

Capturing rainwater for use in the garden or the home is an option available to anyone with legitimate access to a drainpipe. Although rainwater may not be recommended for drinking, it is said to be preferable to tap water for garden irrigation because plants don't like the chlorine residues in drinking water. And, as for toilet flushing, it does seem daft to shower plants with purified water when, first, they would prefer something else and, second, it's an increasingly pressured resource. You can go a lot further than just a simple water butt, though: it is possible to use harvested rainwater for washing clothes and flushing toilets and even, at the extreme end, for drinking and washing.

Rainwater for the garden

This is cheap, simple and will benefit any garden. Water butts storing over 200 litres can be bought for a little over £20: all they need for installation is some space near a drainpipe and a diverter which is easily fitted to the pipe. Such tanks will be quickly emptied during dry periods, so if the garden demands a lot of watering (for example if you are raising lots of seedlings) it's always ideal to buy the biggest possible butt. Recycled tanks up to 1,500 litres and beyond are available and, although large, such monsters can either be buried or disguised with climbing plants.

Rainwater for the house

Even if you live in a relatively dry part of Britain, a lot of water falls on your roof. Over 45,000 litres a year run off the roof of my terraced house in London, of which I could capture around 30,000 litres. If my family went for drastic water-efficiency measures to get our consumption down to, say, 25 per cent of the national average then we could, in theory, supply all our needs from rainwater. But we'd need somewhere for around 4,000 litres worth of storage tanks and some sophisticated filtering equipment. Relying completely on rainwater is an expensive and potentially hazardous business, and highly dependent on where you live and how suitable your roof is. For example, parts of the east and south-east of England receive only 500mm per year, whilst the Lake District and Snowdonia can get soaked by over 2,400mm.

Still, as purified drinking water is an increasingly precious resource, it doesn't seem to make sense that we use it for so many applications where rainwater would do the trick. Most commercially available rainwater harvesting systems are focused on using the water where it needs minimal filtering – i.e. washing clothes, flushing toilets and watering the garden. Together, these take up over 50 per cent of domestic water use. To use rainwater for drinking and washing, however, adds an extra layer of complexity and expense, as filters need to be installed and maintained throughout the system. And to rely exclusively on rainwater you will additionally need to be absolutely sure of your house's ability to capture enough: for many houses, in many parts of the country, it won't be possible.

If you want to be more autonomous in water, or simply feel it is right to invest in using it more efficiently, then rainwater harvesting for the house is possible, albeit at some cost.

What you need for domestic rainwater harvesting

A supply of water: to calculate how much water falls on your roof, you need to know the local annual rainfall, and the area of the roof. These figures are then multiplied with a 'runoff co-efficient' (which relates to how efficient your roof is at delivering water) and a 'filter efficiency' score, relating to losses in the water filter. So for my house, with a reasonably efficient and generously sized pitched roof, the calculation would be:

London rainfall (mm)		Roof area in square metres		Runoff efficient		Filter efficiency	TOTAL
630	x	72	x	0.75	x	0.9	30,918 litres

To calculate how big a tank you might need, assess your daily requirement in litres and multiply this by a guess at what the longest period without rain is likely to be.

So a rough guess for a family of four each using water at the current average level (150 litres per person per day) and wanting to use rainwater for half their needs might be:

Daily usage (litres)		Days without rain		Half of needs		TOTAL
600	×	21	×	0.5		6,300 litres

Which is a monstrous tank; and which illustrates that the current average levels of water use (600 litres a day means 219,000 litres a year) need to be cut radically with water-saving measures before rainwater harvesting becomes viable.

Space for a tank: the rainwater tank will need either to be buried (under the drive or the garden, for example), or installed in a cellar.

Upwards of £2,500: the system will need to be professionally installed and work will be needed to plumb it into your existing water system so that the right water flows to the right appliances (mains to the taps, rain to the toilets and washing machine).

Greywater recycling

'Greywater' is the rather murky term for the murky stuff that swills out of sinks, bathtubs and showers and off down the drain. Recycling greywater can save up to 18,000 litres per person per year, or a third of daily household use, mainly by using it to flush toilets. So why don't we all do it? Because recycling greywater is a tricky business. It needs to be stored somewhere in order to be used; and because it tends to be warm and full of bugs, greywater deteriorates quickly in quality when stored. So to prevent this happening it needs to be filtered and treated; and also pumped high into the house so it can be gravity-fed to the toilets. This means building and plumbing in a sealed system.

Easier ways of recycling greywater are simply to chuck a bowl of washing-up or bath water around plants. However, even this can be problematic because the salts in soap can damage the soil.

On the whole, domestic greywater recycling on anything other than an 'occasional bucketful on the garden' basis is expensive and generally considered impractical for even the greenest of households to consider. If you live in a dry area, pay for mains drainage, and do a lot of gardening, then it may well be worth considering using a reedbed as a way of dealing with greywater: it could reduce your sewage costs and also produce a resource. As Patrick Whitefield points out in the *Earth Care Manual*, reeds are a useful source of mulching material.

Sewage alternatives

In a foreword to Peter Harper and Louise Halestrap's *Lifting the Lid: an ecological approach to toilet systems*, environmental campaigner George Monbiot comments that: 'Every time we pull the chain, the future of the world is sucked a little further down the drain.' He's referring to the fact that conventional flush toilets are designed to use excessive amounts of fresh drinking water to do their job. But the 'bog standard' toilet then goes on to commit an even worse crime: it then contaminates this precious stuff with human waste (that itself could otherwise be turned into a valuable natural resource), mixing all into a vile sludge needing industrial treatment at large, unpleasant facilities.

So as part of creating a more environmentally friendly, self-reliant house, should we automatically look at radical ways of dealing with our waste? Not necessarily. As Harper and Halestrap point out, the flush toilet does a lot of things well: it is hygienic, efficient, reliable and socially acceptable. And for most houses in cities, towns and villages, it is plugged into an existing sewage network which, although ecologically illogical, works well and has preserved public health for many years.

There are many ways of dealing with human waste differently, from the simple to the extreme. Which – if any – you choose to use depends on several things: where you live, your budget, your sensibilities and your personal philosophy.

Basic steps: cheap and easy sewage alternatives for all

Because flushing uses so much of it, many of the things we can do to make our toilets less destructive have to do with saving water. Using displacement devices in the cistern (see p. 185) can save 3–4 litres per flush. And following the axiom: 'If it's brown flush it down; if it's yellow, let it mellow' can save even more, but this is not to everyone's taste.

But what possible way is there of using waste differently without exposing the household to unpleasantness and risk? According to the authors of *Lifting the Lid*, urine is, with the exception of some rare tropical diseases, non-pathogenic and 'almost certainly the best fertiliser you can obtain and it's free'. This isn't a licence to start peeing willy-nilly all over the vegetable beds, because neat urine will 'burn' the plants and contains high levels of sodium they won't like. Diluted at around 1:20, however, its valuable nitrogen content can be delivered directly to growing plants. Application is easy, particularly for men: who is to know that you had a sly pee in the watering can before topping it up from the water butt?

Fresh urine, in modest quantities, is also famed for 'activating' sluggish compost heaps (see p. 49).

Also cheap and easy, but perhaps offending more sensibilities, is a way of 'composting' urine. The 'straw-bale urinal' could lurk in a discreet, shady corner of a larger garden: nothing more than a straw bale with the cut ends uppermost, it is peed on intermittently then left for six to nine months: a fine compost develops in the interior and the rest can be used as mulch or added to a compost heap.

More serious steps: sewage alternatives that cost money and won't suit everyone

If you are refurbishing a house or simply feel it is right to invest in sewage alternatives, then upgrading your existing toilets is an obvious step. Low-flush models cost little more than standard toilets and use a great deal less water (see p. 185). For a household containing males, a more radical step might be to introduce a waterless urinal. Not everyone's idea of a bathroom adornment, these cost upwards of £250 and deal with the 'odour' problem by using air freshener pads. There are also air-flushed models available. Depending on the gender mix of a household, waterless urinals can reduce water usage by up to 20 per cent. In the case of these and low-flush toilets, the extra investment can be offset over the longer term by savings in water charges for metered households.

Further up the sliding scale of complexity and potential offences to sensibility is the composting toilet. The mere phrase strikes fear into many; and the 'black hole' of a dry composting toilet can indeed be an unsettling prospect, particularly for those with small, inquisitive children. On the plus side, though, composting toilets do perform a kind of magic, converting faeces into valuable fertilizer that can be used around, say, fruit trees and bushes. (Although the resulting compost is widely considered to be benign and free of pathogens, it is not recommended to apply it directly to plants that are to be eaten.) And, of course, they produce no sewage, helping your household to be 'waste-neutral'. They don't smell if properly installed and vented and are surprisingly pleasant places to be. Composting systems can also be installed with flush toilets (see case study on p. 195), getting rid of the 'black hole' problem.

Composting toilets are not for everyone, though. Retrofitting one to an existing house, for example, is a serious business. (But it can be done, as the case study shows.) Composting toilets need chambers for the magic to take place: either a large, sloping unit for 'continuous' composting or multiple chambers so that one can be closed when full (the composting process takes a year or so) and a second put into use. Whilst smaller composting toilets are available, ideally you need space: a big cellar or basement space is ideal. They also need not to have too much liquid, meaning ideally that the urine has to be separated out (either by peeing somewhere else or installing urine-separating systems). And as they are, in effect, living ecosystems in their own right, they need looking after: someone, for example, has to indulge in the delightfully named practice of 'peak knocking' from time to time in order to keep the metamorphosing pile of ordure happy.

So unless you have a strong ideological commitment to sewage reduction, a large cellar and either upwards of £2,000 to spare or confident DIY and plumbing skills, composting toilets are probably a step too far for most people looking to 'retrofit' an existing house with eco-friendly features. However, if you are building from scratch, doing an extensive refurbishment of a suitable house, or don't have access to mains sewerage, they merit further investigation and are by far the most environmentally benign way of dealing with human waste.

Water at a glance

	Cost/ hassle	Payback time †	'Green' value	Things you need to know
Changing behaviour	💧	💧💧	💧💧💧 / 💧💧	Anyone can do these and payback is quick.
Buying water-efficient appliances	💧💧💧	💧💧	💧💧 / 💧💧	Low-flush toilets make the biggest difference.
Rainwater for the garden	💧💧	💧💧	💧💧💧 / 💧💧	Easy, cheap and gardens love rainwater. Everyone should have a butt.
Rainwater for the house	💧💧 / 💧💧	💧💧💧 / 💧💧	💧💧 / 💧💧	Need somewhere to put a large tank. Including drinking water makes systems more expensive and complex.
Greywater recycling	💧💧💧 / 💧💧	💧💧💧 / 💧💧	💧💧💧	Too much hassle to be viable for most.
Cost/hassle:	💧 = free and easy or as near as dammit; 💧💧💧💧💧 = possible five-figure sum and professional help needed			
Payback time:	💧 = less than 1 year; 💧💧💧💧💧 = more than 10 years			
'Green' value:	Subjective score rating overall environmental benefit: 💧 = none; 💧💧💧💧💧 = maximum			

† Household payback times for water saving are largely irrelevant unless you have a water meter.

Waste at a glance

	Cost/hassle	'Green' value	Things you need to know
Changing behaviour	🧻	🧻🧻🧻🧻🧻	Anyone can do these and big water savings are achieved.
Urine as fertilizer	🧻	🧻🧻🧻🧻🧻	Discretion is advised.
Straw-bale urine composting	🧻	🧻🧻🧻🧻🧻	Even more discretion is advised.
Low-flush toilets	🧻🧻🧻	🧻🧻🧻🧻🧻	Save water where it is wasted most.
Waterless urinals	🧻🧻🧻	🧻🧻🧻🧻🧻	Use no water but can be culturally problematic.
Composting toilets	🧻🧻🧻🧻	🧻🧻🧻🧻🧻	Stupendously eco-friendly but need an appropriate location. Recommended to contact appropriate public authorities before installing.
Cost/hassle:	🧻 = free and easy or as near as dammit; 🧻🧻🧻🧻🧻 = possible five-figure sum and professional help needed		
'Green' value:	Subjective score rating overall environmental benefit: 🧻 = none; 🧻🧻🧻🧻🧻 = maximum		

Case studies

Nottingham EcoHome: an 'eco-retrofit'

Despite having been 'the worst example of a thermal slum' when they bought it, Gil Schalom and Penney Poyzer's Victorian semi-detached house in Nottingham is now thought to be the best-performing 'eco-retrofit' in Britain. It is highly energy efficient, produces minimal CO_2 emissions and no solid sewage.

As Gil points out, we will never be able to build enough new environmentally friendly houses to correct the energy-inefficiency of Britain's existing housing stock. And even if we could afford to do it, knocking down all the draughty old houses to replace them with new eco-houses would simply bury the nation in rubble: construction waste makes up 70 per cent of all landfill. 'Retrofitting' existing houses with eco-friendly features has the dual advantage of making sustainable living available to any householder and contributing significantly to reducing the country's overall CO_2 emissions.

The philosophy behind Gil and Penney's project was to turn one of the worst-performing houses into one of the best. Their aim was to upgrade the house's thermal performance as much as they could whilst at the same time aiming to be as autonomous as possible in energy, water, sewage treatment and food. To make their project financially viable, their renovation also included accommodation for a lodger.

Saving energy

Every possible energy-saving feature has been incorporated into the house. The roof was rebuilt and given 300mm of Warmcel (recycled paper) insulation. Thick insulation was also added under floorboards for acoustic insulation as well as to keep the heat in. However, the biggest source of heat loss in a house is the walls, which in the case of this (rather tall) house covered an area of 200 square metres and had no cavity to fill with insulation. So the only options were either to clad the house in a 'skin' of insulating material or to add layers of insulation within rooms. Gil and Penney chose a hybrid approach, insulating inside at the front of the house to preserve its appearance, and cladding it in polystyrene and render at the side and rear. This was one of the most expensive pieces of work, costing £12,000. The house also has high-performance double- and triple-glazed windows and is draught-stripped throughout.

Generating heat and energy

As with all such schemes, Gil and Penney's choices for generating heat and energy were dictated partially by the house and its existing systems. The house had expensive electric water and space heating which meant big savings were possible straight away: a single flat-plate solar hot-water panel has been installed on the south-facing roof and has already achieved payback. Despite the superinsulation, the house is too big to heat with just a wood-burning stove and back boiler (the 'greenest' option), so some form of central heating was needed. Keen to minimize CO_2 emissions, Gil and Penney opted for a high-tech, Smoke Control Zone-compliant wood-burning boiler and heat store rather than choosing gas central heating, the obvious and much cheaper option. At £5,000 after grants, this was one of the most expensive items in the retrofit, but it gives them carbon-neutral heating when they need it and the fuel is free if they can scavenge enough discarded pallets. Two 1m-diameter wind turbines bolted to the chimney are being considered as an electricity-generating option for the future, if planning issues can be overcome; if not, there's room on the south-facing roof for photovoltaic panels.

Dealing with water and waste

The EcoHome has a rainwater-harvesting system that feeds the washing machine, toilets and an outside tap for watering the garden. The water is stored in two 1,000-litre tanks in the cellar and pumped directly to the appliances. A small roof means that rainwater supplies only around 30 per cent of the household's needs at the moment and although not currently bringing savings, it is expected to do so if, as is widely anticipated, water costs rise in the future. The rainwater-harvesting system cost a total of £2,000 installed.

Water-saving features in the house include prominent water meters at different points in the system for easy monitoring, and low-flush (2–4 litre) toilets throughout.

Although the house is connected to the sewage system, Gil and Penney were keen, for ideological and ecological reasons, to 'deal with their own shit'. So the EcoHome also features a bespoke composting system, which separates the solids from the low-flush loos and deals with them in a composting chamber in the cellar. Although the system cost £2,000 and needs occasional attention, its use of normal WCs overcomes any issues of social acceptability: and it is likely the EcoHome's fruit bushes will in time be particularly well fertilized!

Tree House, Clapham, London: an 'eco-newbuild'

Keen to build an environmentally friendly house, Will Anderson chanced upon that rarest of things, a building plot with planning permission in central London. The slim site is dominated by a tall mature sycamore tree and Will was captivated by the comparison between trees – built to last, using resources and energy efficiently, recycling everything – and how a house should work. So although high-tech, Tree House has been built with natural principles in mind. The guiding principle of the house is that good design can significantly reduce a house's impact on the environment: in Will's view, cheap fossil fuels are ultimately to blame for much of today's badly designed and inefficient housing.

Building an 'eco-house' from scratch has huge advantages over a retrofit. You are still constrained by the size and orientation of the plot, by surrounding buildings and local regulations; but a new build means you can use the very latest and most efficient techniques and technologies. As Will points out, though, to be truly workable these need to be deployed in a way that is acceptable to everyone involved: his partner Ford was consulted throughout the project.

Saving energy

Tree House is built from a timber frame that allows for a huge thickness of insulation in the walls, between the floors and in the roof. The walls are clad on the outside with wood and insulated with Warmcel (recycled-paper insulation). Windows are high-performance glazed units. Whilst it takes a great deal of effort to insulate an older building effectively, a new build can be completely airtight, providing maximum thermal efficiency. Tree House is airtight and uses 'whole house mechanical ventilation': this takes stale air from places like the kitchen and bathroom and mixes it with fresh air in a heat exchanger to provide heat for living rooms and bedrooms.

Generating heat and energy

Starting with a 'super-insulated' house gives you more options for generating heat and power, because there is much less heat loss. So for space heating, Tree House uses a ground-source heat-pump system, viable only for well-insulated houses. Four 25-metre-deep boreholes were drilled into the ground for pipes which will take the 11–12°C underground heat to a compressor, where it will be concentrated and fed into an underfloor heating system. It's expensive to install (typically from £6,000 upwards) but very cheap to run and the fuel source is free. Electricity for Tree House will be provided by a 5kWp solar photovoltaic array on the south-facing roof. Will anticipates that over the course of a year, the house will produce more electricity than it consumes, making it self-sufficient in energy (but not autonomous, as it relies on the grid when the solar panels are not generating electricity). Hot water will be provided by a solar hot-water system.

Dealing with water and waste

Whilst Will believes that there is value in every householder doing what they can towards generating energy, his view on water and waste is that the infrastructure needed for elaborate technologies such as complete rainwater-harvesting systems can often outweigh their benefits. So Tree House will address the 'demand' side of water use, with features such as low-flush toilets, spray taps and basic rain harvesting for the garden. For sewage, Will believes that the location of Tree House in a high-density urban area – and the site itself – would make an alternative solution such as a composting toilet inappropriate.

What if you've looked through this book and completely failed to heed its warnings about the perils of going 'all the way' towards a completely self-sufficient smallholding lifestyle? You haven't been put off by the expense, the grinding toil, or the knife-edge economics of it all. Rather than being a 21st-Century Smallholder – picking from a menu of lifestyle changes – you want to jack in the job, head for the hills and be a real, full-time smallholder. The romantic lure of such an idea is difficult to resist: a life free of bosses and bills, and a cornucopia in your backyard. What would it take to do this? How would you start?

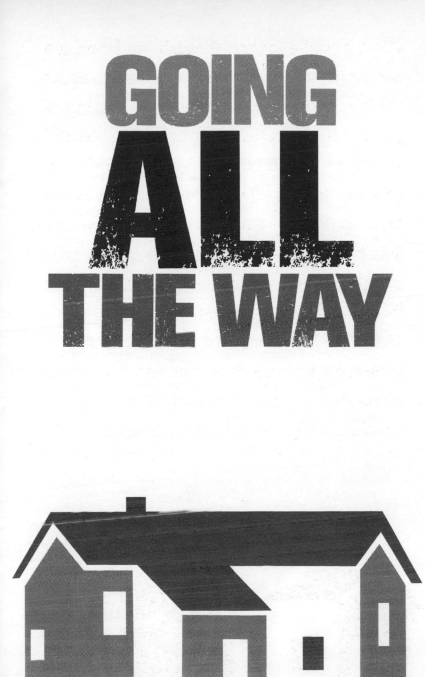

Smallholding is a way of life, not a nine-to-five job. So the best starting point is to ensure that you and your family are prepared to accept a very radical lifestyle change from, say, office workers to modern peasants. And many urban dreamers fail to think about the economics. As land rights advocate and smallholder Simon Fairlie says: 'You can't be self-sufficient in Wellington boots.' No matter how close to total self-sufficiency you get, you will still need money to buy stuff and pay the bills. This either means lots of capital or some form of part-time work, especially in the start-up phase; and then in the longer term, money-making smallholding activities (which are particularly important if you are going to try to live on agricultural land – see p. 203). Still, 60 per cent of farmers today have an additional source of income, illustrating that not many people truly live off the land.

So in the first instance you should ponder the economics and their practicalities: for example, if a vegetable-box scheme will be the cornerstone of your income, then veg-growing skills would be a distinct advantage. If it's going to be small-scale organic dairy products, then there are yet more skills, start-up costs and infrastructure needed. Your chosen money-making route will also partially determine where your smallholding will be: for example, veg-growing wouldn't be ideal on a steep, wooded site.

But despite the need to focus hard on the economics, the most pressing question for most people considering a truly self-sufficient future is: how do I get my smallholding? There are four main ways of going about it.

How to get your smallholding

1. Do it at home

If you are fortunate enough to have some land already, then self-sufficient smallholding can begin at home, depending on how much space you have. In the classic *Complete Book of Self-Sufficiency* (required reading for anyone wanting to go all the way), author John Seymour suggests that one acre of land (quality permitting) could support a diverse holding with chickens, pigs and a cow as well as extensive vegetable-growing. It wouldn't be true 'self-sufficiency', as you would have to buy in food for the animals and buy in your own cereal crops; but otherwise, such an area could provide for much of a family's needs. Move up to 4 acres and you could theoretically provide fodder for the animals and cereal crops for the family too, creating a complete, 'closed-loop' holding with everything grown on site and an occasional surplus for sale. What would the neighbours say? Well, with all that space you could probably design it in such a way that the neighbours wouldn't notice it too much. And as long as there aren't restrictive local bylaws, you could keep livestock too as long as you had the correct permissions and paperwork (see Chapter 2).

2. Buy a smallholding

In the days of the 1970s self-sufficiency movement, which was kick-started by the decade's oil crisis, chucking it all in and buying a smallholding was a viable option for many. A farmhouse with the necessary few acres of land could be had for an affordable sum. Since then, house prices have increased 35-fold and, unless it is in the far north of Scotland, the perfect place for a smallholding is going to cost hundreds of thousands of pounds. Which is fine if you have enough capital tied up in an existing property to make the move with a small or non-existent mortgage. It's important to keep mortgage outgoings to a minimum because, in order to create a viable smallholding operation, you will additionally need to invest in all manner of kit and infrastructure, whether it's polytunnels, food-processing gear, or wind turbines and solar panels. For those fortunate enough to have the money, however, this is the quickest and easiest way into smallholding: 'peasantry for the comfortably-off'.

3. Buy agricultural land and move on to it

For those of us not already in possession of a fortune in land or cash, this is the most financially viable way towards self-sufficiency. Agricultural land is still relatively cheap and it is possible to live on it. However, this approach is fraught with insecurity. On paper, the government supports 'sustainable development' in the countryside, so eco-friendly, low-impact smallholdings would seem to be in favour. But in practice there is, as Simon Fairlie notes, a 'massive, obsessive, neurotic' resistance at government level to dwellings on agricultural land. This has its roots in an attitude neatly summed up by low-impact roundhouse dweller Tony Wrench: 'The planning system was set in legislation in 1948 to preserve a nice view for toffs and landowners." Some planning authorities seem to have a policy of resisting any proposals for residence on smallholdings. In the face of this, many people find that the only approach likely to work for them is to move on, live in a tent, caravan or temporary dwelling, start work on their smallholding, put in a planning application and try to get the local authority's refusal overturned at appeal.

Most well-planned smallholding projects do eventually get planning permission, but it can be a long, stressful slog and the effort and insecurity are not for everyone. The key things you need to be able to prove in the planning process are:

- **Financial viability:** supported by a business plan that shows even a subsistence holding making a profit by the end of year three.
- **A need to be there:** because smallholding is a way of life, of course you need to be there; but the planning authorities are not always receptive to this argument.
- **Ability:** experience or training in your chosen smallholding activity is helpful.
- **No other appropriate accommodation:** showing that there is nowhere else available to live nearby.
- **Sustainability:** any smallholding is likely to be able to provide ample proof of this; local authorities may not give it weight, but appeals inspectors might.

Getting involved with the local community so that they are inclined to support your planning applications is also a highly recommended way to increase your chances of success. The case study of Guilden Gate on pp. 212–13 provides some insight into how to create a sustainable single-family smallholding on agricultural land.

4. Do it with friends or family

Smallholdings work best with a 'polycultural' mix of activities, for example arable farming, livestock and woodland management. So if, say, the crops don't do too well one year, the dairy and timber business can keep you going. And, of course, there's a symbiosis between different activities – such as animals providing fertility for the land – that is lost if your smallholding concentrates on just one thing. The problem is that keeping all this going can be a very tall order for a single family. The livestock side of things alone will tie you to the holding all year unless you have some (skilled) outside help. So a 'community' approach is often more practical. Indeed this is how smallholding was done in the past, at a village or extended-family level, with maybe fifteen or so people involved.

Whether you are buying an existing farm or taking the cheaper but riskier approach of occupying agricultural land, starting out as a community of several families or an extended family has many advantages: shared costs, a mix of skills, many hands making light(er) work. However, a close-knit community is not for everyone, so an alternative is to divide the land into a cluster of more loosely affiliated smallholdings: a 'co-housing' or perhaps 'eco-village' approach. This needs a great deal of co-ordination and agreement between everyone involved; but it offers the benefits of shared effort and expertise without the tight integration of community living.

There are several community smallholdings operating in Britain, each with a different set-up and mix of activities: the case study of Tinker's Bubble on pp. 214–15 shows how one of these works.

What you will need to make your smallholding work

So you've got your smallholding – what next? Our smallholding ancestors had it easy, at least in one sense: they didn't have to set up from scratch. Land, infrastructure, tools and skills were all passed down from generation to generation. The contemporary smallholder will have to learn many skills and buy or build a lot of stuff. The list which follows gives a basic idea of what you will need to make a smallholding work.

The right kind of land: this is something you should obviously check before buying – it's crucial that the land around your holding can support the mix of activities you plan to do. It is, for example, easier to establish woodland than it is to clear it. The richest and most diverse smallholdings have a balance between grass and trees: this will be determined by the balance of livestock and growing/forestry activities you are planning. Some other factors to bear in mind in assessing the land include:

Orientation – how much sun/frost/wind might it get?
Slope – is it a problem or an opportunity? Is there any flat land?
Soil – how good is it; what sort is it?
Drainage – are there problems (or opportunities) with water?
Location – where is it in relation to towns, markets, etc.
Planning issues – is it in an area with a special designation (Site of Special Scientific Interest or Area of Outstanding Natural Beauty)? What's the local authority like?
Infrastructure – what have you got? Fences? Buildings? Hard standing?

A plan: planning is crucial to success. Practitioners of permaculture (see p. 29) suggest observing the land over a full growing season before planning in order to find out where the problems and opportunities lie. There's a great deal of sense in this; however, few will have the leisure to be able to do it in full. But in order to build up the holding in a manageable way, experienced smallholders all recommend putting as much time as you possibly can into planning. This means, for example, deciding what's going to go where and when; which activities you will start first; how you will develop your food-growing operation; how the costs will be spread and how much labour is needed.

Water and sanitation: where's the water supply? If you're on a 'bare-land' (agricultural-land) holding, there's unlikely to be any mains, so you will need a viable supply from a spring, stream or borehole. There won't be any mains sewage either, so you'll need a plan for that too (see pp. 190–3 for sewage alternatives or p. 208 'Building an 'eco-home').

Energy: again, bare-land holdings won't have mains connections, so in these cases generating your own will be the best option (and the most likely to pass the 'sustainability' test). Any woodland on the site could provide fuel for heating; a stream could offer micro-hydro possibilities; a hilltop might suit a windmill and solar is always available as an option, although it's expensive for electricity. (See p. 170 for more on generating energy.)

Equipment: this depends hugely on the type of smallholding. At 'farm level' – over 5 acres – a tractor or multiple horses become necessary; below this, the land could be managed with a small tractor or cultivator or even just a mower, or maybe one horse. Then there are agricultural tools, greenhouses and polytunnels, fruit cages, housing for livestock … smallholders need a lot of stuff to get started.

Infrastructure: do you have a farmyard? If not, build one (or the equivalent of one) to avoid the smallholding turning into a sea of mud. Some form of barn is also essential to keep equipment (and possibly animals) out of the weather.

Somewhere to live: if you've bought an existing farmhouse, this won't be a problem: but if it's seriously dilapidated, maybe it's worth knocking it down and starting again. This gives a much better chance of creating a sustainable, energy-efficient dwelling (see p. 196). On a bare-land holding, your accommodation choice in the short term will be dictated by your means and sensibilities: in ascending order of cost and luxury this could be bender, yurt or caravan. In the longer term, your chances of planning acceptance will be enhanced if the permanent dwelling is as eco-friendly and sensitive to the location as possible.

Paperwork and permissions: depending on the type of smallholding, you may need:

    Business plan – only required if you are applying for residential planning permission or funding (mortgage or loan).

    Land management plan – again, only necessary to support planning applications.

    Environmental health approvals – for any form of food processing for sale.

Organic certification – you can't sell produce as 'organic' without formal certification. It is good for marketing but requires much admin and is expensive for the smallholder.
DEFRA animal paperwork – for livestock.

Making a living

Unless you are wealthy enough for it to be a hobby, smallholding has to pay, either by creating an income from produce sold commercially, or by providing the best part of the smallholders' subsistence needs. The insane economics of modern agriculture mean, however, that only certain activities are commercially viable on a smallholding scale. Whilst – as previously mentioned – property prices have risen thirty-five times since the 1970s, wheat prices, for example, are unchanged. Even the large-scale production of grain, lamb or beef is difficult to make profitable today. However, the smallholder does have an advantage, because the lower volumes of produce mean that he or she can process locally and sell direct, via farmers' markets or box schemes. As a result, smallholders can keep the 80–90 per cent of the retail price that is otherwise creamed off by processors, distributors and supermarkets (albeit at the cost of having to process and sell everything themselves).

The following table shows different activities that are carried out commercially on a smallholding scale and also lists 'subsistence' production activities.

COMMERCIAL	SUBSISTENCE
Frequently profitable Salad bags and polytunnel veg Veg-box schemes and market stalls Nursery plants Free-range eggs Pigs Herbs Apple juice/cider Chick-rearing Coppice Firewood Mushroom logs Hardwood sawlogs 'Horseyculture' (paddocks for ponies, etc.)	Subsistence production on a small-holding goes way beyond home-grown veg and may include many products that have considerable value in the outside world: Food (veg, fruit, grain, meat, fat, honey) Water Sanitation Energy (wood, solar, wind, hydro, horse) Clothing (rarely) Timber and timber products Shelter
Harder to make profitable Dairy (high processing costs) Beef (needs many acres) Sheep (also need many acres) Honey (pest control can be problematic) Field-scale veg Softwood sawlogs	Entertainment
Almost never profitable Arable crops	

Table courtesy of Simon Fairlie.

Building an 'eco-home'

If you are going 'all the way' – as far towards self-sufficiency as possible – then your home will have an impact on your plans. Even though only 3 per cent of household expenditure (around £600 a year) goes on heat and power, such a sum becomes more significant if you are trying to get outgoings down to an absolute minimum. (The similar annual cost of organic accreditation is cited by smallholders as one of their major annual expenses.) It is also highly unlikely that the costs of 'traditional' fossil energy will do anything but rise in the future. And if you are interested in the extremes of self-sufficiency, then chances are you are also interested in consuming minimal amounts of energy for either economic or ideological reasons (or both).

But a home's impact on the environment is not just about energy consumption. A house built from brick, breezeblock and with PVC windows also has high 'embodied' energy, meaning that a great deal of energy has been expended in producing the building materials. And the presence of materials such as PVC or medium-density fibreboard (MDF) mean that the house also has 'embodied toxicity': its materials have been responsible either for environmentally unfriendly industrial processes or for residual pollution ('off-gassing' from the urea-formaldehyde bonding, in the case of MDF).

So a home that is miserly in energy consumption and has a minimal impact on the environment is likely to appeal to smallholders for both financial and personal reasons. It is also integral to achieving true 'sustainability', which has perhaps been best defined by the WWF, the global conservation organization, responsible for the assessment (quoted in the introduction to this book) that the current British lifestyle needs the resources of three planet Earths to sustain it. The WWF also assessed the roundhouse built by Tony Wrench at the Brithdir Mawr community in Wales. Made largely of locally sourced natural materials, heated by a wood stove, with solar electricity but no fridge, freezer or TV, and with a composting toilet, maximum recycling and some food-growing, the roundhouse scored 'one Earth' – but only just. This is a stark illustration of how much our lives have to change for them to be sustainable; and it also shows how our homes are central to this change.

Building an environmentally friendly house is a huge subject to be covered in a tiny section of a chapter and there are plenty of guides and resources available for those wishing to research the subject in depth (see Further Reading). But here are some pointers to pique your curiosity.

Three steps to a sustainable house

1. Design for minimal energy use
Most 'conventional' housing – from modern houses to ancient country cottages – has not been designed with energy efficiency in mind. Retrofitting can help to put this right (see p. 194), but the 'new builder' can use good design to save up to 90 per cent of the energy a house might otherwise use.

※ **Super-insulate:** the ideal is to aim for 400mm of insulation all round, in the walls, the floor and the roof. This can be most easily achieved in timber-framed buildings, where much of the walls' thickness can be made up of insulation, with only thin layers of cladding on the outside and inside.

☀ **Orientate the house for 'passive solar gain':** with the jargon removed, this simply means making sure that the house makes maximum use of the sun for natural solar heating. At its simplest, this means ensuring most windows face south. If internal walls are of heavy masonry, and floors of tile or stone, these can act as a store that releases heat at night. Adding a conservatory on the south side (see p. 167) can make even more use of the sun, as well as offering other advantages.

2. Choose environmentally friendly materials

This won't necessarily affect the energy efficiency of your house, but it will reduce the 'embodied energy' in its construction, may make for a more pleasant place to live and will also make the house easier to recycle, should this be a consideration. There are always some compromises to be made: for example, maximum energy efficiency is achieved when a building is, in effect, 'airtight', with the airflow managed by heat exchangers (see case study on p. 196). Such high-tech efficiency cannot always be achieved in a house build of entirely 'low-tech' materials: however, such a house may have had a lower environmental impact in its construction; and its owner might put up with the odd draught. Some alternative materials to consider:

🌱 **Straw bale:** modern straw-bale houses do not present the vulnerability that did for the first little pig. Typically, the bales are used in conjunction with a timber frame then rendered, or clad in timber. As long as the walls are kept dry at top and bottom ('good boots and a good hat', straw-bale buildings have a long life, are cheap, provide excellent insulation and of course are a renewable, biodegradable resource.

🌱 **Rammed earth:** compressed soil, amazingly, can be turned into bricks or entire walls that are long-lived, environmentally friendly and offer reasonable insulation.

🌱 **Cob:** mud (mixed with a bit of straw) can also make for fine, solid walls that offer good thermal mass and therefore act as heat stores for a 'passive solar' house.

3. Build in features to support a 'low impact' smallholding lifestyle

One of the problems you will encounter as a 21st-Century Smallholder is that the average house or flat doesn't have a lot of the features that are really useful in the business of food-growing, processing and storing. And ultra eco-friendly features like composting toilets are rarely appropriate for retrofits. Bearing in mind the limits of the location, the 'new builder' can design such features in from the start.

- **Cellar or root store:** dark and with a reasonably constant temperature, cellars are ideal for long-term storage of many foodstuffs, but particularly fruit and veg such as apples, potatoes, onions and root crops. If it's too hard to dig one, maybe it's a good excuse to build a small, windowless straw-bale outbuilding.
- **Pantry:** why don't kitchens have pantries any more? Dark but well-ventilated spaces, they are ideal for many of the things that are currently desiccated in the artificial, air-conditioned atmosphere of our fridges.
- **Conservatory:** can also double as a space for raising seedlings if you don't have room for a greenhouse.
- **Workroom:** somewhere to extract and bottle the honey, make the wine (or even the cheese) and store all the kit to do it.
- **Composting toilet:** (see p. 191) if it's appropriate to the site, then it will ultimately help with your fruit-growing and any ambitions towards becoming 'waste neutral'.
- **Rainwater harvesting:** (see p. 187) designing this in from the start will bring savings in the longer term and benefits for the garden too.

Depending on how it is built and which energy features it uses (e.g. solar PV, ground-source heat) an 'eco-home' may be more than 10 per cent more expensive than a conventional house. However, given its potential for keeping financial outgoings (and environmental impact) to a minimum in the longer term, it would seem madness for the smallholder going 'all the way' to build anything else.

Case studies

Guilden Gate organic smallholding

Simon and Jacqueline Saggers established Guilden Gate in 1999 with the aim of 'creating one practical example of what sustainable rural development could look like'. They bought the 2-hectare plot from Simon's family, who have been farming in the village of Bassingbourn for generations. Before starting work on the land, they spent two years planning and researching, learning how to create a farm that is also a diverse, interconnected ecosystem. From a ploughed field they have created a beautiful, richly biodiverse place – a mixture of orchard, woodland, hedges, meadow and vegetable beds – that supports Simon and Jacqueline and their two children and provides a vegetable-box scheme for around twenty-five local customers.

Home and resources

The Saggers took the risky option of building a house on the base of some old battery chicken houses with only temporary planning permission. Surrounded as Guilden Gate is by the giant arable fields of eastern England, their application was unusual and it was six years before they received permanent planning permission to live on their holding. Plans for their house had to be modified along the way, but the result is a highly energy-efficient building that is almost invisible amongst the trees and hedges. The cottage at Guilden Gate is timber-framed, super-insulated with Warmcel and clad in local larch weatherboards. For all but three months of the year, heat is provided by passive solar gain and solar water heating; in the coldest months a wood stove supplements these.

The cycle of water use at Guilden Gate is completely closed. 'Water in' for the household and for irrigation is provided by a borehole and buried rainwater tanks. 'Water out' is either filtered and reused, or purified in a reedbed, flowform pond and willow trench. A composting toilet turns solid wastes into fertilizer.

The energy cycle is also closed on the holding with the recent arrival of a 5kW grid-linked wind turbine that will generate more than the family uses in a year. With a capital cost of £15,000, a third of which was paid by a Clear Skies grant, the turbine is expected to pay back in twelve to fourteen years and to be a net contributor to the grid. All the other energy used at

Guilden Gate is renewable: wood for winter heating comes from coppice in the holding's woodland; otherwise water and space heating are provided by the sun. Guilden Gate is a net zero CO_2 emissions site.

Economics

Guilden Gate's main commercial activity is their own organic 'veggie'-box scheme which runs from Easter to Christmas and supplies around twenty-five local customers. The box scheme has been built up entirely by word of mouth, without any advertising, and has a lengthy waiting list. The scheme's economics are helped by the fact that the majority of customers, all of whom live locally, collect – and sometimes even pick – the produce themselves. For many customers (and their children), the visit to Guilden Gate is an event in itself and this also helps Simon and Jacqueline to build relations with them. Guilden Gate also produces eggs from a flock of around thirty chickens and honey from five beehives. There are also mushroom logs and, in the future, pigs are planned for the woodland. Despite all this, the smallholding's income from the veggie-box scheme is only around £6,000 per year. However, if the holding's provision of fuel, water, electricity and fruit and veg is counted as income substitution, its income rises by at least another £2,500. In addition, Simon and Jacqueline run guided tours of Guilden Gate and do consultancy and part-time work. The holding's biggest overhead is Soil Association certification (official accreditation is essential if you want to call your produce 'organic') which costs around £400 annually and is described by Simon as 'like sitting an A-level every year'.

Simon is keen to stress that smallholding is not an easy life, nor is it going to make one financially rich. The planning and project management was long and complex yet essential to creating the successful enterprise that the Saggers now have. The key to being a smallholder, says Simon, is 'to be jack of all trades, willing to fail at all of them but determined to keep trying!' He is passionate about bringing small 'human-scale' agriculture back to the countryside and points out that one of the greatest pleasures is starting to succeed more often than not, as your experience grows. Simon gets the greatest sense of achievement from walking around the holding with his family, knowing that he and Jacqueline have created something special for their children. After all, he says, 'We were inspired by Gandhi's words: "Be the change you want to see in the world" and we do believe we have created something worth passing on to the kids. We believe that we must work as if we were farming for ever.'

Tinker's Bubble

Tinker's Bubble is a community smallholding set in 16 hectares (40 acres) of rural Somerset. It was established in 1994 by a group of people intent on living a low-impact lifestyle modelled, as member and land rights activist Simon Fairlie puts it, on a 'sustainable iron-age village'. Named after the spring that rises in the middle of the holding, Tinker's Bubble is an extraordinarily beautiful and diverse site, consisting of steep, dense woodland, sloping pasture and orchards. It took five years for the smallholding to get planning permission for twelve adults to live on the land they worked. Today, their operation provides subsistence and a low-cost, sustainable lifestyle for the inhabitants as well as commercial sales of vegetables and timber products.

Home and resources

The original dwellings at Tinker's Bubble were tents: now a small group of buildings, all made from local materials (mainly the Douglas Fir trees that dominate much of the woodland) are tucked away in the holding. A founding tenet of the Tinker's Bubble 'experiment' was that no fossil fuels should be used on the site, a constraint which has demanded low-technology solutions, particularly for the forestry operation. Trees are brought down by hand, then taken to the on-site sawmill by a shire horse called Sam, who also works in the fields when needed (for example at haymaking time). The logs are cut by a steam-powered saw, fuelled by waste wood taken from the site. Much of the agricultural work is done by human power, including the major task of cutting hay, which is done by hand with traditional scythes.

All heating is provided by wood; and cooking happens either on a wood stove in the communal roundhouse or outside on an open fire. The smallholding does use electricity, but only a fraction of what a single modern household would consume. There is no grid connection: the combination of a 750W wind turbine and 300W peak solar PV array, using batteries for storage, provides a supply of electricity through the year that is adequate for lighting, charging cordless tools and powering the odd laptop. There are no washing machines, televisions, dishwashers or other energy-guzzling paraphernalia of the modern world at Tinker's Bubble (although a battery-powered fridge gets occasional use in the hottest days of summer).

Tinker's Bubble is autonomous in water as well as energy. Although there is a mains connection, it isn't used: the spring provides all the holding's water needs, with a ram pump, powered by the spring's flow, taking water up to the main living area. Sewage is dealt with locally by composting toilets and earth closets.

Economics

Most of the income at Tinker's Bubble currently comes from the sale of organic vegetables (at local markets) and timber products. There are also products from the substantial orchard: the apples themselves, then apple juice and cider. There are two Jersey cows, with calves, and a heifer: dairy products are also sold, but most of the dairy output is consumed on the holding. As much as possible, the livestock – the cows and their calves (who eventually go for beef) and the Shire horse – eat fodder produced on-site: fresh grass in the season and hay through the winter months. Organic lucerne is bought in to supplement the cows' feed.

Tinker's Bubble provides for all its members' basic needs for a cost per person of £23 per week. As Simon Fairlie points out: 'When people think about self-sufficiency, they tend to be thinking about growing their own vegetables. But that takes only a tiny fraction of someone's expenditure, maybe 1–2 per cent. Tinker's Bubble is self-sufficient in energy, water, housing, furniture, even entertainment: that's why it can cost relatively little for people to live like this.' Members still need to buy their own clothes, beer (although the holding is self-sufficient in cider!), private motor transport and luxuries, but the basics of life are catered for by the land.

This lifestyle comes at a price: the work is hard and physical, and the dynamics of community living don't suit everyone. But the rhythm of life at Tinker's Bubble – and the beautiful, biodiverse space it occupies – shows that genuinely sustainable rural development is not only possible, but attainable.

FURTHER READING

1 Growing your own food

Books

All About Compost, Pauline Pears, Search Press, 1999.
Grow Your Own Vegetables, Joy Larkcom, first published 1976 as
    Vegetables from Small Gardens, Frances Lincoln, 2002.
Encyclopaedia of Organic Gardening, Henry Doubleday Research
    Association, editor-in-chief Pauline Pears, Dorling Kindersley, 2001.
The River Cottage Cookbook, Hugh Fearnley-Whittingstall,
    HarperCollins, 2001.
Organic Gardening, Pauline Pears and Sue Stickland, Mitchell Beazley, 2000.
Soil, Charlie Ryrie, Gaia Books, 2001.
Pests, Charlie Ryrie, Gaia Books, 2001.
Compost, Charlie Ryrie, Gaia Books, 2001.
The Edible Container Garden, Michael Guerra, Gaia Books, 2005.

Internet publications and websites

Pesticides in your food, available from Pesticides Action Network,
    www.pan-uk.org

2 Raising your own food

Books

Guide to Bees and Honey, Ted Hooper, first published 1976, Marston
    House, 2001.
Bees at the Bottom of the Garden, first published 1983, Alan Campion,
    2001.
Keeping Traditional Pig Breeds: available from www.pigparadise.com
Starting with Chickens, Katie Thear, Broad Leys Publishing Ltd, 1999.

Internet publications and websites

British Beekeepers Association, www.bbka.org.uk – information and links
    to local beekeeping associations
Starting to keep domestic ducks, available from British Waterfowl
    Association, www.waterfowl.org.uk
Pigs: a guide for new keepers, Defra, available from www.defra.gov.uk
Keeping poultry, Low Impact Living Initiative, available from
    www.lowimpact.org

Too hard to swallow: the truth about drugs and poultry, Soil Association, available from www.soilassociation.org

3 Getting the most from your home harvest

Books
500 Recipes for Jams, Pickles, Chutneys, Marguerite Patten, Paul Hamlyn, 1963.

Internet publications and websites
Storage of organically produced crops, MAFF/HDRA, 1997, available from the Henry Doubleday Research Foundation at www.hdra.org.uk

4 Building biodiversity

Books
How to Make a Wildlife Garden, Chris Baines, Frances Lincoln, 2000.
Attracting Wildlife to Your Garden, Michael Chinery, Collins, 2004.

Internet publications and websites
Living Planet Report 2004, WWF, available from www.panda.org

6 Making your home more self-reliant

Books
The Whole House Book, Pat Borer and Cindy Harris, Centre for Alternative Technology Publications, 1998.
Lifting the Lid: an ecological approach to toilet systems, Peter Harper and Louise Halestrap, Centre for Alternative Technology Publications, 1999.

Internet publications and websites
Energy and Climate Change, Friends of the Earth, available from www.foe.org.uk
Small or atomic? Comparing the finances of nuclear and micro-generated energy, Green Alliance, available from www.green-alliance.org.uk

Eco-minimalism: getting the priorities right, Howard Liddell and Nick
    Grant, available from Elemental Solutions,
    www.elementalsolutions.co.uk
Eco-realism: an emerging paradigm? Peter Harper, Centre for Alternative
Technology, available from www.elementalsolutions.co.uk
The Nottingham Ecohome, www.msarch.co.uk/ecohome
Tree House, www.treehouseclapham.org.uk
Micro-hydro power factsheet, Centre for Alternative Technology, can be
purchased from www.cat.org.uk

**Factsheets available from the Energy Saving Trust, at
www.est.org.uk**
Energy Efficient Refurbishment of Existing Housing
Advanced Insulation in Housing Refurbishment
Groundsource Heat Pumps
Biomass
Small Scale Wind Energy
Small Scale Hydroelectricity
Solar PV

**Factsheets available from the Environment Agency,
www.environment-agency.gov.uk**
Conserving water in buildings
Harvesting rainwater for domestic use
Water efficient WCs and retrofits
Conserving water in buildings: domestic appliances
Conserving water in buildings: greywater
Conserving water in buildings: gardening

Micro-hydro power factsheet, CAT

7 Going all the way

Books

The Complete Book of Self-Sufficiency, John Seymour, first published 1975, Dorling Kindersley, 1996.
The Earth Care Manual, Patrick Whitefield, Permanent Publications, 2004.

Internet

Building your own energy efficient house, Energy Saving Trust, available from www.est.org.uk

Background reading: ecology, economics, food, politics

Books

Gaia: a new look at life on Earth, first published 1979, James Lovelock, Oxford University Press, 2000.
Silent Spring, Rachel Carson, first published 1962, Penguin Classics, 2000.
Small is Beautiful, E. F. Schumacher, first published 1973, Vintage, 1993.
The One-Straw Revolution, Masanobu Fukuoka, first published 1978, Other India Press, 2004.
Permaculture One, Bill Mollison and David Holmgren, first published 1978, Tagari, 1990.
Not on the Label, Felicity Lawrence, Penguin, 2004.
Shopped, Joanna Blythman, Fourth Estate, 2004.
The Little Earth Book, James Bruges, Alastair Sawday Publishing, 2004.
Growth Fetish, Clive Hamilton, Pluto Press, 2003.

Internet

Eco-realism: an emerging paradigm? Peter Harper, Centre for Alternative Techology, www.cat.org.uk
Living Planet Report 2004, WWF, www.wwf.org.uk
City Harvest: the feasibility of growing more food in London, Sustain, www.sustainweb.org

INDEX